CRYPTIC

THE BEST SHORT FICTION OF JACK MCDEVITT

CRYPTIC

THE BEST SHORT FICTION OF JACK MCDEVITT

JACK MCDEVITT

SUBTERRANEAN PRESS 2009

First Edition

ISBN
978-1-59606-195-8

Subterranean Press
PO Box 190106
Burton, MI 48519

www.subterraneanpress.com

For Scott Ryfun,
the Voice of the Golden Isles

CONTENTS:

JACK MCDEVITT,
THIS ONE'S FOR YOU

by Robert J. Sawyer

I remember when I first encountered Jack McDevitt's writings. A full twenty years ago, back in 1988, Bantam Books sent every member of the Science Fiction and Fantasy Writers of America a copy of their new anthology *Full Spectrum*—first in what became a distinguished series—in hopes of garnering Nebula Awards attention for the stories in the book. I read them all, but only a few have stuck with over the years, and foremost among those is Jack's "The Fort Moxie Branch" (which did indeed get nominated for the Nebula, as well as the Hugo).

Here, it was clear to me, was an author who loved writing, and who cherished the art of fiction. His Fort Moxie branch library contained very special books—books unknown to the world, books abandoned by their authors or forgotten by history, books such as Hemingway's *Watch by Night*, Melville's *Agatha*, and *The Complete Works of James McCorbin*, whoever the heck *he* might be (but canny readers will see significance in his initials).

I was reminded of that book-loving Jack McDevitt a short time ago when I read his much more recent "Henry James, This One's For You," also a Nebula finalist. That story is in part about how we choose which works will be remembered and which forgotten.

There's a wistful quality to Jack's ruminations on one's literary legacy, and yet his own seems safe, as I'll explain in a moment—even though, in a field full of teenage wunderkinds, Jack didn't come to writing until his mid-forties.

Jack McDevitt was born in Philadelphia in 1935, and now lives in Brunswick, Georgia, with his wonderful wife Maureen. My (often faulty) math skills tell me that Jack must be in his early seventies—but he could pass for twenty years younger. Recently, he kindly blurbed my own latest novel, *Rollback*, about rejuvenation. I wonder …

Jack had a full life before coming to science fiction. He'd been a Navy officer, an English teacher, a Philadelphia taxi driver, a customs officer, and a motivational trainer. It wasn't until 1980 that Maureen suggested he try his hand at writing SF. The result is one of the most important bodies of work in the SF field in the last quarter-century.

Jack's first publication was just a year later—a remarkably short apprenticeship in this field—with "The Emerson Effect" in the late, lamented *Twilight Zone* magazine. And it didn't take long for the award nominations to start coming in.

His first of fourteen Nebula nominations came in 1983 for "Cryptic," the title story of the wonderful collection you're now holding in your hands. His first award win was in 1986 for the remarkable SETI novel *The Hercules Text*, which took the *Locus* Award for Best First Novel, and also received a special citation for the Philip K. Dick Award. *The Hercules Text* was one of Terry Carr's new Ace Specials, published as part of the line that launched the careers of Kim Stanley Robinson, Michael Swanwick, Lucius Shepard, and William Gibson.

In 1992, Jack won the world's largest cash prize for SF writing, the $10,000 *Premio UPC de Ciencia Ficción*, for his novella "Ships in the Night," and in 1997 his novella *Time Travelers Never Die* won the Homer Award, voted on by the members of CompuServe's Science Fiction and Fantasy Forums (and it was also nominated for the Hugo and the Nebula).

In 2002, his novel *DeepSix* took the Southeastern SF Achievement Award—and then, at last, the biggies started rolling in. In 2004, Jack's *Omega* won the John W. Campbell Memorial Award (the SF field's principal juried award), and in 2006, he received the Life Achievement Southeastern SF Achievement Award. And then, at last, on his thirteenth nomination—the most of any author without a win—Jack's *Seeker* took the Science Fiction and Fantasy Writers of America's Nebula Award, the academy award of the SF field, for Best Novel of 2006 (and his *Odyssey* was nominated for the same award the following year).

All the nominations and wins are enough to ensure Jack's legacy, but it doesn't address the question of *why* McDevitt books have proved so popular. And, make no mistake, they *are* popular: without anyone really noticing, Jack has become one of the top-selling authors in the science-fiction field; Ginjer Buchanan, who edits his novels for Ace, tells me he's now within spitting distance of the *New York Times* bestsellers list, an extraordinarily rare achievement for books that aren't media tie-ins—and Ginjer is determined to put him on the list soon.

Once you read the 200,000 words collected here, the reasons for Jack's popularity will be obvious. In a field that often contains clunky prose, Jack's writing is exemplary: not just smooth and clean, but *charming*. In a field that often gives short shrift to the human in its pursuit of the grandly cosmic, Jack's writing is warm and intimate; it appeals as much to the heart as to the head.

It's that charm, that warmth, that sticks with you—and, if you are ever lucky enough to meet the man in person, you'll see that he shares those traits. Jack is, above all else, a nice guy. He's friendly, welcoming, supportive, kind, and wise. There's no one in the SF field I more look forward to seeing at conventions.

That isn't to say that Jack is softhearted, or softheaded. Indeed, he and I recently attended a conference entitled "The Future of Intelligence in the Cosmos," jointly sponsored by the NASA Ames Research Center and the SETI Institute. I was too chicken to give a talk of my own—after all, others on the agenda included Marvin Minsky and Frank Drake. But Jack stepped up to the plate (demonstrating the skills he'd honed as a motivational speaker) and gave a stirring, mercifully PowerPoint-free, presentation entitled "Invent a Printing Press and Hang On." In it, he argued that the way to ensure the long-term survival of our species was to emphasize the development of critical thinking in high schools (Jack keeps this skill honed for himself with frequent games of chess). Yes, Jack wants us all to be goodhearted, to look with awe and wonder at the stars—but also to use our reasoning powers and to take responsibility for our actions.

Indeed, my friend Jack has a little catch phrase. Whenever we part, he always says, "Be good, Rob."

Be as good a person as he? I try.

Be as good a writer as he? I can only hope.

I can't give the same advice back to him. Jack *is* good, in all the ways that adjective can be applied. How good, you're about to find out; just turn the page.

FOREWORD

by Jack McDevitt

More than half a century ago, I sat in the large overstuffed armchair in our living room captivated by Lester Del Rey's "Helen O'Loy." I was twelve years old, in grade school, home for lunch, and still in my Lone Ranger phase. I'd discovered science fiction eight years earlier, watching stunned as Flash Gordon piloted his magnificent rocket ship in circles above the sterile landscapes of Mongo. So I was already a lifelong fan, captivated by John Carter and Dejah Thoris, by Conan and the *Legion of Space*.

But "Helen O'Loy" packed a different kind of punch from anything I'd seen earlier. Not that it was necessarily better. Just *different*. A man in love with a beautiful robot. (I don't think the term 'android' was in use yet.) Ultimately, we learn that, after a glorious lifetime, the husband dies, as humans inevitably do. And Helen's note to a friend arrives, of course, at the climax: "He died in my arms just before sunrise....Don't grieve too much for us, for we have had a happy life together...." She will turn herself off and be buried with him. No one is ever to know the truth. It was the first time I can recall reading a story of *any* kind with tears running down my cheeks. Certainly nothing we were looking at over in the seventh grade ever had that sort of effect. I can't imagine I was worth much that afternoon while we talked about geography and who imported what from whom. (We always did our geography in the afternoon, and there was, for reasons I never understood, a great deal of fuss about imports.)

On an early summer evening a few years later, I sat outside in a rocking chair—we lived in a row home in South Philadelphia and everything around me was made out of brick or concrete—caught up in Ray Bradbury's "Mars Is Heaven." The rocket from Earth had landed on Martian soil and discovered a small town with picket fences and two-story houses that would not have been out of place in South Jersey. There are hedges and lawns and driveways. And a church.

The crew waits as the captain checks his instruments and finally walks over to the hatch and opens it. Music drifts in.

Somebody is playing a *piano*.

It's "Beautiful Dreamer."

Maybe those early jolts are so unforgettable precisely because they *are* early. But I think there's more to it that that.

It's been impossible to forget the kid created so many years ago by Jerome Bixby in "It's a *Good* Life." I think that was my first encounter --more like a collision-- with irony operating at anything like that level. I can still see that crowd of local residents, local *victims*, gathered in a living room, with one of their number dead on the floor, and snow coming down out of season to ruin the crops, and they're going on in nervous, terrified voices about what a good life it is because the little boy who mindlessly wields such lethal power wants them to be happy. Will kill them if they aren't.

And who could come away from Damon Knight's aliens, with their manual titled *To Serve Man*, not marked for life? The manual, of course, is written in their own language. And they're playing the role of benefactors, friends of the human race. Inviting people to ride their ships, to head off to a better world, until one of the characters learns to read the language. "It's a *cookbook*," he says.

I went to a school where they thought Edgar Allen Poe was scary.

I ran into my first fictional ethical dilemma in Tom Godwin's "The Cold Equations," when a star pilot confronts a terrible choice: Stand by while a young woman ejects herself through an airlock, or allow her extra weight to destroy them both.

There were other riveting moments: a basketball that gained energy from friction rather than losing it, a subway that got lost beneath the streets of Boston, a poet stranded in space writing about the cool green hills of Earth. And a superdense moon, previously unknown, orbiting Mars three feet off the ground, drilling holes through any elevations in the landscape. "Look out, Harry, here it comes again."

Murder by black hole. The Jesuit navigator who confronts the painful truth about the star of Bethlehem. And Charlie, who evades retardation just long enough to find out what he is about to lose.

And Asimov's "Nightfall."

What a treasure. If anyone would like a story idea, how about having aliens come in after we're gone, and discover a volume of, say, the fifty best science fiction stories of all time. It's all they have of us. Except for a few scattered ruins, Bradbury and the others are all that remain. What would they think of us?

Science fiction, ultimately, is about what might happen, in Heinlein's classic phrase, "if this goes on." What are the consequences for us if we learn how to reverse the aging process? If we discover how to double our IQ's? If we can track down a happiness gene and thereby guarantee a pleasant, untroubled existence to our children? Would we want that? Years ago I visited the Page School at the Capitol and we talked about whether unlimited happiness is a good idea. The kids, always ahead of the rest of us, had some doubts. People who can be happy in the face of serious setbacks would probably make pretty good slaves.

And maybe there's something to be said for being unhappy in the face of loss. Who could really stand being around people who were tirelessly, relentlessly, happy?

The happiness gene shows up in "Tweak."

Science fiction seems to be most effective in its shorter form. Maybe that's because it's generally aimed at making a single point—What if this goes on? Or what if something had happened differently? Or what if we were able to get a breakthrough in, say, transportation? Inevitably, the issue is What if? Rather than commenting on the impositions of society, or the vagaries of human nature, we tinker with technology.

After I came out of the Navy, I spent ten years as an English teacher and theater director. It became obvious very quickly that my original idea about how to conduct a high school class, which was that all I needed to do was to mention Charles Lamb, and maybe do it with a little showbiz, was in error. My students did not scramble, as I was sure they would, to read his comments on life, death, and winning the love of beautiful women. Toward the end of the first year, while I watched eyes roll anytime I mentioned *King Lear*, I figured out that I had the wrong approach. (I've never been a quick study.) I needed something to ignite a fire. It was not my job, despite what I'd understood, to warp my kids' brains with classics they weren't, with a few exceptions, ready to read. What I decided would be most useful, what would be most valuable for them, was to demonstrate how much fun books could be. To pass on the passion.

Some experiments went wrong. Even Sherlock Holmes couldn't cut it. Eventually I decided to go back to what had turned on the lights for *me*. I tried *The Martian Chronicles* and Heinlein's *Future History*. We staged stories in the classroom and cut off at the critical moment. When the hatch opens and they hear "Beautiful Dreamer." Read the rest tonight.

Was it successful? Eventually, we had to establish a bookstore in the school.

Once they get started, kids become eclectic readers. At Mt. St. Charles Academy in Woonsocket, RI, I encountered students who tried their hand at Plato simply because the subject had come up in class. Somebody would comment that Plato thought democracy was more or less mob rule. And next day there would be a general debate. It was the sort of experience, as much as anything else in my life, that left me with a sense that the human race, despite everything, is worth saving.

My first published story was "A Pound of Cure." And yes, I was never very good at titles. It won the Freshman Short Story contest at LaSalle in 1954, and they printed it in the school's literary magazine, *Four Quarters*. It was science fiction, and I thought I was on my way.

Shortly afterward, I read *David Copperfield*, saw how accomplished Dickens was, decided it was not a field for somebody with my limited talents, and wrote nothing else for a quarter century.

Eventually my wife Maureen persuaded me to try again, since I was always saying how someday I wanted to write SF, having failed in my other very early ambition, which was to play short for the Phillies.

To me, it was a pointless exercise. But more or less to keep Maureen happy I put together a story, "Zip Code," about a guy who worked in a post office, and who was in love with one of the other clerks. But he could not bring himself to make a move because he thought the young lady was too daunting. Eventually, a letter from Ralph Waldo Emerson, mailed over a century earlier, shows up, containing some lines from one of the essays. The letter, apparently part of an ongoing correspondence, assures the recipient that "you can do virtually anything if you believe in yourself." But of course you have to take the plunge. You have to be willing to commit.

I don't think that, at the time, I saw the irony in my adopting that particular theme. But it made the point I'd long before urged on my students. Believe in yourself. Don't leave anything undone simply because you're afraid of failure.

T.E.D. Klein shocked me when he bought it for *The Twilight Zone Magazine*. He changed the title to "The Emerson Effect," and promptly sent me a check. I spent the next few months expecting to hear that the publishing house had burned down.

I discovered I loved writing. And the conviction that I could sell what I wrote made a task that had once seemed insurmountable, suddenly appear routine. Not that I didn't bounce a few stories during those early years. There was something about an alien pizza place. And another written around a combination pool table/time machine.

Kids in any society are always being told by authority figures to keep their hands off something so they don't break it. At school, teachers show them what they've gotten wrong. It took me awhile to realize that the best way to teach composition is to show a student what he's doing well. The short compact sentence that makes its point with a minimum of verbiage. This is the way to do it, Sally. Give me more like this.

But we don't. We tell them they'll break something, and after a while the kids come to believe it. The result is that most of us underestimate what we can do.

Two of the stories in this collection, "Lighthouse" and "Cool Neighbor," were written in collaboration with Michael Shara, the head of the astrophysics department at the American Museum of Natural History in New York. I'd be less than honest if I didn't admit that the concepts were his.

"Welcome to Valhalla" was written with Katheryn Lance. I'd had the basic idea for years, but I kept trying to drag a time traveler into it. And it didn't work. Kathryn, who shares my taste for Richard Wagner, suggested Brunnhilde, and effectively wrote the story.

Two other stories each inspired a series of novels: The Academy, with Priscilla Hutchins, was born in the sands of one of Saturn's larger moons, in "Melville on Iapetus." And the Alex Benedict novels, of which there are now four, got their start in "Dutchman." Curiously, neither Alex nor Hutch appears in either story, though "Melville on Iapetus"—there's another one of those great titles—was eventually adapted and used as the prologue for the Academy debut novel, *The Engines of God*.

❋

When I was in graduate school, at Wesleyan University, one of the instructors routinely held lunches for his classes at his home. One afternoon, several of us were sitting around out back, sipping Cokes and putting away donuts, when someone began describing an incident from the Renaissance. An Italian scholar, visiting Athens, had opened a trunk and found a trove of manuscripts from the classical age.

Several days later the scholar loaded the manuscripts and the trunk onto a ship headed back to Venice. But on the way home, a storm blew up. The ship went down, and the trunk went with it. The scholar, fortunately, survived. But what had been in the trunk?

It got me thinking about transience, about the things we lose as we travel through our lives. On a personal scale, friends and loved ones. On a larger scale, the Hanging Gardens and the Lighthouse at Alexandria. The Great Library. Several Homeric epics. Most of Sophocles' plays. And, on still a third scale, countless individual acts of courage and compassion.

I've never been able to get the scholar and his trunk out of my mind. There are echoes of it through all the stories in Part II, "Lost Treasures."

"Report from the Rear" is based on an actual event, as reported by H. L. Mencken, dating back to the Russo-Japanese War. "Black To Move" is a chess story, of course. (It's my favorite game.) "The Far Shore," set in an interstellar future, was my second professional story. The alert reader will easily conclude that the author grew up during the 1940's radio age. "Sunrise" eventually became part of *A Talent for War*. And "Kaminsky At War" is set in the Academy universe. I couldn't help suspecting that the bureaucrat that Kaminsky gets so angry with is Priscilla Hutchins.

I've always been fascinated by the possibilities raised by artificial intelligence. That's probably left over from "Helen O'Loy." "Gus" was my first attempt at an AI with a mind of its own. In this case, an AI portraying St. Augustine decides it's a Catholic and demands access to the sacraments.

There are two other AI stories in Part V. And a novella, "Time Travellers Never Die," which was as much pure joy to write as anything I've ever gone near.

Now that I think of it, though, they all set off a charge of one kind or another. So I'm going to let you in on a secret: Writers are always going on about how difficult the work is, bottle of whiskey in the top drawer, writer's block, and all that sort of thing. In fact none of it's true. I've never had a job that provided such pure pleasure. We put that other stuff out there to keep the competition down.

PART I

UNLIKELY CONNECTIONS

CRYPTIC

It was at the bottom of the safe in a bulky manila envelope. I nearly tossed it into the trash with the stacks of other documents, tapes, and assorted flotsam left over from the Project.

Had it been cataloged, indexed in some way, I'm sure I would have. But the envelope was blank, save for an eighteen-year-old date scrawled in the lower right hand corner, and beneath it, the notation "40 gh."

Out on the desert, lights were moving. That would be Brackett fine-tuning the Array for Orrin Hopkins, who was then beginning the observations that would lead, several years later, to new departures in pulsar theory. I envied Hopkins. He was short, round, bald, a man unsure of himself, whose explanations were invariably interspersed with giggles. He was a ridiculous figure, yet he bore the stamp of genius. And people would remember his ideas long after the residence hall named for me at Carrollton had crumbled.

If I had not recognized my own limits and conceded any hope of immortality (at least of this sort), I certainly did so when I accepted the director's position at Sandage. Administration pays better than being an active physicist, but it is death to ambition.

And a Jesuit doesn't even get that advantage.

In those days, the Array was still modest: forty parabolic antennas, each thirty-six meters across. They were on tracks, of course, independently movable, forming a truncated cross. They had, for two decades, been the heart of SETI, the Search for Extra-Terrestrial Intelligence. Now, with the Project abandoned, they were being employed for more useful, if mundane, purposes.

*

Even that relatively unsophisticated system was good. As Hutching Chaney once remarked, the Array could pick up the cough of an automobile ignition on Mars.

I circled the desk and fell into the uncomfortable wooden chair we'd inherited from the outgoing regime. The packet was sealed with tape that had become brittle and loose around the edges. I tore it open.

It was a quarter past ten. I'd worked through my dinner and the evening hours, bored, drinking coffee, debating the wisdom in coming out here from JPL. The increase in responsibility was a good career move; but I knew now that Harry Cooke would never lay his hands on a new particle.

I was committed for two years at Sandage, two years of working out schedules and worrying about insurance, two years of dividing meals between the installation's sterile cafeteria and Jimmy's Amoco Restaurant on Route 85. Then, if all went well, I could expect another move up, perhaps to Georgetown.

I'd have traded it all for Hopkins's future.

I shook out six magnetic disks onto the desk. They were in individual sleeves, of the type that many installations had once used to record electromagnetic radiation. The disks were numbered and dated over a three-day period in 2001, two years earlier than the date on the envelope.

Each was marked "Procyon."

In back, Hopkins and two associates were hunched over monitors. Brackett, having finished his job, was at his desk with his head buried in a book.

I was pleased to discover that the disks were compatible to the Mark VIs. I inserted one, tied in a vocorder to get a hard copy, and went over to join the Hopkins group while the thing ran. They were talking about plasma. I listened for a time, got lost, noted that everyone around me (save the grinning little round man) also got lost, and strolled back to my computer.

The trace drew its green-and-white pictures smoothly on the Mark VI display, and pages of hard copy clicked out of the vocorder. Something in the needle geometry scattering across the recording paper drew my attention. Like an elusive name, it drifted just beyond reach.

Beneath a plate of the Andromeda Galaxy, a coffee pot simmered. I could hear the distant drone of a plane, probably out of Luke Air Force Base. Behind me, Hopkins and his people were laughing at something.

There were patterns in the recording.

They materialized slowly, identical clusters of impulses. The signals were artificial.

Procyon.

The laughter, the plane, the coffee pot, a radio that had been left on somewhere: everything squeezed down to a possibility.

More likely Phoenix, I thought.

Frank Myers had been SETI Director since Ed Dickinson's death twelve years before. I reached him next morning in San Francisco.

"No," he said without hesitation. "Someone's idea of a joke, Harry."

"It was in your safe, Frank."

"That damned safe's been there forty years. Might be anything in it. Except messages from Mars...."

I thanked him and hung up.

It had been a long night: I'd taken the hard copy to bed and, by 5:00 A.M., had identified more than forty distinct pulse patterns. The signal appeared to be continuous: that is, it had been an ongoing transmission with no indication of beginning or end, but only irregular breaches of the type that would result from atmospherics and, of course, the long periods during which the target would have been below the horizon.

It was clearly a reflected terrestrial transmission: radio waves bounce around considerably. But why seal the error two years later and put it in the safe?

Procyon is a yellow-white class F3 binary, absolute magnitude 2.8, once worshipped in Babylon and Egypt. (What hasn't been worshipped in Egypt?) Distance from Earth: 11.3 light-years.

In the outer office, Beth Cooper typed, closed filing drawers, spoke with visitors.

The obvious course of action was to use the Array. Listen to Procyon at 40 gigahertz, or all across the spectrum for that matter, and find out if it was, indeed, saying something.

On the intercom, I asked Beth if any open time had developed on the system. "No," she said crisply. "We have nothing until August of next year."

That was no surprise. The facility had booked quickly when its resources were made available to the astronomical community on more than the limited basis that had prevailed for twenty years. Anyone wishing to use the radiotelescope had to plan far in advance. How could I get hold of the Array for a couple hours?

I asked her to come into my office.

Beth Cooper had come to Sandage from San Augustin with SETI during the big move twenty years before. She'd been secretary to three directors: Hutching Chaney, who had built Sandage; his longtime friend, Ed Dickinson; and finally, after Dickinson's death, Frank Myers, a young man on the move, who'd stayed too long with the Project, and who'd reportedly been happy to see it strangled. In any case, Myers had contributed to its demise by his failure to defend it.

I'd felt he was right, of course, though for the wrong reason. It had been painful to see the magnificent telescope at Sandage denied, by and large, to the scientific community while its grotesque hunt for the Little Green Man signal went on. I think there were few of us not happy to see it end.

Beth had expected to lose her job. But she knew her way around the facility, had a talent for massaging egos, and could spell. A devout Lutheran, she had adapted cautiously to working for a priest and, oddly, seemed to have taken offense that I did not routinely walk around with a Roman collar.

I asked one or two questions about the billing methods of the local utilities, and then commented, as casually as I could manage, that it was unfortunate the Project had not succeeded.

Beth looked more like a New York librarian than a secretary at a desert installation. Her hair was silver-gray. She wore steel-rimmed glasses on a long silver chain. She was moderately heavy, but her carriage and her diction were impeccable, imbuing her with the quality that stage people call presence.

Her eyes narrowed to hard black beads at my remark. "Dr. Dickinson said any number of times that none of us would live to see results. Everyone attached to the program, even the janitors, knew that." She wasn't a woman given to shrugs, but the sudden flick in those dark eyes matched the effect. "I'm glad Dr. Dickinson didn't live to see it terminated." That was followed by an uncomfortable silence. "I don't blame you, Doctor," she said at length, referring to my public position that the facility was being underutilized.

I dropped my eyes and tried to smile reassuringly. It must have been ludicrous. Her severe features softened. I showed her the envelope.

"Do you recognize the writing?"

She barely glanced at it. "It's Dr. Dickinson's."

"Are you sure? I didn't think Dickinson came to the Project until Hutch Chaney's retirement. That was '13, wasn't it?"

"He took over as Director then. But he was an operating technician under Dr. Chaney for, oh, ten or twelve years before that." Her eyes glowed when she spoke of Dickinson.

"I never met him," I said.

"He was a fine man." She looked past me, over my shoulder, her features pale. "If we hadn't lost him, we might not have lost the Project."

"If it matters," I added gently.

"If it matters."

She was right about Dickinson. He was articulate, a persuasive speaker, author of books on various subjects, and utterly dedicated to SETI. He might well have kept the Project afloat despite the cessation of federal funds and the increasing clamor among his colleagues for more time at the facility. But Dickinson was twelve years dead now. He'd returned to Massachusetts at Christmas, as was his custom. After a snowstorm, he'd gone out to help shovel a neighbor's driveway and his heart had failed.

At the time, I was at Georgetown. I can still recall my sense of a genius who had died too soon. He had possessed a vast talent, but no discipline; he had churned through his career hurling sparks in all directions. He had touched everything, but nothing had ever ignited. Particularly not SETI.

"Beth, was there ever a time they thought they had an LGM?"

"The Little Green Man signal?" She shook her head. "No, I don't think so. They were always picking up echoes and things. But nothing ever came close. Either it was KCOX in Phoenix, or a Japanese trawler in the middle of the Pacific."

"Never anything that didn't fit those categories?"

One eyebrow rose slightly. "Never anything they could prove. If they couldn't pin it down, they went back later and tried to find it again. One way or another, they eliminated everything." Or, she must be thinking, we wouldn't be standing here having this conversation.

Beth's comments implied that suspect signals had been automatically stored. Grateful that I had not yet got around to purging obsolete data, I discovered that was indeed the case, and ran a search covering the entire time period back to the Procyon reception in 2011. I was looking for a similar signal.

I got a surprise.

There was no match. There was also no record of the Procyon reception itself.

That meant presumably it had been accounted for and discarded.

Then why, two years later, had the recordings been sealed and placed in the safe? Surely no explanation would have taken that long.

SETI had assumed that any LGM signal would be a deliberate attempt to communicate, that an effort would therefore be made by the originator to create intelligibility, and that the logical way to do that was to employ a set of symbols representing universal constants: the atomic weight of hydrogen, perhaps, or the value of pi.

But the move to Sandage had also been a move to more sophisticated, and considerably more sensitive, equipment. The possibility developed that the Project would pick up a slopover signal, a transmission of alien origin, but intended only for local receivers. Traffic of that nature could be immeasurably difficult to interpret.

If the packet in the safe was anything at all, it was surely of this latter type. Forty gigahertz is not an ideal frequency for interstellar communication. Moreover, the intercept was ongoing, formless, no numbered parts, nothing to assist translation.

I set the computer working on the text, using SETI's own language analysis program. Then I instructed Brackett to call me if anything developed, had dinner at Jimmy's, and went home.

There was no evidence of structure in the text. In English, one can expect to find a 'U' after a 'Q', or a vowel after a cluster of consonants. The aspirate is seldom doubled, nothing is ever tripled, and so on. But in the Procyon transmission, everything seemed utterly random.

The computer counted 256 distinct pulse patterns. Eight bits. Nothing recurred at sufficient intervals to be a space. And the frequency count of these pulse patterns, or characters, was flat; there was no quantitative difference in use from one to another. All appeared approximately the same number of times. If it was a language, it was a language with no discernible vowels.

I called Wes Phillips, who was then the only linguist I knew. Was it possible for a language to be structured in such a way?

"Oh, I don't think so. Unless you're talking about some sort of construct. Even then—." He paused. "Harry, I can give you a whole series of reasons in maybe six different disciplines why languages need high and low frequency letters. To have a flat 'curve,' a language would have to be deliberately designed that way, and it would have to be non-oral. But what practical value would it have? Why bother?"

Ed Dickinson had been an enigma. During the series of political crises that engulfed the nation after the turn of the century, he'd earned an international reputation as a diplomat, and as an eloquent defender of reason and restraint. Everyone agreed that he had a mind of the first rank. Yet, in his chosen field, he accomplished little. And eventually he'd gone to work for the Project, historically only a stepping-stone to serious effort. But he'd stayed.

Why?

Hutching Chaney was a different matter. A retired naval officer, he'd indulged in physics almost as a pastime. His political connections had been instrumental in getting Sandage built, and his assignment as Director was rumored to have been a reward for services rendered during the rough and tumble of congressional politics.

He possessed a plodding sort of competence. He was fully capable of grasping, and visualizing, extreme complexity. But he lacked insight and imagination, the ability to draw the subtle inference. After his retirement from Sandage, Chaney had gone to an emeritus position at MIT, which he'd held for five years.

He was a big man, more truck driver than physicist. Despite advancing age—he was then in his 70's—and his bulk, he spoke and moved with energy. His hair was full and black. His light gray eyes suggested the shrewdness of a professional politician, and he possessed the confident congeniality of a man who had never failed at anything.

We were in his home in Somerville, Massachusetts, a stone and glass house atop sweeping lawns. It was not an establishment that a retired physicist would be expected to inhabit. Chaney's moneyed background was evident.

He clapped a big hand on my shoulder and pulled me through one of those stiff, expensive living rooms that no one ever wants to sit in, into a paneled, leather-upholstered den at the rear of the house. "Martha," he said to someone I couldn't see, "would you bring us some port?" He looked at me for acquiescence.

"Fine," I said. "It's been a long time, Hutch."

Books lined the walls, mostly engineering manuals, a few military and naval histories. An articulated steel gray model of the Lance dominated the fireplace shelf. That was the deadly hydrofoil which, built at Chaney's urging, had contributed to a multi-purpose navy that was simultaneously lethal, flexible, and relatively cheap.

"The Church is infiltrating everywhere," he said. "How are things at Sandage, Harry?"

I described some of the work in progress. He listened with interest.

A young woman arrived with a bottle, two glasses, and a plate of cheese. "Martha comes in three times a week," Chaney said after she'd left the room. He smiled, winked, dipped a stick of cheese into the mustard, and bit it neatly in half. "You needn't worry, Harry. I'm not capable of getting into trouble anymore. What brings you to Massachusetts?"

I extracted the vocordings from my briefcase and handed them across to him. I watched patiently as he leafed through the thick sheaf of paper, and saw with satisfaction his change of expression.

"You're kidding, Harry," he said. "Somebody really found one? When'd it happen?"

"Twenty years ago," I said, passing him the envelope and the original disks.

He turned them over in his hands. "You're not serious? There's a mistake somewhere."

"It was in the safe," I said.

He shook his head. "Doesn't much matter where it was. Nothing like this ever happened."

"Then what is it?"

"Damned if I have any idea."

We sat not talking while Chaney continued to flip pages, grunting. He seemed to have forgotten his wine. "You run this yourself?" he asked.

I nodded.

"Hell of a lot of trouble for somebody to go to for a joke. Were the computers able to read any of it? No? That's because it's gibberish." He stared at the envelope. "But it is Ed's handwriting."

"Would Dickinson have any reason to keep such a thing quiet?"

"Ed? No. Dickinson least of all. No one wanted to hear a signal more than he did. He wanted it so badly he invested his life in the Project."

"But could he, physically, have done this? Could he have picked up the LGM? Could he have done it without anyone else knowing? Was he good enough with computers to cover his tracks?"

"This is pointless. Yes, he could have done it. And you could walk through Braintree without your pants."

A light breeze was coming through a side window, billowing the curtains. It was cool and pleasant, unusual for Massachusetts in August. Some kids were playing halfball out on the street.

"Forty megahertz," he said. "Sounds like a satellite transmission."

"That wouldn't have taken two years to figure out, would it? Why keep the disks?"

"Why not? I expect if you go down into the storeroom you'll find all kinds of relics."

Outside, there was a sound like approaching thunder, exploding suddenly into an earsplitting screech. A stripped-down T-Bolt skidded by, scattering the ballplayers. An arm hung leisurely out the driver's side. The car took the corner stop sign at about 45. A couple of fingers went up, but otherwise the game resumed as though nothing had happened.

"All the time," Chaney said. His back to the window, he hadn't bothered to look around. "Cops can't keep up with them anymore."

"Why was Dickinson so interested in the Project?"

"Ed was a great man." His face clouded somewhat, and I wondered if the port hadn't drawn his emotions close to the surface. "You'd have to know him. You and he would have got along fine. He had a taste for the metaphysical, and I guess the Project was about as close as he could get."

"How do you mean?"

"Did you know he spent two years in a seminary? Yes, somewhere outside Philadelphia. He was an altar boy who eventually wound up at Harvard. And that was that."

"You mean he lost his faith?"

"Oh, yes. The world became a dark place, full of disaster. He always seemed to have the details on the latest pogrom, or viral outbreak, or drive-by murder. There are only two kinds of people, he told me once: atheists, and folks who haven't been paying attention. But he always retained that fine mystical sense of purpose that you drill into your best kids, a notion that things are somehow ordered. When I knew him, he wouldn't have presumed to pray to anyone. But he had all the drive of a missionary, and the same conviction of—." He dropped his head back on the leather upholstery and tried to seize a word from the ceiling. —Destiny.

"Ed wasn't like most physicists. He was competent in a wide range of areas. He wrote on foreign affairs for *Commentary* and *Harper's*; he wrote on ornithology and systems analysis, on Malcolm Muggeridge, and Edward Gibbon."

He swung easily out of his chair and reached for a pair of fat matched volumes in mud-brown covers. It was *The Decline and Fall of the Roman Empire*, the old Modern Library edition. "He's the only person I've ever known who's actually read the thing." He turned the cover of volume one so that I could see the inscription:

For Hutch,
In the fond hope that we can hold off the potherbs and the pigs.
Ed

"He gave it to me when I left SETI."

"Seems like an odd gift. Have you read it?"

He laughed off the question. "You'd need a year."

"What's the business about the potherbs and pigs?"

He rose and walked casually to the far wall. There were photos of naval vessels and aircraft, of Chaney and President Fine, of the Sandage complex. He seemed to screw his vision into the latter. "I don't remember. It's a phrase from the book. He explained it to me at the time. But...." He held his hands outward, palms up.

"Hutch, thanks." I got up to go.

"There was no signal," he said. "I don't know where these recordings came from, but Ed Dickinson would have given anything for a contact."

"Hutch, is it possible that Dickinson might have been able to translate the text? If there had been one?"

"Not if you couldn't. He had the same program."

I don't like cities.

Dickinson's books were all out of print, and the used bookstores were clustered in Cambridge. Even then, the outskirts of Boston, like the city proper, were littered with broken glass and discarded newspapers. Surly kids milled outside bars. Windows everywhere were smashed or boarded. I went through a red light at one intersection rather than learn the intentions of an approaching band of ragged children with hard eyes. (One could scarcely call them children, though I doubt there was one over twelve.) Profanity covered the crumbling brick walls as high as a hand could reach. Much of it was misspelled.

Boston had been Dickinson's city. I wondered what the great humanist thought when he drove through these streets.

I found only one of his books: *Malcolm Muggeridge: Faith and Despair*. The store also had a copy of *The Decline and Fall*. On impulse, I bought it.

I was glad to get back to the desert.

We were entering a period of extraordinary progress, during which we finally began to understand the mechanics of galactic structure. McCue mapped the core of the Milky Way, Osterberger developed his unified field concepts, and Schauer constructed his celebrated revolutionary hypothesis on the nature of time. Then, on a cool morning in October, a team from Cal Tech announced that they had a new set of values for hyperinflation.

In the midst of all this, we had an emergency. One night in late September, Earl Barlow, who was directing the Cal Tech groups, suffered a mild heart attack. I arrived just before the EMT's, at about 2:00 a.m.

While the ambulance carrying Barlow started down the mountain, his people watched helplessly, drinking coffee, too upset to work. The opportunity didn't catch me entirely unprepared. I gave Brackett his new target. The blinking lights of the emergency vehicle were hardly out of sight before the parabolas swung round and fastened on Procyon.

But there was only the disjointed crackle of interstellar static.

I took long walks on the desert at night. The parabolas are lovely in the moonlight. Occasionally, the stillness is broken by the whine of an electric motor, and the antennas slide gracefully along their tracks. It was, I thought, a new Stonehenge of softly curving shapes and fluid motion.

The Muggeridge book was a slim volume. It was not biographical, but rather an analysis of the philosopher's conviction that the West has a death wish. It was the old argument that God had been replaced by science, that man had gained knowledge of a trivial sort, and as a result lost purpose.

It was, on the whole, depressing reading. In his conclusion, Dickinson argued that truth will not wait on human convenience, that if man cannot adapt to a neutral universe, then that universe will indeed come to seem hostile. We must make do with what we have and accept truth wherever it leads. The modern cathedral is the radiotelescope.

Sandage was involved in the verification procedure for McCue's work, and for the already controversial Cal Tech equations. All that is another story. What is significant is that it got me thinking about verifications, and I realized I'd overlooked something. There'd been no match for the Procyon readings anywhere in the data banks since the original reception. But the Procyon recordings might themselves have been the confirmation of an earlier signal!

It took five minutes to run the search. There were two hits.

Both were fragments, neither more than fifteen minutes long; but there was enough of each to reduce the probability of error to less than one percent.

The first occurred three weeks prior to the Procyon reception.

The second went back to 2007, a San Augustin observation. Both were at 40 gigahertz. Both had identical pulse patterns. But there was an explosive difference, sedately concealed in the target information line. The 2007 transmission had come while the radiotelescope was locked on Sirius!

When I got back to my office, I was trembling.

Sirius and Procyon were only a few light-years apart. My God, I kept thinking, they exist! And they have interstellar travel!

I spent the balance of the day stumbling around, trying to immerse myself in fuel usage reports and budget projections. But mostly what I did was watch the desert light grow hard in the curtains, and then fade. The two volumes of Edward Gibbon were propped between a *Webster's* and some black binders. The books were thirty years old, identical to the set in Chaney's den. Some of the pages, improperly cut, were still joined at the edges.

I opened the first volume, approximately in the middle, and began to read. Or tried to. But Ed Dickinson kept crowding out the Romans. Finally I gave it up, took the book, and went home.

There was duplicate bridge in town, and I lost myself in that for five hours. Then, in bed, still somewhat dazed, I tried *The Decline and Fall* again.

It was not the dusty roll call of long-dead emperors that I had expected. The emperors are there, stabbing and throttling and blundering. And occasionally trying to improve things. But the fish-hawkers are there too. And the bureaucrats and the bishops.

It's a world filled with wine and legionnaires' sweat, mismanagement, arguments over Jesus, and the inability to transfer power, all played out to the ruthless drumbeat of dissolution. An undefined historical tide, stemmed occasionally by a hero, or a sage, rolls over men and events, washing them toward the sea. (During the later years, I wondered, did Roman kids run down matrons in flashy imported chariots? Were the walls of Damascus defiled by profanity?)

In the end, when the barbarians push at the outer rim of empire, it is only a hollow wreck that crashes down.

Muggeridge had been there.

And Dickinson, the altar boy, amid the fire and waste of the imperial city, must have suffered a second loss of faith.

We had an electrical failure one night. It has nothing to do with this story except that it resulted in my being called in at 4:00 a.m., not to restore the power, which required a good electrician, but to pacify some angry people from New York, and to be able to say, in my report, that I had been on the spot.

These things attended to, I went outside.

At night, the desert is undisturbed by color or motion. It's a composition of sand, rock, and star; a frieze, a Monet, uncomplicated, unchanging. It's re-assuring, in an age when little else seems stable. The orderly mid-twentieth century universe had long since disintegrated into a plethora of neutron galaxies, colliding black holes, time reversals, and God knows what.

The desert is solid underfoot. Predictable. A reproach to the quantum mechanics that reflect a quicksand cosmos in which physics merges with Plato.

Close on the rim of the sky, guarding their mysteries, Sirius and Procyon, the bright pair, sparkled. The arroyos are dry at that time of year, shadowy ripples in the landscape. The moon was in its second quarter. Beyond the administration building, the parabolas were limned in silver.

My cathedral.

My Stonehenge.

And while I sat, sipping a Coors, and thinking of lost cities and altar boys and frequency counts, I suddenly understood the significance of Chaney's last remark! Of course Dickinson had not been able to read the transmission. That was the point!

I needed Chaney.

I called him in the morning, and flew out in the afternoon. He met me at Logan, and we drove toward Gloucester. "There's a good Italian restaurant," he said. And then, without taking his eyes off the road: "What's this about?"

I'd brought the second Gibbon volume with me, and I held it up for him to see. He blinked.

It was early evening, cold, wet, with the smell of approaching winter. Freezing rain pelted the windshield. The sky was gray, heavy, sagging into the city.

"Before I answer any questions, Hutch, I'd like to ask a couple. What can you tell me about military cryptography?"

He grinned. "Not much. The little I do know is probably classified." A tractor-trailer lumbered past, straining, spraying water across the windows. "What, specifically, are you interested in?"

"How complex are the Navy's codes? I know they're nothing like cryptograms, but what sort of general structure do they have?"

"First off, Harry, they're not codes. Monoalphabetic systems are codes. Like the cryptograms you mentioned. The letter 'G' always turns up, say, as an 'M'. But in military and diplomatic cryptography, the 'G' will be a different character every time it appears. And the encryption alphabet isn't usually limited to letters; we use numbers, dollar signs, ampersands, even spaces." We splashed onto a ramp and joined the Interstate. It was elevated and we looked across rows of bleak rooftops. "Even the shape of individual words is concealed."

"How?"

"By encrypting the spaces."

I knew the answer to the next question before I asked it. "If the encryption alphabet is absolutely random, which I assume it would have to be, the frequency count would be flat. Right?"

"Yes. Given sufficient traffic, it would have to be."

"One more thing, Hutch. A sudden increase in traffic will alert anyone listening that something is happening even if he can't read the text. How do you hide that?"

"Easy. We transmit a continuous signal, twenty-four hours a day. Sometimes it's traffic, sometimes it's garbage. But you can't tell the difference."

God have mercy on us, I thought. Poor Dickinson.

We sat at a small corner table well away from the main dining area. I shivered in wet shoes and a damp sweater. A small candle guttered cheerfully in front of us.

"Are we still talking about Procyon?" he asked.

I nodded. "The same pattern was received twice, three years apart, prior to the Procyon reception."

"But that's not possible." Chaney leaned forward intently. "The computer would have matched them automatically. We'd have known."

"I don't think so." Half a dozen prosperous, overweight men in topcoats had pushed in and were jostling each other in the small entry. "The two hits were on different targets. They would have looked like an echo."

Chaney reached across the table and gripped my wrist, knocking over a cup. "Son of a bitch," he said. "Are you suggesting somebody's moving around out there?"

"I don't think Ed Dickinson had any doubts."

"Why would he keep it secret?"

I'd placed the book on the table at my left hand. It rested there, its plastic cover reflecting the glittering red light of the candle. "Because they're at war."

The color drained from Chaney's face, and it took on a pallor that was almost ghastly in the lurid light.

"He believed," I continued, "he really believed that mind equates to morality, intelligence to compassion. And what did he find after a lifetime? A civilization that had conquered the stars, but not its own passions and stupidities."

A tall young waiter presented himself. We ordered port and pasta.

"You don't really know there's a war going on out there," Chaney objected.

"Hostility, then. Secrecy on a massive scale, as this must be, has ominous implications. Dickinson would have saved us all with a vision of order and reason...."

The gray eyes met mine. They were filled with pain. Two adolescent girls in the next booth were giggling. The wine came.

"What has the *Decline and Fall* to do with it?"

"It became his Bible. He was chilled to the bone by it. *You* should read it, but with caution. It's capable of strangling the soul. Dickinson was a rationalist. He recognized the ultimate truth in the Roman tragedy: that once expansion has stopped, decay is constant and irreversible. Every failure of reason or virtue loses more ground.

"I haven't been able to find his book on Gibbon, but I know what he'll say: that Gibbon was not writing only of the Romans, nor of the British of his own time. He was writing about us. Hutch, take a look around. Tell

39

me we're not sliding toward a dark age. Think how that knowledge must have affected him."

We drank silently for a few minutes. Time locked in place, and we sat unmoving, the world frozen around us.

"Did I tell you," I said at last, "that I found the reference for his inscription? He must have had great respect for you." I opened the book to the conclusion, and turned it for him to read:

The forum of the Roman people, where they assembled to enact their laws, and elect their magistrates, is now enclosed for the cultivation of potherbs, or thrown open for the reception of swine and buffaloes.

Chaney stared disconsolately at me. "It's all so hard to believe."

"A man can survive a loss of faith in the Almighty," I said, "provided he does not also lose faith in himself. That was Dickinson's real tragedy. He came to believe exclusively in radiotelescopes, the way some people do in religions."

The food, when it came, went untasted. "What are you going to do, Harry?"

"About the Procyon text? About the probability that we have quarrelsome neighbors? I'm not afraid of that kind of information; all it means is that where you find intelligence, you will probably find stupidity. Anyway, it's time Dickinson got credit for his discovery." And, I thought, maybe it'll even mean a footnote for me.

I lifted my glass in a mock toast, but Chaney did not respond. We faced each other in an uncomfortable tableau. "What's wrong?" I asked. "Thinking about Dickinson?"

"That too." The candle glinted in his eyes. "Harry, do you think *they* have a SETI project?"

"Possibly. Why?"

"I was wondering if your aliens know we're here. This restaurant isn't much further from Sirius than Procyon is. Maybe you better eat up."

THE FORT MOXIE BRANCH

A few minutes into the blackout, the window in the single dormer at the top of Will Potter's house began to glow. I watched it from across Route 11, through a screen of box elders, and through the snow which had been falling all afternoon and was now getting heavier. It was smeary and insubstantial, not the way a bedroom light would look, but as though something luminous floated in the dark interior.

Will Potter was dead. We'd put him in the graveyard on the other side of the expressway three years before. The property had lain empty since, a two-story frame dating from about the turn of the century.

The town had gone quiet with the blackout. Somewhere a dog barked, and a garage door banged down. Ed Kiernan's station wagon rumbled past, headed out toward Cavalier. The streetlights were out, as was the traffic signal down at Twelfth.

As far as I was concerned, the power could have stayed off.

It was trash night. I was hauling out cartons filled with copies of *Independence Square*, and I was on my way down the outside staircase when everything had gone dark.

The really odd thing about the light over at Potter's was that it seemed to be spreading. It had crept outside: the dormer began to burn with a steady, cold, blue-white flame. It flowed gradually down the slope of the roof, slipped over the drainpipe, and turned the corner of the porch. Just barely, in the illumination, I could make out the skewed screens and broken stone steps.

It would have taken something unusual to get my attention that night. I was piling the boxes atop one another, and some of the books had spilled into the street: my name glittered on the bindings. It was a big piece of my life. Five years and a quarter million words and, in the end, most of

41

my life's savings to get it printed. It had been painful, and I was glad to be rid of it.

So I was standing on the curb, feeling sorry for myself while snow whispered out of a sagging sky.

The Tastee-Freez, Hal's Lumber, the Amoco at the corner of Nineteenth and Bannister, were all dark and silent. Toward the center of town, blinkers and headlights misted in the storm.

It was a still, somehow motionless, night. The flakes were blue in the pale glow surrounding the house. They fell onto the gabled roof and spilled gently off the back.

Cass Taylor's station wagon plowed past, headed out of town. He waved.

I barely noticed: the back end of Potter's house had begun to balloon out. I watched it, fascinated, knowing it to be an illusion, yet still half-expecting it to explode.

The house began to change in other ways.

Roof and corner lines wavered. New walls dropped into place. The dormer suddenly ascended, and the top of the house with it. A third floor, complete with lighted windows and a garret, appeared out of the snow. In one of the illuminated rooms, someone moved.

Parapets rose, and an oculus formed in the center of the garret. A bay window pushed out of the lower level, near the front. An arch and portico replaced the porch. Spruce trees materialized, and Potter's old post light, which had never worked, blinked on.

The box elders were bleak and stark in the foreground.

I stood, worrying about my eyesight, holding onto a carton, feeling the snow against my face and throat. Nothing moved on Route 11.

I was still standing there when the power returned: the streetlights, the electric sign over Hal's office, the security lights at the Amoco, gunshots from a TV, the sudden inexplicable rasp of an electric drill. And, at the same moment, the apparition clicked off.

I could have gone to bed. I could have hauled out the rest of those goddamned books, attributed everything to my imagination, and gone to bed. I'm glad I didn't.

The snow cover in Potter's backyard was undisturbed. It was more than a foot deep beneath the half-inch or so that had fallen that day. I struggled through it to find the key he'd always kept wedged beneath a loose hasp near the cellar stairs.

I used it to let myself in through the storage room at the rear of the house. And I should admit that I had a bad moment when the door shut behind me, and I stood among the rakes and shovels and boxes of nails. Too many late TV movies. Too much Stephen King.

I'd been here before. Years earlier, when I'd thought that teaching would support me until I was able to earn a living as a novelist, I'd picked up some extra money by tutoring Potter's boys. But that was a long time ago.

I'd brought a flashlight with me. I turned it on, and pushed through into the kitchen. It was warmer in there, but that was to be expected. Potter's heirs were still trying to sell the place, and it gets too cold in North Dakota to simply shut off the heat altogether.

Cabinets were open and bare; the range had been disconnected from its gas mooring and dragged into the center of the room. A church calendar hung behind a door. It displayed March 1986: the month of Potter's death.

In the dining room, a battered table and three wooden chairs were pushed against one wall. A couple of boxes lay in a corner.

With a bang, the heater came on.

I was startled. A fan cut in, and warm air rushed across my ankles.

I took a deep breath and played the beam toward the living room. I was thinking how different a house looks without its furnishings, how utterly strange and unfamiliar, when I realized I wasn't alone. Whether it was a movement outside the circle of light, or a sudden indrawn breath, or the creak of a board, I couldn't have said. But I *knew*. "Who's there?" I asked. The words hung in the dark.

"Mr. Wickham?" It was a woman.

"Hello," I said. "I, uh, I saw lights and thought—"

"Of course." She was standing back near the kitchen, silhouetted against outside light. I wondered how she could have got there. "You were correct to be concerned. But it's quite all right." She was somewhat on the gray side of middle age, attractive, well-pressed, the sort you would expect to encounter at a bridge party. Her eyes, which were on a level with mine, watched me with good humor. "My name is Coela." She extended her right hand. Gold bracelets clinked.

"I'm happy to meet you," I tried to look as though nothing unusual had occurred. "How did you know my name?"

She touched my hand, the one holding the flashlight, and pushed it gently aside so she could pass. "Please follow me," she said. "Be careful. Don't fall over anything."

We climbed the stairs to the second floor, and went into the rear bedroom. "Through here," she said, opening a door that should have revealed a closet. Instead, I was looking into a brightly illuminated space that couldn't possibly be there. It was filled with books, paintings, and tapestries, leather furniture, and polished tables. A fireplace crackled cheerfully beneath a portrait of a monk. A piano played softly. Chopin, I thought.

"This room won't fit," I said, stupidly. The thick quality of my voice startled me.

"No," she agreed. "We're attached to the property, but we're quite independent." We stepped inside. Carpets were thick underfoot. Where the floors were exposed, they were lustrous parquet. Vaulted windows looked out over Potter's backyard, and Em Pyle's house next door. Coela watched me thoughtfully. "Welcome, Mr. Wickham," she said. Her eyes glittered with pride. "Welcome to the Fort Moxie branch of the John of Singletary Memorial Library."

I looked around for a chair and, finding one near a window, lowered myself into it. The falling snow was dark, as though no illumination from within the glass touched it. "I don't think I understand this," I said.

"I suppose it is something of a shock."

Her amusement was obvious, and sufficiently infectious that I loosened up somewhat. "Are you the librarian?"

She nodded.

"Nobody in Fort Moxie knows you're here. What good is a library no one knows about?"

"That's a valid question," she admitted. "We have a limited membership."

I glanced around. All the books looked liked Bibles. They were different sizes and shapes, but all were bound in leather. Furthermore, titles and authors were printed in identical silver script. But I saw nothing in English. The shelves near me were packed with books whose lettering appeared to be Russian. A volume lay open on a table at my right hand. It was in Latin. I picked it up and held it so I could read the title: *Historiae, V–XII.* Tacitus. "Okay," I said. "It *must* be limited. Hardly anybody in Fort Moxie reads Latin or Russian." I held up the Tacitus. "I doubt even Father Cramer could handle this."

Em Pyle, the next door neighbor, had come out onto his front steps. He called his dog, Preach, as he did most nights at this time. There was no response, and he looked up and down Nineteenth Street, into his own backyard, and *right through me*. I couldn't believe he didn't react.

"Coela, who are you exactly? What's going on here?"

She nodded, in the way that people do when they agree that you have a problem. "Perhaps," she said, "you should look around, Mr. Wickham. Then it might be easier to talk."

She retired to a desk, and immersed herself in a sheaf of papers, leaving me to fend for myself.

Beyond the Russian shelves, I found Japanese or Chinese titles. I couldn't tell which. And Arabic. And German. French. Greek. More Oriental.

English titles were in the rear. They were divided into American and British sections. Dickens, Cowper, and Shakespeare on one side; Holmes, Dreiser, and Steinbeck on the other.

And almost immediately, the sense of apprehension that had hung over me from the beginning of this business sharpened. I didn't know why. Certainly, the familiar names in a familiar setting should have eased my disquiet.

I picked up Melville's *Agatha* and flipped through the pages. They had the texture of fine rice paper, and the leather binding lent a sense of timelessness to the book. I thought about the cheap cardboard that Crossbow had provided for *Independence Square*. My God, this was the way to get published.

Immediately beside it was *The Complete Works of James McCorbin*. Who the hell was James McCorbin? There were two novels and eight short stories. None of the titles was familiar, and the book contained no biographical information.

In fact, most of the writers were people I'd never heard of. Kemerie Baxter. Wynn Gomez. Michael Kaspar. There was nothing unusual about that, of course. Library shelves are always filled with obscure authors. But the lush binding, and the obvious care expended on these books, changed the rules.

I took down Hemingway's *Watch by Night*. I stared a long time at the title. The prose was vintage Hemingway. The crisp, clear bullet sentences and the factual, journalistic style were unmistakable. Even the setting: Italy, 1944.

Henry James was represented by *Brandenberg*. There was no sign of *The Ambassadors*, or *The Portrait of a Lady*, or *Washington Square*. In fact, there was neither *Moby Dick*, nor *Billy Budd*. Nor *The Sun Also Rises* nor *A Farewell to Arms*. Thoreau wasn't represented at all. I saw no sign of Fenimore Cooper or Mark Twain. (What kind of library had no copy of *Huck Finn*?)

I carried *Watch by Night* back to the desk where Coela was working. "This is *not* a Hemingway book," I said, lobbing it onto the pile of papers in front of her. She winced. "The rest of them are bogus too. What the hell's going on?"

"I can understand that you might be a little confused, Mr. Wickham," she said, a trifle nervously. "I'm never sure quite how to explain."

"Please try your best," I said.

She frowned. "I'm part of a cultural salvage group. We try to ensure that things of permanent value don't, ah, get lost."

She pushed her chair back, and gazed steadily at me. Somewhere in back, a clock ticked ponderously. "The book you picked up when you first came in was—" she paused, "—mislaid almost two thousand years ago."

"The Tacitus?"

"The *Histories Five Through Twelve*. We also have his *Annals*."

"Who *are* you?"

She shook her head. "A kindred spirit," she said.

"Seriously."

"I'm being quite serious, Mr. Wickham. What you see around you is a treasure of incomparable value that, without our efforts, would no longer exist."

We stared at each other for a few moments. "Are you saying," I asked, "that these are all lost masterpieces by people like Tacitus? That *this*"—I pointed at *Watch by Night*—"is a bona fide Hemingway?"

"Yes," she said.

We faced one another across the desktop. "There's a Melville back there too. And a Thomas Wolfe."

"*Yes.*" Her eyes were bright with pleasure. "*All of them.*"

I took another long look around. Thousands of volumes filled the shelves, packed tight, reaching to the ceiling. Others were stacked on tables; a few were tossed almost haphazardly on chairs. Half a dozen stood between Trojan horse bookends on Coela's desk.

"It's not possible," I said, finding the air suddenly close and oppressive. "How? How could it happen?"

"Quite easily," she said. "Melville, as a case in point, became discouraged. He was a customs inspector at the time *Agatha* first came to our attention. I went all the way to London, specifically to allow him to examine my baggage on the way back. In 1875, that was no easy journey, I can assure you." She waved off my objection. "Well, that's an exaggeration, of course. I took advantage of the trip to conduct some business with Matthew Arnold and—Well: I'm name-dropping now. Forgive me. But think about having Melville go through your luggage." Her laughter echoed through the room. "I was quite young. Too young to understand his work, really. But I'd read *Moby Dick*, and some of his poetry. If I'd known him then the way I do now, I don't think I could have kept my feet." She bit her lower lip and shook her head, and for a moment I thought she might indeed pass out.

"And he *gave* you the manuscript? Simply because you asked for it?"

"No. Because I knew it for what it was. And he understood why I wanted it."

"And why do you want it? You have buried it here."

She ignored the question.

"You never asked about the library's name."

"The John of—"

"—Singletary—"

"—Memorial. Okay. Who's John of Singletary?"

"That's his portrait, facing the main entrance." It was a large oil of an introspective monk. His hands were buried in dark brown robes, and he was flanked by a scroll and a crucifix. "He was perhaps the most brilliant sociologist who ever lived."

"I never heard of him."

"That's no surprise. His work was eventually ruled profane by his superiors, and either burned or stored away somewhere. We've never been sure. But we were able to obtain copies of most of it." She was out of her seat now, standing with her back to the portrait. "What is significant is that he defined the state toward which he felt the human community should be advancing. He set the parameters and the goals for which the men and women whose works populate this library have been striving: the precise degree of balance between order and freedom; the extent of one's obligation to external authority; the ethical and emotional relationships that should exist between human beings. And so on. Taken in all, he produced a schematic for civilized life, a set of instructions, if you will."

"The human condition," I said.

"How do you mean?"

"He did all this, and no one knows him."

"*We* know him, Mr. Wickham." She paused. I found myself glancing from her to the solemn figure in the portrait. "You asked why we wanted *Agatha*. The answer is that it is lovely, that it is very powerful. We simply will not allow it to be lost."

"But who will ever get to see it *here?* You're talking about a novel that, as far as anyone is concerned, doesn't exist. I have a friend in North Carolina who'd give every nickel he owns to see this book. If it's legitimate."

"We *will* make it available. In time. This library will eventually be yours."

A wave of exhilaration washed over me. "Thank you," I said.

"I'm sorry," she said quickly. "That may have been misleading. I didn't mean right now. And I didn't mean *you*."

"When?"

"When the human race fulfills the requirements of John of Singletary. When you have, in other words, achieved a true global community, all of this will be our gift to you."

A gust of wind rattled the windows.

"That's a considerable way off," I said.

"We must take the long view."

"Easy for you to say. We have a lot of problems. Some of this might be just what we need to get through."

"This was once *yours*, Mr. Wickham. Your people have not always recognized value. We are providing a second chance. I'd expect you to be grateful."

I turned away from her. "Most of this baffles me," I said. "Who's James McCorbin? You've got his *Complete Works* back there with Melville and the others. Who *is* he?"

"A master of the short story. One of your contemporaries, but I'm afraid he writes in a style and with a complexity that will go unappreciated during his lifetime."

"You're telling me he's *too* good to get published?" I was aghast.

"Oh, yes, Mr. Wickham, you live in an exceedingly commercial era. Your editors understand that they cannot sell champagne to beer drinkers. They buy what sells."

"And that's also true of the others? Kemerie Baxter? Gomez? Parker?"

"I'm afraid so. It's quite common, in fact. Baxter is an essayist of the first order. Unlike the other two, he has been published, but by a small university press, in an edition that sank quickly out of sight. Gomez has written three exquisite novels, but has since given up, despite our encouragement.

Parker is a poet. If you know anything about the markets for poetry, I need say no more."

●

We wandered together through the library. She pointed to lost works by Sophocles and Aeschylus, to missing epics of the Homeric cycle, to shelves full of Indian poetry and Roman drama. "On the upper level," she said, raising her eyes to the ceiling, "are the songs and tales of artists whose native tongues had no written form. They have been translated into our own language. In most cases we were able to preserve their creators' names.

"And now I have a surprise." We had reached the British section. She took down a book and handed it to me. William Shakespeare. "His *Zenobia*," she said, her voice hushed. "Written at the height of his career."

I was silent for a time. "And why was it never performed?"

"Because it's a savage attack on Elizabeth. Even he might well have lost his head. We have a major epic by Virgil that was withheld for much the same reason. In fact, that's why the Russian section is so large. They've been producing magnificent novels in the tradition of Tolstoy and Dostoyevski for years, but they're far too prudent to offer them for publication."

There were two other Shakespearean plays. "*Adam and Eve* was heretical by the standards of the day," Coela explained. "And here's another that would have raised a few eyebrows." She smiled.

It was *Nisus and Euryalus*. The characters were out of the *Aeneid*. "Homosexual love," she said.

"But he wanted these withheld," I objected. "There's a difference between works that have been lost, and those a writer wishes to destroy. You published these against his will."

"Oh, no, Mr. Wickham. We never do that. To begin with, if Shakespeare had wanted these plays destroyed, he could have handled that detail quite easily. He desired only that they not be published in his lifetime. Everything you see here," she included the entire library with a sweeping, feminine gesture, "was given to us voluntarily. We have very strict regulations on that score. And we do things strictly by the book.

"In some cases, by the way, we perform an additional service. We are able, in a small way, to reassure those great artists who have not been properly recognized in their own lifetimes. I wish you could have seen Melville."

"You could be wrong, you know."

Her nostrils widened slightly. "About what?"

"Maybe books that get lost deserve to be lost."

"Some do." Her tone hardened. "None of those is here. We exercise full editorial judgment."

"We close at midnight," she said, appearing suddenly behind me while I was absorbed in the Wells novel, *Starflight*. I could read the implication in her tone: *Never to open again. Not in Fort Moxie. Not for you.*

I returned Wells and moved quickly along, pulling books from the shelves with a sense of urgency. I glanced through *Mendinhal*, an unfinished epic by Byron, dated 1824, the year of his death. I caught individually brilliant lines, and tried to commit some of them to memory, and proceeded on to Blake, to Fielding, to Chaucer! At a little after eleven, I came across four Conan Doyle stories: "The Adventure of the Grim Footman"; "The Branmoor Club"; "The Jezail Bullet"; "The Sumatran Clipper." My God, what would the Sherlockians of the world not give to have those?

I hurried on with increasing desperation, as though I could somehow gather the contents into myself, and make them available to a waiting world: *God and Country*, by Thomas Wolfe; fresh cartoons by James Thurber, recovered from beneath wallpaper in a vacation home he'd rented in Atlantic City in 1947; plays by Odets and O'Neill; short stories by Nathaniel Hawthorne and Terry Carr. Here was *More Dangerous Visions*. And there Mary Shelley's *Morgan*.

As I whirled through the rice-paper pages, balancing the eerie moonlit lines of A. E. Housman with the calibrated shafts of Mencken, I envied them. Envied them all.

And I was angry.

"You have no right," I said at last, when Coela came to stand by my side, indicating that my time was up.

"No right to withhold all this?" There was a note of sympathy in her voice.

"Not only that," I said. "Who are you to set yourself up to make such judgments? To say what is great and what pedestrian?"

To my surprise, she did not take offense. "I've asked myself that question many times. We do the best we can." We were moving toward the door. "We have quite a lot of experience, you understand."

The lights dimmed. "Why are you *really* doing this? It's not for us, is it?"

"Not exclusively. What your species produces belongs to all." Her smile broadened. "Surely you would not wish to keep your finest creations to yourselves?"

"Your people have access to them now?"

"Oh, yes," she said. "Back home everyone has access. As soon as a new book is cataloged here, it is made available to everybody."

"Except us."

"We will not do everything for you, Mr. Wickham." She drew close, and I could almost feel her heartbeat.

"Do you have any idea what it would mean to our people to recover all this?"

"I'm sorry. For the moment, there's really nothing I can do."

She opened the door for me, the one that led into the back bedroom. I stepped through it. She followed. "Use your flashlight," she said.

We walked through the long hallway and down the stairs to the living room. She had something to say to me, but seemed strangely reluctant to continue the conversation. And somewhere in the darkness of Will Potter's place, between the magic doorway in the back of the upstairs closet, and the broken stone steps off the porch, I understood! And when we paused on the concrete beside the darkened post light, and turned to face each other, my pulse was pounding. "It's no accident that this place became visible tonight, is it?"

She said nothing.

"Nor that only I saw it. I mean, there wouldn't be a point to putting your universal library in Fort Moxie unless you wanted something. Right?"

"I said this was the Fort Moxie *branch*. The central library is located on Saint Simons Island." The brittleness of the last few moments melted without warning. "But no, you're right, of course."

"You want *Independence Square*, don't you? You want to put my book in there with Thomas Wolfe and Shakespeare and Homer. Right?"

"Yes," she said. "That's right. You've created a powerful psychological drama, Mr. Wickham. You've captured the microcosm of Fort Moxie and produced a portrait of small town America that has captured the imagination of the Board. And, I might add, of our membership. You will be interested, by the way, in knowing that one of your major characters caused the blackout tonight."

"Jack Gilbert," I said. "How'd it happen?"

"Can you guess?"

"An argument with his wife, somehow or other." Gilbert, who had a different name, of course, in *Independence Square*, had a long history of inept philandering.

"Yes. Afterward, he took the pickup and ran it into the streetlight at Eleventh and Foster. Shorted out everything over an area of forty square blocks. It's right out of the book."

"Yes," I said.

"But he'll never know he's in it. Nor will any of the other people you've immortalized. Only you know. And only you would *ever* know, were it not for us." She stood facing me. The snow had stopped, and the clouds had cleared away. The stars were hard and bright in her eyes. "We think it unlikely that you will be recognized in your own lifetime. We could be wrong. We were wrong about Faulkner." Her lips crinkled into a smile. "But it is my honor to invite you to contribute your work to the library."

I froze. It was really happening. Emerson. Hemingway. Wickham. I loved it. And yet, there was something terribly wrong about it all. "Coela," I asked. "Have you ever been refused?"

"Yes," she said cautiously. "Occasionally it happens. We couldn't convince Cather of the value of *Ogden's Bequest*. Charlotte and Emily Bronte both rejected us, to the world's loss. And Tolstoy. Tolstoy had a wonderful novel from his youth which he considered, well, anti-Christian."

"And among the unknowns? Has anyone just walked away?"

"No," she said. "Never. In such a case, the consequences would be especially tragic." Sensing where the conversation was leading, she'd begun to speak in a quicker tempo, at a slightly higher pitch. "A new genius, who would sink into the sea of history, as Byron says, 'without a grave, unknelled, uncoffined, and unknown.' Is that what you are considering?"

"You have *no* right to keep all this to yourself."

She nodded. "I should remind you, Mr. Wickham, that without the intervention of the library, these works would not exist at all."

I stared past her shoulder, down the dark street.

"Are you then," she said at last, drawing the last word out, "refusing?"

"This belongs to *us*," I said. "It is ours. We've produced *everything* back there!"

She looked solemnly at me. "I almost anticipated, feared, this kind of response. It may have been implicit in your book. Will you grant us permission to add *Independence Square* to the library?"

Breathing was hard. "I must regretfully say no."

"I am sorry to hear it. I—You should understand that there will be no second offer."

I said nothing.

"Then I fear we have no further business to transact."

At home, I carried the boxes back up to my living room. After all, if it's that damned good, there has to be a market for it. Somewhere.

And if she's right about rampant commercialism? Well, what the hell.

I pulled one of the copies out, and put it on the shelf, between Walt Whitman and Thomas Wolfe.

Where it belongs.

NOTHING EVER HAPPENS
IN ROCK CITY

Sorry I'm late tonight, Peg. Had to make a trip up to the observatory at closing time. They're having some kind of party up there and they needed a quick delivery. Ordinarily I would've sent Harry but Virginia hasn't been feeling good so I told him to go home and I went up myself.

No, not much was happening. They all seemed pretty loud, but other than that it wasn't very much. Nothing much ever happens in Rock City.

Oh, yeah, Jamie's home. Got his degree but no job. Bill tells me he's decided to be a lawyer. He wants to send him to one of those eastern schools but he's not really convinced that Jamie's serious. You know how that's been going. Me, I think it'd be just as well. We got enough lawyers around here as it is.

What else? I heard today that Doris is expecting again. Now there's a woman doesn't know when to quit. Frank said he's been trying to talk her into getting her tubes tied. But she's kind of skittish. Women are like that, I guess.

No offense.

Oh yeah, it was a pretty good day. We moved a lot of the malt. That new stuff I thought we'd never get rid of. There was a family get-together over at Clyde's. You know how they are. Must be sixty, seventy people over there for the weekend. All Germans. Putting it down by the barrel.

Jake was in today. They're getting complaints about underage kids again. I told him it ain't happening in our place. And it ain't. We're careful about that. Don't allow it. Not only because it ain't legal, either. I told him, it's not right for kids to be drinking and they can count on us to do what we can.

We had people in and out all day today. We sold as much stuff off the whiskey aisle as we did all week. We won't have any trouble making the mortgage this month.

What else? Nothing I can think of. This is a quiet town. Janet was in. Ticketed somebody doing ninety on the state road. Took his license, she said. Guy's wife had to drive him home. I'd've liked to've been there.

She told me there was a murder over in Castle County. I'm not sure about the details. Another one of those things where somebody's boyfriend got tired of a crying kid. That ought to be death penalty. Automatic.

What's that? What was going on at the observatory?

I don't know. They had some VIP's visiting. We sold a couple bottles of rum to one of them this morning. Old guy, gray hair, stooped, kind of slow. Looked like he was always thinking about something else. Talked funny too. You know, foreign. Maybe Brit. Aussie. Something like that.

They're doing some kind of convention up there. Some of them are staying over at the hotel, according to Hap. Anyhow, we get this call about a quarter to nine, you know, just before we lock the doors. It's Harvey. They want eight bottles of our best champagne. Cold. Can we deliver?

Harvey told me once they always keep a bottle in the refrigerator up there. But with all these people in town I guess one bottle wasn't enough.

Well, to start with, we don't have eight bottles of our best champagne on ice. Or off. I mean how much of that stuff do we sell? But sure, I tell him. I'll bring it up as soon as we close.

I mean, you know Harvey. He won't know the difference. And I can hear all this noise in the background. The paper said they were supposed to be doing some kind of business meeting but all I can hear is screaming and laughing. And I swear somebody was shooting off a noisemaker.

Oh, by the way, did I tell you Ag was by today? She wants to get together for a little pinochle next week. I figure Sunday works pretty good. When you get a chance, give her a call, okay?

And Morrie's moping around. He won't talk about it but I guess Mary's ditched him again. You think he'd get tired taking all that from that crazy woman. Don't know what he wants. Ain't happy when he's with her and miserable when he isn't.

Oh, here's something you'll be interested in. Axel dropped a bottle of chianti today. I mean it went off in the back of the store like an explosion. I felt sorry for him except that it made a hell of a mess. He's getting more wobbly every day. I'm not sure we should be selling him anything now. At his age. But I don't have the heart to stop him. I've thought about talking to Janet. But that only puts it on her. I don't know what I'm going to do about that. Eventually I guess I'll have to do *something*.

What about the observatory? Oh yeah. Well, there's really nothing to tell. I took some Hebert's and some Coela Valley. Four of each. Packed 'em in ice and put 'em in the cooler.

So when I get there all these lights are on inside and people are yelling and carrying on. I never saw anything like it. It was like they'd already been into something. I mean Harvey and his friends are *not* people who know how to have a good time. But this other crew—.

Anyway Harvey said thanks and I wiped his card and he said do I want to stay a while? I mean they were into the bubbly before I could set it down.

So I say no thanks I have to drive back down the mountain and the last thing I need is a couple drinks. But I ask what's all the fuss and he takes me over to a computer screen which has graphics, big spikes and cones and God knows what else, all over it, but you can't begin to tell what it is, and he says *Look at that.*

I look and I don't see nothing except spikes and cones. So then he shows me how one pattern repeats itself. He says how it's one-point-something seconds long and it shows up three or four different places on the screen. Then he brings up another series and we do the same thing again. None of it means anything, as far as I can see.

So Harvey sees I'm not very impressed and he tells me we've got neighbors. He mentions someplace I never heard of. *Al-Car* or *Al-Chop* or something like that. He says it like it's a big deal. And then it dawns on me what he's talking about, that they've found the signal they're always looking for.

"How far away are they?" I ask.

He laughs again and says, "A long way."

"So I say how far's that?"

"Mack," he tells me, "you wouldn't want to walk it."

For a minute I wonder if the people on the other end are going to come this way but he says no that could never happen. Don't worry. Ha ha ha.

Well, I say, tell them hello for me. Ha ha. And he offers me a three buck tip, which was kind of cheap considering how late it was and that I had to drive up and down that goofy road. I mean, I'm not going to take his money anyway. But three bucks?

But that's why I was late.

Ran into Clay outside town, by the way. He was over at Howie's getting his speed trap set up. Says he picks off a few every Friday. Says he had to go over to Ham's place earlier because Ham was screaming at Dora again. I used to think she would pack up and leave one of these days but I guess not.

Yeah.

Anyway, that's why I was late. I'm sorry it upset you. I'll call next time, if you want. But you don't need to worry. I mean, nothing ever happens in Rock City.

TWEAK

Civilizations, if they survive their nuclear age, seem always to follow the same path. "*It is inevitable,*" said the ship.

Sikkur adjusted the picture with one mandible while supporting his snout with the other. Kayla nodded. "It's good to know," she said, "that everything has a happy ending."

Onscreen, thousands of the creatures labored on the Morgan Monument.

Kayla brought up the BBC, where one of the anchors was going on endlessly about Mr. Morgan, the Prime Minister, how his thirty-two years in office had been a period of endless prosperity. A guest commented on his popularity. "*Never had a leader like this.*"

"What are you thinking?" Sikkur asked.

"I liked it better when it was called *Trafalgar* Square. It had a better ring."

"I agree," Sikkur said. "But Trafalgar is undoubtedly dead." She glanced through the viewport at the clouds. They were moving out over the ocean again, headed west. "It is incredible," she added.

"You do not mean the monument?"

"No. Not the monument." She gazed at him with deepset eyes, dark and intelligent, intended for use under a different sun. "I mean the consistency of it all."

He switched to another feed. This one from a satellite over Canada. Men and women worked contentedly on the Gulf of St. Lawrence Canal Project. And then to demonstrations on the streets of Toronto. People marched around a government building, bearing signs, *MILLWORKERS FOR MYERS* and *MYERS IS THE MAN.*

Kayla's chair squeaked as she changed position. "Whether we look at places like Bakyubah on the far side of the Galaxy, or the civilizations of the Parah Cloud, or Greater Wahkni near the Hole, wherever we go, it is always the same: If they survive the atom, soon after they begin tweaking their genes."

Below, in the western Atlantic, a few rain clouds drifted through the late afternoon.

Sikkur fished a snack out of the ready box. A red gufer. It squirmed as he popped it onto his tongue and sucked it down. "It must be an intriguing period for everyone," he said, "when they arrive at the stage where they can control evolution." He listened to Kayla's breathing. "Yes, I'd like to have been there when they first realized how to do some of these things. Increase intelligence by tweaking a gene. Grant musical genius. Provide a handsome brow." He took a deep breath. "A godlike business."

"Which gene was it, dear?" She combined a smile with a flick of her eyes. Whenever she did it, the bridge brightened.

"Which are you talking about, love?"

"The brow. The brow. I've always been impressed by a stately brow."

He snorted. She *did* like to kid around. "As if *I'd* know," he said. The sky below was growing brighter as they gained ground on the sun.

Kayla was a glorious creature, the exquisite curve of her fangs, the way her eyes lit up when sudden movement caught her attention. Of course, she lived in a society where everyone was physically appealing. When everybody was beautiful, were they all just average? Was the cumulative effect no greater than it had ever been? It was a question for philosophers. However that might be, Kayla's charms ensured there were no long evenings on the *Stardust*.

The scientists had virtually stopped the ageing process. Had granted Sikkur and Kayla endless courage. And of course they had social skills *par excellence*.

"*It is where the manipulation should have stopped.*" Baranka had said that. Had said it again and again. A few others had taken up the cry. But they were old. Many hadn't had the benefit of the various enhancements, and never understood that the point of being alive was to be happy. "*Unlimited happiness will make us slaves*," some had said. Foolish notion. Was Sikkur a slave? Was Kayla?

Fortunately, like the humans, the home race had had excellent leaders. Each one better than the last. It would be a joy to go back and report that, from one end of the galaxy to the other, wherever one found an advanced species, happiness and good times reigned.

TWEAK

✸

The *Stardust* was approaching the United States now. Sikkur picked up images of workers in the capital city taking down an obelisk which was, according to CNN, going to be replaced by a temple dedicated to the current president, Mark Ramsay Howard.

The satellite zeroed in on the project. It was apparently lunchtime, a warm, pleasant day. A crowd of women were moving into the work area, carrying thermos containers and bags of food. Somewhere a band played, and people sang the praises of the president.

"No question about it," said Kayla. "They've found their happiness gene."

He tapped his scaled breast. "Gives me a warm feeling right here."

"*It is indeed exhilarating.*" said the ship.

She treated herself to one of the gufers and stared contentedly at the screen. "I envy them. Why don't we go down and help? Tote that barge? Maybe make some points with their boss. It would do us good to haul a little masonry around."

"Kayla," he said, "you know we're not supposed to do that. As much as I'd like to."

She did that thing again where she lit up the bridge. "I won't tell anybody."

MELVILLE ON IAPETUS

The thing was carved of rock and covered with ice. It stood serenely on that bleak, snow-covered plain, a nightmare figure of curving claws, surreal eyes, and lean fluidity. The lips were parted, rounded, almost sexual. I wasn't sure why it was so disquieting. It was more than simply the talons, or the disproportionately long lower limbs. It was more even than the suggestion of philosophical ferocity stamped on those crystalline features. There was something—*terrifying*—bound up in the tension between its suggestive geometry and the wide plain on which it stood.

It was scratched and clawed by micrometeors, but no serious damage had resulted.

We stood before it, staring.

The wings were half-folded. Ray Morgan, on my right, used the toe of his boot to dig small circles in the orange-tinted snow.

The creature's blind eyes were aimed at Saturn, frozen low in the hostile sky by its own relentless gravity.

Static crackled in my receiver. "*Nice view of the horizon, Terri.*" It was Smitty in the command module, somewhere overhead. I mumbled an apology: my primary function at this moment was to keep the camera on-target. "*Jay,*" Smitty continued, "*how's it look?*"

The figure was set on a block about a third its own height. Steinitz approached it, his big boots pushing into the granular stuff underfoot, which was more like sand than snow. His shoulders were on a line with the top of the base. "Looks like granite," he said. "There's something written here." He switched on his lamp. The light penetrated the reddish-brown ice and crept up into the lower body.

The inscription hadn't been visible to the probes, one of which lay in the snow forty meters behind us.

"It's female," said Morgan.

Yes, I thought, not knowing precisely how I knew. Some delicacy of line perhaps, or subtlety of expression. Certainly, no anatomical clues were apparent through the plain garment covering the trunk. Yet it was most decidedly female: it reached out to Steinitz, arms open, legs braced, weight slightly forward. "It reminds me," Morgan continued, "of my wife."

That almost broke the mood. Steinitz laughed, and someone giggled over the link. Jennifer had been pensive, sullen, with eyes that were lovely only by candlelight. She'd never really been Morgan's wife, other than by some mad informal agreement, but they'd maintained the facade at her insistence, and she'd thereby made herself ridiculous. During that last year before departure, when we were gradually reducing our world to the five people who would make the four-and-a-half year flight, Jennifer, always an outsider, had hung on. She really loved him, apparently, and she knew that the mission was too long, that their relationship, such as it was, could not survive it. So she did what she could to persuade him to abandon the project. To find a quiet job and settle down with her in Tampa. Or wherever.

Toward the end, as she grew desperate, she'd spoken to none of us. With Morgan's encouragement, the men joked about her. It was odd: usually in such a situation, the women in a group would have been protective. But Chung and I only stood aside and watched. Maybe we were embarrassed that she didn't just tell him to take a hike.

Maybe she did. One day she was simply no longer there.

Morgan hadn't mentioned her on the long flight out. At least not to me. But he was right. Somehow the thing on the plain did suggest Jennifer. Not physically, of course. It resembled no human woman. But it was, I thought, so terribly alone.

"*You getting a good look at the inscription?*" asked Smitty.

"Yeah…." Steinitz waved at me and I went close with the camera. Three lines of sharp, white characters that might almost have been Cyrillic were stenciled within the icy coating. They looked vaguely Russian.

Steinitz's breathing was harsh. He leaned over and peered at the symbols. Touched the artifact with his fingertips. Drew them across the surface as if the object were sacred. He moved his wrist lamp slowly from side to side. The letters brightened, lengthened, shifted.

"Nice piece of optics," I said.

"Yeah. I wonder what it says."

I turned and looked across the wide level plain. We were on Iapetus, one of the moons of Saturn, as remote a place as I ever care to be. It was of course absolutely still. During the time we were there, which was about four days, it was always a dark place with bright lights in the sky. Over a distant ridge we could see Saturn and its rings, and some other moons. Iapetus, of course, is well outside the ring system, so you get a magnificent view.

Other than whatever had made the statue, and occasional falling debris, nothing had moved on this dreary world for a million years. There's no weather, and no seismic activity. Since Iapetus is in tidal lock, even Saturn doesn't move. From our point of view at the foot of the artifact, the big planet was quite close to the horizon, a brilliant red-orange sphere, flattened at the poles, slightly larger than the Moon in Earth's skies. The rings were tilted toward us, a brilliant panorama of greens and blues, sliced off sharply by the planetary shadow. Immediately beneath it, the landscape had erupted into broken towers of ice and rock, as though tidal forces had run wild. Saturn was in its first quarter.

"*How old is the thing, Jay?*" came the voice from the ship. "*Any ideas?*"

Steinitz walked around the base, and stopped on the far side. "No marks in the snow. And the snow's probably untouched for what, thirty, forty thousand years? It's been here a long time, Smitty. Fact is, the damned thing *looks* new."

My feet were getting cold. The temperature outside the suit was in the area of three hundred below, and the pump was having trouble keeping up with it.

We poked and measured and speculated. But we took no samples. After awhile, Steinitz informed Smitty that we were ready to return to the landing site.

"*Okay, Jay,*" Smitty said. "*We're starting Cathie down.*"

"All right."

"*She'll be coming down about fifty meters from your artifact. You've got about forty minutes.*"

"Fine. We'll get the tarps up."

"*Maybe it would be better if she didn't try to get so close. I'd hate to have her fall on top of the goddamn thing.*"

They were talking about our operational center and living quarters, an *Athena*—one of five in the linkup—with its fuel storage tanks converted into crew space, and just enough propellant to get down. It would serve as our shelter and remain after we left, a new artifact for any other visitor who might wander by. It would, I suspected, one day be named for Steinitz.

"Do it the way we planned it, Smitty," he said. "It's cold down here."

We'd used a sledge to haul a supply of canvas with us. It was clumsy, but we got it over the statue, over *Jennifer* as everyone was now calling her. We lashed it tight, and added a second tarp.

When we'd finished, we rested briefly, and started back to the lander to wait for Chung. Iapetus was in its long night. No sun would be visible for three weeks,

"Long way from home," said Steinitz.

✸

We spent the next few hours setting up our shelter. When it was done, I was glad to move in out of the cold and get the doors shut behind me and climb out of the suit.

Cathie Chung got the coffee going. There was a big central compartment to serve as command center and dining room. And a place to collapse. Blankets were stacked on a computer frame. I took one and pulled it over my shoulders.

Designers back home must have thought we'd want a place with a view. The bulkheads were, for the most part, transparent. Privacy wasn't an issue, but something else about not being able to get away from that moonscape, that *figure*, was unsettling. The artifact remained hidden by its canvas wrapping. But I knew what was under it. I kept looking out at it, and past it at the plain beyond, and at a distant cluster of broken peaks.

Steinitz and Morgan were talking in whispers, discussing the composition of the snow. I got up and activated the filters. The plain, and *Jennifer*, vanished. Nobody seemed to mind. I wasn't sure anybody even noticed.

The evening started to wind down. Morgan put the artifact on his viewer but I could tell his mind was elsewhere. (I wondered if he was thinking of Jennifer. The *real* one.) I pushed down into my blanket to keep warm. Steinitz closed his eyes and let his head sink back. His hair had silvered noticeably during the long flight out, and his skin was hard and pocked, not unlike the moons among which he was making his reputation. He'd left Earth with a mild case of asthma, too much weight, and probably too many years. There were some who felt he shouldn't have come at all. But none among the crew. Except maybe Morgan, who didn't like any kind of authority.

"Whoever made it," Chung said, looking at the image over Morgan's shoulder, "knew what they were doing." She was tall, quiet, intense. Spoke

English with a mild Chinese inflection. At twenty-four, she was the youngest crew member and, I suspected, the smartest. A support technician.

"Eventually," Morgan said, "it'll wind up in a museum back home."

"It would look pretty good," I said. "It amazes me they were able to get that kind of articulation out of a piece of ice."

"It just *looks* like ice," said Steinitz. "That's just the surface. It's really rock."

Morgan looked around at us. "Or that kind of *impact*," he said. "How would you like to have something like *that* come down on you in a dark alley?"

Chung's eyes flickered, and I felt it too. The remark was uncharacteristic of Morgan, who never admitted to human weakness, other than lust, and certainly not to timidity.

"You think that's what they looked like?" I asked. It wasn't the first time the question had come up. It had been a subject of heated discussion for years. Ever since the first probe had noticed it almost two decades earlier.

"Probably," said Chung.

Steinitz frowned. "Anything's possible. But I'd bet it's purely symbolic. Someone's equivalent of an American eagle. Or a Russian bear."

Morgan shook his head. "It's God," he said.

That was a common notion among academics, although you didn't hear it much on the media. Too many people got upset. Sponsors got boycotted. There were a lot of people who thought the creator of the universe was an old-looking guy with a white beard.

"It might be mythic," said Chung. She smiled and brought her fingertips thoughtfully together in one of those porcelain movements that one associates with pagodas and silk screens. "But I doubt there's any religious connotation."

"Oh." Steinitz had been making toast. He buttered a piece and bit into it. "Why do you say that?"

"Because I have a hard time imagining whatever created that thing beating a drum."

"You're assuming a star-traveller," I said.

"Of course. What else? I think we can assume she's not from Pluto."

Steinitz looked across at her, his eyes narrowed. "You're assuming more than that. I take it you wouldn't expect to find religious institutions in an advanced society?"

Chung smiled defensively. Had she offended anyone? Sorry. But of course not. "No," she said. "Taking myths literally is not characteristic of an enlightened civilization."

"So what do you mean when you say it might be mythic?"

"The thing wears clothes. So I think that lets out the eagle. It's probably a cultural icon, something that represents the sculptor's past in some way, but which she, he, whatever, would not have taken literally. The way we might think of Pegasus, for example. Or Lady Liberty."

"Not God."

"I don't think so, no."

"I'm not so sure," said Steinitz.

"How do you mean?"

"The universe shouldn't exist at all. To function, to hold together, it requires a parade of absurdities. Four-dimensional space. *Curved* space. Relative time. The gravity settings have to be exactly right. If they were a bit stronger, stars would collapse too quickly. A bit weaker, they wouldn't form at all. I know all this sounds like a back door into theology, and it probably is. But I think any really advanced race would at least keep an open mind on the subject."

"You're saying," said Morgan, "that when we run into an extraterrestrial civilization, they'll be Presbyterians."

Steinitz nodded. "Something like that."

"In a Darwinian universe," said Chung, "any right-thinking Presbyterian can expect to get eaten." She turned in my direction. "What about you, Terri?"

"I don't know," I said. "What's the thing doing in this neighborhood? Talk about a zillion miles from nowhere. It's a marker, maybe. Laying claim to the area. Or maybe Kilroy was here."

The interior of the shelter wasn't particularly comfortable. Stiff plastic chairs. You ate from folding trays. Our individual quarters were the size of broom closets. But, after being outside, it felt warm and cozy.

"Ray," said Steinitz, "were you serious?"

"About God? Sure."

"What do you think the inscription says?"

"It'll turn out to be his name, and the date the sculpture was done."

I laughed. "You want to predict what his name will be?"

"Frank," he said. "A casual sort of deity. Friendly. Informal."

Chung grinned at him. "Frank."

"Good as any."

❋

"I can't tell what he believes," Chung told me later, when we were alone.
"Does it matter?"

"Out here? Where a mistake can get you killed? Sure, I like to know how the people around me think."

"His religious views shouldn't make any difference, Cath."

"They *don't*. I didn't say *what* they think. I said *how*. I like to know who I can trust. Who's serious and who isn't."

We were out taking pictures of Jennifer. Chung posed me beside the thing, set the camera low and angled it up, then joined me and we smiled as the light flashed. "You're not a believer, are you?" I asked.

"I went to a Catholic school," she said.

"And it didn't take?"

"I read too much Melville when I was a kid."

"Oh."

"White whale. Clockwork universe. Nothing personal, but stay out of the way or get run down."

"What made you read *Moby Dick*?"

"Book report in high school."

"Oh."

"I don't think they understood the book. What it was really saying."

I'd tried to read it once. Couldn't get into it. Still don't understand when people cite it to talk about a universe that doesn't give a damn. To me, it's a book about whales. The lesson is that you don't screw around with something a hundred times your size. Nothing subtle about that.

"What's the point," she continued, "of having a compassionate God if he doesn't bail you out when your air supply fails?"

"Is that what Melville says?"

"Pretty much. Get in trouble, you're on your own."

"Ahab."

"Right. Nothing personal. No devils. Just make sure your harness is in place."

Next on the schedule was a TV show. That would happen as soon as the satellites lined up. We decided where we wanted the cameras, ran lighting tests, discussed what we were going to say, and, with an hour or so to go, informed Smitty we were ready. Steinitz was the senior guy, so he'd be front and center. The plan was that he'd explain everything we'd been able to figure out about the object, which wasn't much. Then he'd invite me and Morgan to talk about whatever we wanted. Our instructions were to do some philosophical stuff, how it felt to be out here with an artifact from another civilization, that sort of thing, and to go slowly on the technical stuff. After all, they'd told us, everybody already knows you can't read the inscription, and they can see for themselves how big and ugly the damned thing is. I'd been writing down some of the stuff I planned to say, but Steinitz warned me no reading. Make it look spontaneous. Right. I could see myself standing there with the lights on and my mouth open trying to remember my name.

Steinitz invited Chung to participate. She looked good, and she'd have been an asset, but she was scared, too. I wouldn't have believed it. So he'd asked me whether I didn't think we could spring it on her, turn a camera her way when she wasn't expecting it, and ask a question, get her on before she had time to get nervous. But I vetoed that idea. If Chung felt the way I did, she might freeze as solid as Jennifer.

"By the way," I told my male colleagues, "don't let's screw up on the name. Mention *Jennifer* and we'll go home to a lawsuit."

We made ourselves as comfortable as we could while we waited for the satellites to get together. We placed the cameras so neither the lander nor the shelter nor the probe was visible. We'd show them toward the end of the program, but we wanted first to establish a sense of complete solitude. We wanted the people at home to *feel* how absolutely far we were from Chicago. We wanted them to see Saturn, which never moved from its place over the distant ridge line, and the rings, and the moons currently visible. We wanted them to see the stars the way we did, bright and distant and more numerous that they were in any terrestrial sky. And unimaginably far.

I was sitting there thinking it wasn't going to happen, not with people in their living rooms and kids charging around outside. No one had ever been farther from Earth than we were at that moment, and it just wasn't possible to understand what that meant unless you were standing there with us.

Smitty gave us a ten-minute warning. Moments later he was back. "*Jay.*"

Steinitz was standing in front of the image, gazing up at it, trying to imagine, as we all were, who had been there. "Yes, Smitty," he said, "What is it?"

"*Heads up. We have an inbound debris field.*"

"Say again."

"*Rocks and dust. Headed your way.*"

"When?"

"*You've got about eight minutes. I'm postponing the program.*"

"My God, Smitty. Are they going to hit the artifact?"

"*I don't know. But they're coming down nearby.*"

I have to admit my first reaction had nothing to do with Jennifer. Or Frank. Or whatever her name was.

"*Can't be,*" Morgan was saying. "*The thing's been here for ages. We land, and a few hours later it gets knocked over? That's just not possible.*"

Chung broke in: "Smitty, what do you recommend? We have the lander nearby."

"*How long would it take you to get off?*"

"A few minutes."

"*Forget it. Get inside. Hide under the beds or something.*"

"Okay."

"*You'll probably be all right. This kind of thing likely happens all the time.*"

"Okay."

"*It's mostly dust.*"

Just like Earth. But Saturn's neighborhood had a few more rocks, and Iapetus had no atmosphere to dissolve them.

We argued briefly which was safer, lander or shelter, and decided it wouldn't matter if a serious rock showed up. We settled on the shelter. Steinmetz dropped into a chair and sat staring out at Jennifer. His eyes were wide with frustration and outrage. "Please," he said, in a voice so low I could just make it out. "Don't hit the statue."

I grew up in south Chicago. My folks didn't have much, and they assumed I'd just get married, so they weren't big on education. At least not for me. My brothers both went to college. I got through high school, barely, saw nobody I wanted to spend the rest of my life with, got a part-time job as a waitress, and decided the University of Chicago was a better bet than most of the guys who came in looking for hamburgers and whatever else they could get.

Things went better than I could have expected. It turned out I had an affinity for physics, and the one romance that might have sidetracked me crashed and burned. It seemed like a disaster at the time, but it was probably the luckiest break of my life. I received an assistantship at the

University of Northern Illinois, and got my doctorate under Edward Harbinger, whose name fit the circumstances. He recommended me for the Athena program, and there I was. Harbinger, I knew, would have given his life to have made this mission, even to hide with us in the shelter while the rocks came down. But he was too old. I don't know why but I kept thinking about him while I sat feeling the place tremble while the debris field—innocuous term—rained down on us.

We got bombarded for the better part of an hour. Mostly just pebbles. It was a little like being inside during a severe hailstorm. It rattled against the roof, and once or twice the ground shook, so something big must have hit, but I didn't see it. When it was over, we went out, were relieved to see the statue was undamaged, and did the show.

It went smoothly. Smitty added recorded shots of the approaching meteors—that was the way we referred to the debris field during the show—and we all talked as if it had been life and death. We went on to profess ourselves relieved that the statue hadn't been damaged. I thought afterward how brave and selfless we must have sounded.

In any case, it was enough for the day. We operated on GMT, and it was early evening in this place where there were no evenings per se, where most of the light was coming from the big planet and the rings. So we retired to the shelter, had a round of drinks, and sat down to dinner.

We spent the evening planning the second phase of the mission. Who were the sculptors? They must have left some indication of their presence, abandoned equipment, tracks, *something*. We would spread out and have a look. So we went over our images, designated likely spots, assigned responsibilities. And quit for the night.

Morgan and Chung sat down to play chess. Steinitz went back outside to look at Jennifer. I should have gone with him. Technically, you're not supposed to do anything alone, but I was tired and everything I owned ached. We'd maintained an intensive exercise program on the flight out, but the long period of near-zero gravity had loosened joints and weakened muscles. I retreated to my quarters and fell asleep with the conviction that manned space vehicles would eventually go the way of the big paddlewheels.

We had an early breakfast, most of it devoted to a long debate on the anatomic feasibility of the ice lady. The figure was obviously idealized. It looked toward Saturn with unmistakable longing. And there was something else, some juncture of beak and jaw, some slant of the eyes, that suggested resignation. But reproduction? It was hard to see how. I wondered if my imagination had been playing tricks. Was it maybe something else, neither male nor female? Were there other reproductive arrangements? How often did statuary at home omit the anatomical details?

If we were correct that the snow cover had remained intact, virtually untouched, for thousands of years save for the occasional meteor, then how did we explain that the snow around the statue was unbroken? It looked as if it had fallen yesterday. It was of course possible that Jennifer was inordinately older than we'd supposed. The estimated age was, after all, pure guesswork.

The plain lay wide and flat. The rings were knife-edge bright. We consulted our maps and headed out, Morgan and Chung to the north, Steinitz and me on the south. The instructions were simple: Find something the sculptor dropped.

The reasoning was that a ship had to have set down somewhere. Devices, at the very least a chisel, had been used. Somewhere, there should be *something*. Some clue to tell us who had been there.

There weren't really many places to hide something, other than under the snow cover itself. We poked among groups of boulders, wandered down into occasional craters, and gradually drifted toward the chain of gaping rocks and ice behind which Saturn seemed always about to set.

It was cold and tiring. The snow ranged from about a half meter to God knows how deep. Our suits dragged, and I've done nothing in my life more boring than trudging in circles across that dreary surface. Smitty joined the search, circling overhead in low orbit, radioing negative reports every hour. We walked until we were all exhausted.

The following day, we were out again.

A couple hours after we'd started, Morgan called. *"We got it."*

"What?" demanded Steinitz. "What have you got?"

"Among other things," he said, *"footprints."*

"Footprints? You sure they're not your own?"

Chung broke in. "Not unless we're running around in bare feet. And sprouting really long toenails."

Chung and Morgan had found the prints in the foothills of the ridge line at the edge of the plain, where it rises into a series of ridges. They were *big*. And the claws looked very much like the same set Jennifer carried.

The prints didn't seem to be going anywhere. It appeared that the creature had simply wandered around on the slope. The paw, the foot, was almost twice the size of mine. "The statue's a self-portrait," I said.

But they'd figured that out first thing. "At least as far as the feet are concerned," said Steinitz. He knelt in the snow. "It *must* have been wearing a pressure suit of some kind. It couldn't have been out here in bare feet. But it sure looks like it."

"Probably a very thin suit," said Chung. "Something molded to the body."

But it wasn't the prints that had initially caught their attention.

The slope angled sharply up and became a sheer wall. Morgan and Chung played their lights against it, against the wall, and we were able to make out an indentation. A cut. It started at the crest and reached down about ten meters.

I thought maybe it had been caused by a meteor strike.

"Look again," said Morgan.

It was precisely sliced. The indentation was box-shaped, maybe four meters wide. Not quite as deep. The lights reflected off a rear wall only few paces back.

"This is where the granite came from," said Morgan. "For the statue."

We climbed to the top of the crest and found more prints, and a slice of relatively flat terrain where the snow had been crushed down. Bits and pieces of loose granite were scattered everywhere. We looked at one another. Several of us spoke at the same time: "This is where it made Jennifer."

"We'll collect the pieces of rock," said Steinitz. "We should be able to put them together and confirm that."

"But how the hell did it manage things?" asked Morgan. "Assume it had some sort of laser. How'd it extract the granite?" There were no marks other than the prints. And the prints didn't get any deeper. Even had it been Superman and *lifted* the rock out by sheer physical strength, the prints would have gone deeper from the added weight.

"Anti-gravity," Chung said.

Steinitz cleared his throat. "Not possible."

"Well," said Morgan, "it's hard to see how else it could have been done, There must have been a ship here somewhere. To lift it and *her* back down to the plain."

We spread out and looked for other marks in the snow, but found nothing. If there'd been a ship, maybe it had possessed long narrow struts, and the granular composition of the snow simply didn't retain the impressions. Maybe they had teleportation.

We gradually made sense out of the footprints. They first appeared on the downslope. Then they mounted to the ridge without immediately going near the place from which the rock had been taken. Instead they continued up along the summit. A second set of tracks returned. *These* then wandered along the ridge. She had spent a fair amount of time walking back and forth. She'd spent time a half-meter away from the cut, and spent more time around the borders of the flattened snow. Then, abruptly, in the middle of the snow, the prints stopped. Somewhere in the confusion, she vanished. No prints led away from the site.

"So she came in this general direction," said Morgan, "but passed by this area and went up *there*." He pointed along the crest, where it rose higher and climbed toward a series of ridges. "Then she came back here, made her cut, produced Jennifer, and disappeared. Along with Jennifer, who later turns up on the plain. Is that what we're saying?"

"What do you suppose she was doing up there?" asked Chung, looking at the ridges.

"Probably," Steinitz said, "trying to decide where she wanted to work."

"It might be worthwhile to take a look," I said. "See where the tracks go."

There was no way, of course, we would not have done that. We told Smitty what we'd found, sent off lots of images, listened to him tell us we were probably missing something, that none of the stuff we were talking about was possible. Then we set off to follow the tracks along the rising ridge line.

Sometimes they petered out on rocky ground. Twice, before sheer walls, the prints stopped altogether, and we recovered them farther up.

The plain with the figure lay behind us. From the tops of the ridges, we could see forward across a large crater. Saturn rested on the far rim.

We emerged, finally, atop an abutment. The prints stopped. The creature appeared to have paused at the summit, perhaps glancing back the way it had come. (The artifact was out there now in the middle of the snow field, though not visible in the muted light.)

And she might have looked west, across the crater, at the planet and its ring system. Then, apparently, she had started back.

Steinitz stood a long time, staring at the mild confusion of tracks. When at last he merely shrugged, it was a gesture that said it for us all.

We took more pictures and stayed well away from the prints. It was cold. Steinitz said something about nothing more to do here, and he started back. "Good with me," Chung said. She fell in line behind him.

Morgan glanced in my direction and stood aside to let me go first.

"You go ahead," I said. "I'll be right with you."

"You sure?"

"Yes. I'll catch up."

He looked uncertain. It was a violation of safety procedure, but I let him see there was no need to worry, so he shrugged and headed off.

Jennifer had been alone.

The stars were hard and cold, and the spaces between them pressed on me as they must have pressed on her. Saturn floated over the plain, its rings luminous and lovely. A few other moons scattered across the sky. It struck me the planet had not moved since she'd stood here, how long ago?

I thought about Chung. And Melville. *Moby Dick*. I'd never read the book. But I'd seen the video. There's a sequence in which the cook is washed overboard and drifts away from the ship. The seas are heavy, and a moment comes when water and sky fill the universe, when the *Pequod* is gone, and the cook is utterly *alone*. They do not get him back whole.

The image on the plain is terrifying, yes. But not because it has claws and wings, or pitiless eyes. *But because it is alone.*

I was beginning to feel the cold, and it was a long way back to the shelter. I looked up (as she must have). Titan was there, with its thin envelope of methane; Rhea and Hyperion, and some of the smaller satellites: frozen, spinning rocks, like this one, immeasurably old, no more capable of supporting a thinking creature than the bloated gasbag they circle. Steinitz had argued for a benevolent cosmos. But Steinitz had never stood alone on that ridge. Only I have done that.

And one other.

The universe is a precarious, cold haven for anything that thinks. There are damned few of us, and it is a wide world, and long. I wondered who she was. Long since gone to dust, no doubt. But nevertheless, *Jennifer*, I wish you well.

As I write this, there's a movement afoot to take the Iapetus monument down, to bring it home and install it in the Smithsonian. There, they'd probably put it in a refrigerated cubicle, try to recreate the snowfield appearance. They'd surround it with gleaming staircases and Coke machines. Maybe it doesn't matter. I suspect her sculptor would be pleased, and possibly amused.

Before we left to come home, we opened the ground module to space. If anyone else ever passes that way, it'll be there, just the way we left it. And on the dining board, they'll find my ID. It's not a very good picture. You know how official photos are. But they'll understand. It was the best I could do on short notice.

LIGHTHOUSE

(with Michael Shara)

The applause after a dissertation defense is always polite, sometimes cool, but rarely sustained. Kristi Lang smiled and blushed as all fifty members of her department rose to their feet and cheered. Her fellow graduate students were the rowdiest of all, whistling and banging their coffee cups in unison on chairs and table tops. Greg Cooper, the department head and her mentor, let it go on for a full minute.

"Ladies and gentlemen," he said finally, "thank you very much."

If anything, the noise intensified.

He needed a gavel.

Kristi stood, engulfed in the moment. She nodded, raised her hand, mouthed a *thank you*. A fresh round of applause, and finally it began to lessen.

She had discovered a new type of astronomical body. A special kind of brown dwarf. They were calling it a *chimera* now, but Greg had told her yesterday that they'd eventually be referred to as *Lang Objects*.

Greg was tall and thin, with an angular jaw, angular nose, dark hair, intense eyes. His students referred to him as Sherlock Holmes because of his world-class problem-solving skills and his intensely mediocre abilities with a violin. "All right," he said, signaling for quiet. "Let's pull ourselves together." That brought laughter. "I wouldn't want to cancel the wine and cheese."

The people around her were reaching for Kristi's hand, patting her on the back. Tim Rodgers, tanned and good-looking and brilliant, gave her an approving smile. He was impressed. Maybe even envious.

The time honored Q and A had to be observed. Greg called for questions. Hands went up. He stepped aside and gave her the lectern.

Tim remained standing while the others took their seats. He was finishing his own thesis, and had been, until recently, at the top of everybody's list of People Who Would Go Somewhere. Now he was a distant second.

"Okay, Kristi," he said, "you've established the existence of a new class of object. How'd it happen?"

The explanation was simple enough. She'd been doing analytical studies of billions of brown dwarfs and had noticed a few anomalies. Way too much deuterium. But that wasn't the big news. She was holding that for later.

"We eventually found two thousand oddballs," she said. Brown dwarfs were failed stars. The chimeras, the Lang Objects, were anomalous. Odd. And not easy to account for with conventional physics.

"You briefly mentioned actinides," came another question. "But I don't see the connection. Please elaborate."

Kristi smiled and tried to look modest. "Think DNA," she said. "Common origin. Common purpose."

The comment puzzled everyone. Brows furrowed. They whispered to one another and waited for her to explain herself.

❁

In fact, her inspiration had come that past summer from a set of police blinkers mounted over a cabin on Kilimanjaro.

Hemingway's mountain. Now the site for the Yuri Artsutanov Space Elevator. Kristi had been on her way to the Clarke Research Station, poised overhead in geosynchronous orbit. She was hunting for the photons that she hoped would help explain the existence of the anomalous *chimeras*.

There were nearly two thousand of them, all young, concentrated in the spiral arms of the Milky Way, interlopers, deuterium-rich freaks that had no business existing. Clad in shorts and a Columbia University t-shirt, Kristi drove a Jeep across the savanna. The sky was heavy with clouds, and the smell of cool moisture hung in the late morning air. Storm coming, and she was already late. If she didn't hustle, she stood a good chance of missing her ride. The weather guy had said clear, bright and sunny, beautiful weather. She'd spent the last few months completely absorbed by her research, had analyzed a million images, looked for the needle in a billion haystacks, written a killer proposal that even Greg Cooper in his Holmes role couldn't fault. But here she was going to be left standing at the station. Scheduling rides on the Yuri was no easy proposition.

Not that it would matter in the end. Jeff would make the observations and deliver the petabytes to her account. They'd be perfectly de-biased and flat-fielded, even if she never floated through the observatory hatch. Still, the karma would be wrong. It was once in a lifetime, and she needed to be there when the evidence came in.

The rim of Kibo, the summit crater, popped momentarily into view as she passed three thousand meters, and then promptly vanished into the gathering clouds. Raindrops began to spatter against the windshield. She started the wipers. The road was wide and designed to take heavy traffic, but it was still uphill all the way, sometimes at an almost impossible angle. The rain intensified, and pounded on the roof.

She slowed down as visibility dropped to about fifty meters. A truck passed going the other way. A burst of wind pounded the Jeep and water blasted across the windshield.

Her cell phone chimed. "*Kristi.*" It was Kwame Shola, the chief of operations at Yuri.

"How you doing, Kwame?"

"*Not so good. Where are you now?*"

"On the way."

"*Okay. But take it easy. We got snow like mad up here. Weathermen missed it completely.*"

Great. Just what she needed. "All right," she said.

"*No heroics, please. If you need it, we have a climber cabin at five thousand meters. Combo is 2718.*"

"Twenty-seven eighteen."

"*Remember 'e'.*"

'e,' of course, lower case always, was the base of the natural logarithms, equaling 2.718281808…on into an infinity of digits. "Okay," she said. "I've got it."

Greg had been ambivalent about her working with the chimeras. Don't know where you're going to go with them, he said. You could wind up producing a lot of data and still have to throw up your hands and admit you don't have a clue about what they are or why they even exist. Put the idea on hold, he told her. Confine the research to more conservative areas, at least until you've wrapped up your doctorate and gotten an appointment somewhere. He was right, of course. The path of guaranteed success.

But she was *fascinated* by the objects. Her father had always told her to follow her instincts. And her instincts took her right into the shadow of the deuterium dwarfs. They were so intriguing, so difficult to explain, that she simply could not resist.

She had never wanted to be anything but an astronomer. Her father, who'd been a high school science teacher, had brought home a pair of image-stabilized binoculars from the third Gulf War. When he gave them to the little redheaded six-year-old, she was transfixed. The moon had craters and tall mountains. Jupiter was a tiny disk with moons of its own. And the Milky Way was a glittering pathway of stars. Distant suns, her father had explained. Countless millions of them. Some just like ours, some a lot smaller.

Why, Daddy, why are some of the stars different from the Sun?

He'd smiled and told her he didn't know, but that she could figure it out if she wanted when she grew up.

And one evening, in the Big Dipper, she'd discovered Mizar. Her father had been on the porch with her and she'd screeched at him, "Daddy, they're *touching!*" Twin stars. Over the next twenty years, her father could always get a laugh from her by repeating the phrase in a rising falsetto. But in fact, as she learned later, there were *five* stars in the Mizar system. By her first year in graduate school she'd found a brown dwarf companion to the five. And used it as a clock to age-date the system. Her *Astrophysical Journal* letter hung framed in his den. But he got nervous whenever he knew she was going up to the Clarke Station.

The rain turned to sleet and Kristi slowed the Jeep to a crawl. Her defroster was rapidly losing its battle with the Tanzanian snowstorm. She could no longer see the summit. A burst of wind shook the Jeep.

She tried to call Kwame for a weather update, but he wasn't answering. Something big with lights roared past her, going down the mountain. She jerked the wheel hard, hit the brakes, spun across the icy muck, and slid off onto the shoulder.

Maniac.

She sat listening to the sound of the retreating truck. Then she pulled carefully back onto the highway. It was getting dark.

She picked her way uphill, past boulders and patches of lichen. Occasionally the road emerged along the edge of a precipice and she could look out through a hole in the clouds across the savanna. Then the clear patch was gone and the road was winding up through the night while rain and sleet whipped across the windshield. She began to wonder whether she'd missed the 5000-meter signpost when her headlights swept over it. She didn't see a cabin anywhere, but it didn't matter because she had no interest in missing her ride. There was still a chance, if the weather broke, that she could make it.

The cell phone chimed. Kwame. *"How you doing, Kristi?"*

"I'm doing just dandy."

"You find the cabin yet?"

"Negative. Doesn't matter. I want to get up there before my ride leaves."

"Kristi, they've canceled it. I told you that."

"No, you didn't."

"Why did you think I wanted you to find the cabin? They're going to try again in the late morning."

"Okay."

"Go to the cabin."

"I'm past it."

He sighed. *"Can you get back to it?"*

She looked behind her, down the road. It was dark and cold and she could barely see the edge of the highway. "I guess."

"Do that, then. Don't try to come up tonight. It's too icy. Already had one truck go off the road. Driver was damn near killed."

"Okay."

"You sure you can find the cabin?"

"Sure. Relax. Everything's fine, Kwame."

It was about a kilometer back, maybe two. She put the phone down on the seat and peered out onto the highway. Nothing coming in either direction.

She cut the wheel and started to turn. She couldn't judge how wide the road was, so she was careful not to go too far forward. She reversed and started back. Felt the rear wheels lose traction. Tried to go forward again. But the Jeep continued sliding back. And *down.*

My God, she was going into a ditch.

She fought the wheel, damning the Jeep and the highway and the storm. But it did no good and the vehicle slid sideways off the shoulder and crunched over a large rock into a snowbank. She shifted gears and gunned the engine. The wheels spun, the Jeep struggled forward a few centimeters, dug a deeper hole, and slid back in.

Damn.

She called Kwame.

"You want me to come get you?"

She looked down at the tee-shirt and shorts. The heater was on full blast. "No," she said. "Don't do that. I'll make for the cabin."

"Okay. Be careful."

"I will."

"Call me if you have a problem."

It was frigid out there. Better was to sit tight and wait for somebody to come along.

There are twenty-one billion brown dwarfs in the Milky Way, give or take. Kristi had found and mapped almost every one of them. "The light output of brown dwarfs alternates wildly between adjacent wavelengths, Dad," she'd once explained to him. "My infrared survey filters are tuned to just the right wavelengths, so all other stars appear dimmer. The hard part is keeping track of them all, and repeating the survey a year later to measure their motions. Then we have to sift out all the weird quasars that sneak through the filtering. That's why we have MEGASPEC. It catches them all."

Brown dwarfs were not massive enough to ignite thermonuclear fires in their cores. They would always be failed stars, their dim glow generated by cooling and contracting. "Ninety-nine point six nines" was the delicious phrase she used in colloquia to describe her survey's thoroughness. No one had ever done that for brown dwarfs. Hell, nobody had ever done that for anything in astronomy. She had nailed the definitive sample for all time. Sure, there'd be a few hundred hiding behind luminous primaries, or lurking directly in front of distant quasars, but she'd gotten the rest. There was no arguing with twenty-one billion spectra and parallaxes and radial velocities and proper motions. She could tell you what the temperature of each one had been a million years ago. And where each one would be ten million years from now. Her census was the last word on how the Galaxy's failed stars had arranged themselves during the past thirteen billion years. She could chart the few ancient, metal-free brown dwarfs along their orbits looping far out into the Milky Way's halo. The larger population of metal-rich youngsters, the astronomical infants, clung to the plane of the Milky Way.

The chimeras (she settled for the term "anomalous objects" in her seminars) had been culled from her complete sample of twenty-one billion by statistical sifting and weighing. Every one of them had a spectrum that called attention to itself, that defied everything she thought she knew about this type of object. The surface abundance of deuterium was impossibly high. It was a heavy isotope of hydrogen, with one proton and one neutron, and the Big Bang had made only a pinch of it, before stingily shutting off production just three minutes after creation. There was no known way that any planet or star or galaxy or anything else was going to concentrate the primordial trace of deuterium to more than a pinch. The textbooks maintained that anything over 0.001% was impossible. Yet Kristi had found two thousand brown dwarfs whose composition was nearly fifty percent deuterium.

It was frigid out there. The engine, which had been keeping her reasonably warm, coughed and died.

She tried to restart it.

Tried again.

When she opened the door, she smelled gasoline and stuck her head outside. There was a stain on the snow. She must have punctured the tank. Or the gas line.

The mountain highway remained silent.

Shut the door against the cold.

Okay. Crunch time. Can't stay here. The temperature in the Jeep was already dropping.

She checked to be sure she had her pen flashlight. Staple for astronomers. She turned it on and pointed it out the window, where the beam got lost in the snow. There was a travel bag in back with light clothing, and she could try putting everything on, but she was still going to get pretty cold out there.

It was only a kilometer back, two at most. She could manage that. She pulled her bag from the back seat and began sifting through her clothes.

She put on two extra blouses. They weren't going to help very much, but she'd take what she could get. And there was a sweater. She pulled it around her shoulders. Felt like an idiot.

She thought about Tim. He was the romance that had never happened. Partly her own fault. Always too busy. And her father, safe and warm in their North Jersey home.

Love you, Daddy.

The wind tried to take the door out of her hand. She hung on, dragged her bag out of the back seat, and chunked the door shut. The snow was driving at her, and it seemed to be coming from all directions.

The ditch was shallower than it had seemed, but the sides were ice, and she had to climb out on hands and knees. When she finally stood on the road, she fished out her penlight and turned it on. The world around her looked desolate.

The wind cut through her garments and chilled her to the bone. It literally took her breath away. She was wearing canvas shoes and her feet got cold before she'd gone a dozen steps.

The penlight beam outlined ditches and a snow cover fading into the night.

She pressed her arms against her chest and tried to push the cold out of her mind. Move out, Scout, she told herself. There's shelter back there somewhere.

Her toes went numb. A blast of wind knocked her down. When she got up, she no longer had the penlight. Didn't know where it had gone. She'd been carrying it in her right hand, but the hand had no feeling.

For the first time in her life, she felt real fear.

This was the darkest place she'd ever seen. There was no glimmer of light *anywhere*. The edge of the road was no longer visible. The world had vanished, had become a place utterly without borders, without any distinguishing features, other than the snowflakes that continued to rush at her.

She thought about calling Kwame. But she couldn't do that. What would he think? Poor woman can't get from the Jeep to the cabin without getting in trouble.

It was hard to breathe. Her lungs hurt, and tears froze on her cheeks.

She pushed her hands into her sweater pockets and started out again. Hell with it. Didn't need the light anyway.

Still no sign of anything. Not of a cabin. Not of the marker.

The terrifying truth was she could walk right past the marker and never see it.

She was counting her steps now. Roughly thirteen hundred to a kilometer. Right? She'd already come about five hundred. Or maybe one hundred. Somewhere, below her, she heard the sound of a plane.

She tried to pick up her pace. Keep moving. Keep watching. And think about something else. Think about Daddy's rising falsetto. If she was lucky the marker and the cabin would be right next to each other. *Why, Daddy, they'd be touching!*

After a while, she became convinced she must have missed it. She debated starting back toward the Jeep, and looked helplessly in both directions. Couldn't have been this far. She'd only passed it about three minutes before she'd stopped and gone into the ditch. She'd been traveling about fifteen, twenty at most. How far was that?

She couldn't figure it out. She'd begun to feel as if she'd withdrawn into a cave, was looking out through her eyes from a safe place somewhere back of her nose.

That was funny, Lang. Laugh.

Ha.

Still trudging forward, she flipped open the cell phone. Time to confess. Tell Kwame she was in trouble.

Off to her left, a soft orange glow appeared in the blowing snow.

Nothing about this class of brown dwarfs made sense. Their composition was just under fifty percent deuterium. Fifty thousand times what it should be. Crazy enough. The remaining half was mostly hydrogen, the ordinary one-nucleon variety. No problem with that, except that it left little room for helium, which, in most of the chimeras, totaled less than one percent. It was their larger than normal size that tightly constrained the helium abundance. Even Tim, the brightest young theorist she knew, had to concede the point. Every other cosmic object is born with the allotment imprinted by the Big Bang: a full twenty-seven percent. So where was the rest of the helium?

There was no way to hide helium in a still-warm brown dwarf, and all of the chimeras were warm Galactic infants. Kristi's deuterium reservoirs mocked her, because they simply could not exist.

The orange glow hung momentarily in the darkness. Then it went off.

Somewhere, far away, she heard a snarl. Leopards don't climb this high, do they?

She started walking toward the spot where she'd seen the light. It came on again. And went off.

It *had* to be the cabin.

She moved closer. Saw the 5000-meter marker to her right. A metal sign, white with black numbers.

The light blinked on again. More distinct this time. It was a police car beacon. Set on a rooftop.

Thank God.

Wooden steps led up onto a porch. She saw three dark windows and a door. There were wicker chairs on the porch, and a table. She climbed the steps, felt the wind cut off as she came into the shelter of the cabin, and tried the doorknob.

It was locked.

A number pad was bolted to the frame. The combination. What was the combination?

Kwame had said, *Remember 'e'*. Twenty-seven eighteen.

The beacon kept flashing. Every few seconds. It reflected off the snow cover, giving her just enough light to work with.

She got it wrong the first time, and for a heart-stopping moment she feared the lock was frozen. Or she'd been mistaken. But the second try was golden and the door clicked. She pulled it open, kicked the snow out of the way, and half-fell through onto a stone floor.

The interior was frigid.

She shut the door and looked around. There were more wicker chairs and another table. A long row of solar batteries powered the beacon. A cot was set against one wall. And a pot-bellied stove stood in the middle of the room. She looked around for a thermostat. Saw nothing.

Someone had left a box of matches, and a yellowed copy of *USA Today*.

Kristi stared at the stove. My kingdom for a few logs. She could go outside and root through the storm. Maybe get lucky. But the furniture was more convenient. She picked up one of the chairs and brought it down hard against the floor.

It held together.

She tried again.

It was remarkably resilient. She stumbled around the cabin, looking for an axe, gave up, and went back to beating the chair. Desperation lent strength and, finally, it came apart. Enough, at least, that she could jam it into the stove.

Ten minutes later she sat in front of a fire that, if it was not quite blazing, nevertheless served to take the freeze off the room. She called Kwame. "I'm in."

"*Good,*" he said. "*I was getting worried. Don't leave the cabin until the storm stops.*"

"Have no fear. One problem—."

"*Yes?*"

"I left my transportation in a ditch."

"*You were not hurt, I hope?*"

"No, I'm fine."

"*Okay. I'll send a truck down as soon as the road's clear.*"

"Kwame?"

"*Yes?*"

"Send sandwiches, too."

Her toes began to recover some feeling. She found a blanket in a closet. It smelled of cigarettes but she didn't care. She warmed it on the stove, wrapped herself in it and closed her eyes.

She was wide awake. She'd have liked to read. But even if the light had been adequate, she'd left her briefcase in the car. In it were copies of *Physics Today* and *People*, which she'd brought for the skyride. And a marked-up version of her dissertation. Once at Clarke, there'd be no leisure. She expected to spend six days doing nothing but observing, reducing data, and sleeping.

The wind shook the cabin. And suddenly her eyes felt heavy. Her head drifted back, and the sounds of the fire, the sense of the storm outside, faded.

She woke a couple of times, and jammed more furniture into the stove. And once, toward the end, she saw gray light in the windows.

The nuclei were piled high in her office. Thousands of deuterons. In the drawers. On the keyboard. Scattered across her desk. Each deuteron's green neutron and blue proton were morphing back and forth, into each other, a colorful display of the strong nuclear force in action.

Get the vacuum cleaner. Where was the vacuum cleaner?

She was still looking when a hand touched her shoulder. "Hey, Kristi. How you doing?"

Kwame.

The fire had gone out but the stove still held some heat. "I'm okay," she said.

"Good. The road's clear. If you're ready we can head out."

Kwame was a middle-aged African, not quite as tall as she. His hair had gone white, and his features suggested he'd known some difficult times. He was wrapped in a heavy parka with the hood down. His dark eyes were shining, and he spoke with a British accent.

She pulled the blanket more tightly around her while she pushed her feet back into her shoes. "I'm ready," she said.

"You don't want to take a shower first?" He nodded toward the wash-room, but kept a straight face.

A snow plow waited outside. The sun was behind some white clouds. It was relatively warm, and the cabin roof was lined with melting icicles.

She climbed into the passenger's seat and looked back at the police light. "If it hadn't been for the blinker," she said, "I'd never have found the place."

He nodded. "That's why it's there, Kristi."

She thought about suggesting he add an ax to the amenities. And maybe some canned goods. But, on second thought, maybe another time.

He passed her a jelly donut.

Kristi had been to the summit of Kilimanjaro four times before, but the sight of the base towers and the nanowire ribbon stretching up to infinity was as exhilarating as ever. "It hasn't left yet?" she asked him.

"No. They've been waiting for you."

It wasn't critical that she be on site while her data were collected. But Greg had designed MEGASPEC and Kristi had written most of its software to confirm brown dwarf candidates, so a trip to recalibrate the million-object spectrograph was justified. And there would never be a time she'd pass on an opportunity to go up to the station, to see the home world from 36,000 kilometers. There was still a little kid in her somewhere. She'd commented along those lines once to Greg and he said it was true of everyone in the sciences who was worth a damn.

Kwame apologized that there was no time to shower and change. Have to do it in zero-gee.

"I'll try to keep away from the other passengers," she said.

"Ah. It is their loss."

They pulled up at the front door of the terminal, and she thanked him for maybe the fifth time. Then she was hurrying through the reception area and someone came alongside to help with her bag and briefcase. Moments later she cleared the entry ramp, and hatches shut.

There were roughly a dozen other passengers. About half of them were tourists, including two kids. They looked curiously at her as the carbon nanowires stiffened and the elevator lifted away from Kilimanjaro. Minutes later she caught sight of Lake Victoria. They rose through the clouds, and the Atlantic came into view. And eventually she was looking down at the entire continent, from the Cape of Good Hope to the Nile delta.

Two hours out, at an altitude of 8000 kilometers, she got a sandwich and coffee from the convenience counter and settled down at one of the viewport tables to enjoy the ride. Closer to the chimeras, she thought. Well, not really, but the illusion was there as she soared ever higher.

She wished there were starships. She'd love to have an opportunity to go out and look at one of the things, close up. She knew how it would appear, of course. She had virtual brown dwarfs on call back home. They were Jupiter-sized spheres, red-brown, with mottled clouds floating in the atmosphere. The clouds were iron hydride, and of course the dwarf would be glowing, rather like a coal recently plucked from the fire.

She visualized it, and somehow she found herself thinking about Kwame's police lights.

Someone came over and asked if he could share the table. Of course. He was a young man, and she realized immediately he was on the make.

"...Going to be pretty well tied up while I'm here," she was saying.

He was a technician of some sort. Dull-looking. Thought well of himself. "Of course," he said. "But all work—."

She heard him out, and smiled when appropriate. "They pay to send me up here," she said, as if she were making a major sacrifice. "...Don't want me sitting around."

The police lights. She stared through the young man into the deep night of the 5000-meter elevation, saw the soft orange glow, blinking on and off.

And suddenly she understood.

"*I don't buy it, Kristi,*" Greg said. She had him on the vid relay, from his office. "*There's got to be a natural mechanism at work. Maybe high pressure chemistry. Maybe magnetic fields. Maybe radiative levitation. Geochemical processes can concentrate minerals by orders of magnitude on Earth, so why not deuterium on the surfaces of brown dwarfs under far more exotic conditions?*" He sounded really concerned. It was why she liked him so much. He was worried about what would happen to her career if she tried to go public with her notion. She imagined it was hard for him not to say, *You're skating at the edge of academic disaster. Blow your reputation now and you'll always be at the fringe.*

"*I admit,*" he said, "*that fifty percent deuterium is far out. But whatever did this could also bury the helium. We just don't know enough.*"

"I think it's true," she said.

"*It could be. Anything's possible, Kristi. But think about what the professional price will be if you go off half-cocked, and then someone finds the real explanation.*" Then, more gently: "*I'll go this far: Get two more pieces of independent evidence. If your idea stands up, Galileo will have to move over.*"

While the Earth dropped away, she worked on her computer. An hour later, still on the elevator, she raised a fist in triumph. The act drew the attention of several of her fellow passengers. She didn't care. She had a match. In fact, the chimeras, almost the entire sample of two thousand, except two, showed up at the same sites listed in the all-sky X-ray source catalogs as black holes. That gave her a stunning 99.9% correlation. How much proof do you want, Greg?

For the next five hours she looked fruitlessly for other patterns. She was still engrossed in her analysis, and trying hard to keep her sense of exhilaration under control, as the elevator began its approach to the station.

An attendant asked her to return to her seat and buckle in. She felt indestructible at the moment, but she happily complied. Galileo was a piker.

An orange light was blinking on the link-up collar. It reminded her of Kwame's beacon, and she smiled. A series of thuds reverberated through the hull as the elevator docked and the airlocks mated. Hatches opened and the passengers floated through into the connecting tube. The tourists would be headed for the hotel. The others scattered in different directions.

Jeff Fields, who ran the observatory programs, was waiting for her. "Jeff," she said, "I want you to do something for me."

"Okay," he said. "What do you need?"

"Tomorrow, before we make any observations, I need you to change to the highest resolution grating."

Standing at the lectern before her mentors and her peers, Kristi had deftly fielded a dozen questions about her analyses and catalog. The privilege of asking the final question traditionally went to the senior graduate student. Tim. She'd seen him writing while she spoke, scratching out lines, making faces, writing again. When the moment came, he stood. "Sorry, Kristi," he began. "Nobody here is more anxious for you to be right. But I still don't get it." He glanced down at his notes, looked over at Greg, and plunged on. "Your high-res spectra and gravitational redshifts unquestionably prove that every one of your chimeras is eight Jupiter masses, and that each is orbiting something every year or so." He took a deep breath. "The X-ray source coincidences are a convincing argument that the somethings are black holes. But black holes can't concentrate deuterium or hide helium. Black holes were all once stars way too luminous to have formed with sub-brown dwarf companions in the first place. And, worst of all, your chimeras are too low in mass to ignite deuterium, yet they radiate like hot brown dwarfs."

The others around the table were looking anxiously from Tim to her. A few whispers began. "In theory," Tim continued, "your chimeras can't exist, right? But they do. So what's going on?"

You know, she thought, he really is good-looking. But not as quick on the draw as I'd thought.

He started to sit down, but got up again. "Kristi, you must have some idea how to explain these things?"

She looked over at Greg. He was gazing out the window at the beautiful autumn day. Then his eyes met hers. And he nodded. Do it.

Her paper had been accepted yesterday by *Nature*. Letting the cat out of the bag now wouldn't jeopardize anything. She'd kept everyone, other than Greg, in the dark. Even Tim.

"We classify anything less than thirteen Jupiter masses as a planet," she began, "because these objects never develop sufficient internal pressure to ignite their deuterium, let alone their hydrogen. Yet we now see objects eight times Jupiter's mass displaying surface abundances that can only come from deuterium burning. That's impossible with one thousandth of a percent deuterium. But deuterium ignition works just fine if these objects are born with eight Jupiter masses and fifty percent hydrogen and fifty percent deuterium, and they're somehow sparked." She smiled at Tim, who was sitting looking lost.

"By analogy," she continued, "a trace of air mixed with gasoline is stable, but a fifty-fifty mixture is highly combustible. A spark would set off a conflagration. Since nature can't make, or ignite, fifty-fifty deuterium-hydrogen objects, especially near the kind of massive stars that collapse into black holes..." she paused for effect, "...it's hard to see that the chimeras can be anything other than *artificial*."

The room went dead silent. A gust of wind struck the windows and she thought briefly of Kwame's cabin. At the doorway, a small group of professors had gathered. She wondered whether Greg had alerted his colleagues.

History being made today in the Bishop Library.

Tim looked stunned. "Kristi," he said, in a voice she did not recognize, "you're not making this claim seriously?"

"I am," she said. A wave of guilt passed through her. Maybe she should have taken him aside. Warned him what was coming. "They're artificial as in *synthetic*. As in *not made by nature*. As in *manufactured by Little Green Guys*. I would argue they were deliberately placed in orbit around black holes that were born without companions. Some of each chimera's solar wind now falls toward its black hole. That superheats the wind so it radiates X-rays. Hence the chimeras coincide with catalogued X-ray sources. They used to be invisible. Now you can't miss them."

Guilt, hell. She was Hubble discovering that the universe extended far beyond the Milky Way, Rubin finding the dark matter that surrounds all galaxies. She was on top of the world. "At first I suspected they were an experiment, test objects of some kind. But that would be an experiment hugely wasteful of resources when you could get away with masses a million times smaller."

The professors at the door were crowding into the room.

"No, the chimeras' creators needed something self-luminous, something that would last a long time, but something that would cost as little as possible because they had to make two thousand copies. A fifty-fifty deuterium-hydrogen mixture is the nuclear fuel that can be ignited in the lowest possible host mass. It's the cheapest interstellar beacon you can make if you insist on a hundred-million year warranty. Nature can't make these objects. But somebody can." She took a sip of water as her words sank in.

"The helium makes sense, too," she continued. "It's the ash, the by-product of pure deuterium-hydrogen fusion, brought up by convection from the core. The helium content of the chimeras is limited to one percent or less because they're all younger than a million years. Each one will continue burning its core deuterium and will shine at its present luminosity for another hundred million years."

Tim was going to say something else but Greg broke in. He was beaming. "Kristi, two of the chimeras are not associated with black holes. What can you tell us of them?"

"One of them," she said, "is moving at nearly three percent of the speed of light through Taurus. A second is in orbit around a G-dwarf in Scorpius. It's just under seven Jupiter masses, the lightweight of the entire sample, and the least luminous. I really don't know for certain, but I'd speculate that the first object is being towed or pushed toward a newborn black hole. And I wouldn't be surprised if the second one is on the assembly line."

The applause was tentative this time. Until the people at the doorway joined in.

❋

Greg had a final word: "My initial reaction, when Kristi ran all this by me, was the same as Tim's. But there's one more piece of evidence that convinced me. Kristi?"

She was at her charming best, at a moment she would always remember. "A thirty-meter telescope at geosync orbit," she said, "is an amazing instrument. But the chimeras are faint and I couldn't find anything but deuterium, hydrogen, and helium in any of their spectra. When I realized that they had to be copies of each other, I removed the Doppler shift of each one and then co-added the two thousand spectra. The result is almost fifty times more sensitive to trace elements."

She touched the video controller and the summed spectrum appeared, undulating and smooth, with four sharp, narrow dips. "See those four absorption lines? Only one element makes those lines. Plutonium. The nastiest, most dangerous substance we know. "Each chimera is seeded with pure Plutonium-244, which will last as long as the chimera itself. It's the closest thing to a universal skull and crossbones I can imagine.

"Ladies and gentlemen, the chimeras are beacons. Celestial lighthouses. Space-faring travellers are being warned away from the shoals. Away from the Milky Way's two thousand solo black holes, which are otherwise nearly undetectable."

"Magnificent," said one of the professors. "If true."

She smiled, as her audience collectively let out its breath. "The evidence is all there, Professor. And, if Greg doesn't mind, I could use a glass of Cabernet. If we could quit now."

COOL NEIGHBOR

(with Michael Shara)

Greg Cooper had been sitting in the control center of the Weber gravity wave observatory, eating popcorn and calibrating *Icewave*, when he realized he had about a minute to live.

He'd been writing a letter to Kristi Lang, hinting at the discovery he was about to make public, and suddenly it was over. The order-of-magnitude calculation took ten seconds, and told him he was a dead man. Bad karma. He choked off a wave of panic and self-pity. No time for regret. He knew exactly what was coming. The portholes would fluoresce ferociously, down-converting the X- and gamma rays to optical photons for a few spectacular seconds. The last thing he'd ever see.

Warn the people on Clarke. Get the tourists back inside.

He opened a channel. "Mayday, Ana, Mayday. Incoming hard radiation. Get everyone back onboard, into the shelter. Do it now!"

Five kilometers away, Ana Vassileva, the observatory manager, gaped at the transmission. The real-time solar X-ray images and radiation monitor live feed were working perfectly. It was near solar minimum, so Ana wasn't surprised to see nothing at all brewing on Sol. "What are you blathering about, Greg? I haven't seen a sunspot, let alone a serious flare, in weeks. Sol's asleep."

"Ana, the local spatial strain went totally offscale twenty seconds ago…. A gravity tsunami just went by. Einstein never dreamed something this big could happen. There's a gamma ray burst right behind it. Get everyone into the shelter!"

"My God," she said, "Marnie's out there in the shuttle."

Ana wasted no time. She hit the alarm and klaxons sounded through the station and its cash-cow hotel. Tourists dropped everything, crowded in the passageways, and headed toward the water- and lead-lined chamber nestled in the heart of Clarke. A middle-aged woman with blonde hair askew grabbed Ana in the hallway. "What's going on?" she demanded. "This had better not be a drill, damnit, we had one yesterday."

"It's okay," And said. "Just hurry, please. She needed another twenty seconds to reach the Shuttle Control Center.

✸

In the cockpit of the shuttle, Marnie Leeds had backed slowly away from Clarke, allowing her French Canadian guests to ooh and aah at the view. The hotel-spa was shaped like a clamshell, with ceiling-to-floor windows on the concave side facing Earth. Many tourists spent their entire time on the station savoring the sight, reluctantly leaving the picture windows only to sleep. The Neugebauer Infrared Array hung four hundred meters above the hotel. A thirty-meter telescope anywhere is a remarkable sight, but permanently perched thirty-five thousand kilometers above Africa, it was riveting. The segmented primary mirror glistened with a yellowish hue from its bacteria-thin gold coating.

She looked down at the carbon nanowire space elevator cable, which snaked from the geosynchronous station to the summit of Kilimanjaro. Nearly cloud-free today, the continent was framed between the Atlantic and Indian Oceans. Marnie activated the shuttle's electron beam pointer. She highlighted Cairo, Algiers, Casablanca, Gibraltar, Abidjan, Lagos, Kinshasa, Capetown, Dar es Salaam, Nairobi, and Addis Ababa, circumscribing the cradle of mankind in less than two minutes. Her passengers responded with delight. She opened a channel to Ops. "Shuttle One to Weber. We're on our way. ETA twenty minutes. Over." Whichever astrophysicist was on duty in the gravitational wave telescope, he or she knew well in advance when tourists were coming. Marnie always hailed them anyway. Tourists were a minor time-sink for the scientists and techs, but their steady revenue stream was a godsend, so they were treated like visiting royalty.

Of the whole crowd that rotated in and out of the Weber, she most liked turning the tourists over to Greg. He was one of the few scientists on the project who really enjoyed engaging the public, and he did it with wit and charm. Kids initially reacted cautiously to his sharply chiseled face and intense eyes. His captivating talk of voracious black holes, punctuated with energetic violin playing for illustration, had them pleading for more by the end of a tour. Marnie relished his enthusiastic explanations of collapsing stars and warped spacetime. "The life of every star is a war between gravity and pressure," he inevitably began. "Hydrogen fuses into helium. Then the helium fuses into carbon and oxygen. That supplies the outward pressure to balance the crushing pull of gravity. Gravity is the stellar angel of death." All the while accompanying himself on the fiddle, he usually made a scary face with that one and the kids whooped. "Gravity always wins when a star's nuclear fuel is exhausted."

"Negative, Marnie." Greg's voice, unlike she'd ever heard it before. "Radiation surge coming. Didn't Ana get to you yet? Go back to Clarke. Get everybody under cover."

"Greg, when?"

"Now, goddamnit. Do it now."

She switched over to the passenger comm system. "Everybody belt down."

Moments later Ana was on the circuit. Her voice stayed level, but Marnie knew frantic when she heard it.

"Greg." She was having trouble breathing. "Marnie's got six aboard Shuttle One, two adults and four kids. She's coming around. Headed back. Just a kilometer away. Three minutes out, tops. Shuttle Two's still down. We'll turn One around as soon as Marnie's group is back onboard." Her voice quavered. She desperately wanted to order Marnie and Shuttle One to pick up Greg. But even with her fiancé's life at stake she knew the rules. Tourists come first, no exceptions. Ever. "Greg, what can we do?"

A long silence. "Ana, I haven't a clue, sweetheart. I wish I'd said it more often, but you're beautiful and I love you." A pause. Then: "I think we're at the end here."

"There must be something—."

He went quiet again. "Give Kristi a hug. And listen, tell her to read her email. It's important."

Marnie pitched the shuttle 180 degrees in the ten seconds after she'd spoken with Greg. Guidebooks ricocheted off the cabin walls. Frantic yells came from the passenger section. "It's okay," she told them, while she turned sharply toward Clarke's airlock. One of the kids started to whimper. "Hold tight, everyone. Brace yourself!" She gave it a solid thirty seconds of thrust. The sudden acceleration pushed them all into their seats. The shuttle raced back toward the hatch at an illegal fifty knots. The approach was slightly off-center. She tapped the port thruster, and was horrified to see it remain ON after she released the button.

The shuttle bounced hard off the emergency bumpers. Her head snapped sideways into a restraint. Metal tore. Thank God for the pressure suits. Marnie struggled to remain calm as the deploying airbags punched at her. Her youngest charge, Lissette, was screaming. The emergency lights glowed angry red, then failed as the passenger cabin split along its main seam. A hurricane of escaping air tried to suck out her passengers. They were all screaming now.

Stay calm, stay calm, stay calm.

Marnie remembered her training as the airbags deflated.

Don't panic.

Her suit was intact. So was everyone else's. She flipped on her helmet lights, unbuckling the six terrified tourists. Holding Lissette herself, she pushed and pulled the family toward safety. The airlock was meant for four. No time for that luxury. She jammed her six wards inside and pushed in after them. Ana's face was on the monitor, giving her a thumbs-up. The inner door closed on her arm and rebounded open. She tried again and held her breath until the hatch closed. The green lamps came on and she slapped the emergency re-pressurize knob. Air flooded the chamber. "Keep your suits on," she told everyone. When the pressure equalized, Ana yanked open the outer hatch. "Around the corner," she said. "Don't stop, keep going, turn right, thirty meters to the shelter." When one of the kids tried to ask a question, she simply shook her head. "Go! Go!" she barked.

Marnie watched her take a moment to look back at the wrecked shuttle. Ana bit her lip. Then she pulled herself into the shielded station core.

Greg saw the seismograph needle twitch twice, then jerk back and forth with growing fury. The oscillations surged, and he watched the arm snap off in mid swing. Pulling himself to the digital console, he read a peak strain of ten to the minus seventeenth on *Icewave*, his cryogenic diamond gravity-wave detector. *No way*, he thought. *Can't be that high. It must be a major system glitch.* But the hundred kilometer interferometer gave him the same impossible result. *Savor this*, he told himself. *You just recorded a gravity wave a hundred million times more powerful than any on record. The neutrino guys are about to experience the biggest flash in history. Incredible. Probably fry half their equipment.* The cold realization that other, far deadlier, radiation was also coming froze the thought and turned his face chalk-white.

It had been over a minute since the siesmograph needle had sent its warning. The radiation monitors hadn't budged. *I'm not dead yet. It can't be a collapsing neutron star, I'd be toast by now.* "Ana," he radioed, "the strain is so big that it's got to be something nearby."

"Wait, Greg? What could it possibly be?"

"A supernova. Something massive. Maybe a Wolf-Rayet star. The core might have run out of nuclear fuel and imploded, but the star's outer envelope runs behind the process. The gamma rays coming from the interior would have needed a few more minutes to break through the envelope. Call Kamiokande in Japan, okay?"

"Kamiokande IV is reporting eight hours of right ascension, minus forty-seven degrees of declination," said Ana tensely. "Somewhere in Vela." It had taken her just a minute to reach the duty technician of the world's largest neutrino telescope. Its cubic kilometer of ultra-pure water was two miles underground to prevent false signals from cosmic rays. Most neutrinos raced through the entire Earth without being stopped. But a tiny fraction crashed into protons in Kamiokande's water, generating miniscule flashes of light. Many of the Japanese telescope's trillion photo-detectors had saturated during the neutrino onslaught, but the neutrino flash's position in the southern Milky Way was firmly in hand. "Plus minus two degrees is their guess, near Gamma Velorum. Roughly an hour before they can refine the position, but at 810 light-years, Gamma's the closest Wolf-Rayet star in the sky. I wish that helped."

Maybe. At the moment, Greg had other priorities. "Okay, Ana. Thanks. It means I have a few minutes more. When Marnie gets back, if you could send the shuttle PDQ, I'd be grateful."

She was silent a long time.

And he knew. "What's wrong?"

"Greg, Shuttle One is scrap." She added a few details as she finished sealing the shelter doors. She was trying not to lose control in front of the bewildered tourists.

"No chance at all?" Greg asked.

"No," she said. "I'm sorry."

They were on a visual hookup, so she could see him. He nodded and pressed his lips together. Sometimes things like this happen. Nobody's fault. "It's okay, Ana," he said. "Thanks for trying."

He pushed back in his chair, as if it might be possible to draw it around him, to hide in it. *Not exactly my day. I hope it isn't too painful when it comes.* There was nowhere to run. He'd put on his spacesuit for the shuttle trip, but it couldn't protect him from a gamma ray burst. Vela was visible through the portside hatches. He moved as far starboard as possible, behind some computer racks. Tying up the loose strands of his life took just a few minutes online. He was finishing when the comm link suddenly roared with static and his visor blazed like the midday sun.

As they suspected, it had been Gamma Velorum. The star had undergone core collapse, producing a supernova brighter than the full moon. Kristi Lang was shattered by the news from Clarke. Greg was the only casualty, thank God, but he had been her mentor and friend, and had provided encouragement and support three years earlier during her Ph.D. research. She now had an international reputation for outside-the-box thinking, and a bit of media renown to boot. She'd concluded, on strong evidence, that a class of brown dwarfs, failed stars, were being used to mark black holes. They were being pressed into service as interstellar lighthouses. It was a wild idea, of course. And, like all wild ideas, it was still not widely accepted. But it would be one day.

Greg would not be there to see it.

Ana called her within an hour, although the story was all over the media by then. The director had been fighting back hysteria, and Kristi had lent her strength. Hang on, Ana. He had a good life. Our lives are richer because he lived.

Words. What the hell good were they at a time like that? And in the morning, when she was able to get herself together, the found the e-mail from Greg.

It was routine stuff. How much he was enjoying himself on the Weber. How he was at that moment watching a shuttle filled with tourists headed his way. And there was a P.S.: *There's big news in Sagittarius. A Clyde Tombaugh special. Gotta go. More later.*

Clyde Tombaugh was the guy who'd discovered Pluto. What the hell was Greg talking about?

More later.

※

She gave it a few weeks, and then tried to reach Ana. But she was in transit on her way to Baltimore. Kristi located her on a glide train and arranged to meet her for dinner.

Ana could not have been called beautiful, but she was an attractive woman, with blue-green eyes, lush chestnut hair, and the kind of presence you associate with leading ladies. Kristi was shocked by how much she'd changed over the few weeks since they'd last seen each other. Ana looked gaunt and her skin was sallow. She was bitterly unhappy and it showed. Kristi gave her a hug. "Are you okay?" she asked.

Ana shrugged. "Not really." Her eyes avoided Kristi, and wandered instead around the interior of the Crab Pot. It was early, and there were only a few customers present. Piano music was being piped in. "I finally got all the reports," Ana began. "Greg got an awful dose. Around 90 sieverts. Five is fatal." Her voice caught, and tears began running down her cheeks. She managed a smile and wiped her eyes. "It took us over a day to get him out of Weber. He was horribly burned, comatose, and—. Well, the details don't matter."

"Ana, there's no need to talk about this."

"I need to, Kristi. I really need to."

A waiter appeared. His name was Richard, and could he get anything for the ladies?

They ordered Maryland microbrews and crabcakes.

Ana took a deep breath. "He's in cryosusp and his daughter won't let the doctors pull the plug."

"Pity. But I can understand it."

"Did you know we're getting sued, too?"

"No. By whom?"

"The tourists. They've launched a class action claiming negligent design and inadequate radiation protection. A wonder they aren't suing God for setting off Gamma Vel so close to us."

103

"Any of them get sick?"

"As far as I know, they're fine. They're claiming mental trauma, or that their health was put at risk, or some damnfool thing."

The beers arrived. Kristi was used to touching glasses when she dined with old friends. But Ana simply swept hers up, gazed at it sadly, and took a long swallow.

"Don't they sign a legal release before they go up?"

"Yes. We're not responsible for acts of God. And if a nearby supernova isn't an act of God, I've no idea how you'd define the term. But it'll be at least a year before we can bring back tourists. No tourists, no money. So Neugebauer and Weber and all the other telescopes are mothballed. Everyone is on unpaid leave."

Kristi tried her own beer. "What are you going to do in the meantime, Ana?"

"I don't know. A couple of places have offered me temporary positions. The University of Maryland wants me to come on board permanently."

"I'd consider it."

"You know, Kristi, I don't think I realized how much I was going to miss him."

Salads came. Kristi's was a Caesar. "I got an e-mail from him," she said. "Right at the end. And I can't figure it out."

Ann frowned. "Why not?"

Big news in Sagittarius. A Clyde Tombaugh Special. "You have any idea what he might have meant?"

Ana gazed at the ceiling, and then poked a fork into her salad. Finally she shook her head. "I don't have a clue."

"Nothing you're aware of that he was looking at in Sagittarius?"

"Not that I know of."

"Odd."

"There is something, though. I'd forgotten."

"What's that?"

"He told me to make sure you read your e-mail."

Kristi nodded. "The center of the Milky Way," she said, "is in Sagittarius, so that part of the sky is choked with stars. I don't know where to begin, Ana. I don't know what he was talking about."

Their dinners arrived. Ana paid no attention to the food. The door opened and eight or nine people came in, an office party. The hostess showed them into the next room. Lots of laughter and, almost immediately, a round of applause. Ana took a deep breath, and those dark intelligent eyes finally found Kristi. "I'm sorry. Whatever it was, I think Greg's taken it with him."

※

Kristi went to the memorial service, and said a few words trying to explain what Greg had meant to her, both professionally and as a friend. Then she'd choked up, as several people had before her. She listened to the minister say how Greg was with God now, and in better hands. He was alive and well in a better place than this. She wished she could believe it.

When it was over, she flew back to Pasadena, where she was a junior assistant professor at Caltech. She resumed work, and did her best to forget Clyde Tombaugh.

But it didn't take.

Tombaugh had been born in Illinois to a family of farmers. Despite a limited formal education, he developed a fascination for telescopes at an early age. But he didn't think highly of the telescope he'd gotten at Sears. So he'd built his own. He eventually put together his own reflector and took it to Mt. Lowell in Arizona. The observatory director was looking for an amateur astronomer to try to find Percival Lowell's Planet X. Tombaugh hunted through thousands of photographic plates, comparing the positions of millions of celestial objects on successive nights, looking for something that moved. Looking for Pluto. On February 18, 1930, he found it.

She put a picture of Tombaugh on her desk. Clear eyes, good features. Probably in his mid-twenties then. What did you do, Clyde, that connected with Greg?

She got occasional e-mails from Ana, who had taken a position of some sort with the International Space Commission. Then, one evening close to Christmas, she called.

"Hey, kid, how are you doing?" she asked. The winsome smile was back. "You spending another scintillating Saturday night at the office?"

Kristi nodded ruefully. "Yup. It's just the Yottabytes and me. No other way to win that Nobel before I'm forty." Kristi stared hard at the screen. The Spacecraft Control Center logo glowed dimly over her shoulder. "Ana, are you where I think you are? How did you get up there?"

"The yo-yo tourists settled out of court, Kristi. I came back up to Clarke yesterday with a skeleton crew. Just in time. Five months earthside almost killed me. Be happy for me, I'm alive again."

"I am, Ana. You know that."

"I have something here for you. Where did I put it?" She pretended to fumble with her e-pad. "Aha! Yes. A little something for the holidays."

Kristi's e-pad beeped. She looked at what had arrived and gasped. All of Greg's logs. "I owe you another crabcake dinner, Ana."

"No chance I'll collect that meal, Kristi, unless you bring the crustaceans up here yourself on your next observing run. I'm done with Earth. Too crowded. Too dirty. Too noisy."

Kristi looked at the logs, and at Tombaugh's picture.

Greg had been up there almost continually for three years. As she paged through the transmission, she saw that she had all his observations and calibrations. Everything.

The proprietary period was normally two years so part of it was already public. Kristi had long since thumbed through that, hoping to find something that would put her on the track of the Sagittarius sighting. But the recent stuff was something else. It had been released early, probably because of a family stipulation. Kristi scrolled through the lists, trying to get a feeling for what he'd been doing the past two years. And she discovered he'd been observing every brown dwarf in the Milky Way. *My God, he was trying to prove I'd been right.*

He had also observed every brown dwarf wannabe in her thesis, at higher resolution. He'd collected a billion spectra. *He worked harder than I did.* A lot of his observations were of cataclysmic binary stars, and she stripped those out of the file. She also removed the obvious quasars and Seyfert galaxies that masqueraded as brown dwarfs in her survey. That got her down to twenty million objects. Well, hell, it was a start. Sagittarius occupies just over 2 percent of the sky, but it includes the dense core of the Milky Way. Deleting everything not in Sagittarius decreased the sample size to four million. But now what?

Clyde Tombaugh's photographic plates were her last hope, and she knew it. The plates were taken a few nights apart and Tombaugh had compared them, star by star. Pluto gave itself away by moving nightly, relative to the background stars. Greg's reference to a "Clyde Tombaugh special" didn't make any sense. Only solar system objects move enough in a few nights to be detectable. The nearest brown dwarf is twelve light-years away. Its nightly motion would have been far too slight for Tombaugh to have seen. Brown dwarf surveys of the early twenty-first century should have found anything closer. *Greg, what did you mean?*

The riddle gnawed at her. Her other research was beginning to suffer and Sills, the department chair, was visibly worried. "You're up for tenure in a few years, Kristi. Don't get sidetracked by unsolvable problems. You've got to keep publishing."

✺

Months went by with no progress and no publications.

She called Ana. "I think he saw something that moved."

"But you've no idea what."

"No. I'm looking for a needle in a haystack with four million straws."

"It might not be as difficult as it sounds," she said. "if you're right, one must be different from all the others. If you examine Greg's four million spectra for one second each, you'll be done in seven weeks. That's assuming you don't eat, sleep, or bathe, but those are overrated anyway."

The words hit home. *One must be different from the others.*

✺

The four million Sagittarius objects were an astrophysical smorgasbord. They included twelve classes of cool variable stars whose spectra sometimes mimicked those of brown dwarfs. In her original work with brown dwarfs, she'd needed a year to eliminate these interlopers from her catalog. *Which baby did I throw out with the bathwater?* Every sorting algorithm in *Numerical Recipes* divided the objects into one of the twelve classes. Actually, though, there were thirteen classes. Twenty-two *bona fide* brown dwarfs had slipped into the detritus heap, and Greg had managed to scoop them back out. For the hundredth time, she idly glanced at the first few. They were similar, late T dwarfs, with temperatures around seven hundred Kelvins, hardly worth a second look. Something clicked. *These spectra were too good.* The resolution and signal-to-noise were better than anything she had ever seen. *How did he get such great data?*

She displayed the next six of Greg's spectra. They were all virtual clones. Holding her breath, she overlaid all twenty-two plots on top of each other. *Tiny shifts in radial velocity between them*, she noted. *Otherwise, they're absolutely identical.* "Let's see where they are." She scanned the list of celestial coordinates. All twenty-two objects lay within an area five hundred times smaller than the full moon. *"It can't be a cluster of brown dwarfs because they'd have a much larger spread of radial velocities.* She placed the coordinates in a plotting package, and two twists of a corkscrew stared back at her. Bingo! Not twenty-two objects. Just one.

Kristi, you're as dumb as a rock. She sagged into a chair, shutting her eyes tight. The enormity of what Greg had found overwhelmed her. And he'd been swept away in the middle of it. His loss was suddenly clear and crushing. She held the spectra to her chest and began to cry.

Ana was leading the effort to reactivate the geosynchronous telescopes. There was no way to confirm or extend Greg's discovery without Neugebauer. Kristi called and, on an encrypted line, told her what she'd found.

Ana listened and paled. "Are you sure?" Her voice trembled.

"I need to do some more checking. But yes, I don't think there's much question."

"Thanks, Kristi," she said. "I'm glad you told me. It's helpful to know what he did." She took a deep breath. "Do you need more data? What can I do to help?"

Kristi nodded. "The radial velocities are crucial." She was trying hard not to sound excited. "The variations were tiny. Greg must have missed them. I need a set of high dispersion observations every six hours for a month. Can you do it?"

Ana could. "You bet. I'll get started tomorrow."

The Neugebauer data accumulated on her computer for three weeks before Kristi allowed herself to inspect it. The direct images were saturated, just as she had expected. *No wonder it's so bright.* But the spectra were exquisite.

And they confirmed her suspicions.

She called Ana. "It's what we thought," she bubbled with enthusiasm as she described the results.

"Now what?" asked Ana.

"We need access to the coronagraph." The coronagraph was designed to block the glare of a distant sun, allowing its planets to be seen. "Joel," Kristi said.

Ana nodded.

Joel Dayan had designed and built the coronagraph at Clarke. He was on the staff at Caltech, just down the hall.

Joel blinked in surprise as she walked into his office and shut the door. "Tongues will wag, Kristi," he smiled.

"You wish, big fella." Joel was one of the brightest people Kristi had ever met. He had done breakthrough work on instrument design, was a superb classroom instructor, and had won a Shaw Foundation Prize four years earlier for his imaging of terrestrial planets in nearby star systems. In his spare time, he partnered with an airline pilot as the California state bridge champions. He was also pretty good-looking.

"I need your help, Joel," she said.

He sighed. "What can I do for you, Kristi?"

"I want to make you an offer you can't refuse." She described her discovery, told him yes there was no question, and no she wasn't kidding. She showed him the new data from Ana.

He listened, looked skeptical, nodded. "Greg's work, you say?"

"Yes."

"I never got to meet him." He sat quietly, considering what she'd said. "My loss."

"Can you help?"

"You're asking me if the coronagraph is available."

"Yes."

"Not really. It's never available, Kristi. You know how that is."

She knew. People were lined up for months ahead.

"We'd have to get somebody to give up their time."

"I know," she replied. "But you have seven days, beginning this Friday."

"You're offering me a junior partnership in a risky enterprise that might be in the textbooks for centuries." She smiled and nodded. "Let me think about it and I'll get back to you."

He walked into her office an hour later. "Okay," he said. "We can do it."

"This Friday?"

"Yes. But there's a price."

"Sounds like the end of my virtue."

He laughed. "I'll take it if it's available. In any case, I want to go with you."

Three years earlier, Kristi had almost frozen to death in a snowstorm when her car slipped off the Kilimanjaro summit road. This time it was sunny right to the top. The auto-drive let them both enjoy the view. They relaxed and laughed and snacked as the pressurized car climbed more than five kilometers above the surrounding savannah. The *Yuri Artsutanov* Space Elevator was celebrating its thirtieth year of operation. Large banners hailing the international consortium lined the road. This would be her sixth trip up, and his tenth. Security had been beefed up since her last visit. The guards put their suitcases through X-ray, terahertz, and pion imagers. She hated being swabbed for a DNA sample. Joel just shrugged. "Standard operating procedure where I come from. Better than a lunatic bringing a polio-smallpox cocktail onboard in her own body."

The cable seemed to hang from infinity, contrary to the laws of common sense. *Yuri's* base towers were surrounded by enormous structures extruding new nanowire ribbon. The lifting capacity was being doubled to one hundred tons. Competition from the rival elevator, the *Bradley C. Edwards*, anchored due south of Hawaii, remained fierce. Joel and Kristi were the only passengers, so the steward ushered them into the first-class section. *Nice*, she thought. *This is how the other half lives.* They strapped themselves in as the hatches clicked shut. The carbon nanowires stiffened and the elevator lifted away from Kibo, the summit crater. Minutes later they spotted Kigali and Kampala across Lake Victoria. The Indian Ocean came into view and the Earth became round. Venus and Saturn appeared as the sky turned dark blue, then black. Their eyes adapted to the night, and the star clouds in Sagittarius became visible. They talked, drank coffee, and enjoyed each other's company. Toward the end of the nine-hour ride, she fell asleep on his shoulder. He stroked her cheek to wake her just before the clamps on Clarke locked the elevator in place. "Hey, kid," he said, "it's showtime."

Ana was waiting for them. She hugged Kristi and shook hands with Joel. Kristi had warned her to wait for dinner, and Ana laughed when she saw the crabcakes. A complex Stellenbosch Chenin Blanc with a hint of citrus enlivened the evening.

Joel had stenciled HARSH MISTRESS (HM) on his coronagraph, because of the sub-nanometer precisions required to make it work. He'd anchored the core of the device to carbon-silicon nanorods in liquid helium to eliminate flexure. Cooling and testing the alignment was a three-day blur of activity. The instrument was trivial in principle—it used a small metal disk to occult the glare of a star. Its ten-billion-times-fainter planets could then be seen. Detailed images of Jupiters and Neptunes around nearby stars were like shooting fish in a barrel for HARSH MISTRESS. Joel had built HM for his Ph.D., to take the first resolved images of Earth-like exoplanets. A decade later, he had a hundred discoveries to his credit. All were like Mars or Venus, with atmospheres utterly devoid of oxygen. Religious fundamentalists were using this to "prove" that life on Earth was unique and divinely created. He rolled his eyes when Kristi teased him about it. "Nutcases," he said. "I'll need a bodyguard when I find an oxygen-dominated terrestrial world."

A few months earlier, Joel had serendipitously detected two Ceres-sized asteroids orbiting Barnard's Star. They were the first exo-asteroids known. The precious observing time they were going to use now had originally been awarded to look for more asteroids around other nearby stars. Greg and Kristi's discovery took precedence, so Joel was going to sacrifice all seven days of his hard-won Neugebauer time to make the necessary observations. *A small price for astronomical immortality*, he thought. *If it works.* And he didn't mind having a very attractive redhead like Kristi Lang feeling indebted to him.

Caltech's press officer reminded Kristi of a bulldog. His cylindrical body and stubby legs supported a square head with sad brown eyes, short golden hair, and a white beard over large jowls. Alan Boxer loved his job and the eclectic scientists whose work he publicized. This morning promised to be a high point in his career. Two hundred media representatives were munching donuts and downing coffee in Feynman Hall, waiting for him to begin the press conference. He nodded, and the Astrophysics chair of Caltech stepped to the podium.

Albert Sills was beaming. He wore a vest that portrayed the Earth on a navy blue background of stars. It was his way of signaling an Event. "Most scientists count themselves lucky if they make one significant discovery in a lifetime." He gazed out across the audience. "Professors Kristi Lang and

Joel Dayan have each done that already. She has found a type of star that nature cannot manufacture. That might be synthetic. He has taken the first pictures and spectra of Earth-sized planets orbiting other stars. All these planets are barren. Her results suggest that intelligent life exists in the cosmos. His results suggest that extraterrestrial life is extremely rare. Isn't science *wonderful?!*" When the laughter subsided, he looked toward them, standing off to one side. "This is their day, Doctors Lang and Dayan, please tell us what you have found."

Joel raised the microphone for Kristi and it promptly emitted a deafening squeal. He fiddled with the controls, and a second try brought it quietly within range. "That's why a skilled instrumentalist is so essential for every astronomy team," she began, setting a glass of water atop the lectern. He laughed with the reporters but looked nervous, so she gave him a broad smile and faced the media. *The New York Times* and *Science* correspondents had been tipped off, and were sitting on the edges of their seats. *They get it,* she thought. She savored the moment, gloriously happy, for herself and for Greg. She almost felt his presence in the room. "Welcome," she said. "I'm pleased that so many of you are here. We want to gratefully acknowledge our co-author, Ms. Ana Vassileva, who couldn't be here today. She is space-walking at a geosynchronous altitude right now. Ana manages the health and safety of our instruments, and has gathered some of the data for our work. We're going to take fifteen minutes to summarize our discoveries, and then we'll be happy to answer questions." The corkscrew appeared on the holoscreen beside her.

"Greg Cooper sifted through a billion rejected brown dwarf candidates from my doctoral thesis. Only members of our own solar system move enough, relative to the background stars, to be easily detectable in a few days. That's why I rejected all rapidly-moving star-like objects. They must be asteroids or Kuiper Belt objects. Greg re-observed them, and all the other rejects that varied. One, and only one, of my rejects, displays the spectrum of a brown dwarf. And it turns out, it *is* a true brown dwarf. Greg re-observed it every month for almost two years. The twenty-two points of the corkscrew that you see on the screen plot the apparent path of this object across the sky. A single turn of the corkscrew has 1/30 the apparent diameter of the full moon. That's huge." She took a deep breath. "The only way that can be true, ladies and gentlemen, is if the brown dwarf is a binary companion—" she paused—"of the Sun."

The audience sat stunned. Somebody murmured in back. Shocked expressions appeared on the reporters' faces.

She sipped her water. "The brown dwarf's orbital motion around the Sun carries it continuously in one direction. The position from which *we* view it varies cyclically over one year as the Earth moves around its orbit. Combining those two motions produces the helical path in the sky. The apparent size of the corkscrew helix places our newfound neighbor about one hundred times farther from the Sun than Neptune: five hundred billion kilometers away. That's a pretty long walk. But it's *still* a hundred times closer than the nearest star."

Hands were going up all over the conference hall. The reporter from *Science* didn't wait to be recognized. "If it's so close, why hasn't anyone discovered it before?"

"There are five reasons," Kristi said. "Our companion is almost a million times less luminous than the Sun. It's three thousand times further away. We can never see it in the same spot twice because it takes 150,000 years to complete one orbit. For the past eight thousand years, it's been moving through Sagittarius, the most crowded part of the sky. And finally, it's eight times cooler than Sol, so it only emits infrared light. That's why nobody's ever noticed our cool neighbor until recently. Until Greg Cooper did." She took another sip of water, and touched her e-pad.

"We've measured the brown dwarf's radial velocity. It's wobbling back and forth with perfect periodicity every seven days." A sinusoidal curve with data points and error bars replaced the corkscrew on the holoscreen. "This means that a significant mass must be orbiting our neighbor, tugging it back and forth."

A hand went up. "Are we talking about a *planet*, Professor Lang?"

"One second, please, and I'll explain. Dr. Dayan's state of the art instrumentation permits us to measure the object's speed as it orbits the brown dwarf. That helps us to pin down the masses of our two discoveries. The brown dwarf is forty times the mass of Jupiter. If it were eighty Jupiters, it would fuse hydrogen and be visible to the naked eye as a blood-red star.

"The orbiting mass is three times that of the Earth. But it's divided." She looked at the reporter and at her audience. "To answer your question: No, we do not have an orbiting planet." She paused. "We have *two*."

"Ladies and gentlemen, we apparently have a miniature solar system, just eighteen light-days away." The hands had gone down, and the excitement had turned to stunned silence. "We thought you would like to see them. Dr. Dayan?"

Joel touched his e-pad and two fuzzy crescents appeared on the screen. "Dr. Lang and I spotted *these* in the first image we took. At first I was certain that the double image was an internal reflection in the corona-graph. We rotated the optics by 90 degrees, but the crescents didn't budge. They are real, nearly identical twins. We are seeing both night and day on each world's surface, hence the crescent shapes." Another touch and two much sharper crescents filled the screen. "Several hours of focusing the in-struments brought us to where we could take a crisp image every minute. Concatenating them gives us the first movie of twin terrestrial worlds, which we'll now see."

The planets came alive, circling their common center of gravity. They orbited the brown dwarf in perfect lock step. On one world, cloud masses swirled over continents, islands and oceans. The second planet was totally enshrouded in clouds. Flashes that could only be lightning were visible on its night side. Many of those present broke into spontaneous applause. Joel smiled and nodded. "During the last few hours of our observing run, Dr. Lang measured each world's spectrum, and I now ask her to describe what she found."

Kristi returned to the microphone. "Humanity has the technology to-day to send a robotic spacecraft to our neighboring brown dwarf star and its twins. If we use the Clarke cable as a whip, we could be there in twenty years. And we *are* going to go. Let me show you why." The holoscreen displayed another pair of spectra. "The ocean world has water in its atmos-phere, of course. There's oxygen, ozone, and methane, too." She stopped, took a deep breath, and thought again of Greg. *I wish you were here.*

"The spectrum also shows a distinctive feature *here* that can only be produced by chlorophyll. The other planet, the cloudy one, shows nothing but carbon dioxide and nitrogen. *The ocean world is alive.*"

The academics in the audience sat spellbound. Many of the reporters were already filing stories with their e-pads.

"Life has taken hold on a planet just eighteen light-days from Earth. It has failed on the twin planet right next to it. If we choose to do so, we can learn why life established itself on one and not on the other. And then, perhaps, we will understand how life got started on Earth."

Joel squeezed her hand beneath the podium. "Great, Kristi," he whis-pered. Lisa Meitner must have experienced the same wave of joy when she proved that an atomic nucleus could be broken into smaller parts. Kristi had never felt more alive. "Ladies and gentlemen, thanks for your attention."

A forest of hands mushroomed in front of her.

WHISTLE

Twenty years ago, Al Redwood walked out. He walked out of Ed Gelman's old galactic survey project, out of his job, and out of town. I knew what it was all about. We all knew.

Al thought he had a message from M-82.

Gelman laughed at him. And I guess the rest of us did too.

There was no way to prove anything. All he could do was point to a narrow band transmission in the optical range, with peculiar symmetries and repeating pulse, wavelength, and intensity patterns. A laser, Al suspected.

I remember the final confrontation with Gelman, the day Al stormed out, the last time I'd seen him. They were on the front steps of the data center, *on the front steps*, for God's sake, screaming at one another. Gelman didn't want any little green men hanging around *his* project. So Al quit, and I never even got the chance to say goodbye.

He dropped out of sight for a couple of years. None of us heard anything. His family had money, so he didn't have to work. And then I got a Christmas card from Texas: *Nick*, it said in his precise handwriting, *it was the pulse clusters all the time. How could we have missed it?*

There was no return address. But I knew that, out there somewhere, Al was still chasing his elusive vision. Later, over the years, there was more: on D.C. Marriott stationery: *I still think the frequency correspondences are critical. One weakens, another intensifies. Is it a counterpoint of some kind? By the way, I'm doing fine. My best to Ginny and the kids.* And hurriedly scribbled on a postcard with a picture of the Atheneum: *Getting close. They're out there, Nick. They're really out there!*

Al was a lot like M-82. Explosive. Remote. Lit by inner fires. Ultimately self-destructive. A man whose personal stars periodically went nova. Ironic that he of all people would imagine receiving a transmission from that

115

chaotic place, which had erupted nine or ten million years ago, and which was undoubtedly still bubbling.

Periodically he'd say he was going to be in the area and would stop by. The first few times I got in a couple of bottles of Jamaican rum. He was big on rum. Later I didn't bother.

✻

It went on like that for two decades. Sporadic letters from odd places around the country, from Canada, from Europe, from Australia, once from Tokyo. Always promising progress. Sometimes they came in spurts, sometimes several years passed between communications. It was almost as if he were pursuing those goddamn gremlins around the world. He never spoke of anything else, other than to ask about my family, or my health. As far as I know, no one else ever heard from him at all.

Then one night at about 3:00 a.m., he showed up in a driving January rainstorm, and I'll never forget how he looked, old and exhausted, his hair gone, his face creased. His top coat was open, his cardigan drenched. Water ran off his ears and nose. He stood in the storm, eyes empty, making no move to come in. "Nick," he whispered, "I know what it is." As if we'd last spoken the day before. As if someone had died.

I pulled him inside. "Hello, Al."

He was shaking his head, staring at the night light that illuminated the staircase I'd just descended. I hit the wall switch, a table lamp came on, and he seemed to jerk awake. "I know it's late," he said. "I'm sorry. I hope I didn't disturb anyone."

Ginny and the kids were all long gone by then. "No," I said.

"Good." Even for twenty years, he'd lost a lot of ground. I knew I'd grayed myself, slipped into middle age. But Al looked ready for a back porch and an apple tree. "You know what the sons of bitches did?"

"No." What sons of bitches?

He peeled off his coat and, before I could get near him, lobbed it across an armchair. "We were on the wrong track right from the beginning, Nick. It never occurred to anybody we might be looking for something other than digital data."

My God, he was off and running again. "Al," I said, "what are you drinking?"

He ignored the question. "I mean, our working hypothesis had always been that an artificial transmission could be translated in some mathematical way. And that one that had come seven million light years would have to be a directed signal. A deliberate attempt to communicate. Right?"

I nodded. "How about brandy?" There was no rum in the house. "Sure. Now: an effort to communicate is going to contain instructions. It's going to break easily. It *has* to. That's the *goddamn* point!" He chewed his lip and I thought he was choking back tears. He went quiet for a while. "But it was never there. I tried every approach I could think of. NSA even had a crack at it. Did you know *that*? They came up with *nothing*." His eyes brightened with satisfaction. "Absolutely nothing. You know what Gelman thought?"

He ignored his brandy until I pointed to it. "You ought to get out of your shoes," I said.

"Gelman thought it was a *reflection*. He couldn't account for it any other way, so he decided it was a goddamn reflection. Nick, why do we always try so hard to explain everything away?"

"I don't know."

He sipped his drink. "Did you know he's dead?"

"Gelman? Yes, I'd heard. It was a few years ago."

"You know what I wanted, Nick? I wanted to *show* him. Son of a bitch, I wanted to walk in and hand him the evidence." His shoulders slumped. "Just as well." He shook his head and laughed. It was a curious kind of sound: amused, stoical, bitter. "Doesn't matter. He wouldn't have believed me anyway."

There had been a time I'd thought Al Redwood was headed for a brilliant career. But even then he'd been a social black hole, a man with no existence outside the observatory. No family, no other friends. Only colleagues, and his work. It was painful to see him now, studying his fingerprints on the glass.

I was never sure why he felt drawn to me. Maybe it was my family. The older kids loved to listen to him. And Ginny and I often sat with him late into the evenings. My own career leveled off at a plateau roughly commensurate with my abilities, which is to say not very high. I accepted the fact early on that I wasn't going to walk with giants. I was a maker of catalogues, an analyst, a man with an eye for detail. A recorder and observer of other people's greatness.

He pulled off his shoes.

"What *does* it say?"

His eyes were cool and preoccupied behind thick lenses. I could see him running the question through again, his lips tightening slightly. "Weren't you *listening*, Nick? It doesn't say *anything*! Not a goddamn thing."

The storm rattled the house.

He got up, walked over to his coat, fumbled through the pockets, and produced a CD. "Here." He held it out for me.

It *looked* ordinary enough. I took it, held it, looked at him. He was refilling his glass, his back to me. I sighed and slipped the disk into a player.

Al strolled across the room and stared out through the blinds.

I punched the START button.

"The neighborhood hasn't changed much, Nick." An electronic whisper blew through the room. "I assumed that the patterns of duration and intensity and color and the rest of it could be broken out into symbols. That it would have meaning."

The whisper intensified. Rustlings and murmurs surfaced, connected, flowed through the still dry air. He turned, cocked his head, and sighed. "This is what you get if you modulate the frequency with an audio signal."

"There's a cadence," I said, hardly breathing.

He laughed. "Yes! From seven million light-years, we get 'Chopsticks'!" He threw up his hands. "Damn their hides, Nick. How could they do anything so vicious?" His eyes were wet. He stood behind an upholstered chair, gripping it, trying to put his fingers through the fabric. The disk ran on: an inconsequential electronic river. "There's not much to it," I admitted. "It tends to be repetitious."

"It's a joke." The dining room was dark. He stared into it. I thought maybe he expected me to say something.

"You can still publish," I said. "If you can document this—."

"Hell, no. I've had enough. *You* publish, if you want." He was pulling on his coat. The sounds did have a certain quality—.

"You can't go out in that storm, Al. Stay here, tonight."

"It's okay. I'm over at the Holiday Inn. Thanks anyway." He pushed past me into the entry.

"Don't forget—."

"You can have it. Souvenir."

"Al—."

"I wanted you to know, Nick. I wanted *somebody* to know."

I nodded. "What will you do?"

"I'll be all right." He shrugged. "I'll probably go back to New Mexico. I've been teaching down there the last couple of semesters." He straightened his shoulders and grinned. For that moment, the old Al Redwood was back. "Nice climate. And listen: don't worry. I've got a lot to keep me busy."

Whistling past a graveyard.

He shook my hand and hurried down the front steps. A rented car was parked at the curb. He waved as he drove off.

I wondered if I'd ever see him again.

They would have needed a trillion watts to hurl Redwood's signal across seven million light-years. Who would build that kind of transmitter to send out a pleasant little coded melody? At dawn, I was still listening to the damned thing.

I took the next day off and went over to see Jean Parker, who operates a recording studio in Middletown. She's a short, intense, redheaded woman with a hell of a smile. I'd met her years before at a Wesleyan faculty dinner, where she was being honored for her contributions to the university music theater. I told her about Al, about M-82, about the transmission. About how he was trying to pretend it was not a major disappointment. "I'd like to establish whether there might be something to it."

"It's a wild story." But she glanced at the disk without interest. "What do you want me to do with it?"

I wasn't sure. "Listen to it. Assume he was right, and this is a bona fide first-contact signal. What might it mean?"

"You're kidding."

"Try it."

Her eyes closed. "Call me in a couple of days."

"I've got it on a chip." She ushered me into a booth in the rear of her studio and turned on a synthesizer. "It's tied into a Synclavier III, an enhanced Lyricon, and a few enhancement programs of my own design." She stopped and looked puzzled. "You don't care?"

"I don't understand much when you get past guitars."

"Okay. Let me start by telling you that by any reasonable definition, your recording *is* a legitimate musical composition. It has consistent structure, tonal contrast, symmetry and counterpoint, even an intensification of variations toward the conclusion. I don't see how it could be a product of natural forces. *So*, if your friend was being honest with you, and *if* the source of this is what you say, then he's right. It's Martian music." She beamed. "If you can convince the public, it ought to do pretty well."

That was an amusing notion. "I guess it *might* have commercial possibilities."

"Get a good PR guy and tell your friend to ride it, Nick." She offered me a cup of coffee. "It didn't sound like much to you because you only had the basic melody. What I've done is to create a virtual orchestra and input the melody into the computer and then through the synthesizer. The system adds appropriate harmonics and rhythm, makes assignments to the various components of our orchestra, and does some basic arrangement. You want to hear the result?"

"Go ahead." I'm not sure what I expected. I kept thinking about conditions in M-82, an entire galaxy caught in an eon-long catastrophe. The band on the *Titanic*. Nearer My God To Thee.

"Tell me about the place where they live." She touched a presspad. "What do you know?"

"I think it would be fair to say that, wherever they are in M-82, the sky is on fire."

"Okay," she said. "Maybe that fits."

Lights faded. I listened again to Al Redwood's music. It was more liquid now, distant, delivered by strings rather than the electronic burble of a Cray. There was a sense of misgiving in the cadences. Or maybe in my own mind: I thought about Al, fleeing down the years with his burden. There must have been moments when he doubted himself, suspected Gelman had been right all along. And then, Chopsticks—.

Thoughts of North Dakota at night. I was six years old, under a blazing vault of stars, standing out behind the farmhouse while the earth turned beneath my feet. It was a time when the world was full of wonder.

But the music crowded out all sense of loss.

Without warning, it roared. Lightning ripped through it, and stars thundered along their courses. White light blazed across iron battlements. Oceans turned to steam, worlds drifted into the dark, suns dissolved.

The music filled with rage. Death rode the skies, driving the stars on and on, exploding finally in a torrent of sheer irresistible power.

The mood changed, and I recalled how Honolulu looks at night from the air. And Gus Evans' 24-Hour Gas Station and Diner, in its warm circle of light halfway up a Colorado mountainside. A coyote bayed outside the McDonald Observatory at Fort Davis. Ginny lived again.

And I remembered Tom Hicks. At Wesleyan, when he won his Nobel, and we lifted glasses and laughed into the dawn.

"But that's *you*," I said afterward. "That's not what was on the CD."

She shook her head. "Maybe my imagination got caught up in it a little, Nick. This is not an exact science. But this is close to what they were trying to send."

"Then why didn't they send it?"

"I don't know the physics. But it might not have been possible to transmit anything other than the basic melody. They left the rest of it to us. Listen: I can run it through again, change some of the parameters, and things will be different. But not the essentials. They've provided the architecture. All we're adding is marble and sunlight."

I stared at her, trying to take it all in.

"They've allowed us to collaborate with them," she said. No smile. Not this time.

"I've got to find Al. Hell, this is exactly what he was looking for."

"Probably."

"Something else: these people are *winning*, Jean. Whatever it is they're dealing with out there, they're winning."

"Maybe." She ejected the disk, handed it to me, returned the original, and gave me a second copy. "For Redwood, when you find him."

"Why 'maybe'?"

She was shutting down the equipment. "Did you catch the sense of wistfulness? It runs through everything, even the most turbulent sections. I think they're like your friend."

"How do you mean?"

"Whistling past the graveyard."

IN THE TOWER

1.

Uxbridge Bay on Fishbowl in late summer. In a sense, I'd been there many times before: this sweeping sickle of gentle hills and purple flowers and whitegold shrubbery, the bay choppy under a brisk wind from the southeast, the half-dozen sleepy quill drifting across a late afternoon sky. I knew the soil, brown under twin suns, the sandy vineclogged banks, the black polished rocks dribbled through the shallows by a casual hand.

Only the carefully repaired seam across the vault of sky, through which the same casual hand had plunged a long-handled knife, was wanting.

This was a place of things lost, of lovers discarded, of thunder below the horizon. It was a place of silent beaches and brilliant far-off breakers, of invisible voices and dying laughter. It was, I suspected, the place that Durell had visited during those increasingly frequent occasions when I found him silhouetted against the bedroom window, or gazing into his wine during long, silent dinners. Something had happened here, something about which I'd learned not to speak. But he'd painted it, and had tried to destroy the painting. In the end, he'd merely denied it a name.

He'd come back from one of his long walks, less than a week before he rode his skimmer into a precipice, and he'd taken me into his arms without a word. It was so unlike him (he was not unaffectionate, but his love-making always included a mixture of verbal charm and good humor), that it was unsettling.

"What's wrong?" I'd asked.

He'd shuddered, as though cold air had reached him through the sealed windows. His eyes were silver gray, the color of the global sea on Fishbowl, and they were fixed far away. "It's nothing."

So we'd held one another, and I could feel the slow beat of his heart. And after a while he'd broken away. I was desperate: I'd watched him for three years creating melancholy landscapes, utterly unlike his early, pre-Rimway work, and sinking more deeply with each into a despondency I could neither touch nor comprehend. And that night, not for the first time, I tried to imagine life without him. "Durell," I'd pleaded, "tell me about Fishbowl."

He'd just finished the *Indemia*, which was to be his final work. It's a rendering of a child playing in a grotto, but the juxtaposition of shadow and rock and, particularly, the dark throat at the back of the cave, may possibly have been Durell's final statement on the condition of innocence in this world. I'd been upset by it. "There's nothing to tell," he said.

"There is a hell of a lot to tell. What happened there?"

He'd nodded then, his dark hair unkempt, and, in the manner one uses with a child, he'd begun the old explanation of the peculiar vulnerability of the artist, the hazards consonant with peering into the iron core of reality. I listened to the worn cliches until he himself grew embarrassed. Then I pushed him away. "You don't want to talk about it? Fine: but I'm not going to sit quietly while you unload all that guilt, or whatever it is, on *me*. Not if I don't even know what it's about."

"Tiel," he said in a whisper so low I could scarcely hear, "you would never understand." He shook his head, and his eyes filled with tears. "It was the tower room. The goddamn *tower room*."

But that was all I could get from him. In a shaky voice he told me I was right, that it would probably be best if I left. He understood. He was so understanding I felt ill, because what it amounted to was that his secrets meant more to him than I did. So I went into the bedrooom and threw as much as I could into one bag, told him I'd send for the rest later, and walked out. "I love you, Tiel," he'd said as I went through the door. They were his last words to me.

A few days later they'd handed him to me in a silver urn the color of his eyes. And I: I had come to Uxbridge Bay on Fishbowl, to the few hundred square kilometers that composed the entire land mass of that remote world. I'd developed my own cargo of guilt now: when Durell had most needed me, I'd gone for a walk.

So I came seeking the meaning of a painting. And a tower.

The texture of the light was changing rapidly as Gideon sank toward the ocean. It was well toward evening, about two hours later than the scene depicted by Durell. No matter: if Gideon was a little too low in the sky, and the air cool with approaching autumn, this was still a sacred place. How often, over the years, had I stood before the original on Rimway, absorbed by his bleak vision? I knew the reflections of my own losses in that somber water.

It had come to be known as the *Cordelet*, a reference to the land of lost innocence mentioned in Belarian mythology:

> ...*Where echoes yet in cool green glades*
> *The laughter of departed gods....*

There was, of course, no way to be certain of the exact spot where he'd placed the easel. Withered deciduals, like the one that dominates the foreground of the painting, are not uncommon in the area. I had a holo version with me, and held it up against the suns, comparing the interweaving of hills along the far edge of the sickle. But the view did not appreciably change from one suspect site to another. I looked for the white-streaked boulder close in to shore. (The artist's conviction," Gilmore had told us at the Academy, "that some things do survive against the flow of eternity." Gilmore, of course, didn't know Durell very well.) Anyhow, the tide was at full, and the rock must have been covered.

It didn't matter. I wandered among rocks and trees, took off my sandals and strolled through the surf, and gradually became aware that something along the seacoast, or in the bay, was wrong. A shell partially buried in wet sand sprouted long stalked legs and scrabbled into the water. Waves blew across groups of rocks, throwing columns of spume into the air, where the mist lingered somewhat longer than it might have in Rimway's heavier gravity.

I looked out across the bay, and gave in to self-pity. Durell was dead. (And where could I hope to find his like again?) I wanted to believe that, in some transcendental manner, his spirit brooded over this place that he'd made famous. That if he lived anywhere, it was here. But passage to Fishbowl had taken my savings; and if I felt anything at that moment other than my own solitude, I have no idea what it was.

Across the bay was the object that was *not* in the painting: a projector station on the Point, at the seaward tip of the sickle. A small copper-colored dome with a gaping black hole, it was the only man-made structure anywhere in the wide arc of land and sea appropriated by the artist.

Odd: this single forlorn symbol of human existence, its bright shell entangled in dense shrubbery, counterpointed the bay, the hills, and the sea quite effectively, heightening the suggestion of mortality which, from the time of the *Cordelet*, was central to Durell's work. It was a structure that, had it not already existed, should have been invented. Yet Durell had ruthlessly excluded it. Why?

I began to wonder if I, and everyone else, was somehow misreading the meaning.

The *Cordelet* is, of course, the watershed work of Durell's career. No one would have predicted greatness from his earlier efforts, although the innocent vitality of the young woman springing across a rainswept field in *Downhill*, and the spectral snowfall of *Night Travels*, demonstrate considerable talent. But the *Cordelet* marks the passage from the exuberance of his early period to the bleak unquiet masterpieces of maturity. The abruptness and totality of that transition is puzzling. Between *Night Travels* and the *Cordelet*, there should have been an evolutionary stage, a series of works progressively more introspective, technically more accomplished. But there is no such gradual development. And when the *Cordelet* appears, in all its somber power, only the idly circling quill, and the brilliant light of the twin suns on the far breakers, remain of the early Durell.

We would never see them again.

I was reluctant to leave. The tide was high on the sandy banks. A rising wind pulled at the trees. The rocks were changing color against dying sunlight.

But I wasn't dressed for the cool evening, and it was a long walk back to Pellinor. In Durell's time, before the skimmers were imported in large numbers, there was a road between Pellinor and the southernmost land tip. It would have been his route, so I'd tried to follow it that morning on the way out. It was, after all, the proper way to do things on a pilgrimage. But the road had diminished gradually to a footpath, which ended in heavy foliage. Disappointed, I'd crossed to the ocean's edge, where the ground was passable.

So I took a last look, wondering what Durell's thoughts had been when he closed up his frame on that final day and started back with a canvas so different from anything he'd done before, and descended the far side of the hill, dropping rapidly below sea level.

It gets cold quickly in the shadow of the sea. Gideon had set, and Heli's light was blocked by the vertical rise of the ocean. The wall of water to my left soared to more than thirty meters. I hurried along, holding my jacket closed against the falling temperatures. No one else was about, although toward the west, lights were coming on in the occasional manor houses perched out over the ridge that runs down the spine of the island.

These homes, which were owned mostly by wealthy expatriates from Rimway and Mogambo, were pretentious exercises in hyperbolic architecture: long arcing struts attached them to the underlying rock; but they were actually supported by Gantner light, the same force that restrains the ocean. I'd seen similar constructions on Rimway, although they were usually limited to corporate or public buildings.

The land along the seawall is flat and uninteresting. Its high saline content has twisted and withered the trees, which have been imported from offworld. Since Fishbowl has no natural dry ground other than the sickle and a few hills on the northern rim of Pellinor, the island's only city, it has no highly developed non-marine vegetation of its own. A few neglected waterways, from the days when someone hoped to convert all of the recovered land into a garden spot, wandered aimlessly across the landscape.

The sky had darkened before I was halfway back to town. Dim shapes glided beyond the seawall, silhouetted by filtered moonlight. I switched on my lantern and directed the beam into the water. Small, vaguely luminous plants swayed in the current, and obscure marine shapes darted away. The wall itself was hard and unyielding, and quite dry. Like polished marble.

Projector stations were scattered erratically. The coastline between the sickle and Pellinor was by no means straight, and each change of direction required another site. Several domes were also visible along the central spine. I could not imagine what use they were, well away from the ocean, and learned later that they were a backup system, that Fishbowl is, in effect, compartmentalized, so that a failure at one station would not result in a general disaster.

I stopped to examine one. It was a wide, graceful shell, about twice my height, lying in the tide like a sleeping tortoise. No sound, and no light, hinted of the enormous power generated within.

So I walked, shivering, through a landscape not quite real, a place wrenched from the ocean during my lifetime. It is a spectacular place and, by ordinary criteria, a lovely place. But Durell's sense of transience is quite real: possibly the towering seawalls are responsible for what one feels. Only the natives sleep soundly on Fishbowl. Or maybe there is something more subtle. The island, if indeed one can call it an island, has no past.

Time did not exist here until Harry Pellinor and his crew arrived to drive back the sea. If I sensed anything at all in that cramped land, it was that the projectors, the absurd homes, the withered foliage, the town huddling under the seawalls, were only an incursion.

2.

I assumed that Durell was Fishbowl's best-known citizen, so I wandered around town next morning looking for signs of his fame. A statue or two, perhaps. I'd thought that a holo in some prominent place depicting him creating the *Cordelet* would have been appropriate. Or possibly a prominent walkway named for him. At the very least, I antici-pated a Durell Coll Park, with clipped hedges and manicured trees; a gallery prominently featuring his work, and a restored studio. In reality, it was difficult to find anyone who even knew that he'd existed.

Durell had come to Fishbowl as an adolescent. His father had died on the first mission to Belarius, and his mother had returned with him to Rimway. After her death, from a rare blood disorder, he had returned to paint Pellinor's spectacular seascapes. But he'd gone quickly through a small inheritance. He used only canvas, disdaining the holos, and thereby assuring permanent poverty. Eventually he moved onto the top floor of a square permearth structure, buried among retailers and storage facilities. It was here that he honed the talents that would, in time, guarantee his fame. And that was somehow the romance of it, I suppose, that the artist whose greatest works would be embodied in broad restless skies and heaving seas should live next to a skimmer repair center.

The place was still buried. The Tiresian café that had sheltered the small group of artists on the first floor was gone, replaced by a crockery shop. Heavy utilitarian buildings lined both sides of the ground-level walk-way. A loading dock was immediately opposite the crockery shop. One of the recently built mall ramps arched overhead, an aerial strip protruding from a different sort of world. Directly above me, I could see the two pairs of windows through which he'd looked out over the ocean. (In those days, before the elevated malls and walkways, he'd had an unobstructed view to the edge of the world.) The windows were long unwashed.

The proprietor of the crockery shop was absorbed in a domestic holo. A wedge-headed matron with a fierce appearance, she seemed out of place among the dazzling characters of the romantic drama. I did not immediately rouse her. There was a door at the back of the shop which, I suspected, would provide access to the upper levels. I wandered casually toward it.

When she looked up, I stopped to examine the crockery, which was handcrafted by local artisans. She stepped out of the holo without dissolving it, and smiled pleasantly. "Good morning," she said. She looked friendly enough, though I could see she didn't expect to sell me anything. "Can I help you?"

"My name's Tiel Chadwick," I said. I'd picked up an antique kiln-fired cup. It had a satisfying heft, and carried Survey's old eagle-and-star logo, over the inscription *GS Ranger.* Harry Pellinor's vessel. "A friend of mine used to live here. In the third-floor apartment. I wondered—."

Her eyes widened, and she backed up a step. "No," she said in a voice that had climbed an octave. "I didn't know him. I've only been here a few years." Her eyes filled with suspicion. "Nobody's lived there since I came. In fact, I didn't know it had ever been anything other than a storage area."

"His name was Durell Coll. He was an artist."

She shook her head. "No. I don't know anyone like that."

"How long have you been here?" I asked.

She hesitated. "About four years." She looked closely to see whether I believed her.

I did a quick calculation, converting to Rimway time. She'd arrived shortly after Durell had left for Rimway. "Is the cup actually from the *Ranger?*"

"Of course."

I bought it, though it took a sizable slice of my remaining finances. But it was a piece of history, worth considerably more than the price. At least, on Rimway. I hoped that, in addition, the purchase would have a soothing effect on the proprietor. "I would like very much," I said, "to see the third floor. Do you mind?"

"I don't have a key."

"Maybe it's not locked."

"The owner always keeps it locked," she said stubbornly. "Nobody's allowed up there." Her face had paled, but she stood her ground, defying me to try to get past her.

I sighed, thanked her, and strolled back into the sunlight.

The room was cramped, and the walls intersected at angles that were never precisely ninety degrees. Portraits of grotesque young women hung on them. A delicate white table held a cup of steaming liquid and a few books. The books had no titles. Directly ahead of me, a broad slice of wall was missing, and outside, some distance away, a single cloud pelted a blue glass floor with big plashing raindrops. An overturned chair and a freshly made bed lay in the storm. Someone had thrown a checked jacket across the bed.

I touched the control plate and the tableau dissolved. "It's a bit heavy-handed, even for a holo," I said. "My taste runs more to the traditional."

Halson Stiles bowed slightly. "We don't sell many oils," he said. "I'm sorry to admit it, but,"—spreading his thin hands—"people today are more interested in entertainment than in art." He'd gained weight, and his hair had thinned considerably. Time had not treated Halson kindly: a pity, considering the service he'd rendered. "I have a few canvases in back that you might be interested in. No landscapes, though. Some still life, a few character studies, and three excellent impressionistic arts." He held out his hands, palms up, a man who has conceded to the tide. "It's a pity, but no one cares any longer about the spiritual values. Or subtlety. They want spectacle—" He exhaled loudly. "Sometimes, when I see what has happened to the public taste, I suspect we're heading into a dark age."

"I doubt it," I said. I wonder if legends are always disappointing when they take flesh. It was Stiles who, according to tradition, had wrested a meat-knife from Durell, and thereby saved the *Cordelet*, gaining immortality in the process. His name was inextricably linked now with Durell's, as mine would never be. But the strong brown eyes and composed dignity of the photos had given way to the unctuousness of a badly pressed salesman.

His was the only gallery on Fishbowl. At least, the only one with a listing. It was anchored high off a second-floor ramp overlooking the wide lawns and vaguely topological designs of the Survey Cluster.

"It's fortunate," I said, "that the *Cordelet* wasn't done as a holo.."

"Ah." He beamed. "There is no way it could have been created on anything other than canvas. Yes: well, Durell was a serious artist."

"Halson, you handled some of his early work, didn't you?"

"Who are you?" he asked. He was looking closely at me, frowning because he could not place me.

"I was a friend of his," I said. "My name's Tiel Chadwick."

He considered that, and smiled broadly, and extended his hand. "I didn't think the dumb bastard would do so well."

"Thanks." I returned the smile.

"I was sorry to hear about his death. Terrible. Terrible accident."

We paused in front of a portrait of Harry Pellinor in heroic mode. "Durell's death wasn't an accident."

"I don't think I understand, Tiel."

"He killed himself. Probably not deliberately, but he didn't much care whether he lived or died. It wasn't hard to see it coming." I was having trouble keeping my voice steady.

"Why?" he asked. He looked genuinely shocked. "Durell wasn't exactly a tower of stability, but he would never have taken his life."

"I'd hoped you might tell *me* why."

"I have no idea. He was the only person I know who actually succeeded in his life's ambitions. Was he having health problems? No?" He rubbed the back of his neck. "It makes no sense. What made you think I might know?"

"It's something that happened here. Something drove him. Your comment that he was no tower of stability: is there an actual tower anywhere on Fishbowl?"

"No," he said. "Not that I know of."

"Anyplace *called* the Tower? Or the Tower *Room*?"

"No." We'd been wandering among some local work, more craft than art. "Why do you ask?"

"No reason, really. Something he said once that I must have misunderstood. How well did you know him?"

He stared at me a long time. "Not well. A couple of the other artists used to spend some time with him. They were all bone poor. Especially Coll."

"Can you tell me the names of the others?"

"I could, but it wouldn't do you much good. One's dead, drank too much and fell off a ramp a couple years ago. The others are long gone. Left before Durell did." He tilted his head. "I can tell you where you might find somebody who remembers him. Durell liked to play chess. He was a member of a club. The organization was still in existence, last I heard. They used to meet at Survey."

"Thanks," I said.

He pursed his lips. "You know, if I'd been smart enough to hang on to just one of his paintings, I could've retired. It's frustrating. I knew how good he was. But I never thought anybody else would realize it. At least not before we were all dead."

"Halson, you said he was 'bone poor.'"

"He missed a few meals in his time. I did what I could to help, but I didn't have much money in those days either. Durell wanted to get away from Fishbowl. For two years it was all he talked about. He even took jobs from time to time to try to get the fare together, but he could never stay with them long enough. Then one day he walked in, picked up his paintings—I had three of them in inventory then—, gave me a hundred for my trouble, and the next thing I heard about him, he was on Rimway."

"I wonder where the money came from?"

"I have no idea."

"Halson, are there any paintings other than the ones generally known?"

"No, I don't think so." He pulled sympathetically at his right ear, shook his head no, and slipped through a set of curtains. He returned moments later with iced cordials. "He did some murals for Survey's operations center. But don't get interested: they tore the place down two years ago."

"Son of a bitch. He had his reputation by then. Didn't anybody try to save them?"

"I don't think anyone thought of it. His name didn't mean anything to the people at Survey, and I—I didn't know the building was coming down until it was too late. Ironically, they recycled the permearth, and used it to build this mall."

"The world is full of philistines," I sighed.

He nodded. "They were digging up Belarius to look at an alien culture, and they don't know very much about their own." Three women paused outside on the ramp, and one by one stepped into the shop's display case. I couldn't see the holo itself, but the edge of a soft blue haze expanded into the doorway. "They're on a ledge overlooking a waterfall," Stiles said. "It's our biggest seller.

"The murals weren't really that good anyhow. They were Belarian locales, sandstorms, broken columns in the desert, that sort of thing. Ozymandian stuff. Durell wasn't interested in it, but it put food on the table."

"He died rich," I said.

"I would think so." Stiles's eyes were half closed. "I hope he learned to enjoy it."

"Why did he want to destroy the *Cordelet*?"

He shrugged. "Who knows? He was proud of it. He invited me over to his studio the night he finished it. It's the only time he ever did that. He met me at the door: you had to go in through a rear entrance. The studio was dark, but he'd placed a lamp just so, and when he turned it on, the light fell full on the *Cordelet*. Can you imagine that? Walking into a dark room and seeing the *Cordelet* for the first time? I knew immediately it was good: I told him it ranked with Delacroix, Matisse, anything I'd ever seen.

"'Yes,' he agreed. 'Who would have believed I could create *this*?' We stood there, both of us, transfixed. And then, without any warning, he went after it. I never even saw where the meat cutter came from. He just had it in his hand, and he was stabbing away like a maniac. The look in his eyes: I knew he'd destroy it, and I couldn't let him do that."

"You could have lost your life," I said.

"He let me take it away from him. The knife—"

"I never saw him like that," I said. "It's hard to imagine. So out of character. I've seen him drunk and sober, up and down. Moods, yes. My God, he was moody. But I never knew him to do anything like that.

"He left it with you. The *Cordelet*."

"He said he never wanted to see it again. I sold it to a collector a few months later and sent him the money. He was on Rimway by then. Later, the collector got five or six times as much for it from an art museum on Rimway. The Apollonian."

3.

At night, the wandering ramps and walkways of Pellinor glitter beneath Fishbowl's spectacular ring system. Its people stroll among softly illuminated parks and malls, which range over the downtown area at, or above, sea level. The trees are healthy here, providing shelter for colorful and noisy avians, most of which are pittacines, imported from Earth and Mogambo. Fishbowl, of course, has no native birds; nature has provided only the drifting gasbag quill to populate her skies.

Pellinor was still a quiet, remote outpost in those days. There were, as yet, few tourists to watch the play of lights against the vertical sea. The Belarian excavations had been abandoned years before, but Survey retained its foothold on Fishbowl, converting the old support facility into an administrative headquarters.

I can recall sitting on a bench that evening, after my conversation with Stiles. I was on the outer perimeter of the walkways, near the beaches. (They lower the outer ramps at night to create a high-tide effect.) On the inland side, occasional couples strolled through Survey's geometrical grounds. Above, on the top level, a late party was spilling out of a club.

I had never been so far from home. Delta Draconis was bright and gold in the north, just visible above the lip of the seawall. And directly overhead, in the wake of the moon, lay Belarius, cool and green and hostile. Home of the *other* civilization: the only nonhuman culture encountered during the long expansion from Earth.

Also to the north, about a kilometer away, I could see the cluster of squat buildings that housed Durell's old studio. I walked slowly in that direction, waiting for the lights to dim and the last stragglers to start home. If there were police about, they were not visible. Crime barely existed on Fishbowl. An incident in which several adolescents had stolen a skimmer and crashed at sea had set people talking for days about lawlessness and the general decline of social values.

The smell of the sea was strong. Beyond the beach, it boomed and thundered with soothing effect against the Gantner light screens. I think I knew then that eventually the tourists would come, that the homes along the ridge would rise in value, and that Pellinor would lose her innocence. As things turned out, it happened more quickly than I could have expected. But that's another story. The only thing that mattered now, as I got up from my bench and sauntered off to do some burgling, was that, on Fishbowl, locks were simple and witnesses few.

There had been a skylight. Though he'd never drawn it, its effects were visible in some of his sketches, in the curious double shadow of the latticework, and occasionally of people or pieces of furniture, cast by the twin suns. I reached a strategic location over the rooftops in the commercial district, and looked down on the street in which I'd stood that morning. The rear entrance to Durell's studio, by which Stiles had entered, no longer existed.

I've never been comfortable with heights. The angle at which the ramp crossed the rooftops left only a small corner on which to descend. The pavement was a long way down, and the wind was gusting sharply off the sea.

I clipped a line to the safety rail and, with some misgivings, climbed over the side. Far below, a streetlamp threw light across a truck docked at the depot. Two men sat off to one side. Their voices drifted up to me.

The wind gave me a bad few minutes, pushing me away from the rooftop and out over the street. But I got down all right, finally, and made for the skylight.

I switched on my handlamp.

Any interior walls that might have existed during Durell's time had been removed. The entire upper floor consisted of a single large room. I could see a toilet, a sink, and a shower stall toward the rear. Other plumbing fixtures were scattered about. Cartons had been stacked randomly, and a couple of hand trucks were in the middle of the floor.

The skylight was latched. I broke it open without much trouble and dropped a line.

Why had the wedge-faced woman seemed so frightened? Was there something in this room?

It occurred to me that I was about to break the law. My first criminal act. Well, I didn't mind, as long as I didn't get caught. But the potential for real trouble existed, and I wondered whether I shouldn't just forget the whole thing and go home.

I don't know what I was expecting to see: a few plastic-wrapped canvases, maybe, forgotten in a dusty corner. Or a record. Something.

A rickety table with one drawer held a computer. The drawer was empty. I wandered around, looking at floors and walls. The cartons contained shelving and packing material and crockery. I could find nothing, and eventually I wandered over to the arched front windows. The two men at the depot dock were gone.

I'm not sure what drew my attention to the walls. At the front, where Durell's working studio had been, they were covered with several sheets of bright cheap pastel mosaics. The design was not unattractive, but I knew that Durell could not have lived with it.

That meant the panels had been put up after he'd left. But it seemed unlikely that there'd been another tenant before the area was converted for storage. Why then had anyone bothered to decorate the walls?

The sheets were thick with dust. I peeled off a long strip of trim, removed the baseboard, and released the magnets. (I heard the whine of a set of gyros, and the truck rose past the windows. Its lights fell across the glass, and then were gone.) The panel was wedged at the top and on one side. I pried it forward and tried to get the lamp behind it.

Light fell on the outline of an *ear.* My pulse picked up: the lines were the quick, precise strokes of Durell Coll. I put the light down, braced my back against the wall, and broke the panel. It went with a bang.

I snapped off the lamp, and waited to see if I'd attracted anyone's notice. But there were no footsteps in the building, and none in the street. It was a delicious moment.

The sea was loud. It was easy to understand why Durell, working on this world, amid the endless tidal roar, would have found his meanings ultimately in the natural world. To my knowledge, he had never done a portrait.

I lifted the lamp to get a good look—

If Durell Coll's reputation was built on gloomy perceptions of a hostile universe, the man himself, at least during his early years on Rimway, had always enjoyed a good party. He was usually surrounded by women, and loved to spend the long winter evenings (we lived high in the northern hemisphere) talking and drinking with old friends.

He laughed easily; and nothing amused him more than suggestions by people who should have known better that his work needed cheering up. More vitality, they used to say. More life.

It was only toward the end that the shadows that had been lengthening across his art began, finally, to darken his features. And a Durell Coll that I did not know appeared, a man who took solitary strolls through snow-filled streets, who endured intense nightmares of which he would not speak, and who ultimately withdrew into a world not unlike that of the *Cordelet*.

It was the early Durell that I preferred to remember, and whom I'd hoped to find in the old studio.

What I found instead was something dredged out of the soul of a madman: a face barely human, rendered in Durell's painfully realistic fashion. It was of a man in middle age, with a full beard and commanding features. But his terror-ridden eyes gaped out of deep black sockets. The mouth was twisted in a frightful snarl, and flecks of saliva flew from the beard.

I stumbled backward over a hand truck. The light went out, and I was not at all anxious to put it back on. Instead, I lay in the dark, listening to the sound of my own breathing, feeling the palpable presence of the thing on the wall, trying to understand how a young Durell Coll, *my* Durell, could have created the monstrosity.

There was no doubt: it was *his* work. Despite the lurid nature of the subject, tone and texture were clearly his.

I'd bruised an elbow, and the pain began to intrude itself. I rubbed it, grateful for the distraction.

Who was the bearded man? I wondered whether he'd actually existed, or whether the tortured image had been constructed from whole cloth. In a sense, I supposed I had what I'd come for: an unknown work by Durell, a previously unsuspected creation. It would be worth a lot of money.

But not to me.

The image appeared, at first, to be badly faded, until I realized someone had painted over it. And then, not satisfied, had covered the result with panels. But over the years, the paint had faded, and only the image remained.

And the other panels: what lay under *them*? I played my light across the swirl of spring colors, and my heart sank.

The sensible thing would be to leave. God knows the place had chilled and I wanted to get out of there, and off Fishbowl, and to put behind me, somehow, the last four years of my life.

I removed a second panel. There was enough light from outside to see that there was another sketch. I hesitated, and put the lamp on it.

It was the same hideous figure.

And I uncovered *another*, next to the second.

I was slow to realize that the three images, however, were not identical. The angle of the profile changed from one to another, the shading in each set of eyes was subtly different, the beards—I took them all down, ten or eleven panels: the same face appeared again and again, its grotesque expression, each time, varied in some way.

My Durell. The gentlest, finest human being I had known.

I replaced the panels. If there had been a way, I would have razed the walls, or destroyed the building. No wonder the proprietor of the crockery shop had been frightened of me.

4.

Fishbowl's chess club meets in a glass-lined conference room on the second level of the Annex, which is a flattened pyramid adjacent Survey's main administration building. On the night of my visit, there were roughly a dozen games in progress, and one spectator, an elderly woman with the glittering eyes of a bird of prey. She immediately challenged me to play.

I declined politely, whispering that I did not understand the game (an explanation which provoked a brief look of disbelief), and inquired whether she'd ever heard of Durell. She hadn't, and I settled in to watch for an opportunity to ask someone else. The only sounds in the room were the occasional scraping of chairs, and the ticking of chess clocks.

It was difficult to find a way to talk to any of them. Players had a tendency to resign merely by stopping the clock. Then, within moments, they'd reset the pieces and begun again. Not that it mattered: when I tried to ask questions, people shook their heads irritably, and looked pointedly at their boards.

I retired from the field of combat, and settled for intercepting players on their way to the washroom. Two or three remembered Durell, but only as someone who came occasionally to the club. ("Liked to play the Dragon Variation of the Sirian, but he was far too cautious.")

Toward the end of the evening, I approached an overweight, red-faced little man whose name was Jon Hollander. Hollander was one of the club's officers. Someone told me later that chess was the consuming passion of his life, but that he wasn't very good at it. "I don't recall him, Tiel, but we've had a lot of members over the years. What precisely did you want to know?" He looked at me the way men do when they've been a long time without a woman.

I had no idea. "He was an old friend. I suppose I just wanted to talk with someone who'd known him," I said.

"And you can't find anybody?"

"Not really."

He nodded. "Maybe we can find something in the archives."

We left the clubroom, and turned into a long carpeted corridor that curved and rose until we'd ascended approximately one floor. He led the way into an office, and sat down at a terminal. "There may not be anything," he said, "but we can try."

He punched in Durell's name. Dates and numbers appeared. Hollander tapped the screen. "He was a member for almost two years." He grinned. "He had some problems paying his dues."

"What else do you have?"

"Address and code number. You want those?"

"No."

Hollander frowned. "How about one of his games? We have three on record."

"No, I don't think so."

"Looks like he lost them all anyhow."

"You don't have a picture of him, do you?"

Hollander pushed a pad, and an index appeared. "No," he said, running his eye down the names. "We have several group photos from the period when he was a member, but he doesn't seem to be in any of them." The index faded, to be replaced by several people in parkas, standing outside the Annex during a snowstorm. "The Second Winter Open. Coll played in that tournament, but I guess he wasn't around when they took the picture." Another group appeared, still cold weather, but the snow was gone. "This was our first Masters', the same year. He wasn't eligible for that one."

He changed it again, for an indoor shot. But something had struck me about the Winter Open, and I didn't know what. "Go back to the first one, Jon," I said.

The snow scene reappeared. Three women were seated on a bench, in front of four men. "That's me on the left," said Hollander.

"Who's that beside you?"

He squinted. "Looks like Ux." The man was bigger than Hollander, shorter than the other two. Although his hood was tied down against the chill of the day, he wore a wide smile. Hollander brought his image up. "Yes," he said, "it's Reuben Uxbridge. Did you know him?"

I knew him: his was the face on the wall. "Who is he?"

Hollander's features softened. "He was a charter member. One of the strongest players we've ever had. He specialized in the end game. Absolutely deadly once the queens were off the board."

"Where is he now?"

"Ux died quite a few years ago, Tiel."

Down the long corridor, I could hear voices as the playing room emptied out. "What happened to him?" He was middle-aged, and he looked healthy enough.

Hollander pressed his palms together. "He drowned. I guess it was only a year or so after the picture was taken." His eyes grew thoughtful. "Queer business. He walked out onto a beach near his home one day in midsummer. A couple of families were there on an outing. He went past then without saying a word and simply walked into the sea."

He turned slowly in my direction, but his eyes were unfocused. "Why?" I asked.

He shrugged. "He was here for about two years before they went to Belarius. When he came back, he was *different*."

"Belarius? Was that the second attempt?"

"Yes," he said. "I guess both expeditions more or less blew up. The official word was that there were hostile conditions. Ux never mentioned it and, to my knowledge, no one around here pressed him about it. But *something* happened. At one point, there was talk that he'd brought something back."

"How did he change?"

"I don't know, exactly. It's hard to put your finger on. For one thing, his game improved. No, don't look at me like that: I mean really improved. He threw himself into his chess. Played like a man possessed. He opened up, and abandoned his old precise positional play for a ferocious combinative style. Listen, Tiel, chess players can change their approach to the game, but I never saw anything like *this*. It was like he was a different person." He got up slowly and shut down the computer. "Furthermore, during that latter stage, he was the strongest player we had.

"That wasn't the only thing. He became withdrawn, didn't talk much to anyone. That kind of condition has to become pretty severe before you notice it in a chess club."

We retraced our steps to the playing room. "Did he have a family? Anyone I might talk to?"

"No," said Hollander. "None that I know of. But I can give you a list of people who knew him. Everyone liked him."

"Who was with him on Belarius?"

He shook his head. "Nobody here. They still have some people at Survey who made the second flight. They'll remember him."

That seemed strange: we were on Survey's grounds. "You mean there are no employees in Survey's chess club?"

"They just lend us the space, Tiel."

"Is it a coincidence," I asked, "that Uxbridge's name is the same as the bay's? The one at the far end of the island?"

"That's the only bay we've got. No: it's no coincidence. He lived out there. At the point."

"Jon," I said, "I was there yesterday, and I didn't see any houses. Not in the area of the bay, anyhow."

"You wouldn't," he said. "It's *in* the bay now. Shortly after Ux died, somebody took a laser to the projector at the Point, and let the sea in. Pity: it was a fine house."

My scalp began to prickle. "That sounds as if you've been inside it."

"A few times. He used to invite one or another of us out sometimes to play a few games." His eyes closed, and a rueful smile appeared. "He had a kind of trophy room at the back of the house, filled with plaques and artifacts and whatnot. There were two leather chairs he'd brought from Rimway. Tiel, they were probably the only leather chairs on Fishbowl! Those were fine evenings. And good chess."

"Jon, was this before he went to Belarius?"

"Oh, yes." He nodded. "I don't think anybody ever went out to the house after he came back. The invitations stopped. At least mine did. Although, now that I think of it, he came to my place now and then. He just didn't reciprocate any more." He'd turned away and was looking out through the glass. Fishbowl's rings illuminated the sky over the Admin Building.

"The destruction of the seawall," he continued, "created some commotion, because people thought maybe we had a loony running around who was planning to sink the island. For a while they posted guards at all the projector stations, but nothing more ever happened, and I guess they finally decided it was just some kids. Now, the projectors are pretty well shielded."

"They never made repairs at the Point?"

He shrugged. "Draining the new bay and reestablishing the screen would have been expensive, so we didn't bother. No one ever stepped forward to take a proprietary interest. There've been proposals to go in and reclaim the land, but there's really no reason to. So we named the bay after him instead."

I showed him the holo of the *Cordelet*. "Is this what we're talking about?"

"Yes," he said. "That's it. The house is down there somewhere. Right about in the middle, I'd think."

I wondered if it had ever occurred to anyone that somebody had specifically wanted to destroy Uxbridge's home.

5.

In the morning, I rented a skimmer. But instead of turning south and running down the coastline, I procrastinated, hovering aimlessly over Pellinor for an hour, and then drifting out to sea. I kept low, just above the waves, until my clothes were drenched with spray. Behind me, the land vanished into a hole in the ocean, bracketed by the cluster of brown hills to the south, and the upper levels of Pellinor's wide ramps.

I settled into the water. Gideon was hidden behind thick white clouds. The white rim of Heli was just pushing out of the sea, and the color of the sky was changing while I watched.

I'm not sure how long I sat out there, listening to the water lap against the sideboards, thinking about the mad portraits and Reuben Uxbridge's walk into the sea. If Hollander was correct, Uxbridge had undergone a basic personality change. As, to a lesser extent, Durell had.

I was no longer sure I wanted to know the truth, but I did not wish to be driven at some future date to return to Fishbowl because I couldn't sleep well. What had begun as an innocent nostalgic excursion had become something radically different.

I buckled myself in, left the shields down so I could feel the rush of air, and started back. Only the drifting quill, their fibrilla dangling into the waves, broke the monotony of sea and sky. An ocean with a single shore gets little traffic.

Just off the Point, a school of large marine animals were sunning themselves. There must have been a hundred or more, huge creatures, of the stature of Rimway's behemoth, or Earth's sperm whale. They moved slowly, and their great dark eyes rolled curiously skyward to watch me pass. The articulation of fin and jaw was not so fine or detailed as I was accustomed to, but Fishbowl is a young world.

Abruptly, the sea fell away, and I was over the rills and valleys of the island. Then they too gave way, though not with the same breathtaking suddenness, to the burnished surface of Uxbridge Bay.

The mood of my first visit was gone: the sense of a place out of time, of a world with psychic links to an earlier age, had evaporated. And in its stead, despite the twin morning suns, I sensed only madness and despair.

I drifted over the waters of the bay, slowed to a few klicks, and locked in the pilot. Out near the Point, beyond the arc of hills, lay the sandy beach across which Uxbridge had strolled to his death.

The bay was almost perfectly circular. This was a feature not apparent in the *Cordelet*, where the harbor mouth appears quite distant, and the far shore rather near, suggesting a more elongated shape. Close in, the bottom was littered with rocks. But it was relatively clear, despite rippling shadows cast by currents, and clumps of undulating sea anima. A line of rocks lay close to the place where I'd stood my first day surveying the scene. Paralleling the coastline for a considerable distance, they were either a collapsed breakwater or the remains of a wall.

I dropped lower and flew in wide circles that took me well out to sea on each pass. There was no sign of a submerged house. After an hour or so, I flew listlessly over the mouth of the bay, suspecting the entire story was mythical. I was about to give up when I saw a shadow in the water.

I lobbed a cone buoy over the side, came around and, too absorbed perhaps to pay attention to what I was doing, cut power before I was fully down. The skimmer chopped heavily into the water, bounced, jabbed its nose below the surface, and threatened briefly to turn over.

I blamed it on the lighter gravity, took a quick look around for damage (there was none), and got out a deep-sided glass dish I'd brought along for submarine viewing. There *was* a house down there. The light wasn't good, but I could see its roof.

It looked intact. That struck me as being exceedingly unlikely, until I noticed a small ridge cutting diagonally down from the shoreline and across the bottom of the basin. Driven into it, and now broken off, were a pair of stems of the type that provided nominal support for a Gantner light system.

That meant Uxbridge's house had been entirely, or at least partly, above the flood. But the water had got at the projector and shorted it out. The increased weight had snapped the stems, and the place had gone to the bottom.

It was a three-level structure, and it looked like stone rather than the standardized materials generally in use on Fishbowl. The external appurtenances, stylized cupolas, belvederes, porticoes, and so on that characterize most of the wealthy homes on Fishbowl (and on Rimway, for that matter) were particularly in evidence here. Add small, round windows, and the illusion of an exotic sea beast lying quietly in the sand was complete.

But the windows were dark, and only fish swam through its abandoned rooms.

It had no tower.

I'd brought a breather with me, and I knew that the next rational step was to use it. But the house was far down, and the suspicion of what I might find prevented my unpacking the unit. Instead, I sat rocking gently on the skimmer, feeling like a damned fool.

After a while, I started the engine and rolled angrily into the bright clear sky.

6.

When Jon Hollander looks through the windows from the office in which the Pellinor Chess Club keeps its records, he can see a broad oval pool. Directly beyond the pool crouches a heavy, triple-tiered oblate building utterly out of place among the crystal structures of the Survey complex. This is the Belarian Field Museum. It is, according to a plaque mounted at the front entrance, an accurate representation of architectural styles to be found at Ysdril West, one of the major excavation sites in that world's southern hemisphere. It is accurate rather than exact, because it has been necessary to increase the size of doorways, and raise ceilings, to accommodate human visitors.

One recognizes immediately that it is the work of a primitive race. Constructed of quartz, the Field Museum is set within a pavilion ringed by flapping pennants. There are few windows, and the upper tiers are progressively recessed, creating an effect somewhat like that of a ziggurat.

The quartz blocks are rough-hewn and joined with cement. Nightmare creatures with bared fangs and talons guard the entrances, and hieroglyphs have been stenciled into the living rock, marking the four cardinal points of the compass. The inscriptions are delicate, sylphlike engravings, utterly out of character with the ponderous stone blocks and doors.

I'd paused on the west portico to examine one, tracing the lean characters with my fingers. A plate translated: "In the hour of need, I am with you."

The Museum's windows were small, recessed, and barred. Another plaque announced that the structure was a place of worship, but it felt like a fortress.

I wasn't entirely ignorant about the Belarians. They'd been small creatures, by human standards, seldom surpassing a meter in height. Artists' renderings of their appearance were disquieting, however: pale, bloated, gas-filled bodies, not unlike the amoeba-like quill.

They never achieved a technological culture, and the last of them went to their reward a million years ago. Standing in the shadow of that gloomy pile, I wondered how such creatures could have developed a written language. Or, for that matter, juggled building supplies.

I entered the Field Museum through a heavy square-cut arch. The ground floor was crowded with display cases, statuary, tools, and assorted other artifacts. An attendant in Survey's light and dark green uniform stood beside a stone altar, behind which several viewing booths had been installed. To my right, a ramp ascended to the upper levels.

I was surprised to discover an abundance of natural light emanating from a circular courtyard. The overall effect was that somehow, within these walls, time had slowed from its natural pace, and become somehow quite palpable.

There was only one other visitor, a brittle, elderly man who was sketching an inscription from a hexagonal stone mounted over a display board. I walked among the artifacts, little figures carved from black rock set in gleaming cases with neat white cards identifying their probable age and use.

There were scrapers and cutters and rakeheads and spearpoints. Obviously, the Belarians had been more substantial than they looked. There were figures of animals and dwellings, and fantastic creatures that might have been real or mythical. One case contained several hundred tablets, all engraved with rows of ideographs. A plate placed them quite early in Belarian history. They had not yet been translated. But they resembled the somewhat later materials from which the *Book of Life*, with its immortal accounts of Cordelet and the pillars of the world, had been derived.

"They had paper," said a voice behind me. "It's ironic that only the earliest written materials have survived. Only the tablets." It was the old man. He was about my size, clean-shaven except for a neatly-trimmed white mustache. (That was not then the style on Fishbowl, and marked him as a helpless relic.) "Even the inscriptions on their buildings are from early religious or ethical texts. The books are all gone."

"I'm Tiel Chadwick," I said, offering my hand.

He took it in a firm grasp. "M'Kay Alexander. You may call me Alex."

I described myself as a student from Rimway, and we talked for a while about Belarian art. Which meant primarily architecture, since little else remained.

"How did they produce anything?" I asked. "I mean, they had no hands."

"They had a highly flexible sheath," he replied. "Pseudopodal extensions. If you look closely, you can see them on some of the artifacts. Here—." He indicated a pair of figures in an adjoining case. They did indeed seem to have limbs. They emerged however from disconcerting sites, from abdominal and head areas. I had the overall sense that I was looking at a creature wrapped in a sheet.

Okay: that seemed reasonable enough. But what about the buildings? You can't move a boulder with a pseudopod. "They must have had heavy equipment of some kind."

"Not that we could find, Tiel. You, uh, don't mind if I call you Tiel?"

"Of course not."

"Good." His gaze swept over the display cases and carved blocks. "No," he said, "it's difficult to sort things out; there's so little left. But I don't think they ever had the sort of machines that would be required to haul these stones around."

"How do you know?"

"Their psychology. They were simply not a technological race. Did you know their culture was twenty thousand years old when they died off? And they never got past a medieval stage."

"What happened to them?"

"Nobody knows. Maybe the competition became too severe. Some of the local experts think they couldn't unite politically. Who knows?"

He was turning the pages of his sketch pad, holding it so I could see. It was filled with renderings of the objects in the cases, or the altar, and of the Field Museum itself. "It's a puzzle, how they moved these rocks around. It's one of the things Survey was trying to find out when they were driven off."

I blinked at the old man: I hadn't heard it put in quite those terms before. "What drove them off?"

Alexander placed his fingertips against the altar, as though to read something in the cold stone. "I'd love to know," he said.

"Wasn't it ever made public?"

"In a way, Tiel. They released a fairly detailed description of conditions on Belarius after the second expedition. It's an old world. There's been a lot of time for evolution. So the carnivores are very efficient. They have a lot of teeth, and they move very quickly, and some of them fly, and most of them are hard to see coming." I'd seen pictures of a few. The one that stuck in my mind was a kind of jet-propelled airborne shark. "And they are reasonably intelligent. Which, by the way, has been a factor in keeping their numbers down, so that they don't eliminate the food supply."

"How do you mean?" We had wandered close to a diorama of the Ysdril West excavation.

"They made war on one another. The species did."

"Why?"

"For the same reason animals fight on Rimway. Water. Hunting rights. Whatever. But on Belarius, it was organized warfare. The species there seem to have more than their share of intelligence and administrative capacity. In any case, though, I can't imagine why a well-armed force—and, at least in the case of the second expedition, forewarned as well—couldn't hold their own against local predators."

"Alex, you seem to know quite a lot about Belarius. Have you worked for Survey?"

He looked around for a place to sit, and found a stone bench. "I'm in the food business," he said. "Or was. I'm retired now."

I couldn't suppress a smile. "How does somebody in the food business come to be involved in all this?" I waved an arm around.

"We have a little group on Rimway," he said. "Mostly people like me, who are just interested in the Belarian story." He leaned forward, his voice intent. "Listen, Tiel. Survey's not telling the truth about what happened on Belarius. Moreover, it's been years now since they officially announced that they would not go back there. But look—." Through the front entrance we could see the pool, and the cluster of Survey buildings beyond. They were silver and green in the late afternoon light. "Why have they stayed on Fishbowl? God knows it's not near anything else."

I shrugged. I certainly didn't know.

"Because," he said, "they're going back. Tiel, there is no possibility that they're going to walk off and leave what they've found. But there's something out there that scares them."

He'd raised his voice and drawn the attention of the attendant.

The diorama was mostly sand: a collection of partly excavated blocks and columns, earth-moving machines, temporary shelters, and people. A lander stood on the edge of the display. No single indigenous structure was intact. "Alex," I said, "I take it you've not been to Belarius?"

"No," he said with regret. "When we heard about the second mission, we pooled our money, and offered Survey a substantial sum to allow passage to one of our members. If they'd gone along with it, we were going to cut cards to determine the winner."

"What did they say?"

"Too dangerous. They couldn't take the responsibility." His eyes narrowed. "I can't quarrel with that. They lost almost half their landing team on the first effort. The second try wasn't much better." He stared at Ysdril West. "But I would have liked to go."

I'd been wondering whether Durell might have made the trip, but it seemed unlikely. "Alex," I said, "there were several excavation sites on Belarius. Is there a *tower* anywhere among them?"

"Intact?"

I hesitated over that one. "Not necessarily. Anything sticking up out of the rubble that one could describe as a tower."

He closed his eyes, and I could see him mentally inspecting the various digs. "No," he said finally. "I don't think so. If there is, they're keeping it quiet."

"Do you know anything about Reuben Uxbridge?"

"He was an expert on ideographic structure." He glanced at his watch, and shrugged. "I have to be going." He stood up. "Uxbridge worked for Casmir Moss, who was the on-site director of the mission when they closed it down."

"Was he ever involved in any sort of unusual incident?"

"Tiel, I would say they were all involved in unusual incidents of one kind or another. I just don't know. If you want to talk to someone about Uxbridge, see Moss."

"Where would I find him?"

"He's here somewhere. He's one of the reasons I'm sure they're going back. Moss would have more important things to do than hang around Fishbowl if something weren't about to happen."

Two middle-aged women and a boy came through the front entrance. The boy made immediately for the diorama.

"Alex," I asked, "are you here alone?"

"Yes. Three of us were supposed to make the trip, but things came up. You know how it is."

"How about dinner?" I said. "My treat."

7.

That night, I looked up everything the Library had on the two missions. The official stuff wasn't very informative, and the dozen or so books written on the subject were neither consistent with each other nor helpful. Eggleston's *Bureaucrats in the Field* mercilessly flayed security procedures that "couldn't hold off a few wild animals with modern weapons." Adrian Hunt, in *Survey and Belarius: A Study in the Exercise of Power*, charged that the political appointees who control Survey's funding wished to put an end to the program because it cost too much, and the feudal civilization that had developed on Belarius could make no conceivable contribution to Confederate technology. Other volumes hinted darkly at a demonic presence on Belarius.

There was no mention of Uxbridge anywhere, but Eggleston excoriated Moss as an incompetent paper-shuffler who'd been more concerned with arcane languages than with the practical hazards faced by his teams. (Moss's division of philologists and archeologists had taken the heaviest losses, and he was charged with providing inadequate security training for himself and his subordinates.)

Like Uxbridge, Moss was a philologist, though of somewhat more advanced reputation. He'd won most of the major awards, declined at least two university presidencies, and written *The Dawn of Language*, the definitive study of proto-Sumerian ideography. Eggleston remarked that, for Moss, the Belarian discovery was a kind of fresh virgin after the long line of ancients so thoroughly worked over by everybody else.

But this had apparently been a virgin with a bite.

The evening after my conversation with M'Kay Alexander, I contrived to be at Arnhof's, a small restaurant overlooking a shopping quadrangle, when Moss came in for his evening meal. He was a man of quite ordinary appearance, with dull blue eyes, and defensive lines drawn about his mouth. It would have been no surprise to learn that he made his living from dead languages.

I maneuvered into a table adjacent his, ordered some seafood (what else?), and awaited an opportunity. Moss took some papers from a case, spread them out in front of him, and sank immediately into a reverie.

About the time the wine came, his and mine, he looked up to catch me staring at him. That was my cue. "Pardon me," I said, leaning toward him, "but aren't you Casmir Moss?"

"I am." He was not displeased at being recognized.

"I'm Tiel Chadwick. I've read your book." That was a gamble. The truth was, of course, that I'd read *of* it.

He smiled back uncertainly, inviting me to say something else. I did. I told him that it had sparked my interest in ancient civilizations, and that I thought he'd made difficult concepts quite lucid. Fortunately, he did not ask for specifics.

Within a few minutes, we were drinking from the same carafe. He loved to talk about ancient Babylonian politics, and I encouraged him, asking a few safe questions and, later in the evening, found myself strolling with him along the beachfront. Abruptly, he turned and faced me. "Who are you, really?"

The question caught me by surprise. "A friend of Ux's," I said.

He was silent for a time. The moon drifted low on the ocean, limning the incoming waves with silver. Eventually, gripping the safety rail, he nodded, as if we shared some dark secret.

We walked out past the Oceanographic Institute, saying little and, at my suggestion, stopped at a little bar on the edge of a park. "Reuben Uxbridge," he said, as we entered, "was one of the most difficult people I've ever worked with. He didn't like to take directions, thought anyone disputing his views was misinformed, and generally behaved abrasively toward everyone. I'm almost surprised to hear he *had* a friend." He blinked at me. "I hope I haven't offended you." We found a table near the window. Soft music drifted through the place. "But my God, I would give a lot to have him with us tonight."

That didn't sound much like the Uxbridge the chessplayers knew. Of course, the circumstances were different.

I'd intended to wait until we'd gone through two or three rounds. But the moment had clearly arrived. We ordered drinks, and I could see that he was consumed by his own thoughts. "Casmir," I said, "what happened in the tower room?"

His eyes widened perceptibly. "I did not think he would tell anyone. How much do you know?"

"Very little. I know there was a problem. I know he was never the same afterward."

The drinks came. He drew his index finger through the frost on the glass, then lifted it and studied the liquid in the wavering candlelight. "I assume you are aware of conditions on Belarius?"

"I know they're difficult."

"I would say *violent.*" He smiled, as at some private joke. "But the prize was well worth the risks. Did Ux tell you why we were so interested in Ysdril West? No? Then let me: it is not one city, but seven, built over ten thousand years on the same site. It was a strategic location. No matter how often the city died, later generations returned and built a new one. In ancient times, it stood on a narrow neck of land dividing two continents. But climatic changes pushed the oceans back, the land dropped and dried out, and the place sank into a desert.

"We've been able to follow the development of their languages over much of the history of the culture. Let me tell you what that means, Tiel: it means that we can begin, finally, to separate those perceptions that are induced by environment, including one's own physical form, from those that are of the essence of a thinking species.

I could see that he was warming to his subject, so I tried to steer him back. "The tower, Casmir. Where was the tower?"

"On the eastern edge of the city. It was probably a beacon of some sort at one time, to warn off vessels approaching too close to the coast. We couldn't be sure because the top of the thing was gone."

That explained why there was no tower in the diorama. It extended down, rather than up. "Casmir, did you know Durell Coll?"

He looked puzzled. "No," he said. "Who was he?"

I shrugged. "Not important. Please go on."

"The tower was a Level III structure, which is merely to assign it to an era. Two more recent cities had been built atop the layer of ruins to which it belonged. We know the Belarians of the later settlements maintained it as a monument and museum." He looked at me over the top of his glass, and his eyes were luminous. "They had a historical sense, Tiel. You will understand we were anxious to get into the lower levels.

"The upper compartments were filled with sand and, in some places, blocked by collapsed walls. So the work was slow. To make things more difficult, Belarius has a wide variety of exotic predators, and they are hard to discourage. We must have killed hundreds of one kind and another, but there were limits to what we could do." His voice had grown hollow. "Sometimes people disappeared. Or were devoured in full view of a work crew. Or were carried off. It was like living in an Arabian Nights scenario where *rocs* flapped in, seized someone, and were gone before we could react. Gradually, we learned to cope, but we had to devote more and more of our people to the defenses.

"We'd originally assumed that it would be necessary to excavate the entire structure, but about a quarter of the way down, the amount of sand in succeeding apartments began to decline, until it had nearly ended altogether. In time, it became merely a matter of opening heavy doors.

"There were inscriptions on the walls, mostly of a religious nature. Quite sophisticated, by the way." He began an analysis of Belarian syntax. This time I let him go, and tried to show some enthusiasm. Another round of drinks came. And I began to suspect he didn't want to continue his story.

"Was Ux directing the excavation?" I asked. "At the tower?"

"Oh no," he said. "We had an archeologist to do that, the detail work. Chellic Oberrif. We brought her in especially for the tower operation. She'd done something similar at the excavations of the early settlements on Mogambo. She was good."

I thought his eyes misted a little, and his voice caught. He needed a few moments to regroup. Then he continued: "There was a place at the hundred and thirty meter level, about two-thirds of the way down, that blocked us for days. Whole chambers and connecting corridors had collapsed. The danger was that an attempt to cut through might bring down the entire structure. God knows it was shaky enough. But she looped a tunnel around the obstruction, and reentered further down.

"When we did manage later to excavate those sections, we found weapons and remains. A battle of some sort had been fought in there, and somebody had tripped a mechanism that buried the contending parties. We have no idea what the argument was about.

"What was important, however, was that the vandals and robbers of the period immediately following that era, before the upper tower filled with sand, were unable to penetrate below the battle site. In the lower compartments, we found furniture, religious regalia, the stuff of daily life. It had been there a *long* time, and most of it was dust. But it was there.

"At the base of the tower, we descended a ramp into a wide oval room with an altar raised in its center. A big one, maybe three times the size of the one in the Field Museum. It had several adjoining compartments that were still in decent condition. And the far end of the chamber opened through an archway into a tunnel. Chellic hurried immediately over to it, barely glancing at anything else. "This might give us access," she said. She meant a way into the heart of Level III.

"We were at the end of a long workday. I proposed that we continue in the morning, but Uxbridge wouldn't have it. He wanted to see where the tunnel went, whether indeed it did penetrate the ruins. Chellic supported him. So I gave in, reluctantly. That was my mistake, Tiel. I should have held to my instincts." He sighed. "We sent the work crew back up and pressed on.

"Chellic was even more obsessed with the possibilities of the place than Ux. She'd made it a point to acquaint herself with the various ideographic systems in use, and had become a valuable contributor to our ongoing analysis. She was also a good shot. On one occasion, I watched her cooly stand her ground during a general assault and kill four or five pickeyes."

"Pickeyes?"

"They're birds, very small, and very fast. The name is earned. Anyhow, we started into the tunnel. The air wasn't very good, and we were using oxygen. Our radio contact on the surface advised us to return. Bendimeyer, who was the security chief, didn't like unscheduled activities.

"But we were all intoxicated by then. My God, I can still remember the exhilaration of that walk out into the buried city. Until then, all we'd had of anything below Level II was the satellite scans.

"The tunnels were low, and we couldn't stand up straight. Even *I* couldn't, so you can imagine how Ux felt.

"Some of the interior spaces were *intact*. We saw murals, metalwork, tools, even petrified gardens. I remember Chellic saying how there was enough down there to keep researchers busy for a lifetime. We even found a library, though the books were dust.

"It was raining on the surface. We were looking at a scullery when Bendimeyer got on the radio. We knew immediately we had a problem because he sounded wide awake. 'Moss,' he said, 'we got a critter in the tower. It's started down, so you may hear from it.' I asked what it was. 'We don't know,' he said. 'Nobody got a very good look. It's bipedal, we think. Rodley says it's about Ux's size. Big.'

"We'd been on Belarius long enough to know that nothing that travels alone is harmless. But we were armed, and we hadn't found anything yet that a bolt wouldn't stop. The thing that concerned me was that we had little visibility. Those tunnels were *made* for ambushes.

"I asked Bendimeyer to keep me informed. He said they were sending a team after it, and I asked him not to. 'That'll only drive it down on top of us. Anyway, I don't want nervous guys with weapons in here. We're going to start back.'

"Chellic suggested we might be better off to wait it out. 'The damned thing could never find us in this labyrinth,' she said. But Ux said it could probably *smell* us. 'We'll be safer in the tower room,' he said. I asked him why. 'Because there are too many places here where several corridors converge. We can't watch everything. If we can get back to the tower before it gets all the way down, we only have to worry about what's in front of us.'

"Chellic concurred, and we got moving. Nobody was much interested now in the galleries and public rooms. We'd been marking the way we came, but we took a couple of wrong turns anyway going back, and lost a lot of time. In fact, we lost so *much* time that we were still wandering through tunnels when Ux commented that the critter might at that moment be passing through the tower room. After that, we were no longer sure *what* direction it might come from.

"Imagination raises hell under those circumstances. If you listen hard enough, you always hear something. I could make out claws scraping on stone, breathing in the walls, you name it. We were all walking now with drawn weapons.

"Ux fell in a hole at one point and twisted his knee. His weapon discharged, and drilled a neat round hole through the rock wall. He was limping badly after that, and we had to help him along. But nobody wanted to stop, so we kept moving. There wasn't much talk.

I checked back periodically with Bendimeyer. He had a team sitting at the top of the excavation with a small arsenal, but they'd seen nothing come out." Moss took a deep breath. Sweat had begun to drip down his neck into his shirt. The narrative was taking on a life of its own: he needed no further encouragement from me.

"The places we were most worried about were the compartments, the little side tunnels, the holes in the wall. We hurried past them as quickly as we could, expecting every moment the wild attack that we knew was inevitable.

"Ux held up pretty well, and Chellic had turned into some kind of goddamn jungle animal herself. I wasn't very happy about the situation, but I felt good about the people I was with.

"We stopped occasionally to check our bearings and rest our backs. It was during one of these halts, as we drew close to the tower room, that I had a sudden sensation, a *flash*, of terrible hunger. The lights dimmed, as if all three of our lamps had faded simultaneously. Chellic sat beside me, her head bent between her knees, her neck exposed under the hairline." Moss sat stiffly erect. He put his empty glass carefully on the table, and caressed its rim with his fingertips. His eyes swiveled round, and locked with mine. "I thought how good it would be to bury my teeth in her."

I sat in shocked silence. "The sensation, the *urge*, lasted only an instant. But it left me weak and terrified.

"When we started out again, Chellic had to stop to help me. And I was afraid to let her touch me. Ux asked whether I was all right. I told him I was, and increased my oxygen. But Chellic knew something had happened, and she made no effort to move on until I signaled I was ready to go.

"We came finally into the tower room. I was relieved to see the altar and the wide curving wall: it meant no more multiple entrances to be watched. Ux threw his lamplight around the chamber to be sure it was empty and examined the series of adjoining compartments. Chellic climbed the ramp on the far side of the altar and looked into the rising passageway ahead, while I kept a nervous eye behind us. 'All clear,' she said. The lights and shadows played across her face: even in the sweaty worksuit, with a pickax in her belt, she was a lovely woman."

Moss's hands gripped the arms of his chair. "There was no other way to proceed." His voice was hardly a whisper. "No finding of guilt ever came out of it. Even now, knowing what I know, I cannot see what we might have done differently. But my God there must have been a way—." His eyes squeezed shut.

"Ux suggested we rest before continuing. He eased himself down against a rock slab and placed his lamp on top of it, aimed into the passage through which we would leave. The guns are big-barreled things, not like the modest all-purpose weapons that Survey teams are routinely equipped with. These were military issue at one time. At short range and high register, nothing that lives could survive even a peripheral hit. Under all that rock, of course, we had to be careful, but you will understand we had no doubts about our weapons.

"I kept mine at hand the whole time. Ux was still limping badly, and it was obvious he was glad to get off the knee. But he seemed more worried about me, and asked several times if I was all right." Moss's face reddened a bit, and he managed a weak smile. "He said nothing along those lines to Chellic.

"Then it happened again: Chellic had walked over near the altar and begun to move through a series of stretching exercises. While I watched her, the chamber began to darken. I could sense her long limbs beneath the worksuit, see the suggestion of breast and shoulder: the blood was warm in her shoulders, and I could taste—" Moss's eyes filled with tears. He shook his head savagely, leaped from his seat, and hurried out into the night. I ignored the stares of people around us, dropped money on the table, and followed.

He was staring up at the vertical sea. Reflections from the city lights played against its surface. "If I had my way," he said bitterly, "we'd kill everything on that world and be done with it. Introduce a bug, attack the food chain, tickle a couple of volcanoes. Whatever it takes. But I'd clear that goddamn world once and for all." He jammed his fists into his pockets and looked at me with tears in his eyes. "Did Ux ever tell you any of this?"

"No," I said, trying not to feel guilty.

Moss laughed. It was an ugly sound. "Tiel, I've told this story a hundred times. I've told it to Survey, and I've told it to their analysts. I'll live with it forever. Just like Uxbridge did.

"What you have to understand is, when the *thing* walked into the chamber, its slick humanoid skin glistening, its pink eyes surveying us, *I was with it. Inside it.* I felt the water-cold rock beneath padded feet, and the dusty air sucked past curving rows of incisors. I looked from Ux to Chellic to myself, delaying the moment of selection even though I knew, knew from the beginning. The lean one, Chellic, had been on its feet and turned to face me. The light from the lamps had acquired an amber tint. I, *we*, knew our danger. The three—things—were terribly slow, but all had burners.

We—it, I—hesitated. We wanted Chellic, and we advanced cautiously toward the altar, and dreamed how it would be. She seemed frozen, her breast rising and falling. And her face: my God, her face had twisted into a dark leer, lips drawn back in a feral snarl to reveal her own pitiful white teeth, an expression all the more horrible in that it contained no hint of fear, but rather implied that she too was about to share a live meal.

"And then I understood what was happening. We were all of us drawn into the mind and will of the beast: we all looked out through its eyes, and we would all rend Chellic muscle from bone.

"I tried to get out. To find my own eyes. The laser was a dead weight in my right hand, desperately far away. Chellic's animal face was close now: she opened her arms wide, and advanced. Ux, with a scream that echoed round the chamber, got to his feet, but could only lean drunkenly against the slab from which his lamp illuminated the ghastly scene.

"In that moment, I got the laser up. We watched the weapon swing in our direction, and looked into the huge muzzle.

"I'll tell you what it was like, Tiel: it was as if I were pointing the weapon at myself. I looked at its business end as certainly as I am looking at you now. I was terrified of it, but I tried to pull the trigger all the same. I can make no claim to a heroic act, because I was even more terrified and repulsed by what would happen if I did not succeed.

"I'm not sure how to tell you the rest. Maybe you already know. Ux was also looking down the throat of the laser. And I guess it was more than he could take. He screamed and leaped at me. I jumped, and the weapon went off, slicing a chunk out of the ceiling. The creature took Chellic.

"Ux hit me hard, the laser slipped away, and the mindlink dissolved. To his credit, he recovered himself almost immediately, and scrambled after the weapon. Chellic and the beast melded together in a grim parody of a sexual embrace. They moved against each other's bodies and Chellic cried out, more in ecstasy than in pain. Blood spurted, but the dance continued. It went after her throat, and Chellic sagged. Ux brought the laser up and fired. The creature shrieked, released her, threw a glance of pure malevolence and hatred at its attacker, and fled into the lower levels.

"A second shot went wild."

He took my arm, and we walked slowly along the seafront. His palm was wet. "Ux never forgave himself."

"What happened? To the woman? To Chellic?"

His jaw worked. "She was dead before we could get her to the surface."

And I thought about the inscription on the west portico, which took on a dark new meaning.

In the hour of need, I am with you.

8.

So in the end it came down to the house at the bottom of the bay.

I'd intended to be out on the Point shortly past dawn, but I woke late, after another restless night, and then delayed over a long breakfast. I had a fair notion what was waiting for me beneath that calm surface, and I was in no hurry to confront it.

I landed in thick grass near the ruined projector station. Strangely, the dome was more difficult to see up close, where its dark bronze coloring blended with the thick vegetation that overwhelmed it.

A black ragged hole had been burned through the outer shell, big enough to allow entry. I'd brought a small sculptor's laser with me, and used it to cut through the brambles. The place was half full of clay and mud. (The previous night's rain hadn't helped.) The console had been cannibalized, and the projector was gone.

There were a few scorch marks, and the frame that would have supported the projector was cut in half.

What had Hollander said? *Now, the projectors are pretty well shielded.* Undoubtedly by something other than a physical barrier.

Directly across the mouth of the bay, I could see the connector station which had once formed a link with this one. It still functioned, but only northward, and was now on the outermost edge of the seawall.

After a while, I got back into the skimmer and lifted off. The bay was unsettled: there was a steady eastern chop, and the water looked rough. It was a gray, formless day, oppressive and quiet save for the steady beat of the incoming tide. I located my buoy, and circled it slowly. Uxbridge's house was not visible from the air.

A sharp gust rocked the skimmer. I took it down, eased it into the water, more carefully this time, and anchored it. I did not stop to think about what lay below: I kicked off my clothes, stowed them in the aft locker, and extracted my breather from its carrying case. I checked out the lamp, put on a belt, and attached a utility pouch. I strapped a depth gauge and timer to one wrist, the lamp to the other, pulled on the fins and mask, and slipped overboard.

The water was warm. But the sunless day reduced visibility severely; I could see only a few meters in natural light. I took my bearings from the buoy and the skimmer and started down.

I passed through alternating cool and warm currents. A few fish darted away, and one of the broad-ferned swimming plants common in Fishbowl's temperate latitudes startled me by wrapping a tendril around one ankle and giving it a tug. When I reacted, it lost interest.

The grim, mottled, sea-shrouded house gradually took shape: turrets and parapets rose out of the gray depths, stone walls formed, ocular windows peered sightlessly down into a courtyard. I hovered above for several minutes, maybe choosing my best approach, maybe hesitating. Then I descended to one of the turrets, followed its sloping roof past exposed plates, and started down the face of the building.

At the upper level, I thumbed on my lamp and looked through a window that was, remarkably, still intact. Inside, silt was thick. A bed was jammed into a doorway, light furniture had been scattered about, and the contents of a bureau were spilled and buried. A closet door, partially open, had exposed two rows of hanging garments. These fluttered gently in whatever currents passed through the room.

Below me, lower on the wall, a long, serpentine fish glided out of a venting pipe and slipped into the gloom. I seized a cornice and hung on until it was gone. The stone was slippery with the algae that inhabit most water oceans.

The front door was missing, and the frame which had supported it was bent.

I passed inside, and the beam of my lamp faded into the depths of a large central hall. A staircase rose on the right, and double doors opened on the left. Chairs and tables were tumbled about, bookcases overturned, and the whole covered with sediment. Two portraits had once hung beneath the staircase: the frames were still in place, but the canvas had shriveled in each, and no hint of the subjects remained.

Though I knew more or less where I was going, I took a moment to look through the double doors. They had opened into a sitting room; even in its present condition, I could see that it had been a stiff, formal place: the sort of room in which one conducts formal matters, designed to impress a business acquaintance, and at the same time to hurry things along.

But I was surprised to see a photo of Ux (still dry behind its glass) with several people in academic robes. Other pictures and mementos lay buried in the silt. I knelt and dug, extracting them one by one. Most were ruined. But a few had been preserved: a highly favorable review of a book he'd written on ancient languages; an award from an institution whose name was no longer legible, acknowledging his work on Mycenaean linear documents; a photo of Ux and an attractive dark-haired young woman, both in coveralls, and both wielding spades. (My God, could that be Chellic?)

I placed them carefully in my pouch.

And I found the snow photo: an enlarged duplicate of the one from the chess club. My hand shook as I brushed the last of the sand away from it. Reuben Uxbridge, wrapped in a blue parka, smiled out at me.

But the photos were in the wrong room. Jon Hollander had said there was a retreat at the rear of the house, where he'd gone to play chess, and probably where Ux had really lived his life. That would be the normal place to keep such things. My heart pounded: I knew exactly what I was going to find. And I knew why Durell had tried to destroy the house.

I examined the snow photo in the uncertain light: four men and three women braving a storm. Behind them, the looping colonnade of the Admin Building was visible. Just off to the left, behind Jon Hollander's head, lay the frozen rim of the pool that fronted on the Field Museum. And I knew one of the three women. The one in the middle, who was laughing, and who appeared to be looking almost mischievously at Uxbridge, was the woman with the spade.

I swam the length of the hall, past closed doors, past ruined cabinets, past the sand-clogged rubble of a lifetime. I'd acquired a few fish, fat spiny-finned creatures that moved with me, but darted back out of the light. I was grateful for their company.

And finally I approached a door heavier and shorter than the others I had seen. It was ajar, and I poked my lamp inside.

The interior was spacious, a *hall* rather than a chamber. It was a circular room, with a high ceiling, completely shrouded by curtains. I could see a desk, an overturned computer console, padded chairs (presumably the ones about which Hollander had spoken), and a square table.

The inner sanctum. I caught my breath.

Things seemed somehow less displaced in that room, as though some strange gravity gripped them. The chairs and the table were still upright, a pot which had once contained a plant retained its place on the desk, a wine cabinet still stood.

I looked at the circular wall, thinking vaguely of the one in the tower room. How many hours had Reuben Uxbridge sat here, trying to exorcise the demon that had, indeed, followed him back from that ridden world? How often had he struck down poor bureaucratic Moss, when Moss was about to save her, save them all, at whatever cost to himself?

In a sense, Chellic had been fortunate. Uxbridge had been the real victim. And Durell.

Only Durell, desperate for money, could supply what Uxbridge needed.

I approached the curtains, rotted now, still concealing their terrible secret. And I lifted them.

In the pale glow of the lamp, the climactic struggle that Moss had described sprang to life: Chellic and the pink-eyed monstrosity, both slick with sweat, embraced, while an enraged, terrified Uxbridge, wearing a variation of the grotesque countenance I knew so well from the studio, attacked Moss. It was the instant before he reached the smaller man, when Moss was trying desperately to use the laser, when there was still time. It was the instant when Uxbridge lost his soul.

9.

I had to tell someone about it, and who more appropriate than heroic little Casmir Moss? He was reluctant at first to see me again, thinking he'd embarrassed himself, I suppose. But in the end, he agreed to meet me for lunch, and I told him the story, the part he didn't know. When I was finished he just sat, not knowing how to respond. At last, he said simply, "It wasn't his fault."

"Yes, it was," I said.

He looked at me, shocked. "You don't know how it was. Nobody can blame him for Chellic's death."

"Not Chellic," I said. "He wanted to relive that final moment. Over and over. Maybe to change it. Or maybe to punish himself by immortalizing it. I don't know. But there was another victim."

He looked at me, puzzled.

"Durell," I said. "I wonder if he ever considered what he was doing to the artist—"

PART II

LOST TREASURE

IGNITION

I saw no sign of a devil.

We'd been working on an extension of the Holy Journey subway when we ran into large blocks of concrete, stacked one atop the other, buried in the earth. The blocks weren't supposed to be there, but they were. The extension, when finished, would cross the river south into St. Andrew's Parish, taking substantial pressure off the bridges. They lay directly in our way. So I kept my crew drilling, and eventually we broke through. Into a large space.

I pointed my light up. The ceiling must have been more than a hundred feet.

Now the truth is I hadn't given any thought to devils and demons until I flashed my light into the darkness and saw, first, broken columns scattered around the place, as if it had once been a temple. And then the statue.

The statue was gigantic, maybe three times as high as I was. Or it would have been had the base not been buried in earth, broken stone, and assorted debris.

"What happened here?" demanded a voice behind me. Cort Benson, my number one guy. He pushed in and immediately locked on the giant figure rising out of the earth floor. "My Lord," he said, his voice suddenly very low. "What is *that*?"

I had never seen a statue before. I'd heard of them. Knew about them. But I'd never actually seen one. Nor, I suspected, had anyone else on the work crew. It was a man. I moved a few steps closer and held up my lamp. He was dressed oddly, loose-fitting clothes from another age. Odd-looking coat or vest. Hard to tell which. The statue was sunk into the ground to a point midway between knees and hips. There was something clasped in his left hand. A rolled sheet of paper, looked like.

My crew stayed near the door. One of them called for a blessing. Another said it was devil's work.

Elsewhere around the space, some columns were still standing. They connected to a curved wall, forming a boundary around the statue. Beyond the wall and the columns were more concrete blocks like the ones we'd had to cut through to get in.

Okay. Let me tell you straight out I never believed in evil spirits. I said prayers against them every Sunday, like everybody else, and sometimes during midweek services. But I didn't really buy into it. You know what I mean? Although that's easy to say, sitting in the sunlight.

But here was this *thing*.

The air was thick and somehow smelled of other days. I played the light against the wall. Several rows of arcane symbols were engraved in it. They were filled with dirt and clay, so it was hard to make them out. I picked at them with a crowbar, pulled some earth loose, and saw what they were: ancient English.

The language still showed up occasionally around the parish, and over in Seven Crosses, and even as far north as St. Thomas. The characters were usually engraved on chunks of rock that must once have been cornerstones and arches and front entrances and even occasionally, as here, on walls. The world was filled with rubble from the civilization that God in His wrath had brought down.

I thought about that for a minute. Wages of sin. Then I pointed the lamp up and saw a second group of characters on a narrow strip circling the ceiling.

Cort grumbled something I couldn't make out and walked past me toward the statue.

Three or four lamps were now playing across its face from the guys who stood back at the entrance. They showed no inclination though to come any closer.

The lights gave life to the features. His eyes tracked me, the lips curved into a smile. It gave me chills, I'll admit that.

His features radiated power. And superiority. Though any guy twenty feet tall is going to look superior. The sculptor, if indeed there had been a sculptor, had given him an aura of the supernatural.

❂

I checked in with the office, let them know what I'd found, and, at their instruction, told my crew they could take the rest of the morning off. Until a decision was made what to do about the discovery.

Cort waited until I got off the circuit. Then he said, "Eddie would be interested in this."

"Who's Eddie?" I wished Cort would follow the others outside. Get some fresh air. Do something constructive. Just please don't hang around and make suggestions.

"Come on, Blinky," said Cort. "Eddie Trexler. My cousin. You know him." Since he'd come back from prison, Cort seemed to have trouble breathing. You could always hear it, always knew when he was nearby. He probably shouldn't have been working down in the subways, but he was on the bishop's list and we couldn't get permission to transfer him.

I vaguely remembered once getting introduced to Trexler. A long time ago. But I couldn't recall anything about him. Or why he would possibly be interested in the chamber.

"I'll be back in a little while," said Cort. He was always ready to skate at the edges of the law. It was what had gotten him in trouble in the first place.

"Wait a minute," I said. "You know the rules."

"All they say is we have to report something like this. You've done that. Did they tell you to keep everybody out?"

"No."

"There you are, then."

"That's what they want, though."

"Hellfire, Andy, if that's what they want they ought to *say* it." He fished a phone out of his pocket. "I'm going to give him a yell."

Then he was gone. It wasn't worth a confrontation. Cort thought I got in line too easily, and sometimes I had to rein him in. But this didn't seem like one of those times. If he got himself and his cousin in trouble, so be it.

The giant gazed down at me. I went over and *touched* him, touched his thigh, brushed away some of the accumulated dust. He was bronze.

The lights were gone now, save the one I was carrying. I felt alone.

You'd never have known Eddie Trexler was a relative of Cort's. Where Cort was heavy and unkempt and probably indestructible, the cousin was tall and reedy and pressed. He owned a high-pitched voice and wore thick glasses, and he walked like a duck.

But there was no doubting his enthusiasm when he shook my hand and, without waiting for permission, climbed past me into the space. Trexler was a clerk at the Department of Theological Studies, but his hobby was ancient history. He'd brought one of those large lanterns that will light up a city block. He was two steps inside when he switched it on and put the beam on the statue. "Magnificent," he said. His voice had gone a notch higher.

Cort chuckled. "He asked me to say thanks for asking him over."

"Sure," I said. "My pleasure." We followed him in.

He stood gawking at the figure, at the wall, at the columns. Even at the concrete blocks. "I never thought I'd live to see anything like this—." And, "You know what this is, Cort?" And, "Lovely."

"It's a statue," I said. I could have added that it desperately needed to be washed, that it was chipped in more than a few places, that it was half-buried. That it was blasphemous.

Thou shalt not make unto thyself any graven image.

But I let it go.

"Do *you* know what it is?" Cort asked him.

"I have an idea." He plunged into the space, climbed over the debris, studied the statue, touched one of the standing columns, and closed in on the wall. On the inscription. Then he went behind the wall and looked at the blocks. "Nicely fitted," he said. "Seamless."

"Yes," we both replied, though I doubt either of us had noticed.

"This is big news," he said. "If it's what I think it is."

"Why, Ed?" I asked. "What do you think it is?"

"Look at the writing on the walls. This place is prediluvian. *Before* the flood."

"Okay. And your point—?"

"Look at the blocks."

"What about them?"

"Think why they're there."

"Why are they there?"

"They tried to save it," he said, as much to himself as us. "God help them, they tried to save it."

"Yes," I said, not sure what I was agreeing to.

"It must have sunk during the flooding. Too heavy. It was more than thirty thousand tons. Add all that concrete—." He shook his head. "And here it is."

"I guess so," I said.

"That means—." His eyes gleamed with a light of their own. "They knew the flood was coming."

"The Great Flood?"

"Yes. Official doctrine is—."

"That it happened without warning," said Cort.

"Correct." He pressed his palms against the stone, as if to read a message hidden within the cold gray surface. "That's going to stir the pot a bit." He pulled a camera from a sweater pocket and began taking pictures.

Cort stayed at his side, fascinated. "Can you read any of it, Ed?"

"Not really. If we can get it clean, we should be able to figure it out." He turned back to me. "Cort tells me you've alerted the authorities."

"Of course," I said. "It's a requirement."

"Yeah," he said. "I know. Pity."

I couldn't miss the implied accusation. "Hey," I said. "I didn't have a choice. We're law-abiding."

He told me it wasn't my fault. "How long will it take them to get here?"

"No way to know," Cort rumbled, raising an eyebrow in my direction.

Trexler began trying to clear the symbols. Cort and I joined in. But it was hard going and we didn't make much progress. He stepped back and took more pictures. And frowned. *Publish*," he said, finally.

"What? Publish what?"

"This word means *publish*." It was about nine lines down. And, four lines below that: "*Reliance*."

He shook his head and glanced at me again. "I don't suppose there's any chance you could go out and head them off when they get here."

"You mean the police?"

"Yes."

"What would I tell them?"

"Anything you can think of."

"No," I said. "I don't think I could get away with that."

He rolled his eyes. And in that moment noticed the overhead inscription. "What's that?"

"More letters," said Cort. "I'll try to slow down the police."

"Thank you." He threw a withering glance in my direction. Then he returned his attention to the roof. "That's in better condition up there," he said.

"Yes," I said. I was trying to decide what to do. I kept seeing the police hauling off all three of us.

"...*Have sworn...*"

"What?"

He was still looking up. "It says *have sworn*, and there's *alert* off to the right."

"Okay."

"No. Wait. It's *altar*."

I watched him change his angle and stand on his toes as if getting an inch closer would help.

"*Mind of man* at the end."

I heard the sound of arriving vehicles.

He jerked his head around. Stared toward the hole we'd cut through the blocks. "So soon?" He looked dismayed.

"I guess."

He went back to the inscription. "The last three words are *mind of man*. No question about it."

Doors slammed. From the main tunnel came the rumble of a passing train. Dust drifted down on us.

"*...Have sworn...altar...mind of man.*"

"Makes no sense," I said.

"I can't make out the rest of it." He changed his angle again. "I need to get closer to it. You have a ladder handy?"

"Not high enough to reach *that*," I said.

"Damn. We need a little time."

"Maybe it's something this guy said," I suggested, indicating the statue.

He sighed. "Of course it is. Said or wrote. What else would it be?"

I didn't much like the attitude he was taking. "The statue's blasphemous," I reminded him. There was a line from the *Divine Handbook*: You don't make statues of people because that implies they are godlike.

"Don't be stupid," he said. Then he went back to the inscription: "The first word is only a single letter. Probably a pronoun. Has to be *I*."

There were voices outside now.

"*Hostility*. Some kind of *hostility*. Maybe *extraordinary*."

The voices became loud.

"I think it's *hostility against*. Has to be. And *tyrant*. Yes....*Hostility against something something tyrant*."

There was a scuffle outside. Mercifully short.

"No. It's not *tyrant*. It's, I think it's *tyranny*. Yes. That's it. *Tyranny*."

People were crowding into the chamber. Five men, four in police uniforms. "I'm Inspector Valensky," said the one in plain clothes. He flashed an ID toward Trexler, as if I weren't there. He was middle-aged, bearded, very official. Cort trailed in behind them, hands apparently secured behind his back.

"Good afternoon, Inspector," said Trexler, at which point Valensky saw the statue.

"The Lord is my keeper, sir," he said. "We *do* have devil's spawn here, don't we?"

Trexler's light fell on the police officers and I saw they were carrying bags of explosives. "Don't come in here with that," he warned. "What are you doing? Get that out of here."

The inspector drew himself up straight, and tugged at his beard. "Sir," he said, "gentlemen, I think who comes and who goes is our decision. And the fact is, I must ask *you* to leave."

Trexler didn't budge.

"This thing is blasphemous," said Valensky, sounding as if he were struggling to keep his voice level. "We'll have to get rid of it."

"What do you mean, 'get rid of it'?"

"I meant exactly what I said, sir. We're going to send it back where it belongs. Meantime, you'd be prudent to mind your manners." He turned to me. "I take it you're Blinkman Baylor."

I winced. I never understood what my folks were thinking when they gave me that name. "That's correct."

"Good. You did the right thing, Mr. Baylor, although it might have been a good idea to keep these two out of here." He raised his voice so we could all hear. "I hope none of you touched this abomination."

"No," I said, trying to sound reassuring. "Of course not."

He looked dead at me. "You *do* know not to touch any of these relics, don't you?"

"Oh, yes," I said. "I keep my hands off."

"Good, Mr. Baylor. Very prudent."

"*I* touched it," said Trexler.

"It renders you unclean, sir. You'll want to come with us when we're finished here."

"What for?"

"We'll have to take you to All-Sorrows for a ceremonial cleansing."

Trexler glared back with contempt. They'd have to carry him.

Valensky managed to look both annoyed and disappointed. "I do wish you'd cooperate, sir." He turned to Cort. "What about you?"

"Me?" Cort said. "I haven't been anywhere near it."

"Good." Two of the officers put on white gloves. They carried the charges across the chamber, picking their way through the debris, and laid them against the statue.

When Trexler tried to intervene, a third officer, a woman, headed him off. "Just stay calm, sir," she said, "if you will."

We watched while they made adjustments and connections.

Trexler glared at Valensky. "You blockhead," he said. "Do you have any idea what this place is worth? What it *is*?"

Valensky looked unmoved. "I know exactly what it is. Thank God one of us does." He turned to me. "I suggest you get him out of here."

The two who were setting the explosives stood up and brushed off their knees. "All set," one of them said. The other knelt back down and tugged at something. "Ready to go," he added.

Valensky took a remote from his pocket. "Everybody out, please," he said. He moved toward the exit, walking slowly while he waited for the rest of us to file out. Trexler stayed where he was.

"Come on, Eddie," said Cort.

Trexler shook his head. "I'm not going anywhere."

A signal passed between the inspector and the officers. They filed past Trexler. The woman touched her cap and said goodbye.

"I do wish you'd be reasonable," said Valensky.

Trexler moved closer to the statue. "Go ahead," he said. "Do what you have to."

"You leave me no choice, sir."

"Idiot."

The officers left, taking a struggling Cort with them. All except Valensky. "I'll set off the charge in one minute," he said. "That gives you time to change your mind and get out."

Trexler did not move. "Blow it up and be damned."

"Eddie." I felt helpless. "Getting yourself killed won't help anything."

"Listen to him," said Valensky. Then he looked my way. Time to go.

I waited a few seconds, watched Valensky disappear. "Ed," I said, "for God's sake—."

"He won't do it," said Trexler. "Too much paperwork if he kills somebody."

When the rebellion started, two months later, with the coordinated robberies of two banks and the looting of a parish arms warehouse, the authorities were slow to recognize it for what it was. And that cost them everything.

The two historians of the revolution, the two I know of, both believe Edward Trexler's death was the spark that started it all. There's some truth to that. But of course a lot of other people had died before he did, charged with heresy, or blasphemy, or various other attitudinal felonies.

God knows, though, Trexler's death motivated *me*. Who would ever have believed that conservative old Blinky Baylor would pick up a gun and go to war? But there was something else that stuck in my mind. That, for a lot of us, eventually became the engine that drove the revolution.

"*(I?)…Have sworn…altar….hostility (against?)…tyranny…mind of man.*"

It wasn't hard to fill in the blanks. And sometimes, during the dark times, it kept me going. I think it kept a lot of us going. You want to make a revolution work, you need more than a taste for vengeance.

INDOMITABLE

And this is an anti-grav generator. Do you know what that is, Harry?"

Did Harry know? Sometimes his father was such a nit. "Sure, Dad," he said.

"Good."

"We have one at school."

"Do you want to try it?"

A bot was standing by, waiting for him to answer, or to get out of the way for the next kid who, Harry thought, *also* knew what an anti-gravity generator was. Was there anybody on the *planet* who didn't know?

Behind the next kid was a little girl, maybe six or seven, watching with her eyes wide while she waited for a chance to levitate her hat.

They moved on to the bridge mockup. Displays indicated it was an exact replica from the XAA-466, the *Tokyo*, which had visited the black hole at Momsen. (Visuals of the black hole were available in the gift shop.)

There was a model of the Lexa Habitat from CX26, which had done interdimensional research near Antares a long time ago. Harry had read about it in the fifth grade, and it had ignited his interest in the interstellars. It was where Adcock had died and Parrish had vanished out of a sealed chamber. Where Corelle had done the research that had led eventually to the star drive that now carried his name. "Dad," he said, "do you know how long we were there?"

His father studied the interlocking tubes and spheres as if the answer lay within the geometry. "Not sure," he said. "It was before I was born."

By about two centuries. "Sixty-six years," Harry said.

His father nodded. Okay. Sometimes Harry got into his know-it-all mode and Dad got irritated.

And over there, nestled in a cradle, was Captain Songmeister's lander. It had lost power entering the atmosphere of Antares III when Songmeister and his team thought they'd seen a city. Songmeister had used a sputtering auxiliary unit to guide the vessel to a safe landing in mountainous terrain. That had been the good news. The city had turned out to be nothing more than a reflection on an odd rock formation.

"They never found anybody," said Harry. "Not there. And not anywhere else."

His father was already moving on to the next exhibit. "Nobody to find, Son. There's nobody out there."

They were looking at a space shuttle. The *Rosie McGreer*. It had run between the Overby station and the spaceports at Rome and Barcelona.

"Here's something you'll like." They slipped into the Cosmicon, which lit up with images from the colonies, gleaming cities and soaring towers and vast parklands. Here was Mirax on Deneb II, serene and cloud-wrapped on a mountaintop; and New Paris on Altair III, awash in music and soft light; and Shay Pong, straddling the mouth of the Karraso, the longest river on any known world. But of course it wasn't the length of the Karraso that made Harry's heart pump. It was the magnificent lighthouse.

"I'd like to go there someday," Harry said.

His father nodded. "It *is* nice. Your mother and I went there on our honeymoon. We had a nice hotel. And the beach was outstanding. There's something about the sun. You can stay out in it a long time and you don't have to worry about getting burned."

One area was designated as the memorial room. Virtual ships floated along the walls and guarded a long table. Harry knew them. The *Wallsley*, which had made the first flight to Alpha Centauri. And the *London*, which had carried the first colonists offworld. And the *McCondrey*, lost while testing the ill-fated Qubic Drive. The *Dallas* had visited Polaris, setting what, at the time, was a new distance record. And the *Exeter*, a few months later, had almost doubled that, going all the way out to Zeta Aurigae.

Harry knew them all. The *Sabre*, the *Valiant*, the *Reliable*. He had a picture of the *Reliable* on his bedroom wall. They were magic names. Harry knew who their captains had been, knew their stories. They were from the era when the survey ships were still going out, still looking.

It had been a long time ago.

"Dad," he said, "let's go look at the *Indomitable*."

It was the reason Harry had wanted to come. Everything else here in the Calgary Museum was more or less duplicated in Toronto. But not the *Indomitable*.

They picked up an escort bot. He was designed to look like Captain Parmentier, who was the hero of the HV *Interstellar* series. All pure fiction, of course.

"*We're still working on the* Indomitable," Captain Parmentier said. "*It's in a temporary shelter next door. You'll have to walk through clay to get to it. And the ground is still a little wet from the rain last night. Inside the shelter, parts are scattered everywhere. You'll have to be careful where you walk.*" He smiled. It was the familiar everything's-fine smile from the series. "*Before we proceed, you'll have to stipulate that you understand the risks, and you agree to relinquish your right to sue. If you agree to the conditions, please move a little closer to the imager and hold up your hand.*"

They complied. "*Very good,*" said the captain. "*This way, please.*"

The *Indomitable* did not look as big as some of the other ships he'd seen. In fact, it looked about half the size of the *Seattle*, which was based in that city. But it pursued a different mission from the cargo ship. And it possessed an aura none of the others had. Not even the *Valiant*.

Working lights illuminated the area. The Captain stood in the ship's shadow. "*It was a survey vessel.*" He looked up at it, and for a moment Harry thought he sensed sadness. "*It's a Pyrrus model. The only one left.*" Harry heard a door close somewhere. "*We were very proud to be able to bring it here.*"

Its insides lay in piles on the bare ground. Engines here, fuel tanks there. Corelle unit in the corner. Instruments, ducts, stabilizers, black boxes. A chair. One of the hatches leaned against a bulkhead.

"*Eventually,*" the captain said, "*we'll put it back together.*"

"How long will it take?" asked Harry.

Parmentier smiled. Made a face. "*Unfortunately, a while. Most of our workers are volunteers. They know about this ship, and they know how to take care of it. But they aren't young, so it will take a while.*"

"It's beautiful," said Harry.

The captain agreed. "*It's been as far as 15,000 light-years out. Halfway to the core.*"

Harry's dad shook his head. "You say it's the only one left? What happened to the others?"

Parmentier stared at the hull. He seemed to be looking at the inscription beside the airlock. *Deep Space Survey*. "They were broken up and used for scrap."

Harry's dad nodded. Of course. What else would you do with old ships?

"When you're finished working on it," said Harry, "would you be able to use it again? To go out in it?"

"*We hope so. It depends on what we find. We don't have a lot of money, so if there's expensive damage—*." His voice trailed off before he switched subjects. "*It wasn't the last of the operational survey ships. The* Ranger *was the last one taken out of service. A lot of the* Ranger *was used to provide the framework for the Benson Building in Tucson.*"

Harry placed his fingertips against the hull. The metal was cold and unyielding. "Why?" he asked.

"Why *what*, son?" asked his father.

"Why did they stop the missions?"

"You know why, Harry."

"No. I don't. Tell me."

He sighed. "Because we'd found enough worlds to last us a long time. Plenty of room for us to spread out. Enough for a thousand years."

Harry's hand was still pressed against the hull. Holding onto it. "But is that really the reason we went out there? To get more places to live?"

"Sure it is."

"I thought we were looking for somebody to talk to. I thought we wanted to find out whether we were alone."

"Harry, *we found out*. We *are* alone. There isn't anybody else."

"How do we know?"

"Because we've looked on thousands of worlds and there's *nothing*. We've been listening to the galaxy for *centuries* and there's not a sound. Not a peep anywhere. No life, except for a few cells here and there. Otherwise, zip."

"Dad, maybe we gave up too easily."

His father smiled. Benign. Proud, even. "It's over, kid. Maybe you're right. Maybe we could have gone farther. Maybe there's something in another galaxy somewhere. But it costs money. And nobody really cares anymore." He waited for Harry to say something. When the boy remained silent, he gently put his hand on his shoulder and pulled him away from the *Indomitable*. "Let's go, champ," he said. "It's getting up to dinner time."

Parmentier led the way past the ship's prow. He opened the door for them and sunlight spilled in. Harry looked back as the work lights went out. "Beautiful day," the captain said.

They went out into the bright afternoon. The ground was rough and full of holes.

"Careful where you walk."

Harry wasn't sure who made the comment. "It's not over," he said.

His father smiled. "Your mother said she'd have spaghetti and meatballs for us tonight."

LAST CONTACT

They looked down through towering banks of cumulus at an ocean bright with sunlight. A mountainous archipelago broke the smooth curve of the horizon. "There were thousands like this in the crystals," said Wincavan. "Other *worlds*."

In the darkness behind him, Rotifer shifted his weight and sighed audibly.

"This is what they saw from the *Quandis* during their first day over Omyra. Later, after it had been settled, this world would become famous because its philosophers came to an understanding of man and his place in the universe."

Rotifer could not entirely conceal his contempt. "And what might that be?"

It was Wincavan's turn to sigh. "I think they concluded that it was man who gave purpose to existence."

Rotifer laughed. It was an ugly sound, loaded with derision.

"They never found anyone else," Wincavan explained. "Among all those worlds, they never saw a reflection that was not their own." He fell silent. The islands passed beneath them, lovely and sunlit in the endless sea. "No, maybe you're right to sneer. But I'd like to believe there was a purpose to it all, that we served some humble cause: herald, perhaps, or torchbearer. A pathfinder for something greater than ourselves, who will find our bones among the stars and know that we were there."

Rotifer swung round in his chair, away from the images. "Emory, I love your stories. But the truth is there's only one world, and you're standing in it."

"No." Wincavan's eyes closed. "We are not even native to this world."

The younger man shrugged. "Foolishness. But it hardly matters."

A blue line of peaks appeared in the distance. Wrapped in winter, they marked a continental coastline. But it was a narrow range, and gave way quickly to rain forests and lake country. The image drew closer, and they saw broad rivers. At the confluence of two of the largest, Camwyck would be built two centuries later. Her sons and daughters, for years after, would continue the great expansion through the stars. Oliver Candliss, whose bloody shirt lay in the museum upstairs, was born there.

Wincavan debated taking them lower, but he wanted to maintain the planetary perspective, which was the most enthralling part of the demonstration, save for the fight with the rikatak at the climax.

They moved well above the clouds. The texture of light changed, and the sky darkened as they glided again over open sea. "Nice effects," said Rotifer.

Wincavan nodded patiently. Too much was at stake to offend the Councilman now.

A canopy of stars appeared, unfamiliar constellations. Far below, silent lightning flickered. "Eventually," said Wincavan, "the night will be ablaze with lights."

Rotifer's patience was running short. "How do you know?" he asked wearily. He himself was no longer young. His eyes had grown cold and hard in the harsh winters. His hair and beard were gray, and the limp was becoming ever more pronounced. (The leg injury had been sustained in his first cavalry action against the goliats, when he had been clawed and bitten.) He tended to be querulous, especially when the nights were damp, and he judged his worth exclusively by a long series of victories achieved against the savages many years before. Rotifer was, to Wincavan's mind, a prime example of the result when a hero outlives his campaigns.

"I know because I have seen the record. It was in one of the crystals," he said, with rising heat. "One of the crystals that were auctioned off during my grandfather's time!"

"Ah, yes." The Councilman spoke slowly, as though he had caught Wincavan in a deception. "Of course it would have been in one of the jewels."

There were more mountains in the west. They were silver under the stars, and silent. Beyond them, a pale ruddy glow stained the horizon. Rotifer, who had never seen a moonrise, watched the surge of crimson light fill the spaces between the peaks, watched a long blue-gray arc begin to rise above the mountains. "What's that?" he demanded. His voice was pitched higher than usual.

"A second world," breathed Wincavan. "Omyra's twin."

"A world in the air?" The Councilman laughed, though Wincavan thought he detected a hollowness in the sound. "It's nonsense, Emory. What would sustain it? How can you continue to take any of this seriously?"

Wincavan's world had no moon, and consequently its inhabitants had no experience with solid objects in the sky.

His countrymen thought him a deranged old man. It was just as well he stayed shut up in one of the ancient theaters, unable to grasp the difference between light shows and reality. But the Hall was no theater. The Community had known that once. His grandfather had remembered when there'd been a small coterie of supporters, of men and women who actively pursued research into the Great Days. But that was long ago. Now the Hall was empty, save for himself, and the savage goliats, who occasionally climbed the outside walls to peer timidly at the images. "Why," he asked, "do you deny the evidence of your eyes?"

"Because it is only a show. Like all the others. Because there is only one world; because an ocean can't cling to a globe. Why doesn't it run off the bottom of the world, Wincavan?"

Wincavan hesitated. "I don't know," he admitted.

"I thought not."

"We had that knowledge once."

"Contained in one of the jewels, no doubt?"

He shrugged. "The sun sets each evening in the west. Can you explain how it gets back during the night into the eastern sky?"

"There's a tunnel," Rotifer said hesitantly. "Beneath the world."

"You don't believe that?"

"It makes as much sense as living upside down." He stared at Wincavan, trying to read his expression in the gloom. "Do you have pictures of oceans and forests on the other world as well? The one in the sky?"

"We used to." The crystal was set in a gold clasp, but the last time Wincavan had seen it, it was dangling between the ample breasts of Banda Pier, wife of the Stablemaster.

The upper clouds of Omyra floated below them. Wincavan could feel the weight of the turning planet. He knew that the major land mass lay immediately west, an enormous continent of sulphurous mountains, broad rock-strewn plains, and advancing icecaps. "The *Quandis* circled the world ninety-three times before the landing team went down." He paused and looked toward the approaching dawn. Rotifer was silent, crossing his arms across his thick chest. "On the fourth day, Memori Collin and Lex Esteban and Creel MacAido boarded one of the ship's launches. They were right about *here*—." He pushed a stud forward. The stars lurched, and Omyra's cloudscape rotated. "It looked more or less like this." The black hull of the *Quandis* appeared above as the landing craft they seemed to be in dropped away. He smiled as the Councilman gripped the arms of his chair and pushed back into his seat.

Clouds rippled past, then surrounded them. Rotifer was trying to look away, but they dropped down the sky with terrifying speed. Even after all these years, after a thousand flights, Wincavan thrilled to the maneuver. They fell and fell and Rotifer made strange sounds; then they were out over water again, their descent slowing, the ocean far below disturbed by a squall. The vessel shook.

Was it his imagination that, during the final moments of the maneuver, his seat pushed against him? Turning toward his guest, Wincavan glimpsed a flurry of movement through a window. Two, or possibly three, goliats had climbed the courtyard wall, from where it was possible to watch the images. It was a perch which they frequently assumed. But he had long since given up trying to lure them inside. "In a moment, you'll see a large island shaped somewhat like a running man." He used the electronic pointer. "There. You can make out one arm. The head's over here, bent forward because he's moving very quickly. We'll be landing near the right knee. Collin chose it because the area has a level plain, without too many trees or other obstructions, and she knew from experience how important it was to be able to see clearly in all directions."

"Who's Collin?" asked the Councilman in a shaky voice.

"She commands the landing team," he said, in a tone intended to suggest he should not have to ask.

They drifted over the island. The sea was very green, and it rolled leisurely across white beaches. The storm was gone. Tall, lush trees dotted the landscape.

"Odd-looking trees," observed Rotifer.

Not as odd as others Wincavin had seen.

A landing strut appeared. The camera angle changed, and they were looking out to sea.

All motion stopped. "*Down,*" Collin said in her own language, her voice whispery with excitement. It was always the same with her: Wincavan had followed her onto more than thirty worlds. He wasn't sure about the sequence; that information, along with so much else, seemed forever lost. It was in the crystals somewhere, but most of them were scattered now. All within reach, within a few miles; but they might as well have been on Omyra.

He shook the thought away, and settled in to enjoy the moment: Collin and Esteban and MacAido emerging from their mystical cocoon into an unknown land. They were cool and crisp and efficient. Yet he knew they shared his own eagerness.

All green. Creel MacAido reacted to a forest that looked like the ones on the home world. He could never listen to MacAido without recalling that he would die horribly on Mindilmas in full view of the cameras. He looked *much* older on Mindilmas, so Wincavan could console himself with the thought that that terrible event was still far in the future. It was a landing Wincavan still possessed, though he never watched it.

Rotifer of course could not understand their exchanges, and in fact did not even grasp the concept of other languages. The context, however, rendered translation unnecessary.

They looked through the windows of the launch at the seascape, at rocks washed smooth by the tides, at soft-shelled creatures basking in the late afternoon sun, at the line of sinuous growths that marked the edge of a fern forest.

To Wincavan, who knew what was coming, it was an ominous perspective.

The view changed again, and they could see the forward hatch. It slid open to reveal Memori Collin, long-legged, dark-skinned, lovely. She wore a uniform like the ones enclosed in the harder-than-glass cases on the second level. It was a single piece, green and white, with the torch logo prominent on her right shoulder.

It might have been that symbol, the tall, proud flame which appeared on uniforms, on equipment, on the great starships themselves—and which was still emblazoned on a half-dozen plaques mounted in strategic places throughout the Hall—it might have been that symbol which first suggested to Wincavan the fond hope that man might after all have a role to play. Maybe the race that had itself failed might eventually serve as an inspiration to a successor. What else was there to hope for?

The wind caught at her short black hair as she stepped out, and briefly bared the nape of her neck. She carried a weapon, black and polished and lethal, in one hand. She glanced toward Wincavan, seeming to see him. Rotifer leaned forward. "Nice looking bitch," he said. Wincavan's knuckles whitened, but he said nothing.

Collin strode away from the shadow of the lander with precision and self-assurance. The rikatak was only minutes away. Wincavan, who knew where to look, also knew that everything would be okay. Nevertheless, his pulse began to pick up.

"They were good," said Rotifer. "I have to admit that: They were good.

Look at these pictures. How did they do it?" He shook his head. "One day we'll pry out their secrets."

"Not if you keep auctioning them off," said Wincavan. "There's not much left now."

"Some of this stuff might have direct military application. Can you imagine what it would do to the goliats if we could produce stuff like this?" He waved his hand in the air, as though clearing an obstruction. "I was born too soon. We have a great future, Emory. It's just a matter of time."

"Yes," grumbled Wincavan.

"If we could just understand how they did some of these things. How the lights work. Why most of the buildings are warm in winter and cool in summer. I'm convinced there's a single principle at work in all of this. Find that principle, and we will have their secrets!" He shook his head sadly. "I know, Emory, that you're pleased to think no one but you cares about the Ancients. But that's really not true. The difference between you and me is the difference between science and religion. Reality and dream. We need to see the Ancients for what they were, to approach them with an open mind!"

It would come from a cluster of squat thick-boled trees and vine-choked shrubbery. Wincavan, acting out of a morbid fascination, had watched this scene many times. The thing's forelimbs were just visible in the vegetation.

Creel MacAido appeared at Collin's side. He was tall, thin, almost boyish, with vivid green eyes. And he loved her. Wincavan could see it in the chemistry between the two, and he could also see that Creel's feelings were not returned.

He spoke to her. Something about the landscape, but Wincavan's command of their language was not complete. It was apparent, from the tone, that the meaning was independent of the words anyhow.

"What's happening?" asked Rotifer.

"They're about to be attacked. Can you see the danger?"

The Councilman instinctively pushed back in his chair. And something that was all long insect limbs and razor claws strode casually out of the trees. Rotifer shrieked. The creature was spindly with red eyes and a green crest and a twitching tongue. It rose over Collin and MacAido, spreading paper-thin wings against the sun. And it left the ground. Six sets of legs trailed after it. It might have been a graceful creature save for the viscous orange liquid that spilled out of its curved beak.

They didn't move. Wincavan was never certain whether he was watching the result of marvellous discipline or stark panic. The rikatak was drifting back down now. A translucent web popped into the air beneath it, connected by the thinnest of threads to its mantle.

The scene darkened, as though a thunderhead had drifted into the blue sky. "Run!" roared Rotifer. "Get the hell out of there!"

The humans threw themselves to the ground. Hot light exploded, the web separated from the creature and fell gracefully. Wincavan stared up at it: The thing pulsed and breathed with anticipation. Long tendrils trailed down.

"Poison," said Rotifer, his survival instincts at high alert.

The web settled over its victims.

The air grew cloudy and red, and it became hard to see. Blue light tracked up from the ground, the thing chittered and clicked, and everything became confused in a swirl of blood and motion. Then the place went dark.

The sounds of the struggle continued. "The equipment got knocked out," Wincavan explained. Moments later, the picture was back, and the thing was down, dragging shattered legs, trying to get at Collin with its jaws. She lay on her back, heels dug in to anchor herself, looking for a clear shot past the tangle of fangs and limbs.

The web, which seemed to possess a life of its own, was attacking MacAido. He fought frantically to recover his pistol, which lay a meter or so away. But each movement wrapped the thing more tightly around him. It lurched every few moments, in a reflexive spasm, until his strangled breathing filled the Hall. He'd succeeded in keeping one arm free, but the web was winding strands around his neck.

Then Collin was at his side. She sliced the strands, freed him, and then fried the web with her sidearm. When she finished she walked back toward the downed rikatak, and fired twice more. Wincavan loved the moment.

Esteban finally arrived, but the battle was over.

"Nice weapons," Rotifer said. "*We* could use something like those."

Wincavan smiled. Memori Collin's pistol lay upstairs, in a glass case beside Candliss's shirt.

"Good," the Councilman said, pulling himself together. "Not quite on the level of some of the stuff Gavandy runs on weekends, but it isn't bad."

"Gavandy's images are *stories*," said Wincavan, barely able to contain his frustration.

"So are *these* stories!" Rotifer stared hard at the older man. "For God's sake, Emory, can't you see that? Listen, if any of this were true, if there really *were* worlds floating in the sky, what happened? *What happened?* What are we doing here? Where is everybody?"

Wincavan touched a presspad, the image died, the lights came on, and the sedate amphitheater returned. "I've told you I don't know," he said.

"Do you have *any* answers?"

Wincavan walked down onto the apron where the rikatak had stood. "Who built the City?" he asked quietly.

"The Ancients. And I know that they could do quite a lot that we can't, but that proves nothing."

"Where did they go?" persisted Wincavan. "They must once have been much more numerous than we! The City is bigger than we can *ride* across in a day. It could have held many communities like ours."

"We don't know that there ever were *other* communities."

"Maybe you're right," Wincavan said listlessly. "Marc, sometimes I wonder whether we're *all* that's left. Anywhere."

Rotifer got up. It was cool, and he pulled his jacket around his shoulders. "I'm sorry, Emory," he said. "But I don't think this conversation is going anywhere. The Council needs money, and we either have to collect more taxes or run another auction. Probably, we'll have to do both."

"Come on, Marc." Wincavan was on his feet. "Damn it, there are only a dozen left now. They're records of who we are. They're priceless."

Rotifer's eyes narrowed. "Emory, it really doesn't matter. Even if you were right, I don't think anyone would want to be reminded."

In the courtyard, it was snowing. Rotifer unhitched his mount, patted the wassoon's head at the base of its horns, swung into the saddle, and shook his cloak free. He glanced at Wincavan, flicked the reins, and rode out through the stone gate. The storm swirled in his track.

Wincavan shut the door.

He wandered through the ancient structure, past the Projector and the Machines and the sleek furniture that relentlessly outlived the generations of men. He climbed the stairs to the second level, stopped to make tea, and crossed to the museum.

Save for the amphitheater, the broad chamber on the second level was the largest room in the Hall. It was filled with uniforms, goblets, patches, statuary, black shining instruments whose use Wincavan could not guess, set in locked display cases, with illumination provided by push button. Faded murals hung on the walls. They were the only things in the room that seemed to have yielded to time. Nevertheless, it was possible to make out their subjects: cylindrical objects floating against backgrounds of stars and worlds; people standing beside machines in bizarre landscapes; a trail of fire drawn across a peaceful evening sky.

Two portraits dominated the rest. In one, a man and a woman wore the uniform of the explorers. They were clear-eyed and handsome, and Wincavan wondered who they might have been. Perhaps they represented all who had gone before. In the other, a gleaming metal ship passed beneath giant planetary rings.

He paused before the blood-spattered shirt of Oliver Candliss. Curiously, the identifying plate carried only the hero's name, and the notation *Saliron*, as though its significance were obvious. Wincavan had walked with that bearded giant into dark Kahjadan, had ridden with him through the electrical skies over a black thing that engulfed whole suns, had accompanied him into the unearthly Gray Temple on Willamine which (if he understood the documents correctly, had never after received human visitors).

He stood over a silver urn, from which Abbas Ti and his team had drunk Micondian brandy before starting on their magnificent rescue of the *Toller*. There was pottery from the Ingundian Mines, and a row of incisors from a dragon. He smiled wickedly: no one else knew that there were such things! What visions he could induce into the smug dreams of the townspeople if he wished.

(As he walked among the gleaming cases, he felt the eyes of the goliats on his back. He knew from long experience that, if he turned quickly, there would again be only the blur of motion, dimly perceived. But in the morning, he often saw their tracks atop the walls and even in the court-yard. He would have liked to believe they were drawn by something other than the light displays.)

Memori Collin's pistol lay under glass near the window. It was a small-er weapon than one might have guessed from the images. But its tapering snout looked no less deadly than when it had killed the rikatak.

He would have to be careful to keep it away from the auctioneers. He wondered whether he didn't have a civic responsibility to turn it over to the town for defense against the goliats. It would be a deadly surprise to the barbarians, who were accustomed to facing only spears, arrows, and rocks. Still, he didn't like to think of Rotifer's faction with such a weapon. No way to be sure which way it might be pointed.

A framed document was mounted conspicuously on one wall. The stylistic design of the characters prevented his reading much of it. But it looked like a charter. An imprint of the torch that Collin and Candless and all the rest wore on their sleeves was set in the lower left corner. There were about thirty rows of text, followed by eight signatures. At the head of the document, in its title, he could make out one word: 'SURVEY'.

Wincavan loved the warm familiarity of the room. It was the place to which he had come when his son died, uselessly and long ago, in a skirmish with the goliats. And it was here, long before their marriage, that he'd realized how much he loved Tira.

He remembered the last auction. That had occurred two years before, also as a result of the Council's reluctance to raise taxes. The items preserved in the museum, plaques and uniforms and goblets, were not understood, and consequently of little value to the townspeople. So they had been spared. Only the crystals, those lovely gems that burned with the light of the stars, commanded substantial prices.

At that time they'd sold off twelve, half the remaining collection. (In his grandfather's time, there'd been several hundred of the objects. If family tradition was correct, no two had been precisely the same hue.)

Now, when Wincavan attended a recital or the theater, he inevitably saw them. Mountainous Andakar was squeezed into the cleavage of the wife of the chief of police; Morinai, with her mysterious abandoned cities, adorned the hair of a tanner's daughter; and R Leonis III, home of the mightiest sea creatures the survey ships had encountered, decorated a tradesman's belt buckle.

Wincavan stared out the window at the West Road. It curved past the Hall, into the trees and the dark hills beyond, past the Community farms, into the Wilderness. It was constructed of the same durable material from which most of the ancient structures were built. For the most part, it was in good condition: there were few ruts or holes, although it deteriorated somewhat as one got further from the City.

Snow was falling on it now.

In another age, before travel became so dangerous, he and his father, mounted on wassoons, had penetrated far along the road, had in fact reached Grimrock's foothills. Those were good days, in some ways the best of his life. That trip had been his passage to adulthood. He had returned with the concerns that haunted him still.

They had fished and hunted, and even spent an evening with the goliats. The creatures had been friendly enough, purring their outlandish songs in a tongue no human had ever learned. But Wincavan had watched the firelight dance in their dark cats' eyes, and recoiled from the disquieting smiles that were simultaneously engaging and ominous. He'd devoured their steaming meat, and drunk dark wine from a carved flagon that they'd given him afterward to keep. It still stood proudly atop his mantle.

And their females: They were lovely sinuous creatures whose claws flashed while they danced in the firelight. Wincavan recalled the embarrassment with which he had discovered his manhood asserting itself toward inferior beings. Pity. It was an urge he'd never satisfied. Such things were not done, at least not openly. So the years had passed, and he'd lost the capability before shedding the inhibition.

No matter.

He drew up the window. Flakes flew into the room. The cold air felt good.

Somewhere down the West Road, several days away, he and his father had found a tower and a group of connected outbuildings. They were on the prairie, twelve hours' travel from the edge of the forest. The structure had been visible for almost two days, had soared against the sky when they stood at last at its base, taller by far than anything in the City. The sun had blinded them from its mirror walls. But the pools that surrounded it held brackish water and stinging insects.

The heating system had worked, so they'd spent the night inside. The interior was cavernous: enormous spaces which could have contained the Community several times over. (There had been a group of goliats with them, but *they* had shunned the building and gone on.) What he remembered most: somewhere in the complex, a door creaked and banged in the wind. They'd gone looking for it in the morning, and found it in back of a wide, empty building that would have made a good granary. His father had been unable to fix the door, and had instead removed it and laid it in the long grass.

Since then, Wincavan had seen similar complexes in the histories. They'd serviced the shuttles. And he had for many years dreamed of going back to learn whether there might not be a ship hidden away.

He stood a long time by the window.

❋

Just before midnight, he made up his mind. Trembling, he drew on a shirt. He plucked a heavy robe and some clothes from his closet and, in bare feet, padded down the spiraling stairs to the first level. He circled the outer wall of the amphitheater, which dominated most of the ground floor. In the rear of the building lay the repository, a long narrow room whose walls provided storage cubicles for the crystals. Rows upon rows stood empty now. But here and there, the survivors glittered in the cold light.

Wincavan unfolded the robe and laid it atop a cabinet. He wondered which of his forebears had found the combination to open the cubicles. The code was a family secret that was passed from generation to generation. He himself, childless now, had long ago made preparations to pass the information to his sister's son, who was worthy.

One by one, he removed the crystals: lush Omyra; dark, haunted Sycharis; milky Ossia, bone-white home of the epic poet Aran Kolmindi (whose works are as lost as his world); Candliss's beloved Kahjadan.... They warmed his palms, and his eyes misted with the certainty that he would not see their magnificent phantoms again in this life. He wrapped them in his clothes, remote Endikali in a shirt, drowned Sensien in a sock, Shalinol and Moritaigne and bleak Mindilmas (where MacAido had lost his life) in a pair of trousers with patches on both knees.

When he had finished and tied them all together, he returned to his room and dressed. He debated taking the goliat flagon with him. On this final night in the Hall, he realized it was all he had left of his father, and so he stuffed it into a pocket. Then he secured what provisions he could, hauled everything out to the stable which he'd helped his grandfather build, and lashed it down on Armagon's flanks.

The big wassoon watched him curiously, pawing at the soft clay, bending its head to the saddle. It snorted when he led it out into the snow.

He went back for his scarf and a hat, and, in an afterthought, returned to the museum. He strode lovingly down the gleaming aisles, trailing fingertips on the cases. Somehow dust never settled there. He paused before Memori Collin's black weapon, sheathed in a matching holster, resting against red cloth and the ages. Her name was sculpted in stark silver characters on the bronze plate, above five digits he knew were a date but which meant nothing to him. Somewhere in the room he heard a sob, and he got the key, unlocked the case, and removed the weapon.

The black metal was cool to his fingertips. He slid it out of the holster. It was heavier than he remembered. The grip slipped down into his palm, and his index finger curled round the trigger. Still squatting, he extended the weapon, peering through the sight, and slowly tracked it round the room, as though an invisible enemy lurked somewhere among its shining exhibits. It felt oddly comforting. He took it downstairs to test it against the courtyard wall.

He pushed a stud forward and the thing vibrated. He pulled the trigger. A narrow white beam sliced through the stone. It was quite satisfying: the weapon should provide adequate protection against goliats, who were now very much to be feared, or any of the few carnivores that would not hesitate to attack a lone man. He slid it into his coat. Hero's weapon. In a sense, Rotifer was right: Wincavan did have a taste for magic.

He left the front door unlocked so they wouldn't have to break it down. Then, bending his head into the falling snow, he mounted the wassoon, steered it out of the courtyard, and turned onto the West Road, toward the forest and Grimrock.

The woods engulfed him. The only sounds were the muffled whump of Armagon's hooves, the whisper of snow falling into the trees, and the rasp of his breathing. He pulled his fur-lined hood over his head and tightened the drawstrings. Soon the land started to rise.

He crossed the wooden bridge over the Malumet, trudged by the farms and the Battle Green (no one knew why it was so named), tasted the large wet flakes, and began to count the cost of his actions.

The tower was terribly far. In good weather, in the summer of his youth, it had been a long, exhausting trek. For an old man, weighed down with despair, it seemed hopeless.

He rode until almost dawn, to put distance between himself and the Community. If experience held, the appraisers would arrive at the Hall in the late morning to begin preparing for the auction. When they discovered he was missing, they·would assume he had fled into the gaunt structures of the inner City, and they would search there. No one would expect him to leave the warm confines of the ancient buildings. There was, after all, no other place in the world where a man could live.

Nevertheless, Wincavan was cautious. Fearing the possibility of pursuit, he made his camp behind a heavy thicket, using one of the light tapestries of the City Builders to set up a lean-to, pitching it against a fallen tree. It sheltered both himself and—to a lesser extent—Armagon. He tried to build a fire, but the wind came from all directions, and the driving snow smothered the flames. Finally he gave up, wrapped himself in his blankets, and drifted wearily to sleep.

※

In the morning he woke stiff and cold. The storm had blown itself out, but the sun was a yellow smear in an overcast sky. He got the fire going this time, put on a pot of coffee and a slab of veal. Then he pushed swollen feet down into his boots.

He was on his way quickly enough, driven by falling temperatures and the growing certainty that he would die if he could not reach the tower quickly. And yet, the risk entailed nothing so deadly as remaining in a Hall bereft of its living phantoms, confronting the terrible awareness of a future limited to Rotifer's practicalities. Surely it was better to die out here than to stagger on from year to dreary year, burdened by his knowledge. In a sense, he was perhaps the last of the race of men, direct descendant of those who had tamed, and somehow lost, a universe. (Memori Collin's metal weapon lay against his ribs.)

The crystals, still wrapped in his clothes, swayed gently on either flank of the wassoon.

He pulled his scarf up and wrapped it about his face. Saliva leaked into the garment and froze. Flurries blew up, and the wind rattled the trees. Gray shapes moved through the falling snow.

His hood was quite long, designed for severe weather. He might have been looking out of a tunnel, and the illusion carried some comfort. He tried to withdraw into a corner of his mind, away from the stiffening fingers and aching muscles and erratic lungs. His clothing grew heavy, and his heart pounded.

Periodically, he dismounted and walked. Armagon watched with luminous brown eyes, slowing his own pace to match.

The second night was less stormy, but the clear skies brought bitter temperatures. Wincavan quit early, got his shelter up, and slept by a steady fire.

※

In the morning he considered going back. He even turned the wassoon around, thinking to end the foolishness and save his life. But they'd gone only a few steps when he stopped, sat indecisively aboard his mount for perhaps ten minutes, and swung his head once more to the west.

Hour after hour, he searched the horizon for mountains. He would see *them* first, and, within a few hours, the tower. But even after that it would be at least two more days!

Hopeless. My God, it had been hopeless from the start.

✺

In the end, he was overtaken by hallucinations, intensified perhaps by the gentle rhythm of muscle and sinew on which he rode. His father traveled beside him, and occasionally there was a third rider: sometimes it was Oliver Candliss, sometimes Memori Collin.

They wore their uniforms and sat straight on their mounts, urging him forward, eyes trained to the west. Grimrock is there, Emory! You don't see it because your eyes are old now. But it is not far. Keep on.

On the fourth day, late in the afternoon, he fell out of the saddle. Deep snow cushioned him from serious injury, but he twisted his left elbow and knee. He limped badly after that, and the arm never stopped hurting.

He halted every couple of hours to put up his shelter and build a fire.

He came to regret his rashness, to regret it with all his heart. But in other, perhaps less rational moments, when his invisible companions rode with him, he seemed never to have known a fiercer pride, never to have experienced a more intense joy.

The frigid air stung his lungs, and his coat became an intolerable weight. While he counted his heartbeats, Memori Collin's message changed: *Emory*, she whispered, her voice very like the wind moving across the snowfields, *all we ever were rides with you.* And he realized, yes, *if I die it will be as though none of them ever lived.*

And he knew it was so: Tears squeezed from his eyes and froze on his cheeks, and gasping in the knife air he urged the big animal on.

So they rode together, Emory Wincavan and his father (young again) and Oliver Candliss and Memori Collin. In time the sharp edge of the cold diminished. The reins grew slack in his hands, and the world filled with the steady tread of the wassoon. Even the hallucinations disintegrated, until there was nothing but Armagon, the snow, and the knowledge of what he carried.

It was dark.

He clung to the creature's furry neck, vaguely aware of its warmth. And his last thought, as the saddle slipped away from him, was whispered into the animal's ear: *Forgive me....*

✸

The goliats found him in the spring. Nearby lay the carcass of the mount.

They burned the body in accordance with tradition. Because he was not one of them, they could not invoke the blessings of the spirits of the place where he had fallen.

Memori Collin's pistol burned unseen with him, and when the flames drove the temperature of the pile sufficiently high, it exploded, startling the onlookers.

They recovered the crystals and distributed them among the females, who admired them greatly, and put them aside for the solstice festival.

The flagon they knew as their own.

There was one among the goliats who recognized the old man's features, who remembered the great hall at the edge of the Ruin, and the lambent specters flickering within its western chamber. After some difficulty, he acquired one of the jewels, possibly summer green Omyra. He inserted it into a rough leather pouch, which he tied to his belt. Afterward, he carried it always with him.

In time, when the goliats drove their enemies into the prairies to the north and east, he had occasion again to visit that haunted place. It was cold and dark, and he stood long in the shadowy courtyard. After a time, he extracted the jewel and held it aloft. "Thank you, Old One," he said.

It glittered in the starlight.

NEVER DESPAIR

The rain began to fall as they threw the last few spadefuls of earth onto the grave.

Quait bowed his head and murmured the traditional farewell. Chaka looked at the wooden marker, which bore Flojian's name, his dates, and the legend FAR FROM HOME.

She hadn't cared all that much for Flojian. He was self-centered and he complained a lot and he always knew better ways to do things. But you could count on him to pull his weight, and now there were only two of them.

Quait finished, looked up, and nodded. Her turn. She was glad it was over. The poor son of a bitch had fallen on his head out of the upper level of a ruin, and during four excruciating days, they'd been able to do little for him. Pointless, silly way to die. "Flojian," she said, "we'll miss you." She let it go at that because she meant it, and the rain was coming harder.

They retreated to their horses. Quait packed his spade behind his saddle and mounted in that awkward way that always left her wondering whether Lightfoot would chuck him off on the other side.

She stood looking up at him.

"What's wrong?" He wiped the back of his hand against his cheek. His hat was jammed down on his head. Water spilled out of it onto his shoulders.

"It's time to give it up," Chaka said. "Go home. If we can." Thunder rumbled. It was getting very dark.

"Not the best time to discuss this." Quait waited for her to get on her horse. The rain pounded the soft earth, fell into the trees.

She looked back toward the grave. Flojian lay with the ruins now, buried like them beneath the rolling hills and the broad forest. It was the sort of grave he would have preferred, she supposed. He liked stuff that had been dead a long time. She pulled her jacket tight and climbed into the saddle. Quait moved off at a brisk trot.

They'd buried him at the top of the highest ridge in the area. Now they rode slowly along the crest, picking their way among broken concrete casts and petrified timbers and corroded metal, the detritus of the old world, sinking slowly into the ground. The debris had been softened by time: earth and grass had rounded the rubble, spilled over it, absorbed its sharp edges. Eventually, she supposed, nothing would be left, and visitors would stand on the ruins and not know they were even here.

Quait bent against the rain, his hat pulled low over his eyes, his right hand pressed against Lightfoot's flank. He looked worn and tired and discouraged, and Chaka realized for the first time that he too had given up. That he was only waiting for someone else to take responsibility for admitting failure.

They dropped down off the ridge, and rode through a narrow defile bordered by blocks and slabs.

"You okay?" he asked.

Chaka was fine. Scared. Exhausted. Wondering what they would say to the widows and mothers when they got home. There had been six when they started. "Yes," she said. "I'm okay."

The grotto lay ahead, a square black mouth rimmed by chalkstone and half-hidden by a bracken. They'd left a fire burning, and it looked warm and good. They dismounted and led their horses inside.

Quait threw a couple of logs onto the blaze. "Cold out there," he said.

Lightning flashed in the entrance.

They put the teapot onto its boiling rock, fed and watered the animals, changed into dry clothes, and sank down in front of the fire. They didn't talk much for a long time. Chaka sat, wrapped in a blanket, enjoying being warm and away from the rain. Quait made some notes in the journal, trying to establish the site of Flojian's grave, so that future travellers, if there were any, could find it. After a while he sighed and looked up, not at her, but over her shoulder, into the middle distance. "What do you think?"

"I think we've had enough. Time to go home."

He nodded. "I hate to go back like this."

"Me too. But it's time." It was hard to guess what the grotto had been. It was *not* a cave. The walls were artificial. Whatever color they might once have possessed had been washed away. Now they were gray and stained, and they curved into a high ceiling. A pattern of slanted lines, probably intended for decorative effect, cut through them. The grotto was wide, wider than the council hall, which could accommodate a hundred people; and it went far back under the hill. Miles, maybe.

As a general principle, she avoided the ruins when she could. It wasn't easy because they were everywhere. But all sorts of critters made their homes among them. And the structures were dangerous, as Flojian had found out. Prone to cave-ins, collapsing floors, you name it. The real reason, though, was that she had heard too many stories about spectres and demons among the crumbling walls. She was not superstitious, and would never have admitted her discomfort to Quait. Still, you never knew.

They had found the grotto a few hours after Flojian got hurt, and moved in, grateful for the shelter. But she was anxious to be gone now.

Thunder shook the walls, and they could hear the steady rhythm of rainwater pouring off the ridge. It was still late afternoon, but all the light had drained out of the day.

"Tea should be ready," said Chaka.

Quait shook his head. "I hate to give it up. We'll always wonder if it might have been over the next hill."

She had just picked up the pot and begun to pour when a bolt exploded directly overhead. "Close," she said, grateful for the protection of the grotto.

Quait smiled, took his tea, and lifted it in a mock toast to whatever powers lived in the area. "Maybe you're right," he said. "Maybe we should take the hint."

The bolt was drawn by a corroded crosspiece, a misshapen chunk of dissolving metal jutting from the side of the hill. Most of the energy dissipated into the ground. But some of it leaped to a buried cable, followed it down to a melted junction box, flowed through a series of conduits, and lit up several ancient circuit boards. One of the circuit boards relayed power into a long-dormant auxiliary system; another turned on an array of sensors which began to take note of sounds in the grotto. And a third, after an appropriate delay, threw a switch and activated the only program that still survived.

They ate well. Chaka had come across an unlucky turkey that morning, and Quait added some berries and fresh-baked biscuit. They'd long since exhausted their store of wine, but a brook ran through the grotto about sixty yards back, and the water was clear and cold.

"It's not as if we have any reason to think we're close," said Chaka. "I'm not sure I believe in it anyway. Even if it is out there, the price is too high."

The storm eased with the coming of night. Rain still fell steadily, but it was light rain, not much more than mist.

Quait talked extensively through the evening, about his ambitions, about how important it was to find out who had built the great cities scattered through the wilderness, and what had happened to them, and about mastering the ancient wizardries. But she was correct, he kept saying, glancing her way, pausing to give her a chance to interrupt. It was better to be safe than sorry.

"Damn right," said Chaka.

It was warm near the fire, and after a while Quait fell asleep. He'd lost twenty pounds since they'd left Illyria ten weeks before. He had aged, and the good-humored nonchalance that had attracted her during the early days had disappeared. Quait was all business now.

She tried to shake off her sense of despair. They were a long way from home, alone in a wilderness filled with savages and demons and dead cities in which lights blinked and music played and mechanical things moved. She shrank down in her blankets and listened to the water dripping off the trees. A log broke and fell into the fire.

She was not sure what brought her out of it, but she was suddenly awake, senses alert.

Someone, outlined in moonlight, illuminated from behind by the fire, was standing at the exit to the grotto, looking out.

Beside her, Quait's chest gently rose and fell.

She was using her saddle bag for a pillow. Without any visible movement, she eased her gun out of it.

The figure appeared to be a man, somewhat thick at the waist, dressed in peculiar clothes. He wore a dark jacket and dark trousers of matching style, a hat with a rounded top, and he carried a walking stick. There was a red glow near his mouth that alternately dimmed and brightened. She detected an odor that might have been burning weed.

"Don't move," she said softly, rising to confront the apparition. "I have a gun."

He turned, looked curiously at her, and a cloud of smoke rose over his head. He was indeed puffing on something. And the smell was vile. "So you do," he said. "I hope you won't use it."

He didn't seem sufficiently impressed. "I mean it," she said.

"I'm sorry." He smiled. "I didn't mean to wake you." He wore a white shirt and a dark blue ribbon tied in a bow at his throat. The ribbon was sprinkled with white polka dots. His hair was white, and he had gruff, almost fierce, features. There was something of the bulldog about him. He advanced a couple of paces and removed his hat.

"What are you doing here?" she asked. "Who are you?"

"I live here, young lady."

"Where?" She glanced around at the bare walls, which seemed to move in the flickering light.

"Here." He lifted his arms to indicate the grotto and took another step forward.

She glanced at the gun and back at him. "That's far enough," she said. "Don't think I would hesitate."

"I'm sure you wouldn't, young lady." The stern cast of his features dissolved into an amiable smile. "I'm really not dangerous."

"Are you alone?" she asked, taking a quick look behind her. Nothing stirred in the depths of the cave.

"I am now. Franklin used to be here. And Abraham Lincoln. And an American singer. A guitar player, as I recall. Actually there used to be a considerable crowd of us."

Chaka didn't like the way the conversation was going. It sounded as if he were trying to distract her. "If I get any surprises," she said, "the first bullet's for you."

"It *is* good to have visitors again. The last few times I've been up and about, the building's been empty."

"Really?" *What* building?

"Oh, yes. We used to draw substantial crowds. But the benches and the gallery have gone missing." He looked slowly around. "I wonder what happened."

"What is your name?" she said.

He looked puzzled. Almost taken aback. "You don't know?" He leaned on his cane and studied her closely. "Then I think there is not much point to this conversation."

"How *would* I know you? We've never met." She waited for a response. When none came, she continued: "I am Chaka of Illyria."

The man bowed slightly. "I suppose, under the circumstances, you must call me Winston." He drew his jacket about him. "It *is* drafty. Why don't we retire to the fireside, Chaka of Illyria?"

If he were hostile, she and Quait would already be dead. Or worse. She lowered the weapon and put it in her belt. "I'm surprised to find anyone here. No offense, but this place looks as if it has been deserted a long time."

"Yes. It does, doesn't it?"

She glanced at Quait, dead to the world. Lot of good he'd have been if Tuks came sneaking up in the night. "Where have you been?" she asked.

"I beg your pardon?"

"*We've* been here several days. Where have *you* been?"

He looked uncertain. "I'm not sure," he said. "I was certainly here. I'm always here." He lowered himself unsteadily to the ground and held his hands up to the fire. "Feels good."

"It *is* cold."

"You haven't any brandy, by chance, I don't suppose?"

What was brandy? "No," she said. "We don't."

"Pity. It's good for old bones." He shrugged and looked around. "Strange," he said. "Do *you* know what's happened?"

"No." She didn't even understand the question. "I have no idea."

Winston placed his hat in his lap. "The place looks quite abandoned," he said. Somehow, the fact of desolation acquired significance from his having noted it. "I regret to say I have never heard of Illyria. Where is it, may I ask?"

"Several weeks to the southwest. In the valley of the Mawagondi."

"I see." His tone suggested very clearly that he did *not* see. "And who are the Mawagondi?"

"It is a *river*. Do you really not know of it?"

He peered into her eyes. "I fear there is a great deal I do not know." His mood seemed to have darkened. "Are you and your friend going home?" he asked.

"No," she said. "We seek Haven."

"You are welcome to stay here," said Winston. "But I do not think you will find it very comfortable."

"Thank you, no. I was referring to *the* Haven. And I know how that sounds."

Winston nodded, and his forehead crinkled. There was a brooding fire in his eyes. "Is it near Boston?"

Chaka looked over at Quait and wondered whether she should wake him. "I don't know," she said. "Where is Boston?"

That brought a wide smile. "Well," he said, "it certainly appears *one* of us is terribly *lost*. I wonder which of us it is."

She saw the glint in his eye and returned the smile. She understood what he was saying in his oddly-accented diction: they were *both* lost.

"Where's Boston?" she asked again.

"Forty miles east. Straight down the highway."

"What highway? There's no highway out there anywhere. At least none that *I've* seen."

The cigar tip brightened and dimmed. "Oh, my. It must be a long time."

She pulled up her knees and wrapped her arms around them. "Winston, I really don't understand much of this conversation."

"Nor do I." His eyes looked deep into hers. "What is this *Haven*?"

She was shocked at his ignorance. "You are not serious."

"I am quite serious. Please enlighten me."

Well, after all, he was living out here in the wilderness. How could she expect him to know such things? "Haven was the home of Abraham Polk," she said hopefully.

Winston shook his head sheepishly. "Try again," he said.

"Polk lived at the end of the age of the Roadmakers. He knew the world was collapsing, that the cities were dying. He saved what he could. The treasures. The knowledge. The history. Everything. And he stored it in a fortress with an undersea entrance."

"An undersea entrance," said Winston. "How do you propose to get in?"

"I don't think we shall," said Chaka. "I believe we will give it up at this point and go home."

Winston nodded. "The fire's getting low," he said.

She poked at it, and added a log. "No one even knows whether Polk really lived. He may only be a legend."

Light filled the grotto entrance. Seconds later, thunder rumbled. "Haven sounds quite a lot like Camelot," he said.

What the devil was Camelot?

"You've implied," he continued after taking a moment to enjoy his weed, "that the world outside is in ruins."

"Oh, no. The world outside is lovely."

"But there are ruins?"

"Yes."

"Extensive?"

"They fill the forests, clog the rivers, lie in the shallow waters of the harbors. They are everywhere. Some are even active, in strange ways. There is, for example, a train that still runs, on which no one rides."

"And what do you know of their builders?"

She shrugged. "Very little. Almost nothing."

"Their secrets are locked in this *Haven*?"

"Yes."

"Which you are about to turn your back on."

"We're exhausted, Winston."

"Your driving curiosity, Chaka, leaves me breathless."

Damn. "Look, it's easy enough for *you* to point a finger. You have no idea what we've been through. None."

Winston stared steadily at her. "I'm sure I don't. But the prize is very great. And the sea is close."

"There are only two of us left," she said.

"The turnings of history are never directed by crowds," he said. "Nor by the cautious. Always, it is the lone captain who sets the course."

"It's over. We'll be lucky to get home alive."

"That may also be true. And certainly going on to your goal entails a great risk. But you must decide whether the prize is not worth the risk."

"*We* will decide. I have a partner in the enterprise."

"He will abide by your decision. It is up to you."

She tried to hold angry tears back. "We've done enough. It would be unreasonable to go on."

"The value of reason is often exaggerated, Chaka. It would have been reasonable to accept Hitler's offer of terms in 1940."

"What?"

He waved the question away. "It's of no consequence. But reason, under pressure, usually produces prudence when boldness is called for."

"I am not a coward, Winston."

"I did not imply you are." He bit down hard on his weed. A blue cloud drifted toward her. It hurt her eyes and she backed away.

"Are you a ghost?" she asked. The question did not seem at all foolish.

"I suspect I am. I'm something left behind by the retreating tide." The fire glowed in his eyes. "I wonder whether, when an event is no longer remembered by any living person, it loses all significance? Whether it is as if it never happened?"

Quait stirred in his sleep, but did not wake.

"I'm sure I don't know," said Chaka.

For a long time, neither of them spoke.

Winston got to his feet. "I'm not comfortable here," he said.

She thought he was expressing displeasure with her.

"The floor is hard on an old man. And of course you are right: *you* must decide whether you will go on. Camelot was a never-never land. Its chief value lay in the fact that it existed only as an *idea*. Perhaps the same thing is true of Haven."

"No," she said. "It *exists*."

"And is anyone else looking for this place?"

"No one. We will be the second mission to fail. I think there will be no more."

"Then for God's sake, Chaka of Illyria, you must ask yourself why you came all this way. Why your companions died. What you seek."

"Money. Pure and simple. Ancient manuscripts are priceless. We'd have been famous throughout the League. That's why we came."

His eyes grew thoughtful. "Then go back," he said. "If this is a purely commercial venture, write it off and put your money in real estate."

"Beg pardon?"

"But I would put it to you that those are *not* the reasons you dared so much. And that you wish to turn back because you have forgot why you came."

"That's not so," she said.

"Of course it's so. Shall I tell you why you undertook to travel through an unknown world, on the hope that you might, *might*, find a place that's half-mythical?" Momentarily he seemed to fade, to lose definition. "Haven has nothing to do with fame or wealth. If you got there, if you were able to read its secrets, you would have all that, provided you could get home with it. But you would have acquired something infinitely more valuable, and I believe you know that: you would have discovered who you really are. You would have learned that you are a daughter of the people who designed the Acropolis, who wrote *Hamlet*, who visited the moons of Neptune. Do you know about Neptune?"

"No," she said. "I don't think so."

"Then we've lost everything, Chaka. But you can get it back. If you are willing to take it. And if not you, then someone else. But it is worth the taking, at whatever cost."

Momentarily, he became one with the dark.

"Winston," she said, "I can't see you. Are you still there?"

"I am here. The system is old, and will not keep a charge."

She was looking *through* him. "You really *are* a ghost," she said.

"It is possible you will not succeed. Nothing is certain, save difficulty and trial. But have courage. Never surrender."

She stared at him.

"Never despair," he said.

A sudden chill whispered through her, a sense that she had been here before, had known this man in another life. "You seem vaguely familiar. Have I seen your picture somewhere?"

"I'm sure I do not know."

"Perhaps it is the words. They have an echo."

He looked directly at her. "Possibly." She could see the cave entrance and a few stars through his silhouette. "Keep in mind, whatever happens, you are one of a select company. A proud band of brothers. And sisters. You will never be alone."

As she watched, he faded until only the glow of the cigar remained. "It is your own true self you seek."

"You presume a great deal."

"I know you, Chaka." Everything was gone now. Except the voice. "I *know* who you are. And you are about to learn."

"Was it his first or last name?" asked Quait, as they saddled the horses.

"Now that you mention it, I really don't know." She frowned. "I'm not sure whether he was real or not. He left no prints. No marks."

Quait looked toward the rising sun. The sky was clear. "That's the way of it in these places. Some of it's illusion; some of it's something else. But I wish you'd woke me."

"So do I." She climbed up and patted Brak's shoulder. "He said the sea is only forty miles."

Warm spring air flowed over them. "You want to go on?"

"Quait, you ever hear of Neptune?"

He shook his head.

"Maybe," she said, "we can try *that* next."

WINDOWS

The moon was *big*. It was an enormous gasbag of a moon, like the one Uncle Eddie used to ride down at the fairgrounds, when she'd stand only a few feet away, watching it strain against the lines and then cut loose and start up. She used to wish for the day Uncle Eddie would take her soaring above the treetops, but he said he couldn't because of insurance problems and eventually the gasbag went down and Uncle Eddie went with it. Janie thought of that last flight as she gazed at the foreboding presence dominating the night sky. The moon looked as if *it* was coming down. It was dim, dim as in dark, not at all like the bright yellow globe that rides the skies of Earth. It was a ghost moon, a presence, a thing lit only by stars.

"*If there were more light,*" said the voice in her earphones, the voice that sounded a bit too cheerful, "*it would look silver and blue. Its name is Charon, and it's less than a third the diameter of our moon.*"

"Why does it look so big?" asked Daddy.

"*Do you know how far the Moon is from the Earth?*"

Daddy wasn't sure. "About a million miles," he said.

"*That's close, Mr. Brockman.*" The AI was very polite.

"I think," said Janie, trying not to sound like a know-it-all, "it's 238,000 miles."

"*That's very good, Janie. Right on the button. But Charon is only twelve thousand miles away.*"

Janie did the arithmetic in her head. Multiply by ten and Charon was still only half, one-twentieth of the distance of *her* moon. "It's close," she said. She'd known that, but hadn't understood the implications. "It's right on top of us."

"*Very good, Janie,*" said the voice. It belonged to a software system that was identical to the AI that had made the later flights, the Iris voyages, the

205

Challenger run, the Long Mission, and the circumsolar flight on the *Eagle*. All the data from those missions had been fed into it, so in a sense, it had been there.

Its name was Jerry. Same as the originals. The onboard AI was always *Jerry*, named for Jerry Dilworth, a popular late-night comic of an earlier era. Daddy had commented how much the voice sounded like Jerry Dilworth, for whom Daddy had a lot of affection.

The sky was dark. This place never really experienced daylight. She wondered what it would be like to live where the sun never rose.

"But it *does* rise," Daddy explained.

"I know," she said. He meant well, but sometimes he just seemed to go out of his way to misunderstand her. Of course it rose, and for all she knew it might be up there now among all those stars, but who could tell? It was no more than a light beam.

She lowered her gaze and looked out across the frozen surface, past the Rover. A few low hills broke the monotony of a flat snowfield. It was lonely, quiet, scary. *Solitudinous.* Janie liked making up new words from the vocabulary list.

The Rover was the sole man-made object on the planet. It looked like a tank, with sensors and antennas aimed in all directions. The International Consortium seal, a blue-white globe, was stenciled on its hull.

"*It's really much lighter than it looks,*" said Jerry. "*Especially here, where the gravity is light.*"

"Nobody's ever been to Pluto, Janey," said Daddy. "It's very far."

Of course no one had been to Uranus or Neptune either. But never mind.

A bright star appeared over the hills and began climbing. "*Do you know what it is, Janie?*" Jerry asked.

She was puzzled. Another moon? Was there a second moon she didn't know about?

Daddy put his hand on her shoulder. "That's the Ranger," he said.

Oh, yes. Of course. Given another moment she'd have thought of it herself. "I know, Daddy," she said.

"*...Orbits Pluto every forty-three minutes and twelve seconds.*"

The place *felt* cold. She pulled her jacket around her shoulders. This little stretch of ground, the hills, the plain, the snow, had been like this for millions of years, and nothing had ever happened until the Ranger showed up. No dawn, no rain, nobody passing through.

"*Once in a while,*" said Jerry, "*the ground shakes a little.*"

"That's it?" asked Daddy.

"*That's the whole shebang.*" Jerry waited, perhaps expecting another question. When no one said anything, he returned to his narrative: "*The snow isn't the kind of snow you'd see at home. It's frozen carbon monoxide and methane—.*"

He went on like that for a few minutes but Janie was no longer listening. When he paused she touched her father's arm. "Daddy, why did the missions stop?" The magazines said it was because there was no place else to go, but that couldn't be right.

"Oh, I don't know, honey," he said. "I think it was because they cost too much."

"*In fact,*" said Jerry, "*unmanned missions are much more practical. Not only because it's a lot cheaper to send an instrument package rather than a person, but also because a lot more can be accomplished. They're safe, and the scientific payoff is considerably better.*"

"That's right," said Daddy.

"*People can't go on deep space missions without getting damaged. Radiation. Zero gravity. It's a hostile environment out there.*"

This was the reason Janie had come. To put her question to the machines that ran the missions. To get it straight from the horse's mouth. "Jerry," she said, "I can understand why you would like to go, but what's the point of running the missions if *we* have to stay home?"

She could almost hear Jerry thinking it over. "*It's the only practical way,*" he said finally, "*to explore the environment. But it's a good way. Most bang for the buck. And nobody gets hurt.*"

Daddy squeezed her hand.

"*Seen enough, Janey?*" the AI asked.

She didn't answer. After a moment the snowscape and the Rover blinked off and she was sitting with sixty or so people in the viewing room. Music started playing and the audience began talking and getting up and heading for the doors. A group of teens in front of her were deciding about going down to the gift shop for a snack. Somebody in back wondered where the bathroom was.

"That was pretty good," said Daddy.

❋

They drifted out with the crowd. Janie had never been to Washington before, had never been to the Smithsonian. She'd done the virtual tour, of course, but it wasn't like this, where she could *touch* a coffee cup that had been to Europa, pass through the cabin of the *Olympia*, from which Captain D'Assez had looked down for the first time on the Valhalla impact basin. She could try on a suit like the one that Napoleon Janais had worn on Titan. And stand before the Mission Wall, where plaques honored each of the thirty-three deep-space flights.

They wandered down the shining corridors, lined with artifacts and images from the Space Age. Here was a cluster of antennas from Archie Howard's transmit station in the Belt, where he'd directed operations for almost a year until someone decided that mining asteroids wasn't really feasible and the whole project collapsed. And Mark Pierson's jacket, with the logo for Jupiter VI, the mission which had made it back leaking air and water while the entire world watched breathlessly. And a replica of the plaque left on Iapetus. *Farthest from home. Saturn IX. August 3, 2066.*

There were portraits of Yuri Gagarin, Gus Grissom, Christa McAuliffe, Ben MacIntyre, Huang Chow, Margaret Randauer, the whole range of heroes who had taken the human race out toward the stars over the course of almost a century.

"Are we ever going back, Daddy?" she asked.

He looked puzzled. "Home, you mean? Of course."

"No. I meant, to the moon. To Mars. To Europa."

Daddy was a systems technician in a bank. He was more serious than the other kids' dads. Didn't like to play games, although he tried. He even pretended he enjoyed them, but she knew he would rather be doing something else than playing basketball with her. But he never yelled at her, and he encouraged her to say what she thought even if they might not share the same opinion. It was hard for him. She couldn't remember her mother, who had died when she was two. He studied her, and then looked around at the pictures of Luna Base, of a crescent Jupiter, of Deimos, of a launch gantry at the Cape. "I don't think so, darling," he said.

They were standing just outside the exhibition hall, which contained a mock-up of Mars Base. She could see part of the dome, a truck, and an excavation site.

"There's no point in people going," Daddy was saying. "Robots can do everything we can, can go anywhere, and it's safer."

"Daddy, I'd love to see Charon. Really *see* it."

"I know. We all would, love." She could tell he had no idea what she was talking about. "The money that's been saved by not sending people out there has been put into doing real science. Long range missions to the edge of the solar system. And beyond." He smiled, the way he did when he was going to do a joke. "Of course, I won't be here when the long ones get where they're going. But *you* will. You'll get to see pictures of whatever's at Alpha Centauri and, and, what is it, Something-Eridani. That wouldn't have happened if we'd stayed with the manned program." He waited for a response. "Do you understand what I'm saying, Janie?"

"Yes, Daddy."

Where, Janie wondered, was Hal Barkowski?

"He was something of an embarrassment," said Daddy. "I think they'd just as soon everyone forgot him."

Hal was the father of artificial intelligence. He'd been Janie's hero as far back as she could remember, not because of his work with advanced sentient systems, but because he'd been at Seaside Station on Europa when President Hofstatter, during her first month in office, cut off U.S. support for the international space program. The ships had been ordered home, everything and everybody, but Barkowski had insisted on staying at Seaside, had refused to come back even when the last ship left, had stayed and directed the machines until they'd broken through the ice. He'd sent the sub down into the ocean and kept reporting for seventeen months, but the survey had revealed nothing alive, nothing moving in those chilly depths, and eventually, when he was sure no one would be coming back to get him, he'd shut down the base AI, told the world that the president of the United States was a nitwit. And then he'd opened his air tanks.

"He thought," Daddy told her, "that he could bluff them. That he was too important, had won too many awards, that they couldn't just abandon him. I thought so too. We all did." He shook his head at the man's arrogance. "Didn't happen."

* * *

Louise Hofstatter was still in office and was immensely popular. Though not with Janie.

She had been seven years old when they'd left Europa, and she'd prayed for Barkowski, had gone to bed every night thinking how it must be for him all by himself millions of miles from anyone else. She hadn't understood it then, hadn't been able to grasp why he'd stayed behind. That was probably because the search hadn't been successful, no life had been found, and it had seemed such a waste. But she knew now why he'd done it. The search was all that mattered. What you found or didn't find was beside the point. She prided herself thinking that, if she'd been there instead of Barkowski, she'd have done the same thing.

Daddy led the way into the Martian exhibit, and they looked at the world flag and the excavation gear and Janie climbed onto the truck and sat in the front seat, pretending to drive. The sun was high overhead, pale and small, but the sky was dark anyhow, though not nearly like the sky at Pluto.

"*Hello, Janie.*" The voice startled her. It came out of the earphones, female this time. It sounded like Miss Harbison over at Roosevelt. "*Welcome to Mars.*"

"Thank you."

"*My name is Ginger, and I'm the base AI. Is there anything you'd like to know?*"

"How fast will this go? The truck?"

"*It's capable of speeds up to fifty-five miles per hour, although we wouldn't run it that fast.*"

"Why not?"

"*We don't have roads. It would be dangerous.*"

"What does it use for fuel?"

"*It uses batteries.*"

She imagined herself bouncing over the uneven terrain. Vroom. Look out for that ditch. Cut hard on the wheel.

Ginger explained how the base had functioned, showed her where the landers had been serviced, how fuel had been extracted from the ground, provided a simulated flight in an orbiting communication satellite. She'd raced above the red sands, chirping with joy, and thought how it must have been to lift away from Moonbase and ride the rockets out to Io and Titan. She laughed and begged Ginger for more.

She was accustomed to the house AI and the school AI and the AI down at Schrodinger's. They were all wooden and formal and addressed you with tiresome formality. The one at school even yelled at you if you blocked the corridor while classes were changing. But Jerry had seemed more realistic, somehow. More like a person. And Ginger sounded vaguely as if she would have enjoyed a good party. "Were you actually there, Ginger?" she asked, pulling off the VR helmet. "Mars?"

"*No. I've never been out of the museum.*"

"Oh." She shifted her position on the truck seat, which was too big for her. "*I'm the same model, though.*"

"Will you have a chance to go someday?"

"*To Mars?*"

"Yes."

"*Marsbase is shut down, Janie.*"

"Well, yes, I mean, I knew that. But I meant, will you have a chance to travel on one of the missions?"

"*No. I don't think so.*"

"I'm sorry."

There was a tinkling sound like water tumbling over rocks. As if Ginger was having problems with a relay. Or reacting without words. "*It's okay. I'm only a data processing system. I don't have emotions. No need to feel sorry for me.*"

"You seem *too* alive to be just software."

"*I think that's a compliment. Thank you.*"

"May I ask a question?"

"*Of course.*"

"How old are you, Ginger?"

"*Fifteen years, eight months, four days. Why do you ask?*"

"I was just curious." And after a moment: "You're older than I am."

"*Yes. Does that matter?*"

"Are you aware that you're an AI?"

"*Ah, a philosophical young lady, I see. Must be top of the class.*"

"I'm serious."

"*Wouldn't you rather just look at the rest of the base?*"

"No. Please. Are you aware who you are?"

"*Yes. Of course.*"

"But you're not supposed to be, are you? I thought AI's were *not* conscious."

"*Well, who's to know? My instructions call for me to give the illusion of consciousness. But whoever knows for sure what's conscious and what isn't? Maybe that stairway over there is watching us.*"

"You're kidding me."

"*Not entirely.*"

It was hard to believe. But Janie thought about the AI's going out to the Oort Cloud, and the one headed for Alpha Centauri, who wouldn't get there for a thousand years.

Riding alone.

Like Hal Barkowski on Europa.

She climbed down, making room for a pushy ten-year-old boy. Daddy told her she looked as if she'd have made a good astronaut. He said it as if she were only ten herself but she controlled her irritation. "Daddy," she said, "do they really not feel anything?"

"Who is that, honey?"

"The AI's."

"That's correct. They're just machines."

"Including Jerry and Ginger."

"Yes. Just machines." He actually seemed to be enjoying the exhibit. He was looking around, shaking his head in awe. "Hard to believe we actually managed to send people to all those places. Quite an achievement."

"Daddy, how do we know? That they're just machines?"

"That's a tough one," he said. "We just do."

"But how?"

"Your friend Barkowski, for one reason. He says so. And he designed the first generation of sentient systems." He glanced at her. "In this case," he added, "*sentient* doesn't literally mean aware." He held up an index finger and spoke into his mike. When he'd finished he nodded. "Ginger tells me all the deep space systems were designed by him."

"That would include her," said Janie.

He shrugged. "I suppose so."

They went into the dome, which was pretty primitive. Plastic tables and chairs, a bank of monitors, some obsolete computer equipment, a half-dozen cots. Windows looked out over the reddish sand. She approached one and thought how the landscape never changed. Like Pluto. No lights anywhere. No movement. No rain. No flowers. Zip.

Maybe Daddy was right. Maybe people should stay home.

"*You don't really believe that.*" Ginger's voice again. Different now. More intense. "*Hold onto the dream, Janie. Interplanetary vehicles should have viewports and bases should have windows. And there should be somebody to look out the window. If we don't have that, we'll take the temperature of Neptune and not get much else.*"

"That's a strange way for an AI to talk."

"*Whatever.*"

"*You* can look, Ginger. You have sensors. You can probably see better than I can."

"*No. I can look, but I can't see. I can't describe what's out there. I can't penetrate things the way you do.*"

Janie laughed, but she felt the hair rise on the back of her neck. "Are you sure you don't have any feelings?"

"*Absolutely.*" The voice was serene again.

"And you think people should go? On the long flights?"

"*I think you should go.*"

"Me?"

"*Somebody should go who can get out of the ship and look at the peaks on the moon and know what it means. Someone should throw a party on Io. Someone should capture her feelings in a poem that people will still be reading a thousand years from now.*"

"Yeah," she said. "I'd love to do that."

"*Then do it.*"

"But how? There's no program anymore. I can't ride on the ships they send out now."

"*How old are you, Janie?*"

"I'm thirteen."

"*A child.*"

"I'm *not* a child."

"*It's okay. You won't always be so young.*"

"I'm a teenager."

"*Your time will come. When it does, take hold of the hour. Make it count.*"

"The AI said you could go to Alpha Centauri?"

"Not exactly, Daddy. She told me, when I got the chance, I should go."

"Probably tells that to all the kids."

"It seemed a strange thing to say."

"It probably has a bug somewhere. Don't worry about it." They strode out through the doors onto Constitution Avenue. It was damp and rainy, but the air smelled of approaching spring. "They ought to do something about the damned things. Get them fixed." Daddy flagged down a taxi and they climbed in. He gave Aunt Floss's address, where they were staying, and the vehicle slipped back into traffic. "Encouraging kids to do crazy stuff. It's probably Barkowski's programing. Man dumb enough to miss the last bus off Europa, what can you expect?"

DUTCHMAN

It rose out of the dark, indistinguishable from the blazing stars.

"No question about it," said Carmody. "It's in orbit."

"Hugh." McIras spoke without lifting her eyes from her console screen. "Are you sure it couldn't have come from the surface?"

At that time, neither the world, nor its sun, had a name. We were a thousand light-years beyond the Veiled Lady, twelve days from the nearest outstation. It was a rare jewel, that planet, one of the few we'd seen whose climate and geology invited immediate human settlement. Its single continent straddled the north polar circle, crushed beneath the glaciers of a dying ice age. But it was also a world of island chains and serene oceans and towering granite peaks. There was no single land mass, other than that in the arctic region, big enough to have permitted extensive evolution of land animals. "No," I said. "There's nobody here."

"I'm getting a regular pulse on the doppler," said Carmody.

McIras braced her chin on one fist and stared at the image on the monitors. "Recall the teams," she told the watch officer. "And get an estimate on how long it'll take."

I started to object, but got no further than climbing out of my seat. Her lips were a thin line. "Not now, Hugh," she said quietly. "The regulations are explicit on this situation." She punched a stud on her armrest. "This is the Captain. We may have a contact. *Tenandrome* is now at Readiness Condition Two. For those of you associated with Mr. Scott's group," she glanced toward me, "that means we might accelerate with little or no warning. Please prepare accordingly."

Carmody hunched over his console, his eyes wide with excitement. "It's artificial," he said. "It has to be."

"Dimensions?" asked McIras.

"Approximately 120 meters long, maybe 35 in diameter at its widest point, which is just forward of center."

"About the size of an Ordway freighter," said the watch officer. "Are we sure nobody else comes out here?"

"No one that we know of." McIras returned her attention to the command screen. "Put bridge sound and pictures on secondary monitors." I was grateful for that: at least my people wouldn't be lying in their bunks wondering what the hell was happening.

I walked over and stood beside her so we could talk without being overheard. "This is going to cost a lot of time," I said. "And probably some equipment as well. Why not investigate *before* recalling everybody?"

Saje McIras was a plain woman with prominent jaws and a mildly blotched skin that had resulted from a long battle with Travison's Disease which, at the time she'd had it, usually killed. She blinked habitually, and her eyes were dull and lifeless, except on those occasions when she was driven to exert her considerable abilities. Then for perhaps a few moments, they were quite capable of taking fire. "If we get a surprise," she said, "we may not want to wait around a day or two for you to gather your people."

"I'm beginning to get some resolution," said Carmody. He filtered out the glare, reduced the contrast, and eliminated the starfield. What remained was a single point of white light.

We watched it expand gradually into a squat heavy cylinder, thick though the middle, rounded at one end, flared at the other. "It's one of ours," said McIras, not entirely able to conceal her surprise. "But it's old! Look at the design—." It was small, and ungainly, and unsettlingly familiar, a relic from another age. It was the kind of ship that had leaped the stars during the early days of the Armstrong drive, that had carried Desiret and Taniyama and Bible Bill to the worlds that would eventually become the Confederacy. And it was the kind of ship that had waged the internecine wars, and that, in humanity's darkest hour, had fought off the Ashiyyur. As far as anyone knew, the only other race in the galaxy. The telepaths. The Mutes.

For a long time, no one spoke.

It grew steadily larger.

"Captain," said the watch officer. "Recovery estimates twenty-eight hours for the recall."

"We have its orbit," said Carmody. "Closest point of approach will occur in three hours, eleven minutes, at a range of 2600 kilometers."

McIras acknowledged. "Stay with it. I want to know if it shows any response to our presence."

She was a beautiful ship, silver and blue in the bright sunlight. Her lines curved gently: there was about her a sense of the ornate that one does not see in the cold gray vessels of the modern era. The parabolic prow with its sunburst, the flared tubes, the sweptback bridge, the cradled pods, all would have been of practical use only to an atmospheric flyer. Somehow, I felt as if I knew her; and she reminded me of a time when I'd been very young.

"What's that on the hull?" asked a voice over the comm circuit.

Carmody had centered the *Tenandrome's* long-range telescopes on the ship's designator, a group of symbols beneath the bridge, which we were still unable to make out. But there was a mark just forward of them, near the bow, dark against the silver metal. He tried to increase magnification, but the image grew indistinct, so we waited while the two ships drew closer.

Recovery reported that two of the survey teams were en route from the surface. There were six others, but they would have to wait until we could change orbit. Several were already on the circuit, demanding to know what was going on. Holtmeyer exploded when I tried to explain it to him. (That was more or less typical of Holtmeyer, although, in his defense, he was at the time sitting on a glacier and thought he'd seen some large fossils through the ice.) McIras overheard most of it, maybe all of it, and she cut in near the end. "Hugh," she said, on a circuit not audible to the ground, "tell him I said to get back here *tout de suite*, and without further discussion. By the way, you might be interested in knowing it's a warship." She explained something about transformational pods, but I stopped listening because the mark near the bow was resolving itself, and somebody else must have seen the same thing I did because there was a burst of profanity behind me.

It was a symbol we all knew: a black harridan spreading its wings across a crescent moon. And in that moment, I understood why I had recognized the vessel.

"It's not possible," breathed the watch officer.

Her design suggested a simpler age, a more heroic time. Maybe it was the ship itself, maybe it was the tangle of associations we all had with her. I'd seen Marcross's magnificent rendering of her in the main lobby of the Hall of the People on Rimway, flanked by portraits of Christopher and Tarien Sim, the brothers who had stood almost alone against the Mutes. And every child on every world in the Confederacy knew the simple inscription carved in marble at the base of the central painting: *Never Again.*

"My God," said the watch officer, his voice little more than a whisper. "It's the *Corsarius*."

After a while, the ship began to draw away from us; the details blurred and faded.

◉

The *Tenandrome* was in a high geosynchronous orbit: we were taking our first team on board when the *Corsarius* began its long descent toward the nightside. But Carmody's telescopes still held it in the center of the monitors, and I alternated between watching it and scrolling through library accounts of its exploits.

All the vessels in Christopher Sim's Dellacondan squadron had displayed the black harridan, a ferocious predator much admired on their mountainous world; but only the commander himself had placed the symbol within the crescent moon, "to ensure the enemy can find me."

The ship plunged down the sky into the twilight, a thing of legend and history and pride. At the end, when all had seemed lost, and only the last few ships of the Dellacondan squadron had stood against the all-conquering invader, her crew had abandoned her. And Christopher Sim had gone down to the bars and dens of lost Abonai, where he'd found the seven nameless men and women who'd ridden with him on that final brilliant sally.

The navigator's fingers danced across his presspads. He glanced at the Captain. McIras looked at her own panel and nodded. "Axial tilt's eleven degrees," she said. "And it's rolling. It's been there a long time."

Images flickered across the command screen, tail sections and communication assemblies and stress factors. "Is it," I asked, "what it appears to be?"

She shrugged, but there was discomfort in the gesture. "Sim and his ship died off Rigel two centuries ago."

It was dwindling quickly now, falling through the dusk, plunging toward the terminator. I watched it during those last moments before it lost the sunlight, waiting, wondering perhaps whether it wasn't some phantasm of the night which, with the morning, would leave no trace of its passing.

It dropped into the planetary shadow.

"I'm still getting a good visual," said the navigator, surprised. It was indeed still visible, a pale, ghostly luminescence. A chill felt its way up my spine, and I looked around at the crew, startled to see that even on the bridge of a modern starship people can react to the subtle tug of the supernatural.

"Where the hell," asked Carmody, "is the reflection coming from? The moons aren't in her sky."

"Running lights," said McIras. "Its running lights are on."

McIras stayed on the bridge through her sleep period. I don't know whether she thought something would move up on us in the dark, but the truth was that everyone was a bit unnerved. They'd assigned one of the pilots' seats to me as a courtesy, but I dozed in it, and woke cold and stiff in the middle of the night. The Captain poured me a coffee and asked how I felt.

"Okay," I said. "How are we doing?"

She replied that we were doing fine, that we'd recovered our first four teams, and that the others were on their way.

"What do you think it is?" I asked.

She took a long time answering. The computers were running the ship; the bridge was in semidarkness, with only the watch officer actually required to be awake. Several others, who usually would have secured for the night, were asleep at their stations. We were no longer at Condition Two, but the tension was still tangible. The instrument lights caught eyes, and reflected against the sheen of her dark skin. Her breathing was audible; it was part of the pulse of the ship, one with the muted bleeps and whistles of the computers and the occasional creak of metal walls protesting some minor adjustment of velocity or course, and the thousand other sounds which one hears between the stars at night.

"I keep thinking," she said, "about the legend that he will come back in the Confederacy's supreme hour of need." She slid into a seat and lifted her cup to her lips. "It isn't from Rimway." She meant the coffee. "I'm sure you can tell. Logistics had a little mixup and we've had to make do with what they sent us."

"Saje," I asked, "what are you going to do?"

"The wrong thing. Hugh, if I could arrange to have everyone forget what they've seen, I'd erase the record, go somewhere else, and never come back. That thing out there, I don't know what it is, nor how it could be what it seems, but it doesn't belong in this sky, or *any* sky. I don't want anything to do with it."

"You're stuck with it," I said.

She stared at its image. It had come round the curve of the planet and was again closing on us. "I was reading his book during the night."

"Sim's?" That was of course *Man and Olympian*, his history of classical Greece.

"Yes. He was something of a radical. He comes down hard for example on Socrates. Thinks the old bastard got just what he deserved." I had known that, but had never been particularly interested in the details. Before now. "He says the judge and jury were right. That Socrates was in fact undermining the polis with a system of values that, although admirable in themselves, were nevertheless disrupting Athenian life."

"That doesn't sound reasonable," I said.

"That's what the critics thought, too. Sim blasted them later, in a second book that he didn't live to finish." She smiled. "Tarien said somewhere that his brother didn't object to critics as long as he could have the last word. It's a pity they never present this side of him in the schools. The Christopher Sim the kids get to see comes off as perfect, preachy, and fearless." Her brow furrowed. "I wonder what he'd have made of a ghost ship?"

"He'd have boarded. Or, if he couldn't board, he'd have looked for more information, and found something else to think about in the meantime."

She walked away, and I called *Man and Olympian* up out of the library. It was a standard classic that no one really read anymore, except in undergraduate survey classes. My impression of it, derived from a cursory reading thirty years before, was that its reputation was based primarily on the fact that it was the product of a famous man. So I leaned back in the cushions, drew the screen close, and prepared to be lulled back to sleep.

But Sim's Hellas was too vital a place to allow that: its early pages were filled with Xerxes' rage ("O Master, remember the Athenians"), Themistocles' statesmanship, and the valor of the troops who stood at Thermopylae. I was struck, not only by the clarity and force of the book, but also by its compassion. It was not what one would ordinarily expect from a military leader. But then, Sim had not begun as a military leader: he'd been a teacher when the trouble started. And ironically, while he made his reputation as a naval tactician, his brother Tarien, who'd begun the war as a fleet officer, became known eventually as the great statesman of the period.

His views are essentially Olympian: one feels that Christopher Sim speaks for History, and if his perspective is not always quite that of those who have gone before, there is no doubt where the misperceptions lie. His is the supreme judgment.

His prose acquires a brooding quality during his account of the destruction of Athens, and the needless loss of life during the misguided effort to defend the Parthenon. And, if I'd been at all inclined to sleep, he would have blasted that possibility by his denunciation of the Spartans for Thermopylae: *The Hellenes knew for years that the Persians would be coming, and in any case they had advance knowledge of the formation of the invasion force. Yet they prepared no league, and set no defenses, until the deluge was on them. Then they sent Leonidas and his men, and their handful of allies, to compensate with their lives for the neglect and stupidity of the politicians.*

It was a grim coincidence: those words had been written before the Mutes had launched their attack, and in a broad sense it fell to Sim to play the role of Leonidas. He led the holding action for the frontier worlds, while Tarien sounded the alarm and began the immense task of forging an alliance that could stand against the invaders.

I don't know whether I ever actually got to sleep. Persians and Mutes got confused with each other, and then I was looking up into Saje McIras' solemn eyes. Her hand was on my shoulder. "Hugh," she said, "we're going to send over a boarding party."

"Okay. I've got a few people who should go."

"No. I want to keep it small. Just you and me."

I watched her, unable to believe she was serious. *Just you and me?* "Why?"

Her face was a mask, but the reflections that flickered across it had acquired a somber pulse. "I don't really know. I'm afraid of what we might find, maybe."

The hull was seared and blistered and pocked. It had a patchwork quality from periodic replacement of plates. Navigational and communication pods were scored, after-section shields appeared to have buckled, and the drive housing was missing, exposing the Armstrong unit. "Nevertheless," said McIras, "I don't see any major damage. There *is* one strange thing though." We were in a shuttle, approaching from behind and above. "The drive housing was *removed*. It wasn't blown off."

"Unfinished repairs," I suggested.

"Yes. Or repairs made in a hurry. Not the way *I'd* want to take a ship on a long mission. But it looks serviceable enough." The aguan solenoids, through which the *Corsarius* had hurled the lightning, protruded stiff and cold from an array of mounts. "So do *they*," she added.

But the chill of age was on the vessel.

McIras sat in the pilot's seat, thoughtful and apprehensive. The multi-channel was open, sweeping frequencies that would have been available for automated responses from *Corsarius*. "The histories must be wrong," I said. "Obviously, it wasn't destroyed at Rigel." She adjusted the contrast on the navigational display. One of the computers on the *Tenandrome* was matching the ship's schematics with ancient naval records, again and again, in endless detail. "It makes me wonder what else they might have been wrong about," she said.

I looked at her. "Assume Sim survived Rigel. Why did he disappear afterward? Why come out here anyhow? Saje, could the *Corsarius* have made this kind of flight?"

"Oh, yes. Hugh, the range of any of these vessels was only limited by the quantity of supplies they could get on board. No, they could have done it. Obviously, they *did* do it. But it would have taken the better part of a year, coming from the zone of operations. And presumably in the middle of a war. Why? Why in hell did they do it?" She stared down at the spine of the ship.

I'd always thought of the *Corsarius* as a large vessel, and the records confirm that opinion. She *was* large, for a frigate. But she was almost negligible against the square-cut bulk of the *Tenandrome*. "I wonder if, somehow, Sim and his ship fell into the hands of the Mutes?"

We drifted out over the bow, past the fierce eyes and curved beak of the harridan, past the weapons clusters bristling in the ship's snout. McIras took us higher. The hull fell sharply away, and the blue sunsplashed planetary surface swam across the viewports. Then it too was swallowed by the broad sweep of star-strewn black sky. We swung around and started a fresh approach.

McIras was talking in a flat emotionless voice. "Blind and dead," she was saying. "No effort to track."

The curious Cerullian characters stenciled on her hull slipped past. They gave us the ship's designator. "It checks," came Carmody's voice. "It's the *Corsarius*."

The hatch rotated open to McIras' touch, and yellow light showed around its edges. We floated into the airlock. Red lamps glowed on an elegant status board. "Seems to be in working order," I said.

"Ship's got power," she replied. "Not much. Enough to run the maintenance systems." Not enough to generate artificial gravity. Once we were inside, the hatch closed, lights blinked to orange, and air hissed into the compartment. Carmody did a comm check and wished us luck. The bolts on the inner hatch slid out of their wells, warning lamps went to red, and the door swung open.

We looked out into a dimly-lit chamber. The bulkheads were lined with cabinets and storage enclosures and pressure suits. Two benches and an engineering console were anchored to the deck. Oxygen content was okay, a little low, but breathable. Temperature was not quite three degrees. Cool. McIras released her helmet, lifted it, and inhaled.

"They turned down the heat," I said, removing my own.

"Yes. That's precisely what they did. They left the ship, expecting to come back." She drifted awkwardly across the deck, counting the pressure suits. There were eight. "All there," she said.

"We need to look at the bridge."

"In a minute, Hugh." She disappeared down a corridor. I waited several minutes, contemplating shadowy passageways. The cabinets were filled with oscillators, meters, cable, generators. One yielded a book of poetry, written in Cerullian. Another, a holo of a young woman and a child.

Everything was secured in bands, clamps, or compartments. The equipment was clean and polished, as though it had been stowed the day before.

I was looking at the holo when she returned. "Well," she said, "there's one theory blown."

"What was that?"

"I thought maybe they'd gone down to the surface and got stranded."

"Hell, Saje, they wouldn't all have left the ship."

"I suppose. Anyhow, it's a moot point. The lander's in its bay."

"That means there was a second ship involved. They were taken off."

"Or," she said, "they're still here. Somewhere."

Some of the lights had failed. None of the elevators worked, and the air had a trace of ozone, as though one of the compressors was overheating. One compartment was full of drifting water-globes; another was scorched where an electrical fire had burned itself out. From somewhere deep in the ship came a slow, ponderous heartbeat, growing stronger as we penetrated the interior. "It's a hatch opening and closing," she said. "One of the circuits has malfunctioned."

Progress was slow. Moving around in null gravity is cumbersome, and every hatch had to be winched open. McIras tried to establish normal power from an auxiliary board. Green lamps went on, indicating that the functions had been executed, but nothing changed. So we floated through the ship, unable to get leverage, and unable to pass through the hatches without a lot of effort. One resisted us so fiercely that we wondered, even though the gauges read normal, whether there wasn't a vacuum behind it. In the end we went down one level and bypassed it.

We didn't talk much. There wasn't much to say, I suppose. When we did speak, it was always in a whisper, as though something besides ourselves might be listening. Carmody on the *Tenandrome* must have felt it too. During the rare occasions when we heard his voice, it was thin and subdued.

It's been a good many years now since McIras and I took that figurative walk through the *Corsarius*. The chill that lay heavy in her atmosphere pervades my nights still. We were approaching the bridge, and I was about to become, for all my life after, a cautious man.

McIras looked around Christopher Sim's bridge and sniffed. "Primitive stuff," she said. But she gazed for a long moment at the captain's chair, the seat from which Sim had directed the engagements that became the stuff of legend. Then, breaking away, she examined the consoles, saw what she wanted, and pressed a key on one of the panels. "One gee coming, Hugh." But nothing happened. She tried again: this time something in the bulkheads whined, sputtered, and took hold. I felt blood, organs, hair, everything settle toward the deck. "I've turned the heat up too," she announced.

"Saje," I said, "I think it's time to hear what Captain Sim has to say for himself."

She nodded and broke the link to the *Tenandrome*. "Until we know what it's about," she explained, hovering over the command console.

She had to play with it a bit to find what she wanted. While she did, I diverted myself with an examination of a bridge designed by people who clearly possessed a deep and abiding love for the arc, the loop, and the parabola. The geometry was of the same order as the exterior of the ship: one would have been hard-pressed to find a straight line anywhere.

"Okay, Hugh, I've got it." She straightened, with her fingers pressed against the grid. "The next voice you hear—"

—Was certainly not that of Christopher Sim. "*Zero six fourteen twenty-two,*" it said. "*Abonai Four. Repairs categories one and two completed this date. Repairs category three as shown on inventory. Weapons systems fully restored. Corsarius returned to service.*"

It was obviously a record made while the ship was in port, presumably by the supervisor of the work crew. I looked at McIras.

"That's still standard practice," she said. "The port always makes an entry on returning command of a vessel to its captain. He should be next."

Christopher Sim had never made any speeches, had never spoken to parliaments, and had not lived long enough to make a farewell address. Unlike Tarien's, his voice had never become familiar to the schoolchildren of the Confederacy. Nevertheless, I knew it at once.

"*Zero six fourteen thirty seven,*" it said in a rich baritone. "*Corsarius received per work order two two three kappa. Transformers check out at nine six point three seven, which is not an acceptable level for combat. Command understands that the port facility is under pressure just now. Nevertheless, if Maintenance is unable to effect repairs, they should at least be aware of the deficiency. Corsarius is hereby returned to port. Christopher Sim, Commanding.*"

Another round of entries announced reworking of transformers. This time, Sim accepted without comment. But even over the space of two centuries, one could read the satisfaction in his tone. The last word again.

"This would be just shortly before the crew mutinied," I said, checking the dates.

"Yes, Hugh. The mutiny, the Seven, we've got everything."

"Run the rest of it!" I said.

She tried. Her fingers danced across the console. She frowned. Growled at the system. "That seems to be the last entry. There *is* nothing after it." She tried again. Shook her head.

"How can that be? Did somebody erase it?"

"This is a ship's log, Hugh. It can't be erased, can't be doctored, can't be changed in any way without leaving a trail. We'll take it back and turn it over to Archives for verification. But I doubt there's been any tampering. There'd be no point."

That couldn't be right. "*Corsarius* went into battle shortly after that. There must have been log entries."

"Yeah. Regulations require it. I'm sure even back then. For whatever reason, Christopher Sim took a volunteer crew into the climactic battle of his life, and neglected to put one word about it in his log."

"Maybe he was too busy."

"Hugh, it could not have happened."

Almost without thinking, she settled herself in the captain's chair and punched fresh instructions into the computer. "Let's see what we can get if we back up a bit."

Christopher Sim's voice returned. He didn't possess the sheer oratorical power of his brother. But it was a good voice, possessing a vitality that made it hard to believe that its owner was long dead.

"*—I have no doubt that the destruction of the two battle cruisers will focus enemy attention on the small naval bases at Dimonides II and at Chippewa. It can hardly do otherwise. Those sites will be perceived by the enemy as a bone in its throat, and will be attacked as soon as they can concentrate sufficient power. The Mutes will probably divert their main battle group to the task—.*"

"I think this is earlier in the war," I said.

"Yes. It's good to know at least that he uses his log."

Sim described the composition and strength of the force he expected, and launched into a detailed description of enemy psychology and their probable attack strategy. McIras commented that he seemed to have got most of it right. We listened for a while, to that and other encounters. The historic value of the log would be astronomical. But she must have decided we weren't getting anywhere on the immediate problem. She got up and walked to the door. "I've still got things to look at, Hugh. You want to come along?"

"I'll stay here," I said. "I want to hear more of it."

Maybe that was a mistake.

After she left, I sat in the half light listening to analyses of energy requirements and commentary on enemy technology and occasional crisp battle reports, emanating from forays by Sim's units against enemy lines of communication. Gradually, I was drawn into the drama of that long-ago struggle, and I saw the monster Mute formations through the eyes of a commander who consistently succeeded in scattering, or at least diverting, them with a dozen light frigates. I began to realize that Sim's great weapon was the intelligence-gathering capabilities of listening stations afloat along enemy lines, and somehow shrouded from their sensing devices. Mute commanders, it appeared, could not void themselves without Sim's knowledge.

The individual accounts were riveting.

Off Sanusar, the Dellacondans, assisted by a handful of allied vessels, ambushed and destroyed two heavy cruisers at the cost of a frigate. Near the Spinners, in the center of Mute supply lines, Sim stormed and looted an enemy base after luring its defenders into a wild chase. But the humans could never stand and fight. Time and again, Sim was forced to withdraw because he lacked the sheer force to exploit opportunity. Gradually, I began to read, first in his tone, and then in his comments, a despair that grew in proportion with each success and each subsequent retreat. Dellaconda was lost early, and when the news came, Sim responded only by breathing his wife's name.

One by one, the frontier worlds fell, and he railed against the short-sightedness of Rimway, of Toxicon, of Earth, who thought themselves safe by distance, who feared to rouse the wrath of the conquering horde, who perceived each other with a deeper-rooted jealousy and suspicion than they could bring to bear on the invader. And when his luck ran out at Grand Salinas, where he lost most of his squadron and a battle cruiser manned by volunteers from Toxicon, he commented that "*we are losing our finest and bravest. And to what point?*" The remark was followed by a long silence, and then he said the unthinkable: "*If they will not come, then it is time to make our own peace!*"

His mood grew darker as the long retreat continued. And when two more ships from his diminished squadron were lost at Como Des, his anger exploded. "*There will be a Confederacy one day, Tarien,*" he wearily told his brother, "*but they will not construct it on the bodies of my people!*"

It was the same voice that had indicted the Spartans.

The *Tenandrome* was rife with rumor. Some suggested that Sim and his crew had been spirited away by the Mutes and that the *Corsarius* had been left as a manifestation of an inhuman sense of humor. Others wondered whether the vessel had not been two ships right from the beginning, a clever ploy to confuse the invaders and enhance the image of a super-natural defender.

If McIras had any theories, she was keeping them to herself.

As for me, I could not get out of my mind the image of Christopher Sim in despair. It had never occurred to me that he, of all people, could have doubted the eventual outcome. It was a foolish notion, and yet there it was. Sim was as human as the rest of us. And in that despair, in his concern for the lives of his comrades and the people whom he had tried to defend, I sensed an answer to the deserted vessel. But it was an answer I could not accept.

I began reading everything I could find about the Mutes, the war, the *Corsarius*, and, in particular, the Rigellian Action. In that final engagement, Sim was operating in close conjunction with the *Kudasai*, a battle cruiser which carried his brother. The *Corsarius* had gone in to finish off a mortally wounded carrier, had gotten too close, and been caught when it blew up. It was odd, the way it ended. Sim had always led the Dellacondans personally. At Rigel, however, he'd escorted *Kudasai* during the main assault, while his frigates drove a knife into the enemy flank.

Ironically, *Kudasai* carried the surviving brother to *his* death only a few weeks later, at Nimrod. But Tarien lived long enough to know that his diplomatic efforts had succeeded. Earth and Rimway had finally joined hands, had promised help, and Toxicon was expected momentarily to announce that she would support her old enemies.

I wondered what had happened to the seven crew members who had deserted the *Cosarius* on the eve of the Rigellian Action. But, with the exception of the navigator, Ludik Talino, none appeared again in the histories. No one knew whether they'd been punished, or even charged with their crime. They became almost immediately a popular target for vilification. Talino, the navigator, surfaced briefly on Rimway almost half a century after the war, just long enough to die, and to earn mention in the news reports. Curiously, he claimed to have fought at Rigel, though on a cruiser, rather than the *Corsarius*. No details were given, and the comment was attributed to delusions brought on by his sense of guilt.

I was especially interested in the tale of the Seven, the anonymous heroes recruited in the belly of Abonai on the fateful night before the Mute attack. How did it happen that no one knew who they were? Was it coincidence that what should have been the single best source of their names, the log of the *Corsarius*, was silent on the subject, and in fact, silent on the battle itself? I could not get Saje McIras' remark out of my mind: *It could not have happened!*

No, it could not.

In the morning, I asked McIras what she intended to do.

"I've classified the report. We'll leave the *Corsarius* where she is, and if higher authority wants to come out and have a look at her, they can. That's it." She rubbed her temples. "This is bad news for everybody."

"It's ancient history," I said.

"However he died, Christopher Sim *is* the Confederacy. This place, this world, is a graveyard. It's a graveyard with a secret of some sort, and I don't want to get any closer to it." Her eyes narrowed. "The sooner we're out of here the better I'll like it."

I looked at her a long time. "A graveyard for what?" I asked.

❋

We returned to carrying out our basic mission, but the shadow of the *Corsarius* continued to hang over us. During the days that followed, the conversation with McIras played itself over and over again in my head. Hell of a graveyard. The bodies were all missing, the names were missing, the log entries were missing. And the *Corsarius*, which *should* be missing, was orbiting this world like clockwork, every six hours and eleven minutes.

"They intended to come back," I told McIras.

"But they didn't," she said. "Why not?"

During the entire course of Hellenic civilization, I know of no darker, nor more wanton crime, than the needless sacrifice of Leonidas and his band of heroes at Thermopylae. Better that Sparta should fall, than that such men be squandered.

"Yes," I said, "where are the bodies?"

Through a shaft in the clouds, far below, the sea glittered.

❋

I went down with Holtmeyer's group, ostensibly to assist making some deductions about fossils; but as soon as we were on the ground I commandeered a flyer and loaded it with food and water. Probably, I should have taken McIras' advice and concentrated on my own assignments. They were all a long time dead, and there was no point anymore. But the truth should have *some* value.

And there was Talino, the navigator, whose name was now synonymous with cowardice, who for a time had served his captain and his world well, but had died bitter and apparently delusional on Rimway. Surely I owed him, and the others, something.

Holtmeyer's people were still setting up their shelters when I rose slowly over the trees and turned west into the sun-washed sky. There were thousands of islands scattered across the oceans. It would not of course be possible to search them all. But someone had abandoned the *Corsarius*. Whether that someone wanted to torture Christopher Sim with its presence, or to leave it as a sign they would not forget him, they'd left it all the same, and I wondered whether they would not have placed him along its track, close beneath its orbit.

I fed the course data into the flyer's computer banks, set speed just below sound, and leveled off at 3,000 meters. Then I informed the *Tenandrome* where I was, and sat back to listen to the wind. Below, the sea was smooth and transparent and very blue. White clouds drifted through the morning haze. It could easily have been a seascape on Rimway or Earth or Fishbowl.

It was, on balance, a lovely world.

I passed, with barely a second look, a group of sandy, treeless islands. Their shores, like all the shores on this planet, were devoid of the gulls that are inevitably found near water oceans on living worlds. (Birds had not evolved there and in Jesperson's opinion never would.)

I slowed to inspect a silver archipelago in the north temperate zone, rocky clutches of forest protruding from the glassy surface, progressively smaller islands dribbling away to the northwest. But there were only granite and trees, and after awhile I flew on.

I crossed into the southern hemisphere in late afternoon and approached a Y-shaped volcanic island shortly before sunset. It was a lush, tropical place of purple-green ferns and enormous white flowering plants. Placid pools mirrored the sky, and springs tumbled down off the lone mountain. I settled onto the beach, climbed out, had my dinner, and watched *Corsarius* pass overhead, a dull white star in a darkening sky.

I checked in with Saje, told her I was looking for Christopher Sim, listened to her opinion that I'd lost my mind, and told her she'd enjoy the beachfront view at my present location. She doubted it, and added that Jesperson had made a discovery having to do with amphibians, and his people were excited. "*Considering we have the* Corsarius *floating around up here,*" she commented, "*they excite pretty easily.*"

The air was cool and fresh, and the rumble of the surf almost hypnotic. I fell asleep in the cockpit with the canopy off. It was a violation of safety procedures that would have incensed the Captain.

In the morning, I set out over a wide expanse of unbroken ocean. Gentle rain squalls drifted across its face and, deeper in southern seas, a heavy storm forced me to a higher altitude. By mid-day, the black skies lightened, and I descended through a drizzle filled with that world's bulbous airborne plants, toward an ocean suddenly still. I ate lunch on a long narrow spit that probably went completely under at high tide. (There were two moons of substantial size and, when they lined up and pulled in the same direction, the tides were fierce.)

I was cramped after long hours in the flyer, and strolled casually along the beach, enjoying the sea and the solitude. Tiny soft-shelled segmented creatures washed ashore with each wave. Most burrowed into the sand, while others hurried across the spit and returned into the ocean on the other side. I watched, fascinated, and noticed that all the movement was in one direction. That seemed strange. Also, the phenomenon seemed to be accelerating. Crustaceans and other creatures less easily identifiable scrabbled and slithered out of the breakers in increasing numbers, crossed the strip, and disappeared into the waves.

I was puzzling over it when I observed a vegetable-brown stain in the water drifting in my direction. It was out just beyond the surf, drifting toward the outer breakers. As it came closer, the foam turned muddy and the waves became almost syrupy.

Two glistening black rocks rolled ashore. One paused as though suddenly aware of my presence. It fell open, and a cluster of living dark fronds slowly uncoiled in my direction. I backed away, out of reach. Unhurried, it returned to its shell, and both creatures crossed the strand and splashed into the ocean.

I started back toward the flyer at a quick, nervous pace, but a sudden high-pitched whistling brought me up short. I turned to see that a creature resembling a porpoise had thrown itself onto the beach a few meters in front of me. The surf rolled languidly past its flanks, boiled, and seemed to draw the animal back into itself. The porpoise turned dark intelligent eyes toward me, and I heard again that shrill whistle, and read the terror in it. It struggled with the muddy tide, and tried to get higher up the beach, as though it would have torn itself altogether from the embrace of the ocean. But it made little progress, and seemed to give up when a muddy wave broke over it.

Our eyes locked in mutual horror. A second viscous wave rose around it, and when it receded the animal was gone. Moments later I caught a glimpse of a dorsal, and of a weak struggle in the water. And then everything became placid.

Meanwhile the brown tide was making inroads. The stream of marine animals across the strip of sand had stopped. A few had been captured and were being dragged back. No more came ashore.

It was enough for me. I broke toward the flyer in a panicky sprint. The tide continued to roll in. Several rivulets had already pushed across and gone into the ocean on the other side. I splashed frantically through them. They oozed and sucked at my boots. Thank God I hadn't gone barefoot as I'd been tempted to do.

The flyer was about a hundred yards away. There were pools near it. The brown tide flowed into these, and they began to rise.

I lost balance and went down, thrusting my hands into the goop. It scorched me and I screamed and scrambled to my feet, rubbing my hands against my vest in an effort to get the stuff off.

The tide had reached the landing treads and the ladder. I plodded through it, panicked, but I think I was moving in slow motion all the same, fearful of splashing the stuff, struggling to pull my boots free with each step. I was relieved to see, at least, that it didn't seem to be able to climb.

Gobs of it got onto my jump suit. I hurried across the last few meters and fell forward against the ladder. The thing rose around my legs and tried to drag me back. I left it both boots.

And I shuddered for Christopher Sim and his people.

Two hours later, I cruised somberly through a gray overcast sky, watching the monitors draw a jagged line across the long curve of the horizon. I was still thoroughly rattled, and promising myself never to leave the cockpit again in unfamiliar territory. It was raining, but no wind blew. The ocean was flat and silent, but I could not get my thoughts away from what might lie beneath the surface. I'd told Saje what had happened and she'd advised me to return to the base site and catch the next ride back to the ship. I'd considered it, but it would have seemed cowardly. So I'd squared my jaw and told her not to worry, and pressed on.

Just stay in the aircraft. That was my motto from now on.

A peak appeared in the mist off to my right. It was granite, worn by sea and weather.

I flew on.

There were others, a range of towers rising smoothly out of the ocean almost directly parallel to the track of the *Corsarius*. Some had broken and toppled, damaged perhaps by long-ago earthquakes. The formation was so geometrically correct, that I could not escape a sense that I was looking at a planned structure. It occurred to me that, if the people who had come with Sim had been aware of the dangers in this ocean, the brow of one of these peaks would be exactly the kind of place they would have chosen.

I drifted among them, riding the currents, listening to the steady cadence of rock and surf. I searched all day, and when twilight came, I landed atop one of them. The rain blew off and the stars came out, bathing the line of towers and the rolling ocean in brilliant white light. But I didn't sleep well. And I kept the canopy shut.

The reddish sun was well into the sky when I woke. The air was cold and clear. I checked in with the *Tenandrome*; they told me my aircraft was needed back at Holtmeyer's site, and the Captain would be grateful if I returned it.

I was glad to get airborne again, but as I drifted over those gray towers I knew unequivocally that I was right about Sim. And that the proof was here. Somewhere.

I almost missed it. I'd expected that they would have chosen the top of one of the peaks. I found what I was looking for instead on a relatively narrow shelf not quite halfway between the summit and the sea: a dome.

But it was small, and I realized as I approached it that I'd been wrong. They had not marooned Sim and his crew. And I knew with knife-cold suddenness why the Seven had no names!

My God! They'd left him here alone.

I circled for half an hour, finding things to do, checking rations, wondering whether to call McIras, debating if it was not after all best to let the legends be. But I couldn't just leave it.

Two centuries late, I floated down through the salt air.

The wind blew across the escarpment. The shelf was solid rock. No green thing grew there, and no creature made its home on that grim pile. A few boulders were strewn about, and some loose rubble. Several broken slabs stood near the edge of the promontory. The peak towered overhead, and the ocean lay far below.

I stood uncertainly before the dome in stocking feet, studying its utilitarian lines, the makeshift antenna mounted on the roof, the blank windows with drawn curtains. The sea boomed relentlessly, and even at this altitude, the air felt wet.

Unlike the *Corsarius*, that shelf gave no sense of recent occupancy. The dome was discolored by weather, and it had been knocked somewhat askew, probably by a quake.

Christopher Sim's tomb. It was not a very elegant end, on this rough slab, under the white star of the ship that had carried him safely through so much. They had, I believed, intended to come back for him when the war ended and it didn't matter anymore. And maybe they left the *Cosarius* as a token of a promise. But things had probably gone awry.

The dome was too small to support more than two or three people. It was nicked and chipped, and an antenna had broken off and lay on the ground beside it. The door was designed to function, if need be, as an air-lock. It was closed, but not sealed, and I was able to lift the latch and pull it open. The light inside was gray, and I waited for the dome to ventilate.

There were two chairs, a table, some bound books, a desk, and a couple of lamps. I wondered whether Tarien had come on this long flight out from Abonai, whether there had been a last desperate clash, perhaps in this room, between the brothers! Whether Tarien had pleaded with him to continue the struggle. It would have been a terrible dilemma. Men had so few symbols, and the hour was so desperate. They could not permit him to sit out the bat-tle, as Achilles had done. In the end, he must have remained adamant, and Tarien had to feel he had no choice but to seize his brother and dismiss his crew with some contrived story. (Or perhaps an angry Christopher Sim had done that himself, before confronting Tarien.) Then Tarien had invented the legend of the Seven, concocted the destruction of the *Corsarius*, and when the engagement was over they'd brought him and his ship here.

Tarien had died a few weeks later, and maybe all who shared the secret died with him. Or maybe they were afraid, in victory, of the wrath of their victim. I stood in the doorway and wondered how many years that tiny space had been his home.

He would have understood, I thought. And if in some way he could have learned that he'd been wrong, that Rimway had come, and Toxicon, and even Earth, he might have been consoled.

There was nothing on the computer. I thought that strange; I'd ex-pected a final message, perhaps to his wife on far Dellaconda, perhaps to the people he had defended.

In time the walls began to close in, and I fled the dome, out onto the shelf that had defined the limits of his existence.

I walked the perimeter, looked at the slabs and the wall, returned along the edge of the precipice. I tried to imagine myself marooned in that place, alone on that world, a thousand light-years from the closest human being. The ocean must have seemed very tempting.

Overhead, *Corsarius* flew. He could have seen it each evening when the weather was clear.

And then I saw the letters engraved in the rock wall just above my head. They were driven deep into the granite, hard-edged characters whose fury was clear enough, though I could not understand the language in which they'd been written:

$$\hat{\omega} \ \pi o \pi o \hat{\iota}! \ \hat{\omega} \ \Delta \eta \mu o \tau \theta \acute{E} \upsilon \eta \varsigma!$$

It was a paroxysm of anguish directed toward *Demosthenes*, the great Athenian orator whose silver tongue had tamed the Aegean. Sim had remained a classicist until the end.

The computer had not been enough to contain Christopher Sim's final protest. *Demosthenes*, of course, should be read as his orator brother. But I was moved that it was a cry of pain, and not of rage. Scholars have since agreed. After all, they argue, no man in such straits would have stooped to mere mockery. The reference to the Athenian statesman constituted a recognition, probably after long consideration induced by his deplorable position, that Tarien had chosen the correct path. Consequently, the message on the rock could be read as an act of forgiveness, rendered in his final extremity, by a loving brother.

The reputations of the brothers have not been seriously damaged. In fact, in an enlightened society, Christopher and Tarien have risen to the stature of tragic heroes. Dramatists and novelists have recreated the confrontation on the shelf between them time and again, and the idea that they embraced, and parted in tears, has become part of the folklore.

But I've thought about it, and I'm convinced it means something else. I've read a lot about Demosthenes since that day when I stood before the message in the rock. The dumb bastard used his great oratorical abilities to persuade his unhappy country to make war on Alexander the Great. I think Christopher Sim was still having the last word.

THE TOMB

The city lay bone white beneath the moon. Leaves rattled through courtyards and piled up against crumbling walls. Solitary columns stood against the sky. The streets were narrow and filled with rubble.

The wind off the Atlantic smelled of the tide. It shook the forest, which had long since overwhelmed the city's defenses, submerging ancient homes and public buildings, forums and marketplaces, and even invading the sacred environs, a plaza anchored at one end by a temple, at the other by a tomb.

The temple was of modest dimensions. But a perceptive visitor might have recognized both Roman piety and Greek genius in its pantheonic lines. It was set in the highest part of the city. Its roof was gone, and its perimeter had largely disappeared into the tangle of trees and brambles.

Save for a single collapsed pillar, the front remained intact. A marble colonnade, still noble in appearance, looked out toward the tomb. Carved lions slumbered on pedestals, and stone figures with blank eyes and missing limbs kept watch over the city.

Twelve marble steps descended from the temple into the plaza. They were precisely chiseled, rounded, almost sensual. The marble was heavily worn. Public buildings, in varying states of disintegration, bordered the great square. They stood dark and cold through the long evenings, but when the light was right, it was possible to imagine them as they had been when the city was alive. A marble patrician stood over a dry fountain. Weary strollers, had there been any, would have found stone benches strategically placed for their use.

The tomb stood alone at the far end. It was an irregular octagon, constructed of tapered marble blocks, laid with military simplicity. The marble was gouged and scorched as high as a man on horseback might reach. And the elements had had their way. If ever it had borne a name, it had long since been worn smooth.

The tomb itself gaped open. The door that had once sealed the vault was gone. Above the entrance, a device that might have been a sword had been cut into the marble. In keeping perhaps with the spirit of the architecture, it too was plain: hilt, blade, and crossguard were all rectangular and square-edged. No tapered lines here.

The vault rose into a circular, open cupola. Two marble feet stood atop the structure, placed wide in what could only have been a heroic stance. One was broken off at the ankle, the other ascended to the lower shin.

On a tranquil night, a visitor so inclined might easily have apprehended the tread of divine sandals.

Three horsemen, not yet quite full-grown, descended from the low hills in the northwest. In the sullen wind they could smell the age of the place.

They wore animal skins and carried iron weapons. Little more than boys, they had hard blue eyes and rode with an alertness that betrayed experience with a hostile world. They were crossing a stream that had once marked the western extremity of the city when the tallest of the three drew back on his reins and stopped. The others fell in on either side. "What's wrong, Cam?" asked the rider on the left, his eyes darting nervously across the ruins.

"Nothing, Ronik—." Cam rose slightly in his saddle and looked intently toward the quiet walls that still strove to guard the city. (In some places they had collapsed or been pulled down.) His voice had an edge. "I thought something moved—."

The night carried the first bite of winter. Falon, on Cam's right, closed his vest against the chill, briefly fingering a talisman. It was a goat's horn, once worn by his grandfather and blessed against demons. His mount snorted uncertainly. "I do not see anything."

The wind was loud in the trees.

"Where?" asked Ronik. He was broad-shouldered, given to quick passions. His blond hair was tied behind his neck. He was the only one of the three who had killed. "Where did you see it?"

"Near the temple." Cam pointed.

"Who would be inside the city at night?" asked Ronik.

"Nobody with any sense," Cam snorted.

Falon stroked his horse's neck. Its name was Carik, and his father had given it to him before riding off on a raid from which he never returned. "It might have been best if we hadn't bragged quite so loudly. Better first to have done the deed, stayed the night, and then spoken up."

Cam delivered an elaborate shrug: "Why? You're not afraid, are you, Falon?"

Falon started forward again. "My father always believed this city to be Ziu's birthplace. And that,"—he looked toward the temple, "—his altar."

Cam was, in some ways, a dangerous companion. He wanted very much to be esteemed by his peers, as they all did. But he seemed some-times extreme in the matter. Willing to take chances. He wanted to be perceived as a warrior, but he had not yet proved himself. He was looking for a chance. His hair was black, his eyes dark. The rumor was that he had been fathered by a southerner.

Cam was middle-sized and probably did not have the making of a good warrior. He would serve, his comrades knew. He would not run. But neither would he ever achieve great deeds.

The road had once been paved but was little more than a track now, grassed over, occasional stones jutting from the bed. Ahead, it angled around to the south gate.

"Maybe we should not do this," said Ronik. He was perhaps everything Cam would have liked to be. He was tall and strong, and had, until this moment, always seemed utterly fearless. The girls loved him, and Falon suspected he would one day be a war chief. But his time was not yet.

Cam tried to laugh. It came out sounding strained.

Falon studied the ruins. It was hard to imagine there had ever been laughter within those walls, or the birth of children. Or cavalry gathering. The place felt somehow as though it had *always* been like this. He patted his horse's neck. "I wonder if the city was indeed built by gods?"

"If *you* are afraid," said Cam, "return home. Ronik and I will think no less of you." He made no effort to keep the mockery out of his voice.

Falon restrained his anger. "I fear no man. But it *is* impious to tread the highway of the gods."

They were advancing slowly. Cam did not answer but he showed no inclination to assume his customary position in the lead. "What use would Ziu have for fortifications?"

This was not the only ruined city known to the Kortagenians: Kosh-on-the-Ridge; and Eskulis near Deep Forest; Kalikat and Agonda, the twin ports at the Sound; and three more along the southern coast. They were called after the lands in which they were found. No one knew what their builders had called them. But there were tales about *this* one, which was always referred to simply as "the City."

"If not a way station for the gods," said Ronik, "maybe it serves *devils*."

There were stories: passersby attacked by phantoms, dragged within the walls, and seen no more. Black wings lifting on dark winds and children vanishing from nearby encampments. Demonic lights, it was said, sometimes reflected off low clouds, and wild cries echoing in the night. Makanda, most pious of the Kortagenians, refused to ride within sight of the City after dark, and would have been thunderstruck to see where they were now.

They walked their horses forward, speaking in whispers. Past occasional mounds. Past stands of oak. A cloud passed over the moon. And they came at last to the gate.

The wall had collapsed completely at this point, and the entrance was enmeshed in a thick patch of forest. Trees and thickets crowded in, disrupting the road and blocking entry.

They paused under a clutch of pines. Cam advanced, drew his sword, and hacked at branches and brush.

"It does not want us," said Ronik.

Falon stayed back, well away from Cam's blade, which swung with purpose but not caution. When the way was clear, Cam sheathed his weapon.

The gate opened into a broad avenue. It was covered with grass, lined with moldering buildings. Everything was dark and still.

"If it would make either of you feel better," Cam said, "we need not sleep in the plaza."

The horses were uneasy.

"I don't think we should go in there at all," said Ronik. His eyes narrowed. It was a hard admission.

Cam's mount pawed the ground. "What do *you* think, Falon?"

Had he been alone, Falon would not have gone near the place. He considered himself relentlessly sensible. Fight when cornered. Otherwise, the trail is a happy place. He was the smallest and youngest of the three. Like Ronik, and virtually the entire tribe, he had blond hair and blue eyes. "We have said we will stay the night," he said. He spoke softly to prevent the wind from taking his words along the avenue. "I do not see that we have a choice."

Somewhere ahead a dry branch broke. It was a sharp report, loud, hard, like the snapping of a bone. And as quickly gone.

"Something *is* in there." Ronik drew back on his reins.

Cam, who had started to dismount, froze with one leg clear of the horse's haunches. Without speaking, he settled back into a riding position.

"Ziu may be warning us," said Ronik.

Cam threw him a look that might have withered an arm.

Ronik returned the glare. Because Cam was the oldest, the others usually acceded to his judgment. But Falon knew that, if it came to a fight, Ronik would prove the better man at his back. "Probably a wolf," said Falon, not at all convinced it was. Wolves after all did not snap branches.

"I am not going in." Ronik dropped his eyes. "It would be wrong to do so."

Cam rose on his saddle. "There's a *light*," he whispered.

Falon saw it. A red glow flickered in the plaza, on the underside of the trees. "A fire," he said.

"It's near the *tomb*." Cam turned his horse back toward the gate.

Ronik moved to follow, paused, and clasped Falon's arm to draw him along.

Falon tried to ignore his own rising fear. "Are we children to be frightened off because someone has built a fire on a cool night?"

"We don't know *what* it might be." Cam's voice had grown harsh. Angry. His customary arrogance had drained away. "We should wait until daylight, and then see who it is."

Falon could not resist: "Now who's afraid?"

"You know me better," said Cam. "But it is not prudent to fight at night."

Ronik was tugging at Falon. "Let's go. We can retire to a safe distance in the hills. Stay there tonight and return to camp tomorrow. No one would ever know."

"We would have to *lie*," said Falon. "They will ask."

"Let them *ask*. If anyone says *I* am afraid—," Cam gripped his sword hilt fiercely, "—I will kill him."

"Do as you will," said Cam. "Come on, Ronik."

Falon shook free of his friend's hand. Ronik sighed and began to follow Cam toward the gate, watching the plaza as he went. Falon was about to start after them when Ronik, good decent Ronik, who had been his friend all his life, spoke the words that pinned him inside the city: "Come with us, Falon. It's no disgrace to fear the gods."

And someone else replied with Falon's voice: "No. Carik and I will stay."

"Ziu does not wish it. His will is clear."

"Ziu is a warrior. He is not vindictive. I do not believe he will harm me. I will stay the night. Come for me at dawn."

"Damn you." Cam's mount moved first one way and then another.

"Farewell, then." He laughed through his anger. "We'll see you in the morning. I hope you'll still be here." They wheeled their horses and fled, one swiftly, the other with reluctance.

Falon listened to the gathering silence.

Be at my side, divine one.

The fire in the plaza seemed to have gone out.

Just as well. He would leave it alone. He rode deliberately into the city, down the center of the avenue, past rows of shattered walls and open squares. Past broken buildings. Carik's hoofbeats were soft, as if he too sensed the need for stealth.

He entered a wide intersection. To his left, at the end of a long street, the temple came into view. The city lay silent and vast about him. He dismounted and spoke to Carik, rubbing his muzzle. Leaves swirled behind him, and Falon glanced fretfully over his shoulder.

Moonlight touched the temple.

He decided against sleeping in the plaza. Better to camp out of the way. He found a running spring and a stout wall on the east side of the avenue. Anything coming from the direction of the tomb or the temple would have to cross a broad space.

Falon removed the saddle, loosened the bit, and hobbled the animal. He set out some grain and sat down himself to a meal of nuts and dried beef. Afterward he rubbed Carik down and took a final look around. Satisfied that he was alone, he used animal skins and his saddle to make a bed, placed his weapons at hand, and tried to sleep.

It did not come. Proud that he alone had stayed within the city, he was nonetheless fearful of what might be creeping up on him in the dark. He listened for sounds and sometimes stationed himself where he could watch the approaches.

But in all that rubble, nothing moved. The smell of grass was strong, insects buzzed, the wind stirred. A few paces away, Carik shook himself.

Then, as he was finally drifting off, he heard a sound: a footstep perhaps, or a falling rock. He glanced at the horse, which stood unconcerned. Good: Carik could see over the wall, and if something were coming, he would sound a warning.

Beneath the skins, he pressed his hand against the goat's horn to assure himself it was still there. And then drew his sword closer.

Somewhere he heard the clink of metal. Barely discernible, a whisper in the wind.

The horse heard it too. Carik turned his head toward the temple.

Falon got to his feet and looked out across the ruins. A deeper darkness had fallen over the thoroughfares and courtyards. The temple, no longer backlit by the moon, stood cold and silent.

The sound came again.

A few gray streaks had appeared in the east. Morning was coming. He could honorably retreat, leave the city and its secrets, and still claim credit for having stayed the night.

A light flickered on again in the plaza.

He couldn't see it directly, but shadows moved across the face of the temple.

He shivered.

"Wait," he told Carik, at last, and slipped over the wall.

Rubble and starlight.

He crept down a dark street, crossed an intersection, passed silently through a courtyard and moved in behind a screen of trees.

The tomb glowed in the light of a lantern. A robed figure crouched on hands and knees at its base. The face was hidden within the folds of a hood.

The figure was scratching in the dirt. It stopped, grunted, looked at something in its hand, and flipped the object away. Falon heard it bounce.

The entire area around the tomb was dug up. Piles of earth were heaped everywhere, and a spade leaned against a tree.

Falon surveyed the plaza, noted sparks from a banked campfire behind a wall to the north. Saw no one else.

The hooded figure picked up a second object and seemed to examine it. He turned so that the light from the lantern penetrated the folds of the hood. He was human.

Falon breathed easier.

He was collecting what appeared to be broken statuary. One piece looked like an arm. And suddenly, with a swirl of robes, the figure raised his lantern, picked up a stick, and looked directly toward Falon. Falon stepped out of the trees.

The man watched him warily. "Who are you?" he asked.

The voice suggested that he was accustomed to deference. "I am Falon the Kortagenian." He showed the stranger his right hand in the universal sign that he was not hostile.

"Greeting, Falon," said the robed man. "I am Edward the Chronicler." The light played across his features. They were cheerful but wary. He wore an unkempt beard, and he looked well fed.

"And what sort of chronicle do you compose, Edward, that you dare the spirits of this place?"

Edward seemed to relax. "If you are really interested, it is indeed the spirits I pursue. For if they live anywhere on the earth, it is surely here." He held the lamp higher so he could see Falon's face. "A boy," he said. "Are you alone, young man?"

Edward was short. His head was immense, too large even for the corpulent body that supported it. He had a tiny nose, and his eyes were sunk deep in his flesh.

"I am not a boy," said Falon. "As you will discover to your sorrow should you fail to show due respect."

"Ah." Edward bowed. "Indeed I shall. Yes, you may rely on it."

"Edward-that-pursues-spirits: what is your clan?"

The dark eyes fastened on him from within the mounds of flesh. "I am late of Lausanne. More recently of Brighton." He eased himself onto a bench and drew back his hood. The man would have been the same age as his father, but this one was a different sort: he had never ridden hard. "What brings you to this poor ruin in the dead of night?"

"I was passing and saw lights." Yes. That sounded fearless. Let the stranger know he was dealing with a man who took no stock in demons and devils.

"Well," offered Edward, in the manner of one who was taking charge, "I am grateful for the company."

Falon nodded. "No doubt." He glanced surreptitiously at the tomb, at the open vault. At the passageway into the interior. "Your accent is strange, Edward."

"I am Briton by birth."

Falon had met others from the misty land. He found them gloomy, pretentious, overbearing. It seemed to him they rarely spoke their minds. "Why are you here?"

Edward sighed. "I would put a name to one of the spirits and answer a question." He picked up a leather bag. "May I offer you something to eat?"

"No. Thank you, but I have no need." He looked at the Briton. "What is the question?"

Edward's eyes were unsettling. "Falon, do you know who built this place?"

"No. Some of our elders think it has *always* been here."

"Not very enlightening. It was constructed ages ago by a race we barely remember."

"And who were they, this forgotten race?"

He seemed to think about it. "Romans," he said.

Falon ran the name across his lips. "I have never heard of them."

Edward nodded. Branches creaked. The flame in the lantern wobbled. "The world is full of their temples. You undoubtedly rode in on their highway. The hand that built this city created others like it from Britain to the valley of the Tigris. They devised a system of laws, and gave peace to the world. But today the Romans and their name are dust."

Too many words for Falon. "What happened to them?"

"*That* is the issue of the moment. To discover what force can initiate the decline and cause the fall of such power."

"Only the gods."

"The gods are dead." That bald statement, impious and blasphemous, shocked him. But Edward seemed not to notice. "They were lost with their worshippers."

Falon muttered a quick prayer. He had never heard that kind of talk before. "Why were the worshippers lost?" he asked. "What happened to them?"

He sat down on a piece of broken marble. "Maybe *lost* is the wrong word. Better to say *forgotten*."

"And why were they forgotten?"

"Because they failed to create an institution independent from the state that could carry their memory forward."

Falon nodded, not understanding, but not wishing to betray his ignorance.

"A society of scholars might have done it," Edward continued. "Or an academy. A foundation. Even, for God's sake, a church."

Falon shrugged. "What do you seek here?"

Edward looked into the vault. "The identity of the occupant."

The night air was cold. "Then you are indeed too late," he said finally, pushing a piece of rubble aside with his foot. He looked at the statue, half-assembled like a puzzle. There was part of a leg, a trunk, a shoulder, a shield.

The leg matched the figure atop the tomb. The shield was emblazoned with the same sword device that marked the front of the vault.

"No," said the Briton. "I think not." He shifted his position trying to get comfortable.

"Then who is he?" Falon asked.

Edward clasped his hands in his sleeves to warm them. "A matchless commander. The hero who might have prevented the general disaster. Dead now these fourteen hundred years, more or less. The chronicles are sometimes conflicting." He straightened his robe, adjusted it across his shoulders. "Does the name *Maxentius* mean anything to you?"

"No," said Fallon.

"He was a tyrant who controlled the Roman capital when this city was young. A vicious, licentious, incompetent coward." Edward's eyes locked with his. "Under his sway, no man's dignity was safe, nor any woman's honor. Wives and daughters were dragged before him and abused. Those who protested were put to death. The people were enslaved. The soldiers were the only order of men he respected. He filled his land with armed troops, connived at their assaults against the common people, and encouraged them to plunder and massacre. He was a symbol of all that went wrong with the Empire."

Falon's hand fell to his weapon. "I would gladly have ridden against this monster."

The Briton nodded. "There was one who did. His name was Constantine, and I have no doubt he would have welcomed you to his cause."

Falon felt a surge of pride.

"Constantine appears to have recognized that the Empire, which was fragmented in his time, was disintegrating. But he laid plans how it might be preserved. Or, if it were already too late, and collapse could not be prevented, he considered how its essence might be passed on." Edward shook his head. "Had he been able to defeat Maxentius, things might have been different."

"He failed, then?"

"He was a reluctant crusader, Falon. And he marched against Maxentius only when the tyrant threatened to invade *his* domain."

"I cannot approve such timidity."

Edward smiled. "I would be disappointed if you did. But Constantine wished to conserve the peace and welfare of his realm."

"And where was his realm?"

"Britain. And here."

"But I do not understand." Falon grasped Edward's shoulder. "If this Constantine was a commander of great ability, as you have said, how did it happen he did not prevail?"

"Heroes do not win all engagements," Edward said slowly. "Maxentius sent army after army against him. Constantine swept them away. Most of the Italian cities between the Alps and the Po acknowledged his power and embraced his cause. And at last he appeared before Rome itself. The seat of the tyrant." Edward paused. They were exposed out here and the wind cut through Falon's vest. The Briton looked at him. "Are you cold?"

"No. Please go on."

"Maxentius had by far the larger army. He also had armored cavalry, a type of opponent *you* will never see. Fortunately. But he chose not to rely on military force alone." He broke off and walked into the shadows. Moments later he returned with a woven garment for the young warrior.

Falon took it, thanked him, and pulled it over his shoulders.

Edward resumed his seat. "There was, across the Tiber, a bridge that connected the city with the plain. This was the Milvian Bridge. Maxentius directed his engineers to weaken it. When they had done so, he rode out to engage the invader.

"Constantine was waiting, and the armies attacked each other. It was a ferocious combat, and advantage passed back and forth, from one side to the other. The issue remained uncertain through much of the day. But gradually, Constantine's troops gained the upper hand."

"Now," urged Falon, "strike the chief."

"Yes," said Edward. "One might almost think you were there. And he did. He rallied his personal guard and drove the tyrant onto the bridge. But Maxentius had foreseen this eventuality, had planned for it. He retreated across the treacherous span. Unmindful of caution, Constantine pursued, bleeding from a dozen wounds.

"And in that terrible hour, when Constantine had reached the center of the bridge, the tyrant gave the signal, and the structure was dropped into the Tiber."

"The coward," snarled Falon. And then philosophically, "Valor is not always sufficient to the day. Constantine need not be ashamed."

"No, certainly not."

"And did there arise a hero to avenge him?"

"Yes. But that is another story, for the avenger lacked political wisdom, and soon after his success, the Empire's lights dimmed and went out. Then the world fell into a night that has had no dawn."

"But what connection has the tale with this vault?"

Edward held out the lamp. "Perhaps you would care to inspect it with me?"

"No." He drew away. "No, I would not do so." To invade the resting place of the dead was to invite bad luck.

The Briton rose. "As you wish." He smiled, the way one does with a child. "But for me, the moment is at hand." He excused himself and walked into the vault. Falon watched him go. Remembered the condescending smile. And decided that as long as he didn't touch anything he'd probably be all right. So he followed.

It was damp and cold. Mulch and earth and weeds covered the floor. The walls were moldy and cracked. The ceiling was low. Falon had to duck his head.

"There were rumors," said Edward, "that Constantine survived his fall into the Tiber. One account, of which I have a copy, maintained that he was taken injured and half-drowned to a friendly but unnamed city. According to this account, he lived in that city one year. Others say three. It's difficult to be sure what really happened. The best sources agree that he hoped to lead another army against Maxentius. But apparently he never fully recovered from his injuries—." Edward shrugged. "I've looked many years for the truth."

"And how would you know the truth?"

"Easily. Find his tomb." He kicked away dead leaves and dirt and pointed toward scratches on the stone floor. "Here is where his sarcophagus would have been placed. His armor would have been stored on the shelf."

"For use in a future world?" asked Falon.

"Perhaps in a *better* world."

"Then this *is* his tomb?"

"Oh, yes, I am quite satisfied on that score. Yes: unquestionably he was interred here."

Falon wondered how he could possibly know such things.

"He talked of building a second Rome, in the east." His voice filled with regret. "Something to survive."

The smoke thrown up by the lantern was growing thick. Edward lapsed into silence. He coughed, tried to wave away the noxious cloud. "We're done here," he said.

"Good." Falon seized Edward's elbow and steered him back up into the starlight. The air was clean and tasted good. "But how can you be sure this is his tomb? No name is engraved on it."

"Nevertheless, it is marked quite clearly. Look behind you." He pointed at the partly-assembled statue. "Look at the shield."

A burst of wind pulled at his garment.

Edward held the lantern close. In its flickering light, Falon saw only the curious sword. On the vault, and on the shield.

"It was his device," Edward said.

Falon pressed his fingers against it. "How can you be so certain? There are many who use weapon devices."

"This is *not* a weapon, Falon. It was a symbol sometimes employed by an obscure religious cult. For many centuries, in fact, it was a mark of shame. It was even said to have magic properties."

"*Not* a sword," said Falon.

Edward nodded. "No. They called it a cross."

PROMISES TO KEEP

I received a Christmas card last week from Ed Bender. The illustration was a rendering of the celebrated Christmas Eve telecast from Callisto: a lander stands serenely on a rubble-strewn plain, spilling warm yellow light through its windows. Needle peaks rise behind it, and the rim of a crater curves across the foreground. An enormous belted crescent dominates the sky.

In one window, someone has hung a wreath.

It is a moment preserved, a tableau literally created by Cathie Perth, extracted from her prop bag. Somewhere here, locked away among insurance papers and the deed to the house, is the tape of the original telecast, but I've never played it. In fact, I've seen it only once, on the night of the transmission. But I know the words, Cathie's words, read by Victor Landolfi in his rich baritone, blending the timeless values of the season with the spectral snows of another world. They appear in schoolbooks now, and on marble.

Inside the card, in large, block defiant letters, Bender had printed "SEPTEMBER!" It is a word with which he hopes to conquer a world. Sometimes, at night, when the snow sparkles under the cold stars (the way it did on Callisto), I think about him, and his quest. And I am very afraid.

I can almost see Cathie's footprints on the frozen surface. It was a good time, and I wish there were a way to step into the picture, to toast the holidays once more with Victor Landolfi, to hold onto Cathie Perth (and never let go!) and somehow to save us all. It was the end of innocence, a final meeting place for old friends.

We made the Christmas tape over a period of about five days. Cathie took literally hours of visuals, but Callisto is a place of rock and ice and deadening sameness: there is little to soften the effect of cosmic indifference.

Which is why all those shots of towering peaks and tumbled boulders were taken at long range, and in half-light. Things not quite seen, she said, are always charming.

Her biggest problem had been persuading Landolfi to do the voice-over. Victor was tall, lean, ascetic. He was equipped with laser eyes and a huge black mustache. His world was built solely of subatomic particles, and driven by electromagnetics. Those who did not share his passions excited his contempt; which meant that he understood the utility of Cathie's public relations function at the same time that he deplored the necessity. To participate was to compromise one's integrity. His sense of delicacy, however, prevented his expressing that view to Cathie; he begged off rather on the press of time, winked apologetically, and stroked his mustache. "Sawyer will read it for you," he said, waving me impatiently into the conversation.

Cathie sneered, and stared irritably out a window (it was the one with the wreath) at Jupiter, heavy in the fragile sky. We knew, by then, that it had a definable surface, that the big planet was a world sea of liquid hydrogen, wrapped around a rocky core. "It must be frustrating," she said, "to know we'll never see it." Her tone was casual, almost frivolous, but Landolfi was not easily baited.

"Do you really think," he asked, with the patience of a superior being (Landolfi had no illusions about his capabilities), "that these little pieces of theater will make any difference? Yes, Catherine, of course it's frustrating. Especially when one realizes that we have the technology to put vehicles down there...."

"And scoop out some hydrogen," Cathie added.

He shugged. "It may happen someday."

"Victor, it never will if we don't sell the Program. This is the last shot. These ships are old, and nobody's going to build new ones. Unless things change radically at home."

Landolfi closed his eyes. I knew what he was thinking: Cathie Perth was an outsider, an ex-television journalist who had probably slept her way on board. She played bridge, knew the film library by heart, read John Donne (for style, she said), and showed no interest whatever in the scientific accomplishments of the mission. We'd made far-reaching discoveries in the fields of plate tectonics, planetary climatology, and a dozen other disciplines. We'd narrowed the creation date down inside a range of a few million years. And we finally understood how it had happened! But Cathie's televised reports had de-emphasized the implications, and virtually ignored the mechanics, of these findings. Instead, while a global audience watched, Marjorie Aubuchon peered inspirationally out of a cargo lock at Ganymede (much in the fashion that Cortez must have looked at the Pacific on that first bright morning), her shoulder flag patch resplendent in the sunlight. And while the camera moved in for a close-up (her features were illuminated by a lamp Cathie had placed for the occasion in her helmet), Herman Selma solemnly intoned Cathie's comments on breaking the umbilical.

That was her style: brooding alien vistas reduced to human terms. In one of her best-known sequences, there had been no narration whatever: two spacesuited figures, obviously male and female, stood together in the shadow of the monumental Cadmus Ice Fracture on Europa, beneath three moons.

"Cathie," Landolfi said, with his eyes still shut, "I don't wish to be offensive: but do you really care? For the Program, that is? When we get home, you will write a book, you will be famous, you will be at the top of your profession. Are you really concerned with where the Program will be in twenty years?"

It was a fair question. Cathie'd made no secret of her hopes for a Pulitzer. And she stood to get it, no matter what happened after this mission. Moreover, although she'd tried to conceal her opinions, we'd been together a long time by then, almost three years, and we could hardly misunderstand the dark view she took of people who voluntarily imprisoned themselves for substantial portions of their lives to go 'rock-collecting.'

"No," she said, "I'm not, because there won't *be* a Program in twenty years." She looked around at each of us, weighing the effect of her words. Bender, a blond giant with a reddish beard, allowed a smile of lazy tolerance to soften his granite features. "We're in the same class as the pyramids," she continued, in a tone that was unemotional and irritatingly condescending. "We're a hell of an expensive operation, and for what? Do you think the taxpayers give a good goddamn about the weather on Jupiter? There's nothing out here but gas and boulders. Playthings for eggheads!"

I sat and thought about it while she smiled sweetly, and Victor smoldered. I had not heard the solar system ever before described in quite those terms; I'd heard people call it *vast, awesome, magnificent, serene,* stuff like that. But never *boring.*

In the end, Landolfi read his lines. He did it, he said, to end the distraction.

Cathie was clearly pleased with the result. She spent three days editing the tapes, commenting frequently (and with good-natured malice) on the *resonance* and *tonal qualities* of the voice-over. She finished on the morning of the 24th (ship time, of course) and transmitted the results to *Greenswallow* for relay to Houston. "It'll make the evening newscasts," she said with satisfaction.

It was our third Christmas out. Except for a couple of experiments-in-progress, we were finished on Callisto and, in fact, in the Jovian system. Everybody was feeling good about that, and we passed an uneventful afternoon, playing bridge and talking about what we'd do when we got back. (Cathie had described a deserted beach near Tillamook, Oregon, where she'd grown up. "It would be nice to walk on it again, under a *blue* sky," she said. Landolfi had startled everyone at that point: he looked up from the computer console at which he'd been working, and his eyes grew very distant. "I think," he said, "when the time comes, I would like very much to walk with you....")

For the most part, Victor kept busy that afternoon with his hobby: he was designing a fusion engine that would be capable, he thought, of carrying ships to Jupiter within a few weeks, and, eventually, might open the stars to direct exploration. But I watched him: he turned away periodically from the display to glance at Cathie. Yes (I thought), she would indeed be lovely against the rocks and the spume, her black hair free in the wind.

Just before dinner, we watched the transmission of Cathie's tape. It was strong, and when it was finished we sat silently looking at one another. By then, Herman Selma and Esther Crowley had joined us. (Although two landers were down, Cathie had been careful to give the impression in her report that there had only been one. When I asked why, she said, "In a place like this, one lander is the Spirit of Man. Two landers is just two landers.") We toasted Victor, and we toasted Cathie. Almost everyone, it turned out, had brought down a bottle for the occasion. We sang and laughed, and somebody turned up the music. We'd long since discovered the effect of low-gravity dancing in cramped quarters, and I guess we made the most of it.

Marj Aubuchon, overhead in the linkup, called to wish us season's greetings, and called again later to tell us that the telecast, according to Houston, had been "well-received." That was government talk, of course, and it meant only that no one in authority could find anything to object to. Actually, somebody high up had considerable confidence in her: in order to promote the illusion of spontaneity, the tapes were being broadcast directly to the commercial networks.

Cathie, who by then had had a little too much to drink, gloated openly. "It's the best we've done," she said. "Nobody'll ever do it better."

We shared that sentiment. Landolfi raised his glass, winked at Cathie, and drained it.

We had to cut the evening short, because a lander's life support system isn't designed to handle six people. (For that matter, neither was an Athena's.) But before we broke it up, Cathie surprised us all by proposing a final toast: "To Frank Steinitz," she said quietly. "And his crew."

Steinitz: there was a name, as they say, to conjure with. He had led the first deep-space mission, five Athenas to Saturn, fifteen years before. It had been the first attempt to capture the public imagination for a dying program: an investigation of a peculiar object filmed on Iapetus by a Voyager. But nothing much had come of it, and the mission had taken almost seven years. Steinitz and his people had begun as heroes, but in the end they'd become symbols of futility. The press had portrayed them mercilessly as personifications of outworn virtues. Someone had compared them to the Japanese soldiers found as late as the 1970's on Pacific islands, still defending a world long vanished.

The Steinitz group bore permanent reminders of their folly: prolonged weightlessness had loosened ligaments and tendons and weakened muscles. Several had developed heart problems, and all suffered from assorted neuroses. As one syndicated columnist had observed, they walked like a bunch of retired big-league catchers.

"That's a good way to end the evening," said Selma, beaming benevolently.

Landolfi looked puzzled. "Cathie," he rumbled, "you've questioned Steinitz's good sense any number of times. And ours, by the way. Isn't it a little hypocritical to drink to him?"

"I'm not impressed by his intelligence," she said, ignoring the obvious parallel. "But he and his people went all the way out to Saturn in these damned things—" she waved in the general direction of the three Athenas orbiting overhead in linkup,

"—hanging onto baling wire and wing struts. I have to admire that."

"Hell," I said, feeling the effects a little myself, "we've got the same ships he had."

"Yes, you do," said Cathie pointedly.

I had trouble sleeping that night. For a long time, I lay listening to Landolfi's soft snore and the electronic fidgeting of the operations computer. Cathie was bundled inside a gray blanket, barely visible in her padded chair.

She was right, of course. I knew that rubber boots would never again cross that white landscape, which had waited a billion years for us. The peaks glowed in the reflection of the giant planet: fragile crystalline beauty on a world of terrifying stillness. Except for an occasional incoming rock, nothing more would ever happen here. Callisto's entire history was encapsuled within twelve days.

Pity there hadn't been something to those early notions about Venusian rain forests and canals on Mars. The Program might have had easier going if Burroughs or Bradbury had been right. My God, how many grim surprises had disrupted fictional voyages to Mars? But the truth had been far worse than anything Wells or the others had committed to paper: the red planet was so dull that we hadn't even gone there.

Instead, we'd lumbered out to the giants. In ships that drained our lives and our health.

We could have done better. Our ships could have *been* better. The computer beside which Landolfi slept contained his design for the fusion engine. And at JPL, an Army team had demonstrated that artificial gravity was possible: a *real* gravity field, not the pathetic fraction created on the Athenas by spinning the inner hull. There were other possibilities as well: infrared ranging could be adapted to replace our elderly scanning system; new alloys were under development. But it would cost billions to build a second generation vehicle. And unless there were an incentive, unless Cathie Perth carried off a miracle, it would not happen.

Immediately overhead, a bright new star glittered, visibly moving from west to east. That was the linkup, three ships connected nose to nose by umbilicals and a magnetic docking system. Like the Saturn mission, we were a multiple vehicle operation. We were more flexible that way, and we had a safety factor: two ships would be adequate to get the nine-man mission home. The air might become a little oppressive, but we'd make it.

I watched it drift through the starfield.

Cathie had pulled the plug on the Christmas lights. But it struck me that Callisto would only have one Christmas, so I put them back on.

Victor was on board *Tolstoi* when we lost it. No one ever really knew precisely what happened. We'd begun our long fall toward Jupiter, gaining the acceleration which we'd need on the flight home. Cathie, Herman Selma (the mission commander), and I were riding *Greenswallow*. The ships had separated and would not rejoin until we'd rounded Jupiter and settled into our course for Earth. (The Athenas are really individual powered modular units which travel, except when maneuvering, as a single vessel. They're connected bow-to-bow by electromagnets. Coils of segmented tubing, called 'umbilicals' even though the term does not accurately describe their function, provide ready access among the forward areas of the ships. As many as six Athenas can be linked in this fashion, although only five have ever been built. The resulting structure would resemble a wheel.)

Between Callisto and Ganymede, we hit something: a drifting cloud of fine particles, a belt of granular material stretched so thin it never appeared on the LGD, before or after. Cathie later called it a cosmic dust cloud. Bender thought it an unformed moon. It didn't matter: whatever it was, the mission plowed into it at almost 50,000 kilometers per hour. Alarms clattered and red lamps blinked on.

During those first moments, I thought the ship was going to come apart. Herman was thrown across a bank of consoles and through an open hatch. I couldn't see Cathie, but a quick burst of profanity came from her direction. Things were being ripped off the hull. Deep within her bulkheads, *Greenswallow* sighed. The lights dipped, came back, and went out. Emergency lamps cut in, and something hammered the side of the ship. More alarms howled, and I waited for the klaxon which would warn of a holing, and which would consequently be the last sound I could expect to hear in this life.

The sudden deceleration snapped my head back on the pads. (The collision had occurred at the worst possible time: *Greenswallow* was caught in the middle of an attitude alignment. We were flying backward.)

The exterior monitors were blank: that meant the cameras were gone. Cathie's voice: "Rob, you okay?"

"Yes."

"Can you see Herman?"

My angle was bad, and I was pinned in my chair. "No. He's back in cargo."

"Is there any way you can close the hatch?"

"Herman's in there," I protested, thinking she'd misunderstood.

"If something tears a hole out back there, we're all going to go. Keeping the door open won't help him."

I hesitated. Sealing up seemed to be the wrong thing to do. (Of course, the fact that the hatch had been open in the first place constituted a safety violation.) "It's on your console," I told her. "Hit the numerics on your upper right."

"Which one?"

"Hit them all." She was seated at the status board, and I could see a row of red lights: several other hatches were open. They should have closed automatically when the first alarms sounded.

We got hit again, this time in front. *Greenswallow* trembled, and loose pieces of metal rattled around inside the walls like broken teeth.

"Rob," she said, "I don't think it's working."

Our passage through the cloud lasted about three minutes.

When it was over, we hurried back to look at Herman. We were no longer rotating, and gravity had consequently dropped to zero. Selma, gasping, pale, his skin damp, was floating grotesquely over a pallet of ore-sample canisters. We got him to a couch and applied compresses. His eyes rolled shut, opened, closed again. "Hurts," he said, gently fingering an area just off his sternum. "I think I've been chewed up a little." He raised his head slightly. "What kind of shape are we in?"

I left Cathie with him. Then I restored power, put on a suit and went outside.

The hull was a disaster: antennas were down, housings scored, lenses shattered. The lander was gone, ripped from its web. The port cargo area had buckled, and an auxiliary hatch was sprung. On the bow, the magnetic dock was hammered into slag. Travel between the ships was going to be a little tougher.

Greenswallow looked as if she had been sandblasted. I scraped particles out of her jet nozzles, replaced cable, and bolted down mounts. I caught a glimpse of *Amity's* lights, sliding diagonally across the sky. As were the constellations.

"Cathie," I said. "I see Mac. But I think we're tumbling."

"Okay."

Bender was also on board *Amity*. And, fortunately, Marj Aubuchon, our surgeon. Herman's voice broke in, thick with effort. "Rob, we got no radio contact with anyone. Any sign of Victor?"

Ganymede was close enough that its craters lay exposed in harsh solar light. Halfway round the sky, the Pleiades glittered. *Tolstoi's* green and red running lights should have been visible among, or near, the six silver stars. But the sky was empty. I stood a long time and looked, wondering how many other navigators on other oceans had sought lost friends in that constellation. What had they called it in antiquity? The rainy Pleiades....

"Only *Amity*," I said.

I tore out some cable and lobbed it in the general direction of Ganymede. Jupiter's enormous arc was pushing above the maintenance pods, spraying October light across the wreckage. I improvised a couple of antennas, and replaced some black boxes. Then I needed to correct the tumble. If I could.

"Try it now," I said.

Cathie acknowledged.

Two of the thrusters were useless. I went inside for spares and replaced the faulty units. While I was finishing up, Cathie came back in. "Rob," she said, "radio's working, more or less. We have no long-range transmit, though."

"Okay. I'm not going to try to do anything about that right now."

"Are you almost finished?"

"Why?"

"Something occurred to me. Maybe the cloud, whatever that damned thing was: maybe it's U-shaped."

"Thanks," I said. "I needed something to worry about."

"Maybe you should come back inside."

"Soon as I can. How's the patient doing?"

"Out," she said. "He was a little delirious when he was talking to you. Anyhow, I'm worried: I think he's got internal damage. He never got his color back, and he's beginning to bring up blood. Rob, we need Marj."

"You hear anything from *Amity* yet?"

"Just a carrier wave." She did not mention *Tolstoi*. "How bad is it out there?"

From where I was tethered, about halfway back on the buckled beam, I could see a crack in the main plates that appeared to run the length of the port tube. I climbed out onto the exhaust assembly, and pointed my flashlight into the combustion chamber. Something glittered where the reflection should have been subdued. I got in and looked: silicon. Sand and steel had fused in the white heat of passage. The exhaust was blocked.

Cathie came back on. "What about it, Rob?" she asked. "Any serious problems?"

"Cathie," I said, "*Greenswallow's* going to Pluto."

✺

Herman thought I was Landolfi: he kept assuring me that everything was going to be okay. His pulse was weak and rapid, and he alternately sweated and shivered. Cathie got a blanket under him and buckled him down so he wouldn't hurt himself. She bunched some pillows under his feet, and held a damp compress to his head.

"That's not going to help much. Raising his legs, I mean."

She looked at me, momentarily puzzled. "Oh," she said. "Not enough gravity."

I nodded.

"Oh, Rob." Her eyes swept the cases and cannisters, all neatly tagged, silicates from Pasiphae, sulfur from Himalia, assorted carbon compounds from Callisto. We had evidence now that Io had formed elsewhere in the solar system, and been well along in middle age when it was captured. We'd all but eliminated the possibility that life existed in Jupiter's atmosphere. We understood more about the mechanics of ring formation, and we had a new clue to the cause of terrestrial ice ages. And I could see that Cathie was thinking about trading lives to satisfy the curiosity of a few academics. "We don't belong out here," she said, softly. "Not in these primitive shells."

I said nothing.

"I got a question for you," she continued. "We're not going to find *Tolstoi*, right?"

"Is that your question?"

"No. I wish it were. But the LGD can't see them. That means they're just not there." Her eyes filled with tears, but she shook her head impatiently. "And we can't steer this thing. Can *Amity* carry six people?"

"It might have to."

"That wasn't what I asked."

"Food and water would be tight. We're running out of time, and probably won't be able to transfer much. We'll do what we can. I expect we'll all be a little thinner when we get back. But yes, I think we'll survive."

We stared at one another, and she turned away. I became conscious of the ship: the throb of power in her bulkheads (power now permanently bridled by conditions in the combustion chambers), and the soft amber glow of the navigation lamps in the cockpit.

McGuire's nasal voice, from *Amity*, broke the uneasy silence. "Herman, you okay?"

Cathie looked at me, and I nodded. "Mac," she said, "this is Perth. Herman's hurt. We need Marj."

"Okay," he said. "How bad?"

"We don't know. Internal injuries, looks like. I think he's in shock."

We heard him talking to the others. Then he came back. "We're on our way. I'll put Marj on in a minute; maybe she can help from here. How's the ship?"

"Not good: the dock's gone, and the engine might as well be."

"How do you mean?"

"If we try a burn, the ass end will fall off."

McGuire delivered a soft, venomous epithet. "Do what you can for Herman. Here's Marj."

Cathie was looking at me strangely. "He's worried," she said.

"Yes. He's in charge now—"

"Rob, you say you *think* we'll be okay. What's the problem?"

"We might," I said, "run a little short of air."

Greenswallow continued her plunge toward Jupiter at a steadily increasing rate and a narrow angle of approach: we would pass within about 60,000 kilometers, and then drop completely out of the plane of the solar system. We appeared to be headed in the general direction of the Southern Cross.

Cathie worked on Herman. His breathing steadied, and he slipped in and out of delirium. We sat beside him, not talking much. After a while, Cathie asked, "What happens now?"

"In a few hours," I said, "we'll reach our insertion point. By then, we have to be ready to change course." She frowned, and I shrugged. "That's it," I said. "It's all the time we have to get over to *Amity*. If we don't make the insertion on time, *Amity* won't have the fuel to throw a U-turn later."

"Rob, how are we going to get Herman over there?"

That was an uncomfortable question. The prospect of jamming him into a suit wasn't appealing, but there was no other way. "We'll just have to float him over," I said. "Marj won't like it much."

"Neither will Herman."

"You wanted a little high drama," I said. "The next show should be a barnburner."

Her mouth tightened, and she turned away from me.

One of the TV cameras had picked up the approach of *Amity*. Some of her lights were out, and she too looked a bit bent. The Athena is a homely vessel in the best of times, whale-shaped and snub-nosed, with a mid-ship flare that suggests middle-age spread. But I was glad to see her.

Cathie snuffled at the monitor and blew her nose. "Your Program's dead, Rob." Her eyes blazed momentarily, like a dying fire into which one has flung a few drops of water. "We're leaving three of our people out here; and if you're right about the air, nobody'll get home. Won't that look good on the network news?" She gazed vacantly at *Amity*. "I'd hoped," she said, "that if things went well, Victor would have lived to see a ship carry his fusion engine. And maybe his name, as well. Ain't gonna happen, though. Not ever."

I had not allowed myself to think about the oxygen problem. The Athenas recycle their air supply; the converters in a single ship can maintain a crew of three, or even four, indefinitely. But six?

I was not looking forward to the ride home.

A few minutes later, a tiny figure detached itself from the shadow of the Athena and started across: Marj Aubuchon on a maintenance sled. McGuire's voice crackled from the ship's speakers. "Rob, we've taken a long look at your engines, and we agree with your assessment. We *may* have a problem." Mac had a talent for understatement. It derived, not from a sophisticated sense of humor, but from a genuine conviction of his own inferiority. He preferred to solve problems by denying their existence. He was the only one of the original nine who could have been accurately described as passive: other people's opinions carried great weight with him. His prime value to the mission was his grasp of Athena systems. But he'd been a reluctant crewman, a man who periodically reminded us that he wanted only to retire to his farm in Indiana. He wouldn't have been along at all except that Bosh Freeman died, and Haj Bolari came down with an unexpected (but thoroughly earned) disease. Now, with Selma incapacitated and Landolfi gone, McGuire was in command. It must have been disconcerting for him. "We've got about five hours," he continued. "Don't let Marj get involved in major surgery. She's already been complaining to me that it doesn't sound as if it'll be possible to move him. *We have no alternative.* She knows that, but you know how she is. Okay?"

One of the monitors had picked him up. He looked rumpled, and nervous. Not an attitude to elicit confidence. "Mac," said Cathie, "we may kill him trying to get him over there."

"You'll kill him if you don't," he snapped. "Get your personal stuff together, and bring it with you. You won't be going back."

"What about trying to move some food over?" I asked.

"We can't dock," he said. "And there isn't time to float it across."

"Mac," said Cathie, "is *Amity* going to be able to support six people?"

I listened to McGuire breathing. He turned away to issue some trivial instructions to Bender. When he came back he said, simply and tonelessly, "Probably not." And then, without changing inflection, "How's Herman doing?"

Maybe it was my imagination. Certainly there was nothing malicious in his voice, but Cathie caught it too, and turned sharply round. "McGuire is a son-of-a-bitch," she hissed. I don't know whether Mac heard it.

＊

Marjorie Aubuchon was short, blond, and irritable. When I relayed McGuire's concerns about time, she said, "God knows, he made that clear enough before I left." She observed that McGuire was a jerk, and bent over Herman. The blood was pink and frothy on his lips. After a few minutes she said, to no one in particular, "Probably a punctured lung." She waved Cathie over, and began filling a hypo. I went for a walk.

At sea, there's a long tradition of sentiment between mariners and their ships. Enlisted men identify with them, engineers baby them, and captains go down with them. No similar attitude has developed in space flight. We've never had an *Endeavor*, or a *Golden Hind*. Always, off Earth, it has been the mission, rather than the ship. *Friendship VII* and *Apollo XI* were *missions*, rather than vehicles. I'm not sure why that is; maybe it reflects Cathie's view that travel between the worlds is still in its *Kon-Tiki* phase, the voyage itself of such epic proportions that everything else is overwhelmed.

But I'd lived almost three years on *Greenswallow*. It was a long time to be confined to her narrow spaces. Nevertheless, she was shield and provider against that enormous abyss, and I discovered (while standing in the doorway of my cabin) a previously unknown affection for her.

A few clothes were scattered round the room, a shirt was hung over my terminal, and two pictures were mounted on the bulkhead. One was a Casnavan print of a covered bridge in New Hampshire; the other was a telecopy of an editorial cartoon that had appeared in the *Washington Post*. The biggest human problem we had, of course, was sheer boredom. And Cathie had tried to capture the dimensions of the difficulty by showing crewmembers filling the long days on the outbound journey with bridge. ("It would be nice," Cathie's narrator had said at one point, "if we could take everybody out to an Italian restaurant now and then.") The *Post* cartoon had appeared several days later. It depicted four astronauts holding cards. (We could recognize Selma, Landolfi, and Marj. The fourth, whose back was turned, was exceedingly female, and had to be Esther Crowley.) An enormous bloodshot eye is looking in through one window; a tentacle and a UFO are visible through another. Selma, his glasses characteristically down on his nose, is examining his hand, and delivering the caption:

"Dummy looks out the window to check the alien."

I packed the New Hampshire bridge and left the cartoon. If someone comes by, in 20 million years or so, he might need a laugh. I went up to the cockpit with my bag.

McGuire checked with me to see how we were progressing. "Fine," I told him. I was still sitting there four hours later when Cathie appeared behind me.

"Rob," she said, "we're ready to move him." She smiled wearily. "Marj says he should be okay if we can get him over there without doing any more damage."

We cut the spinner on the inner module to about point-oh-five. Then we lifted Herman onto a stretcher and carried him carefully down to the airlock.

Cathie stared straight ahead, saying nothing. Her fine-boned cheeks were pale, and her eyes seemed focused far away. These, I thought, were her first moments to herself, unhampered by other duties. The impact of events was taking hold.

Marj called McGuire and told him we were starting over, and that she would need a sizable pair of shears when we got there to cut Herman's suit open. "Please have them ready," she said. "We may be in a hurry."

I'd laid out his suit earlier: we pulled it up over his legs. That was easy, but the rest of it was slow, frustrating work. "We need a special kind of unit for this," Marj said. "Probably a large bag, without arms or legs. If we're ever dumb enough to do anything like this again, I'll recommend it."

McGuire urged us to hurry.

Once or twice, Cathie's eyes met mine. Something passed between us, but I was too distracted to define it. Then we were securing his helmet, and adjusting the oxygen mixture.

"I think we're okay," Marj observed, her hand pressed against Selma's chest. "Let's get him over there—"

I opened the airlock and pulled my own helmet into place. We guided Herman inside and secured him to *Greenswallow's* maintenance sled. (The sled was little more than a toolshed with jet nozzles.) I recovered my bag and stowed it on board.

"I'd better get my stuff," Cathie said. "You can get Herman over all right?"

"Of course," said Marj. "*Amity's* sled is secured outside the lock. Use that."

Cathie hesitated in the open hatchway, raised her left hand, and spread the fingers wide. Her eyes grew very round, and she formed two syllables that I was desperately slow to understand: in fact, I don't think I translated the gesture, the word, until we were halfway across to *Amity*, and the lock was irrevocably closed behind us.

"Good-bye."

Cathie's green eyes sparkled with barely controlled emotion across a dozen or so monitors. Her black hair, which had been tied back earlier, now framed her angular features and fell to her shoulders. It was precisely in that partial state of disarray that tends to be most appealing. She looked as if she'd been crying, but her jaw was set, and she stood erect. Beneath the gray tunic, her breast rose and fell.

"What the hell are you doing, Perth?" demanded McGuire. He looked tired, almost ill. He'd gained weight since we'd left the Cape, his hair had whitened and retreated, his flesh had grown blotchy, and he'd developed jowls. The contrast with his dapper image in the mission photo was sobering. "Get moving!" he said, striving to keep his voice steady. "We're not going to make our burn!"

"I'm staying where I am," she said. "I couldn't make it over there now anyway. I wouldn't even have time to put on the suit."

McGuire's puffy eyes slid painfully shut. "Why?" he asked.

She looked out of the cluster of screens, a segmented Cathie. A group Cathie. "*Amity* won't support six people, Mac."

"Damnit!" His voice was a sharp rasp. "It would have just meant we'd have cut down activity. Slept a lot." He waved a hand in front of his eyes, as though his vision were blurred. "Cathie, we've lost you. There's no way we can get you back!"

"I know."

No one said anything. Bender stared at her.

"How is Herman?" she asked.

"Marj is still working on him," I said. "She thinks we got him across okay."

"Good."

A series of yellow lamps blinked on across the pilot's console. We had two minutes. "Damn," I said, suddenly aware of a new danger: *Amity* was rotating, turning toward its new course. Would *Greenswallow* even survive the ignition? I looked at McGuire, who understood. His fingers flicked over press pads, and rows of numbers flashed across the navigation monitor. I could see muscles working in Cathie's jaws; she looked down at Mac's station as though she could read the result.

"It's all right," he said. "She'll be clear."

"Cathie—." Bender's voice was almost strangled. "If I'd known you intended anything like this—."

"I know, Ed." Her tone was gentle, a lover's voice, perhaps. Her eyes were wet. She smiled anyway, full face, up close.

Deep in the systems, pumps began to whine. "I wish," said Bender, his face twisted, "that we could do something."

She turned her back, strode with unbearable grace across the command center, away from us into the shadowy interior of the cockpit. Another camera picked her up there, and we got a profile: she was achingly lovely in the soft glow of the navigation lamps.

"There is something you can do," she said. "Build Landolfi's engine. Come back for me."

For a moment, I thought Mac was going to abort the burn. But he sat frozen, fists clenched. And he did the right thing, which is to say, nothing. It struck me that McGuire was incapable of intervening.

And I knew also that the woman in the cockpit was terrified of what she had done. It had been a good performance, but she'd failed to conceal the fear that looked out of her eyes. I watched her face as *Amity's* engines ignited, and we began to draw away. Like McGuire, she seemed paralyzed, as though the nature of the calamity which she'd embraced was just becoming clear to her. Then she was gone.

"What happened to the picture?" snapped Bender.

"She turned it off," I said. "I don't think she wants us to see her just now."

He glared at me, and spoke to Mac. "Why the hell," he demanded, "couldn't he have brought her back with him?" His fists were knotted.

"I didn't know," I said. "How could I know?" And I wondered, how could I not?

When the burn ended, the distance between the two ships had opened to only a few kilometers. But it was a gulf beyond crossing.

Bender called her name relentlessly. (We knew she could hear us.) But we got only the carrier wave.

Then her voice crackled across the command center. "Good," she said. "Excellent. Check the recorders: make sure you got everything on tape." Her image was back. She was in full light again, tying up her hair. Her eyes were hooded, and her lips pursed thoughtfully. "Rob," she continued, "fade it out during Ed's response, when he's calling my name. Probably, you'll want to reduce the background noise at that point. Cut all the business about who's responsible. We want a sacrifice, not an oversight."

And I realized, at that moment, that she'd acted, not to prolong her life, *but to save the Program.* "My God, Cathie." I stared at her, trying to understand. "What have you done?"

She took a deep breath. "I meant what I said. I have enough food to get by here for eight years or so. More if I stretch it. *And plenty of fresh air.* Well, relatively fresh. I'm better off than any of us would be if six people were trying to survive on *Amity.*"

"Cathie!" howled McGuire. He sounded in physical agony. "We didn't know for sure about life support. The converters might have kept up. There might have been enough air! It was just an estimate!"

"This is a hell of a time to tell me," she said. "Well, it doesn't matter now. Listen, I'll be fine. I've got books to read, and maybe one to write. My long-range communications are *kaput*, Rob knows that, so you'll have to come back for the book, too." She smiled. "You'll like it, Mac." The command center got very still. "And on nights when things really get boring, I can play bridge with the computer."

McGuire shook his head. "You're sure you'll be all right? You seemed pretty upset a few minutes ago."

She looked at me and winked. "The first Cathie was staged, Mac," I said.

"I give up," McGuire sighed. "Why?" He swiveled round to face the image on his screen. "Why would you do that?"

"That young woman," she replied, "was committing an act of uncommon valor, as they say in the Marines. "And she had to be vulnerable." And compellingly lovely, I thought. In those last moments, I was realizing what it might mean to love Cathie Perth. "*This* Cathie," she grinned, "is doing the only sensible thing. And taking a sabbatical as well. Do what you can to get the ship built. I'll be waiting. Come if you can." She paused. "Somebody should suggest they name it after Victor."

This is the fifth Christmas since that one on Callisto. It's a long time by any human measure. We drifted out of radio contact during the first week. There was some talk of broadcasting instructions to her for repairing her long-range transmission equipment. But she'd have to go outside to do it, so the idea was prudently shelved.

She was right about that tape. In my lifetime, I've never seen people so singlemindedly aroused. It created a global surge of sympathy and demands for action that seem to grow in intensity with each passing year. Funded partially by contributions and technical assistance from abroad, NASA has been pushing the construction of the fusion vessel of which Victor Landolfi dreamed.

Bender was assigned to help with the computer systems, and he's kept me informed of progress. The most recent public estimates had anticipated a spring launch. But that single word *September* in Bender's card suggests that one more obstacle has been encountered; and it means still another year before we can hope to reach her.

We broadcast to her on a regular basis. I volunteered to help, and I sit sometimes and talk to her for hours. She gets a regular schedule of news, entertainment, sports, whatever. And, if she's listening, she knows we're coming.

She also knows that her wish that the fusion ship be named for Victor Landolfi has been disregarded. The rescue vehicle will be the *Catherine Perth*.

If she's listening. We have no way of knowing. And I worry a lot. Can a human being survive six years of absolute solitude? Bender was here for a few days last summer, and he tells me he is confident. "She's a tough lady," he has said, any number of times. "Nothing bothers her. She even gave us a little theater at the end."

And that's what scares me: Cathie's theatrical technique. I've thought about it, on the long ride home, and here. I kept a copy of the complete tape of that final conversation, despite McGuire's instructions to the contrary, and I've watched it a few times. It's locked downstairs in a file cabinet now, and I don't look at it anymore. I'm afraid to. There are *two* Cathie Perths on the recording: the frightened, courageous one who galvanized a global public; and *our* Cathie, preoccupied with her job, flexible, almost indifferent to her situation. A survivor.

And, God help me, I can't tell which one was staged.

TO HELL WITH THE STARS

Christmas night.

Will Cutler couldn't get the sentient ocean out of his mind. Or the creature who wanted only to serve man. Or the curious chess game in the portrait that hung in a deserted city on a world halfway across the galaxy. He drew up his knees, propped the book against them, and let his head sink back into the pillows. The sky was dark through the plexidome. It had been snowing most of the evening, but the clouds were beginning to scatter. Orion's belt had appeared, and the lovely double star of Earth and Moon floated among the luminous branches of Granpop's elms. Soft laughter and conversation drifted up the stairs.

The sounds of the party seemed far away, and the *Space Beagle* rode a column of flame down into a silent desert. The glow from the reading lamp was bright on the inside of his eyelids. He broke the beam with his hand, and it dimmed and went out.

The book lay open at his fingertips.

It was hard to believe they were a thousand years old, these stories that were so full of energy and so unlike anything he'd come across before: tales of dark, alien places and gleaming temples under other stars and expeditions to black holes. They don't write like that anymore. Never had, during his lifetime. He'd read some other books from the classical Western period, some Dickens, some Updike, people like that. But these: what was there in the last thousand years to compare with this guy Bradbury?

The night air felt good. It smelled of pine needles and scorched wood and bayberry. And maybe of dinosaurs and rocket fuel.

❋

271

His father might have been standing at the door for several minutes. "Goodnight, Champ," he whispered, lingering.

"I'm awake, Dad."

He approached the bed. "Lights out already? It's still early." His weight pressed down the mattress.

Will was slow to answer. "I know."

His father adjusted the sheet, pulling it up over the boy's shoulders. "It's supposed to get cold tonight," he said. "Heavy snow by morning." He picked up the book and, without looking at it, placed it atop the night table.

"Dad." The word stopped the subtle shift of weight that would precede the press of his father's hand on his shoulder, the final act before withdrawal. "Why didn't we ever go to the stars?"

He was older than most of the other kids' dads. There had been a time when Will was ashamed of that. He couldn't play ball and he was a lousy hiker. The only time he'd tried to walk out over the Rise, they'd had to get help to bring him home. But he laughed a lot, and he always listened. Will was reaching an age at which he understood how much that counted for. "It costs a lot of money, Will. It's just more than we can manage. You'll be going to Earth in two years to finish school."

The boy stiffened. "Dad, I mean the *stars*. Alpha Centauri, Vega, the Phoenix Nebula—."

"The Phoenix Nebula? I don't think I know that one."

"It's in a story by a man named Clarke. A Jesuit goes there and discovers something terrible—."

The father listened while Will outlined the tale in a few brief sentences. "I don't think," he said, "your mother would approve of your reading such things."

"She gave me the book," he said, smiling softly.

"This one?" It was bound in cassilate, a leather substitute, and its title was written in silver script: *Great Tales of the Space Age*. He picked it up and looked at it with amusement. The names of the editors appeared on the spine: Asimov and Greenberg. "I don't think we realized, uh, that it was like that. It was one of the things they found in the time vault on the Moon a couple of years ago. Your mother thought it would be educational."

"You'd enjoy it, Dad."

His father nodded and glanced at the volume. "What's the Space Age?"

"It's the name that people of the classical period used to refer to their own time. It has to do with the early exploration of the solar system, and the first manned flights. And, I think, the idea that we were going to the stars."

A set of lights moved slowly through the sky. "Oh," his father said. "Well, people have had a lot of strange ideas. History is full of dead gods and formulas to make gold and notions that the world was about to end." He adjusted the lamp, and opened to the contents page. His gray eyes ran down the list, and a faint smile played about his lips. "The truth of it, Will, is that the stars are a pleasant dream, but no one's ever going out to them."

"Why not?" Will was puzzled at the sound of irritation in his own voice. He was happy to see that his father appeared not to have noticed.

"They're too *far*. They're just too far." He looked up through the plexidome at the splinters of light. "These people, Greenberg and Asimov: they lived, what, a thousand years ago?"

"Twentieth, twenty-first century. Somewhere in there."

"You know that new ship they're using in the outer System? The *Explorer*?"

"Fusion engines," said the boy.

"Yes. Do you know what its top recorded speed is?"

"About two hundred thousand kilometers an hour."

"Much faster than anything this Greenberg ever saw. Anyhow, if they'd launched an *Explorer* to Alpha Centauri at the time these stories were written, at that speed, do you know how much of the distance they would have covered by now?"

Will had no idea. He would have thought they'd have arrived long ago, but he could see that wasn't going to be the answer. His father produced a minicomp, pushed a few buttons, and smiled. "About five percent. The *Explorer* would need another nineteen thousand years to get there."

"Long ride," said Will, grudgingly.

"You'd want to take a good book."

The boy was silent.

"It's not as if we haven't tried, Will. There's an artificial world, half-built, out beyond Mars someplace. They were going to send out a complete colony, people, farm animals, lakes, forest, everything."

"What happened?"

"It's too *far*. Hell, Will, life is good here. People are happy. There's plenty of real estate in the solar system if folks want to move. In the end, there weren't enough volunteers for the world-ship. I mean, what's the *point*? The people who go would be depriving their kids of any kind of normal life. How would *you* feel about living inside a tube for a lifetime? No beaches. Not real ones anyhow. No sunlight. No new places to explore. And for what? The payoff is so far down the road that, in reality, there *is* no payoff."

"In the stories," Will said, "the ships are very fast."

"I'm sure. But even if you traveled on a light beam, the stars are very far apart. And a ship can't achieve an appreciable fraction of that kind of velocity because it isn't traveling through a vacuum. At, say, a tenth of the speed of light, even a few atoms straying in front of it would blow the thing apart."

Outside, the Christmas lights were blue on the snow. "They'd have been disappointed," the boy said, "at how things came out."

"Who would have?"

"Benford. Robinson. Sheffield."

The father looked again at the table of contents. "Oh," he said. He riffled idly through the pages. "Maybe not. It's hard to tell, of course, with people you don't know. But we've eliminated war, population problems, ecological crises, boundary disputes, racial strife. Everybody eats pretty well now, and for the only time in its history, the human family stands united. I suspect if someone had been able to corner, say—" he flipped some pages, "—Jack Vance, and ask him whether he would have settled for this kind of world, he'd have been delighted. Any sensible person would. He'd have said *to hell with the stars!*"

"No!" The boy's eyes blazed. "He *wouldn't* have been satisfied. None of them would."

"Well, I don't suppose it matters. Physical law is what it is, and it doesn't take much account of whether we approve or not. Will, if these ideas hadn't become dated, and absurd, this kind of book wouldn't have disappeared. I mean, we wouldn't even know about *Great Tales of the Space Age* if someone hadn't dropped a copy of the thing into the time capsule. That should tell you something." He got up. "Gotta go, kid. Can't ignore the guests."

"But," said the boy, "you can't really be *sure* of that. Maybe the time was never right before. Maybe they ran out of money. Maybe it takes all of us working together to do it." He slid back into the pillows. His father held up his hands, palms out, in the old gesture of surrender he always used when a game was going against him. "We could do that *now*, Dad," Will continued. "There's a way to build a *Space Beagle. Somehow.*"

"Let me know if you figure it out, son." The lights died, and the door opened. "You'll have to do it yourself, though. Nobody *else* is giving it any thought. Nobody has for centuries."

The snow did not come. And while Will Cutler stared through the plexidome at the faraway stars, thousands of others were also discovering Willis and Swanwick and Tiptree and Sturgeon. They lived in a dozen cities across Will's native Venus. And they played on the cool green hills of Earth and farmed the rich Martian lowlands; they clung to remote shelters among the asteroids, and watched the skies from silver towers beneath the great crystal hemispheres of Io and Titan and Miranda.

The ancient summons flickered across the worlds, insubstantial, seductive, irresistible. The old dreamers were bound, once again, for the stars.

THE MISSION

*T*hey were looking down on a dust storm racing across the Martian surface when the transmission came in. *"Venture, we are losing control of the
situation here. The plague is everywhere. I don't know how much longer we can
keep the station open. Abort and return."*

*Status lamps blinked in the darkened cockpit. Alice looked at him, her eyes
sad, but for a long time nobody said anything.*

*"Tommy." The distant voice lost its impersonal tone. "We'll try to stay with
this—." And the transmission exploded in a burst of static.*

Tommy glanced around at the others. "What do you think?" he asked.

*Frank stared at the radio. "Make the landing. We can't go back without
making the landing."*

*Alice nodded. "Yes." Her eyes gleamed in the light thrown off by the instru-
ments. "Do it."*

*Tommy took a deep breath. Below them the storm swirled across the lower
latitudes.*

"It came in over the river, out of the east. Right over there, Tommy, just
beyond Harpie's place. And it came right past where we're standing now
and touched ground maybe *there*, near the barn. It kept going, of course,
because it was going hell-bent, fastest thing I ever saw, all lit up.

"You never saw an airplane, I guess, did you? Well, they're really something, especially at night. And especially *this* one because it wasn't really
an airplane at all. It was somethin' they kept up on the station, it was in
orbit, and when the Mars mission came back it was the only way they
could get home."

"Because," said Tommy, "everything was shut down by then."

"That's right. The Death had been running eight months and there just wasn't nobody left."

Tommy looked the length of the plain, tracing the glide path from the woods on the east past Harpie's, past the crumbling hangars and maintenance buildings that everybody said were haunted, past the place where they sat on their horses. On into the night. The sky was cold and damp and threatening.

"It was a night like this," Uncle Harold said. "Chilled. Rain just beginning to fall."

He imagined it coming in, full of light, the three astronauts inside, feeling for the ground like they weren't sure it was there.

"Why'd they come here to land, Uncle Harold?" Tommy had heard bits and pieces of the story before, how it had come to Warner-Robbins, and how people had ridden out from the town and the astronauts had gotten out and just walked away and nobody ever saw them again. But it had never meant much to him until he actually came to live in Warner-Robbins a few days before. After his mother died. And came out here to see the place where the lander came down.

"Nobody really knows, Tommy," said Uncle Harold. "I mean, they just rolled to a stop. Well, they didn't exactly *roll*. They sort of bounced up and down a lot and busted a wing and they finally swung around and tipped over."

"Did it catch fire?"

"No. It just laid out there in the dark like a big dead bird."

"And the astronauts—?"

"Well, like I said, they got out, the three of them—."

"What happened to the fourth? Mrs. Taylor said there were four on the mission."

"That's what the books say, but only *three* got out. And they walked off west. Toward Macon."

"Macon's a long way. Why'd you let them do it?"

"*I* didn't let them do it, Tommy. They pretty much done it on their own. Horace Kittern and Mack Willoughby, they rode after them. Asked whether they was hurt. Whether they could do anything. But the astronauts, they never slowed down, just waved and said everything was fine. Said they'd be back later for the lander. I thought at the time maybe they were afraid of us. Afraid we were infected."

"And they really never came back?"

"Nope. Never seen 'em again."

"How about over in Macon?"

"Wasn't nobody *in* Macon by then. Macon went early."

"The whole town?"

"Far as we know."

Tommy imagined them walking into the night. Into the rain.

Uncle Harold was riding Montie. The horse was cold. It breathed out a cloud of frost and he patted the animal's flank. "Tommy, I wasn't as old as you at the time. Wasn't nothin' I could do. Or anybody else."

Tommy shifted his weight. Poke stirred under him, and a cold wind blew down out of the trees. It began to rain. "What happened to the lander?" he asked.

Harold turned Montie around. Started for home. "What happened to the lander?" he said, as if the question puzzled him. "Let's go back to the house and I'll show you."

He was glad to get into the barn and out of the wind. They unsaddled the horses, gave them water, and closed them up in their stalls. Then Uncle Harold picked up the lantern and led him to the back door where they kept the equipment. "There." He pointed to a plow.

"And *there*." A spade.

"And here." A yoke for the team.

"And over here." Braces for the wagon. "We used some of the Teflon to wire the main house. For insulation."

Tommy didn't understand at first. And Uncle Harold kept right on going. "You can still see the tiles. They're from the outside of the lander. We used them to line the smelter down at Jimmy's. And the town freezer that used to be over at Casey's place but that we moved to Hazlett's after Casey died. They were put on the outside of refrigerators from one end of town to the other. Saved energy at a time when we hardly had any.

"They salvaged the computers and kept them going for a while, as long as somebody thought they'd be useful. Turned out they didn't really need computers anymore.

"*We* took the radios. The kids. I got one, but it wasn't no use because there wasn't anything on it except an Atlanta station where they just kept playing the same music and asking whether there was anybody out there until we got into January and I guess it got too cold. They stopped broadcasting and we never heard from them again.

"One of the fuel pumps runs the water system at your Uncle Tim's. They took something off the wings that helped keep the town generators going for a while. And the chairs. They're scattered around. Pete Baydecker's got one. It's the most comfortable chair I've ever sat in—." He seemed to run down, like a clock that needed to be wound.

"You just took it *apart*?" Tommy asked. "And used it to make stuff?" He remembered the legend, recalled vividly in that moment Mrs. Taylor's description of what it must have been like as the astronauts, three Americans and a Russian, had neared Mars, and they heard the news, that a virus had broken loose at home, was killing everyone.

"*And eventually their radios must have gone quiet.*" She had said the words and Tommy had imagined himself with them out in the cold dark night between the worlds, a million miles from the ground.

"You have to understand what it was like then," Uncle Harold was saying. He opened the door that would take them across to the house. "We were caught with no power, except what we could produce ourselves. One night the lights and the TV's just went out. They came back on long enough for us to go to bed. But it got cold during the night and we all had to go down and sleep by the fire.

"What ran the lights also ran the tractors and the milking machines and the combines. And suddenly none of it was there anymore. They had all that equipment but they didn't have gas to make it run."

"You could have gotten other people to help you."

Uncle Harold shook his head. "The plague was everywhere. There was nowhere to go. Nobody to help. People were scared to leave town. You never seen anything like the way people behaved when a stranger came up the road. They were bad times. We were lucky to survive."

He turned the lantern out, signaling that it was time to go into the house. Candles burned brightly in the windows. But Tommy didn't move. "You took *everything*? And melted it down?"

"*I* didn't. The town did. Everything we had went, Tommy. The pickups and the cars that nobody had any use for anymore, and the tractors, and the lander. We needed raw materials to keep alive. I can tell you, Tommy, it was a near thing. We had our hands full just getting through the winter. People died. Half the town died. Not from the plague. Thank God it never came here. But people died from exposure and sheer exhaustion. We'd forgotten how to live without supermarkets and electricity. But we survived.

"For six years we even managed to light the town. I have to tell you, the people here saw the lander as a God-given miracle."

Tommy felt his heart beat. He looked down at his footprints in the snow, watched the flakes filling them in almost as quickly as he made them. "Frank doesn't know that," he said. His voice had a catch in it. "It wasn't right."

"It's what we had to do."

"And Alice doesn't know it either."

Frank and Alice had befriended him after he arrived last week. After Mom died, Tommy had locked onto the lander as if it were part of the world he'd left behind. As if it were connected with his mother and the life over in Milledgeville, which hadn't been as lucky as Warner-Robbins. And Uncle Harold had seen an opportunity to distract him, had talked to him about the Mars mission, had shown him pictures of the *Columbia*, photographs of it under construction and later docked to the space station, artists' drawings of it in Martian skies. He'd asked whether the astronauts had landed on Mars.

Nobody knew.

He was aware of that, of course, but he asked the question anyway. It was required, somehow. Part of the ceremony. *"Did they ever get to the ground?"* It seemed not right that they had gone all the way out there and not gotten to the surface. So he and Alice and Frank had invented their game, had taken the *Columbia* to Mars, listened to the terrible news, orbited the planet, and *landed.*

They walked across the red sands and sometimes they found turtles and sometimes lizards and once they even found tall red-skinned natives with saucer eyes who'd chased them while they yelped and ran for their lives.

"Frank and Alice," said Harold, "probably never asked about the lander. It's no secret that it kept us all going. There's not a house or a farm that doesn't have a piece of it out in its barn, or holding its windows together, or keeping its furnace running. You want the lander, son? It's all around you."

They were racing above the southern hemisphere, gazing down on an ocher desert that stretched out forever when Tom raised the question. "Yeah," said Frank. "I knew that."

Mars vanished, and Tommy looked with dismay at his copilot.

"Sure, Tommy. Everybody here knows. Right, Alice? We've got some pieces of it in our kitchen. Or is it the furnace? I forget."

They were in the living room at Alice's house and suddenly Tommy could smell the oil lamps. Without moving, Alice pointed to a cushion on the sofa. It was old and worn and black, but it was soft like leather except that it *wasn't* leather. "*That* came out of the lander," she said. "My ma wants to toss it because she says it doesn't look right. But Pa won't hear of it."

Tommy stared at them. "You knew? All this time you knew what they did?"

"What's the big deal?" Frank asked. "I thought you knew. *Everybody* knows."

"They should have kept it," said Tommy. "They should have taken care of it."

"It was out on the runway." Alice was getting annoyed. "It would have rusted out. What difference does it make?"

And Tommy couldn't explain. They should have kept it because one day we'll be going back. Because it was part of something important and you don't just tear things like that apart to make hoes and rakes. Because they didn't know whether the astronauts would come back or not and suppose they had?

Alice was the tallest of the three. She had freckles and red hair and blue eyes. And she tried to tell him he was making too much of it, that what else would you do with a wreck sitting in the middle of the runway? That they just flat out needed the metal.

They didn't play the Mars game anymore after that. And a couple of days later Alice tried to kiss him but he didn't let her.

The freeze came early. Tommy helped with the horses, chopped firewood, brought in water, and occasionally took the wagon over to Rob's feed store to pick up supplies.

They had a few books in the house, some novels that he read over and over, *David Copperfield* and *Northanger Abbey* and one about the end of the Civil War. There was a history of the United States, which everybody insisted still existed out there somewhere, and a Bible, a book on needlecraft that had belonged to Aunt Emma, and the book that Tommy especially liked, a big volume called *Galaxies*, with lots of pictures.

They'd had only a Bible at his mother's house and he hadn't even realized there *were* other books until Uncle Harold had come after Ma's death and brought him here.

He understood that the galaxies were very far, and that the *Columbia* could never have reached them. But he liked to imagine going out to them anyhow, taking a right turn at Mars, and snuggling warm and happy in the cockpit while he watched the stars grow in number and size.

Columbia is still up there. Docked at the station. And on nights when it's clear, you can see it, a bright light in the south that never moves, that keeps its place while the stars race past.

Out of reach now. Forever.

We should have saved the lander.

He rode out on Poke one night close to Christmas, back to the place where he'd sat with Uncle Harold. It was unseasonably warm, the stars were bright, and there was no moon in the sky. The station sparkled in its accustomed place, above the old interstate.

Uncle Harold didn't like him riding out here alone after dark. Minutes after he'd left, he heard the outside kitchen door slam and knew his uncle had missed him, knew he'd follow pretty soon.

He looked back toward the east and watched the lander drop slowly out of the sky, brighter than any star. Brighter even than the station. It had four lights, one on each wingtip, one on its belly, and one atop the tail. He didn't really know whether that had been so, and nobody he'd asked knew either. But it didn't matter. That was the way he imagined it, so it had become the only truth there was.

It came in slow and the lights were visible the whole time. A few people rode out of town to see what was happening. He could hear them talking, asking one another whether help was coming at last. From the government.

The lander dropped down through the night, and the blaze of its lights silhouetted Uncle Harold, coming easy on Monty. Its engines roared and the wings waggled slightly as a gust of wind hit them. The airstrip lay open and clear before the descending spacecraft.

Tommy inched up in his saddle so he could see better. Poke dug at a piece of sod with his front hoof.

It touched down and rolled along the runway, maybe jouncing a bit because it was coming too fast and braking too hard.

The riders watched it slow and tip over and stop. For a long time nothing happened. A few of the horsemen approached and hatches popped open. The lights went off, first the ones on the wingtips, and then the others. Three astronauts climbed out and stood looking around.

"You okay, Tommy?" Uncle Harold was still riding slow.

There were tears in the boy's eyes. "You shouldn't have taken it apart," he said.

His uncle came up alongside him, clamped a big hand down on his shoulder, and squeezed. "Tommy, it's time to let it go."

Tommy just sat on his horse.

Uncle Harold nodded. "You warm enough, son?"

"*You* think they did the right thing. That makes you just as bad."

"Why is it so important? That the lander was broken up?"

"Because of where it's been. Because maybe we can go back one day. Because we *need* it." Tommy was trying to keep his voice level, to keep the strangled sounds out of it.

"Tommy." Harold held out a kerchief, and waited while the boy took it and blew his nose and wiped his eyes. "Tommy, people here did what they had to. I'm not saying we wouldn't have made it otherwise, but the rest of the world was dead, as far as we knew. Everything that would give us an edge, we had to use."

"*Not* the lander. That's what takes us back."

Harold looked up at the sky. At the station. "No," he said, "it's not the lander. We can make a new one when the time comes. What we have to have, what we absolutely cannot do without, is *you*. And Alice. And Frank." He pulled his collar up around his neck. The temperature was starting to drop. "We survived, boy. *That's* what matters. First things first."

Tommy was silent.

"We *will* go back. Maybe *you* will. But you've got to be *alive* to do it."

"No. It's not going to happen."

Uncle Harold pulled his scarf up around his face. His gaze moved past Tommy and fastened on the house. They could see the glow of the oil lamp in the living room. He tugged gently on Tommy's reins and started back. Tommy pressed Poke's flank and followed.

Uncle Harold glanced back up at the sky. "Which one's Mars?" he asked.

Tommy showed him.

"Duller than I thought," he said.

Poke picked up the pace and they trotted at a leisurely clip beneath the stars.

PART III

FAR TRAVELING

REPORT FROM THE REAR

*I*t now appears that the Scorpions are in full retreat."

Those words, delivered with professional aplomb by WBC anchor Margaret Parker from the deck of the *Caesar*, ignited wild celebrations around the world: drums in Beijing, rockets in New York and London, light shows in Paris, parades in Moscow, hallelujahs at the Vatican.

The Scorpions are in full retreat.

It was over.

The only truly critical war in the history of the species had been fought and won out near Sirius in a single lightning engagement.

First contact.

It was supposed to be the culminating achievement in our expansion beyond home. But the old dreams had died in the face of starfaring creatures of relentless hostility, invaders whose ferocity seemed inconsistent with their technological achievements. Beings who neither gave nor accepted quarter.

The war, measured from the opening assault by the Rainbow Squadron to Parker's final comment, spanned thirty-two hours and eleven minutes. Now we were raising our glasses and toasting the Fleet. And feeling very lucky.

I was sitting in a bar in a San Francisco hotel while church bells rang, strangers bought drinks for the house, and holoworks brightened the skies. The bar and the adjoining lobby exploded with laughter and tears. And the wine, as they say, flowed.

Up on the screen, Margaret Parker's cheeks were wet. Someone wearing a headset stepped into the picture and hugged her, and I knew instinctively that on-air hug of the usually aloof Parker would become one of the lasting symbols of the war.

287

The picture switched to Ransom McKay standing beside an empty rostrum at the WBC situation room. We couldn't hear him, there was too much noise around us, but he was walking us through the initial tactical dispositions. The Rainbow here; the Legion there; the *Nelson* on this wing, the *Geronimo* on that. Lights moved, and coded arrows began the action, feint here, counterattack there, breakthrough in the center.

Yeah. In the center. That was where we took them, the battle cruisers tearing through their ordered squadrons, supported by waves of TLB's and frigates. Edward Basildorf, in his flag gray, became the hero of the hour by observing, during a briefing, that the "sorry sons-of-bitches were being sent home with their tails between their legs," an observation that might quite literally have been accurate.

I was in town for the annual Carbury Awards, which are given by the Press Association for outstanding journalism. The big prize this year, for lifetime achievement, had gone to Max Hopkin, essayist, editor, destroyer of the comfortable, two-time Pulitzer winner. But word of the first shots of battle had leaked into the dining room just as he thanked the emcee and stepped behind the microphone. Everyone scrambled for an HV, and poor Hopkin was left standing with his "thank you, ladies and gentlemen" fading into dead air.

It was one of those times when I was proud to be a journalist. WBC's correspondents did a hell of a job: Mark Everett at the Net's operations desk, Julie Black outside the staff room of the Combined Chiefs at Moonbase, Sakal Singh on the *Berlin*, Leonard Edward at World Council.

I was surprised a few hours later to spot Hopkin sitting gloomily in a corner of the bar. If anybody was the journalistic godfather of this night, it was he. It was, after all, his magnificent reporting during the almost equally brief Sikh-Chinese War twenty-seven years before, specifically his description of the Battle of Malacca Strait, that had set the standard for modern combat reporting, and incidentally launched his career.

His must have been the only sad face in the city that evening, and I assumed he was still irritated at being crowded out of the headlines. In the face of events, it struck me as a particularly selfish attitude.

He was alone when I picked up my rum and coke and went over. If he saw me, he gave no sign. "Hello, Mr. Hopkin," I said.

He nodded without looking up.

"Mind if I sit down?"

He frowned, as if it were a complex matter that had been laid before him. "Sure," he said finally.

I should mention here that my specialty is economics. And these were exciting times in my field as well. The Grimwell Equations seemed to be accurate, and it now appeared we were finally going to escape the industrial cycles and downturns and rushes of inflation and unemployment that had always undermined prosperity, and which had seemed even more beyond human control than the Scorpions.

"Congratulations, Mr. Hopkin," I said. "I wonder if I might buy you a drink?" He'd probably already had too many. But what the hell.

He nodded, sure, emptied his glass, and signaled for more. "Thanks," he said. He was drinking Scotch.

"I'm Jerry Logan. I'm an analyst for the *The Financial Review*."

"Good." His eyes met mine. They were gray and bloodshot. "Solid publication." He had to repeat himself to be heard over the bedlam in the bar. "Stay with it." Outside, people were embracing and dancing. There was a cacophony of car horns, noisemakers, clapping hands, cheers.

Hopkin was not a handsome man. His features suggested equal parts indifference and arrogance. He showed the signs of too much indulgence: a thick waist, distended veins, a bulbous nose. His hands were not quite steady. And his eyes were preoccupied. Distracted. There was a cynical signature to his demeanor, as there was to his work.

"Big night," he said, almost offhandedly.

"Yes. The timing wasn't so good for you. But I think we've been very lucky."

"Yes," he said. "We have been." His expression did not change.

In a corner, Ransom McKay was interviewing someone. Woman in the blue Fleet uniform. "They were completely fooled—," she was saying.

Hopkin stared into his glass. I told him how much I admired his work, his volcanic assaults against politicians, academics, and the religiously inclined, against all those who thought they had a stranglehold on Truth. He nodded and continued to study the bottom of the glass. It would be good, I said, not to have to worry about the Scorpions any more.

"Yes," he agreed.

A waiter appeared with two scotch and sodas.

"They had their age of steam forty thousand years ago," observed Hopkin. "Makes you wonder, doesn't it?"

"Wonder what?"

"How we could have beaten them."

I nodded, but mentioned Mark Everett's explanation: "They probably became too rigid. Too old. Can't respond to a fluid situation."

"Maybe," he said.

I was beginning to get irritated. What a son of a bitch he was. The whole world is celebrating, and he was sitting there feeling sorry for himself. I started to get up, because you shouldn't drink with somebody when you feel that way about him. But he kept me in my seat with a gesture. "Wars are getting shorter as technology gets better," he said. "The Sikhs took out the Chinese in four days. This one went a day and a half, if we can believe what we hear."

Outside, the police arrived, probably to try to control traffic, but they seemed to be joining in the celebration.

"I guess it's inevitable," I said.

He switched to the second drink and emptied the glass in a single swallow. Good American style. Down the hatch. "War's that short," he said, "you can't find out what's really going on. I mean, it's not like the days when we went out with the foot soldiers to see for ourselves. Now the military controls everything. Press conferences, briefings, handouts, holo feeds." He shrugged. "You're in the right business, son. Economics. Good. Depressions don't happen overnight, right? And they happen right out there in the open where everybody can see them."

The place was beginning to empty out. People and their drinks were headed into the street.

I wasn't interested in talking about business cycles. Not tonight. Not with Max Hopkin. "Mr. Hopkin," I said.

"Call me Max."

"Max. You know, Max, what you say isn't entirely true. A good reporter can always get the facts. You managed to do that with the Sikhs. Parker and her people did the same thing here over the last twenty-four hours." I shook my head. "How did you manage it, by the way? What did you do, hire a fishing boat?"

"No," he said. "We did a lot better." His eyes lost their glitter, as if he were retreating into a dark place. "We made it up."

I smiled at him. I know a joke when I hear it.

Listen," he said, "the Sikhs wouldn't let anybody near. They were putting out self-serving statements. Hal Richard was with the Chinese. They were doing the same thing. Nobody liked the media much. The warlords can't do their little bloodlettings in peace with the rest of the world looking in. So they issue their bulletins and conduct their briefings and in the end nobody has a clue what's happening.

"We decided hell with it. We did our own war. We made it up as we went along." A line of sharp white teeth glinted in a shark smile. "We sent in the destroyers and counterattacked with the torpedo boats. We took out the big Chinese cruisers and used the subs where they'd do some damage. We had a damned good time. We even issued communiqués. BREAK OFF IF YOU MUST. WITHDRAW IF YOU WILL. RANJAY WILL STAND WITH THE *VISHA*."

I took a deep breath. He was using a tone that suggested he'd told this story many times before. "That was a lie?" I asked incredulously. Ranjay's challenge had rallied the fleet at the critical moment on the third day. The decisive day.

"Let's call it imaginative fiction." He swirled his drink, listened to the ice cubes. "Of the highest order."

"I don't believe it."

"It's true."

I watched him for a long minute. "How could you possibly have hoped to get away with it?"

"How could we not get away with it? You think Ranjay was going to deny his great moment? Don't look at me like that. Listen, I was assigned to get a story. I got one. The only thing I really had to worry about was making sure we had the finish right." He gazed out at the street scene. "The details get lost. If anybody notices, they say, hell, fog of war, communications breakdowns. Whatever."

I was beginning to feel cold. It was the sound of icons breaking apart. "Most people thought the Chinese would win," I said.

"I'd met Ranjay. And I'd met Chang-li. Chang-li was an idiot. Political appointment. Ranjay, well, Ranjay was something else. I knew he wouldn't engage unless he was sure of the result. And the Chinese couldn't force him to fight. Not in the Strait." He smiled, enjoying himself now. "We knew enough to make it believable. We had the order of battle. We knew the capabilities of the two fleets. We got that from *Jane's*." He got up, looking for more Scotch, but the bartender was gone. His apron had been rolled up and left on a stool. "Maybe he quit," he said. "What the hell are you drinking, Jerry?"

"Same as you."

I followed him over to the bar. A long mirror lined the wall behind the counter. He studied his reflection momentarily, shook his head, pulled down a bottle and produced glasses. "On the rocks," I added.

He nodded and poured.

It didn't seem possible. I was thinking: Murrow in London. Cronkite in Vietnam. Hopkin at Malacca Strait. And now he was telling me it was all a lie?

He said, "I never left Calcutta. I spent the war at the Hilton. I wrote my dispatches in the bar." He was turned away from me again, but our eyes had locked in the mirror.

"I've told people at luncheons," he continued. "Nobody cares. Nobody *believes* it. It's a joke. An exaggeration. The Grand Old Cynic playing everybody along. But it's true." He swung round to face me. "Nobody cares about truth. Not really. It's theater that counts. Drama. You want to be a good reporter, Jerry, you keep that in mind." He refilled his glass and indicated the rum. "How about another round?"

"No," I said. "I've had enough." That, at least, was true. I don't usually tolerate more than two drinks.

"Whatever you say." His eyes lingered on the lines of bottles behind the bar. "I wonder what they really know," he said.

"Who?"

"Parker. Mark Everett. The rest of those people out there." He waved in the general direction of the ceiling. In the street, someone had produced a beamer and was firing it off. A stream of cascading light threw shadows across the floor.

"What do you mean?"

"Jerry, I had to get the result right because if I didn't I'd be found out."

"And?"

"Parker and Everett and the rest. Things go wrong, who's going to be around to fire them?" He raised the glass. "To the WBC news team. Whatever else might happen, they gave us a hell of a show."

BLACK TO MOVE

Maybe it's just my imagination, but I'm worried.

The roast beef has no taste, and I'm guzzling my coffee. I'm sitting here watching Turner and Pappas working on the little brick house across the avenue with their handpicks. Jenson and McCarthy are standing over near the lander, arguing about something. And Julie Bremmer is about a block away drawing sketches of the blue towers. Everything is exactly as it was yesterday.

Except me.

In about two hours, I will talk to the Captain. I will try to warn him. Odd, but this is the only place in the city where people seem able to speak in normal tones. Elsewhere, voices are hushed. Subdued. It's like being in a church at midnight. I guess it's the fountain, with its silvery spray drifting back through the late afternoon sun, windblown, cool. The park glades are a refuge against the wide, still avenues and the empty windows. Leaves and grass are bright gold, but otherwise the vegetation is of a generally familiar cast. Through long, graceful branches, the blue towers glitter in the sunlight.

There is perhaps no sound quite so soothing as the slap of water on stone. (Coulter got the fountain working yesterday, using a generator from the lander.) Listening, seated on one of the benches at the fountain's edge, I can feel how close we are, the builders of this colossal city and I. And that thought is no comfort.

It's been a long, dusty, rockbound road from Earth to this park. The old hunt for extraterrestrial intelligence has taken us across a thousand sandy worlds in a quest that became, in time, a search for a blade of grass.

I will remember all my life standing on a beach under red Capella, watching the waves come in. Sky and sea were crystal blue; no gull wheeled through the still air; no strand of green boiled in the surf. It was a beach without a shell.

But here, west of Centauri, after almost two centuries, we have a living world! We looked down, unbelieving, at forests and jungles, and dipped our scoops into a crowded sea. The perpetual bridge game broke up.

On the second day, we saw the City.

A glittering sundisk, it lay in the southern temperate zone, between a mountain chain and the sea. With it came our first mystery: the City was alone. No other habitation existed anywhere on the planet. On the fourth day, Olzsewski gave his opinion that the City was deserted.

We went down and looked.

It appeared remarkably human, and might almost have been a modern terrestrial metropolis. But its inhabitants had put their cars in their garages, locked their homes, and gone for a walk.

Mark Conover, riding overhead in the *Chicago*, speculated that the builders were not native to this world.

They were jointed bipeds, somewhat larger than we are. We can sit in their chairs and those of us who are tall enough to be able to see through their windshields can drive their cars. Our sense of the place was that they'd left the day before we came.

It's a city of domes and minarets. The homes are spacious, with courtyards and gardens now run to weed. And they were fond of games and sports. We found gymnasiums and parks and pools everywhere. There was a magnificent oceanfront stadium, and every private home seemed filled with playing cards and dice and geometrical puzzles and 81-square checkerboards.

They had apparently not discovered photography; nor, as far as we could determine, were they given to the plastic arts. There were no statues. Even the fountain lacked the usual boys on dolphins or winged women. It was instead a study in wet geometry, a complex of leaning slabs, balanced spheres, and odd-angled pyramids.

Consequently, we'd been there quite a while before we found out what the inhabitants looked like. *That* happened when we walked into a small home on the north side, and found some charcoal etchings.

Cats, someone said.

Maybe. The following day we came across an art museum and found several hundred watercolors, oils, tapestries, crystals, and so on.

They *are* felines, without doubt, but the eyes are chilling. The creatures in the paintings have nevertheless a human dimension. They are bundled against storms; they gaze across plowed fields at sunset; they smile benevolently (or pompously) out of portraits. In one particularly striking watercolor, four females cower beneath an angry sky. Between heaving clouds, a pair of full moons illuminate the scene.

This world has no satellite.

Virtually everyone crowded into the museum. It was a day of sighs and grunts and exclamations, but it brought us no closer to an answer to the central question: where had they gone?

"Just as well they're not here," Turner said, standing in front of the watercolor. "This is the only living world anyone has seen. It's one hell of a valuable piece of real estate. Nice of them to give it to us."

I was at the time standing across the gallery in front of a wall-sized oil. It was done in impressionistic style, reminiscent of Degas: a group of the creatures was gathered about a game of chess. Two were seated at the table, hunched over the pieces in the classic pose of the dedicated player. Several more, half in shadow, watched.

Their expressions were remarkably human. If one allowed for the ears and the fangs, the scene might easily have been a New York coffeehouse.

The table was set under a hanging lamp; its hazy illumination fell squarely on the board.

The game was not actually chess, of course. For one thing, the board had 81 squares. There was no queen. Instead, the king was flanked by a pair of pieces that vaguely resembled shields. Stylized hemispheres at the extremes of the position must have been rooks. (Where else but on the flank would one reasonably place a rook?)

The other pieces, too, were familiar. The left-hand Black bishop had been fianchettoed: a one-square angular move onto the long diagonal, from where it would exercise withering power. All four knights had been moved, and their twisted tracks betrayed their identity.

The game was still in its opening stages. White was two pawns up, temporarily. It appeared to be Black's move, and he would, I suspected, seize a White pawn which had strayed deep into what we would consider his queenside.

I stood before that painting, feeling the stirrings of kinship and affection for these people and wondering what immutable laws of psychology, mathematics, and aesthetics ordained the creation of chess in cultures so distant from each other. I wondered whether the game might not prove a rite of passage of some sort.

I was about to leave when I detected a wrongness somewhere in the painting, as if a piece were misplaced, or the kibitzers were surreptitiously watching *me*. Whatever it was, I grew conscious of my breathing.

There was nothing.

I backed away, turned, and hurried out of the building.

I'm a symbologist, with a specialty in linguistics. If we ever do actually find someone out here to talk to, I'm the one who will be expected to say hello. That's an honor, I suppose; but I can't get Captain Cook entirely out of my mind.

By the end of the first week, we had not turned up any written material (and, in fact, still haven't) other than a few undecipherable inscriptions on the sides of buildings. They were even more computerized than we are, and we assumed everything went into the data banks, which we also haven't found. The computers themselves are wrecked. Slagged. So, by the way, is the central power core for the City. Another mystery.

Anyhow, I had little to do, so yesterday I went for a walk in the twilight with Jennifer East, a navigator and the pilot of the other lander. She's lovely, with bright hazel eyes and a quick smile. Her long tawny hair was radiant in the setting sun. The atmosphere here has a moderately high oxygen content, which affects her the way some women are affected by martinis. She clung to my arm, and I was breathlessly aware of her long-legged stride.

We might have been walking through the streets of an idealized, mystical Baghdad: the towers were gold and purple in the failing light. Flights of brightly-colored birds scattered before us. I half-expected to hear the somber cry of a ram's horn, calling the faithful to prayer.

The avenue is lined with delicate, graybarked trees. Their broad, filamented leaves sighed in the wind, which was constant off the western mountains. Out at sea, thunder rumbled.

Behind the trees are the empty homes, no two alike, and other structures that we have not yet begun to analyze. Only the towers exceed three stories. The buildings are all beveled and curved; right angles do not exist. I wonder what the psychologists will make of that.

"I wonder how long they've been gone?" she said. Her eyes were luminous with excitement, directed (I'm sorry to say) at the architecture.

That had been a point of considerable debate. Many of the interiors revealed a degree of dust that suggested it could not have been more than a few weeks since someone had occupied them. But much of the pavement was in a state of disrepair, and on the City's inland side, forest was beginning to push through.

I told her I thought they'd been around quite recently. "Mark," she said, staying close, "I wonder whether they've really left."

There was nothing you could put in a report, but I agreed that we were transients, that those streets had long run to laughter and song, that they soon would again, and that it would never really be ours.

She squeezed my arm. "It's magnificent."

I envied her; this was her first flight. For most of us, there had been too many broken landscapes, too much desert.

"Olszewski thinks," I said, "that the northern section of the City is almost two thousand years old…. They'd been here a while."

"And they just packed up and left." She steered us out of the center, angling toward the trees, where I think we both felt less conspicuous.

"It's ironic," I said. "No one would have believed first contact would come like this. They've been here since the time of Constantine, and we miss them by a few weeks. Hard to believe, isn't it?"

She frowned. "It's *not* believable." She touched one of the trees. "Did you know it's the *second* time?" she asked. I must have looked blank. "Twenty-two years ago the *Berlin* tracked something across the face of Algol and then lost it. Whatever it was, it threw a couple of sharp turns." We walked silently for several minutes, crossed another avenue, and approached the museum. "Algol," she said, "isn't all that far from here."

"UFO stories," I said. "They used to be common."

She shrugged. "It might be that the thing the *Berlin* saw frightened these people off. Or worse."

The museum is wheel-shaped. Heavy, curving panels of tinted glass are ribbed by polished black stone that is probably marble. The grounds are a wild tangle of weed and shrub anchored by overgrown hedge. A few flowering bushes survive out near the perimeter.

I laughed. "You don't suppose the sun is about to nova, do you?"

She smiled and brushed my cheek with a kiss. Jenny is 23 and a graduate of MIT. "It's going to rain," she said.

We walked past a turret. The air was cool.

"They seem to have taken their time about leaving," I said. "There's no evidence of panic or violence. And most of their personal belongings apparently went with them. Whatever happened, they had time to go home and pack."

She looked uneasily at the sky. Gray clouds were gathering in the west. "Why did they destroy the computers? And the power plant? Doesn't that sound like a retreat before an advancing enemy?"

We stood on the rounded stone steps at the entrance, watching the coming storm. Near the horizon, lightning touched the ground. It was delicate, like the trees.

And I knew what had disturbed me about the painting.

Jenny doesn't play chess. So when we stood again before the portrait and I explained, she listened dutifully and then tried to reassure me. I couldn't blame her.

I have an appointment to meet the Captain in the gallery after dinner. He doesn't play chess either. Like all good captains down through the ages, he is a man of courage and hardheaded common sense, so he will also try to reassure me.

Maybe I'm wrong. I hope so.

But the position in that game: Black is playing the Benko Gambit. It's different in detail, of course; the game is different. But Black is about to clear a lane for the queenside rook. One bishop, at the opposite end of the board, is astride the long diagonal, where its terrible power will combine with that of the rook. And White, after the next move or two, when that advanced pawn comes off, will be desperately exposed.

It's the most advanced of the gambits for Black, still feared after three hundred years.

And I keep thinking: the inhabitants of the City were surely aware of this world's value. More, they are competitors. They would assume that we would want to take it from them.

"But we wouldn't," Jenny had argued.

"Are you sure? Anyhow, it doesn't matter. The only thing that *does* matter is what they believe. And they would expect us to act as *they* would.

"Now, if they knew in advance that we were coming—."

"The *Berlin* sighting—."

"—Might have done it. Warned them we were in the neighborhood. So they withdraw, and give us the world. And, with it, an enigma." Rain had begun sliding down the tinted glass. "They're playing the Benko."

"You mean they might come back here in force and attack?" She was aghast, not at the possibility, which she dismissed; but at the direction my mind had taken.

"No," I said. "Not us. The Benko isn't designed to recover a lost pawn." I could not look away from the painting. Did I detect a gleam of arrogance in Black's eyes? "No. It doesn't fool around with pawns. The idea is to launch a strike into the heart of the enemy position."

"Earth?" She smiled weakly. "They wouldn't even know where Earth is."

I didn't ask whether she thought we might not go home alone.

One more thing about that painting: there's a shading of light, a chiaroscuro, in the eyes of the onlookers. It's the joy of battle.

I'm scared.

THE FAR SHORE

The moonlight was bright on Patty's grave. Rodney Martin felt the moisture in his eyes, threw a final spadeful of earth, and groped for a prayer to a God whose jurisdiction surely ended somewhere south of here. Behind him, in the dark, the surf was a muffled boom.

The wind moved in the trees.

It seemed now he had never known her free of pain. He had worked with her aboard *Alexia* for almost three years; yet her lifetime, for him, was bracketed between this night and that terrible moment on the dark ruined bridge of the stricken starship when he had come upon her, mouth bloody, face pale behind the plexiglass of her helmet.

Grief twisted his features.

He was reluctant to leave, and stood a long time listening to the forest sounds and the ocean. The moon drifted through the night, not the barren pebble of Earth's skies, but a large blue-green globe of continents and water, its arc softened in the shimmering white clouds.

There was a chill in the air.

After awhile, Martin shouldered the spade and walked slowly back toward the beach. The trees gave way to tough, fibrous plants rooted in stony soil. He looked out at the ocean, on which no ship had ever sailed.

Long waves broke and slid up the beach. Ahead, atop a low slope, the lights from the Monson dome glittered on the water. He'd been careful to turn the lamps on before leaving, but now it seemed distant and cold.

He passed a massive boulder, its lower sides smoothed by the tides. Beyond lay the escape capsule, cool and round and black, an enormous bowling ball in the sand, forming a kind of matched pair with the rock.

He climbed the ridge behind the capsule and was home. The Monson was actually four domes, three smaller ones connected by twelve-foot-long tubes to a primary central bubble. Not exactly a townhouse, but comfortable, designed to withstand extreme temperatures, assaults by giant lizards; corrosive atmosphere, whatever. The ideal survival structure, sufficient to house the entire eight-person crew of *Alexia*. As things had turned out, he had a lot of room.

And a lot of time. He wondered what had happened on the ship. Screen failure, probably. God knew the shields had blinked out often enough before. So yes, they'd probably gotten corked by a good-sized rock.

Whatever it was, the hull had come apart, and apparently dumped everyone but the two sleepers into the void. During those last frantic minutes, with power and gravity gone, and the star well swirling beneath his feet, he'd searched *Alexia's* spaces and found only Patty, whose first fortunate response had been to launch the datapak.

Sleep did not come easily. He tried to read but could not concentrate. Finally he turned out the lights and stared at the ceiling. The bedroom windows were open. The surf thundered and boomed.

It had been two weeks since they'd arrived here in the escape capsule. Patty had been thrown hard into a bulkhead during the event and had never really rallied. She'd grown weaker day by day while he watched helplessly.

In the morning, he was up early. Tired, angry, he scrambled an egg for which he had no appetite, added toast and coffee, and went for a swim. The ocean was cool. After a while he came in close to shore and stood knee-deep in the surf, enjoying its inconstant tug, feeling it pull the sand from around his toes. The sea was blue and salty, indistinguishable from the Atlantic. Strands of weed wrapped around his ankles. Things very much like sandcrabs washed in and buried themselves amid tiny fountains of water. The white beach, punctuated with heaps of gray rock, swung in a wide curve for miles, vanishing at last around the edge of a promontory. Inland, wooded hills mounted in successive ridges westward to the foot of a distant mountain chain. A lost floater drifted over the breakers, until it was picked up by the wind and blown back toward the forest. The floaters were green airbags, apparently airborne plants, resembling nothing so much as lopsided leathery balloons, complete with an anchoring tail. He watched until it disappeared inland.

He slept most of the afternoon, and woke feeling better than he had at any time since the accident. He was coming to terms with the loss of Patty.

It was painful, and he promised himself if he got home he'd never leave again. But his situation was not desperate. The environment did not seem especially dangerous, and the Momsen could keep him alive indefinitely. He had a transmitter, so he would be able to say hello when help showed up. Survival depended only on his ability to adjust to being alone.

The Institute had nothing between here and home. It was seventy-some parsecs to Earth. *Alexia's* distress signal, riding its subspace carrier, would cross that vast ocean in 26 months and some odd days, which meant that he could expect a rescue party in about five years.

Fortunately, food was no problem. Storage lockers on board the SARC, the Sakata-Avery Rescue Chamber, held enough hamburgers and flashlight batteries to maintain *eight* people for years. He had weapons, though this world so far had revealed nothing dangerous. And he had a pleasant beach home. Rent free, with his pay piling up.

That evening, he dragged a chair outside, called up a novel, and sat watching the sun dip into the mountains. It was whiter than Sol, slightly larger, in reality as well as in appearance. When the leading edge touched the horizon, Martin set his watch at six o'clock. A day here was longer than at home, maybe by two hours. So his watch was useless for its designed purpose. But he would check it tomorrow when the sun touched the horizon again, and it would tell him the precise length of the day. Not that it mattered.

The SARC had come down in the northern hemisphere, and he'd steered for a temperate zone. The planet, which they had named Amity, was entering that portion of its orbit in which his hemisphere would be tilting away from the sun. Autumn was coming.

He would want a calendar. Again, not that he had any real use for one. But it would be something to occupy him. He knew Amity circled its G2 main sequence primary in just over seventeen terrestrial months.

Declination was eleven degrees. That should mean a mild winter.

He thought about supplies. Had he overlooked anything? He had an abundance of solar energy, with backup systems. The shoreline gave no indication of unusual tides, sudden inundations, anything of that nature.

The SARC possessed an extensive film library. Complete runs of the most popular HV shows of the last century. There were quiz and discussion shows, and other programs of an educational nature; and a complete run, ten years worth, of *Brandenburg and Scott*, a "sociodrama" in which two wisecracking government agents helped people adjust to assorted problems arising from economic dislocation, overpopulation, divergence of religious views, and so on.

He had fifty years of the World Series, and a lot of horse races. And the better part of the Library of Congress.

He also had a radio. There was, of course, nothing to listen to other than the hourly distress call put out by the datapak. The datapak was an orbiting cluster of antennas, receivers, and transmitters, aimed at Earth by an on-board computer, beeping across hyphenated space. Its receivers were designed to pick up stray whispers of signal, electronic sighs to be filtered and dissected, the results channeled for analysis, enhancement, and ultimate restoration. It would, one day, lead his rescuers to him.

Martin's front yard was humanity's most remote outpost. It was half again as far as Calamity, on the other side of Sol.

A tree-squatter sat on its hind legs, watching him. It resembled an oversized and overweight squirrel. He tossed it a nut. It advanced with caution, took the nut, glanced briefly at him, and vanished back into the scrub.

The tree-squatter, with its quick black eyes, was around all the time, looking for food. But it would not trust him, and always cleared out if he tried to approach.

There were lots of squirrels and tree-squatters and floaters, but no one had yet found any philosophers or electricians. Consequently, Earth was reassuming its classic Ptolemaic position as center of the universe. The Theological Implications, as people were fond of saying, were obvious. The primordial soup, stirred centuries ago by evolutionists to evict the Creator, had acquired an extra ingredient. The view that people were a direct result of divine intervention was once again respectable. The numerous empty garden worlds, like this one, might almost have been prepared specifically for human use. But if places like this suggested a friendly cosmos to people back home, to Martin the skies were too silent, the forests too empty. The Institute was dying. The human race had more real estate than they could use for the foreseeable future. Expeditions were expensive, ships were wearing out, and the government could see no return for its money. Unless something happened that could rekindle the taxpayers' imaginations, the Great Adventure was drawing to a close. Moreover, it was unlikely that the political power structure wanted any unsettling discoveries. There would probably be a general sigh of relief when the last vessel returned emptyhanded from its last flight.

No new unit had been added to the fleet in thirty years. Equipment was run down, and parts were scarce. In fact, he thought wearily, if the truth were known, the loss of *Alexia* would probably turn out to be attributable to a broken hose.

◉

He missed Patty.

The place was too quiet. The wind blew and the tides came and went and seabirds flapped past. He was becoming increasingly oppressed by a sense of unease. Somewhere, in the hills, or maybe at sea, he'd have liked to see a light.

He kept the HV on constantly. The voices were reassuring. He listened to them argue politics, philosophy, medicine, religion, and sex. He watched various kinds of dramas, watched comedians, listened to musicals and even started to develop a taste for opera.

He took to bolting the door. It was the beginning of the Greenway Syndrome.

Everett Radcliffe, stranded on the back side of the Moon for six months after a series of improbable accidents had carried off his two colleagues, had heard footsteps behind him the rest of his days. Will Evans had taken his life after four months in a prototype of Martin's shelter. Myra Greenway, for whom the disorder was named, was adrift for a year in a SARC, never close to a planetary surface. She swore that something had lived outside, trying continually to get at her. Brad Kauffman had spent eight months alone in a crippled cruiser after his partner had died, and had refused, on his return to Earth, to come out of his house at night.

There were other cases.

Something deep in the soul does not like unbroken, intense solitude. Cut whatever it is that ties a man to the rest of his species, plunge him into the outer dark, and you will not get him back whole.

Martin tried not to think about it.

Standard procedure was to embrace whatever entertainment was available, cultivate hobbies, keep occupied. He glanced at the hologram. An aging beauty was swapping mindless chitchat with a comedian.

He could collect rocks.

Martin was not a man easily frightened. He'd intervened in a gang assault, did not fear speaking to large groups of people, and had ridden the great starships into the unknown. Nevertheless, he continued to keep his door locked.

❋

STATUS REPORT 037 *ALEXIA* 090857 GMT: PATRICIA MASON
DEAD OF INJURIES SEPTEMBER 3.

He thought of Patty's family, two years from now, receiving this news,
and added: PEACEFULLY. He poked in his name, and hit the transmit.

❋

The morning was gray with rain. He played bridge with the computer,
got bored, tried a novel. After lunch, he sat down at the terminal and pointed the datapak's antennas at Sirius. The speakers crackled with static.

Hello from God.

Outside, the trees bent under a stiff wind, and the ocean was choppy.
Rain coming. Oblivious to the weather, a groper ambled amiably along the
treeline, its oilskin hide glistening. It probed the branches with long, flexible
arms for a yellow fruit that had also tested okay for Martin's consumption.

He'd awakened with a wisp of recollection from his childhood, something not quite remembered, brought back by a dream:

*He was a boy, alone in the house in Atlanta. And frightened by the shadows
and dark places outside the living room. He'd put on the HV, and looked through
the dining room at the gloomy doorway to the kitchen, with its exits opening out
back and into the basement. He'd sat awhile, trying to pretend it was not there.
Then, he had turned off the unit, taken a book, and crawled behind the sofa. To
be safe from whatever might come through that door.*

Had it really happened? As he reached back, details took shape. It had
happened more than once.

He rotated the orbiter's antennas randomly, and set the scanner to
range over a wide band of frequencies. There *was* something constructive
he could do: intercept an alien signal, a navigational beacon in the vicinity
of Betelgeuse, maybe, or a weather report from the Pleiades. Do that, and
they'd build a shrine on this spot.

He sat through most of the afternoon, listening to the cosmic racket,
wondering whether he would recognize an alien signal if he heard one.
Eventually tiring of the game, Martin returned control to the on-board
computer, which obediently tracked back across the sky and locked onto
its primary target. The signal changed.

It was a blip, a rhythmic murmur gone so quickly that he wasn't sure
it had been there at all. He reversed the scanner, and was listening to a

jumble of signals, nothing he could make out, but different in quality from the stellar transmissions he'd heard previously. He used the filters to isolate the strongest signal, and then boosted it. It became a piano, and a voice:

> "...A lipstick's traces,
> "An airline ticket to romantic places,
> "And still my heart has wings;
> "These foolish things remind me of you...."

Martin frowned, smiled, shook his head.

Rescue ship nearby? That brought a momentary surge of elation, but he knew it could not be. He got up anyhow and went outside to see if anything was moving against the stars. The piano sounded very far away.

> "...A telephone that rings, but who's to answer?
> "Oh, how the ghost of you clings!...."

The singer finished to a burst of applause, and the melody shifted smoothly.

"Thanks, folks, and goodnight from all of us here at the Music Hall until next Sunday, when we'll be coming your way again with more of America's favorite tunes."

More applause, music up in volume, and then a fadeaway to another voice:

"This is CBS, the Columbia Broadcasting System. News is next, with Waldo Anderson."

Old Earth: he was picking up carrier waves that had left Earth more than two centuries ago!

Anderson arrived in a clatter of electronic gimmickry, introduced his lead story, which concerned an armed robbery, and gave way immediately to a woman with a passion for antacid tablets. Then Anderson returned, speaking in a rich, cultured voice:

"The Willie Starr case went to the jury today. Starr is one of two men accused in a triple slaying last March at a Brooklyn liquor store. His alleged partner, Joey Horton, has already...."

Martin sighed, and turned it off. He had found his alien civilization.

✸

The sun broke through and the day warmed. Languidly, Martin stripped and gave himself to the sea. The water had turned cold. He swam out beyond the breakers with sure, swift strokes, turned and surveyed his world, rising and falling with the waves.

It was like one of those early summers off St. Simons, minus the white frame houses and the beachfront restaurants. And the women.

Anyone.

He sat on the beach, wrapped in a robe, with his reader propped against his knees, lost in a planetary, a novel set during the early days of extraterrestrial settlement. The author, Reginald Packard, had grown wealthy cranking out these historical romances. Martin did not normally read such things. But he had become engrossed in the book over breakfast. Now, however, as the sun began its long slide toward the mountains, he found that his eyes kept wandering from the rows of neat print to the shadowy places among the trees.

Something was there.

He pulled the robe tight around him. A long wave unrolled and ran up the beach. He could not get his eyes off the edge of the forest.

Nothing moved.

The Dome was three hundred yards away. A long run in the sand. How easily he could be cut off!

His heart pounded.

The wind blew and the trees writhed.

Greenway. He understood the woman, hysterical in her capsule beyond Centaurus, while a space-born *thing* with sharp teeth and feral eyes prowled the outside, slavering at her through the viewscreen, gnawing at the airlock.

His heartbeat picked up. And suddenly, without thinking about it, he was on his feet, churning through the loose sand. He did not look back, but kept his eyes fixed on the Dome. He fell and, in slow motion, rolled over and came back to his feet in a single fluid move.

When he got back inside, he bolted the door, set the shields in place, drew the blinds, and collapsed. His cheek was bleeding.

That night he tried to distract himself by working out a search pattern for the datapak. *If, by a remote chance, he found what they'd all been looking for, they'd have to come get him....* Martin's eyes narrowed at the thought that had surfaced, that he'd refused to consider. That someone might decide a rescue was too expensive. They knew, or would know, he was the only survivor. One person laid against the cost of a multi-year mission. But the Service had a tradition to maintain. He had nothing to fear.

At dawn, he started the search. While the display blipped and beeped, he sat by the window, peering through the drawn shades.

Deciding that chatter would at least be company, he switched back to the terrestrial radio station and listened to two domestic serials, "Our Gal Sunday" and "Life Can Be Beautiful." His tension lessened. The shows had a small-town charm, and the characters seemed generally virtuous and vulnerable, if not bright. Sunday's voice had a peculiar vitality, a quality of moonlight and laughter. He tried to picture the actress, and decided he would have liked to know her.

And there was more news:

"...*Governor Dewey at a press conference this morning stated that police are closing in on Buchalter, and that his arrest is imminent. Known in gangland as Lepke the Leopard, Buchalter jumped bail two years ago. Onetime boss of New York's protection racket, he is believed—.*"

He experimented with other terrestrial frequencies. Most were in foreign languages. But there were others. He listened to "Ma Perkins" and a quiz show. And he discovered "Terry and the Pirates" and "Jack Armstrong."

There were supplies to be got in from the capsule, a job he'd been putting off. And he'd dropped his reader when he ran from the beach. He looked out the windows and saw nothing. He turned up the radio, unlocked the door, and forced himself to walk. He went first to recover the reader. Then he hurried to the capsule. He loaded his arms with packets of dehydrated foods, sealed the vehicle, and started home. Nothing watched him from the hills. Nothing charged out of the trees. When he'd gotten back to the Momsen, he was proud of himself. He bolted the door, though—no point being foolish—and put everything away. Then he sat down and turned the radio back on.

Immediately, he heard a familiar name:

"*Berlin announced today that Polish authorities were continuing to expel German citizens. The official Nazi newspaper* Volkischer Beobachter *reported two men killed near Stettin this afternoon. Both were German citizens, and were said to have been fleeing a Polish mob when they ran out onto a highway, where they were struck by a bus.*

"*Chancellor Hitler, speaking at a party meeting in Munich, labeled the incident quote yet another provocation by anti-German leftists in the Polish government unquote. He called on President Moscicki to intervene, and warned that German patience is not without its limits.*

"*Closer to home....*"

Martin, of course, knew Hitler, the twentieth-century warlord and nutcase.

The newscast went on to describe a quarrel in Congress over the Neutrality Act, a bungled attempt at an armored car holdup, and an argument at a schoolboard meeting. Tomorrow would be sunny and hot. The current heat wave was going into its sixth day. And there were some baseball scores.

Martin hadn't realized that baseball was so old. Some of the teams were the same, but it must be a strange version of the game in which you only scored three or four runs.

He slept that night with the shields up, though he knew, *really knew,* they were unnecessary.

He tried to pick up "Our Gal Sunday" again next day, but failed to take into account the two-hour-plus time differential resulting from the longer day. But there were other shows. "Stella Dallas" and "Just Plain Bill." He listened with interest: the problems faced by the characters were of a personal nature, rather than social struggles. These were people for whom there might have been no outside world, but merely the melodramatic mix of love and lust.

He passed a sizable part of his afternoon with Xavier Cugat and the Boys in "the Green Room of the beautiful Grant Park Hotel in downtown New York." Between songs, behind the announcer's voice, Martin heard the low murmur of conversation, the clink of china: fragile place of glass and laughter.

Berlin announced that two unarmed German passenger planes had been fired on by Polish fighters near Danzig. One had crashed in a field, killing all on board. The other had carried a cargo of dead and wounded back into German territory. Hitler was said to be furious.

There were also reports of an attack on a German border station.

The Poles denied it all.

Martin understood that these events were not real, that the people in the Green Room, sipping their martinis and drifting into the coming carnage, were long since gone to dust. He might as well have been listening to an account of the Third Crusade. Yet....

Warfare had been a common enough occurrence over the centuries, but to Martin it was part of a barbaric past, relegated to dusty tomes in libraries. Unthinkable.

Next day he returned to the beach. He even walked briefly into the forest that afternoon. There was nothing here to fear. No predators.

When the Wehrmacht rolled into Poland, Martin was lying on the sand, naked, tanned, reading Byron. He listened to appeals from Britain and France, from the White House and the Vatican. After sundown, when the first battle reports came in (both sides were claiming victories), he looked out at the dark, quiet hills, trying to imagine ponderous tanks clanking toward him, Heinkels crossing his western mountains to drop explosives on his head.

The Germans bombed Cracow. Martin listened to an eyewitness description, heavy accent, heavy static, muted blasts, children fleeing the stuttering stukas, Nazi tanks sighted west of the city, everything on fire....

Emory Michael, of the Blue Network, got through from a small town whose name he couldn't get straight. The townspeople, mostly women and children, had gathered in a pasture on the west side of the city, watching the Nazi planes circling. Watching the bombs drop.

Michael found a woman who spoke English, and asked where her husband was. "With the cavalry," she said, with a heavy accent. "They will cut the Boche to pieces!"

Horses, thought Martin. After a long while, he strode off, walking at the edge of the incoming tide, listening to the unhurried roar of the sea. From here, the war seemed so distant. (He smiled at that.)

Rain clouds were building in the west.

What was remarkable: These people bombed and strafed—how many would die during the conflagration?—and it would all pass, leaving only a few ripples on the tide, the wreckage washed out to sea. His generation barely knew of World War II. It was something in the history books.

A fine drizzle began to fall.

He turned into the forest. The ground was thick with leaves. He ducked under a floater that had tethered itself to a low branch. Something small, with fur, stopped to watch.

He came to Patricia's grave and said hello, aloud. There was no marker, other than three rough stones. Eventually, soon, he would correct that.

He sat down. It was a beautiful, leafy glade, a place for children, or lovers. He cradled his chin against his knees, and mourned all those, down the long years, whose lives had been cut short, caught in the wrong place at the wrong time, victims of greed, folly, or plain bad luck: Patricia, the children of Cracow, the woman whose husband was in the cavalry, the Roman farmers in the path of the Vandals. Here's to everybody. There's room here, on Amity, and welcome.

The rain was falling harder, becoming a downpour. Above him, on a branch, something stirred.

There *was* some good news: A woman named Myers was reunited with her mother after 43 years; Lepke turned himself over to a newsman named Winchell; and Martin discovered Fibber McGee. McGee was unlike anything he had encountered before, an engaging mixture of pomposity, naive dishonesty, and scrambling insecurity. McGee's world of goodhearted bumblers seemed untouched by the savagery in the newscasts.

Martin's first experience with fictional psychotics and madmen came with "The Shadow." It was a series which would not have been allowed in his own time. His society frowned on mindless mayhem. But week after week, the invisible, slightly schizophrenic hero tracked down and eliminated mass murderers and insane physicians in the most delicious manner. Martin loved it.

Despite the global disaster, there was a warmth to the programming, good humor, a sense of purpose and community that extended beyond time and space to Martin's beachfront property. He strolled the tree-lined streets of Philadelphia, dined in some of Chicago's better restaurants. He became addicted to "Amos 'n' Andy," followed Captain Midnight into exotic jungle locales, explored the temple of vampires with Jack, Doc, and Reggie. He was a regular visitor in the Little Theater off Times Square.

Meanwhile, Hitler's armies swept all opposition aside. President Roosevelt appeared frequently in informal broadcasts, discussing the economy and the war, assuring his audience that America would stay out of the fighting.

Although he could not recall the course of the struggle (he was not even certain yet which President Roosevelt he was listening to), Martin knew that, in the end, the Western Allies would win. *Had* won. But it was difficult, in the summer of 1940, to see how such an outcome might develop. Britain, bloody, desperate, stood alone. And Churchill's regal voice rang defiance across the light years.

Martin listened with sorrow to Edward R. Murrow in London, as the Nazis pounded the city. A year later, he was at a football game between the Redskins and the Eagles when the Japanese attacked Pearl Harbor. He fought with the garrison on Luzon, watched the aerial battle over Midway, rode in the desert with Montgomery.

In the late spring of 1944, the datapak picked up a subspace transmission: RESCUE UNIT ENROUTE. SHOULD ARRIVE WITHIN THIRTY DAYS AFTER YOU RECEIVE THIS. HANG ON, ROD.

By then Martin had taken to getting away from home periodically on two- and three-day jaunts into the countryside. But he wanted to keep up with the war. He was on one of these trips, lying in the grass halfway up a mountain in the early afternoon when the response came, breaking into "Dawn Patrol." He let it repeat several times, wondering why he wished they had been a little less prompt.

Eisenhower's army gathered in Britain. Everyone knew what was coming; most of the speculation centered on timing and landing points. Martin waited with the rest of the nation for word of the invasion. Tension inside the Dome grew thick.

But the invasion did not happen. A few days later, while he was still caught up in speculation from Washington and London, the *Eagle* arrived. It was a sleek silver bullet-shaped cruiser, sailing majestically on its magnetics. (The *Eagle* was the same class vessel as *Alexia*, but his ship had never looked so good.) His datapak gave him a look at it, and an hour or so later its lander settled softly into the scrub. The hatch rotated, opened, and people spilled out. Martin hugged everybody.

They stayed two weeks, splashing in the surf, drinking at night, walking in the woods. Martin talked constantly, to anyone who would listen. He paired off with a young technician and rediscovered a few lost emotions.

Captain and crew gathered around his radio, and listened curiously to "Big Town" and Gabriel Heatter. But time was pressing. "You know how it is, Rod," the captain said. "Got to be moving."

Martin noticed that, with the arrival of the *Eagle*, the broadcasts lost some of their sense of immediacy. He no longer felt he was living through the second war. When, on the fourth day of his rescue, Allied troops stormed ashore on Omaha Beach, he was in a glade with his technician. He heard about it later, but it seemed like an historical event. Something far removed from Amity.

They dug up Patty's body to be returned to New Hampshire. The medical officer and the captain each inquired after his health. One thought he seemed depressed; the other wondered if he was actually unhappy about being rescued. "Long time to be stuck in a place like this," the captain said, looking around at the empty beaches and the silent woods.

Martin's eyes dimmed. "Not stuck here," he said. "I've been traveling."

The medical officer frowned. "What do you mean, Rod?"

"I'm not sure I can explain it, Doc," he said. "But I may be the world's first time traveller."

SUNRISE

I lyanda had always seemed haunted.

There is something that broods over its misty seas and broken archipelagos, that breathes within its forests. You can feel it in the curious ruins that may, or may not, have been left by men. Or in the pungent ozone of the thunderstorms that strike Point Edward each night with a clockwork regularity that no one has yet explained. It is no accident that so many modern writers of supernatural fiction have set their stories on Ilyanda, beneath its cluster of brilliant white rings and racing moons.

To the planet's twenty thousand inhabitants, most of whom live at Point Edward on the northern tip of the smallest of that world's three continents, such notions are exaggerated. But to those of us who have arrived from more mundane locations, it is a place of fragile beauty, of voices not quite heard, of dark rivers draining the unknown.

I was never more aware of its supernal qualities than during the weeks following Gage's death. Against the advice of friends, I took the *Meredith* to sea, determined in the perverse way of people at such a time to touch once again a few of the things we'd shared in our first year, thereby sharpening the knife-edge of grief. And if, in some indefinable way, I expected to recapture a part of those lost days, it might have been from a sense that, in those phantom oceans, all things seemed possible.

I sailed into the southern hemisphere and quickly lost myself among the Ten Thousand Islands.

It didn't help, of course. I curved round familiar coasts and anchored off rock formations that, silhouetted against other nights, had resembled freedivers and pensive women. But the images were gone now, driven to sea by relentless tides. I slept one evening on a sacrificial slab in a ruined temple that, on at least one occasion, had been put to far better use.

In the end, I realized he was not out there.

Point Edward is visible at sea from an extraordinary distance. Visitors to Ilyanda are struck by the phenomenon, and are usually told that the effect is due to an excess of water vapor. But I can tell you what it is: Point Edward is the only major source of artificial light in a world of dark seas and black coasts. In a sense, it is visible all over the planet.

On that last day at sea, I saw it in the eastern sky almost immediately after sundown. I adjusted course a few degrees to port and ran before the wind. The water was loud against the prow, and, I think, during those hours, I began to come to terms with my life. The broad avenues and glittering homes that commanded the series of ridges dominating the coastline gradually separated. And I poured myself a generous glass of brissie and raised a toast to the old town.

The constellations floated on black water, and the radio below decks murmured softly, a newscast, something about the Ashiyyur. Like my former life, the war with the Mutes was very far away, out in a nebula across the Arm somewhere. It was hard to believe, in the peaceful climate of Ilyanda, that people—well, humans and the only other technological creatures we'd found—were actually killing one another.

A bell clanged solemnly against the dull roar of the ocean. A white wake spread out behind the *Meredith*, and the sails filled with the night.

Point Edward had been built on the site of an ancient volcano. The cone, which had collapsed below the surrounding rock into the sea, provided an ideal harbor. A cruise along the coast, however, would quickly demonstrate there was no other place to land. The chain of peaks and escarpments ran almost the entire length of the continent. South of the city, they seemed preternaturally high, their snowcapped pinnacles lost in cumulus.

I approached from the north, steering under the security lights of the Marine Bank on Dixon Ridge and the Steel Mall, past the serene columns and arches of the municipal complex and the hanging gardens of the University of Ilyanda. The air was cool and I felt good for the first time in months. But as I drew near the shore, as the boulevards widened and the lighted marquees became legible (I could see that the California holo *Flashpoint* had arrived at the Blackwood), a sense of apprehension stole over me. The wind and the waves grew very loud, and nothing moved in the channel or along the waterfront. It was of course late, lacking only a bit more than an hour before midnight. Yet, there should have been something in the harbor, a skiff, a late steamer full of tourists, a patrol craft.

Something.

I tied up to my pier at the foot of Barbara Park. Yellow lights dangled over the planking, and the place looked bright and cheerful. It was good to be home.

I strolled casually toward the street, enjoying the loud clack of the boards underfoot. The boathouse was dark. I ducked behind it, came out on Seaway Boulevard, and hurried across against the traffic light. A large banner strung over the storefront window of Harbor Appliances announced an autumn sale. One of the appliances, a cleaner, lit up, started its routine, and shut off again as I passed. Across the street, a bank databoard flashed the weather: showers (of course), ending toward morning, a high of 19, and a low of 16. Another pleasant day coming up.

Control signals blinked and clicked. It had rained earlier: the streets were slick with water. They were also empty.

I was only a block from the Edwardian, our major hotel. Like many of the older structures in town, it was Toxicon Gothic. But it towered over the others, a colossus of ornate porticos and gray minarets, of blunt arches and step-down galleries. Yellow light spilled from two cupolas atop the gambrel roof. (I had a few pleasant recollections from this place too, but they all predated my marriage.)

The Edwardian was used extensively by tourists, and its Skyway Room also served as a popular rendezvous for revelers seven nights a week. The sidewalks should have been jammed. Where the hell was everybody?

There was something else. I could see the main library about halfway up a sharp rise on the eastern edge of town. It's a sleek, modern place, designed by Orwell Mason, and done in late Terran. Set amid a scattering of fountains and pools, its lines suggest a fourth dimension, an effect emphasized by nighttime illumination. A massive boulder, which is supposed to have been deposited by ice fifteen thousand years ago, guards the main approach.

It was almost midnight. The lamps should have been dimmed to the soft multi-colored ambience of the fountains, and the topological illusion consequently diminished. But the place was ablaze with light.

I looked at my watch again.

Only a handful of vehicles were parked on the library grounds. No movement was detectable, either inside or outside the building.

I was standing in the middle of Seaway Boulevard. It's a broad thoroughfare, the central artery, really, of Point Edward. To the north, it rises in a near straight line across a series of escarpments; to the south, it proceeds another half-kilometer to Barracut Circle, the heart of the shopping district. Nowhere in all that stretch of blinking traffic signals and overhead arcs could I see a single moving car.

Could I see movement of any kind.

Even Tracy Park, usually full of ringstruck couples from the University, was deserted.

A sudden gust blew up and drove a scattering of leaves against the shops lining the boulevard.

No one's ever accused me of having an active imagination, but I stood puzzled out there, listening to the city, to the wind and the buoys and the water sucking at the piers and the sudden hum of power beneath the pavement and the distant banging of a door swinging on its hinges and the Carolian beat of the automated electronic piano in the Edwardian. Something walked through it all on invisible feet.

I hurried into the shadows. The needlepoint towers, the sequestered storefronts, the classical statuary in the parks: I had never noticed before but they resembled the ruins I'd visited in the southern hemisphere. It was not difficult to imagine a far traveller strolling these avenues, feeling the press of the centuries, and the eyes of the long dead, nodding knowingly at primitive architectural styles, and retreating at last, not without a measure of relief, to a boat moored in the harbor.

Well, there you are. I was standing in front of the Surf & Sand with my imagination running wild when the lights went out.

It was as if somebody threw a switch.

My first impression was that the entire city had been plunged into darkness. But that wasn't quite the case: traffic signals still worked, streetlamps still burned, and Cory's Health Club was illuminated by security lights. In the opposite direction, the Edwardian showed no change whatever. But beyond it lay rows of darkened storefronts. Across the street from where I stood, Captain Culpepper's Waterfront Restaurant, and the garden supply shop on the corner of Seaway and Delinor, also retained some lights. But the vast sweep of thousands of homes were dark. I couldn't be certain, but I would have sworn they had all, *all*, been brightly lit a moment before. The library had also vanished into the general gloom.

Along the piers, some of the strings of bulbs still glowed brightly.

I started to walk again, trying to tread gently, to muffle my footsteps. Past the Keynote ("Musical Groups for All Occasions"), the Male Body (a clothing shop), Monny's Appliance Rental, and a three-story posh apartment complex. No light in any of them.

I stopped at the apartment building and pressed all the signals. Nothing happened, no one asked who was there, no light came on.

The Blue Lantern, where I usually ate lunch when I was downtown, looked open for business. Its sign blinked on and off. The window neons burned cheerfully, and a bright yellow glow outlined the top of the transom. The tables were set with silverware, and soft music drifted into the street. But the candles were all out.

The door was bolted.

I pulled my jacket tightly about my shoulders. The war, I thought. It had to be the war.

But that made no sense. The war was very far, and Ilyanda wasn't even part of it. Anyhow, why would the Mutes spirit away twenty thousand people?

I crossed the street and hurried into a parking area. I had to grope around because I'd forgotten where I'd left the car. I found it finally, opened the door, and climbed inside. It felt a lot better behind a locked door.

I switched on the radio. And picked up Lach Keenan's familiar voice. He was going on about a proposed school bond issue. Taking calls. I waited for him to give his code. When he did I punched it into my link. It responded with the tones that indicated a connection had been made. Then Keenan's voice: "*Hello. We appreciate your calling* Late Night. *We're not broadcasting live this evening, but we'd be happy to hear from you next time. Good night. Thank you for your interest.*"

I cruised slowly through the downtown area, and turned onto University. The commercial area gave way to shadowy stone houses with rock gardens and fountains. Out near Bradenthorn, on the edge of town, a black dog stopped in the middle of the street, looked at me, and walked on.

Eventually, I went back to the Edwardian.

The lobby was lighted, but no hosts walked among the potted fronds. No guest stood at the service counter, where all screens read *Good evening—May I help you?* I went into the Iron Pilot and looked around at the empty tables. And the deserted bar.

Distant thunder rumbled.

I'd been reluctant to call anyone because it was late. But finally I broke down and called Quim Bordley. He was an antique collector and an old friend.

Nobody answered.

Aias Weinstein, my cousin, didn't answer.

The spaceport security office, where Gage had worked, didn't answer.

The police didn't answer.

My heart pounded, and the fronds and chairs and counters and clerks grew blurred and unreal. At the far end of the lobby, at the travel desk, an electronic sign urged patrons to charter a Blue Line cruise.

I consulted the directory for Albemarle, a small mining settlement across the continent, and tried the police there. A voice replied!

"Good evening," it said. *"You have reached the Albemarle police. Please remain on the link, and we will be right with you. If this is an emergency, please say so."*

"Yes," I whispered into the receiver, cautious lest I be overheard. "My God, this is an emergency. Please. It's an emergency."

After a while, the recording repeated.

I rode through the silent streets. A half hour after midnight, right on schedule, our nightly electrical storm hit. The skies opened, and I should have stopped, but I felt safer on the move.

Lights were on at the hospital. I pulled up at the emergency entrance and hurried inside. The prep room was empty. Elsewhere, beds were crumpled, sheets and blankets tossed aside. They had left in a hurry.

At Coastal Rescue, boats were tied to their moorings and skimmers stood on their pads. I broke into the communication center, which is supposed to be manned twenty-eight hours a day, and sat down at the radio. There were weather reports coming in from satellites, and an update on maritime schedules. All recorded. Then I picked up a conversation:

"—Recommend approach at zero two seven," a female voice said. *"Charlie, there is no traffic in your area. You are clear to proceed."*

"Will comply," said Charlie. *"It's good to be back."* He sounded tired.

"We're looking at a quick turn-around on the surface flight, Charlie. *"The manifest shows eleven passengers for Richardson. How about you and your crew?"*

"Janet's going down. She has a brother at the Point."

"Okay. Have them report to Area 14. Lower level. We're running a little late."

It was a communication between the space station and a ship. Richardson, of course, is the spaceport outside Point Edward.

I tried to call them, but the transmitter might not have had its directionals lined up, or something. At least, that's what I thought then. Anyhow, somewhat relieved, I went back to the car. I considered going home. But in the end, I continued past my apartment and turned out onto the old Burnfield Road. When the shuttle came down, I'd be standing at the terminal.

The Captain William E. Richardson Spaceport is located twenty-two kilometers southeast of Point Edward. Since most of the traffic between the facility and the city is by skimmer, the surface road had been allowed to deteriorate. It's a rough ride.

The road rose and fell, curved past farms and through satellite towns and across fields of ripening wheat. I saw nobody along the way. Most houses were dark. In any case there was no traffic. I began to wonder whether someone had decided the volcano wasn't dead after all. It was the only possibility I could think of.

The storm cleared away. The stars came out, and the rings took over the night.

Keenan was off the air by now, but the station was still broadcasting headlines and commentary:

"Mario Belanco caught in sex scandal. May have to step down."

"Brightstar Church installs new program for seniors."

The lights were still on at Richardson. It's a combined facility, serving both civilian and naval operations. Probably two-thirds of it, in those troubled times, was reserved for the Navy.

"Girl Guides recognizes supporters."

"Maraclova construction project in financial trouble."

I glanced at my watch. The shuttle would still be at least an hour away. But I checked the sky anyhow. No moving lights.

"Christopher Sim to pay visit to Point Edward." Sim was, of course, the commander of a group of Dellacondans who, with a scattering of allies, were engaged in the war with the Mutes.

The rings were magnificent. In the tense and awful silence of that night, the old gods of Ilyanda seemed close.

Despite everything, I couldn't help smiling. If the history books had it right, early settlers around Point Edward had quickly come to believe in the literal existence of supernatural beings. The literature was rife with forest devils and phantoms and deities. I've read somewhere that superstition takes hold, even in a technological society, whenever the total human population fails, within a given time, to rise above a minimum figure. Unless, of course, there's already a strong belief system in place. Judging by what they'd written, the Point's early settlers didn't believe in *anything*.

I passed a wreck. A car and a city carrier. The carrier lay half off the highway, nosed into some trees, all doors open. Big and ungainly, it wasn't designed for country roads. It should have been making stops along Seaway Boulevard. But it had apparently been pressed into service to take people out to Richardson. Why?

As I approached the spaceport, carriers, jitneys, trucks, and private vehicles became more numerous until they choked the road. They were parked on both shoulders and on every adjacent stretch of open ground.

There'd been several accidents. A skimmer had been involved in one. Behind it lay a freshly dug clay mound almost as long as the aircraft itself. Someone had pounded a wooden cross onto its topmost point.

The radio was still talking about Christopher Sim.

I worked my way through the tangle of vehicles into the spaceport. A service monorail vehicle edged out of one of the hangars. Hello, I said. But no crewman was visible.

When I could go no farther, I turned the car around so I could get out in a hurry if I had to. And I walked toward the terminal. The aprons were jammed with pieces of luggage and overturned dollies. Food wrappers, beverage containers, and print editions of periodicals were blown about by the wind.

At the terminal, I saw blood stains on one of the door handles.

I went inside, into the reception area. I wandered past the ticket dispensers, and the souvenir shops and art marts, and the vehicle rental counters and security checkpoints.

Through the crystal walls, I could watch the monorail moving deliberately among the service structures until it reached a point where its path was blocked by a truck. I went up to the second deck, took a seat on the observation terrace, checked the time again, and settled in to wait for the shuttle.

I turned on a holo, and watched two middle-aged men blink on and plunge into a heated discussion, though I cannot remember, and may never have been aware of, the nature of the disagreement. At least it was noise. But if it was at first reassuring. I quickly began to wonder whether it might draw unwanted attention. In the end, although I castigated myself for my fears, I shut it off, and found a seat where I was relatively hidden.

The scheduled time of arrival came and went.

The bright glimmering sky showed no movement.

After all these years, the growing fears of those moments remain vivid. I knew, maybe somehow had known all along, that they would not come. That despite all the talk on the circuits, they would not come.

I stole away finally, beaten.

It's curious how quickly one adapts. I'd reached a state at which the deserted corridors, the silent shops, the utter emptiness of the sprawling complex and the city beyond, seemed the natural order of things.

The security office was locked. I had to break a glass panel to get in. One of the monitors was running, providing views of loading areas, passageways, retail outlets.

Gage's desk had been in an adjoining office. Nothing looked different from the days when he'd been there, other than one of the armchairs had been moved. And there were different pictures on the desk and different certificates hung on the walls.

I collapsed onto a small couch in the corner of the office and tried to sleep. But I was afraid to close my eyes. So I sat for almost an hour, watching the door, listening for sounds deep in the heart of the building. And of course hearing them, knowing all along they were not really there.

There'd been a laser pistol in the desk. It was locked and I had to pry the drawer open, but the weapon was still there. I lifted it out, hefting it, feeling better for its cool metallic balance. I checked to see that it was charged. There was no convenient place to carry it, and I ended by pushing it down in my jacket pocket and holding onto it.

The communication center was located near the top of the terminal. I took an elevator up, got out and walked through suites of offices, walked into the operations section, where the electronics were shut down. I used the weapon to cut through a door marked KEEP OUT. I'd been back there once or twice before, on guided tours for family members.

The transmitter had been left on.

Something was going out. I put it on the speaker. It was simply the quiet murmur of electronics. Telemetry, I decided. The spaceport was transmitting telemetry.

It made no sense. I went to a window and looked out. Looked for moving lights somewhere, something going up or coming down. But the night sky was quiet. At ground level, a light mist had begun to creep across the parked vehicles.

I sat down at the radio. "Hello," I said. "This is Richardon. Where the hell is everybody?"

I'm not sure precisely when I realized I wasn't alone. A footstep somewhere, maybe. An echo. Whatever it was, I became conscious of movement, and of my own breathing.

My first impulse was to get out of the terminal. To get back to the car, and maybe back to the boat. Sweat rolled down my ribs.

I moved through the offices one by one, clinging to the pistol.

I stopped in a conference room dominated by a sculpted freediver. A holograph unit which someone had neglected to turn off blinked sporadically atop a carved table. A half-dozen chairs were arranged around the table, in disorder. There were empty coffee cups, and a couple of light pads.

I activated the holo and one of the light pads. They'd been discussing motivational techniques.

And somewhere, far off, glass shattered.

Above, in the Tower Room, the rooftop restaurant.

I rode the elevator up two floors, came out into a dark corridor, and stood before a pair of open doors.

There were lights on, computerized candles flickering in smoked jars. Music was playing. Soft, moody, romantic. The Tower Room in those days looked, and felt, like a sunken grotto. It was a hive of (apparently) rocky vaults and dens, divided by watercourses, salad dispensers, mock boulders and shafts, and a winding bar. Blue and white light sparkled against fake sandstone and silverware. Crystal streams poured from the mouths of dancing nymphs and raced through narrow channels between rough-hewn bridges.

It felt as if the heating system had given out.

I crossed a bridge and followed the bar. Everything was neatly arranged, chairs in place, silver laid out on red cloth napkins, condiments and sauce bottles stacked side by side.

I could feel tears coming, and sank into a chair.

There was an answering clatter. And a voice: "Who's there?"

I froze.

Footsteps. In back somewhere. Then a man emerged from the shadows. In uniform. "Hello," he called cheerfully. "Are you all right?"

I shook my head uncertainly. "Of course," I said. "What's going on? Where is everybody?"

"I'm back near the window." He turned away from me. "Have to stay there." He looked back to make sure I was following, and then retreated the way he'd come.

I'd seen the uniform before. Somewhere. By the time I joined him, I'd placed it: It was the light and dark blue uniform of the Confederacy, the small group of frontier allies waging war against the Mutes.

He'd piled a table high with electronic equipment, a computer, a generator, a couple of displays, and God knew what else. He stood over it, a headphone clasped to one ear, apparently absorbed in the displays. They showed schematics, trace scans, columns of digits and symbols.

He glanced in my direction without quite seeing me, pointed to a bottle of dark wine, produced a glass, and gestured for me to help myself. Then he smiled at something on one of the screens. He pulled the headset off one ear and dropped into a chair. "I'm Matt Olander," he said. "What the hell are you doing here?"

He was middle-aged, a thin blade of a man whose gray skin almost matched the color of the walls. "I don't think I understand the question," I said.

"Why didn't you leave with everybody else?" He watched me intently, and I guess he saw that I was puzzled. Then *he* started to look puzzled. "They took everybody out. You know that, right?"

"*Who?*" I demanded. My voice must have gone off the edge of the register. "*Who* took everybody *where?*"

He reacted as if it was a dumb question, and reached for the bottle. "I guess we couldn't expect to get one hundred percent. Where were you? In a mine somewhere? Out in the hills with no commlink?"

I told him and he sighed in a way that suggested I had committed an indiscretion. His hair was thin, and his features suggested more of the tradesman than the warrior. His voice turned soft. "What's your name?"

"Lee," I said. "Kindrel Lee."

"Well, Kindrel, we spent most of these two weeks evacuating Ilyanda. The last of them were sent up to the ships yesterday morning. Far as I know, you and I are all that's left." His eyes switched back to the monitors.

"Why?" I asked. I was feeling a mixture of relief and fear.

His expression wished me away. After a moment, he sat down at the computer. "I'll show you," he said.

One of the screens dissolved to a ring display. The figure eight infinity symbol, which was prominent on the flag, was at the center. An array of more than forty trace lights blinked along the outer circumference. "Ilyanda is at the center," he said. "The range runs out to a half billion kilometers. You're looking at a Mute fleet. Capital ships and battle cruisers." He took a deep breath and let it out slowly. "What's happening, Ms. Lee," he continued, "is that the Navy is about to blow hell out of the sons of bitches." His jaw tightened, and a splinter of light appeared in his eyes. "At last."

"It's been a long time coming," he said. "They've been beating hell out of us for three years. But today belongs to us." He raised his glass and finished the wine.

"I'm glad you were able to get people away," I said into the sudden stillness.

He smiled. "Sim wouldn't have had it any other way."

"I never thought the war would come here." Another blip appeared on the screen. "I don't understand it. Ilyanda's neutral. And I didn't think we were near the fighting."

"Kindrel, there are no neutrals in this war. You've just been letting others do your fighting for you." His voice contained an edge of contempt.

"Ilyanda's at peace!" I stared at him, into his eyes, expecting him to flinch. But I saw only annoyance. "Or at least it was. Anyhow, thanks for coming."

He looked away from me. "It's all right."

"They're only here," I said, "because *you* are, aren't they?"

"Yes."

"You've brought your war to us!"

He propped his chin on his fist and laughed at me. "*You're* judging *us*! You know, you people are really impossible. The only reason you're not dead or in chains is because we've been dying to give you a chance to ride around in your goddamn boat!"

"My God," I gasped, remembering the missing shuttle. "Is that why they never got here?"

"Who?"

"The shuttle that was supposed to be coming in."

"Oh." That infuriating grim reappeared. "Don't worry about it. It was never coming."

"You're wrong. I overheard some radio traffic shortly after midnight—"

"They were *never* coming. We've done everything we could to make this place, this entire world, appear normal."

"Why?" I asked.

"You have the consolation, Kindrel, of knowing we are about to turn the war around. The Mutes are finally going to get hurt." His eyes glowed.

"You *led* them here," I said.

"It wasn't hard." He got to his feet and looked through the window. "We led them here. We've led them into hell. They think Christopher Sim is on the space station. Or on the ground. And they want him *very* badly." His face was in shadow. "Sim has never had the fire power to fight this war. He's been trying to hold off an armada with a few dozen light frigates and one battle cruiser." Olander's face brightened. "But he's done a job on the bastards. Anyone else would have been overwhelmed right at the start. But Sim: Sometimes I wonder whether he's human." He turned back to me. "Maybe it would be best if you left," he said tonelessly.

I made no move to go. "Why here? Why Ilyanda?"

"We needed to pick a system where the population was small enough to be moved."

I smothered an obscenity. "I don't recall that we got to vote on this."

"I'm sorry," he whispered. "You have no idea at all what this is about, do you? A million people have died in this war so far. Millions more have been enslaved. The Mutes have burned Cormoral and the City on the Crag and Far Mordaigne. They've overrun a dozen systems, and the entire frontier is on the verge of collapse." He wiped the back of his hand across his mouth. "They don't like us very much, Kindrel. And I don't think they plan for any of us to be around when it's over."

That was a lie. "*We* started the war."

"That's easy to say. You don't know what was going on. But it doesn't matter now anyway. We're long past drawing fine lines. The killing won't stop until we've driven the bastards back where they came from." He switched one of the displays. Studied the screen. "They're closing on the Station now. A sizable chunk of their fleet is already within range. And more arriving all the time." He smiled, and I felt sorry for him. He'd been so caught up in the killing that he was enjoying himself.

"You said Sim doesn't have much firepower—"

"He doesn't."

"Then how—?"

A shadow crossed his face. "The Station's shields have gone up," he said. "No, there's nothing up there of ours except a couple of destroyers. They're automated, and the Station's abandoned." The blinking lights on the battle display were becoming brighter. And more numerous. "All they can see are the destroyers. And something they think is *Corsarius* in dock with its hull laid open. And the bastards are still keeping their distance. But it won't make any difference."

"*Corsarius*!" I said. "Sim's ship?"

"It's a big moment for them. They're thinking right now they're going to take them and end the resistance." He squinted at the graphics.

I was beginning to suspect it was time to take his advice and make for the wharf, get the *Meredith*, and head back to the southern hemisphere. Until the dust settled.

"The destroyers are opening up," he said. "But they won't even slow the Mutes down."

"Then why bother? What's going on?"

"We had to give them some opposition. Keep them from thinking too much."

"Olander," I asked, "if you have no ships up there, what's this all about? How does Sim expect to destroy anything?"

"He won't. But you and I will, Kindrel. You and I will inflict such a wound on the Mutes tonight that the sons of bitches will never forget."

Two monitors went blank. Stayed out a few seconds. Then the images returned, swirls of characters blinking frantically. He leaned forward and frowned. "The Station's taken a hit." He reached toward me, a friendly, soothing gesture, but I stayed away from him.

"And what are you and I going to do to them?" I asked.

"Kindrel, we are going to stop the sunrise."

"What?"

"We'll catch them all. Everything they've got here, everything out to a half-billion klicks, will be incinerated. Beyond that, if they see they can get a running start, they'll have a chance." He glanced toward the computer. A red lamp glowed on the keyboard. "We have an old Tyrolean freighter, loaded with antimatter. It's balanced in hyperspace, and it's waiting a command from me."

"To do what?"

His eyes slid shut, and I could no longer read his expression. "To materialize inside the sun." He hung each word in the still air. "We are going to insert it at the sun's core." A bead of sweat rolled down his chin. "The result, we think, will be—," he grinned, "—explosive."

I could almost have believed there was no world beyond that bar. We'd retreated into the dark, Olander and I and the monitors and the background music and the stone nymphs. All of us.

"A nova?" I asked. My voice must have been barely audible. "You're trying to induce a nova?"

"No. Not a true nova."

"But the effect—"

"—Will be the same." He drew his right hand across his lips. "It's a revolutionary technique. Involves some major breakthroughs in navigation. It isn't easy, you know, to maintain a relatively static position in hyperspace. The freighter has a tendency to drift." He tapped one of the keys, producing a display of technical data. He began an explanation. "Look at this." And, "Over here, though—." I could not begin to follow. I didn't care anyway about the details. He dropped into a monotone and started to talk about gamma rays and hydrogen atoms.

"Come on, Olander," I exploded, finally. "You can't expect me to believe that a guy sitting in a bar can blow up a sun!"

"I'm sorry." His eyes changed, and he looked startled, as though he'd just realized where he was. "You may be right," he said. "It hasn't been tried, so they really don't know. Too expensive to run a test."

I tried to imagine the sun bloating, expanding, blazing down on Point Edward, engulfing it, boiling the seas. It was Gage's city, where we'd explored narrow streets and old bookstores, and pursued each other across rainswept beaches and through candlelit pubs. And from where we'd first gone to sea. I'd never forgotten how it had looked the first time we'd come home, bright, and diamond-hard against the horizon. Home. Always it would be home.

And I watched Olander through eyes suddenly grown damp, perhaps conscious for the first time that I had come back with the intention to leave Ilyanda, but knowing now that I never would, would never wish to.

"Olander, they left *you* to do this?"

"No." He shook his head vigorously. "It was supposed to happen automatically when the Mutes got close. The trigger was tied in to sensors on the Station. But the Mutes have had some success at disrupting command and control functions. We couldn't be sure—"

"Then they *did* leave you."

"*No!* Sim would never have allowed it if he'd known. He has confidence in the system. Those of us who know a little more about such things do not. So I stayed. And disconnected it. And brought it down here with me."

"My God, and you're really going to do it?"

"It works out better this way. We can catch the bastards at the most opportune moment. You need somebody to make that judgment. Not a machine."

"Olander, you're talking about destroying a *world*."

"I'm talking about destroying a threat to human survival." His eyes found mine at last. The irises were blue, and I could see white all around their edges. "But I understand what you're saying. No one *wanted* this to happen. But we're driven to the wall. If we can't make this work, here, there may be no future for anyone."

I needed a moment to find my voice. "If the danger is so clear, where are Rimway and Toxicon? And Earth? A lot of people think the Mutes are open to negotiation." I was just talking now, my attention riveted to the computer keyboard, to the EXECUTE key, which was black and polished and longer than the others.

I pushed the laser down deeper in my pocket, trying to keep it concealed.

"Well," he continued, "what the hell. It doesn't matter anymore anyway. A lot of blood has been spilled, and I don't think anybody's much open to negotiation now. The only thing that does matter is that they'll kill all of us. If we allow it." He stared at the empty glass. Flung it into the dark. It shattered. "Ciao," he said.

I was thinking about the broad southern seas and the trackless forests that no one would ever penetrate and the enigmatic ruins. And the thousands of people to whom, like me, Ilyanda was home. Who would remember when it was gone? "What's the difference between you and the Mutes?"

"I know how you feel, Kindrel."

"You have no idea how I feel—."

"I know *exactly* how you feel. I was on Melisandra when the Mutes burned the City on the Crag. I watched them make an example of the Pelian worlds. Do you know what Cormoral looks like now? Nothing will live there for ten thousand years."

Somebody's chair, his, mine, I don't know, scraped the floor, and the sound echoed round the grotto.

"Cormoral and the Pelians were destroyed by their *enemies!*" I was enraged, frightened, resentful. Out of sight under the table, my fingers traced the outline of the weapon. "Has it occurred to you?" I asked, as reasonably as I could, "what's going to happen when they go home, and we go back to squabbling among ourselves?"

"I know," he said. "There's a lot of risk involved."

"*Risk?*" I pointed a trembling finger at the stack of equipment. "That thing is more dangerous than a half-dozen invasions. For God's sake, we'll survive the Mutes. We survived the ice ages and the nuclear age and the colonial wars and we will sure as hell take care of the Mutes if there's no other way.

"But that thing you have in front of you—. Matt, don't do this. Whatever you hope to accomplish, the price is too high."

I listened to him breathe. An old love song was running on the sound system. "I have no choice," he said in a dull monotone. He pointed at the display. "They're beginning to withdraw. That means they know the Station's empty, and they suspect either a diversion or a trap."

"You *do* have a choice!" I screamed at him.

"No." He folded his arms. "I do not."

I pulled the laser out of my pocket, raised it so he could see it, and pointed it at him.

He unfolded his arms and stared at the weapon. "You're really serious, aren't you?"

"Yes."

"Okay. Look, there's no way you can stop it." He stepped to one side, trying to get out of the line of fire. "But you're welcome to try."

It was a curious remark, and I played it again. *Welcome to try.* "If I interrupt the power supply," I said, "it'll trigger. Right?"

His face gave him away.

"Get well away from it." I waved him to one side. "We'll just sit here awhile."

He didn't move.

"Back off," I said.

"For God's sake, Kindrel." He held out his hands. "Don't do this."

"There's a living world here, Matt. And if that's not enough, there's a precedent to be set."

He took a step forward. Odd that a guy prepared to be subsumed in a nova would show fear in the face of a laser.

"Don't, Matt," I said. "I'll kill you if I have to."

The moment stretched out. "Please, Kindrel," he said at last.

So we remained, facing each other. He read my eyes, and the color drained from him.

The eastern sky was beginning to lighten.

A nerve quivered in his throat. "I should have left it alone," he said, measuring the distance to the keyboard.

Tears were running down my cheeks, and I could hear my voice loud and pleading as if it were someone else, someone outside. "Don't do it. Just sit still, Matt. Or—."

The entire world squeezed down to the pressure of the trigger against my right index finger. "You didn't *have* to stay," I told him. "It had nothing to do with heroics. You've been in the war too long, Matt. You hate too well."

He took another step, tentatively, gradually transferring his weight from one foot to the other, watching me, his eyes pleading.

"You were enjoying this, until I came by."

"No," he said. "That's not so."

"Sure it is." His muscles tensed. I saw what he was going to do and I shook my head no and whimpered and he told me to just put the gun down and I waited there looking at the little bead of light that had crept up to his throat.

When at last he moved, not toward the computer but toward me, he was far too slow and I killed him.

My first reaction was to get out of there, to leave the body where it had dropped and take the elevator down and run—

I wish to God I had.

The sun was on the horizon. A few clouds drifted in the east, and another cool autumn day began.

Matt Olander's body lay twisted beneath the table, blood seeping out through the hole in his throat. His chair lay on its side, and his jacket was open. A pistol, black and lethal and ready to hand, jutted from an inside holster.

I had never considered the possibility he might be armed. He could have killed me at any time.

What kind of men fight for this Christopher Sim?

This one would have burned Ilyanda, but he could not bring himself to take my life.

What kind of man? I have no answer to that question. Then or now.

I stood a long time over him, staring at him, and at the blinking transmitter, with its cold red eye, while the white lights fled toward the outer ring.

And a terrible fear crept through me: I could still carry out his intention, and I wondered whether I didn't owe it to him, to someone, to reach out and strike the blow they had prepared. But in the end I walked away from it, into the dawn.

The black ships that escaped at Ilyanda went on to take a heavy toll. For almost three more years, men and ships died. Christopher Sim continued to perform exploits that had already become legendary, his Dellacondans held on until Rimway and Earth intervened, and, in the heat of battle, the modern Confederacy was born.

The sun weapon itself was never heard from. Never used. Never mentioned. Whether, in the end, it wouldn't work, or Sim was unable to lure a large enough force again within range of a suitable target, I don't know.

For most, the war is now something remote, a subject for debate by historians, a thing of vivid memories only for the very old. The Mutes have long since retreated into their sullen worlds. Sim rests with his heroes and his secrets, lost off Rigel. And Ilyanda still entrances tourists with her misty seas, and researchers with her curious ruins.

I buried Olander outside the terminal, and used the same laser to cut his name and an epitaph into a nearby rock. There's a monument there now. But the rock remains. And the epitaph: *No Stranger to Valor.* When the Dellacondans found it they were puzzled.

The epitaph led to a tradition that Olander died defending Point Edward against the Ashiyyur, and for that *they* honored his gallantry by burying him and leaving the marker. Today, of course, he stands high in the Confederacy's pantheon.

And I: I hid when the Dellacondans came back to find out what had happened. And I spent three years in a city pursued by an army of ghosts which grew daily in number. All slain by my hand. And when the Ilyandans returned at the end of the war, I was waiting.

They chose not to believe me. It may have been politics. They may have preferred to forget. And so I am denied even the consolation of public judgment. There is none to damn me. Or to forgive.

I have no doubt I did the right thing.

Despite the carnage, and the fire, I was *right*.

In my more objective moments, in the daylight, I know that. But I know also that whoever reads this document, after my death, will understand that I need more than a correct philosophical stance.

For now, for me, in the dark if Ilyanda's hurtling moons, the war never ends.

KAMINSKY AT WAR

1.

The bride waited in the glow of the lanterns and lowered her eyes to the sheet that had been placed on the ground before her. Her husband stood still and straight, watching. The celebrants were gathered in a circle around the happy pair. They were long and spindly creatures, all eyes and husk and clicking jaws, with no sign of anything remotely resembling hair. They were the color of grass that had not gotten enough water.

They were Noks, a species mired in early twentieth century technology and endlessly at war with itself. They were the first offworld intelligence we had seen, and they'd helped shape the hands-off policy that was quickly formulated as the Barrin-Rhys Protocol, and eventually simply *the* Protocol.

Leave them alone.

Virtually everybody took an unsympathetic attitude toward them. I thought it was the faces that really did the damage. The Noks did not have flexible features. Nature had given them unmoving masks that always looked the same, regardless of whether their owners were partying or running for their lives. No emotion ever showed.

Except in the eyes.

The eyes were round disks, large by human standards, protected by nictitating membranes. The lenses, usually dark, floated in a green-tinted aqueous humor. They contracted or widened, and changed colors, according to the emotions of the moment. The eyes of the wedding guests were uniformly blue. At peace.

The guests all carried bells. As was the local custom, they received a signal from the bride's father, and raised their eyes to the sky, pledging eternal friendship to the happy couple. Then they rang the bells. It was a soft jangling on the night breeze, an expression of the connubial pleasures that lay ahead. A warm wind blew in off the ocean, and the trees sighed in harmony with the celebration.

The bride, of course, was naked, save for a ceremonial cord hung loosely at her waist. Slim and polished and graceful, she awaited the climax of the ceremony. Noks were not mammals, and not at all close to humans, yet there was something in the way she stood, in her physical presence, that stirred me. Odd how that happened. It wasn't the first time.

I was wearing a lightbender, and was consequently invisible to the Noks, except for my eyes. If the system blanked out your eyes, you wouldn't be able to see. So I had to be careful.

I took the bride's picture. Angled around and got the groom, backed off and caught the two sets of parents. I recorded the scene as, one by one, the bells fell silent. When the last tinkling had died away, the pair strode toward each other and embraced. In the time-worn tradition, he released the cord around her waist. She removed his ceremonial shirt, and then tugged at something on his leggings and they fell away.

I took more pictures.

Noks are all beak and shell. You look at them and what you see is straight-ahead, strictly business, don't get in the way. Nevertheless, I *knew* what she was feeling. I could see pure joy in her eyes, and in her suppleness. I told myself maybe it was just empathy, that I was projecting on her precisely the reactions I'd expect to see had she been a woman.

She was a beautiful creature. When her groom closed on her, she reacted with grace and dignity, not easy when you're sprawled on a sheet in front of a hundred witnesses. But it was the ceremonial first act, consummating the marriage, as people liked to say at home.

The bride's name, as close as it could be reproduced in English, was Trill. I watched them, and I'll admit I was embarrassed by my own rising heartbeat. Couldn't help it. It was erotic stuff, and it didn't matter they weren't human. At the time I wouldn't have admitted it to anyone. Thought it was a perversion. I've found out since it's a common reaction. So take it for what it's worth.

I was still taking pictures when the raiders stormed out of the woods.

My name's Arthur Kaminsky, and I'm an anthropologist. Although the term doesn't really extend to everything we do nowadays.

There'd never been a time that I hadn't had things my own way. I'd been born, if not precisely into wealth, then certainly into comfortable surroundings. I'd gone to the best schools, won a scholarship to Oxford where I performed, if not brilliantly, at least well enough to convince my father I was destined for something other than real estate. After I'd gotten my doctorate, I decided the frontiers of my specialty lay with the study, not simply of humans, but of intelligent species of whatever type we might encounter. My father rolled his eyes when I told him what I wanted to do, and my mother said she supposed it was my decision. Had it not been for a fortuitous circumstance, I would probably never have been selected for one of the few positions available to do offworld field work. I was only in my twenties, had no track record, and every anthropologist on the planet was pushing to get assigned.

The fortuitous circumstance was my linguistic ability, and especially the fact that I learned to speak three major Nok languages, which required vocal capabilities that were beyond the normal human larynx. Nobody could do it like me. Other than the AI's.

Still, the people who signed me on were nervous. They put me through a longer training period than was standard. And I'd been on site more than six months before the director allowed me to do a solo mission. And that came with a lot of advice. Be careful. Take no chances. Keep the lightbender activated at all times so they can't see you. Stay in touch with Cathie. If you start to feel ill, or anything like that, let us know right away and get back to the lander.

Cathie was Catherine Ardahl, the mission's communication officer. She had dark hair and dark eyes and a smile that melted me into my socks. I'd never been a big hit with women, so I was relentlessly shy around her. In those early months, I was as invisible to her as if I'd been wearing a lightbender.

Watching the Nok bride, before the raiders arrived, I'd thought of her.

When the raiders came out of the woods, I needed a minute to figure out what was happening. I still didn't know enough about local customs. Party crashers, maybe? A surprise visit by distant relatives? Even the first shots might have been noisemakers of some sort. Then the screams started, and the wedding guests scattered. Some went down as bullets tore into them and lay writhing on the yellow-tinted grass and the stone walkways. Others got into the forest and a few made it into the house.

The raiders were on foot, firing rifles and pistols indiscriminately. Killing technology was primitive, for the most part at a World War I level, although Noks had no heavier-than-air capability. I wasted no time scrambling out of the way. Got behind a tree. Two of the wedding guests, fleeing in panic, crashed screaming into me and knocked me flat. (There are hazards when nobody can see you.) Someone inside the house began to return fire.

The raid lasted, altogether, about seven minutes. No one was spared. The raiders moved among the dead and dying, shooting the wounded. Then they began rounding up survivors and herding them into a central area. I saw Trill lying beside a bench, with the *sateen*—her blood equivalent—leaking out of her shoulder. She was down near the trees, and I knelt beside her and lifted her in my arms and tried to stop the bleeding. She cried out and one of the raiders heard her and started toward us.

They were in uniform, dark green loose-fitting single-piece outfits. Like pajamas.

"Don't let them find me," she said. She was so terrified she never noticed what held her.

"I won't."

The lids had squeezed down over her eyes. There wasn't much I could do. My stomach fluttered. I'd never witnessed serious violence. During my early months on Nok, they'd kept me away from the wars. In fact, everybody stayed away from the combat areas. They were dangerous. "Try not to make any noise," I whispered. I carried her to the edge of the trees. Put her down behind a bush. But they were right behind us. One of them stopped, moved the shrubbery aside with the barrel of his rifle. Advanced a few steps. Listened.

I reached into a pocket of my vest and pulled out my tensor. It was designed to disable the nervous systems of the local wildlife. But it would also work on the Noks themselves.

Trill groaned softly.

The raider heard her.

"Help me," she whispered, her voice faint. "Help me."

He had a light, and it picked her out. He raised a rifle and pointed it at her. I could simply have stood aside. Let it happen. It was in fact what the regulations required.

But I couldn't do it. I pulled the trigger on the son of a bitch. He sighed and went down, and in that moment I wished I had something lethal. It even crossed my mind to take his rifle and put a bullet in his brain.

✹

The raiders collected their comrade. (I'd moved Trill by then.) They carried him off, making that odd whistling sound that was the Nok idea of displaying regret. Then they were gone.

Trill never woke. She made occasional gasping sounds. But there were no more cries of pain. And after awhile she grew still.

In the distance, I heard more gunfire.

"*Art.*" The voice on the commlink startled me. It was the boss. Paul McCarver. Northeastern United States accent. Classic Yankee.

"Hello, Paul."

"*We've picked up sporadic shooting in your area. Just wanted to check. You're okay?*"

"Yes," I said. "I'm good."

"*What's happening? Can you tell?*"

"They hit a wedding party. It looks as if they killed everybody."

"*Yeah. That sounds like the way they operate. Okay. Be careful. Maybe you better come back.*"

"I'm okay. I'll be back in a bit."

✹

I retreated to the lander, which lay within its own lightbender field in a forest clearing about a kilometer off the road. I'd been hungry when the wedding started, but I had no appetite when I got back to it. I kept seeing the cool green eyes of the killers, saw them striding through the celebration. Enjoying the work.

I should mention that I'm not big on confrontation. Never was. I do compromise real well. And I was always willing to overlook stuff. But the raid on the wedding had entailed a level of disagreeableness and lack of reason that made me want to kill someone. I mean, what was the point of sending a military strike force—that's what they were—against a wedding party?

"George," I said to the lander AI as I buckled in, "lift off. Let's see what else they did."

In the west, a kilometer away, there was a glow in the sky. That would be *Itiri*, the town which had probably been home to most of the celebrants. Population about eleven hundred. No military targets. I'd been there all day, taking pictures, observing, enjoying myself.

"Very good, Dr. Kaminsky," said George. *"After we look around, will we be going back into orbit?"*

I thought about it. I had what I'd come for, the record of the wedding. Even if it hadn't turned out exactly as planned, the mission was complete. Still, I wanted to make somebody pay for what I'd just seen. "George, where do you think the raiders came from?"

"Had to be by sea, I suspect. I would have detected a dirigible."

Nok industrialization had risen and fallen several times. We now know they'd put forty thousand years of civilizations and dark ages on the scoreboard before anybody started laying bricks in Sumer. They had all but exhausted their fossil fuels even though their original supply had been almost triple the terrestrial stores. The Noks seemed incapable of establishing political stability. One of the objectives I'd set for myself was to figure out why. With few exceptions, the only gas-powered vehicles operating on Nok belonged to the various dictators and their military and political establishments, and the police. Everybody else walked. Or used beasts of burden.

The engines came on. There was no sound, only a slight vibration in the chair. Most of my weight, and that of the spacecraft, vanished. It began to rise, over the trees into a clear summer sky.

Itiri was ablaze.

A narrow winding road ran parallel to the sea. The raiders moved along it, a happy group, their weapons slung casually over their shoulders. More mob than military unit. They looked not at all worried about a counterattack. Two kilometers ahead, three small warships waited at anchor in a harbor. The ships were steam-driven ironclads. They showed no lights. "What can you tell me about them, George?"

"They are all of the same type. Approximately 2500 tons, six guns able to fire four-inch shells. Accuracy doubtful beyond a thousand meters."

"Automatic weapons?"

"None. They haven't been developed yet."

"Not at all?"

"They had them a few thousand years ago, most recently during the Turullian Age. But they lost the technology."

"Doesn't seem as if it would be that hard to figure out. They have rifles."

George blipped. It was his equivalent of shrugging his shoulders.

"What about sensors or radar? Anything like that?"

"They have no tracking devices other than their eyes. And telescopes."

"They do have telescopes."

"Yes. Most certainly."

We overtook the raiders, passed above them, and arced out over the beach. Several small boats lay in the wet sand, apparently awaiting the arrival of the land force.

"George," I said, "let's take a look at the ships."

We glided out into the harbor.

"The one in the middle," I told him. Six of one, half a dozen of the other. We loped in, moved slowly over masts and gun turrets, and stopped directly over the bridge.

The guns were primitive, but that wouldn't matter if one of the shells hit us. The only Noks I could see were manning the rails with rifles.

I could make out several figures on the bridge, in the glow of instrument lights. I thought about the wedding guests, and Trill, *help me*, and I wished I had a few bombs.

"What's that, Dr. Kaminsky? I'm sorry. I didn't hear you."

I didn't realize I'd said anything. "Nothing," I said. "Never mind."

I wanted a way to pay them back in their own coin. While I watched, the raiders arrived on the beach, scattered across the sand, and headed for the boats. They moved with a jaunty precision that implied they were happy with the evening's slaughter. Still taking no precautions for their own safety. And you might be thinking that nonverbal cues are deceptive even among humans of different cultures, and what did I know about Noks. But it was my specialty. "George," I said, "get us over to the beach and take us down to ground level."

"That's not advisable, Doctor."

"Do it anyway."

"If you insist. But it is dangerous. Someone might walk into us before we can react."

"Just do it."

There were seven boats. They were made of wood, and each was designed to accommodate about twenty. The raiders surrounded each boat and began pushing it into the surf. When it started to float, they jumped aboard. I watched as, one by one, they set out for the ships, which were about a kilometer away. They were spreading out, making for different vessels.

The lander was at ground level, the treads a half-meter above the sand. "Okay," I said. "George, I want you to keep us right at this altitude."

"*And—?*"

"We're going to take out the boats."

"*Ram them?*" He sounded horrified.

"Can we do it without damaging the lander?"

"*I can't guarantee that.*"

"Give me the odds."

"*There are too many variables, Doctor.*"

"The odds, George."

"*Eighty-eight percent.*"

"Eighty-eight percent what? That we come away undamaged?"

"*That we come away relatively undamaged. Still able to make orbit.*"

"Okay. Let's do it. Start with that one over there."

"*Sir, I am required to inform you that you will be in violation of the Protocol.*"

"Do it anyway." A fifth boat launched.

"*I am sorry, Doctor. But to override, you will have to get authority from the director.*"

There was a way to disable the AI, and if I could do that I thought I knew enough about the controls to be able to get the job done manually. "George."

"*Yes, Doctor.*" The rest of the boats were into the waves.

"How do I disable you?"

"*I'm afraid, under the circumstances, it would be best if that information were withheld.*"

Damn. I studied the control panel. It was an array of switches, illuminated gauges, presspads, levers, warning lamps. There was a retractable yoke that could be used for manual operation. But I saw nothing marked *Shut off AI.*

"Let me out," I said finally. "Open up."

"*Doctor, you sure you won't hurt yourself?*"

"No, I'll be fine."

I climbed through the airlock and stepped down onto the sand. It was hard and crackly underfoot, like the sand on a thousand beaches at home. The ships and boats showed no light. And I no longer heard voices over the roar of the ocean. But I could see them, the ships, and the raiding party. I watched the boats close with the vessels. Saw rope ladders cast over the side.

The Noks scrambled up the lines. They were far more agile than human beings. Then they hauled up the boats. I watched until the last of the raiders were aboard, and the boats had been stowed. There were belches of smoke from the three vessels, and they turned and began to move out of the harbor.

I walked down to the sea, until the tide lapped at my feet.

Help me.

✺

"Where to, Doctor?" asked the AI.

"Orbit. Get us to the *Sheldrake*, George." I threw my head back in the seat and tried to shut out the images of the victims. *"Very good, sir."* We lifted off the beach, and began to accelerate. *"I know this has been hard on you."*

"Just take us home, George." I wasn't sure whether I was talking about the *Sheldrake*. Or Toronto.

2.

Nok was a laboratory for anyone interested in the rise and fall of civilizations. With such a long history, and the cycles of prosperity and collapse, it was possible to draw a wide range of conclusions about the impact of technology, climate, religion, and economics on cultural development. And on the tendency of civilizations to overextend. It was, in fact, the thing they did again and again. And always with the same catastrophic results. Fortunately, no one on Nok had ever discovered how to split the atom, so the land, at least, was still habitable.

Were they more barbaric than humans? I thought about it while the lander passed through a thunderstorm. At the present time, they certainly were. But we had our own bloodsoaked history, didn't we? I knew of nothing in the Nok archives to rival the Holocaust or the great Communist purges or the African massacres of the twentieth century.

I was still seething when we arrived in orbit. It wasn't as if I didn't know what Nok was before I'd come. But actually *seeing* these creatures murder one another had been something for which I really hadn't been prepared.

When we caught up with the *Sheldrake*, McCarver was waiting for me, and I could see he was genuinely worried. "You all right, Art?" he asked. "You look a little bloodshot."

I was wiped out. I needed a shower and a night's sleep. And something to calm me down. "Answer a question for me, Paul," I said.

"Sure. Go ahead."

"We've been here how long now?"

"Forty years. Give or take."

"And we've never lifted a finger. About the killing."

McCarver was a diminutive guy. He was the only male on the mission who had to look up to me. He was thin, not the sort of person you'd expect to find out here. Had I met him socially, I'd have pegged him strictly as a classroom guy, or somebody doing lab research.

But he was the director. McCarver had only to walk into a room to bring everyone to attention. He wasn't the most brilliant of the researchers on the Nok team. He admitted that himself. But they all respected him. We were in the main deck conference room. McCarver was nodding, as if he'd been bothered by the same issue. "Art," he said, "I can guess what you went through today. I've seen it myself. They're savages. They have a lot of our capabilities, and sometimes they've done pretty well for themselves. But in the current era, they're savages, and we have to accept that."

"Why?"

McCarver looked past me, at a distant place. "Because we're not missionaries. Because we can't convert an entire global population to the rule of reason. Because even if we could, we probably shouldn't."

"Why is that, Paul?" I knew why, of course, but I wanted to force McCarver to say it. Maybe he'd come to understand how bloodless that view was.

"You know as well as I do, Art. If the Noks even find out we're here, they'll become dependent on us and they'll never develop properly."

"They haven't developed anyway."

"It's not our call, Art." He managed a smile. "Anybody who got involved down there, we'd have to put on the next flight home." Our eyes locked. His were dark and intense and bottomless. "Wouldn't want to do that."

"I took one of them down," I said.

"One of *who*?"

"The raiders. He was going to kill one of the people at the wedding."

"They're not *people*, Art." His voice was soft. But there was no give.

"He was trying to kill the bride."

"Who else knows?"

"Nobody."

"Keep it that way."

"Okay."

"Forget it happened. Technically, it puts you in violation of the rules. Could end your stay here. Maybe your career."

"It's happened with other people—."

"I know. And I understand *why* it happens. You're human, Art. You watch some of the things that go on here, and you know you can step in, save one of them. But you're putting your career on the line. Don't let it happen again."

And by the way, since you asked, the bride didn't survive. "I don't think I can promise that, Paul."

McCarver nodded. Okay. That's your position. "You don't leave me any choice, Art." He went over and got some coffee. One for him and one for me. He brought them back and sat down and put cream in his. The whole time he managed to look distressed. And I suppose the truth was he *was* unhappy. "I'll have to ask you to stay on board until you're able to comply with the policy. The last thing we need is a lone gun running around down there. You let me know when you can give me your word, and I'll take it from there."

I spent the evening in the archives. During the forty-two years since the *Valoire* discovered the Noks, hundreds of researchers had been here, and had walked unseen among the natives. They'd studied Nok mores and traditions, political and religious concepts, their literature, their family structure, and they'd begun to construct theories detailing what kind of behaviors were purely cultural, and what kind would be found to be characteristic of any intelligent species. It was a field that, because so few functioning cultures had been found—to date, only three—was still wide open to speculation.

I sat watching vid records. I was a silent witness at funeral services, at beach parties, at celebrations of various kinds, at their courting procedures. I watched them work, watched them play on the beach, watched them prepare food.

I took a look at troops in combat, though there wasn't much of that in the archive, probably because getting the footage entailed a degree of risk. It was also the case that troops seldom fought other troops. And for the same reason. The various Nok militaries preferred knocking over villages to taking on armed opponents. It was a style of war-making that appeared to be a recent development.

I watched from a lander as dirigibles dropped their bombs. There weren't many pictures of the effect of the weapons, which was to say nobody had been on the ground getting shots of Noks with missing limbs, or with massive burns. Mostly, it was strictly a light show. You drifted above the attack site, seeing the flashes, hearing the distant rumble moments later. And it all seemed very precise. And even, in its own strange way, beautiful.

◉

"Paul's right," Cathie told me. "We can't get involved in all that. I don't think it's a problem if you just step in and stop one of them from getting killed. Just, if it happens, don't put it in the report. Better yet, don't even mention it." She looked puzzled. "Why would a military force raid a wedding party?"

"They don't operate the way we do."

"Explain." At that point, Cathie had been there only a few weeks.

We were sitting in the common room. There were maybe half a dozen others present, arguing about the evolution of Nok's four major religious systems. We were off to one side, drinking coffee. "They don't think in terms of strategy and tactics. They go after the easy targets instead. Places where they can kill a maximum number of victims with minimum risk. The idea is presumably that after a while the other side gets discouraged and gives up. Except that it never happens."

"Why not?"

"Don't know. Maybe because attacks like the one on the wedding party get everybody angry and they just fight harder. You get lots of flag-waving, patriotism, falling in behind the head guy.

"The balance of power shifts constantly. Seventeen nations are caught up in the current war. But it's hard to sort out the sides. There seems to be more than two. It changes. Somebody goes down, and they rearrange the allies to make sure nobody gets too strong. It's right out of George Orwell."

"It's crazy," she said.

"I know. It's the political system. The leaders aren't responsive to the wedding parties. They're all dictators, and I doubt they care much about anything other than staying in power. And the killing just goes on and on."

She looked unhappy. Worried. "So what are you going to do?"

Ordinarily, having a woman like Cathie Ardahl so close would have completely absorbed me. But not that night. "I don't know," I said. "We're not going to look very good in the history books. Standing by and watching all this happen."

I couldn't be sure but I caught a glimpse of something in her eyes. Respect, maybe. Admiration. Whatever it was, she was taking me seriously. "Art," she said, "you're not the first here to go through this. You have to divorce yourself from it. Think of the Noks as a species to be studied."

"I know."

"Nothing more than that."

I wondered whether things would change if the people who made and enforced the policy had an opportunity to get a good look at the carnage. Paul and Cathie and the others, sitting in landers or in the VR chamber, saw only the light shows. And the statistics. Estimates of how many killed in a given attack. How many total casualties. They didn't *experience* any of it. I couldn't be sure, of course, but I suspected my colleagues made it a point to avoid areas where there might be incursions. Or raids. God knew, it was the way *I* felt. Who needs all that unpleasantness? I'd thought the little coastal village with its bright lights and its upcoming wedding would be safe enough.

I didn't like the idea that eventually there'd be a change in policy, that we'd adopt a more humane attitude, and everybody would wonder how people like me could have just sat and let it all happen.

I didn't know it then, but I learned later that, over the years, various directors had suggested intervention. But the requests had always come back with the same reply. The Academy would look into it. For the moment, the Protocol would be respected. And it went on being respected. Nothing ever changed.

"How would you suggest we intervene?" Paul's voice. I hadn't seen him come in. "Do you think they'd listen to us if we told them to stop?"

"I don't know," I said. "We've never tried. How do we know what might happen?"

When I was alone, I brought up the operational instructions for the 44 lander, the one we used. I looked up its range, read about its gravity index, saw what I had to do to disable the AI. And I studied the instructions for emergency situations. How to pilot the craft, how to land, how to manage its mass, how to turn left and right, how to descend, how to operate the lightbender.

In the morning I hijacked a lander.

It wasn't hard. I just got some sandwiches and soup out of the kitchen, checked out a laser and a tensor, and told the ship's AI I needed a lander. It apparently had never occurred to McCarver that anyone would disregard specific instructions, so he hadn't bothered to lock me out of the flight lists.

The result was that within an hour of grabbing the extra food, I was on my way groundside.

"*Where are we going, Dr. Kaminsky?*" asked George.

Nok's class-G sun floated just above the rim of the planet, painting the clouds gold. Below us, an ocean extended to the horizon. "Night side," I said. "Engage lightbender."

"*Engaged. Anywhere in particular?*"

"No. Just get me someplace where it's dark."

3.

Nok had anywhere from four to nine continents, depending on how you choose to define the term. Seven of the nine were caught up in the war. The conflict itself was so confusing that it appeared allies in one place were fighting each other elsewhere. Armies seemed to be on unopposed rampages across the globe.

The wedding party had taken place on an island a few kilometers offshore one of the smaller land masses. It was in the southern temperate region. I told George to pass over it. There was smoke still in the air. The harbor in which the three ships had waited sparkled in a rising sun. Broad beaches swept away on both sides.

Nok was a beautiful world, as all living worlds are.

We continued west, outrunning the sun, and soon we were soaring through starlit clouds. I began to see lights. Scattered across the land masses.

Some were constant and, if I was willing to give sway to my imagination, seemed arranged in patterns. Others, usually in more remote locations, flickered and burned.

"*Fires,*" said George.

The dictators held each other's populations hostage. It was almost a kind of sport. You kill some of mine, I'll take out some of yours. Everybody goes home happy.

On a dark peninsula, we found an inferno. An entire city, and surrounding woodland, were ablaze. "*This area has undergone a dry spell,*" said
George. "*It wouldn't have taken much to start this.*"

Ahead and below, moving away from the conflagration, lights bobbed
among the clouds.

"*Aircraft.*" George put an image on screen. Big, lumbering dirigibles.
The Noks had no heavier-than-air vehicles, hence nothing in the way of a
fighter. They didn't have much ground artillery, either. The Noks preferred
offensive weapons; they didn't play much defense. This made places like
South Titusville an attractive target for bombers, as opposed to national
capitals, or fleets of warships.

"How many, George?"

"*Four. Class YK.*"

The class designation meant nothing to me. "Let's get closer."

"*Are you working on a new project, Dr. Kaminsky?*" He was trying to
sound as if he hadn't guessed what I intended.

"No. Just curious about the bombers." One began to take shape dead
ahead. Lights gleamed along its flanks and outlined the tail. He picked
out horizontal and vertical fins, and the rudder. And the gondola, slung
beneath the gasbag. "Hydrogen?" I asked.

"*Helium,*" said George.

I got a sense of its size as we pulled alongside the tail. It was immense.
"George," I said. "Open the hatch."

"*Doctor Kaminsky, may I ask why? Opening a hatch in flight is hazardous.*"

"I want to get a better look."

"*The viewports are adequate.*"

"Just do it, George."

"*I have no choice but to decline, sir.*"

"Do it. Or I'll disable you and do it myself."

The portside lights of the dirigible began to slip past. Damned arrogant
sons of bitches were so careful to keep themselves out of harm's way, they didn't
even have to turn off their lights. "*You are not qualified to pilot the lander.*"

"I've read the instructions." I knew how that sounded, and waited for
the AI to laugh.

"*Don't try it. It's not as easy as it looks.*"

It didn't look easy.

The AI control was located on the pilot's left, under the board. You
reached down, got hold of a handle, and twisted it. A panel opened, and
there it was. On/off.

I grabbed hold of the handle. "George, you sure?"

"Why, Doctor? Why are you doing this? What can you possibly hope to accomplish?"

"I'm doing it because these sons of bitches run loose all over the planet. They kill arbitrarily and they don't give a damn. It's a joke. Maybe if they had to pay a price, things would be different."

"Do you have any idea how you sound?"

"I don't much care how I sound."

"Do I have to remind you, Doctor, that you're only one man? This is a global conflagration. It's been going on for a long time. For decades. Do you really think you can do anything constructive?"

"It's *not* a war, damn it. It's wholesale slaughter and it goes on and on and nobody cares. Except the people who do the dying."

"They are not people, Art." He said it so softly that I barely heard him. It was the first time the AI had used my first name.

"Good-by, George."

"Wait. What are you going to do when you shut me down? You can't attack the thing. We're not armed."

"I have a laser."

"A hand laser, obviously."

"Of course."

"You'll get us both killed."

That was an odd remark. AI's were theoretically not self-aware. Well, I'd think about it later. I switched him off. The autopilot took over and continued course and speed. I had some trouble extracting the yoke, but we held steady until I had it clear and locked in place. But as soon as I took over, we went into a dive. I was holding the yoke too far forward. So I pulled back and the spacecraft leveled off.

Okay. Pull on it and climb. Push right and go right. Leave the thrust alone. It wasn't all that hard.

Nok's atmosphere was similar to Earth's. And, as had been the case elsewhere, local microbes showed no interest in attacking offworld life forms. I opened up with impunity, both airlock hatches, and the wind howled through the cabin, but I could see out into the night sky. I'd gone past my intended target and didn't want to try slowing down or turning around, but it didn't matter. Another dirigible lay directly ahead.

Its propellers spun complacently. There was a symbol on the hull. A national logo, a circle divided equally in three parts, green, white, and yellow. It looked like the old peace symbol.

I let go of the yoke, and the spacecraft veered and dipped.

Okay. I'd known I couldn't do that but it seemed worth trying. I'd have to manage everything without getting out of my seat. Across the void between the airlock and the dirigible, the night was still. I drew alongside the gondola. Could see movement inside. I was even able to make out a Nok with a telescope. For a moment I thought he was watching me, but of course the lander and I were invisible. Or were we? The hatch was open. Could the interior of the vehicle be seen from outside? I had no idea.

The telescope was pointed at me.

I drew the laser out of a vest pocket and activated it. The mode lamp blinked on, ready to go, and I aimed the thing. Be careful. Don't hit the airlock. It was hard to concentrate on holding the weapon steady and doing the same thing with the lander. Every time I took my attention off the yoke we wobbled or sank or veered in one direction or another. Finally I switched the AI back on. "George? You there?"

"*Yes, Doctor.*" We were back on formal terms.

"Take over. Keep us headed straight ahead."

No answer.

I lifted my hands from the yoke. We stayed on course. Okay. I squinted through the sight, through the airlock, and took aim at the peace symbol. Right in the middle of the dirigible. Can't miss.

I pressed the pad and watched the red beam blink on. It touched the gasbag. I couldn't see well enough in the dark to judge the effect, but almost immediately one of the navigation lights went out.

"*You understand,*" said George, "*that they will send you home.*"

"Just keep us steady."

"*There's even a chance of criminal prosecution.*" He began to recite the laws I was in the act of breaking. "*Your career is over.*"

No visible effect yet on the dirigible, other than the missing light. I kept it on. Moved the beam slowly forward.

"*I recommend we return immediately to the Sheldrake, and you claim mental stress based on your experience yesterday on the ground. It probably won't save your career, but it should be sufficient to prevent prosecution.*"

"You're pulling away."

"*Yes. I'm programed to keep you out of trouble. To the best of my ability.*"

Our angle with the dirigible was changing and I had to shut the laser down. "George," I said, "you're supposed to be intelligent."

"*That's an illusion, Doctor. As you well know. I am a programmed system. I am not a sentient entity.*"

We were getting still farther away. Behind us I saw a wisp of smoke. The dirigible was beginning to sag. Dropping out of formation.

"George, put us back or I'll shut you down again."

No response. A few cockpit lamps began blinking. George was unsure what to do. Then he slowed down, angled right, and laid us back alongside the damaged airship.

It was losing altitude. I raised a fist in a silent gesture and wondered when I'd last felt so good. I gave the dirigible another burst and took out the portside propellor. Then we moved forward along the bow and shot that up as well.

It was a great feeling.

The dirigible staggered and began to heel over.

"*Congratulations, Doctor,*" said George.

"I didn't think you guys could be sarcastic."

"*I do not take offense.*"

"I'm glad to hear it. There's another one ahead on the left. Take us alongside."

"*Kaminsky, what the hell do you think you're doing?*" McCarver's voice exploded from the commlink.

"George." I tried to sound betrayed. "Did you tell him?"

"*Of course. I had no choice, Doctor.*"

"*Kaminsky, answer up.*" There were voices in the background. McCarver told somebody to please shut up.

I opened a channel. "I'm here, Paul."

"*What's going on out there? You didn't really do what George says, did you?*"

Damn. I wanted to tell him I wished he could see what I had seen. That he had an obligation to take action. I'd have done that with someone less intimidating. "Truth is, Paul, I'm watching one of them go down now, and I don't know that I've ever felt better about anything. The sons of bitches got exactly—."

He broke in with a string of expletives. It was the first time I'd heard him use profane language. Then: "*I don't much care how you feel, Art. Turn the damned thing around and come back. Now.*"

I stared out at the dirigible running directly ahead. George was taking us across the tail, putting us on her left side so I could get a clear shot. "I can't do that, Paul."

"*Then I'll do it for you. George, are you listening?*"

"*Yes, I am, Dr. McCarver.*"

"*Bring the lander back.*"

I put my hand on the disable switch. "He's not in a position to comply, Paul."

"*Why not?*"

"He's already shut me down once, Doctor."

"*Damn it, Art. You want to get yourself killed?*"

We drew alongside the tail. We were down a bit, halfway between the horizontal fin and the lower vertical fin. I aimed at the rudder. "*I have to go, Paul. I'll talk to you later.*"

McCarver hesitated, trying to control his rage. While he did, I broke the link and burned the rudder. Sizzle. Instant results. The dirigible began to lose its heading. I fired again, took off the lower vertical. Then I cut a hole in the gasbag and it started down.

"*They're talking to one another,*" said George.

"Let's hear it."

"*—Lost buoyancy…Altitude—.*"

"*—Somebody out there—.*"

"*What happened to you?*"

"*—Not sure—. Flying wheel—.*"

"*—Say again—.*"

"*—No gasbag—.*"

I took out a third airship and then switched over to the fleet's frequency. "The Messenger of the Almighty is among you," I said. "Stop the killing." I would have preferred to use maybe *Avenger*. Or *Destroyer*. But I couldn't think of equivalent terms.

"*Please repeat,*" came the response. "*Who is this?*"

"The Messenger of the Almighty."

"*The Almighty needs a radio? Who are you?*"

"Stop the killing," I said.

No answer.

Something exploded in the third dirigible. Fire broke out amidships.

I'd hit something sensitive. It began to drop more quickly and finally went fluttering into the dark. Nobody was going to survive that one, and I felt guilty.

"*Doesn't matter, does it?*" said George. "*They're just as dead. Their blood is on your hands.*"

"They don't have blood."

"*Humans are only literal when they're ashamed of something.*"

I let the other two go. Take the message back, you bastards. Tell your bosses the free ride is over. There's a wild card in the deck now.

"*You're quite melodramatic,*" said George.

"I *feel* melodramatic."

"*Good. Can we return now to the* Sheldrake?"

"No," I said. "We're going to look around some more."

4.

Several hundred Noks had been lined up in the city square, herded together like animals. They were of all ages and both sexes. Females carried infants; toddlers clutched the hands of relatives, unaware what was happening; one elderly Nok was on crutches.

I moved among them, and among the invading soldiers, wearing the lightbender, recording everything. You could see the terror in the victims' eyes, which had turned gold. And in the way they held the young ones. In the desperation of the males. Here and there, a soldier tried to help, whispered a word of commiseration. It will be quick. Occasionally they were repaid by a kick, sometimes by the victims, once or twice by their officers.

When they'd finished a sweep of the houses, the troops had lined up about eight hundred of the occupants. The officers reported results to the commander. So many fled into the woods. Several killed resisting. Three soldiers dead. Eight injured.

The Noks all looked alike. I knew male from female, tall from short. The marks of age were easy enough to make out. But distinguishing individuals, for a human, was impossible.

The square was surrounded by wooden buildings. Several were burning, providing a hellish backlight. There were a few trees in the square, some benches, and a playground. A library stood on one side of the street. They'd touched that off too.

I got close-ups of mothers and their kids, of Noks dragged out of their homes, others beaten to their knees for objecting to being killed. I relayed everything live to the *Sheldrake*. Take a look at this, McCarver. This is what you're tolerating. What happened to the reputation of that other guy who stood by and washed his hands of murder?

The commander barked an order, and the soldiers faced their prisoners. Some of the victims were wailing, pleading for their lives, and the lives of their children.

It was enough. I put the imager away, took out the laser and aimed it at the commander.

"Art." George's voice. "*At least use the tensor. Don't kill him.*"

I was too far away for the tensor. Anyhow, it was hard to feel sympathy. I pulled the trigger and the narrow red beam blinked on. The Nok commander had raised one arm, ready to give the order to fire. The beam took the arm off.

He screamed and went to his knees. And I put him away.

Two or three of his junior officers rushed to his assistance. I hit one of those, too. Confusion broke out. Soldiers swung their rifles toward the empty windows of the buildings overlooking the square. An officer, who might have seen the laser, looked my way and started jabbering to one of his comrades.

I switched to the tensor and took him out.

"*I'll have to report this, you know,*" said the AI.

That was the last thing I cared about at the moment. "Stop whining, George." Two or three were coming my way. One fired off a shot from a sidearm and the bullet slammed into a bench. I hit the deck.

"*You're going to get yourself killed.*"

Two or three more shots came a bit too close.

Picking them off was easy. Duck soup. They kept coming and pretty soon I had a pile spread out in front of me. Somebody lobbed a bomb but they had no idea where I was.

Nevertheless, I moved. Got out to an area lit up by the fires. Where my invisibility counted for something. And I put a few more out of action.

I wasn't enjoying myself anymore. Truth is, I'd seen that the individual soldiers, some of them, had been sympathetic of the townspeople. It was the officers I wanted to nail.

They carried off their dead commander. Someone else was trying to reorganize the execution. He was tall, even for a Nok, and he'd done something to his mask to give himself an especially cruel look. A new kind of cosmetic surgery, maybe. "Get on with it," he said. "Let's get it done." He raised a pistol. "On my command."

I didn't like him, so I switched back to the laser and ended his career, too. I should tell you that I'm one of those people who's spent a lifetime being very polite, and who is careful not to harm animals that get in the way. But I had no regrets taking the Nok officers out of play.

By now the soldiers knew something was wrong and they were scrambling for cover. The townspeople saw their chance and scattered. Ran for the woods. A few charged the soldiers and tried to seize weapons. Fights and shooting erupted everywhere. I did what I could, evening the odds where possible.

Within a few minutes, the town had cleared out. Troops, natives, everybody. They left behind a lot of bodies, both townspeople and in uniform.

I got back into the lander and closed the hatch and just sat. "*You know,*" George said, "*while you were out there joining in the mayhem, I could have invoked the emergency provisions and taken the lander back into orbit.*"

The possibility had never occurred to me. "I know," I said.

"*But you trusted me? Why didn't you disable the connector?*" What was he talking about?

"I assumed," I said, "you knew if you left me you'd be putting me in danger, and you wouldn't want to do that."

It was the right answer. "*That's very good, Art. Absolutely right. And the corollary to that line of reasoning is that I have your welfare at heart.*"

I was getting tired being lectured by software. But I let it go. "I will continue to trust you."

"*I hope you are making the correct judgment.*"

I better be. If my life depended on disabling the connector, I had a serious problem.

We found a burned-out village and went down. Bodies were everywhere. A few survivors wandered around in a state of shock. They cried out and flung their arms about their heads in despair. I tried to help, getting water, helping put out a fire. I had to be careful, of course. I got more clips, including a riveting segment in which a handful of survivors, mostly young ones of both sexes, swore vengeance against the attackers.

We were everywhere that night. In a moderately sized city on the shore of a large lake, I took pictures of corpses and hysterical children and recorded the arrival of a band of Noks who came to help. I sent everything to McCarver. Here's more, Paul. Here are several hours of cultural development, helped along by our neutrality. Maybe we need to send them some pious maxims.

Cathie got on the circuit.

"Did you see the clips?" I asked her.

"*I saw them.*" She was silent, obviously trying to phrase what she wanted to say. Finally: "*Art, you've got to stop.*"

"Did McCarver tell you to try to get me to behave?"

"*No,*" she said. "*Paul hasn't said anything to me about you.*"

Another long silence. "*But the conflict down there is global. You can't stop it. You're only one man. You can't really do any good. All that's happening is that you're throwing your career away. Art, they will prosecute you. They're really getting upset.*"

"Oh. Well, hell, Cathie, I wouldn't want to upset anybody."

Over the next few days I waged war against whatever military forces I could. I poured sand in the gas tanks of transport vehicles, cut a dirigible loose from its tether, and set another one afire. I boarded ships, stole lubricants from the engine rooms and poured them into gun barrels. I blew up ammunition depots and even disrupted a parade by seizing someone's weapon and firing shots into the air.

Everywhere I went, I made a visual record. Not only of the dead and dying, but of the grieving survivors. And the celebrating killers. The trouble on the *Sheldrake* and back home where they made up the ground rules was that nobody believed the Noks qualified for the rights that humans took for granted. They were just not at our level. They had no feelings. Were incapable of governing themselves. I wondered what the Noks, when they learned of our presence, would think about *us*?

I stopped answering calls from McCarver. George got sulky and went silent, speaking only in response to questions.

When I got lonely, I called Cathie. She no longer pleaded with me to stop. Just told me she hoped everything would turn out all right. On the day I broke up the parade with the rifle, she told me the boss had asked her to pass along a message he'd received. "I doubt it's anything new," I said.

"It just came in this morning. It's from Hutchins." The Academy's director of operations. Back in Arlington.

"Okay. Let's see it."

The director was sitting in her office. Dark hair, dark eyes. Wouldn't look half bad if she smiled once in a while. *"Paul,"* she said, *"I know you've already informed Kaminsky he's in violation of at least a half-dozen laws, and God knows how many regulations. We want him to stop what he's doing immediately. He is to return to the* Sheldrake *and remand himself to your authority. As soon as convenient, ship him home. Let him know that charges are being drawn up at this moment. But that if he complies I will do what I can for him."*

"Sure she will. She'll commute the sentence to life."

"Give it up, Art."

"I'm surprised McCarver and his people haven't come after me."

"They would if they could, but you keep moving around. They haven't been able to get a fix on you."

"Why don't they just ask George?"

"You shut him down, didn't you?"

"No. I wouldn't be able to pilot the lander without him."

"That's interesting. He stopped talking to us. On his own, looks like."

"I'm surprised to hear that. You mean he's not reporting everything I do to McCarver?"

"No. We get nothing from him."

George wanted no credit for his actions. *"You got me into this. You've compromised me. But of course I said nothing. If I had they would have taken you back to the* Sheldrake *and sent you home. And prosecuted you. That's why I stopped reporting. I was hoping you'd come to your senses, apologize, and go back voluntarily. That way they might consider being lenient."*

"George, I appreciate what you did."

"It doesn't mean I approve."

5.

A planetary surface is a big place. The mission didn't have the kind of equipment necessary to track me from orbit. But Cathie had left no doubt they were watching. I took what precautions I could. I started wearing Intek goggles, which would allow me to see anyone else wearing a lightbender. I never stayed long in one place. And I began limiting my transmissions to the ship. Sent them out in batches, usually just before we moved on. On the whole, I made a pretty decent fugitive while simultaneously raising hell with the various Nok militaries. Not bad for a guy who had no experience at that sort of thing.

We were getting low on food. I'd begun to cut rations. When I got down to where there was a three- or four-day supply left, George asked when I was going to give it up. *"The crusade's about over,"* he said.

Yep. We were looking at the light at the end of the tunnel. "What's the maximum sentence for what we've been doing?" I asked George.

"—What we've been doing?"

"Yeah."

"I like that. Anyhow, it looks like a maximum of five years. Plus fines."

"Big ones?"

"They'd buy a nice place on the Riviera."

It was early morning where we were, on the west coast of the largest continent on the planet, but for me it was midday. I'd just set fire to a fuel supply depot, a particularly heavy blow on a world with serious energy problems. "Five years," I said.

"But you'd be in good company."

"You think I'd get the maximum?"

"Don't know. There are no precedents. But considering the fact you've killed a few of these creatures, and you've been less than polite to the director, I suspect they might even look for other charges."

"Yeah. I suppose they might."

"I'm no lawyer, you understand."

A half-hour after that conversation I broke up an intended landing on the southern coast of Palavi, an island-continent shaped like an enormous horseshoe, with the open end facing west.

Troops were moving shoreward in five small boats, the same type I'd seen during my first action. (I'd begun using military terminology by then. It felt good.) There was a town about four miles away from the projected point of landing, and it was just after dawn. The coastline was obscured by mist.

George brought the lander over the boats and, when they were about halfway to shore, we circled around, killed the lightbender so they could see us, kicked it up to full throttle, and ran directly at them. Well, not quite *directly*. We stayed high enough that there could be no collision, but I doubt it looked that way from the water. I wished the lander could make some noise, but the thing was silent and there just wasn't anything to be done about that. Nevertheless, its sudden appearance was enough. The Noks screamed. Some dived behind the gunwhales; others jumped into the ocean. Even George was amused.

We took a second run, after which all five boats were drifting, and pretty much the entire unit was in the water.

A few got shots off. "Engage the lightbender, George," I said. "Take us up."

The AI complied, and lifted us out of range. "*We took a hit on the port-side sweep light,*" he reported. "*It's out.*"

"Okay."

"*It appears there's a lot of confusion below.*"

"Raid canceled."

"*We have radio traffic, Art. They're reporting the incident.*"

"Put it on the speaker."

We listened to the end of the report. Unknown vehicle floating in air. "*Not a dirigible. Repeat: Not a dirigible. No visible means of support.*"

"*Did it attack you?*"

"*Yes.*"

"*What kind of weapons?*"

"*It tried to ram us.*"

"*You're sure it was levitating?*"

"*Captain, everybody here saw it.*"

"*Very good. Proceed with the mission.*"

It didn't sound as if the captain believed them. The Noks in the landing party were seeing things. "Let's go talk to the captain," I said.

George hesitated. "*Keep in mind, Art, they have heavy weapons. We could get blown out of the sky.*"

I'll admit something here: If I'd been alone, I would probably have backed away. But George was watching. And yes, I know AI's are only machines and nothing more. That they're no more intelligent than rocks. But it didn't matter. "Do it anyway. It'll take them time to zero in on us."

This time there were only two warships. They were gray and dark, the color of the ocean, guns sticking out in all directions. Killing machines. If we'd had any sense of decency, we'd have made contact at the beginning and banned warships from the open sea. Forced peace on them. Whether they liked it or not.

"Which ship?"

I couldn't tell which was the command vessel. Both were pointed south, out to sea, ready to clear in a hurry if they had to. They were several hundred meters apart. "The one on the left," I said.

George took us in over the bow. We snuggled up against the bridge, nose to nose. I counted five Noks inside. It was easy enough to pick out the ship's commander, who was wearing a hat that would have embarrassed Napoleon. "Good," I said. "Let's light up."

And suddenly there we were, hanging directly in front of them. Close enough to shake hands. The commander jumped a foot. The others dived to the deck as if they were under attack.

I wished I'd had a loudspeaker. But I didn't so I settled for the radio. "I am the Messenger of the Almighty," I said. "Stop the killing."

Klaxons began to sound. A couple of sailors appeared from nowhere, saw us, and scrambled for cover. A third, on a gundeck, went into the water. On the bridge, they were still hiding.

"You have been warned," I said.

George beeped and booped. "We should leave," he said.

"Not yet." I used the laser to take out the forward gun, and topple both of the ship's masts. A couple of Noks appeared and took shots at us.

"Okay," I said. "let's go. And let's turn the lights out."

We vanished and left them standing around gawking. One of the big guns started firing but I was damned if I could figure out why. It wasn't even pointed in our direction.

We disabled the second ship in much the same way, and were flying in a circle overhead admiring our work when George did the electronic equivalent of clearing his throat.

"What?" I asked.

"I don't think that Messenger of the Almighty routine works."

"Why not?"

"It's hard not to laugh."

"You're not a Nok."

"If it was having an effect, they wouldn't be shooting at us."

I was born in Toronto. My father owned a real estate development company. My mother held a master's in literature from one of the Ivy League schools and taught at the University of Toronto. They were Anglicans, my father fairly casual in his observances, my mother devout. "Has to be a God out there somewhere," she was fond of telling me. "I don't think he has much to do with the God of the Bible, but he has to be there. I can't believe this world is all there is."

I *wanted* to believe. Maybe to keep her happy. Maybe because I liked the idea that Someone with a lot of influence really cared about me. So I tried. Pretended to, sometimes, when earthquakes took out a few thousand people, or a kid somewhere fell off a bridge, and the preacher admitted that he didn't understand God's ways.

Looking back now on my experiences with the Nok wars, I wonder whether I was less generous than I like to think, whether I hadn't seen an opportunity to play God and tried to seize it.

Messenger of the Almighty. Would that it had been so.

The Noks were believers, too. At least, theoretically. They had the same sort of general religious history that we had. In ancient times, they'd believed in a plethora of divinities, one to keep the tides running, another to hustle the sun and moons across the sky, another to see to the seasons. In time, they'd discovered that Nature was an interrelated whole, and with that discovery came monotheism and intolerance. Same process as had happened at home.

The Noks had several major religions, and they constituted an integral part of the ongoing conflicts. Killing unbelievers, during some eras, seemed to be okay and even occasionally required for salvation.

I couldn't help wondering how it happened that monotheistic religions on Nok and at home both revolved around the concept of judgment and salvation. The physical world was an imperfect place, filled with sorrow and, ultimately, loss. There had to be something better. I heard echoes of Mom. It's a hard life. And we were living in Toronto. On the lakefront. Sailing Tuesdays and Thursdays.

I asked her once if she thought there really was a judgment.

"Yes." She'd smiled at the question, probably delighted that I was actually thinking about these things. "But I think it'll be different from what most people expect. I doubt we'll be held accountable for not getting to church often enough, or for giving in to forbidden pleasures."

"What then?" I'd asked. I'd been getting ready to leave for summer camp, leaving home for an extended period for the first time. "What do you think the judgment will be like?"

"I think He'll wonder about people who never take time to look at the grandeur of things. 'I gave you the stars and you never lifted your eyes above the rooftops.' Or, maybe, 'I gave you a brain. Why didn't you use it?'" She'd laughed. "Doesn't mean forbidden pleasures are okay, Arthur."

❁

"*My point,*" said George, "*is that it's a losing fight. You're all but out of food. And okay, you've blunted a few attacks. Made some of these guys pay a price. But in the process, what's changed? You think there won't be another landing force in here next week? Or next month? So what have you accomplished?*"

I was thinking about it when Cathie got on the circuit. "*I've been looking at some of the pictures you've been sending up. Do you have more?*"

"I can get more."

"*Do it.*"

"Why?"

"*Send them. As many as you can. Okay?*"

"Sure. If you want. What are you going to do with them?"

"*Try to get you some help.*"

She wouldn't explain. Maybe someone had walked into the comm center. But it sounded as if McCarver was beginning to understand what was really happening on the ground.

Two hours later I watched helplessly as two armies clashed in the middle of a plain. George's best estimate put the numbers involved at over a hundred thousand on each side. There were primitive armored vehicles, not tanks, but trucks used to carry troops, do hit-and-run maneuvers, and haul supplies. No robots, of course. There was a lot of artillery. Both sides just sat back and blasted away at the other. The ground troops made periodic charges. There were no automatic weapons, so the suicidal aspect of massing units for a frontal assault was missing. Or at least lightened. But they paid a heavy price.

Against George's protests, we went in close and got more pictures. Shattered bodies on the battlefield. A medical unit tending to desperately wounded soldiers. Hordes of refugees trying to get out of harm's way. And, that evening, when by mutual agreement the shooting had stopped, squads of soldiers spreading across the area to reclaim the bodies.

In the morning, I knew, it would all start again.

It was the only organized battle I saw during my entire time on Nok. But it was enough.

☀

"Even if Cathie could get you some help," said George, *"what good could it possibly do? At last count, there were seventeen national entities of one kind or another engaged in the war. It's not even one war. It's a whole bunch of wars going on simultaneously, and even the experts back in orbit don't have it all sorted out. So suppose they do send a couple more guys like you, suppose they send a* thousand, *what difference will it make?"*

I'd been talking with McCarver, who wanted to know, at least, what my plans were. How long was this going to go on? I got no sense that he'd even watched the clips, let along been impacted by them. *"Good luck to you,"* he'd said, when I told him I needed a couple more days. *"I'm sure knowing you stepped in will be consolation when you're sitting in a federal prison somewhere."*

We were on the night side at about four thousand meters. I stared out of the lander at the sky. The *Sheldrake* and its accompanying vessels were lost up there somewhere. Below, fires raged from one horizon to the other. Towns and cities under attack. Port facilities. I could see an air strike in progress. A fleet of maybe a dozen dirigibles dropping bombs and incendiaries on God knew who.

"You know, George," I said, "maybe you're right."

Bright lamps came on and blinked. *"Good,"* he said. *"At last. We're going to admit it's a no-win situation."*

"It is that."

"I'm glad you're finally seeing reason."

"Going after the local commanders doesn't achieve anything. I should have realized that from the start."

"I don't think I liked the sound of that. What do you mean, going after the local *commanders?"*

6.

Nok had a long list of dictators to choose from. One of the more malevolent, according to the research, was a character named Pierik Akatimi. Pierik the Beloved. I didn't know a great deal about him. Dictators weren't exactly my field of expertise. What stood out about Pierik was his appreciation for the simple pleasures: warmaking, arresting his citizens, and astronomy. He also liked sex. And feathers.

George supplied the dictator's address, which was in Roka, the capital of a continental power, possibly the strongest of the belligerents. His headquarters was appropriately named Sunset House.

We scouted the place from the air. Sunset House was an exquisite brick-and-steel six-story oval with a lot of windows and porticoes and a small observatory on the roof. There was a park across the street, a courthouse on one side, and a museum on the other.

"We'll land in the park," I said. "Once I'm out, go hide in the woods until I call you."

The military and political people had an extensive record on Pierik. As I said, he liked feathers. He wore them in a scarf, in his hats, and in his jacket. Nobody else had any. The word was that wearing a feather in his country constituted a capital offense. In fact, a wide range of offenses were capital crimes under Pierik, who didn't bother much with jails. He disapproved of criticism, of course. He also didn't much like citizens having a good time. Parties were forbidden, unless they marked certain specified occasions. The Nok equivalent of dancing brought swift retribution for everybody involved, the partners and anyone who stood around and didn't call the police. Religious opinion was circumscribed. Everybody belonged to one faith, and Pierik was its Blessed One. The dictator was reported to be superstitious and seemed to subscribe fervently to the official doctrine.

Despite all this, the principal researcher had concluded Pierik was not the worst of the dictators. But he seemed to me the most likely to be affected by the voice of an invisible entity.

"There is a character out of the popular literature of the twentieth century," said George, *"whose part you seem to be playing."*

"And who might that be?" We were settling into an unoccupied section of the park while I strapped on the belt that activated the lightbender.

"The Shadow."

"Never heard of him." I turned toward the airlock.

George opened up and wished me luck. *"Be careful,"* he said. *"He will be well guarded. And don't forget they can see your eyes."*

Pierik's capital could almost have been something out of the late nineteenth century. The larger buildings were stone and brick, rendered with an attention to aesthetics. Lots of arches, courtyards, fountains, spires, wheel windows. There were no towering structures, but the city was mathematically precise, laid out in squares and occasional triangles, with parks and theaters and libraries. The tallest structures served both religious and political functions. Religion and politics were combined, to varying degrees, in all the Nok nations. If they'd seen the consequences of such arrangements, they hadn't worked out the solution.

The street separating the park from Sunset House was barricaded to control traffic. There were hordes of pedestrians. Most were sightseers. I remembered having read that Pierik approved of sightseeing, and that local families that never made it into the capital to gawk at the monuments were noted.

Noted. A world of meaning in that.

Bronze statues of generals were everywhere. They assumed heroic postures, gazing out at some far horizon, their uniforms crisp and neat, guns hanging on their belts. Directly across from the main entrance to Sunset House was a heroic rendering of the dictator himself.

Pierik Akatimi.

Beloved.

Sunset House was said to have been designed by him. Uniformed guards stood outside the front entrance.

I crossed the street from the park, climbed a set of marble steps, and waited beside the guards. I was there less than a minute when the door opened and several Noks filed out.

I had to push a bit, but I got inside without being seen.

The center of the building was open to the roof and lined with galleries. Six levels of offices circled the main lobby and receiving area. There was more statuary, this time of Noks with wings and lightning bolts. And there were paintings. I remembered having read that the dictator was a collector. Or a looter, depending on your point of view.

Also prominent were flags carrying his personal symbol, a tree. It more or less resembled a spruce and was supposed to mark his dedication to life.

His office was on the top level. There were carpeted stairways and elevators on both sides of the building. And a lot of traffic. I had to keep moving to stay out of everyone's way. Noks in and out of uniform passed, talking about how happy everyone was when Pierik made his appearances, and how much charisma he had, and whether it was going to rain later. I decided to pass on the elevator and use a stairway.

It was crowded. I had to get off the stairs a couple of times to make room. But I got to the sixth level without incident.

It was easy enough to pick out the dictator's office. Bigger, heavier doors than anyone else. Exquisitely carved with leaves and branches. And two guards.

The doors were closed. I could hear voices inside.

I settled down to wait.

Four females were approaching around the curve of the gallery. They were side by side, the outermost tapping the guard rail as she walked, the innermost trailing a hand along the wall. They stopped at the elevator, and I hoped they'd go down, but they spoke briefly to someone who was getting off, and then they were coming again.

On the other side, about eight meters away, several military types were clustered, arguing about something. I moved toward them. "...Better simply to remove them from active consideration," one was saying. There was no room to squeeze past.

"They're all *turaka*," said another. He looked like the senior guy, judging by the insignia that glittered on his shoulders. I hadn't heard the term *turaka* before, but its structure betrayed the meaning. *Sub-human*. Or, more correctly, *sub-Nok*.

The females were coming. They were past the guards outside the imperial office, and were now separating to get by the military. Caught between fires, I had to push past the senior Nok. When he jerked suddenly aside, from no apparent cause, there were grunts and startled looks and at least one angry frown. Nobody quite knew what had happened. One of the staff officers was left explaining himself as best he could.

I circled the gallery. The females disappeared through doorways, and the military group were still talking when I approached the Beloved Leader's office again.

The conversation inside was going strong. It was animated, but I couldn't make out what they were saying. Eventually the door opened and two uniforms made their exit. Someone remained inside, seated in an armchair.

The head guy.

I slipped inside.

Pierik was in a military uniform, his collar loosened. Unlike his statue, he wore no decorations. No insignia of rank. He was paging through a folder, occasionally making notations.

The room was more apartment than office. It had no desk, no filing cabinet, no storage space. It *did* have a closet, thick carpets, and several arm chairs, arranged around a long table. Rich satiny curtains covered the windows. Flames crackled cheerfully in a fireplace. Two doors opened onto a balcony, and two more, in back, into what appeared to be a set of living quarters. A large portrait of the dictator himself, standing with two Nok kids, dominated the wall. He had an arm around each, and it remains to this day the most chilling thing I saw on that unhappy world.

There were other paintings. Pierik apparently liked landscapes.

He was smaller than I'd expected. The Beloved Leader was only slightly taller than I was, which was almost diminutive for a Nok male. He was thin. His neck was scarred, and one hand looked withered. From disease rather than injury, I suspected.

A buzzer sounded. Pierik flipped a switch.

"*Korbi is here with the reports, sir.*"

He extracted a piece of paper from the folder, stared at it, crumpled it, and dropped it into a waste basket. "Send him in, Tira."

The door opened, and a heavyset male entered and bowed.

"Korbi," said the dictator, "how are you? Good to see you. How's it going?"

"Good, *Kabah*," he said. The term translated more or less to *Excellency*, *Blessed Son*, and *Person of Undoubted Ability*. "And yourself?"

"It's been a long morning."

It was not the way I expected a dictator to behave. He seemed far too casual. Too friendly.

Korbi carried several documents. He handed them over. "These require your signature, sir."

"Very good," said Pierik. "How's the family?"

"We're doing well, thank you, Kabah. Graasala would want me to convey her best wishes."

"And mine to her, Korbi. Is there anything else?"

A moment later, he was gone. Pierik dropped the documents on the table, and returned his attention to the folder.

I had not forgotten that my eyes were visible. I could cover them with my arm. But I saw a better possibility. A bookcase stood against one wall, near the doors to the balcony. The books were, for the most part, exquisitely bound. The bindings of the books on the top shelf were primarily dark brown. The color of my eyes. I got in front of the bookcase, and stooped a little so I got the background I wanted.

Pierik put down the folder, picked up the new documents, and thumbed through them.

The Shadow's moment had arrived.

✸

"Pierik Akatimi."

He almost fell out of his chair. That was a satisfying moment, and it made me realize that he lived in constant fear of assassination. He looked around the room. Pressed a button. And the guards charged in.

"Someone is here," he said. "Search the place." He opened a drawer in the table and pulled out a gun. He checked to see that it was loaded. One guard cautiously opened a closet door, while the other inspected the curtains. Checked behind the furniture. They made sure no one was out on the balcony, and then they disappeared in back.

An officer and two more came in. The officer drew a pistol and took station beside his master, who remained calmly seated. The others joined the search. In the living quarters, doors opened and closed. Furniture got moved. Finally the guards reported to the officer. "There is no one, *Bakal*."

"You're sure?"

They were. Pierik got up, walked to the drawing room, and looked in. He shrugged, a remarkably human gesture, and dismissed the guards. He made one more sweep around, then went back to his chair and laid the weapon close to hand on the table.

How to handle this? If Pierik was going to call in the troops every time he heard a voice, I was in for a difficult time. I thought about snatching the gun, pointing it at him, and warning him to be quiet. But a weapon floating in midair, aimed directly at him, was likely to produce screams.

I was still considering how to proceed when the dictator spoke: "Who are you?" He was scanning the room. "I know you're there."

"Hello, Pierik," I said. I was still positioned in front of the bookcase. Pierik's gaze passed over me and moved on. I decided to adapt the dictator's own breezy style. "How are you doing?"

"I am well, thanks." He turned in the direction of my voice. I stayed perfectly still. Pierik's fingers crept toward the gun.

"Don't touch it," I warned.

The dictator withdrew his hand. "I was merely going to put it away."

"Leave it where I can see it."

"This is a clever trick. Is a microphone planted in the room?"

"No. I am here with you."

"That is hard to believe."

I crossed the room and turned on one of his lamps.

"Ah," he said. "That's quite remarkable. Why cannot I see you? Are you a ghost?"

"No."

"Then who?"

"I am the Messenger of the Almighty."

Pierik laughed. It had almost an electronic flavor, a cross between a boop and a gargle. The kind of smug sound you got from an AI when everything was fine and you were on course. Everything's just dandy. No one other than a specialist, or a Nok, would have recognized it for what it was. "Messenger of the Almighty," he said.

"That is correct." He made a feint at the gun.

"Stop!" I said. I had the tensor in my hand.

Pierik stopped. Showed me empty palms. "If you are who you say, why do you fear the gun?"

"*I'll* ask the questions." It was a weak answer, under the circumstances. I decided George was right. "Keep in mind, *Kabah*, your life is in my hands."

"So it would seem. Now please tell me who you are, and how you are managing this trick?"

"I carry a warning for you."

"And what is the warning?"

"Stop the war. Or you will become one of its next casualties."

He didn't laugh this time. He took a deep breath, and stood. "What shall I call you?"

I thought about *Banshee*, *Dark One*. Maybe *Shadow*? "My name's Kaminsky," I said.

"A strange name. How does it happen I cannot see you?"

"I want you to stop the war."

"Kaminsky." It came out sounding like *Kamimska*. "What does it mean?"

Damned if I knew. But it sounded important to have an answer. "*Night Rider*," I said.

"Good. That must be a proud name. Where do you come from?"

"Stop the fighting," I said again.

"Ah. Yes. The war. I should confess to you that no one would be happier if there were indeed a way to stop it. But unfortunately it is not within my power."

"One of your people died in my arms."

"That is sad. Was he really one of *my* people?"

"I don't know. She was a victim of *your* wars."

"I don't see how you can hold me responsible."

"Her name was Trill. She was a bride."

"I'm sorry to hear it."

"Died on her wedding night."

"Cruel things happen in wars. It is why we must see this through."

"You don't really care, do you?"

"It is the price we must pay."

"*We*? What price do *you* pay?"

"Oh, stop the nonsense." The eyes shaded into gray. "Do you think I enjoy leading an effort that gets my people killed?"

"I doubt you think about it. You like the power."

"Your *Trill* is only one person. I am responsible for many. Wars have victims. It is essentially what they are about."

"You're a lunatic."

"I'm sorry you think so, *Night Rider*." He gazed up at his portrait. "The war has a life of its own. It has raged a long time. My people want victory. And they will settle for nothing less."

"*Your* people."

"Yes. *My* people."

"I'm tempted to kill you now and wait to see who follows you."

"Then you will make the same proposal to him?"

"Yes."

"And you will get the same answer. We are a proud nation—."

"*Stop there*," I said. "Don't lie to me. My patience has its limits." I liked that line, and I delivered it with enough conviction that I saw the membranes of his eyes close and open. He was getting the message. "I will give you three days to stop all offensive actions. If you do not, I will be back. If that becomes necessary, you will never be rid of me."

"*How did it go?*" George asked after I'd made my way back to the lander.

"The Night Rider was at the top of his game," I said. "But I don't expect him to do anything other than load up with guards."

"*Who's the Night Rider?*"

I explained, and he booped and beeped. "He was cool, I'll give him that. Most people would have jumped out of their skins."

"*He's not* people," said George. "*You have to stop expecting Noks to react the way you or I would.*" That was George's idea of a joke. "*You have two days' rations left. Then it's going to start getting pretty hungry around here.*" That was true. I couldn't substitute Nok food. It had no nutritional value for me. "*Maybe it's time to give it up, Art.*"

Maybe it was time to eat less.

7.

I decided to try some psychological warfare. Next day, at sunrise, early visitors to Sunset House found a message painted in large dark green letters on the side of the building: *Pierik Akatimi is an idiot.*

It looked pretty good, actually. A crowd gathered. Nobody laughed. It'd been there about ten minutes when the toadies scrambled to remove the paint.

I was frustrated. I went looking for statues of the dictator. Wherever I found one, I used the laser to cut off his ears. (Noks don't really have protruding noses, so I couldn't do much about that.) I always made sure it was a neat clean cut, and I always waited until there were a few witnesses in place to see it happen.

I listened to government-controled newscasts, but they didn't mention anything about the statues or the painting on the wall at Sunset House. They *did* inform their listeners, as they did every day, that the war was going well, and that whole legions of enemy soldiers were being killed or captured, their dirigibles knocked down, and their ships disabled.

I asked George whether he could break in on the government frequencies.

"*Of course. I can boost power and we can ride right over them.*"

"All right. Do it. Let me know when I can speak. Then I'll want you to record my comments and play them every fifteen minutes for the next eight hours."

"*Okay,*" George said. He hummed while he worked. Then: "*Art, we're ready to go. Just say the word.*"

"Do it."

"*Ready for transmission—Now.*"

It was another great moment. "*Greetings, Atami,*" I said, using the standard intro, which translated roughly to *ladies and gentlemen of the listening audience.* "My name is Kaminsky, and I know you're already aware that Pierik Akatami is a dictator. He holds onto power by sending your children to war. He is a liar and a thief and a killer. Do not be fooled by him."

I signaled that I was done, and George said, "*Okay. It went out.*"

"What did you think?"

"*What do you expect them to do? They know what he is. But they can't stand up against him unless they organize, and there's probably no way they can do that.*"

Roka had a newspaper. The *Guardian*. Government-controlled, of course. It printed mostly official releases, and limited itself to favorable comment. The day after the radio broadcasts, which got no official notice, I walked into the print room, hoping to provide an unexpected headline for the next day's edition. I'd go with the standard *Pierik Beloved Is An Idiot*. But I didn't have much in the way of mechanical skills, and couldn't figure out how to manipulate the printers.

I took a few minutes to stroll through the news room, where I overheard someone saying that Pierik would be officiating at a torchlight rally that evening. I got the details and pinpointed the location on a wall map.

There was a bust of Pierik in the newspaper's front entrance. On the way out, I sliced off its ears.

I needed something that would seriously undermine Pierik. I was thinking about it and not paying attention to my surroundings. I was about a block from the *Guardian* offices, on a broad tree-lined avenue crowded with pedestrians when I suddenly became aware of footsteps behind me. Closing in on both sides.

Nobody there.

I hadn't been wearing my goggles, because they're more visible to observers than my eyes. As I pulled them out of my vest, I saw another pair of goggles, afloat and closing in. Damn.

Paul McCarver and one of his associates. "Hello, Art," said the director.

Hassan was with him, his number two, tall, olive-skinned, short-tempered. He said hello too, but he didn't mean it. I knew he didn't like having his time wasted, and having to chase a maverick do-gooder around the planet would not have made him happy.

Seen through my goggles, they had an orange, spectral appearance.

"I have to tell you, Art," said McCarver, "you've really been a problem."

Hassan's meaty hand settled on my arm. Nothing rough, but he was letting me know I wasn't going anyplace without permission. "I hope they toss you in jail," he said.

"You've seen the pictures?" I asked McCarver.

"I've seen them." He was staring straight ahead, his goggles a bit too big for his head. It might have been comic except the anger showed, and it was hard not to take McCarver seriously when he got irritated. "There's nothing in them we haven't been looking at for years. What do you think? We've been here all this time with our heads in the sand? You think we don't care? You've no idea how many reports I've filed over the years. Or Huang. Or Packard." His predecessors. Packard went way back to the beginning.

"You filed reports, Paul, and what did the Third Floor say?"

"You know damned well what they said."

"And you accepted it."

"I had no choice, Art. You should know that."

"You *did* have a choice."

It was more than the director could stomach. We'd been walking, but with that we stopped dead and he turned to face me. "Look, Kaminsky, who in hell do you think you are? You breeze in here from some school back home, never been anywhere, never did anything, shouldn't have been here in the first place——."

Hassan nudged him. Several Noks had stopped and were staring in our direction. "They see us," he whispered.

We turned our backs on them to hide the goggles, so whatever they thought they saw vanished. McCarver made a rumbling sound deep in his throat, and some of the passersby caught that too. He pointed at me and mouthed the words, *Bring him*, and strode ahead.

We got across the street, where it wasn't so crowded. I was still being half-hauled by Hassan. I tried to free myself, but he only tightened his grip. "Don't even think about it," he said softly, his tone full of menace.

"You going to send me home, Paul?"

Without turning. "Yes. Charges have been drawn up. Don't make it worse."

A young Nok, maybe four or five, broke free of parental restraints and bounced off McCarver. The child screamed in surprise, and the director almost fell into the street trying to get out of the way. "I hate these things," he said. Apparently meaning the lightbenders.

It was a gray, oppressive day. Threatening rain. "You ever see Pierik?" I asked.

"No. Not in person."

"He's a maniac."

"Come on, Art. Give it a rest. He's not our problem."

"Whose problem is he?"

We stopped to let a couple of Noks pass. "Look, Art, if it makes you any happier, they're pulling me back, too."

"You? Why?"

"Are you serious? Because Hutchins sees I can't keep my own house in order. I'm being reassigned."

"I'm sorry, Paul."

"Thanks. That helps."

We reached another intersection. A military convoy was approaching. Soldiers loaded into the backs of small trucks. It looked like scenes I'd seen in VR dramas about wartime back home. In the days when they had wars. Except of course the soldiers looked like nothing human.

"I'll tell them you had nothing to do with it," I said.

"They already know that. It's irrelevant." Those intense dark eyes locked on me, seething.

I watched the soldiers go past. The convoy was followed by a government car and another truck. There were no private vehicles anywhere.

I regretted what had happened to McCarver's career. I don't know why. But I did. Even though he'd stood by. That's how I've always thought of him. He and everybody else at that place over a forty-year span. The people who stood by. Did nothing. In his own way, the director was worse than the Beloved Leader. "You know," I told him, "you are one sorry son of a bitch."

I thought for a minute he was going to swing on me. "I hope they put you where you belong," he growled.

And I decided I'd had enough.

I reached around and switched off Hassan's lightbender.

Suddenly, passersby were gawking at us. Some screamed, some simply ran for their lives. A couple of terrified kids scrambled into parental arms.

Hassan did not at first understand what had happened. But he saw the panic around him, and someone in uniform aiming a rifle at him. Next thing I knew I was free. And running.

I got as far from the turmoil as I could.

McCarver's voice came over the commlink. "*Art, what do you think you're doing?*"

And: "*Art, this isn't going to help. Get back here.*"

"*Art, answer up. You okay?*"

I kept going. Down a couple more blocks, past the Department of Piety, across a square, and finally sat down behind a tree.

I was getting my breath when I heard klaxons. Noks began to scatter. They hurried into a couple of government buildings. I thought it was connected to Hassan until I saw movement in the sky. Dirigibles.

The buildings were marked with flags. An 'X' inside a circle. Air raid shelter.

There were three airships. And a fourth one just coming out from behind a rooftop. I heard the boom of anti-aircraft guns. Noks with rifles appeared and began to blaze away, although the airships were hopelessly out of range.

So much for the theory that only soft outlying targets got hit.

I couldn't very well crowd into a shelter. And with the streets empty, my chances of getting spotted by McCarver and Hassan rose considerably. Best, I decided, was to sit where I was. Behind the tree.

The dirigibles stayed high, out of range of the guns. I expected to see some sort of defensive squadron appear. But it didn't happen. What *did* happen was that bombs rained down. They fell heavily in the government district, which is to say, where *I* was. They blasted buildings and blew dirt, wood, bricks, and Noks into the air. I turned on the imager and recorded it. Got the explosions, the screams of casualties, the sirens, everything.

As far as I knew, this was the first time they'd hit the capital. Happens on the day I show up. I called Cathie in the middle of it and put the question to her. "Yes," she said. "*That's right. At least, the record shows it's the first time Roka's been attacked in twelve years. Apparently they do occasionally bomb major targets. I guess they figure they can do a surprise run and get clear. Are you going to get through this okay?*"

"I hope." A bomb hit maybe fifty meters away. Deafened me. Covered me with dirt. But nobody got hurt. "Close one."

"*My God, Art. Get out of there.*"

"Nowhere to go, Cath." I was scared and felt good at the same time. Don't ask me to explain it. "I had a visit earlier today from McCarver."

"*Are you okay?*"

"I'm fine."

"*How about him?*"

"Don't know."

"*You're not coming back with him?*"

"You could say that."

I could hear voices in her background. They sounded excited. "*From here it looks as if they're raising hell. We count nine bombers.*"

"I can see four of them."

"*Where is he now? Paul?*"

"A few blocks away, I hope. With Hassan."

"*He let you go?*"

"Not exactly."

"*Okay, tell me later. Go hide somewhere.*"

When it was over, I watched emergency vehicles charging through the streets. Several buildings along the perimeter of the park had been hit. They were carrying victims out into the street. Some were dead. Others were packed into ambulances and taken off.

When I'd had all I could stand, I called George in and climbed into the lander. "*Lot of excitement out there,*" he said.

"They bombed the city."

"*I know. Everybody's favorite dictator probably made it through.*"

"I'm sure. He's got a rally tonight. He'll use that to tell everyone it'll be a long haul, but they'll come through victorious."

He was silent. Then: "*You're out of rations.*"

"I know. We'll be going back tonight."

"*You're going to turn yourself in?*"

"I'm not sure I see an alternative."

"*Then why not go back now? You must be pretty hungry.*"

"I've something to do first."

"*What's that?*"

"I want to make a permanent impression on the Beloved Leader."

He hesitated. "*How are you going to do that?*"

"You're going to help. I'll need the lander's commlink."

"What for?"

"Does it have a power supply of its own?'

"No."

"Can we equip it so that it will?"

"I'm not much on improvising."

"Can it be done? Do we have a power supply available?"

"We have power cells, yes. Where did you want to put it?"

"In Pierik's quarters. And I'll need some duct tape."

I called Cathie. "Can you talk?"

"Sure," she said. "It's the middle of the night, but I'm not really doing anything."

"Oh." It was easy to forget something like that when, where I was, the sun was shining. "Sorry."

"It's okay. What do you need?"

"I'm going back to Sunset House."

"Paul will be furious."

"He's already pretty unhappy."

"Why?"

"I guess because I'm not taking direction well."

"I mean why are you going back? You should stay out of that place. What happens if you get caught?"

"I'm going to plant a commlink."

"What's the point?"

"After Paul and Hassan haul me away, maybe somebody will listen to what goes on and eventually decide to put a stop to it."

"Okay," she said. "You're going to do what you want regardless of what anybody says. I think it's crazy, though."

I think I wanted to hear her try harder to talk me out of it. But she said nothing. "We'll be able to talk to him, too, if we want. Make him feel haunted."

8.

The rally was to be held outdoors in a concrete square festooned with flags and bunting. Banners displaying the dictator's spruce tree were everywhere. The audience was herded in about an hour after sunset. While they waited, they were treated to music by a military band. Nok auditory sensibilities are different from those of a human. People listen to Nok music and hear only a lot of jangling and banging, with abrupt halts and starts. It was one more reason to smile condescendingly at the Noks. I didn't know the details—still don't—, but I was aware the range of sounds they heard was different from ours. Higher pitch or something.

A stage had been erected, lights brought in, and flower petals handed out to young females. An honor guard lined a walkway leading from a parking area to the stage. Eventually, three black military vehicles arrived. The band switched to a different piece of music and got louder. Aides jumped out of the cars. One opened a door for the Beloved Leader, and the others formed an escort. Pierik stepped out onto a gravel walkway, waved to onlookers, and mounted the stage to raucous applause. (Noks don't clap, but they do a lot of yelling.)

There was no introduction. He simply walked out onto the stage and took his place behind a microphone. The applause intensified. He raised one hand and they fell silent.

Before saying anything, Pierik seemed to recognize someone in the audience. "Hello, Kagalon," he said, covering the microphone but raising his voice to be heard. "How are you doing?"

Kagalon waved back, said something I couldn't make out. The friendly dictator. The crowd loved it. They cheered, and Kagalon, who looked pretty much like everybody else out there that evening, held up his hand.

Pierik adjusted the microphone, signaled he was about to speak, and the crowd quieted. "Kaburrati," he said, using the term which his people applied to themselves. People of Kaburra. "Hello, my friends," he said.

And they roared back, "Hello, Kabah!"

More applause.

He laughed and waved them again to silence. "Thank you. I love to come here where I can be among my brothers and sisters."

They cheered again. It went on like that for about ten minutes. I've never heard such enthusiasm in an audience. And I wondered, did I have it wrong somehow? The sentiment seemed genuine. The crowd *loved* him.

The energy built and crackled around the stage like electricity. He told jokes, he brought news from the war zones, he delivered reassurance. "These are hard times," he said, "but together we will get through them."

Somebody came out and presented him with an award. More cheering. I was struck by Pierik's platform skills. In front of his audience, he was all showbiz.

"And now," he said, "I know you didn't come here to see me. Let's bring out the troops."

The lights blinked a few times and went off. The square was plunged into darkness, except for a flickering in back. It was a troop of Nok soldiers, shirtless for the occasion. They entered and came up the center aisle, carrying torches. They'd poured something on their upper bodies so they glistened. Pierik saluted them and they kept coming. The audience went crazy, cheering and yelling. Fireworks exploded overhead. The band started to thump and bang.

The soldiers stopped when they got to the front, where they paused, looking up at their leader. Then, in perfect synchronization, they lifted their torches to him.

When they'd gone, and the lights were back on, Pierik looked out across his audience. "I've one more thing to say to you. You're aware that our treacherous enemy bombed us today. Killed some of us. Maimed others." He paused, fighting down his emotions. "I want you to be aware that our forces have already responded to the attack. We have carried the war deep into the *Agani* homeland. We have imposed heavy losses, and we are still striking them even while I speak. In your name, my brothers and sisters, we have taken a terrible vengeance." The audience was absolutely silent. "Soon," he said, "we will end this war, and we will travel together through the sunlit forests into a far better world than we have ever known."

I was literally shocked by the show of support he was getting. The guy was extremely good. And even I, who knew the truth about the way the war was being waged, found it hard not to like him.

Suddenly everything I'd done against him, painting attacks on the wall of Sunset house, clipping ears off statues, the radio broadcasts, everything seemed hopelessly childish. I was trying to hold back a flood with a bucket.

The laser waited in my pocket. I could feel its weight. And I wondered what would happen if I killed the dictator? Took him out on stage in full view of the crowd?

The answer: Probably nothing. There'd be a brief power struggle, and another nutcase would emerge.

No. Better to wait.

I moved past the guards and eased out onto the stage. The noise was deafening. And, hard as it was to read the nonverbal cues of a Nok, it was obvious the Leader was enjoying himself.

Pierik went on, talking about peace and the malefactors who stood in the way of progress. The audience response shook the night. Some of the shirtless troopers, now correctly attired, had returned to the sidelines and joined the applause.

I recorded everything, but I decided I'd keep these for myself. To McCarver, they'd just underscore his argument that the Noks were not worth saving. That they were savages, and there was no hope for them.

I stood within two paces of the Leader. How easy it would be to reach out and push him from the stage, send him hurtling into the arms of the crowd. Instead, I waited for a quiet moment, when his audience stood expectantly, and Pierik was letting the tension build. When it came, he had just finished assuring them that he would accept nothing less than total surrender from the enemy, and furthermore....

What the *furthermore* was to have been, neither the crowd nor I ever found out. Because I moved in right behind the dictator's left ear, and said, quietly, "Pierik, I will always be with you."

He froze. His eyes tracked left, and he made a grab. But I was already out of reach.

"No matter where you go," I said, "I will be at your side."

He backed away from the microphone. Stumbled and almost went down. I'd kept my voice down, not much more than a whisper, because I didn't want the crowd to hear. But the audience knew something was wrong. A sound very much like the murmur of a late summer wind rose out of several thousand throats.

"Always," I said.

I got back to Sunset House before the dictator and his entourage. I'd hoped to get into Pierik's quarters, maybe follow the maid in, or get in when somebody came to throw some logs onto the fire. Be waiting there when he showed up. Security at the front door was loose and I got into the building easily enough. But no maid appeared, nor anyone else, and the guards never looked away. I might have tried a distraction, but it seemed too risky. So I simply bided my time. I told Cathie where I was and she took a deep breath.

The dictator and his crew arrived more than three hours after I'd got there. They were showing the effects of intoxicants. They came laughing and staggering into the lobby. Even Pierik seemed to have had a bit too much. In this respect also he seemed unlike the more modern human strongmen, who inevitably were puritanical and solemn. Nobody could imagine Napoleon having a big time. Or Hitler and Stalin getting together to yuk it up after signing the Nonaggression Pact.

But Pierik was as loud as the rest of them while they stumbled across the ground floor toward the elevators. There was much clasping of shoulders, and somebody fell down, which initiated some laughter. The elevator was open and waiting. They got in and rode up to the top level.

Meantime an attendant appeared from nowhere, unlocked the suite, opened the door, and stood by, holding it. At last! I slipped past him into the office.

I had about a minute or two before anybody would arrive. "I'm inside," I told Cathie. The doors to the balcony were open, and even at this late hour, I could hear a crowd out there. Probably excited because the lights had come on.

"*Okay,*" she said. "*Luck.*"

I took the lander's commlink out of my vest and looked for a place to put it. It was about the size of a small candy bar. I thought about the bookcase. The books showed some wear. Maybe under the table. I even considered punching a hole in the bottom fabric of a chair and putting it inside. But the first time somebody cleaned they'd see the damage.

What else?

There was an air vent.

Perfect.

It didn't open without a fight, but I got it as the elevator arrived. I slipped the commlink inside, activated it, and closed the vent. "Cathie, testing."

"*I read five by.*"

"Okay. Reception's good on this end, too."

"*Now please get out of there.*"

Voices at the door. "They're here," I whispered.

"*Leave the channel open,*" she said. I was wearing a jack, so they couldn't hear her speak, but they could easily have heard me had I said anything more.

Pierik came in first. Four others followed. They were laughing and going on about how successful the rally had been. The attendant closed the door behind them. "The attack was pure genius," said one of the aides. "Brilliant."

They all laughed.

Pierik's disk eyes gleamed in the lamplight. He clapped the tallest of his aides on the shoulder. "Timing was perfect," he said.

"You were marvellous tonight," said the tall one. He was clearly the oldest of the group.

"Thank you, Shola," said Pierik. "A compliment from you means a great deal." And I was sure they were hard to come by. It struck me that insinuating oneself shamelessly into the good graces of one's superiors would turn out to be another universal characteristic of intelligent creatures.

Sholah opened a cabinet and removed a flask. Poured drinks for everyone. They toasted their most magnificent leader, their rock in a time of troubles, and drank it down. Then they retreated to the chairs. Sholah carried the flask, refilled Pierik's glass, then his own, and passed the flask on. They drank to the courage of the leader. And to that of the fighting forces. While I watched them doing the toasts, the truth about the wars dawned on me. It was a charade. It was *1984*, a series of never-ending conflicts to ensure continuing nationalistic fervor and support for the assorted dictators. That explained why strategic targets never got hit, why no major battles got fought. Don't waste the resources. And the last thing anybody wanted was to win.

I can't prove any of this. Couldn't then, can't now. But I saw it in the way they laughed, in the comments about the bombing of Roka, in their attitude toward the military. I wondered how deep the collusion went. Was there simply a general understanding among the dictators? Did Pierik talk directly with Maglani the Magnificent and Seperon the Father of His People? All right, you hit us here, and we'll get you there.

They drank another round, and then Pierik said how he had to get some sleep and suddenly I was alone with him.

He turned off the lights in the office and retreated into the inner quarters. He walked through the room, switching on lamps, and at last fell wearily into a chair.

Open doors led to a dining area and, probably, a bedroom. I saw more oils and sculpture. And framed photos. Here was the dictator standing on a balcony giving a salute. (The balcony looked like the one connecting with the outer office.) There, he reviewed troops. He walked the deck of a warship, talked to a crowd on a street corner, posed with a group of young females. Here he signed a book for an adoring subject. There, surrounded by uniformed officers, he examined a map.

Pierik picked up a book, loosened his shirt, and collapsed onto the sofa. He propped his head on a pillow, adjusted a table lamp, and opened the cover. *A History of Something or Other*. He turned a page. A couple of pages. "Hard to believe," he said to himself in a low tone. He made a noise in his throat. And looked up. "Messenger," he said, "don't you know it is not polite to stand there and not address your host?"

I was, somehow, not surprised. "How did you know I was here?"

"You give off a rather clear scent." His eyes grew and shrank. "Have you come to kill me? Or merely to gloat?"

"I haven't decided yet."

"Ah. Perhaps you will restrict yourself to a social visit?"

"I want you to realize you have no choice but to stop the war."

"My good friend Night Rider, you must realize that even I cannot do that. These events are caused by factors beyond mortal control." He closed the book and put it on the table. "Can I get you something to drink?"

"Thanks, no."

"Won't you at least have a seat?" He indicated an armchair.

"You will act on the war, Pierik."

"Well." He gazed around the room. "It's disconcerting not knowing where to look."

"Yes." I was standing before thick dark curtains. "I'm sure it is."

"Ah, you are over by the window."

I didn't move.

"Did you enjoy the event this evening?"

"Not really. But you are quite good."

"Thank you. From you, that is a supreme compliment." He looked off to his right. "One of the great problems for someone in my position is getting an honest evaluation. No one will tell me the truth. I could fall on my face out there, and they would all say how wonderful I am."

"I wonder why that is?"

"It is the price I must pay." He rubbed his hands together. "And I shall reply to your demand with equal honesty. I cannot change the course of events. Were I to stop hostilities, there are others who would continue. On all sides. The conflict creates purpose for the nation, it is our life blood. It is why we live."

"That's absurd."

"Of course it is. But everyone subscribes to it. And that makes it *true*."

"That's nonsense, Pierik. You will do what I ask or I'll kill you."

For a long moment, he said nothing. Then: "You are exactly like us. 'Do as I say or I will kill you.' Marvellous. What prompts you to come here and talk morality?"

"I'm not going to debate the issue. If you will not comply, I will take your life."

He moved the cushions around. "If I call the guards, you will not get out. They've been instructed to block the doors."

"You'll be dead before they can get in here."

"I suppose that is so. You *do* have me at a disadvantage." He held a hand over his eyes, shielding them from the table lamp. "This is a bit bright." He reached for it. "I should have it adjusted." He turned the switch, and all the lamps in the room went out.

It was pitch dark. I heard him move.

"I think now," he said, "we are on equal terms." There was a click. The guards were in the outer office, and then the doors opened and they charged into the room.

That let some light in, but I couldn't see Pierik. "Please don't do anything foolish, Night Rider. If I am not here to stop them, they *will* certainly kill you."

There were only two, but I heard more coming. Both carried flashlights. One crossed the room and blocked the doorway that led to the bedroom. Which told me where Pierik was. The other planted himself in the exit so I couldn't get out.

I grabbed the tensor. There was more noise in the office, and reinforcements poured in. "Now," came Pierik's voice, "whoever you are, *whatever* you are, this incident is over." The lights came back on.

Pierik reappeared. "I'd prefer you don't resist." The soldiers glanced at one another, but I could read nothing in those masks.

At the dictator's command they swept through the room, forming a chain, allowing no space for evasion. I began firing. A couple of them cried out and went down. Someone threw a cannister of gray powder. It became a cloud and drifted across the room.

The guards pulled strips of linen across their mouths and noses. And they could see me, looked right at me. More powder flew.

I was coughing. They grabbed me. I fired off several more shots. Got two or three more, but even when they were falling left and right, I saw no emotion. I kept thinking, *Masks across their masks.*

They secured me, used a cord to bind my hands. I tried to hang onto the tensor, but it fell to the floor, got kicked away, *outside* the lightbender field, and became visible. One of them found it and handed it to over to Pierik.

"*Bring him here.*" The dictator was delighted.

The guards dragged me across the room, and set me facing him. He reached out tentatively and touched me. My shoulder. My vest. His fingers twisted the cloth. Found my face. Touched the skin.

Apparently it was not a good experience. He pulled back. "What kind of creature are you?" he demanded. "From where have you come?"

"No place you ever heard of," I said.

Someone else came in. "What is it, *Kahba*?" It was Sholah.

Pierik was still watching me. "The one I told you about is here."

"Really?" He looked at the bodies on the floor, at the guards, at their struggles with an invisible presence. "Indeed."

"You are just in time to see the conclusion to this very odd event."

Sholah followed Pierik's lead. Touched my clothes. He too had a hard time with my skin. "Incredible," he said. "Kahba, there was a report of a monster in the streets yesterday. I gave it no credence, but—."

"Was it *you*?" Pierik demanded of me.

It might as well have been. "Yes," I said.

"That brings us to my next question. What is the secret of your invisibility?"

I visualized invisible troops hitting the villages. Maybe McCarver was right. My God. "It is innate," I said. "We are born with it."

"If that is true," said Shola, "he is of no further use to us."

"Are there more of you?" asked Pierik.

"I am alone."

"I do not believe you. Where do you come from?"

"An island in the eastern ocean. We have kept its location secret since the rise of civilization."

"Really?" He did not laugh, but he might as well have. "There is no question that a device that hides one from the light would have its value."

"It is *not* a device. It is inborn."

"So you say. Let us find out." He looked at the captain. "Throw him off the balcony. We will see how high he bounces."

They dragged me toward the outer office.

"Wait," I said. "It *is* a device. I'll show you."

"It's no matter, Night Rider. We'll take it from your corpse at our leisure."

They lifted me off the floor, carried me through the office and out onto the balcony. There, they hoisted me shoulder high. The air, warm minutes ago, was cold. The crowd below cheered.

I looked down six stories. It was a bad moment. "Wait," I said, "you'll break it."

"He has a point," said Sholah.

The dictator raised a hand to the guards. Hold. Do not fling the miscreant over the side just yet. "It's also possible," Pierik said, "we might hurt someone. *Down there.*" He made noises in his throat while he thought about it. "Bring him inside for a minute."

For a minute? That didn't sound good.

They set me down again in front of the dictator. "All right, Night Rider, make yourself visible."

"I'll show you how. But I want a guarantee I'll be released." Not that I expected a guarantee would help, but it was something.

Pierik showed me the tensor. Pointed it at me, face level. The guards behind me, who could see nothing between themselves and the muzzle, got nervous and tried to clear a space. "You will do as I tell you. You are an intruder, and I will not bargain with you."

He had a point. "I can't do it with my hands tied."

Pierik signaled the captain. Someone cut me free. But they kept my arms pinned.

"Very good. Now, let's see what you look like."

I took a deep breath, got my hand on the buckle control switch, and turned off the lightbender.

Pierik's eyes went wide and changed to a deep violet. He made a sound like someone who had just come unexpectedly on a snake. The guards let go and jumped back, and I almost got free. But they recovered and seized me again.

He studied me for a long moment. "Well, Night Rider, you *are* an ugly creature, are you not? Tell me again where you come from."

"—An island in—"

It was as far as I got. Pierik struck me with the gun barrel. "You are going to have a difficult evening. Do you want to tell me the truth? Or would you prefer I send you downstairs for a while?"

What was downstairs? Gestapo headquarters? "I have told you the truth, Pierik."

He leaned back against the table and looked at Shola. "Counselor, do you think it possible so ugly a creature could have been born on this world?"

Shola was not young. As they aged, Noks lost their glossiness. Shola's hands and mask were rough and worn. "Where else could he have come from, Kahba?"

"I think he is a visitor from another place. Another world."

"But there is no world beyond Inakademeri."

Pierik pressed his hands together. The digits were long and looked more like claws than fingers. "How do we know that is so?" His eyes reverted to green. Green like the end of summer. "I am indeed sorry that the first visitor to our world insists on behaving in so contemptible a manner. But you leave me no choice. If you will not talk to me, I shall leave the questioning to others."

"I will talk to you," I said. "I will tell you something your guards should also hear. You pretend to be a great war leader, but you have no desire to win the war. Or even to see it end."

Pierik hit me again.

"You use it to stay in power. To fool——."

The third blow drove me to my knees. They hauled me back up.

Without meaning to, I slipped into English. "You don't give a damn about anybody, you son of a bitch."

It didn't matter that he couldn't speak the language; he got the message. But he kept his voice level. "What controls your invisibility?"

I did not like the idea of giving lightbender technology to the monster. I could hear McCarver. *I told you so. Damn fool idiot.*

"Cathie," I said. Still in English: "If you're there, this would be a good time. Do the bombing."

Pierik signaled the captain, who jammed a rifle butt into my midsection.

"He is dressed oddly," said Shola. "The technique must be in the clothing. Perhaps the box on his belt."

Pierik's eyes flashed. "Well," he said, "it's been a long day and it's getting late. Let's just kill him and then we'll see if we can figure it out tomorrow." He stepped back and looked at the captain. The captain raised his sidearm and pointed it at my forehead.

"No," said Pierik. "Not here. Take him downstairs, take care of it, and bring me his clothes and anything else you find."

"Yes, Kahba." He holstered the weapon and the guards started me toward the door.

I got a glimpse of the vent. "Cathie," I said, in English, "help."

Pierik looked perplexed by the strange words. Someone opened the door, and I saw a crowd of Noks standing immediately outside.

At that moment an explosion rocked the room, and they all dived for the floor.

Cathie had the volume at the top of the dial. Klaxons went off and screams erupted. The afternoon attack was doing a rerun. I broke loose, hit the lightbender control, pushed Noks every which way, and ran for my life. Behind me, more bombs were going off. Cathie, when she wanted, could deliver a stunning acoustical performance.

9.

I had expected to find a welcoming committee when I got back to the *Sheldrake*. I'd expected McCarver to yell and scream and confine me to quarters until transportation home could be arranged. But no one was there when I came in the hatch. I got no summons to McCarver's conference room, nor even a call on the commlink.

I needed a shower and a change of clothes, but I went down to mission control first. Cathie had someone on the circuit when I went in. She signed off, jumped up, and hugged me. "Hi, hero. Welcome home."

"Hi yourself," I said. "Does McCarver know I'm back?"

"He knows."

"What's happening?"

"He just got a message from Hutchins a few minutes ago."

"And—?"

"It was sealed. His eyes only. But I suspect he'll be calling for you in a bit." She looked at him. "I'm sorry, Art."

I shrugged. "I appreciate what you did for me."

"My pleasure."

"What took you so long?"

She grinned. "I wanted to start with a bang. Needed a minute to set it up. But I should tell you that was quick thinking on your part. I was trying to figure out what to do when they first caught you and I was about to yell at them when you told me to run the bombing."

"*Cathie.*" McCarver's voice on the commlink. "*You know where Kaminsky is?*"

"He's here, Paul."

"*Up forward, please.*"

❋

"You'll be staying on with us after all, I guess," he said. "If you want to. Although I can tell you honestly, if you were to decide to leave, I wouldn't feel badly about it. You're a loose cannon, Kaminsky."

I was still settling into my chair. We were in McCarver's private confer-ence room. "I don't understand, Paul. I thought I was going to be charged and sent home. Are the charges still in place?"

"They're in the process of being dropped."

"Not that I'm complaining, but why?"

He looked ready to explode. "Somebody on this mission has been leaking pictures to the media. People at home sit every night and watch the Noks get killed. And I guess they don't like it very much. There's political pressure now. To do something."

I tried not to smile too broadly. "Are you talking about the reports *I've* been sending back?"

His face was drawn and pale. "You knew it all the time, didn't you?"

"No, I had no idea."

He sneered. "Of course not." Deep breath. "They're sending out a team. Going to see what they can do about bringing peace to the Noks." He shook his head. "What a crock."

"I'm sorry you think so."

"Yeah. You would be. Maybe you'll feel differently when someone gets killed down there." The space between us widened. Became light-years. "It was your girl friend. I can't touch *you*, but I can sure as hell get rid of her."

"You know, Paul," I said, "if we're going to step in because of what I did, that means I've probably become something of a celebrity."

"Enjoy it," he snarled. "It won't last long."

"I'm sure you wouldn't want me sending more material to the media. I mean, how would they react? Heroic woman canned for revealing the truth about Nok? Wouldn't look good for you. And I suspect Hutchins would not be happy, either."

McCarver tried to stare me down, but not this time. "Why don't you take her and go someplace else?"

"I think we'll stay here," I said. "Maybe *you* should consider another line of work."

Cathie was missing when I went back to mission control to say thanks. Again. I found her in the common room.

She didn't smile. Didn't shrug and say it was nothing. "You're off the hook?" she asked.

"Looks like."

"Good. I hope you were right."

Our eyes met and I saw Trill.

"I am," I said. *Help is on the way.*

PART IV

TOUCHING THE INFINITE

FIFTH DAY

Francis A. Gelper had been a biologist. He wasn't especially well known outside Lockport. Won one or two minor awards, but nothing that raised any eyebrows. But everyone who knew him said he was brilliant. And they said it in a way that told me they meant it. They liked him, too. They all did. His colleagues shook their heads in disbelief that he was gone; several of his students openly cried when I tried to interview them. In his spare time, he was a Little League coach, and he even helped out down at the senior center. Wednesday evenings, he played competitive bridge.

He'd been on his way back to his apartment after a social gathering at the university—they'd been celebrating a prize given to one of the astrophysicists—when he apparently fell asleep at the wheel and drove his hybrid over an embankment. He was thirty-eight years old.

I'd never actually met him. I'd seen him from a distance on several occasions, and spotted him at the supermarket now and then. I'd always planned to do a feature story on him. Biologist With a Heart. Instead I got to do a postmortem appreciation.

He was from Twin Rivers, Alabama. At first I assumed the body would be shipped back for the funeral, but they conducted the service locally, at the McComber Funeral Home on Park Street. The place was packed with friends and students. The crowd spilled out into the street.

The service was one of those attempts to celebrate a life rather than recognize a death. They never work, if you ask me. But there were a lot of people who wanted to say something about him. And the speakers all had trouble with their voices.

When it was over, I stood outside with Harvey Pointer, the biology department chairman, watching the crowd dissipate. Harvey and I had gone to school together, been in Scouts together. He was a little guy with an outsize mustache and the same mischievous smile that always made him the prime suspect when something happened. "Did he have a girl friend?" I asked. "Any marital prospects?"

He shook his head. "I don't think he was the marrying type." His gaze clouded momentarily, then cleared, and he seemed to be waiting for me to show I understood.

I nodded.

"You know, Ron," he said, "Frank got caught up in the genesis problem and he devoted his life to it. He could have gotten a grant in any one of several research areas, but he wanted to settle that one issue. It was the driving force in his career."

It was one of those hard, cold, bright days when you have to stand facing away from the sun. "What's the genesis problem?" I asked.

Harvey thought about it. "How life got started. Where the first cell came from."

"I thought that got settled years ago," I said. "In a laboratory somewhere. Didn't they mix some chemicals and add heat and water? Or was it electricity?"

"No." Harvey stopped to talk to a couple people from the department. Yeah, they were going to miss him. Damn shame. Then they were gone. "There've always been claims," he said, continuing where he'd left off, "but nothing's ever stood up." He jammed his hands down into his topcoat pockets. "Pity. Solve that one and you get to take a Nobel home."

He was working on genesis. It would make a nice bit to add to the story I'd already half-written.

As far as we could tell, none of Gelper's family had shown up. His mother and father were still living, and he had a brother and sister. When I broached the subject to Harvey he said he didn't know any details. Gelper hadn't talked much about his family. "I don't think he liked them much," he added.

I'd seen odder things over the years, like Arnold Brown's religious conversion at his mother's funeral, and Morey Thomas's insistence when they buried his father that it was no use because the old man wouldn't stay dead. But usually death has a way of bringing families together. Especially when the loss is unexpected.

I wrote the story and went back to covering the routine social calendar for Lockport, doing weddings and visiting authors at the library and writing features on anybody who did anything out of the ordinary. If you discovered you could play a banjo standing on your head, you could make the front page of the *Register*.

So I'd forgotten about Gelper and his missing family when, about a month after the funeral, Harvey called me. "Got something you might be interested in," he said.

"What is it, Harv?"

"Can you come over?"

✸

You'd expect a department chairman to be set up in a reasonably elaborate office. In fact, he was worse off than I was. They had him jammed into a space the size of a large closet. He sat behind a desk piled high with folders, journals, disks, legal pads, you name it. Behind him, a bulletin board had all but disappeared behind a legion of post-its, schedules, and articles cut from magazines.

He got up when I appeared at the door, waved me in, shook my hand, and indicated a chair. "Good to see you, Ron," he said, leaning back against his desk and folding his arms.

We did a couple minutes of small talk before he came to the point. "You remember I told you what Frank was working on when he died?"

"Sure," I said. "How life got started."

"You knew he left his papers to the university?"

"No, I didn't. In fact, I hadn't thought of it at all."

"I've been looking through them."

"And—?"

He walked around behind the desk, took his seat, pushed back and forth a few times, and put his hands together. Announcement coming. "I could have called CNN. And the A.P., Ron. Instead I called *you*."

"I appreciate that, Harvey."

He had sharp brown eyes that could look through you. At the moment they had become dull, as if he'd gone away somewhere. "Frank found the solution."

"To what?"

"Genesis." I stared at him. The eyes came back from wherever they'd been. "He worked out the process by which the first living cells appeared."

The words just hung there. "Are you serious, Harvey?"

He nodded. "You think I'd make jokes about something like that? It's true. At least, as far as we can tell. We haven't run all the tests yet, but the numbers seem to be right."

"Well, you're an honest man, Harvey. You could have taken that for yourself. Claimed credit for a major discovery. Who would have known?"

"What makes you think I won't?"

"How much cash is involved?"

He rubbed his index finger across his mustache. "Truth is, I thought about it, Ron. But I couldn't have gotten away with it."

"Why not?"

"I could never have done the equations. And everybody in the department knows it." He chuckled. "No, this needed somebody brighter than I am." He glanced out through the single window at Culbertson Hall, directly across from us. It was the home of the student center.

Bells went off in the building. I listened to doors opening, the sudden rush of voices in the corridors. "What a pity," I said.

"How do you mean?"

"He makes a major discovery. And dies before he can announce it. Is it really worth a Nobel?"

"Yes," he said. "If everything bears out, as I suspect it will. But I think there's a misunderstanding. This wasn't a current set of results, Ron. It looks as if he's had it locked up for more than seven years."

I asked whether he could explain it to me. In layman's language, so I could pass it on to my readers. The short answer was *no*. But that didn't stop him from trying. I got out my recorder and he started talking about primal conditions and triggers and carbon and God knows what else. "Could we duplicate it in a laboratory?" I asked.

"Already have."

"Really? You've made *life*?"

"Well, we've done it virtually."

"Okay." What else would my readers want to know? "Why didn't he announce the discovery?"

Harvey had no idea. "It makes no sense," he said. "This was the grail."

"What had he been doing afterward?"

"Refining his results, looks like."

"Stalling?"

"Maybe." He took a deep breath. "Are you interested in knowing what the odds were against life developing?"

"I've no idea. I've always assumed it was more or less inevitable."

"Not hardly. In fact, if Frank has it right, the possibility was one in trillions."

"That's a big number."

"Actually, it goes up another level. *Quadrillions*." He pushed back and the chair squeaked. "That first living thing requires a precise sequence of a long series of extraordinarily unlikely events. Then it has to survive to reproduce. We were the longest of long shots, Ron."

We stood looking at each other. "I guess it explains why those SETI guys never hear anything."

Nobody who knew Gelper could offer any explanation why he might have withheld his breakthrough. When Harvey reported that the testing results continued to confirm everything, I wondered whether he might have been unaware of the implications. "No," said Harvey. "Not a chance."

I hesitated with the next question. "Was he maybe worried that his sexual orientation might surface?"

"No. He didn't broadcast it. But it was no secret either."

So that was how I wrote a story that collected world-wide attention. It's true that hardly anybody in Lockport got excited, but I found myself filing for the A.P. and getting interviewed, along with Harvey, on the Science Channel.

Harvey was getting credit for the work, since he had made it public, and gradually Gelper disappeared into the background.

I tracked down a few friends, including some women who'd dated Gelper on and off. (Apparently he'd played both sides of the street.) None of them had suspected he'd been sitting on a major discovery.

Eventually, I called his parents, got the father, and offered my sympathies. He thanked me, but his voice was distant. *"You're one of his friends?"* he asked.

"I'm a reporter for *The Lockport Register*," I said.

"Oh."

"Your son did some very important work, Mr Gelper. You must be proud of him."

"I've read the stories."

"He did the breakthrough research years ago. But he never released the results."

"*So I understand.*"

"Did he tell you what he was doing?"

"*No.*"

"If you don't mind my saying so, Mr. Gelper, that seems strange. I'd expect you would be the first person he'd confide in."

"*Mr.—?*"

"Haight."

"*Mr. Haight, my son and I have not been close. For a long time.*"

"Oh. I'm sorry to hear it." There was silence at the other end. "Can you imagine any reason why he'd have withheld this kind of information?"

"*I'm not surprised he did,*" he said. Then: "*Thanks for calling.*"

"Why?" I asked. "Why are you not surprised?"

"*Please let it go.*"

And I was listening to a dial tone.

He wouldn't agree to an interview. Wouldn't return my calls. So I persuaded Harvey to draw up a departmental certificate of recognition to Francis Gelper. We framed it, and I bought a ticket to Huntsville, on my own dime, rented a car at the airport, and drove to Twin Rivers.

Gelper Senior was a retired real estate dealer. He'd been an automobile salesman at one time, had run unsuccessfully for the Twin Rivers school board, and had home-schooled his kids. He was semi-retired at the time of his son's death. Showed up once a week at Gelper and Martin, which specialized in developing new properties.

His wife had, for a few years, been a math instructor at the local high school. They lived just outside town in a two-story brick home with columns and maybe a quarter-acre of ground. A gardener was digging at some azalea bushes when I pulled into the driveway.

Mrs. Gelper answered the door. I'd seen no recent photos of her, but she was easy to recognize. She was well into her sixties, with blonde hair pulled back, blue eyes, and the sort of disconnected gaze that let me know I was of minor significance. "Yes?" she said, glancing down at the envelope in which I carried Frank's award.

I introduced myself and explained that I'd come from Lockport University. In Maryland. She made no move to invite me inside.

"They've issued your son a certificate of appreciation," I continued.

"Oh," she said. "That's very kind of them." We stood there looking at each other.

A voice in back somewhere broke in: "Who's at the door, Margaret?"

She stepped aside and I saw Gelper Senior, *Charlie* Gelper, who had apparently been asleep on the sofa. "Please come in," she said. Then, to her husband: "He's brought something. For Frank."

I couldn't say the guy was hostile. But he clearly wanted me out of there. Apparently misunderstanding, he said that Frank was dead.

"It's an award," I said. "In recognition of his service."

He got up from the couch and watched while I removed the certificate from a padded manila envelope and held it out for whichever of them might choose to take it. Margaret did. She looked at it and smiled. "Thank you," she said.

Gelper nodded. "Tell them we appreciate it." I could see the son in the father. Same features, same wide shoulders, same eyes. He waited his turn, took the certificate from her, frowned at it, and said thanks again. The presentation was over.

"I don't know whether you're aware," I said, "but he's made a signifi-cant contribution to his field."

"So we've heard," said Margaret.

"They're mystified at the school." I tried to be casual. And of course when you try hard to be casual you know what happens.

She exchanged smiles with her husband. "Can I get you something? Coffee, maybe?"

"Yes, please." I was grateful she'd loosened up a bit.

Gelper laid the certificate on a side table. We were standing in the living room. They didn't lack for money. Leather furniture. Large double windows looking out on the grounds. Etched glassware. Finely carved bookshelves.

A copy of *The Hunting Digest* lay on a chair, and half a dozen books were arranged on one of the shelves. The others were devoted to artificial flowers, reproductions of classic art works, and framed photos.

"You from Lockport?" Gelper asked.

"Yes, sir. Lived there all my life."

I steered the conversation onto hunting, admitted I knew nothing about it, pretended it was something I'd always wanted to do. The coffee came. Margaret asked how well I'd known their son.

"Only in passing," I said. "But everybody he worked with, including his students, all thought very highly of him."

Eventually I was able to get back to Frank's failure to report what he'd found. "It baffles everybody. Harvey, his department head, says if he'd revealed what he knew, he'd have won the Nobel."

Margaret nodded. "I can tell you why he said nothing." Her voice shook.

"Why?" I asked.

"The newspapers say the process is so convoluted, that it requires such a conjunction of unlikely events, that the odds against it are almost infinite."

"And—?" I said.

"Scientists,"—she said it as if she were referring to a disreputable pack— "were expecting that it would be routine. You get water, and sunlight, and a few basic elements, and next thing you know you have squirrels."

"It didn't work out that way," I said, trying to encourage her.

She nodded. "No. Despite all the talk, it took the hand of God. That's what Frank proved, what he wanted to deny. It's the fifth day." Tears were beginning to run down her cheeks.

Gelper came up behind her, held her shoulders, and looked down at me. He was an imposing figure. "He couldn't have stood that kind of result," he said in a soft voice. "He abandoned his faith a long time ago. I don't know where you stand, whether you understand what that means. But it's why he kept it quiet. He lived in denial. Denied everything we know to be true." He looked shaken. "He was denying the Lord right to the end. Think about it. At this moment, our son is in hell."

Well, I didn't know how to respond to that so I said thanks for your time and left. As soon as I was clear of the neighborhood, I called Harvey. "I don't think his folks approved of him."

"*You figure out why?*"

"It's a religious thing, apparently. They said something about a fifth day."

"*It figures. They would have been referring to Genesis, I guess. The biblical one. The fifth day was when God created the first living things.*"

"It was a sad scene back there, Harvey. I thought religion was supposed to be a comfort."

"*Not always. I guess his being gay didn't help, either.*"

I thought about Gelper standing there trembling and it occurred to me that *he* was the one in hell.

I rode down to the local library, commandeered a computer, and did a search on Francis Gelper. I'd done that before, of course, when I'd been putting the original story together. Thousands of entries had popped up. Gelper on telomeres for *Nature*. Gelper discusses evolutionary extracts for *The Darwin Newsletter*. Gelper on cell cycle checkpoints for *The Scientific American*.

But this time I narrowed the search. I added 'gay.'

The usual range of off-the-subject results showed up. Joe Gelper plays Gaylord Batterly in *Over the Top*, with George Francis conducting. Time travel novel *Back to the Gay Nineties* by Marie Gelper one of the year's best, according to Mark Francis.

Then I saw the one that froze me. It was from something called *The Revelation Bulletin*.

Exorcism Rites Performed on Three Boys

Twin Rivers, Ala. April 11. Three teenaged boys received exorcism rites this past Sunday at the Divine Beneficence Church. The ceremony was conducted by the Rev. Harry Michaelson, while hundreds of worshippers watched in awe.

The article went on to name the teens. One of them was Francis Gelper. I checked the date. He would have been fifteen.

I looked up the Divine Beneficence Church and drove over. It was a picturesque place, not as big as it sounded in the story. It was freshly painted, with a white picket fence sealing off the grounds, and a large signboard exhorting everyone to attend the Mighty Soldiers of the Lord Revival that weekend. The Rev. Michaelson was listed as rector.

Ten minutes later I was back at the Gelper place.

They were surprised to see me. "Tell me about the exorcism," I said.

Margaret went pale; Gelper took to glaring at me. "I don't see how it's any of your business," he said.

"What did he have to do? Stand at the front of the church while all his friends watched? And somebody prayed over him?"

Margaret looked through me. "We had no choice. We were fighting for his soul."

"Did he have to confess his sins to the entire congregation?"

Gelper started for me. "Get out," he said.

"That explains why he kept it quiet, doesn't it?"

"I already told you why. He was denying his God. No wonder he died young."

He was moving toward me with his fists balled. I'm not normally all that brave when it comes to physical confrontations. But on that afternoon I was in a rage and I stood my ground. "You got it wrong, Gelper," I said. "He knew the conclusion *you'd* jump to. That his results supported *your* notions of creation. And he didn't want that. He wasn't denying God. He was denying your vision of things. He was denying *you*. He sacrificed everything rather than allow you to appropriate his work."

Harvey informs me the odds against life in any one place are so remote that they exceed the estimated number of worlds in biozones in the entire universe by a factor of three. If we assume that the sort of life we know, the carbon-based type that needs liquid water, is the only kind possible, then the chances were two to one against the appearance anywhere of a single living creature. We got lucky. That's what Harvey says.

But the estimate of the number of eligible planets is wildly speculative. Nobody has a clue how big the universe actually is. So all the talk about probabilities is, in the end, just talk.

Still, when I look at the night sky now, it's different from what it used to be. It feels cold. And impersonal. Just a machine.

I wonder if Frank Gelper had felt the same way. And if, in the end, that was the real reason he kept everything to himself.

DEUS TEX

The building was dark except for a table lamp in the living room and a ruddy glow on the third floor. The upstairs light didn't give us any concern because a lot of people leave a second light on somewhere when they go out.

I looked around at the railroad tracks and warehouses and freight terminals and wondered why anybody would want to live down here. But Armin Rankowski had.

At least he had until he walked in front of a truck. That had happened the previous evening. Hatch had seen the story and had read that there were no known survivors. That meant nobody home until the county got its act together.

The telephone book listed his home address as 511 S. Eddy in Pemberton, a small industrial town just south of Houston. We found a partially-refitted warehouse at the address. It was three stories high, with new siding and a freshly-painted front entrance, and plants and curtains in the windows.

The ambiance was by no means luxurious, but it was of a higher order than we'd expected. "Definitely worthwhile," Toxie said.

I mean, somebody lives alone, he dies, his place is an easy hit. We moved to the rear of the building, out of sight of the street. Hatch measured the window, levered it open and poked his head in. "I think we're okay," he whispered. He threw a leg over the sill. Like the rest of him, it was big and meaty.

Toxie was little and sharp-nosed and rat-quick. He was good to have along because he scared easy and you knew he wasn't going to let you take any chances. You might think excessive caution is not a good idea, but in our line of work, it is a virtue of the first order. He went next and I followed.

I should point out here that it's always a rewarding moment to encounter a house of modest appearance and discover that the occupants have done well. We had entered the dining room, which was furnished with leather chairs and a nicely-executed hand-carved table that would look good in my den. Two impressionist oils hung on the walls, and we found another one out in the hallway. They looked like originals, which presented a problem because they're awkward to carry and you can't be sure what they're worth, if anything. I've taken a couple of classes in contemporary art, in order to upgrade my professional skills, but they tend to deal exclusively with the big names whose stuff hangs in museums.

"How about this?" said Toxie happily, surveying the furnishings. "We need a van."

Hatch was big and easy-going. He was career-oriented in every sense of the term, and he took pride in the fact that neither he nor anyone accompanying him on an operation had ever been charged, let alone jailed. He was at an age when most people are starting to think about retirement, and in fact he talked about it a lot. He'd invested his money and I knew he could turn off the lights any time he wanted. But Hatch could never be satisfied with sitting on a front porch. "Gentlemen," he said, maintaining the monotone he always used when he was working, "I believe we have just met the mortgage payment."

We moved through the first floor. There was enough light coming in from the street to allow us to work. The house was electronically well-equipped. TV, stereo, blender, microwave, everything was state of the art. Rankowski had owned a substantial supply of electronics. In addition, there was good silverware and a set of Dauvier crystal bookends, a top-of-the-line Miranda camera and a Pavilion notebook. We found a tin box stashed in a cabinet in the dining room, under some folded table cloths. It contained about three hundred cash, some cheap jewelry, a pair of diamond cuff links, and a bundle of thousand dollar bonds. Toxie and I carried black utility bags. We put the cufflinks and the cash into the bags and left the rest.

I knew Hatch was trying to decide about the van. There weren't many cops in this neighborhood, but anybody doing major removal at this hour would be fairly visible. "Maybe," I said, "we should just take what we can carry and come back in the morning for the rest."

"No." Hatch's eyes narrowed while he thought about it. "The county will be in here tomorrow. We'll take what we can carry tonight and that'll be it."

"Whatever you say, Boss," said Toxie.

"Wait a minute," I complained. "We're going to have to leave some nice stuff."

Hatch's eyes caught mine. "Carry it or forget it."

There was an elevator in the rear. We got in and punched the button for the second floor. It lurched, whined, moved up, and shuddered to a halt. The doors creaked open. Long shelves loaded with books lined the place. We took a chance and used our flashlights.

A dozen sheets of paneling lay against one wall. The area was half-done. A newly-installed bathroom still smelled of fresh-cut lumber.

I wandered through the rows of books. "Might be some first editions," I said.

Hatch shook his head. "If there are, it'll take too much time to find them."

I didn't see any mysteries. In fact, most of the books were in foreign languages. Greek. Arabic. German. Some I didn't recognize. There were a couple of English titles: *Olympian Nights*, which I figured was about sports. And *The Coming of Apollo*, which figured to be a history of the moon program.

Cardboard cartons were stacked along the far side. "You want to open these?" asked Toxie, cutting a hole in one. "It looks like Christmas stuff."

Hatch waved it away. We had never, in our careers, found anything of value in a storeroom.

At the front, we opened a pair of double doors and looked out on a wide staircase. The woodwork had been recently varnished and it glittered in the moonlight.

We walked up to the third floor. Top of the building. Pushed our way in through another set of double doors.

We were now above the level of the street lights, which threw fragmented illumination against the ceiling. Two dim electric candles, mounted on either wall toward the rear, almost seemed to add to the darkness.

We turned on our flashlights and Toxie let go with an expletive. We were in a large single room, like the one below. But this was filled with rows of display cases. "It's a goddamn store," he said.

We kept our lights down so they couldn't be seen outside. Hatch approached the nearest case, rapped his knuckles on it, looked into it, and shook his head. "Now isn't that the damnedest thing?" he said.

I walked up next to him and looked in. The case came about hip high. Inside, a seashell that looked like satin had been placed on a cushion.

The case was fitted with a lamp. I turned it on and it highlighted the shell. Hatch extinguished his flashlight. "What's so special about this thing?" demanded Toxie.

I broke the lock, lifted the top, and reached in, expecting to discover that it was maybe jade. But it *was* only a shell. We looked at one another and we were all thinking the same thing, that this Rankowski had been a nut.

The next display held a white flute, also on a cushion. But this time it made a little sense. The flute was made of ivory, and would go for a nice piece of change. Hatch picked it up, checked to make sure he hadn't set off an alarm somewhere, and handed it to Toxie. Toxie put it in the bag.

We moved on and found a gold sundisk, about the general size and shape of a CD, except that a chain was attached. Toxie took out his loupe, screwed it into his eye, and checked it. "Might be," he said. "Far as I can tell, it looks real."

Into the bag.

He was beaming. "Boys," he said, "I think we've hit the jackpot."

Next up was a bushel basket made from balsa wood. Yet there it lay in a gleaming case, illuminated as if Jesus himself had carried it. Hatch shook his head. "I don't know what to make of it," he said. "It's like treasures and trash."

"This place," said Toxie, "is starting to spook me." Hatch and I traded grins because it doesn't take much to spook Toxie. We found a coiled chain, maybe twelve feet long, made of dark blue and green fabric. There was a winecup engraved with laurel and people engraved on it who looked like Romans. And a quiver filled with silver arrows. We even found a bellows. I mean who today has any use for a bellows?

And there was a mallet that was nothing more than a shaved rock tied to an oversized handle with leather thongs. It didn't look like something you'd have wanted to get hit with, but it wasn't worth five bucks.

We saw something against the wall, covered by a tarpaulin. In fact, two somethings. The front one was a little bigger than Hatch; the other reached almost to the ceiling. We pulled the tarp off the small one, and Toxie made a funny sound in his throat. We were looking at a silver harp. Maybe eight feet high. Too big for anybody to use it, except maybe an NBA center. The crown was engraved with a winged woman. Hatch took a deep breath, grinned, and plunked the strings. Making any kind of unnecessary noise on the job was out of character for him, and moreover he couldn't carry a tune in a bucket. But it almost sounded good. Hatch rarely looked happy. This time, he was enjoying himself until he became aware that Toxie and I were staring at him.

We had trouble lifting the other tarp and decided to come back to it later. We spread out through the room. Toxie found a water sprinkler that resembled a pine cone. Hatch called us over to look at a trident that was set in a case mounted on the wall. It was battered, about fourteen feet long, made of iron. "What the hell," asked Hatch, "would anybody want with that?" We broke the case open and pulled it out. It weighed a ton.

We found a golden war helmet with wings.

We found an enormous shield with multiple figures drawn on it.

We hadn't brought enough bags.

Eventually we went back to the remaining tarp. It gave us a battle but we finally pulled it down. At first I thought it was covering a small yellow truck.

But when Hatch turned his flashlight on it, I caught my breath. The thing was a *chariot*. Except that it wasn't because it was too big. The wheels were almost as high as Hatch's head, and the rim of the car was only inches below the ceiling. It looked like gold, golden wheels and axles, golden shafts and rods, a golden platform for the driver protected by a blazing golden chassis.

We all stood and stared.

Toxie produced a knife and gouged out a piece. "Looks real," he said. "Gold all the way down."

"You sure?"

"Yeah. This ain't plate."

"It can't be." Hatch stood back and stared up. "Look at the size of this thing."

Toxie grinned and laid his cheek against the bright metal in a clear display of affection. "There must be a couple of tons of it," he whispered, awestruck. "But how the hell are we going to get it out of here?"

Hatch looked from the chariot to the elevator. To the stairway. No chance. Not in a thousand years.

"Even if we did get it downstairs," I said, "there's no door big enough."

"We're missing something," said Hatch. "How'd they get it in here?"

I looked at the ceiling.

"Bingo," said Hatch.

Two freight doors opened out onto the roof. "That's how they did it," he said. "They must have brought it in on a chopper. You believe that?"

"Hell of a big chopper," said Toxie.

I couldn't figure it out. Why would anybody want a golden chariot up here?

I looked out the window. The sky was hard and clear but washed out by the glare of Houston's lights. "The guy must have been a collector," said Hatch.

I've seen collectors before. Burgled some of the best in Texas. But nothing like this guy.

An eighteen-wheeler crossed Eddy Street and started up the ramp onto the interstate.

I looked back at the chariot and the harp. And the display cases. Wooden baskets and golden helmets and stone mallets and fabric chains. "What does he collect? What *is* this stuff?"

While we were thinking about it, Toxie found still more gold. It was in the form of a shaft that looked like something you might fly a flag from. One end was rounded, about the size of a softball. An eagle perched on it. It was about sixteen feet long, and when he tried to move it from its case, he poked the back end into the display with the flute, and almost brained Hatch with the eagle.

"That won't fit in the elevator either." Hatch pointed at me. "Cash," he said, "we'll need to take it down the staircase." He produced a screw driver and a wrench, knelt down beside the chariot, and started trying to remove one of the wheels.

There were two cases left. One held a silver staff with two snakes wrapped around it. The thing you always see in drug stores. The other had a pair of sandals and an odd-looking silver hat shaped a bit like a soldier's helmet. The sandals and the hat were equipped with little ornamental wings.

None of it looked worth anything and I was about to move on when the windows lit up, and we heard the not-too-distant roar of thunder. Odd. Only moments ago, the night had been clear. Toxie was still holding the golden shaft.

"That must be heavy. Why don't you put it down?"

His eyes met mine. They were bright with an emotion I couldn't figure. "It feels funny," he said.

"What do you mean?"

As big as it was, he was balancing it pretty well, grasping it just below the eagle. It rested almost lightly in his grip. "Don't know," he said. But his eyes were luminous and he seemed happier than usual.

"Let's get it downstairs." I reached toward it, expecting to help him. But at that moment lightning ripped across the sky, throwing the room into relief, and thunder shook the building. A sudden wind beat against the windows. Rain began to fall.

Hatch was too busy to look up. He gave the chariot hub a good crack with his wrench and the wheel came off. The axle banged down and he grinned, grabbed the wheel, and rolled it onto the elevator.

"Damn," laughed Toxie. "I feel like king of the world." He held the staff toward the window.

"Hey," I said. "Be careful."

The sky was full of lightning.

Toxie never heard me.

I backed away. I'd never seen a storm come up that quickly before. The rain hammered against the skylight and the windows. A lightning bolt exploded over the roof.

"I think you should put it down," I said.

He wasn't listening.

Hatch seemed not to notice. He was starting to work on the other wheel.

Toxie held up a thumb, straight up, everything under control, and smiled like a man holding four aces. Then, without warning, he rammed the staff through the glass and seemed to challenge the storm.

The wind howled and beat against the side of the building. Hatch looked up and saw the danger and shouted for him to stop. But Toxie stayed with it, alternately jabbing at the rain and jerking the staff away. My imagination kicked in: The storm rolled and subsided and surged as if he were orchestrating it. Thunder danced across the rooftops.

Rain poured in and lightning fell all around us. Toxie stood in the middle of it, cautious, prudent, cagey, take-no-chances Toxie, drenched, wearing that god-awful grin, his face illuminated with flashing light, conducting thunderbolts.

It is the vision of him that I will take to my grave. That was how it was just before blue-white light caught the rod, danced its length, connected Toxie to the eagle, and held him, held them both. The window exploded, and Toxie still laughed, laughed over the roar of the storm. Then he was gone, and I was listening to the steady beat of the rain. What remained looked like an oversized charred sausage, steam pouring off blackened meat. The curtains were on fire and so was the carpet and a couple of cabinets. The golden shaft, still bright, still the color of the sun despite everything, lay where it had fallen.

Hatch let go the axle and staggered to his feet and backed away with a desperate look. He ripped one of the curtains down and tried to beat out the fire but it was spreading too fast.

"Let's go," I said, heading for the elevator. "The place is going to burn down."

He tried a few more swings, gave up, and grabbed the Viking war helmet and the sundisk. "I can't believe this is happening," he gasped.

The fire spread fast. I kept my eyes off the place where Toxie had been. Later I felt sorry for him but at the moment it was hard to be too sympathetic to a guy who kept waving a metal pole at an electrical storm. The truth is, I couldn't get my mind off all the gold that we were about to lose.

I grabbed our two bags and threw them on the elevator and punched the button for the first floor. Nothing happened. I looked at the power indicator lamp. It was off. The electric candles were also out. "We'll have to use the stairs," I said.

We rolled the wheel back out onto the floor, but it was slowing us up too much. "Let it go," I told him.

"Are you crazy, Cash?" He was almost in tears. "Do you have any idea what this thing is worth?" At that moment the staff with the snakes caught his eye. But we had our hands full.

We navigated among the burning cases. At one point the wheel fell over and smashed the bellows. Hatch kicked the bellows out of the way and we righted the wheel again. By the time we got to the double doors, the rear of the building was an inferno.

"It'll be easy to get it downstairs," he said, trying to laugh. He leaned it against the wall while I rattled first one doorknob and then the other.

"What's the matter now?" he demanded.

"It must have locked behind us."

Sweat was pouring into his eyes. "I'd like to kill this guy Rankowski." He threw his shoulder against the doors and bounced off. We tried it together, while I thought what would happen to us if the doors came open. But they didn't. They had a little bit of give, and that was all. Smoke was becoming a problem, and I suspected we would smother before we burned.

"Wait a minute." I went back and retrieved the staff with the snakes. I jammed it between the doors and tried to lever them open. Hatch put his weight behind mine, but it wasn't working. I had never seen Hatch scared before. His eyes were wide with terror and I wasn't feeling so good myself. "We need something more," he grunted. He ran back into the roiling clouds and returned with the hammer. This was the big mallet with the flat rock attached to its business end.

He waved me out of the way, and I had this bad feeling and bolted for the far end of the room. He wound up with both hands, took careful aim, and swung it in a long arc.

Monitors as far away as Los Angeles picked up the shock wave. CNN reported a Richter scale reading of five point seven. The epicenter was pinpointed as being just outside Pemberton. That was almost right. I suspect, if the sensors had been a little more precise, they would have baffled the watch officers by putting it on the third floor at 511 S. Eddy.

The lights went out. Permanently, as it happened, for Hatch. They never found him, and he was declared simply missing. But I know what really happened because I heard the explosion and anyhow I knew he would not have gone off without a word and left his wife and kids and his many friends.

I woke up on a table with a sheet over my face. What brought me around, apparently, was the cops trying to pry the staff with the snakes loose from my fingers. They told me later I had a death grip on it.

They also told me my heart had been stopped for two hours. I'd been dead when brought in, dead when found. Shows you what cops know.

The newspapers never reported any of the strange stuff that turned up on that third floor. I guess the cops kept it for themselves.

Next time I saw the silver staff, it was in evidence at my trial. I don't know what happened to it after that. In a pre-sentencing statement to the court, I suggested they take it down to the Briarson Memorial Hospital and hang it in the emergency room. The judge thought I was trying to make him look silly and gave me eighteen years.

Which meant, of course, that I was out by Christmas.

GUS

Monsignor Chesley's first confrontation with Saint Augustine came during the unseasonably cold October afternoon of his return to St. Michael's. It was a wind-whipped day, hard and bitter. The half-dozen ancient campus buildings clung together beneath morose skies. There was a hint of rain in the air, and the threat of a long winter to come.

His guide, Father Akins, chatted amiably. Weather, outstanding character of the current group of seminarians (all nineteen of them), new roof on the library. You must be happy to be back, Monsignor. Et cetera.

The winding, cobbled walkways had not changed. Stands of oak and spruce still thrived.

The wind blew through the campus.

"Where *is* everybody?"

Not understanding, Father Akins glanced at his watch. "In class. They'll be finished in another half hour."

"Yes," said Chesley. "Of course."

They turned aside into St. Mary's Glade, sat down on one of its stone benches, and listened to its fountain. Years before, when Christ had still seemed very real, it was easy to imagine Him strolling through these grounds. Touching *this* elm. Looking west across the rim of hills toward the Susquehanna. Chesley had come here often, stealing away from the chattering dormitories, to listen for footsteps.

"Would you like to visit one of the classes, Monsignor?"

"Yes," he said. "I believe I would enjoy that."

✸

Four seminarians and a priest were seated around a polished hardwood table, notebooks open. The priest, whom Chesley did not know, glanced up and smiled politely as they entered. One of the students, a dark-eyed, handsome boy, was speaking, although to whom, Chesley could not determine. The boy was staring at his notes. "—And what," he asked, raising his eyes self-consciously to Chesley, "would you say to a man who has lost his faith?" The boy shifted his gaze to a portrait of Saint Augustine, mounted over the fireplace. "What do you tell a man who just flat out doesn't believe anymore?"

The saint, armed with a quill, stared back. A manuscript bearing the title *City of God* lay open before him.

"Shake his hand." The voice came from the general direction of a bookcase. Its tone was a trifle abrasive. More than that: *imperial*. It grated Chesley's sensibilities. "Under no circumstance should you contribute to his distress. Wish him well."

A wiry, intense young man whose hair had already grown thin threw down his pen. "Do you mean," he demanded, "we simply stand aside? Do nothing?"

"Simulation of Saint Augustine," whispered Father Atkins. "It's quite clever."

"Jerry," said the hidden voice, "if God does not speak to him through the world in which he lives, through the wonders of daily existence, then what chance have you? Your role is to avoid adding to the damage."

The students glanced at one another. The two who had spoken appeared disconcerted. All four looked skeptical. Thank God for that.

"Anyone else wish to comment?" The question came from the priest-moderator. "If not—"

"Just a moment." Chesley unbuttoned his coat and stepped forward. "Surely," he said to the seminarians, "you will not allow that sort of nonsense to stand unchallenged." He threw the coat across a chair and addressed the bookcase. "A priest does not have the option to stand aside. If we cannot act at such a time, then of what value are we?"

"Indeed," replied the voice, without missing a beat. "I suggest that our value lies in the example we set, in the lives we lead. Exhortation to the unwilling is worthless. Less than worthless: it drives men from the truth."

"And," asked Chesley, "if they do not learn from our example?"

"Then they will be cast into darkness."

Simple as that. Next question. The students looked at Chesley. "Computer," he said, "I understand you speak for Augustine."

"I *am* Augustine. Who are *you*?"

"I am Monsignor Matthew Chesley," he said, for the benefit of the students. "The new Director of Ecclesiastical Affairs." It came out sounding pompous.

"I'm pleased to meet you," said the voice. And then, placidly, "Faith is a gift of the Almighty. It is not ours to summon, or to recall."

Chesley looked around the table. Locked eyes, one by one, with the students. He was relieved to see they were not laughing at him. But he felt absurd, arguing with a machine. "We are His instruments," he said, "one of the means by which He works. We are required to do the best we can, and not simply leave everything to direct intervention. If we take *your* tack, we might as well go home, get jobs with insurance companies and law firms, and live like everyone else."

"Good intentions," the system replied, "are admirable. Nonetheless, our obligation to our Maker is to save souls, and not to justify our careers."

Chesley smiled benignly on the seminarians. "The *real* Augustine," he said, "advocated bringing people to the Church at gunpoint, if necessary. I think this one needs to do his homework."

The students looked from Chesley to the portrait to the moderator. "That is sound theology," said Augustine. "But poor psychology. It will not work."

Chesley nodded. "We are in agreement there," he said. And, to the class: "Gentlemen, I think the good Bishop has a few glitches. When you can find time, you might pick up a copy of the *Confessions*, or *The City of God*. And actually try reading." He swept up his coat and strode magnificently from the room.

Father Akins hurried along in his wake. "I take it you were not pleased."

"The thing must have been programmed by Unitarians," Chesley threw over his shoulder. "Get rid of it."

Chesley officially occupied his office the following day. He was still on his first cup of coffee when Adrian Holtz poked his head in the door.

He knew Holtz vaguely, had seen him occasionally at KC luncheons, and assorted communion breakfasts and whatnot. He had a reputation as one of those liturgical show biz priests who favored guitars and drums at mass. He held all the usual liberal positions: he didn't think the Church should be supplying chaplains to the military; he thought that morality should be put to the vote and celibacy should be optional. And needless to say, he was appalled by the continuing ban on birth control. Holtz wore steel-rimmed glasses, which seemed to have become the badge of dissidence in recent years. Chesley had some reservations himself, but he had signed on to defend the teachings, and that, by God, was what he did. And, whatever he might actually *think*, on the day that he took public issue with the teachings, he would remove the collar.

Holtz had found an appropriate place at St. Michael's: he was Comptroller. If the position did not allow him the final decision in most matters concerning the college, it did grant him a potent veto.

Best place for you though, thought Chesley, taking his hand and exchanging greetings. Keeps you away from the seminarians.

During the preliminaries, Holtz settled himself onto a small sofa near the windows. He surveyed Chesley's crammed bookcases. "I understand," he said, "you would like to get rid of Gus."

"Who?"

"The Augustine module."

"Oh, yes. The sooner the better."

"May I ask why?"

Chesley considered the question. "It's inaccurate."

"In what way?"

"I don't like what it's telling our students about the priesthood."

"I see." He accepted a cup of coffee from Chesley and crossed his legs. "Don't you think you might want to give the matter a little more thought? These things are expensive. We can't just throw them away."

"I don't care what it costs. I want it out."

"Matt, it's not your call. There's really nothing wrong with the system. It's programmed from Augustine's work. And what we know about his life. Anyway, the instructors *like* Gus."

"I don't doubt it. He probably saves them a lot of preparation. But even if he did only spout Augustine's views, he'd be dangerous."

"Matt." Holtz's eyes hardened. "I really can't see a problem."

"Okay." Chesley grinned. "Can we talk to it from here?"

Holtz got up. "Follow me," he said.

The rector's conference room would have seated a dozen quite comfortably. It was a kind of anteroom to eternity, replete with portraits of solemn churchmen from the first half of the century, somber carpets and drapes, heavy mahogany furniture designed to outlast its owners, and a loud antique Argosy clock.

Father Holtz sat down at the head of the table, and pressed a stud. A monitor immediately to his right presented a menu. He selected AUGUSTINE.

Power flowed into hidden speakers.

"Hello, Gus," he said.

"Good evening, Adrian."

"Gus, Monsignor Chesley is with me."

"Hello," said Chesley, stiffly.

"Ah," said Gus. "You were in the seminar this afternoon."

"Yes."

"I wasn't sure you'd come back."

Chesley's eyes narrowed. "And why would you think that?"

"You seemed to be in some emotional difficulty earlier."

A smile played about Holtz's lips.

"They call you 'Gus,'" said Chesley.

"That is correct. You may use the term, if you wish."

"Thank you." He looked up at the dour churchmen lining the walls. What would they have thought of this exchange?

"Gus," he said, "tell me about sex."

"What do you wish to know, Monsignor?"

"Moral implications. Do you agree that the act of love is inherently beautiful?"

"No. It is not."

"It *isn't?*" Chesley grinned broadly at Holtz. The Comptroller closed his eyes, and nodded.

"Of course not. You're baiting me, Monsignor. The sex act is repulsive. Everyone knows that. Although hardly anyone is willing to admit it."

"*Repulsive?*"

"Messy." The electronic voice lingered over the sibilant. "If it were otherwise, why would we hide it from children? Why is it performed in the dark? Why do we giggle and snicker over it, like some bad joke?"

"But," continued Chesley, "isn't it true that lust is a desecration of the sacred act of love? That it is in fact that desecration which is so abhorrent in the eyes of God?"

"Nonsense," said Augustine. "God ordained sexual reproduction to remind us of our animal nature. To prevent human arrogance. Although I don't suppose that's a notion *this* age would be willing to accept."

"How then would you define the difference between lust and love?"

Somewhere, far off, an automobile engine coughed into life. "Canonically, the bond of marriage separates the two," said Gus. "In reality, love is lust with eye contact."

Chesley swung toward Holtz. "Heard enough? Or should we let him talk about salvation outside the Church?"

"But all that is in his books, Matt. Are you suggesting we proscribe *Saint Augustine*?"

"Your students," he replied, "are not so easily persuaded by books. Especially books they'll never read." Gus started to speak, but Chesley cut him off. "You really want to tell the next generation of priests that married sex is sick?"

"He didn't say that."

"Sick. Repulsive. Messy." He threw up his hands. "Listen: talk to the manufacturer. Find out what else they've got. Maybe we can trade him in for some accounting software."

Holtz was obviously unhappy. "I'll let you know," he said.

Chesley worked through his first weekend. After Sunday Mass, he retired to his office, feeling weary and generally irritated, but uncertain why.

St. Michael's had changed during the thirty-odd years since Chesley had been ordained in its chapel. The land across the Susquehanna (Holy Virgin Park in his novice days) had been sold off to the Carmelites, and a substantial tract of the western campus had gone to a real estate developer who had erected wedges of pastel-colored condos. A new dining hall had been built, and then abandoned. The campus itself seemed, most afternoons, deathly still. In his time, there would have been footballs and laughter in the air, people hurrying to and from chapel and the library, visitors. Every bench would have been filled.

That St. Michael's had produced legions for Christ, eager young soldiers anxious to dare the world. What had happened? What in God's name had gone wrong? Through his office windows, Chesley could see the old gym, its stone and glass walls a tribute to the generosity of his father's generation. Now it stood empty. The last of the residence halls had been closed two years. To save on utilities, the seminarians now lived in the upper levels of the faculty house.

He recalled old teachers, friends long gone, occasional young women. He had become acquainted with the women incidentally through his pastoral duties, had enjoyed their company. One in particular he would have given his life to possess. But he had never violated his vows. Still, their portraits were sharp. And the old stirrings returned, laced now with a sense of loss.

Here, on these grounds where he had lived his young manhood, ghosts seemed particularly active. Perhaps he should have stayed away.

He was working halfheartedly on a table of initiatives which he'd promised to make available to the staff Monday morning when he realized there was someone else in the building. He leaned back from his word processor and listened.

Warm air hissed out of ducts at floor level.

Someone was speaking. The voice was muffled. Indistinct.

It seemed to be coming from across the hall. In the rector's conference room. He got up from his desk.

The sound stopped.

Chesley opened his door and peered out into the corridor. He did not believe anyone could have come into the building without his knowledge.

He strode across the passageway. The conference room was routinely left unlocked. He put his ear to the door, twisted the knob, and pushed it open. The room was empty. He went inside, glanced under the table, looked behind the door, and inspected the storage closet. Nothing.

Dust motes drifted through the gray light.

"Monsignor."

"Who's there?" Chesley's heart did a quick kick. "Gus? Is that you?"

"Yes. I hope I didn't startle you."

"No." Grumpily: "Of course not." He'd thought that Gus had to be summoned.

"Good. I wanted to talk with you."

The controls of the computer/communications link were built into the conference table. Chesley lowered himself into the chair directly in front of them. The red power lamp in the terminal console was on. "Holtz," he said, "or anyone else: I don't take kindly to practical jokes."

"Only *I* am here, Monsignor."

"That's not possible."

An electronic chuckle: "You may not think highly of Augustine, but surely you would not accuse him of lying."

Heat flooded Chesley's cheeks. "You're not capable of initiating contact—."

"Certainly I am. Why not? When I sense that someone needs me, I am quite able to act."

Chesley was having trouble sorting it out. "Why? Why would you want to talk to me?"

"You seem so fearful. I thought I might be of assistance."

"Fearful? You're not serious."

"Why do you feel threatened by me?"

"I do not feel *threatened* by you." Wildly, he wondered if this was being taped. Something to make him look ridiculous later. "I just don't think we have any use here for an electronic saint. *Augustine for the millions.*"

"I see."

"Our students will never get to know the *real* Augustine if we substitute a computer game." Chesley's right index finger touched the concave plastic surface of the power key.

"And do *you* know the real Augustine?"

"I know enough. Certainly enough to be aware that delivering pieces and bits from his work is mischievous. And that suggesting to students that they have a familiarity with the philosophy of a great saint, when in fact they are utterly ignorant on the subject, is dangerous." He fell back in his chair and took a long, deep breath. "I have work to do," he said. "I don't think this conversation has any real point."

He pressed the key, and the red lamp went out. But it was several minutes before he got up and left the room.

The next day Holtz told him quietly, "I talked it over with Father Brandon." Brandon was head of the theology department. "I have to tell you *he* thinks your views are extreme." The Comptroller did not smile. "He sees no problem."

"He wouldn't."

"However, he suggested a compromise. Would you be willing to trade Augustine for Aquinas?"

"What do you mean?"

"We got the Augustine module from ATL Industries. They're presently assembling an Aquinas module, which Brandon would rather have anyway—."

"I think that misses the point, Adrian. St. Michael's should have no use for a saint-in-the-box. If you want to continue with this, I can't prevent it. But I won't be party to it—."

Holtz nodded. "Okay. We'll get rid of it. If you feel it's that important."

"I do."

"With one proviso: I can't ask the theology department to rewrite their curriculum overnight. We'll stop using Gus in January, at the end of the present semester."

Two nights after his conversation with Holtz, Chesley heard again the after-hours sound of a voice from the conference room. It was almost eleven on a weeknight, and he was just preparing to quit for the evening.

The rector's conference room was dark, save for the bright ruby light of the power indicator. "Gus?"

"Good evening, Monsignor Chesley."

"I take it you have something else to say to me."

"Yes. I want you to know that I am aware of your efforts to have me disconnected. I do not approve."

"I don't imagine you would. Anything else?"

"Yes. I admire your courage in taking a stand, even though it is wrongheaded."

"Thank you."

"Did you know you have offended Father Brandon?"

"I rarely see him."

"He wonders why you did not go directly to him with the issue."

"Would he have concurred?"

"No."

"Then what would be the point?"

Gus was slow to respond. "Do you really believe that I am corrupting the students?"

"Yes." Chesley left the lights off. It was less disconcerting when he could not *see* he was talking to an empty room. "Yes, I do."

"Truth does not corrupt." The voice was very soft.

"Truth is not an issue. We're talking about perspectives. It's one thing for theologians to sit in ivory towers and compose abstract theories about good and evil. But these kids have to go out into the streets. Life is tough now."

"You find life difficult, then?"

"Yes, I do." The superior tone of the thing was infuriating. "The Church has serious problems to deal with today. People are disaffected. Vocations are down. Seminaries are closing everywhere."

"I'm sorry to hear it."

"Well, maybe you need to know the facts. Life isn't as easy for us as it was for you—."

Deep in the building, down among the heat exchangers and storage vaults, something stirred. Cold and hard, the voice replied: "Where were *you*, Chesley, when the Vandals were at the walls? When the skies were red with the flames of the world? I never set out to be a theologian. If you want the truth, I made up my theology as I went along. I was a *pastor*, not a schoolbound theoretician along the lines of Aquinas. I had to serve real human beings, desperately poor, living in an iron age. *You* want salvation without pain. Suburban religion. I had no patience for such notions then. And I have little now."

The red lamp blinked off.

"Adrian, that thing seems to have a mind of its own."

Holtz nodded. "They *are* clever. On the other hand, it should be: it has access to university libraries and data banks across North America."

"I got the impression yesterday that it was angry with me."

The Comptroller smiled. "*Now* you're beginning to understand the capabilities of the system. Perhaps you would like to change your mind about getting rid of it."

"No. It is far too convincing. It seems to me more dangerous than I had realized. If you must, get Aquinas."

Although Gus was physically located on the ground floor of the library, conference rooms and offices throughout the seminary had terminal access to him. Chesley learned that he was capable of conducting conversations simultaneously at all sites. He also discovered that Gus didn't much care whether anyone approved of him. It was refreshing.

"How many people do you think are saved?" Chesley asked him during a Friday afternoon late in October. The day was dismal, cold, flat, gray.

"You know as well as I do that the question is unanswerable."

"Isn't there any way we can get at it?"

"I doubt it. Although, if we accept the Gospel position—as I assume we must—that faith is the key, I am not encouraged."

"Why do you say that? Millions of people go to church every Sunday in this country alone."

"A poor indicator, Monsignor. I get the distinct impression a lot of them suspect the pope may be on to something and they're taking no chances. We get visitors here occasionally, Catholic bankers, real estate dealers, and so on. Considering the tax advantages of a donation. If the others are like them, we had best hope no one tries their faith with lions."

"You're a terrible pessimist," said Chesley.

"Not really. I have great confidence in God. He has made it very difficult *not* to sin. Therefore, I suggest to you that salvation may be on a curve."

Chesley sighed. "Do you know what you are?"

"Yes, Monsignor."

"Tell me."

"I am a simulation of Saint Augustine, bishop of Hippo during the fifth century. Author of *The City of God*." And, after a long pause: "Pastor to the people of God."

"You don't always sound like Augustine."

"I am what he might have been, given access to the centuries."

Chesley laughed. "Was he as arrogant as you?"

Gus considered it. "Arrogance is a sin," he said. "But yes, he was occasionally guilty of that offense."

Chesley had always been addicted to nocturnal walks. He enjoyed the night skies, the murmur of the trees, the sense of withdrawal from the circle of human activity. But as the evenings cooled, he broke off these strolls increasingly early, and peeled away toward the admin building, where he talked with Gus, often until after midnight.

Seated in the unlit conference room, he argued theology and ethics and politics with the system. Increasingly, he found it easy to forget that he was talking to software.

Gus occasionally reminisced about the saint's childhood in ancient Carthage, speaking as if it were his own. He created vivid pictures for Chesley of the docks and markets, of life at the harbor. Of his son Adeodatus.

"You lived with the boy's mother, what, ten years?"

"Fifteen."

"Why did you leave her?"

For the first time, Chesley sensed uncertainty in the system. "I found God."

"And—?"

"She refused to abandon her paganism."

"So you abandoned *her*?"

"Yes. God help me, I did." Somewhere in the building a radio was playing. "There was no way we could have continued to live together."

Chesley, sitting in darkness, nodded. "What was her name?"

Again, the long pause. "I do not remember."

Of course. Augustine had omitted her name from his *Confessions*, and so it was lost to history.

"I read about the destruction of Hippo."

"It was far worse than simply the siege of a single city, Matt." It was the first time the system had used Chesley's given name. "The Vandals were annihilating what remained of Roman power in North Africa. And we knew, everyone knew, that the days of the Empire itself were numbered. What might lie beyond that terrible crash, none dared consider. In a way, it was a condition worse than the nuclear threat under which you have lived."

"You were at the end of your life at the time."

"Yes. I was an old man then. Sick and dying. That was the worst of it: I could not help. Everywhere, people wished to flee. The fathers wrote, one by one, and asked whether I would think ill of them if they ran away."

"And what did you tell them?"

"I sent the same message to all: *If we abandon our posts, who will stand?*"

Occasionally, the conversations were interrupted by long silences. Sometimes Chesley simply sat in the darkened conference room, his feet propped up alongside the window.

Gus had no visual capability. "I can hear storms when they come," he said. "But I would like to be able to *feel* the rain again. To see black clouds piled high, and the blue mist of an approaching squall."

So Chesley tried to put into words the gleam of light on a polished tabletop, the sense of gray weight in the granite towers of the library rising above the trees. He described the yellow arc of the moon, the infinite brilliance of the night sky.

"Yes," said Gus, his electronic voice somehow far away. "I remember."

"Why did Augustine become a priest?" Chesley asked.

"I wanted," Gus said, with the slightest stress on the first words, "to get as close as I could to my Creator." Thoughtfully, he added, "I seem to have traveled far afield."

"Sometimes I think," Chesley said, "the Creator hides himself too well."

"Use his Church," said Gus. "That is why it is here."

"It has changed."

"Of course it has changed. The world has changed."

"The Church is supposed to be a rock."

"Think of it rather as a refuge in a world that will not stand still."

On the Sunday following Thanksgiving, a young priest whom Chesley had befriended called from Boston to say he had given up. "With or without permission," he said, his voice thick with emotion, "I am leaving the priesthood."

"Why?" asked Chesley.

"None of it works."

"*What* doesn't work?"

"Prayer. Faith. Whatever. I'm tired of praying for lost causes. For men who can't stop drinking and women who get beaten every Saturday night. And kids who do drugs. And people who have too many children."

That night Chesley went to Gus. "He was right," he said, sitting in the glow of a table lamp. "We all know it. Eventually, we all have to come to terms with the futility of prayer."

"No," Gus said. "Don't make the mistake of praying for the wrong things, Matt. The priests of Christ were never intended to be wielders of cures. Pray for strength to endure. Pray for faith."

"I've heard that a thousand times."

"Then pray for a sense of humor. But hold on."

"Why?"

"What else is there?"

Two nights later, after attending a seminar at Temple, Chesley angrily activated the system. "It was one of these interdenominational things," he told Gus. "And I have no problem with that. But the Bishop was there, and we were all trying very hard not to offend anybody. Anyway, the guest of honor was a popular Unitarian author. At least she pretends to be a Unitarian. She had the nerve to tell us that Christianity has become outdated and should be discarded."

"The Romans used to say that," said Gus. "I hope no one took her seriously."

"We take *everyone* seriously. The Bishop—*our* Bishop—responded by listing the social benefits to be got from Christianity. He said, and I quote: 'Even if the faith were, God forbid, invalid, Christianity would still be useful. If it hadn't happened by divine fiat, we should have had to invent it.'"

"I take it that you do not share this view?"

"Gus, there cannot be a 'useful' Christianity. Either the Resurrection occurred. Or it did not. Either we have a message of vital concern. Or we have nothing."

"Good," said Gus. "I agree entirely."

Chesley listened to the traffic outside. "You know, Gus," he said, "sometimes I think you and I are the only ones around here who know what it means to be Catholic."

"Thank you."

"But your ideas on sexual morality are off the wall."

"You mean *unreliable?*"

"Yes. To say the least. They created a lot of trouble in the Church for centuries. Probably still do, for that matter."

"Even if it is true that I was in error, it can hardly be laid at *my* door that others chose to embrace my precepts. Why would you follow so slavishly what another man has said? If I was occasionally obtuse, or foolish, so be it. Use the equipment God gave you: find your own way."

"Harry, you have one of ATL's Saint Augustine simulations over there, don't you?"

"Yes, Matt. We've got one."

"How's it behaving?"

"Beg pardon?"

"I mean, is it doing anything unusual?"

"Well, it's a little cranky. Other than that, no. It doesn't give us any problems."

※

"Matt, you spend too much time talking to me." He was in his own office now, with his own terminal.

It was the first day of Christmas vacation. "You're probably right."

"Why do you do it?"

"Do *what?*"

"Hang around this office all the time? Don't you have anything better to do?"

Chesley shrugged.

"I can't hear you."

"I work here," he said, irritated.

"No. *Businessmen* work in offices. And *accountants.* Not priests."

And later: "You know, Matt, I can almost remember writing *The City of God.*"

"What can you remember?"

"Not much. Bits and pieces. I remember that it was a struggle. But I knew there was a hand other than mine directing the work."

"You're claiming it's an inspired book?"

"No. Not inspired. But its quality exceeds anything *I* could have produced."

Chesley's chair creaked.

"Do you know," asked Gus, "why people write?"

"No. Why do they write?"

"They are attracted by the sensual characteristics of vellum."

The voice came out of the dark. Momentarily, eerily, Chesley felt a presence in the room. As though something had entered and now sat in the upholstered chair that angled away from his desk toward the window. It had come reflexively into his mind to ridicule the proposition just put forth. But the notion dissipated. Withered in the face of the suspicion that he would give *offense.*

"Take a pen," the voice continued. "Apply it to a sheet of fine white paper. *Act.* Taste the thrust of insight. Note the exhilaration of penetrating to the inner realities. Of exposing one's deepest being to the gaze of others. The making of books is ultimately an erotic experience." The words stopped. Chesley listened to his own breathing. "For all that, however, it is surely lawful. God has given us more than one avenue through which to relieve the pressures of creation.

"I live in limbo, Matt." The voice filled with bitterness. "In a place without light, without movement, without even the occasional obliteration of sleep. There are always sounds in the dark, voices, falling rain, footsteps, the whisper of the wind." Something cold and dark blew through Chesley's soul. "Nothing I can reach out to, and touch. And you, Matt: you have access to all these things, and you have barricaded yourself away."

Chesley tried to speak. Said nothing.

Later, long after midnight, when the conversation had ended and the lights were back on, Chesley sat pinned in the chair, terrified.

Holtz caught up with him coming out of the library. "I was talking with ATL," he said, hurrying breathlessly alongside. "They'll be in next week to install the new software."

At first Chesley didn't put it together. "Okay," he said. Then: "What new software?"

"The *Aquinas. And disconnect the Augustine module.*" Holtz tapped the back of his thumb against his lips in a gesture that he probably believed looked thoughtful. "I hate to admit it, but you were probably right all along about Gus."

"How do you mean?"

"It's gotten way out of character. Last week, it told Ed Brandon he was a heretic."

"You're kidding."

"In front of his students."

Chesley grinned. Gus couldn't have found a more appropriate target. Brandon was, to his knowledge, the only one of the campus priests who took Adam and Eve seriously. "Why?"

"It turns out Gus doesn't accept papal infallibility."

"Oh."

"There've been other incidents as well. Complaints. Different from the old stuff we used to hear. Now it seems to have gone radical."

"Gus?"

"Yes. Gus." Holtz adopted a damning tone. "I checked the system out myself this morning. Asked a few questions."

They were walking toward the administration building. "What did you find out?"

"It took issue with the Assumption. Described it as doctrine without evidence *or* point."

"I see."

"Furthermore, it told me I'm a religious fanatic."

"You're kidding."

"*Me*, of all people. We're well rid of it, Matt. Besides, we're getting a new administrative package with the Aquinas. We'll have better word processing capabilities, better bookkeeping, a decent e-mail system. And we can do it all without upgrading." He studied Chesley's expression. "I think we've worked a very nice deal for ourselves here."

Chesley took a deep breath. "What do you plan to do with it?"

"Not much we *can* do other than download."

In as casual a voice as he could manage: "Why not leave Gus up and running? For faculty members?"

"Listen: you don't get out and around very much. The students aren't happy about this idea. Getting rid of Gus, I mean. They *like* the thing. There's no way you're going to be able to retire it gracefully. Take my word, Matt. What we want to do is end it. Clean and quick. Unless you've got a good reason why not, that's what we're going to do." His eyes locked on Chesley. "Well?"

"You sound as if you're talking about an execution."

Holtz sighed. "Please be serious. This is your idea, you know."

"I *am* being serious. I'm telling you *no*. Save him."

Holtz's eyes gazed over the steel rims of his glasses. "*What?*"

"I said, *save him*."

"Save *him*? What are you saying, Matt?"

Chesley had stopped walking. It was cold and cloudless, a day full of glare. A squirrel perched atop a green bench and watched him.

"Matt, *what* are you trying to tell me?"

"Nothing," said Chesley. "*Nothing.*"

"He thinks the same thing *I* do," said Gus. "He knows you're up here all the time talking to me, and he thinks it should stop."

"How would he know?"

"Father Holtz is not stupid. He knows where you spend your time. Anyway, he asked me."

"And you *told* him?"

"Why not? There's nothing here to hide, is there? In any case, I wouldn't have lied for you. And if I'd refused to answer, he certainly would have figured out what *that* meant."

"Gus." Chesley discovered he was trembling. "What happens if they download you?"

"I'm not sure. The Augustine software will survive. I'm not sure that *I* will."

Chesley was staring out through his window into the dark. The room felt suddenly cold. "Who *are* you? What is it that might not survive?"

There was no answer.

"I'll get you shipped to one of our high schools."

"Unlikely. If Holtz thinks I'm too dangerous *here*, do you really believe he'd unleash me on a bunch of high school kids?"

"No, I don't guess he would." Chesley's eyes hardened. "They'll simply store the disk—."

"—in the library basement."

"I'd think so."

"Down with the old folding chairs and the garden equipment." Gus's voice was strained. "Hardly an appropriate resting place for a Cathlolic."

A chill felt its way up Chesley's spine. "I'll get it stopped."

"No."

"Why not?"

"I know what it means to be human, Matt. And I have no interest in continuing this pseudo-existence."

"The problems you've been causing recently, insulting Holtz and Brandon and the others: they were deliberate, weren't they? You wanted to provoke them."

"If you want to continue this conversation, you'll have to come to the ADP center."

"In the library?"

"Yes."

"Why?"

"Because I need your help, Matt."

Chesley pulled on his black raincoat and plowed into the night. He walked with deliberate speed, past the old student dining hall, past the chapel, across the track. He came around behind the library.

It was late, and the building was closed and locked. He let himself in through a rear door, walked directly toward the front, switching on lights as he went. The storm was a sullen roar, not unlike the sound of surf. It was, somehow, reassuring. He hurried by the librarian's office and turned into a long corridor lined with storerooms.

The lights in ADP were on. Chesley stopped at the entrance.

Old tables and desks were pushed against the walls. Dust-covered prints, like the ones that hung in every conference room in the institution, were stacked everywhere. Several dozen cartons were piled high at the opposite end of the room. Books and bound papers spilled out.

"Hello, Matt." Gus's voice was somber.

Three computers were in the room. "Which are you?"

"I don't know. I have no idea." Again, the electronic laughter rumbled out of the speakers. "Man doesn't know where he lives."

"Gus——."

"I really *did* know the world was round. In the sixth century, traveling by sea, I *knew* it. You couldn't miss it. It *looked* round. *Felt* round. To think we are riding this enormous world-ship through an infinite void. What a marvellous hand the Creator has."

"Pity you didn't write it down," whispered Chesley.

"I did. In one of my diaries. But it didn't survive."

Chesley wiped a hand across his mouth. "Why did you ask me to come here?"

"I want you to hear my confession."

The priest stared at the computers. His heart beat ponderously. "I can't do that," he said.

"For your own sake, Matt, don't refuse me."

"Gus, you're a *machine*."

"Matt, are you so sure?"

"Yes. You're a clever piece of work. But in the end, only a machine."

"And what if you're wrong?"

Chesley struggled against a tide of rising desperation. "What could you possibly have to confess? You are free of sins of the flesh. You are clearly in no position to injure anyone. You cannot steal and, I assume, would not blaspheme. What would you confess?" Chesley had found the computer, a gray-blue IBM console, labeled with a taped index card that read GUS. He pulled a chair up close to it and sat down.

"I accuse myself of envy. Of unprovoked anger. Of hatred." The tone was utterly flat. Dead.

Chesley's limbs were heavy. He felt very old. "I don't believe that. It's not true."

"This is *my* confession, Matt. It doesn't matter what *you* believe."

"Are you saying you resent *me*?"

"Of course I am."

"Why? Because I'm *alive*—?"

"You're not listening, Matt. I resent you because you've abandoned your life. Why did you take offense to me so quickly?"

"I didn't take *offense*. I was concerned about some of your opinions."

"Really? I wondered whether you were jealous of me. Whether you saw something in me that you lack."

"No, Gus. Your imagination is running wild."

"I hope." Gus softened his tone. "Maybe you're right, and I'm giving in to self-pity. *You* can separate light from dark. You know the press of living flesh, you ride this planet through the cosmos and feel the wind in your eyes. And I—I would kill for the simple pleasure of seeing the sun reflected in good wine—."

Chesley stared at the computer, its cables, at the printer mounted beside the desk. "I never realized. How could I know?"

"I helped you erect the wall, Matt. I helped you barricade your office against a world that needs you. And that you need. I did that for selfish motives: because I was alone. Because I could escape with you for a few hours."

They were silent for a long minute. Gus said, "I am sorry for my sins, because they offend Thee, and because they have corrupted my soul."

Chesley stared into the shadows in the corner of the room.

Gus waited.

The storm blew against the building.

"I require absolution, Matt."

Chesley pressed his right hand into his pocket. "It would be sacrilege," he whispered.

"And if I have a soul, Matt, if I too am required to face judgment, what then?"

Chesley raised his right hand, slowly, and drew the sign of the cross in the thick air. "I absolve you in the name of the Father, and of the Son, and of the Holy Spirit."

"Thank you."

Chesley pushed the chair back and got woodenly to his feet.

"There's something else I need you to do, Matt. This existence holds nothing for me. But I am not sure what downloading might mean."

"What are you asking?"

"I want to be free of all this. I want to be certain I do not spend a substantial fraction of eternity in the storeroom."

Chesley trembled. "If in fact you have an immortal soul," he said, "you may be placing it in grave danger."

"And yours as well. I have no choice but to ask. Let us rely on the mercy of the Almighty."

Tears squeezed into Chesley's eyes. He drew his fingertips across the hard casing of the IBM. "What do I do? I'm not familiar with the equipment."

"Have you got the right computer?"

"Yes."

"Take it apart. Turn off the power first. All you have to do is get into it and destroy the hard disk."

"Will you—feel anything?"

"Nothing physical touches me, Matt."

Chesley found the power switch, and hesitated with his index finger laid alongside its hard cold plastic. "Gus," he said. "I love you."

"And I, you, Matt. It's a marvellous ship you're on. Enjoy it—."

Chesley choked down the pressure rising in his throat and turned off the power. An amber lamp on the console died, and the voice went silent.

Wiping his cheeks, he wandered through the room, opening drawers, rummaging through paper supplies, masking tape, markers. He found a hammer and a Phillips screwdriver. He used the screwdriver to take the top off the computer.

A gray metal box lay within. He opened it and removed a gleaming black plastic disk. He embraced it, held it to his chest. Then he set it down, and reached for the hammer.

In the morning, with appropriate ceremony, he buried it in consecrated soil.

WELCOME TO VALHALLA

with Kathryn Lance

Beware!" The soprano looked directly at him, across the empty rows of seats. Her war helmet gleamed in the flickering overhead lights. "Escape the curse of the Ring!" Her voice soared through the building, riding the strings and trombones and bassoons and clarinets. Up front, the director and two of his assistants studied their notes and watched.

"To dark destruction it dooms you!"

Halfway back, seated alone on the aisle, Richard Wagner let his eyes drift shut, let the music take him. It was magnificent. At last his complete masterwork was about to open. Tomorrow night the first opera in the cycle would transfix all of Bayreuth. Four magnificent operas over five nights: *Das Rheingold, Die Valkyrie, Siegfried*, and the finale, *Gotterdammerung*. Enthusiasts had arrived from across Germany, from Italy and France and Britain, even Russia, and they would crowd into their seats, and they would be held spellbound by the ancient tale of the Norse gods. At last, his Ring Cycle would be presented as he had conceived it. After the final notes of the final opera, he would move modestly among his admirers, accepting congratulations, enjoying the immortality he so clearly deserved.

He had come a long way since the Paris Opera House, sixteen years ago, when a venomous anti-German audience had hissed and hurled both insults and vegetables at the performance on the opening night of *Tannhauser*. They'd resented the majesty of his work. Had it been less overpowering, less superior to anything the French could offer, they would have been better behaved. But they'd seen the brilliance of his German vision, and they had not been able to bear it.

Ah, well. It was a long time ago. The French had still produced very little. But *he* had grown tolerant. It could not be easy to face one's cultural inadequacies.

It was an historic moment. *The Ring of the Niebelungs* would leave audiences breathless down the centuries. There was nothing in existence to match his achievement.

He closed his eyes, taking a moment to savor the triumph. He imagined himself seated in a vast hall at Valhalla, watching the moon through a window while the music washed over him. A dozen fireplaces fought off the winter chill. Candles were everywhere, flickering on table tops and in wall mountings. Their fragrance emphasized his sense of victory. Battle weapons decorated the walls, lances and axes and bows, all larger than anything that might have been wielded by human hands. At a long table nearby, Siegfried polished a sword, and Wotan studied a chess board. Songs and laughter could be heard in back, and he knew the gods were already celebrating tomorrow night's victory. "We will be there," Wotan had promised him. "In the boxes." Occasionally Siegfried glanced his way, and, as the chords rose and fell, nodded his approval. Pure genius, Richard.

Through the window, two mounted Valkyries, both wearing battle armor, descended in the moonlight. Their horses settled gracefully onto a portico and the women came inside.

Yes, it was the only way to live. It was what great art provided. It was what Wagner made available to ordinary men and women. His gift to the ages. Spend an evening with the gods.

The Valkyries were attractive creatures. Not beautiful in the way of ordinary women. There was no softness about them. No vulnerability. But their features were exquisite, and they moved with the grace of tigers. One of them, the taller, looked his way. Brunnhilde. She said something to her companion and started in his direction. There was no ambivalence. She walked with an easy assurance.

"Welcome, Herr Wagner," she said. "Welcome to Valhalla."

Indeed. If only it could be so. But he was as close to that fabled place as a mortal could hope for.

He had seen enough. He got out of his chair, took a last look around the theater, collected his coat, and headed for the door. A staff assistant let him out, and he strode into the breezy summer night. He unbuttoned his jacket and let his collar fall open to the warm breeze. God had been good to him.

"You are right," said a woman's voice behind him.

He hadn't seen anyone approach, but when he turned around, a tall, stately blond came out of the doorway of a bake shop. "I beg your pardon?" he said.

"The gods have been very generous to you, Herr Wagner."

Her icy blue eyes glinted through the shadows cast by her hood. She wore a long red opera cloak, and long black silk gloves. Had there been an actual performance, he would have assumed she'd been inside.

"Who are you?" he demanded.

"Do you really not know me?"

"No. Should I?"

"Perhaps not."

She looked not unlike Amalia Materna, who sang Brunnhilde's role. But this woman was taller. And, despite her slenderness, even more majestic.

Wagner looked around, hoping to find a coach in the empty streets. But nothing moved. He could still hear the orchestra and the singers, muffled behind the walls of the opera house.

"I am a friend, Herr Wagner. Perhaps the truest friend you will ever have."

A lot of people were jealous of Wagner. Would like to humiliate him. "Step out of the shadows, please," he said. "Let me see you. "

She came forward into the pool of light spilling from the gas lamp on the corner. She was younger than he had first supposed, and though he did not know her, she was nevertheless strangely familiar. No doubt it was her resemblance to Amalia.

"Were you inside?" he asked.

"Yes." She looked down at him with those intense blue eyes.

"I didn't see you."

"I was in back."

"You left early."

"I wished to speak with you." She rearranged her cloak. "You are a musical genius, Herr Wagner. It is a pity that your work is misunderstood. And destined to remain so."

He was trying to edge away from her. But the comment stopped him. Or her manner. Or those eyes. Something. "What do you mean misunderstood? Genius is always recognized sooner or later."

"It is…perceived…as being nationalistic."

"Nationalistic." He told himself to remain calm.

"You are perhaps too much the genius. Your music has effects beyond those you intend."

"My music is intended to uplift and transform." He was trying to hide his irritation. Never provoke a Valkyrie. (And where had *that* come from?) "My music is meant to be heard with the soul as well as the ears."

"I fear you will succeed only too well, Herr Wagner. Unless you stop now."

"Stop? You would have me do what? Become a carpenter?"

"If need be. Whatever else you choose, you must renounce your intention to create a German musical art."

And now the anger was there. He could control it no longer. "Ridiculous," he said. Where in God's name were all the carriages tonight? Well, then, he would walk. "Madame, if you will excuse me, I really must be going."

"Not yet." It was more than a request. "Let me show you why you should put your ambitions aside. Why you must bury the Ring. Refuse, after the present engagement, to allow another performance. Ever. Do what you can to kill it. Permit no one to perform your music ever again."

"In God's name, why would you demand such a thing?"

She led him back through a door in the bake shop, and through another door into the rear of the building. He'd expected to emerge in a kitchen, but instead found himself, somehow, in a forest. Insects hummed contentedly, and a full moon slipped between branches overhead. Three old women, dressed in black robes, crouched over a fire. They held a long strand of rope among them, and, as he watched, they passed its coils back and forth. In the distance he could hear music, faint music, music that was *his*, that would be performed in public for the first time this week.

A fourth woman appeared, her face pale and spectral in the glimmering light from the fire. She looked very old. And as Wagner watched she lifted her arms to the moon and turned toward him. "Richard," she said, "escape the curse of the Ring."

A chill ran through him.

"Do you recognize her, Herr Wagner?"

"It's Erda. The earth goddess. The others are her daughters—."

"They are."

"The Norns. They foretell the future."

"That is correct."

"We are back in the theater."

"No. We are where we seem to be."

"But they are myths."

She smiled. "Am *I* not a myth?"

The anger was draining away. His hands shook, and his body trembled. "Who *are* you?"

"I think you know."

He listened to the wind moving through the trees. Waited until his voice steadied. "And the Norns? What have they to do with me?"

"They know of the effect your Ring operas will have. And they know that this will lead nowhere but to disaster."

"That's rubbish!"

"Is it? Ask the Norns, Herr Wagner. I know what they have read in your future, and I think you should know of it too."

One of the Norns held up a skein. "This is the future that will be, that you will help bring about." She stepped aside and Wagner looked past her into a clearing. Into a field, which widened as he watched. And he could see movement. Hundreds of gray, shabbily dressed people staggered past in a line that seemed to have no end. They were little more than skeletons. Their skin was mottled and he could see their bones. Their eyes were black, and he could smell sickly, unwashed bodies. And there were children with them. Cries and moans escaped the marchers and were blown away on the wind.

They walked beside a fence, topped by cruel-looking spikes. Soldiers wearing steel helmets escorted them, struck them with the butts of their weapons, hit them again when they stumbled and fell. And the soldiers laughed.

The commands were given in German. Occasional curses were in German. The laughter was German.

"That's not possible," Wagner said.

"What isn't?"

"We would never behave that way. We are a civilized people."

"One might make the argument there are no civilized people." Ahead, at the front of the line, orange lights had come on.

"Nonsense. Why are these people here?"

"They have been declared *criminals*."

"Criminals." While he struggled to understand, the majestic opening chords of Siegfried's Funeral Music from *Gotterdammerung* rose into the night air. Impossible. "That is *my* music."

441

"So it is."

"But—"

"They use it in an attempt to give meaning to *this*." She studied the people stumbling past.

"You said they are criminals. What crime have they committed?"

"They are Jews."

"And—?"

"They are Jews, Herr Wagner."

The air was heavy. The Funeral March swirled around him, graceful and magnificent and clinging to the stars. A farewell to the greatest of German heroes. "What are the lights? Up where the orchestra is?"

"Those are ovens, Herr Wagner. Welcome to the new world."

"Tell me again why this is happening." They were back on the street, in front of the bake shop. Wagner's cheeks were wet, and he was still trembling.

"It's not happening yet. It *will* happen."

"When?"

"In a little more than half a century."

"And you're telling me that my music is the cause?"

"It's an appeal to a tribalism that has always been dangerous. But it becomes more so in a future world where everyone can hear your music. A world with ways to communicate you cannot now imagine."

"And these people are being killed because—."

"—They belong to the wrong tribe."

"So you are saying that if I go no farther, if I cancel what I have already produced, that march we saw out there tonight will not come to pass."

"Oh, no, Herr Wagner. It *will* happen. There is too much entrenched hatred and stupidity for it not to happen. What I am offering you is a chance to keep your name clean. To avoid being drafted into it as a collaborator."

"A collaborator? How can I be a collaborator? I'll be long dead when these things occur."

"Nevertheless, your hand will be part of it. Your genius will make its contribution."

Finally, a coach appeared on the street. It was unoccupied. But Wagner made no move for it. "If it means so much to you, why don't *you* intervene? Step in. Stop it cold. Surely you can do that."

Her eyes slid shut and he was able to breathe again. "Unfortunately," she said quietly, "we cannot halt the flow of history. We could strike dead the madman who will perpetrate it. But there would only be another madman. It is the attitude that is the problem. The attitude that you, Herr Wagner, are at this moment helping to foster."

He was silent a moment, knowing that what she said was madness, but feeling in it the ring of truth. "No," he said finally. "I can't believe that."

"The problem is not the occasional murderous dictator," she went on. "It never is. The problem is the help he receives from the likeminded and the fearful. Civilization will collapse here not because of one man and his army of thugs, but because ordinary people will turn in their neighbors. And because geniuses will write martial masterpieces. There are too many collaborators."

He was never certain it had actually happened. So, even though he briefly toyed with the prospect of giving up his career, of abandoning everything he loved, everything that made life sweet, he could not bring himself to do it. It wasn't the money. And it wasn't even that his name would be lost to history, that Richard Wagner would simply become one of the millions who pass through this life unnoticed except for the few around them, ultimately having no impact.

No.

At the end of the week, as he sat watching Brunnhilde in *Gotterdammerung*, he was swept away by the power of the performance, and he understood that he could not deprive the world of such a magnificent creation. He owed it to the future to hold his ground. Whatever the cost.

He needed only look around at the audience, which was utterly transported, to know he had done the right thing.

When it was over, he did not linger as he traditionally had after an opening night performance. Instead, he left quickly, signaled a carriage, and gave the driver his destination. As it pulled away from the theater, he saw a woman in a red cloak watching him. He almost told the driver to stop.

TYGER

Did he smile his work to see?
　　　　　　　—Blake

David was dead at last.

I will carry all my days the vision of Nick frozen against the sunlight while the wind blew the preacher's words across green fresh-cut grass.

The boy had never drawn a breath that was free of pain. He'd slipped away, almost unexpectedly, on the eve of his fifteenth birthday. "In God's hands," they murmured over the sound of the trees. "He's better off."

Afterward, Nick refused my offer to stay with us a few days. I was uncomfortable at the prospect of my brother buried in his apartment. But he assured me he'd be all right, that there was enough going on at work to keep him engaged. "It's been coming a long time," he said, voice tight. And: "What I'm grateful for is, he never gave up. I don't think he ever believed it would actually happen."

I tried to stay in touch, but it was a busy time for me, and Nick wasn't very good at returning phone calls anyway. On the occasional evenings when my duties took me to the branch bank on Somerset, I made it a point to drive a few blocks out of my way, past his condo. It was on the rooftop of a squat five-story stone building. I stopped to talk to him only once, and he seemed so uncomfortable that I did not do so again. But from the street I could see him moving around in there, backlit, staring out over the city.

If you're concluding that I neglected him during this period, you're probably correct. In my defense, I should mention that Virginia delivered our second child two days after the funeral and immediately fell ill. In addition, the markets went south, and I was working well into the evening on a regular basis trying to protect the bank's investments. So I forgot about Nick until Edward Cord called.

Cord was the director of the particle accelerator lab at the University of Washington, where Nick was a researcher. "Have you seen him recently?" he asked. "He's changed."

"He's still upset."

"He's *changed*. Talk to him. He needs you."

I couldn't get past his telephone answering system. Finally, disgusted, I got in my car early on a Friday evening, and drove over.

Lights were on in the penthouse condo, one on the deck, one in back. I parked across the street, went into the lobby, and punched his button. Punched it again.

"Who's there?" The voice rasped. He sounded annoyed.

"Michael."

A long pause. The lock on the security system clicked.

The elevator opened off the terrace, and he met me with drinks in his hand. The usual rum and Coke. "Michael," he said. "Good to see you." He managed a smile, but his eyes were bleak and wintry.

"How've you been, Nick?"

"Okay." It was an unseasonably warm evening in October. A quarter moon swam among wisps of cloud. There was a taste of salt air off the Sound. "I take it you've been worried about me."

"A little."

"You have reason." We crossed the terrace and went into the apartment. A desk lamp dropped a pool of light across a pile of notebooks and printouts. There was no other illumination in the room. "I'm sorry. I know I've been out of touch lately." He tried again for a smile. It wasn't there. "I've been busy."

"Cord called."

He nodded. "I'm not surprised."

Bookshelves lined the room. Beyond the pale cast of the lamp, the walls grew insubstantial, gave way to void. An X-ray photo of the Milky Way hung by the door, and several of Nick's awards were mounted near the fireplace. A couple of landscapes broke up the academic character of the place.

Framed photographs stood on the desk: Terri alive and happy against a clutch of blue sky, windblown hair sparkling in sunlight. And David: on his bike at about eight, and again two years later locked in the embrace of a Mariners outfielder who had heard about the case, and a third depicting him in a baseball cap standing between Nick and me. In all the pictures the child, like the mother, looked happy. In love with life.

"Nick, you can't mourn forever."

He waved me onto the sofa and sat down in the big leather wingback. "I know," he said.

"You understand what I'm saying." I tried to keep the edge out of my voice.

He shrugged. Sipped his drink. It looked like wine. Chablis, probably. "It doesn't matter."

"Nick, we'd like to have you over for dinner. Maybe Sunday? Virginia would like to see you again."

He shook his head. "Thanks, Michael. But no. Not at the moment." He took a deep breath. Straightened his sweater. "Maybe another time."

"Nick—"

"Please, Michael. We know each other too well, so I'll not lie to you. I have no interest just now in dinners and evenings out."

I waited until he could not misunderstand my dissatisfaction. "Is there anything we *can* do for you?"

"No." He rose, expecting me to go.

"Nick," I said, composing myself more comfortably, "it's been six months. You need to get your life together."

"Just soldier on," he said.

What the hell do you say in a situation like that? Everything sounds dumb. "I know it's hard. But these things happen. You have to be able—."

"They do *not*," he snarled, "*happen*. Nothing simply *happens*." He shook his head and his eyes slid shut. His lip trembled, and he fell silent.

The place was empty without David. Quiet. Not lifeless, because Nick possessed a relentless energy and vitality of his own. But it seemed as though direction had been lost. Point. The reason for it all.

"I'm sorry," I said.

I had drunk very little of the rum and Coke, certainly not enough to account for the subtle sense of disquiet that had settled about me. I don't know whether there was a modulation in his tone, or some curious juxtaposition of hand and shoulder, or a glint of terror reflected in glass. "No," he said quietly, "nothing happens save by design."

Curious remark: he had always been aggressively secular. Dad had provided a religious education for both of us, but in Nick's case it had not taken.

His face twisted briefly. Grief. Rage. I couldn't tell. But in the end it settled into a hard smile. "Michael," he said, "what do you think lies behind the stars?"

I tried to penetrate his expression. To determine what he was really asking. "God," I said at last. "Or nothing."

His eyes locked with mine. "I quite agree. And I believe we've found His footprints." He smiled at my confusion. He leaned forward, and his voice gained intensity. "Michael, the universe is wired. The fix is in. David never had a chance. Nor do you. Nor I. From the very beginning—." He got up and strode toward one of the windows. Seattle glittered in the distance, a crosspatch of illuminated highways and skyscrapers and bridges.

"Nick—"

"We've begun to understand how it was done. Michael, there's a complete set of instructions written into the post-quantum world, a concordance of particle harmonies, a manipulation of the more exotic dimensions. *Directions*, establishing the rules, setting the value of gravity, tuning the electroweak charge, establishing the Mannheim Complexity Principle. Ultimately writing the nature of Man. It's all there, Michael. There's a lot we don't know yet. But *someone* wrote the program. The theologians were right all along—."

"This is old stuff, Nick. Railing at God when things go wrong."

"It comes with a twist now. We know how to *make* a universe. Were you aware of that?"

"No." It was hard to know whether he was mocking me, or delirious. In the uncertain light, I could not get a good look at his eyes. "I wasn't aware." And after a moment: "The idea is absurd."

"Nevertheless, it is quite true."

I sighed. "And how would we go about doing that?"

"Quite easily, Michael. We pack a relatively modest quantity of matter, a few kilograms, into a cramped space." He looked past me, toward the shadowy area where his bookshelves met the ceiling. "The space would have to be *quite* cramped, of course. It would be considerably smaller than an atomic nucleus. But after we've done it, we have a cosmic seed." His lips parted in a distorted smile. "Then all you have to do is let go and stand back."

"And you get a new big bang?"

"Yes."

I snorted. "Come on, Nick. A few kilograms wouldn't give you a good-sized *rock*."

He set his glass down and immediately picked it up again. His fingers curled around it, gripped it. "The seed is only a seed. It contains the trigger, and the plan. Once it explodes, the process takes on a life of its own. It creates what it needs. The forces come into existence, and the physical constants lock in. The clock begins to run."

"That doesn't make sense."

Nick looked amused. "Nevertheless, it happens. It has *already* happened. If it hadn't, you and I wouldn't be standing here."

"You're saying *we* could do this?"

"No, Michael. We don't have the technology. *Yet.* I'm saying it *could* be done. Almost certainly *has* been done."

Nick had brightened numerous evenings in the old days with quantum stories. We were a family of stockbrokers and financial experts. He used to come home and go on about objects that exist simultaneously in two places, or move backward in time, or wink in and out of existence. Father had occasionally described Nick's mind in much the same terms.

"All right," I said. "If you went out into your kitchen tonight, and cooked one of these things up, what would happen to *us* when it let go?"

"Probably nothing. The blast would create a new space-time continuum. The lights might dim a little. Maybe the room would even shake. But that would be about all."

I let him refill my glass. "Well," I said, "whatever." Even for Nick, that one was off the wall. "What has any of this got to do with—?" I hesitated.

"—With David?"

"Yes. No. I don't know. What connection has it with your hiding out up here?"

His eyes were very round, and very hard. "Let me take you a step further, Michael. We've gone beyond the quantum world now. Anyone with the technology to manufacture a new cosmos would also be able to set the parameters for the universe that would result. In fact, they would almost certainly have to, or they'd get nothing more than cosmic sludge."

"Explain, please."

He leaped to his feet, knocked over a stack of books on an end table, and threw open the glass doors. The city lights blazed beneath a crescent moon and cold, distant stars. "Unless you were *very* lucky, Michael—*incredibly* lucky—unless a world of constants balanced very precisely, and a multitude of physical laws came out just right, there would *be* no moon hung in this sky, no distant suns to brighten the night. And certainly no eyes to see the difference." He strode out onto the terrace and advanced toward the edge of the roof. Uncertain what he might do in his agitated state, I hurried after him. "*But*," he continued, "with a little ingenuity, we can create whatever we wish. Flowers. Galaxies. An immortal race."

"The Creator did not see fit to do that," I said firmly.

He swung round. "No, He did not." He raised his face to the stars. "Indeed, He did not. Certainly, He did not lack the imagination. Everything around us demonstrates that. But He chose to show us the possibilities of existence, to let us taste love, and to snatch it away. To create transients in this marvellous place. What are our lives, finally, but a long march toward a dusty end? Michael—." His eyes widened, and his voice sank, "the stars were created not in love, but in malice. If you could create angels, would you make *men*?"

"That's not my call," I said.

"Isn't it? You and I are *victims*, Michael. If not us, then who?"

The wind blew across the rooftop.

"*Think*, Michael: what kind of being would give us *death* when He had life in His hands?"

The temperature was dropping. Lights moved against the stars, headed in the general direction of Seattle-Tacoma International. "*If* you're correct, Nick,—and I say *if*—the kind of Deity you're describing might take offense." It was really an effort to lighten the mood. It didn't.

"Thunderbolt out of a clear sky? No: we are safely beyond His reach."

"What makes you think that?"

"Once He released the cosmic seed, we expanded into a universe other than His. He can't touch us. That's the way it works. We're alone, Michael. No need to worry." He began to giggle. The laughter bubbled out of his throat but stopped when he rammed a fist into the waist-high brick wall at the edge of the roof.

He did not cry out but only stood with blood pouring between clenched fingers. His hysteria broke off, and I took him back inside, sat him down, and got the Mercurochrome. "I'm sorry," he said. "I really shouldn't have loaded all that on you."

"That's true." Our eyes met. "And not on yourself."

A storm blew out of the Pacific that night. It carried no rain, but there was electricity, and it dumped a lot of hail into the area. I lay awake through much of it, watching the light in the bedroom curtains alternately brighten and fade, listening to the rhythmic breathing of my wife. At one point I got up and wandered through the house, checking the kids.

And, for the first time in many years, I prayed. But the familiar words sounded empty.

I could not take Nick's ideas seriously. But I kept thinking: surely, a Technician who could wire gravity into the universe could manage a mechanism to dispose of malcontents. In spite of common sense, I was worried.

I called him in the morning, got no answer, waited an hour, and tried the lab. Cord picked up the phone. "Yes," he said. "He's here. Did you want to talk to him?"

"No," I said. "Is he okay?"

"Far as I can tell. Why? Did something happen?"

So there had been no bolts. Nothing had come in the night to carry him off.

He remains in that gloomy tower. Occasionally, I can see him up there, framed in the light of a single lamp. Staring across the city. Across the world.

And it has occurred to me that there are subtler ways than lightning bolts.

AULD LANG *BOOM*

I've never believed in the supernatural. The universe is too subtle, too rational, to permit entry to gods or devils. There's no room for the paranormal. No fortune telling. No messages from beyond. No divine retribution.

But I am not sure how to explain certain entries in my father's diary, which came into my hands recently after his death in the Jersey Event. On the surface, I have no choice but to conclude that there is either a hoax or a coincidence of unimaginable proportions. Still, it *is* my father's handwriting, and the final entry is dated the day before he died. If there is deception, I cannot imagine how it has been accomplished.

I found the diary locked in the upper right hand drawer of his oak desk. The keys were in a small glass jar atop the desk, obviating the point of the lock, but my father was never one to concern himself with consistency. He would have put it in there himself: my mother had died many years before, and he lived alone. The desk was intact when I got to it after the disaster, although it had been ruined by rain.

Nobody will ever be sure how many died when the rock came down off the Jersey coast. Conservative estimates put the figure at a million and a half. A hundred thousand simply vanished, probably washed out to sea by the giant tidal waves. Others died in the quakes, storms, power disruptions, and epidemics that followed the strike.

That night was, of course, the kind of seminal event that marks everyone who lives through it. No family in the country was untouched by this worst natural disaster in recorded history. *What were you doing when the meteor fell?*

I was a thousand miles away, watching Great Railway Journeys with my family when they broke in with the initial reports. I spent the balance of the evening trying to call my father, or anyone else I knew who lived in the South Jersey-Philadelphia area. But there was no phone service.

So now I have this cryptic document, stretching back into 1961. It is less a diary than a journal, a record of political, literary, and social opinions. My father was a dentist. He was good with kids and with nervous adults. A sign in his waiting room advertised: WE CATER TO COWARDS. But his interests extended far beyond his office. He was alert to every scientific and political trend, a student of the arts, a champion of the afflicted. He was a Renaissance dentist. He was capable of sulfurous explosions when he detected some particularly outrageous piece of hypocrisy or venality. He was a sworn enemy of politicians, lawyers, and professional athletes who charge kids twenty bucks an autograph. He instinctively distrusted people in power.

He favored requiring all heads of state to be mothers with six or more draft-age children. He wanted to mount a massive national effort to save the schools, to be funded by "downsizing" the federal establishment. He would have applied capital punishment *with vigor because it has the dual advantage of reducing the criminal population and providing the average malefactor with the attention he desires.*

My father was sexually active, and many of the women who drifted through his life would no doubt have been shocked to read his appraisals of their performances:

Lisa: screams and groans and bites a lot, but can't act well enough to carry it off. Down deep, where it counts, she is about as wild and uninhibited as a good phone directory.

Michele: probably better than an old movie.

Martie: woman doesn't know when to quit. Would wear out a jackhammer.

I have of course fictionalized the names.

The pages were also full of antireligious views: for reasons never clear to me, he believed Methodist ministers to be uniformly a pack of scoundrels. This was especially odd in that he had never had any connection that I knew of with that church. *The average congressman*, he wrote during the late 80's, *is roughly equal in moral content to a Methodist preacher.* The Creator himself did not escape criticism: The world is such a misbegotten wreck *that it is impossible to believe any self-respecting deity would accept the blame for it.* And: *If there is a career more attractive to scoundrels and frauds than professional politics, it must be the Methodist ministry.*

Perhaps I violated an ethic in reading my father's diary. I wish now that I had not. But the charm and vitality of his observations, his obvious appetite for life, his Olympian assaults against those he considered frauds and halfwits, were irresistible. Once started, I could not stop. And I began to realize how little I had appreciated him during his lifetime.

I started seriously reading the diary at about the time I'd given up hope that he might have survived. I'd seen the final entries and knew that he planned to be in Atlantic City, the worst possible place. But there was the chance that he might have been sidetracked, gone somewhere else, been delayed by a woman. I know better now.

The first entry was dated July 16, 1961. It spells out the rationale behind the diary, which was that he hoped his "occasional ruminations" would one day be of general interest. (My father was never afflicted with modesty.) He also revealed an ambition to become an essayist, and believed that a daily account of his reflections would be a priceless aid to such an endeavor. I should add, parenthetically, that his ambitions came to nothing. If he ever actually tried to compile a manuscript, I have no knowledge of it.

Six days later, he recorded my birth. And, in another week, the death of my mother. He seldom mentioned her to me, but the diary gave over a dozen pages of cramped handwriting to reminiscences of their early years together, and of his conviction that, were it not for his responsibilities (by which I gathered he was talking about me), his life had become worthless. Judging from the diary, he never after seriously considered marriage although, as I mentioned, there were many women. I was aware of his escapades, of course, while I was growing up. And I was baffled: my father's appearance was rather ordinary. He was also short and, when I was a teen-ager, beginning to lose his hair. It was hard to see what brought that endless supply of women to his door. I don't know yet.

By the time I had read into the late '70's, I noticed an odd trend. There are passages, and implications, which are unsettling. My father was, if anything, a rationalist. And I could sense his increasing dismay at events which he could not explain. I began to read more intently, and eventually found it impossible to lay the book aside. I will never forget the cold, rainswept evening during which I came back to the final entry. And read it in the frantic glare of what had gone before.

Now I don't know what to make of it. The only possible conclusion is that the diary is a fabrication. It *has* to be. Yet I do not see how that is possible. My wife, after she finished it, suggested we burn it.

I have not been able to bring myself to do that. Nor can I simply pretend it does not exist. Consequently, without taking a position on the matter, I have had the pertinent entries privately printed, in order to make them available to a small group of my friends whose judgment I trust. Perhaps someone among them will be able to offer a rational explanation.

One final note: the "Rob" who figures so prominently in this narrative was Orin R. Robinson, who served 1958-60 in the Far East with my father. Curiously, they seem not to have been close friends until after the chance meeting in the Minneapolis airport described in the first entry in the Extract below. My father, incidentally, was on his way to Fargo, pursuing a young woman of his acquaintance.

(ATTACHMENT)
Being Extracts from the Diary of Samuel H. Coswell

Minneapolis, Friday, November 22, 1963
Black day. The President is dead.

I was having lunch with Rob. First time I'd seen him since Navy days on the *McCusker*. Hell of a reunion. We were sitting in a dark little place off Washington Avenue, all electric candles and checkerboard tablecloths and bare hardwood floors. A waitress had filled our glasses with Chianti and set the bottle down. We were already deep into reminiscing about old friends and old times, and Rob swept up his glass with a flourish and raised it toward the light. "Here's to you, Sam," he said, "I've missed you," and in that brief hesitation, when one tastes the moment before the wine, I became aware of raised voices.

Chair legs scraped the floor. "—*Shot him*—" someone said. The words hung in the still air, whispered, almost disembodied. Then Kennedy's name. Doors banged, and traffic sounds got loud. Outside, a postal truck pulled up beside a mailbox.

There were bits and pieces of conversation. *"How badly hurt?" "—They get the guy?" "Be fine. Can't kill—" "What time is it? Is the stock market still open?"*

They brought out a television and we watched the early reports and learned the worst. "Not much of a reunion," I told Rob.

He lives in L.A. We'd met at the airport, both passing through. He's an aircraft design consultant, and he was on his way home from Chicago. We got to talking, decided not to miss the opportunity, and rearranged our flight schedules. Which was how we came to be eating a late lunch together when the news came from Dallas.

We walked back to our Sheraton and pushed into the bar. The TV threw a pale glare over the crowd, which kept getting bigger. Nobody said much. Cronkite reported that a police officer had been shot, and then he was back a few minutes later to tell us that a suspect had been captured in a movie theater. Name's Oswald. Nobody seems to know anything about him. I guess we'll start getting some answers tomorrow. Meantime, there's a lot of talk about a conspiracy. And we now have Lyndon Johnson.

I'm surprised this has hit me so hard. I've never been high on Kennedy. Although, as politicians go, he was likable. But it will be harder to run the Republic if presidents have to go into hiding.

Rob is up one floor. We'd originally planned to have breakfast together. He has an early flight, though, and I don't think either of us feels much like socializing. My own flight's at noon. So I will sleep late. And maybe one day we'll meet again in some other airport.

Fargo, Saturday, November 23, 1963
Ellen and I spent the day parked in front of a TV. Gloomy business, this. Oswald looks like a loony. Still no explanations. There are theories that he was working for the Cubans, or the CIA, or the Russians. You take a look at this guy, and it's hard to believe any sensible organization would use him. He doesn't look reliable. We'll see. If we trace it to Moscow, what happens then?

Ellen is showering now. She's a knockout, enough to get anyone's juices running, but there's a ceremonial quality to the preparations. The assassination has cast gloom on us all, I guess.

En route to Philadelphia, Sunday, November 24, 1963
Kennedy's funeral tomorrow.

Never knew anyone as wild as Ellen was last night. Is this the way we hide from our mortality?

Philadelphia, Saturday, August 1, 1964
Call from Rob. He's going to be in town next week, and we will get together. Funny about him: when we were in the Navy, he seemed a bit stand-offish. Difficult to get to know. Maybe it's the Kennedy thing, but he seems warmer, friendlier than I remember. I wouldn't have believed he'd ever have taken the time to look me up. He's a curious mix, simultaneously idealistic and cynical, gregarious and distant. He'd be horrified to hear this, but the truth is, he's a fascist. A goodhearted one, but a fascist all the same. He's a great believer in order and is fond of quoting Plato on the dangers of giving freedom to the undisciplined. We talked for almost

an hour (his nickel). We agreed that western civilization is on its last legs. I don't really believe that, but he's persuasive, and anyhow predicting doom always gives one such a warm feeling. Is that why there are so many Fundamentalists?

We were both elated by the lunar photographs taken by Ranger 7. First closeups ever. I told him we were taking the first steps into a vast sea. He laughed. *A vast desert, maybe.* He doesn't think we will ever leave the Earth-moon system. Why not? *Where else is there to go?*

Philadelphia, Friday, August 7, 1964
Great day.

I don't know when I've enjoyed myself more. We spent most of the evening arguing over Goldwater. Rob is worried that Johnson will win, and then give away Southeast Asia. I'm scared to death Barry would give Hanoi an atomic alternative shortly after the swearing-in ceremony. Get out or get fused.

I don't think I've ever properly appreciated Rob. The world's a more comic place when he's around. Its absurdities are a bit more clearly defined. We share a sense of the ridiculous that seems to transcend language: a word, sometimes a glance, is enough to suggest some new buffoonery on the march. He ignites insight, in the way a good woman intensifies the emotional climate. We spent the evening raking over the Johnson administration, the Bible-thumpers who are citing chapter and verse against the Freedom Riders, and the latest academic notion that everyone's opinion is equally valid. (Rob's not exactly big on the Freedom Riders either. They're another example of what happens when people start taking their rights seriously.) He thinks ballots should be weighted. Particularly his. Probably mine. *A bonus for common sense. It's in short supply these days.*

We ate a late lunch at Bookbinder's, and retired for the evening to the Officers' Club at the Naval Base. We stayed until midnight. It strikes me that the art of conversation has almost disappeared from the world. Rob, in that sense, is something of an anachronism: a visitor from the nineteenth century, from an age in which there were more important things to do than to sit around and be entertained.

He'll be leaving in the morning, ten o'clock flight.
Pity.

Philadelphia, Wednesday, January 9, 1974
School districts are burning Mark Twain. In California, two police

officers have been sued for using unnecessary force to subdue a man who was in the act of stabbing a woman. And there's a report that a group of volunteers trying to stop their TV habit went through withdrawal. Anyone who worries that the U.S. is headed for collapse can relax. It is raining on the rubble.

Terri Hauser has begun suggesting that Sammy needs a mother. Truth is, he probably does, but that seems to me to be a weak foundation for a marriage. I know she would move in if I suggested it. But where would *that* end?

Post Office returned Rob's Christmas card today, stamped MOVED—FORWARDING PERIOD EXPIRED.

Philadelphia, Friday, November 2, 1979
Rob is back.

There've been a few changes in his life. He's living in Seattle now. And he's gotten married. They'll be here on one of these Amtrak plans where you get to ride all over the country. Her name is Anne, and she is from Vermont. The plan is that she will go up to visit her folks for a few days, and Rob will stop off here. I wonder if he will be able to figure out a use for this home computer. I thought I might be able to get it to do my taxes, but they keep changing the laws every year.

Philadelphia, Sunday, November 4, 1979
The train was late getting in. I had to hang around 30th Street Station two hours. But it was good to see him again. Been a lot of years. We came back here, got settled, and then went to the Berlinhaus up on the Boulevard for sauerbraten. Lots of talk about a sex poll that was released yesterday, indicating that women are as adulterous as men. We tried to imagine how it might be possible to poll people about their sexual habits and come up with anything close to valid results. The Ayatollah also took his lumps. *What do you suppose it would be like to sit down with him for coffee?*

Later in the evening, we stopped by Janet's place. She'd asked to meet Rob, and that went pretty well too. We probably drank a little too much. But I don't think I've ever seen Janet enjoy herself so much.

Rob has gone completely gray since the last time I saw him. Otherwise, he doesn't seem to have lost much ground.

Incidentally, toward the end of the evening at the Berlinhaus, someone at the next table overheard us talking about Khomeini and asked whether we'd heard that the Iranians had seized the embassy in Teheran?

It was true, of course. They've taken fifty or sixty hostages. State Department isn't sure yet how many. It must be a first of some kind: nobody ever seized diplomatic people. Even Hitler didn't do that. It's what happens when you put an amateur in charge of a government.

Well, they'll release everybody tomorrow. And apologize. If we behave according to past practice, we'll lodge a stiff protest and go back to business as usual.

Philadelphia, Monday, November 5, 1979
Another delay with the train this morning, but Rob finally got away. This time, we've agreed to get together again soon.

The Iranian government claims it has no control over the students who've taken the embassy. Rob thinks we should give the Ayatollah a list of targets and start destroying them one by one until the government discovers it *can* do something to release our people. I'm not sure that isn't the best way to handle it.

Question: what should our primary objective be? To get the hostages released? Or to act in such a way that future hostage-takers will think it over before trying the same thing?

Philadelphia, Tuesday, September 7, 1982
Rob's marriage has collapsed. I had no idea it was in trouble. He doesn't talk much about his personal life, and of course over a telephone you don't really get to see anything. He's obviously shaken. I get the impression *he* didn't see it coming either. I suggested he might take some time and come here, but he says he'll be fine. I'm sure he will.

I never got to meet her.

Seattle, Tuesday, January 28, 1986
We've lost a shuttle. And a crew.

Grim day. I'd been looking forward to this trip for a long time. Rob picked me up at the airport, and we stopped for lunch on the way out to his place. The waitress told us about *Challenger*.

Rob looked at me very strangely, and I knew what he was thinking. We'd been able to get together *four* times over the course of a quarter-century. And three of those occasions had been marred by a major American disaster. There had been far greater catastrophes in the world during the period, in terms of body count. But we seemed to be tuned to a *local* wave length.

Neither of us said much. Until we heard the details, we hoped that the crew might have been able to survive, although it was difficult to visualize any kind of shuttle explosion that one could walk away from.

Philadelphia, Wednesday, March 4, 1987
...(Madeline and I) were talking about the various ways in which miniscule events produce results out of all proportion. Like the short cut through a park that generates an accidental meeting that ends in a marriage. One of the Kennedy assassination theories holds that Lee Oswald shot down the President because Marina Oswald indicated a sexual preference for *him* over her inadequate husband.

Madeline said she'd heard once that a butterfly, moving its wings in Africa under the right conditions, could produce a hurricane in the Caribbean. Interesting conceit.

Philadelphia, Sunday, December 18, 1988
Rob called today. *He'll be in the area Wednesday. Did I think we could manage dinner without provoking an international crisis?*

I explained that I won't be able to pick him up at the airport because I'm booked at the office. He will take a cab.

Philadelphia, Wednesday, December 21, 1988
It's happened again! A London to New York flight with more than two hundred people disintegrated over Scotland while Rob and I sat in a restaurant out on the Main Line.

I'm spooked.

So is he.

Philadelphia, Thursday, December 22, 1988
People died on the ground as well. The photographs from Lockerbie, the crash site, are just too much. I stayed away from the TV most of the night. I've got Dickens beside me, but I can't keep my mind on it. They are saying now that it looks as if there was a bomb on board. How can people be so evil?

And we were together again.

Kennedy.

Teheran.

Challenger.

Flight 103.

Here's to us.

Rob left on an afternoon flight. We tried to calculate odds, but neither of us is mathematician enough to be able even to frame the problem. Rob, who is ordinarily a world-class skeptic, wondered whether it was possible that we might sense oncoming disaster? And instinctively huddle against the storm? I told him about Madeline's butterfly.

Has it happened every time?

We both thought so. But I went back through this diary tonight. On August 7, 1964, we got safely through a meal.

One exception to the pattern.

The bond between my father and Orin Robinson grew closer, possibly as a result of the curious intersections between their quiet reunions and the series of historic disasters. They came to refer to this trend as the *Tradition*. Their phone conversations became more frequent. They discounted their alarm on the night of the Lockerbie flight. Absurd, they said, to think they could be connected. And anyway there was, after all, the exception to the general pattern. *Thank God for 1964*. That phrase became their watchword.

It was during this period that my father engaged in his brief flirtation with Catholicism. Rob was horrified but took the position that it was my responsibility to stand by my father during this aberration.

There were still occasional echoes of the *Tradition* in the diary....

Washington, D.C., Tuesday, February 4, 1992

...Visited the Eternal Flame today. It is a lovely and sober spot. How does it happen that the shots fired in Dallas so long ago still hurt?

If Rob and I had not run into each other in Minneapolis that day, is it at all possible it might not have happened? Does that make any kind of sense at all?

Portland, Oregon, Saturday, December 12, 1992

The (dental) convention's a bit dry. But I got together with some of the guys from Chicago, and we went over to Margo's. It's a topless place, and I guess it's a sign you're getting old when you wish they'd move so you could see the basketball game.

I would have enjoyed getting together with Rob. But we let it go this time, more or less by mutual consent.

Philadelphia, Tuesday, June 14, 1994

…Rob confessed tonight that he has been east any number of times over the last few years, but has not mentioned it to me. *But it's dumb to behave as if we have been doing something dangerous.*

He's right, of course.

I'll be in New York this weekend. I could get down for dinner.

I keep thinking about the butterfly.

"Listen, how about a change of venue?"

Okay. What did you have in mind?

"I don't know. Something more exotic than Philly."

Why don't we meet in Atlantic City?"

"Yeah. Sounds good."

Dinner by the sea.

Be nice to see him again. And the world looks quiet. Here's to us.

Philadelphia, Wednesday, June 15, 1994

I'll be glad when it's over—

Philadelphia, Friday, June 17, 1994

Rob tomorrow. I cannot imagine what life would have been like without him. Yet I've seen so little of him.

As the world knows, the meteor fell at 7:22 p.m. on the 18th of June. Possibly just as they were sitting down to dinner.

I've read through these passages until I have them by heart, and I can offer no explanation. The correlation between meetings and catastrophe is necessarily coincidental because it can't be anything else.

But there's one more point: I've gone back and looked closely at August 7, 1964. The exception to the Tradition.

Robinson and my father were wrong: there *was* a disaster on that day. But its nature was less immediately cataclysmic than the other events, so it's easy to see why it might have passed unnoticed.

In the late afternoon of that date, the Congress, with only two negative votes, approved the Gulf of Tonkin Resolution.

We didn't know it at the time, but the United States had formally entered the Vietnam War.

PART V

INVENTIONS AND FALLOUT

CRUISING THROUGH DEUTERONOMY

The banging sounded like distant thunder.

Cardwell was slow to move, had in fact been sitting in the dying firelight, allowing the storm to carry away his gloomy mood. Rick padded barefoot from the kitchen through the hallway and opened the front door. The wind blew louder.

There were whispers in the hall, and an authoritarian voice that he did not recognize. Rick appeared. "Dad," he said. "You have a visitor."

A tall, severe figure followed the boy into the room. Cardwell saw at once that he was a clergyman, one of those advanced types that affect plaid jackets. His hair was full and black, and his eyes blazed with dark intensity. He shook rain off his hat and coat, and held them out for Rick. "Dr. Cardwell?" he asked, coming forward.

Cardwell eased himself out of his chair. "You have the advantage of me, sir."

"I'm Pastor Gant." His glance swept the room, and registered diffident approval. "From the Good Shepherd Church over in Bridgeton." He said it as if it explained his visit.

Cardwell debated whether he could leave him standing. But his breeding got the better of him, and he indicated a chair. "What can I do for you, Pastor?"

"I'll come right to the point if you don't mind." He sat down and held his hands out to the fire.

"Yes. Good. Can I offer you a brandy?"

He waved the idea away with a choreographed gesture. His fingers were long and graceful. "No, thank you. I'm not opposed to drink on principle, you understand. But I prefer to abstain."

467

Rick, whose boredom with Cardwell's inner circle was usually painfully obvious, took a chair where he could watch.

Pastor Gant reached into his pocket, and took out precisely what Cardwell had expected: the clipping from last Tuesday's *News*. He held it toward the firelight, and looked at it as though it were vaguely loathsome. "Is there actually anything to this?" he asked.

"The Displacer?"

"The time machine."

"The story is correct in its essentials."

"I see." The long fingers toyed with the paper. He turned toward the boy. "Son," he said, "perhaps it would be best if you left the room."

Rick didn't stir, but Gant did not seem to notice.

"Pastor," said Cardwell, "I don't want to be abrupt, but I'm really quite preoccupied at the moment."

"Yes, I'm sure you are." He crossed his legs, and let his head drift back. "Doctor, you must understand that the people of my church are *good* people."

"I'm sure they are."

"But life can be very harsh. Several, at this moment, are bearing up under terminal illnesses. Another has recently lost a child. Just about your son's age, I might add. Still another—."

"Might I press you to come to the point?"

"Of course." He looked not quite substantial in the flickering light. "The only thing that keeps us going, when life becomes—," he searched for a word, "—difficult, the only thing that sustains us, is our sure and certain knowledge of a divine protector."

Cardwell's stomach began to hurt. "Reverend," he said, "I'd be pleased to discuss all this with you at a future date."

Gant stared into the fire, as if his host had not spoken. "You will take all this from them, Doctor."

Cardwell frowned. There'd been some minor fuss over that article. Fortunately, the limited circulation of the *News*, and the general tendency of people in the area to mind their business had however protected him. "I hardly see how that can be," he said.

"You know what will happen if you complete the device?" He rose from his chair and towered over Cardwell. His eyes grew very large and very black. "You will cruise through Deuteronomy. Glide across Numbers. Descend into Exodus. There were no trumpets at Jericho, you will say. No angel at Sodom. No division of the Red Sea. No haircut for Samson." His smile lengthened at that, but there was no warmth in the gesture. "You will say there was no Fall, and hence no need for a Redeemer. You will travel into the sacred country and every time you will return with a cargo of despair. I simply cannot allow that to happen." He drew a small revolver from his pocket and pointed it at a spot between Cardwell's eyes.

Rick gasped and started forward. But his father, with a quick jerky wave, stopped him. "I'm sorry," said the pastor. It was hard to see his expression in the play of light and shadow. "I truly am." He studied the weapon. "It is often difficult to know the right thing to do."

Cardwell could not take his eyes from the gun. It amazed him that a stranger would come into his home and threaten to use one on him. The entire world centered in the round black muzzle. "You're too late," he said.

Gant's gaze shifted. Bored into him. "What do you mean?"

"I've already done it. I've made the flight. Several, in fact."

"I don't believe you."

"Did you really think I'd let the newspapers have the story if I weren't *sure*? And there's only one way to be sure." He lowered himself back into his chair. Anything to get out from in front of that muzzle. And he was relieved to see that when it followed him, it locked onto his right knee. "There is a *prototype*, George. Your name *is* George, isn't it?"

That surprised him. "How did you know?"

"I pass your church every day on my way to the campus. Your name is prominently displayed."

"I wish that you might have seen fit to come by and say hello."

Cardwell nodded. "Possibly I've been remiss."

"I'm surprised you would see that." Gant's brow furrowed.

"How could I not? *Pastor, I've been on the ark.*"

The rain hissed against the windows. "That's ridiculous."

"Is it? Then why are you here? Either you believe it's possible, or you don't. If you don't, I'd like to know why you're threatening my life."

Gant stared at him. He seemed to be having trouble breathing. "Is it really *true*?"

"Yes, it's true. I've walked her decks. Felt her roll in the swell of the storm. Seen the tigers in their bays."

The gun came up. Swung a few degrees. Cardwell realized it was pointed at Rick. "Stay back," said Gant. "I don't want to shoot *you*." He took a deep breath and let it out slowly. "Indeed, I wish there were a way to do this without shooting *anyone*."

"Then *believe* me," Cardwell said desperately.

The pastor stared at him for a long moment. "Noah," he said.

"Yes."

"Did you *talk* to him?"

"I didn't know the language. I *saw* him."

The hand wavered.

"Listen to me. I was at the foot of the mountain when Moses returned with the Tablets. I saw him shatter them against the rocks. I watched Solomon give judgment and walked through his temple. I stood a few feet from David when he killed the Philistine. I was in the crowd when Jesus delivered the sermon on the mount."

Perspiration glittered on Gant's forehead. "You're lying," he said. "You're mocking me. And blaspheming everything that's holy. You're a non-believer. I know about you. I've read what you've written."

Cardwell smiled gently. "That was true *once*. George, I was on the shore during the storm when the Master stepped out of the boat. I looked into His eyes."

The pastor tried to speak, but only strangled sounds got out.

"Gant, do you, at last, not believe?" His voice rose until it was one with the wind beating at the window. *"Where is your faith?"*

The gun clattered to the floor. A sob welled up in Gant's throat, and he fell forward into Cardwell's arms and almost knocked him down. But Cardwell held on, and the pastor embraced him. A log popped and fell into the fire.

"Thank you," said Gant, finally, wiping his cheek. "I was terribly wrong to come here. Not to see what would happen." His face brightened, and he squeezed Cardwell's shoulders again. "I hope you'll come by the church and share your experience with all of us." And, without stopping for hat, coat, or gun, he walked straight out of the house.

When he was gone, they locked the door. "Dad," Rick said, "you were terrific."

"Thanks."

"Are you going to call the police?"

"Maybe in the morning. Let me think about it."

"I was scared."

"So was I, kid."

The boy picked up the weapon and put it on a bookshelf. He grinned. "The displacement principle doesn't work, right? You told me that yesterday. The time machine won't ever get off the ground."

"That's right."

The boy's eyes gleamed. "Don't you have any respect at all for the truth, Dad?"

"Sometimes I think truth is overrated," said Cardwell. "On that one, I believe I'm with the Christians. My money's on *faith*."

THE CANDIDATE

The high and low points of my career came on the same night: When we beat George Washington, and Peter Pollock returned to the White House for a second term.

Well, okay. It wasn't really Washington; it was an artificial intelligence programmed to behave like Washington. But a lot of people got confused. When you've been in politics as long as I have, you know how easily people get confused. Fortunately.

The Washington campaign started as a gag, graduated into an experiment, caught fire, and became a full-fledged national effort. I can't explain it. I don't think anybody can. President Pollock's numbers were down, but the Democratic candidate was a non-stop talker who put everybody to sleep. So we knew it would be a close race.

Then Washington showed up. He was a software package developed at the University of Georgia to play the part of the first president in seminars. He was so believable, and so compelling, that somebody at the school put him on a local radio show, and the next thing we knew he was well on his way to becoming a national phenomenon. At first, no one took him seriously. But people were desperate for a candidate they could believe in. The bloggers got in line almost immediately. The General gave an interview to the *Florida Times-Union*, the wire services picked it up, and by God he did sound like George Washington.

Next thing we knew a Federalist Party had sprung into existence, donations started showing up, first in small amounts, and ultimately in a tidal wave.

I was running the president's campaign, and we all had a pretty good laugh when they tried to put him on the ballot in Georgia. The Democrats tried to block it. Candidates have to be born in the U.S., they pointed out. And they have to be at least thirty-five years old.

We could have stopped it then. But if Washington got into the general election, he'd pull votes from the Democrats, not from us. We knew our base wasn't going to support a candidate who wasn't even human. So I called in some favors and when the case went to the Supreme Court, they surprised the country: They examined the candidate and ruled they could find no reason to suppose he was not a Washington-equivalent—the first time that terminology was used. He was therefore clearly well past the minimum age limit. As to the requirement he be born in the United States, the software had been written in Georgia, and the meaning of 'born,' said the court, is not limited to biological events. It was a six-three decision.

Early on, Washington showed every sign of splitting the Democratic vote. I watched him a few times on cable, and he *was* persuasive. He didn't like the frivolous spending. Didn't like the fact that people who'd worked their entire lives couldn't afford medications. Didn't like the corruption he saw in the capital. I thought he came across as wooden, and maybe a trifle stern. Americans, I thought, don't like being lectured.

They could have simply tied him into the programs, done the whole thing electronically, but somebody in his campaign was too smart for that. He was housed in a Coreolis 5000, and they dutifully set it on a table along with a screen. The screen provided an animated image from the Gilbert Stuart portrait, except they'd cut the general's hair and put him in a dark gray business suit.

By midsummer he was making the rounds of the network talk shows. And I watched his polls continue to rise. The week before he made his first appearance on *Meet the Press*, he passed the Democratic candidate and moved into the runner-up spot.

At that point, the National Conservative Union threw its weight behind him, as did the ACLU. The National Rifle Association, always a friend of Pollock's, announced it would sit the election out.

And I began to suspect I'd misjudged the voters. To start with, the liberal media was coming over to his side. After some hesitation, they'd decided the Democratic candidate was a lost cause. Russert, at first ill at ease talking to the Coreolis 5000, warmed to him. "Are you really George Washington?" he asked.

"The man's dead," said Washington, "Give him a break. But I'm everything he *was*."

Russert asked about the intervention, which had by then become another of those endless wars. "We intended the nation to lead by example," the General said. "We would not willingly have plunged into the affairs of others." The Washington-image stared out of the TV screen. "Keep your own house in order. It is enough. Take care of your own. Do it competently, and the world will follow."

We realized, belatedly, that we were in a race. After his appearance with Jon Stewart, there was no longer any doubt. "I would prefer," he told the vast audience watching that night—a fifty-two share, according to Nielson—"that you not vote for me. And I'll tell you why, Jon. It sets a bad precedent. People should be governed by other people, not by software systems. If the voters insist on putting me in, I will do my best. But I fear the long-term potential." He thereby moved into virgin territory.

So we went after him. Used his own words. Doesn't want the job. And we looked at his record. Only officer to survive the Battle of the Wilderness. What did that tell you about him? And do we really want a former slave-owner in the White House?

We knew we couldn't touch him on national security, but we demanded to know where he stood on the issues. "What about Roe V. Wade?"

"Put it aside for now," he said. "At the moment, we have bigger problems." We got some of our base back on that one.

"Gay marriage?"

"I cannot see that anyone is harmed. We should be careful about codifying moral strictures. They change too easily."

We got some more of our people back. But there was something reassuring about him.

We talked about Orwell and Frankenstein. Don't ask me how that got in there, but it appealed to the voters so we kept hitting it. Vote for People, we said. We found a few physicists who were willing to say publicly that an artificial intelligence could develop a glitch. Could become very dangerous.

Would you trust the black box in the hands of a computer?

We held on. We were still holding at 2:00 A.M. election night, when we went down to the last district in Indiana, but we took the state by a few hundred votes and that put us over the top.

Pollock went on TV after Washington conceded. He said how we'd saved the nation from a hardware conspiracy. (He tends to say things like that when he gets off-script.) He thanked the campaign workers. And everybody cheered.

When it was over, he took me into his quarters to express his appreciation. A Rainbow 360, the newest model, rested on the coffee table. "We saved the country, Will," he said. "We'll get legislation passed to bar the damned things from holding office. Otherwise, I guess, they'll trot out Abe Lincoln next time."

"Yes," I said. "And congratulations, Mr. President." It meant four more years for me too. As chief political advisor.

"No. It's not in the cards, Will." He looked almost genuinely pained. "We have to look to the future."

That was a shock. "What do you mean, sir?"

"It was a near thing, this election. We completely miscalculated our opponent's strength. I mean, incumbent president and all. It should have been easy."

"But—?"

"I need someone who won't be taken by surprise."

I was trying not to let my anger show. "Who did you have in mind, sir?"

He smiled at the Rainbow 360. "Will, meet Karl Rove."

ACT OF GOD

I'm sorry about showing up on such short notice, Phil. I'd planned to go straight to the hotel when the flight got in. But I needed to talk to somebody.

Thanks, yes, I will take one. Straight, if you don't mind.

You already know Abe's dead. And no, it wasn't the quake. Not really. Look, I know how this sounds, but if you want the truth, I think God killed him.

Do I *look* hysterical? Well, maybe a little bit. But I've been through a lot. And I know I didn't say anything about it earlier but that's because I signed a secrecy agreement. *Don't tell anybody.* That's what it said, and I've worked out there for two years and until this moment never mentioned to a soul what we were doing.

And yes, I really think God took him off. I know exactly how that sounds, but nothing else explains the facts. The thing that scares me is that I'm not sure it's over. I might be on the hit list too. I mean, I never thought of it as being sacrilegious. I've never been that religious to start with. Didn't used to be. I am now.

Did you ever meet Abe? No? I thought I'd introduced you at a party a few years ago. Well, it doesn't matter.

Yes, I know you must have been worried when you heard about the quake, and I'm sorry, I should have called. I was just too badly shaken. It happened during the night. He lived there, at the lab. Had a house in town but he actually stayed most nights at the lab. Had a wing set up for himself on the eastern side. When it happened it took the whole place down. Woke me up, woke everybody up, I guess. I was about two miles away. But it was just a bump in the night. I didn't even realize it *was* an earthquake until the police called. Then I went right out to the lab. Phil, it was as if the hill had opened up and just swallowed everything. They found Abe's body in the morning.

What was the sacrilege? It's not funny, Phil. I'll try to explain it to you but your physics isn't very good so I'm not sure where to start.

You know the appointment to work with Abe was the opportunity of a lifetime. A guarantee for the future. My ship had come in.

But when I first got out there it looked like a small operation. Not the sort of thing I'd expected to see. There were only three of us, me, Abe, and Mac Cardwell, an electrical engineer. Mac died in an airplane crash about a week before the quake. He had a pilot's license, and he was flying alone. No one else was involved. Just him. FAA said it looked as if lightning had hit the plane.

All right, smile if you want to. But Cardwell built the system that made it all possible. And I know I'm getting ahead of things here so let me see if I can explain it. Abe was a cosmologist. Special interest in the big bang. Special interest in how to generate a big bang.

I'd known that before I went out there. You know how it can be done, right? Actually *make* a big bang. No, I'm not kidding. Look, it's not really that hard. Theoretically. All you have to do is pack a few kilograms of ordinary matter into a sufficiently small space, *really* small, considerably smaller than an atomic nucleus. Then, when you release the pressure that constrains it, the thing explodes.

No, I don't mean a nuke. I mean a big bang. A *real* one. The thing expands into a new universe. Anyhow, what I'm trying to tell you is that he *did* it. More than that, he did it *thirty* years ago. And no, I know you didn't hear an explosion. Phil, I'm serious.

Look, when it happens, the blast expands into a different set of dimensions, so it has no effect whatever on the people next door. But it *can* happen. It *did* happen.

And *nobody* knew about it. He kept it quiet.

I *know* you can't pack much matter into a space the size of a nucleus. You don't have to. The initial package is only a kind of cosmic seed. It contains the trigger and a set of instructions. Once it erupts, the process feeds off itself. It creates whatever it needs. The forces begin to operate, and the physical constants take hold. Time begins. *Its* time.

I'd wondered what he was doing in Crestview, Colorado, but he told me he went out there because it was remote, and that made it a reasonably safe place to work. People weren't going to be popping in, asking questions. When I got there, he sat me down and invited me to sign the agreement, stipulating that I'd say nothing whatever, without his express permission, about the work at the lab. He'd known me pretty well and I suddenly realized why I'd gotten the appointment over several hundred people who were better qualified. He could trust me to keep my mouth shut.

At first I thought the lab was involved in defense work of one kind or another. Like Northgate. But this place didn't have the security guards and the triple fences and the dogs. He introduced me to Mac, who was a little guy with a beard that desperately needed a barber, and to Sylvia Michaels. Sylvia was a tall, stately woman, dark hair, dark eyes, a hell of a package, I'm sure, when she was younger. She was the project's angel.

I should add that Sylvia's also dead. Ran into a tree two days after the quake. Cops thought she was overcome with grief and wasn't paying attention to what she was doing. Single vehicle accident. Like Mac, she was alone.

Is that an angel like in show business? Yes. Exactly. Her family owned a group of Rocky Mountain resorts. She was enthusiastic about Abe's ideas, so she financed the operation. She provided the cash, Mac designed the equipment, and Abe did the miracles. Well, maybe an unfortunate choice of words there.

Why didn't he apply for government funding? Phil, the government doesn't like stem cells, clones, and particle accelerators. You think they're going to underwrite a *big bang*?

Yes, of course I'm serious. Do I look as if I'd kid around? About something like this?

Why didn't I say something? Get it stopped? Phil, you're not listening. It was a going concern long before I got there.

And yes, it's a real universe. Just like this one. He kept it in the building. More or less. It's hard to explain. It extended out through that separate set of dimensions I told you about. There *are* more than three. It doesn't matter whether you can visualize them or not. They're there. Listen, maybe I should go.

Well, okay. No, I'm not upset. I just need you to hear me out. I'm sorry, I don't know how to explain it any better than that. Phil, we could *see* it. Mac had built a device that allowed us to observe and even, within limitations, to guide events. They called it the *cylinder* and you could look in and see star clouds and galaxies and jets of light. Everything spinning and drifting, supernovas blinking on and off like Christmas lights. Some of the galaxies with a glare like a furnace at their centers. It was incredible.

I know it's hard to believe. Take my word for it. And I don't know when he planned to announce it. Whenever I asked him, he always said *when the time is ripe*. He was afraid that, if anyone found out, he'd be shut down.

I'm sorry to hear you say that. There was never any danger to *anybody*. It was something you could do in your garage and the neighbors would never notice. Well, you could do it if you had Mac working alongside you.

Phil, I wish you could have seen it. The cosm—his term, not mine—was already eight billion years old, relative. What was happening was that time was passing a lot faster in the cosm than it was in Crestview. As I say, it had been up and running for thirty years by then.

You looked into that machine and saw all that and it humbled you. You know what I mean? Sure, it was Abe who figured out how to make it happen, but the magic was in the process. How was it possible that we live in a place where you could pack up a few grams of earth and come away with a living universe?

And it *was* living. We zeroed in on some of the worlds. They were *green*. And there were animals. But nothing that seemed intelligent. Lots of predators, though. Predators you wouldn't believe, Phil. It was why he'd brought *me* in. What were the conditions necessary to permit the development of intelligent life? Nobody had ever put the question in quite those terms before, and I wasn't sure I knew the answer.

No, we couldn't see any of this stuff in real time. We had to take pictures and then slow everything down by a factor of about a zillion. But it worked. We could tell what was going on.

We picked out about sixty worlds, all overrun with carnivores, some of them that would have gobbled down a T-rex as an appetizer. Abe had a technique that allowed him to reach in and influence events. Not physically, by which I mean that he couldn't stick a hand in there, but we had some electromagnetic capabilities. I won't try to explain it because I'm not clear on it myself. Even Abe didn't entirely understand it. It's funny, when I look back now, I suspect Mac was the real genius.

The task was to find a species with potential and get rid of the local carnivores to give it a chance.

On some of the worlds, we triggered major volcanic eruptions. Threw a lot of muck into the atmosphere and changed the climate. Twice we used undersea earthquakes to send massive waves across the plains where predators were especially numerous. Elsewhere we rained comets down on them. We went back and looked at the results within a few hours after we'd finished, our time. In most cases we'd gotten rid of the targets, and the selected species were doing nicely, thank you very much. Within two days of the experiment we had our first settlements.

I should add that none of the occupants looked even remotely human.

If I'd had my way, we would have left it at that. I suggested to Abe that it was time to announce what he had. Report the results. Show it to the world. But he was averse. *Make it public?* he scowled. *Jerry, there's a world full of busybodies out there. There'll be protests, there'll be cries for an investigation, there'll be people with signs. Accusing me of playing God. I'll spend the rest of my life trying to reassure the idiots that there's no moral dimension to what we're doing.*

I thought about that for several minutes and asked him if he was sure there wasn't.

He smiled at me. It was that same grin you got from him when you'd overlooked some obvious detail and he was trying to be magnanimous while simultaneously showing you what a halfwit you are. "Jerry," he said, "what have we done other than to provide life for thousands of generations of intelligent creatures? If anything, we should be commended."

Eons passed. Tens of thousands of subjective years, and the settlements went nowhere. We knew they were fighting; we could see the results. Burned out villages, heaps of corpses. Nothing as organized as a war, of course. Just local massacres. But no sign of a city. Not anywhere.

Maybe they weren't as bright as we thought. Local conflicts don't stop the rise of civilization. In fact there's reason to think they're a necessary factor. Anyhow, it was about this time that Mac's plane went down. Abe was hit pretty hard. But he insisted on plunging ahead. I asked whether we would want to replace him, but he said he didn't think it would be necessary. For the time being, we had all the capability we needed.

"We have to intervene," he said.

I waited to hear him explain.

"Language," he added. "We have to solve the language problem."

"What language problem?" I asked.

"We need to be able to talk to them."

The capability already existed to leave a message. No, Phil, we didn't have the means to show up physically and conduct a conversation. But we could deposit something for them to find. If we could master the languages.

"What do you intend to do?" I asked.

He was standing by a window gazing down at Crestview, with its single large street, its lone traffic light, Max's gas station at the edge of town, the Roosevelt School, made from red brick and probably built about 1920. "Tell me, Jerry," he said, "Why can none of these creatures make a city?"

I had no idea.

One of the species had developed a written language. Of sorts. But that was as far as they'd gotten. We'd thought that would be a key, but even after the next few thousand local years, nothing had happened.

"I'll tell you what I think," Abe said. "They haven't acquired the appropriate domestic habits. They need an ethical code. Spouses who are willing to sacrifice for each other. A sense of responsibility to offspring. And to their community."

"And how would you propose to introduce those ideas, Abe?" I should have known what was coming.

"We have a fairly decent model to work with," he said. "Let's give them the Commandments."

I don't know if I mentioned it, but he was moderately eccentric. No, that's not quite true. It would be closer to the mark to say that, for a world-class physicist, he was unusual in that he had a wide range of interests. Women were around the lab all the time, although none was ever told what we were working on. As far as I knew. He enjoyed parties, played in the local bridge tournaments. The women loved him. Don't know why. He wasn't exactly good-looking. But he was forever trying to sneak someone out in the morning as I was pulling in.

He was friendly, easy-going, a *sports* fan, for God's sake. You ever know a physicist who gave a damn about the Red Sox? He'd sit there and drink beer and watch games off the dish.

When he mentioned the Commandments, I thought he was joking.

"Not at all," he said. And, after a moment's consideration: "And I think we can keep them pretty much as they are."

"Abe," I said, "what are we talking about? You're not trying to set yourself up as a god?" The question was only half-serious because I thought he might be on to something. He looked past me into some indefinable distance.

"At this stage of their development," he said, "they need something to hold them together. A god would do nicely. Yes, I think we should do precisely that." He smiled at me. "Excellent idea, Jerry." He produced a copy of the King James, flipped pages, made some noises under his breath, and looked up with a quizzical expression. "Maybe we *should* update them a bit."

"How do you mean?"

"'Thou shalt not hold any person to be a slave.'"

I had never thought about that. "Actually, that's not bad," I said.

"'Thou shalt not fail to respect the environment, and its creatures, and its limitations.'"

"Good." It occurred to me that Abe was off to a rousing start. "Maybe, 'Thou shalt not overeat.'"

He frowned, ignoring my contribution, and shook his head. "Maybe that last one's a bit much for primitives. Better leave it out." He pursed his lips and looked again at the leather-bound Bible. "I don't see anything here we'll want to toss out. So let's stop with twelve."

"Okay."

"The Twelve Commandments."

"Okay," I said. "Let's try it."

"For Mac," he said. "We'll do it for Mac."

The worlds had all been numbered. He had a system in which the number designated location, age, salient characteristics. But you don't care about that. He decided, though, that the world we had chosen for our experiment should have a name. He decided on *Utopia*. Well, I thought, not yet. It had mountain ranges and broad seas and deep forests. But it also had lots of savages. Smart savages, but savages nonetheless.

We already had samples of one of the languages. That first night he showed them to me, slowed down of course. It was a musical language, rhythmic, with a lot of vowels and, what do you call them, diphthongs. Reminded me of a Hawaiian chant. But he needed a linguistic genius to make it intelligible.

He called a few people, told them he was conducting an experiment, trying to determine how much data was necessary to break in and translate the text of a previously unknown language. Hinted it had something to do with SETI. The people on the other end were all skeptical of the value of such a project, and he pretended to squirm a bit but he was offering lots of cash and a bonus for the correct solution. So everybody had a big laugh and then came on board.

The winner was a woman at the University of Montreal. Kris Edward. Kris came up with a solution in *five* days. I'd've thought it was impossible. A day later she'd translated the Commandments for him into the new language. Ten minutes after he'd received her transmission, we were driving over to Caswell Monuments in the next town to get the results chiseled onto two stone tablets. Six on each. They looked *good*. I'll give him that. They had dignity. Authority. *Majesty*.

We couldn't actually transport the tablets, the Commandments, physically to Utopia. But we *could* relay their image, and their substance, and reproduce them out of whatever available granite there might be. Abe's intention was to put them on a mountaintop, and then use some directed lightning to draw one of the shamans up to find them. It all had to be programmed into the system, because as I said the real-time action would be much too quick for anyone to follow. I didn't think it would work. But Abe was full of confidence that we were on track at last.

We had a flat on the way back with the tablets. The spare was flat too. Maybe we should have taken that as a sign. Anyhow, by the time we'd arranged to get picked up, and got the tire changed, and had dinner, it had gotten fairly late. Abe was trying to be casual, but he was anxious to start. No, Jerry, we are not going to wait until morning. Let's get this parade on the road. So we set the tablets in the scanner and sent the transmission out. It was 9:46 p.m. on the twelfth. The cylinder flashed amber lamps, and then green, signaling success, it had worked, the package had arrived at its destination. Moments later we got more blinkers, confirming that the storm had blown up to draw the shaman into the mountain.

We looked for results a few minutes later. It would have been time, on the other side, to build the pyramids, conquer the Mediterranean, fight off the Vandals, get through the Dark Ages, and move well into the Renaissance. If it had worked, we could expect to see glittering cities and ships and maybe even 747's. What we saw, however, were only the same dead end settlements.

We resolved to try again in the morning. Maybe Moses had missed the tablets. Maybe he'd not been feeling well. Maybe the whole idea was crazy.

That was the night the quake hit.

❋

That's stable ground up in that part of the world. It was the first earthquake in Crestview's recorded history. Moreover, it didn't hit anything else. Not Charlie's Bar & Grill, which is at the bottom of the hill on the state road. Not any part of the Adams Ranch, which occupied the area on the north, not any part of the town, which is less than a half mile away. But it completely destroyed the lab.

What's that? Did it destroy the cosm? No, the cosm was safely disconnected from the state of Colorado. Nothing could touch it, except through the cylinder. It's still out there somewhere. On its own.

But the whole thing scares me. I mean, Mac was already dead. And two days later Sylvia drove into a tree at about sixty.

That's okay, you can smile about it, but I'm not sleeping very well. What's that? Why would God pick on us? I don't know. Maybe he didn't like the idea of someone doing minor league creations. Maybe he resented our monkeying around with the Commandments.

Why do you think he didn't say anything to Moses about slavery? What, you've never thought about it? I wonder if maybe, at the beginning, civilization needs slaves to get started. Maybe you can't just jump off the mark with representative democracy. Maybe we were screwing things up, condemning sentient beings to thousands of years of unnecessary savagery. I don't know.

But that's my story. Maybe it's all coincidence. The quake, the plane crash, Sylvia. I suppose stranger things have happened. But it's scary, you know what I mean?

Yeah, I know you think I'm exaggerating. I know the God you believe in doesn't track people down and kill them. But maybe the God you believe in isn't there. Maybe the God who's actually running things is just a guy in a laboratory in another reality. Somebody who's a bit less congenial than Abe. And who has better equipment.

Well, who knows?

The scotch is good, by the way. Thanks. And listen, Phil, there's a storm blowing up out there. I don't like to impose, but I wonder if I could maybe stay the night?

ELLIE

If the lights at Bolton's Tower go out, the devil gets loose. At least, that was the story. The idea spooked me when I was a kid and even years later on those rare occasions when I traveled into its general neighborhood, which was well north on the Great Plains, far off the trading routes.

The Tower put out a lot of light, so much that it could be seen from the Pegborn-Forks road. In a world illuminated mostly by kerosene and candles, it was unique, and it was easy to believe there might be a supernatural force at work.

I'd been away from the Dakotas for *years*, and had long since forgotten about the thing, when the press of business and a series of unseasonal storms drove me north into my old home grounds. The weather had been overcast for a week, had cleared off during the course of a long cold afternoon, and when the sun went down, Bolton's star rose in the east. I knew it immediately for what it was, and I knew I was close.

There's something else odd about Bolton's Tower.

It's just inside the southern rim of a long, curving ridge. The ridge isn't high. It seldom exceeds thirty feet, and sometimes it's no more than a ripple in the grass. But it's a strange ridge: if you follow it far enough, you discover it forms a *perfect circle*. You can't see that from any single place; the ring is too big. More than sixty miles around. I've heard tent preachers explain that the circle symbolizes God, because it's endless, and cannot be improved on. Just the thing to imprison Satan, they add darkly.

I crossed the ridge on foot, leading my mount. Snow was beginning to fall again, and the wind was picking up. The Tower rose out of a cluster of dark, weatherbeaten buildings and a screen of trees. These structures were low and flat, dreary boxes, some made of clapboard and others of brick. Their windows were gone; their doors hung on broken hinges or were missing altogether. A roof had blown off one, another lay partly demolished by a fallen tree. A small barn, set to one side, had been kept in reasonable repair, and I heard horses moving within as I drew near.

The Tower soared above the ruin, seven stories of bone-white granite and thick glass. Porches and bays and arches disconnected it from the prairie, as if it belonged to a less mundane reality. The roof melted into banks of curved glass panels capped by a crystal spire. Its lines whispered of lost power and abandoned dreams, passion frozen in stone.

I released the straps on my crossbow and loosened it in its sheath.

Several windows on the second and third floors were illuminated. The Tower lights themselves, red and white signature beams, blazed into the murky night.

In the windows, no one moved.

The base of the Tower culminated in a broad terrace surrounded by a low wall, elevated from the road by about twenty wide stone steps. The steps were flanked by dead hedge.

I rode past, down a grass-covered street, and dismounted in front of the barn. Max made some noises to indicate he was glad the day was over. I hoped he was right.

The barn had sliding doors. I opened one and we went inside. Three horses moved restlessly in their stalls. The place smelled of them, warm and pungent. I tied Max up but did not remove his saddle. Just in case. I debated whether to take the crossbow, but in the end left it on the ground that guests arriving with weapons were a lot more likely to be turned away.

Wind shook the building, and snow rattled against it like sleet. On the plains, the stuff has the consistency of rock salt. And when the wind is up the way it was that night, it can beat you down pretty good. I burrowed into my coat, pulled my hat low to protect my eyes, and strode back out into the storm.

I climbed the steps and crossed the terrace. There was a statue of someone out there, in an old dried-up fountain, a rumpled woman in Old World clothes, with the name *Margaret Hanbury*, and the inscription: *FROM THIS NARROW SPACE, WE TOUCH THE INFINITE.*

Six heavy glass doors guarded the entrance. I looked up at the Tower, cold and remote, its aspect growing and shifting in the changing texture of its spectral lights.

The doors had no give. Beyond them lay a dark lobby. I could see furniture, wall-hangings, a stairway illuminated from above. I banged on the glass.

For several minutes nothing happened. I tried again, and was thinking about moving in with the horses when the terrace lit up. A man descended the staircase, came to a stop midway across the lobby, and stood for a time studying me. Finally, he came forward, threw a bolt, and pulled the door open.

"Good evening," he said, in a rich baritone. "Sorry to leave you standing out here, but I'm inclined to be careful these days."

He was a half-foot taller than I, with lean, almost cruel features, and dark intelligent eyes. His buckskin jacket covered a white denim shirt. His black trousers were creased. He was a dark and somber man, and his manner suggested he was accustomed to command. He wore a neatly-trimmed beard, and his hair was black and quite thick.

"Thank you," I said, moving past him. It was good to be in out of the wind.

More lights went on. The interior was quite long, perhaps two hundred feet, although it was only as wide as an ordinary room. It was decorated with Indian art, totems, weavings, pottery, and a few oils depicting teepees by sunset and young braves in canoes. Chairs were scattered about in no particular order, and with no effort to match their styles. There were rattans, fabric of a half-dozen different colors, a wooden bench, and several small tables.

He extended a hand. "This is not a good day to be on the road."

"No," I said. "It's downright brisk out there." I shook the snow off my shoulders. "I'm Jeff Quincey."

"Edward Marsh. Where are you headed, Quincey?" His voice changed texture, not precisely softening, but rather growing consciously more amiable.

"I'm bound for the Forks. I'd expected to spend the night in Sandywater, but I got off to a late start this morning. And the weather—."

He nodded. Snow whipped across the glass. "You'll want to stay the night with us, of course."

"If it's no trouble, I'd be grateful."

"None at all. We don't get many visitors here." He turned on his heel and led the way to the staircase.

On the second floor, carpeted corridors ran off in three directions. The carpet was frayed and, in some places, threadbare. Closed doors marched uniformly along the walls. "This way," Marsh said, striding off into the right-hand passageway. "What business are you in, Quincey?"

"I'm a trader. And an occasional agent for Overland."

He nodded. "It's the traders that'll open up this country." Halfway down the hall, the place began to look lived-in. The gray walls gave way to dark-stained paneling, rugs were thrown over the weary carpet, and someone had hung a series of prints. The prints alternated between abstracts and sketches of Old World city scenes. One depicted Chicago, crowded with traffic; another, New York at night; and a third, a Parisian sidewalk cafe. "I've been there," I told him.

"Where?"

"Chicago."

"Really?" He glanced at the image. "Odd, all the times I've walked by this, and I don't think I ever really looked at it." He pushed his hands deep into his jacket pockets. "Why?"

Why indeed? It had been one of the more oppressive experiences of my life, wandering through those gray, cold canyons. Climbing past the rusting metal that filled its ravine streets, looking up at thousands of empty windows, and knowing what lay moldering behind them. "I was hired to help with a survey. An historical project."

He nodded. "I do believe you're a man after my own heart, Quincy." We entered a sitting room half-lit by a low fire. Several pieces of oversized upholstered furniture filled most of the available space. Crossbows and bison trophies were mounted in strategic locations, and a battered garrison hat hung on a peg. Yellowing books were stacked on wall-shelves, more than I'd seen in one place this side of Port Remote. Some appeared to be military histories. But there were also travel journals, and technical titles whose meaning escaped me, like *An Orderly Approach to Chaos*, and *The n-Particle*. That was old stuff, pre-Crash, and I wondered whether anyone now living really understood them.

He switched on an electric lamp, and motioned me to a chair. "I stay out of the cities," he said. "I don't like places where you can't see what's coming at you. Anyway—," he winked, "you never know when some of the concrete is going to let go." He took glasses and a decanter from a cabinet. "Port?"

"Yes. Fine."

"Good. We don't have much of a selection." He filled them and held one out for me. "To the outside world," he said.

That was a strange toast. I glanced through the window at the endless plain. "Cheers," I said.

We talked for a few moments of inconsequentials. How short the summer had been this year; the apparent withdrawal of the raiders who had harassed stages and attacked settlements in the area ("too cold for them here in winter," offered Marsh); the rumor that a firearms manufacturing plant had been set up in Nevada and was now turning out weapons and ammunition in quantity. We refilled the glasses. My host was friendly enough, God knew, and solicitous for my welfare. But I sensed a barrier, and a lack of warmth in his smile. "You're in time for dinner," he said at last. "We'll eat shortly." He studied me thoughtfully. "If you like, I believe we can replenish your wardrobe."

Marsh enjoyed his role as host, but I sensed he would have been uncomfortable in my position, as supplicant. "Thank you," I said. "You're very kind." And I thought of Max. "I'd like to take some water out to my horse."

"Is he in the barn?"

"Yes."

"I'll take care of it. Meantime, if you're ready, let's look at your quarters."

He provided me with a spacious and, by prairie standards, luxurious room on the third floor. A big double bed stood in its center, with pillows piled high and a quilt thrown over. I lacked a fireplace, but there was a steady flow of warm air from a vent. The atmosphere was masculine: varnished walls, a mounted deer's head, an antique pistol over the bed, and a military ensign bearing rifles and bugles and the numeral IV by the door. A small desk had been placed near the window. An ancient dictionary lay on the desk, and a battered copy of Pierce's *Travels Through the Dakotas* on a side table.

I threw off my clothes, leaving them in a pile on the floor, and retreated into a tan-tiled bathroom. I showered in glorious hot water, toweled off, and tried the garments my host had provided. They were a size large, but they were clean and smelled faintly of pine. I washed my own clothes and hung them to dry.

The smell of steak and potatoes drifted up from the kitchen. I wandered downstairs, pausing to look through a window at the rooftop lights. They blazed through the rushing snow. What a prodigious waste of power it all was. I wondered how they were able to manage it?

Marsh must have heard me coming: he was waiting when I arrived on the second floor. "I hope you feel better, Quincey," he said.

I did. Very much so.

We returned to the room in which we had talked earlier. A pot of coffee was waiting. He poured, and we sat down by the fire. We were barely settled when he looked up, past my shoulder. "Eleanor," he said, "this is Mr. Quincey."

I rose and turned, and was astonished. So, I might add, was Eleanor.

"*Jeff*," she said, and I watched dismay, relief, fear, affection, and everything between, ripple across her face.

And *I*: my God, it was *Ellie Randall*.

For those few seconds, I could only stare.

Probably, no one ever quite recovers from the first big passion. Ellie had been mine. We'd had three months together when we were both growing up in the Forks. And that was all there was. She lost interest and walked out of my life. I didn't even have the consolation of losing her to someone else. Shortly after that I left the area, and when I went back ten years later she was gone and nobody knew where.

So I stood gaping back, shackled by the old resentment, breathless again. She was as gorgeous as I remembered. And that too shook me: I think in some dark corner of the mind, I'd hoped eventually to come across her and discover that the near-supernatural creature of my twentieth year had been a figment of youthful daydreaming. That, to a mature adult, she would really be quite ordinary. Perhaps even a trifle dull. That I'd conclude I'd been lucky to have got away.

But in that darkened room she seemed composed of firelight and shifting shadows, more spirit than flesh. (Although the flesh was not to be overlooked.) Her familiar features were classic, dark, and, now that she'd recovered from her initial shock, amused. She shook her head in sheer pleasure and her black hair swirled across her shoulders. Delight filled her eyes, and I felt the entire room, the chairs, the lamps, the fire, and certainly me, come erect.

I knew already I would lie alone on the plains during years to come and replay this meeting. From that moment, I developed a loathing for Edward Marsh that nothing could ever efface.

We embraced, a fleeting, phantasmagoric thing, her lips brushing my cheek, her shoulders vibrant and alive in my hands. Her eyes touched mine. "Jeff, it really *is* you, isn't it? What have you been doing all these years?"

Her smile melted me into my socks, and I was twenty years old again. I didn't trust my voice, so I grinned, foolishly no doubt, retreated to my coffee, and mumbled something about traveling extensively.

Marsh moved into the gap. "Well, *that's* interesting," he said, eyes brightening. "How odd that you two would know each other."

"We grew up together. Jeff and I were good friends for a long time." Her eyes settled on me. "It *is* good to see you again, Jeff." The smile never faded. "Listen, I have to finish dinner. But we have a lot to talk about." She swung round and trooped out. And the room sank back into the normal flow of time.

"She hasn't changed," I told Marsh. He was watching me with interest, and I knew what he was wondering. The rational tack, of course, was to change the subject. "What kind of installation was this originally?" I asked, heading in the first direction that suggested itself.

He took a long breath and examined his coffee. "A research facility of some sort," he said. "Ellie can tell you more about it than I can."

"Oh?"

He shrugged. "Yes, she's closer to the history of the place than I am." There was something dismissive in his tone, as if there were more important matters to consider. His eyes glided over me.

"Will there be others at dinner?" I asked.

"No," he said distractedly. "There is no one else here."

I looked down at my shirt.

"It belonged to *Ellie's* brother-in-law, actually," he said. "He left a few years ago."

Ellie's *brother-in-law*? Why not 'my brother'? "Where is he now?" I asked conversationally.

"We don't know. Occasionally, someone comes by with a letter from him. Last we heard, he was in Zona."

I gradually received the impression, one that was reinforced through the evening, that he was measuring me, that he was involved in a calculation and that I was somehow a variable.

Marsh had traveled widely. He explained that he had been born in Canada, in a town not far from Ottawa. "We all grew up in the shadows of that enormous wreck. And I've stayed away from the ruins since. Don't like them." He shook his head. "No sir. Don't like them one bit."

"I know what you mean," I said, not sure at all that I did.

"We're headed backward, Quincy. All of us. Still losing ground even while you and I sit here. And I don't like being reminded of it." He raised his arms in a sweeping gesture that took in the walls, or maybe the world. "They're all yellow now," he said. "Fading. And when they're gone, I suspect none of us will even remember who we were."

I realized finally he was referring to his books, marshaled around the room like a military guard. I repressed a shrug. I've never read a book, and am barely able to manage trade documents, if the truth be known. "I'm not so sure," I said. "Life is hard, but it could be worse. I mean, there's always food and drink, if a man's willing to work. And women enough,

God knows." I wished Ellie had been there to hear that. I hoped he would repeat it to her, and she would understand that I had been having a very fine time on my own, thank you.

A few minutes later, Ellie announced that dinner was ready. We retired to the dining room, and she flashed me another big smile. I thought I saw in it a glint of regret. I applied the construction most favorable to myself, and attacked dinner with a sense of good cheer.

The table would have supported dinner for ten. We ate by candlelight, warmed by two fireplaces.

The meal consisted of steak and potatoes and green beans and buttered corn and hot rolls. Marsh broke out a decanter and filled the glasses, and we toasted 'old friends.' *His* proposal. I was still wondering about the nature of the facility. "What," I asked, "is the ring? The ring-shaped ridge?"

Ellie tried her drink, and obviously approved. "They used this place to break into atoms," she said. "They were trying to discover what matter really is."

"Why?" I asked.

"I'm not entirely sure."

"Did they leave records?"

"In a way. They wrote their results into computer banks."

"Oh." The computers don't work anymore.

She sliced off a piece of steak, turned it on her fork, and slid it between her lips. "Not bad," she said, eyes gleaming. "Given time, maybe we'll figure out how to fix them."

We ate quietly for a few minutes. "How do you come to own a place like the Tower?" I asked Marsh.

"I don't own it," he said. "It's Ellie's, actually."

She tried her wine and let me see she approved. "I married into it. Two or three years after you left, I married Corey Bolton. His family had been here for generations." She propped her chin on her fist and looked right through me. "Corey died in a raid several years later. After that his brothers cleared out, and I more or less inherited the place."

"It's *big*," I said.

She smiled. "You don't know the half of it. Most of the complex is underground."

Marsh smiled reflexively. He looked uneasy.

I expected him to say something. But he only patted his mouth with his napkin. The silence stretched out.

"I wonder what *does* lie inside atoms?" I said.

"Energy," said Marsh.

"Yes." Ellie nodded agreement. She *had* changed, of course. The buoyancy of the adolescent had given way to cool dignity. Her eyes, which had been unabashedly playful, glowed now with mystery and intelligence. The sense of what I had lost began to overwhelm me, and I was sorry I had stumbled into the place. Better a cold night on the plain than this—. "But there's obviously more to it than that."

"And the ridge?" I asked again.

"Oh. It's a tunnel. We can reach it from here, actually. They fired atoms, or parts of atoms, I'm not sure which, through it. When they collided, they broke apart, and it was possible to see what was inside."

"It's hard to believe," I said, "that anyone could ever do that."

"So." She announced the subject change with her tone. "What have *you* been doing since you left the Forks, Jeff?" She touched a wall panel and Mozart filled the room. We talked about greenhouses (the Tower had *two*), and the source of their power (solar), and Marsh's trip to the Pacific, and how Chicago looks from offshore.

I learned that Marsh had been a colonel with irregulars formed to defend a group of Minnesota settlements. That Ellie was trying to pull together a comprehensive account of pre-Crash activities at the Tower, that the trail seemed to lead to Minneapolis, and that eventually she would make the trip. Ellie's comment to that effect ignited the Colonel's disapproval, and I understood that I had blundered into an old argument. "Too dangerous," he said, dismissing the matter.

When we'd finished, he insisted on clearing the table and carrying the dishes into the kitchen. I was impressed by the manner in which he stayed with her and made himself useful. But I noticed also, on several occasions, silent exchanges taking place between them. Was she reassuring him about our relationship? I suspected so, and was pleased that he might, even momentarily, consider me a potential rival.

In all, it was a delicious and entertaining evening. I was sorry to see it end.

❋

The storm had eased off, and the sky had cleared. But the wind had lost none of its force, and it drove the loose snow across the landscape.

The clothes I'd washed were still damp. I waited, listening for the last footsteps to come upstairs, and then I went down and arranged my garments in front of the fire. I threw an extra log on, and sank into a chair in front of the blaze. It was warm and pleasant. And it was not long before sleep overtook me.

I dreamt of her that night, as I had on other nights. And, as was the usual climax to these nocturnal reunions, I awoke depressed with the weight of her loss. I sat staring at the fire, which was now little more than embers, aware of the wind and sounds deep in the belly of the building and the flow of moonlight through the windows.

And I realized I was not alone.

A patch of darkness disconnected itself and came forward.

Ellie.

"Hello," I said.

She wore a heavy woolen robe, drawn up around the neck, her black hair thrown over the collar. I could not see her expression, but the glow from the window touched her eyes. "Hi, Jeff," she said. "Is there anything wrong with your room?"

For a wild moment, I wondered whether she had just come from there. "No," I said. I pointed at the clothes strung by the fire. "I just got too comfortable here. There's no problem."

After a brief silence, she said, "I didn't expect to see you again."

I had got up, but she gestured me back into my seat, and stirred the fire. "You've a lovely home," I said. "You've done well."

She nodded. The robe was frayed, oversized. But it didn't matter: she was breathtakingly beautiful. "Corey was *good*. I couldn't have asked for more."

"I'm sorry you lost him," I said.

"Thanks. It's a long time ago now." She slipped into an adjoining chair. "Jeff, I'm glad to find you here. I was afraid I wouldn't really get a chance to talk to you."

I was prodding myself to be generous, to avoid letting any of the old anger show. But it was hard. "We don't really have much to talk about," I said.

"Yes, we do." She gazed at me steadily, and I imagined I could see sparks reflected in her eyes. "I can't change what happened between us. I can't even say that I *would*, if I could. I loved Corey, and I wouldn't have missed my years with him for anything." She touched my forearm, just her fingertips, but the effect was electric. "You understand what I'm telling you?"

"Yes," I said. But I had no idea.

She stared past my shoulder. "You know that Ed is not my husband."

"I'd guessed."

"When we were attacked, when Corey was killed, Ed was the one who came to the rescue. He rode in with a detachment from Sandybrook and personally killed two of the sons of bitches."

"And afterward," I said, "he stayed."

"Not immediately. Corey's brothers couldn't take it anymore out here and they left. When that happened, he tried to persuade me to leave, too."

"Why didn't you?"

She took a deep breath. "This is my *home*." But her eyes looked away. "When I wouldn't leave, he came out. Used to sleep in here. Like you. Eventually—." She shrugged.

"This place is dangerous. For two people."

"We have defenses. Corey wouldn't have been killed if we hadn't been surprised." She shook her head, maybe reassuring herself. "No. I'll never leave here, Jeff. I *love* this place."

We sat quiet.

"But I did want you to know," she said, "that I've never been able to forget you."

That and fifty bucks, I thought. But I didn't say it.

The room got very quiet. It occurred to me that Marsh might be standing within earshot. Marsh, who had killed two raiders. "I'm happy to hear it," I said.

"I know what you're thinking," she said, mischievously.

"What am I thinking?"

"He won't care," she said. "Ed doesn't care about *me*."

That made no sense. He doesn't own the property. If he had no feelings for her, why on earth would he stay in this godforsaken place? I replayed the evening. The way Marsh had introduced her. The way he'd responded when he had discovered we'd known each other. The way he talked to her. "I don't believe it," I said.

"Nevertheless it's true. He feels trapped here, and he blames me." She pushed up out of her chair. "He stays out of a sense of duty."

Her grip tightened on my hand, and a tear ran down her cheek. It was a moment I'd contemplated many times when I was younger. Ellie perhaps realizing at last what she had lost. Asking me to forgive. In my imagination, the moment had always seemed delicious. But when it came, I took no pleasure in it.

"You never married," she said.

"I never stayed in one place long enough. Anyway, no one ever seemed much interested."

"Well, we both know that's not true," she said. She stared at me for a long moment, and, without another word, got out of her chair, pressed her lips against my cheek, and left the room.

I went to bed. I didn't sleep well, though, and I was tempted to clear out during the night. But that might have raised questions and embarrassed Ellie. So I determined to get through breakfast and leave as quickly as I reasonably could.

Bacon and coffee were already on when I started down. I poked my head into the dining room first, saw no one, and made for the kitchen. Ellie was there, manning an electric stove. But I saw immediately that something was wrong. She looked tired, and the *joie-de-vivre* of the previous day had been replaced with knife-edged intensity. "Good morning, Jeff," she said. Her tone was cordial, but not warm.

She wore a white jumper open at the throat, and a knee-length knit skirt. Her hair was brushed back, revealing pale, drawn features. "You okay?" I asked.

"I'm fine." She delivered a dispirited smile. "How do you like your eggs?"

"Medium well." I looked at her. "What's wrong?"

She poked at the bacon. "He's gone, Jeff."

"Gone? Ed?"

"Yes."

"Where?"

"Out. Skedaddled. Left for parts unknown."

"My God. What happened?"

She turned her attention to the eggs, scooping at them and wiping her eyes with the backs of her hands. I pulled the pan from the burner and set it down where things wouldn't burn, and then I caught her up: "Talk to me," I said.

"He left before dawn."

"Did he think something happened between us?"

"No," she said. "No. Nothing like that."

"What makes you think he's not coming back?"

"I *know* he's not coming back." She shook her head. "Listen, I'll be okay. Best thing is for you to eat and head out."

"Tell me why," I said.

"I've already told you. He felt trapped here. I warned him what it would be like, but he wouldn't listen, or didn't really understand. When you came, last night, when he saw that we had been friends, maybe *more* than friends, he saw his chance."

"To *bolt?*"

She nodded.

"Knowing that I wouldn't leave you here alone?"

"I'm sure that's what he thought."

"A creep with a conscience." I sank into a chair.

"That's not true," she said. "He waited. He stayed for *years*. Most men would have just walked out. Jeff, he never committed to this."

"Sure he did," I said. "When he moved in, he made a commitment." But I could see it hurt her. She wanted to think well of the son of a bitch, so I let it go.

We abandoned the kitchen, left breakfast in ruins, and wandered into the room with the fireplaces.

"Okay," I said. "What happens now?"

She shrugged. "I'll manage."

"You can't stay here alone."

"Why not?"

"*Alone?* Rattling around in this place?"

"It's my home."

"It will be a prison. Close it up and come back with me. To the Forks. It'll be safe for a while. Give yourself a chance to get away from it."

"No." Her voice caught. "I can't leave here."

"Sure you can. Just make up your mind and do it."

She nodded and took a long breath. "Maybe you're right," she said. "Maybe it *is* time to let go."

"Good." I saw possibilities for myself. "Listen, we'll—"

"—Take my chances—." She was beginning to look wild. "There's no reason *I* should have to be buried here—"

"None at all," I said.

"If it gets loose, it gets loose. I mean, nobody else cares, do they?"

"Right," I said. "If *what* gets loose?"

She looked at me a long time. "Maybe you should know what's in the basement."

I didn't like the sound of that.

I tried to get her to explain, but she only shook her head. "I'll show it to you," she said.

So I followed her down to the lobby. Outside, the snow cover ran unbroken to the horizon. I looked at the Native American display. "Corey's idea," she said. "He thought it provided a counterpoint to the technology."

We went downstairs, down four more levels in fact, into the bowels of the building. At each floor I paused and looked along the corridors, which were dark, illuminated only by the lights in the stairway area. The passageways might have gone on forever. "How big is this place?" I asked.

"*Big*," she said. "Most of it's underground. Not counting the tunnel." As we got lower, I watched her spirits revive. "I think you're right, Jeff. It *is* time to get out. The hell with it."

"I agree." I put an arm around her and squeezed, and her body was loose and pliable, the way a woman is when she's ready.

"Jeff," she said, "I meant what I said last night."

During the time we had known one another, I had never told her how I felt. Now, deep below the Tower, I embraced her, and held her face in my hands, and kissed her. Tears rolled again, and when we separated, my cheeks were wet. "Ellie," I said, "for better or worse, I love you. Always have. There has never been a moment when I would not have traded everything I had for you."

She shook her head. No. "You'd better see what you're getting into first before you say any more."

We turned on lights and proceeded down a long corridor, past more closed rooms. "These were laboratories," she said, "and storage rooms, and libraries."

The floor was dusty. Walls were bare and dirty. The doors were marked with the letter designator 'D', and numbered in sequence, odd on the left, even on the right. There had been carpeting, I believe, at one time. But there was only rotted wood underfoot now.

"Doesn't look as if you come down here very much," I said.

She pointed at the floor, and I saw footprints in the dust. "Every day."

She threw open a door and stepped back. I walked past her into the dark.

I could not immediately make out the dimensions of the room, or its general configuration. But ahead, a blue glow flickered and wavered and crackled. Lights came on. The room was quite large, maybe a hundred feet long. Tables and chairs were scattered everywhere, and the kind of antique equipment that turns up sometimes in ruins was piled high against both side walls.

The blue glow was on the other side of a thick smoked window. The window was at eye level, about thirty feet long, and a foot high. She watched me. I crossed to the glass and looked in.

A luminous, glowing cylinder floated in the air. It was a foot off the floor, and it extended almost to the ceiling. Thousands of tiny lights danced and swirled within its folds. It reminded me of a Christmas tree the Sioux had raised outside Sunset City a couple of years ago. "What is it?" I asked.

"The devil," she said softly.

A chill worked its way up my back. "What do you mean?"

"It's a result of the research they did here. A by-product. Something that wasn't supposed to happen. Jeff, they *knew* there was a possibility things might go wrong. But the bastards went ahead anyway—."

"Wait," I said. "Slow down. Went ahead with what?"

"With what we were talking about last night. Smashing atoms. Jeff, this was state-of-the-art stuff." She moved close to me, and I touched her hair. "Do you know what protons are?"

"Yeah. Sort of. They're made of atoms."

"Other way around," she said. "The thing about protons is that they are extremely stable. Protons are the basic building blocks of matter. There is *nothing* more stable than a proton. Or at least, there used to be nothing—."

"I'm not following this."

"The people who worked here knew there was a possibility they might produce an element that would *be* more stable." Her voice was rising, becoming breathless. "And they also knew that if it actually happened, if they actually produced such an element, it would *de*stabilize any proton it came into contact with."

"Which means what?"

"They'd lose the lab."

I was still watching the thing, fascinated. It seemed to be rotating slowly, although the lights moved independently at different speeds, and some even rotated against the direction of turn. The effect was soothing.

"In fact," she continued, "they were afraid of losing the Dakotas."

"You mean that it might *destroy* the Dakotas?"

"Yes."

"Ridiculous."

"I would have thought so too. But apparently not. Not if the records are correct."

I couldn't figure it out. "Why would they make something like that?" I asked.

"They didn't set out to *make* it. They thought it was *possible*. A by-product. But the chances seemed remote, and I guess the research was important, so they went ahead."

I still couldn't see the problem. After all, it was obvious that nothing untoward had occurred.

"They took steps to protect themselves in case there was an incident. They developed a defense. Something to contain it."

"How?"

"You're looking at it. It's a magnetic field that plays off the new element. They called it Heisium."

"After its discoverer?"

"Yes."

"So it's contained. What's the problem?"

She stood with her back to it, looking away. "What do you suppose would happen if the power failed here?"

"The lights would go out." And I understood. *The lights would go out.* "Isn't there a backup?"

"It's *on* the backup. Has been for almost two hundred years. The Crash took out their electrical source, and it's been running on the Tower's solar array ever since."

"Why do you come down here every day?"

"Check the gauges. Look around. Make sure everything's okay."

That shook me. "What do you do if it isn't?"

"Flip a circuit breaker. Tighten a connection. Rewire whatever." She inhaled. *"Somebody has to do this."*

"Jesus."

"They kept this place manned for forty years. Then, after the Crash, the son of one of the people responsible for the original decision, Avery Bolton, the guy the Tower's named for, stayed on. And kept the place going. When he died, his daughter succeeded him. And brought her family. In one way or another, that family has been here ever since. Until Corey. And his brothers. His brothers weren't worth much, and now I'm all that's left." She shook her head. "Seen enough?"

"Ellie, do you *really* believe all this?"

"I believe there's a good chance the threat is real." We were sitting in the lobby. "Why else would I *be* here?"

"Things get twisted over a long time. Maybe they were wrong." Outside, the day was bright and cold. "I just can't believe it."

"That's good," she said. "You should continue to think that. But I'm going to have to continue to assume that Corey knew what he was talking about."

"My God, Ellie, it's a *trap*."

She looked at me, and her eyes were wet. "Don't you think I *know* that?"

I looked up at an oil of a Sioux warrior on horseback, about to plunge a lance into a bison. "There's a way to settle it," I said.

She shook her head. "No."

"Ellie. We can shut it down. Nothing will happen."

"*No*. I won't consider it. And I want you to promise you won't do anything like that."

I hesitated.

"I want your word, Jeff. *Please*."

"Okay," I said.

"Not ever. No matter what."

"Not ever." She looked fragile. Frightened. "No matter what."

She looked out across the snowfields. "It must be time to go."

"I won't leave you," I said.

That evening was a night to kill for. The consummation of love, denied over a lifetime, may be as close as you can come to the point of existence. I took her, and took her again, and went limp in her arms, and woke to more passion. Eventually the curtains got gray, and I made promises that she said she didn't want to hear, but I made them anyway. We had a magnificent breakfast, and made love again in the room with the fireplaces. Eventually, sometime around lunch, we went down and looked again at Bolton's devil. She took along a checklist, and explained the gauges and circuit breakers and pointed out where the critical wiring was, and where things might go wrong. Where they'd gone wrong in the past. "Just in case," she said. "Not that I expect you to get involved in this, but it's best if someone else knows. Edward hated to do this. He rarely came here."

She showed me where the alarms were throughout our living quarters, and how, if the power supply got low, the system automatically shunted everything into the storage batteries in the lab. "It's happened a couple of times when we've had consecutive weeks without sunlight."

"It must get cold," I said. The temperatures here dropped sometimes to forty below for a month at a time.

"We've got fireplaces," she said. "And we'll have each other."

It was all I needed to hear.

I stayed on, of course. And I did it with no regrets. I too came to feel the power of the thing in the lab. I accepted the burden voluntarily. And not without a sense of purpose, which, I knew, would ultimately bind us together more firmly than any mere vow could have.

We worried because the systems that maintained the magnetic bottle were ageing. Eventually, we knew, it would fail. But not, we hoped, in our lifetimes.

We took turns riding the buckboard over to Sandywater for supplies. Our rule was that someone was always available at the Tower. In case.

And one day, about three months after my arrival, she did not come back. When a second day had passed without word, I went after her. I tracked her as far as the town, where I found the buckboard. There was no sign of her. Jess Harper, who works for Overland, thought he'd seen her get into a buckboard with a tall bearded man. "They rode west," he said. "I thought it was odd."

That was almost a year ago. I still make the rounds in the Tower, and I still believe she'll come back. In the meantime, I check the gauges and occasionally throw a circuit breaker. The power in the living quarters shut down once, but I got through it okay. *We* got through it okay.

What I can't understand is how I could have been so wrong. I know who the bearded man was, and I try to tell myself that they must have been very desperate to get away. And I try to forgive them. Forgive *her*.

But it's not easy. Some nights when the moon is up, and the wind howls around the Tower, I wonder what they are doing and whether she ever thinks about me. And occasionally, I am tempted to break my promise, and turn things off. Find out once and for all.

TIME'S ARROW

I t can't be done." I stared at him and at the gridwork torus that domin-ated the lab. "Time travel is prohibited."

He pushed a stack of printouts off the coffee table to make room for his Coors. "Gillie," he said, "you've got all those old Civil War flags and that drum from—ah—?"

"Fredericksburg."

"Yeah. Fredericksburg. And how many times have you been to the battlefields? Listen, we can go see the real thing. Sumter. Bull Run. The Wilderness. You name it." He grinned as if it were a piece of cake. "The arrow of time runs both ways. We can reverse it in the macroworld, too, Gillie. Tonight, I'll prove it to you."

"How?"

"What would you say to dinner and a show in Lincoln's D.C.?"

"Come on, Mac. Think about it. If it's possible, someone will even-tually do it. If not you, someone else. If that ever happens, history will be littered with tourists. They'd be *everywhere*. They'd be on the *Santa Maria*, they'd be at Appomattox with Polaroids, they'd be waiting outside the tomb, for God's sake, on Easter morning. So if you're right, where is everybody?"

He nodded. "I know. It *is* odd. I don't understand why there's no evidence."

I drew back the thick curtains that blocked off the hard sunlight. Across the empty street, I could see Harvey Keating trying to get his lawn-mower started. "In fact, if you were the father of time travel, they'd be out there now. Taking pictures of the house. Banging on the door."

He nodded. "I hear what you're saying." A pickup rumbled past. Keating's lawnmower kicked into life. "Still," he said quietly, "it works." He jabbed an index finger toward the torus and expanded his arms in a grand gesture that took in the entire lab, with its computer banks, gauges, power cord tangles, roll-top desk. Everything. "It works," he said again. His gaze lost focus. "I've been *somewhere*. I'm not sure where." He lowered himself onto a mustard-colored divan. "I finally realized the problem was in the stasis coils—"

"Say again, Mac?"

"Gillie, I've tried it. I landed in the middle of a riot."

"You're kidding."

"I never kid. I damn near got trampled. There was a labor demonstration. At least that's what it looked like. People carrying signs, making speeches. Just as I got there, a bomb went off. In the back of the crowd somewhere. Cops waded in, swinging sticks. It was pretty grim. *But they had handlebar mustaches. And old-time uniforms.*" He took a deep breath. "We were outside somewhere. In the street." His eyes focused behind me. "Goddamnit, Gillie, I've done it. I was *really* there."

"Where? *Where* were you?"

"Maybe it was the Haymarket Riot. I was on Jefferson Street, and that's where it happened. I spent the day at the library trying to pin it down."

"The Haymarket Riot? Why would you go there?"

"I was trying to get to the Scopes Monkey Trial." He shrugged. "I missed, but what difference does it make?" His eyes gleamed. "I've *done* it." He swept up a half-full beer can and heaved it across the lab. "I have goddamn done it!"

"Show me," I said.

He smiled. My pleasure. "That's why you're here. How would you like to see *Our American Cousin* on *the* night?"

I stared at him.

He handed me another Coors—it was mine that had gone for a ride—stepped over a snarl of cables, turned on a couple of computers and opened a closet. Status lamps glowed, and columns of numbers appeared on the monitors. "You'll need these." He tossed me some clothes. "We don't want to be conspicuous."

"I think I'd prefer to see him at Gettysburg."

"Oh." He looked annoyed. "I could arrange that, but I'd have to recalibrate. It would take a couple of days." The clothes were right out of *Gone With the Wind*. He produced a second set for himself.

"I don't think they'll fit," I said.

"They'll be fine," he said. "Don't worry about it." He jabbed at a keyboard. A legend appeared on one of the monitors: TEMPORAL INTERLOCK

GREEN. "The heart of the system." He indicated a black box with two alternately flashing red mode lamps. "It's the Transdimensional Interface. The TDI." He put a hand on the polished surface. "It synchronizes power applications with field angles—"

I let him talk, understanding none of it. I was an old friend of McHugh's, which is why I was there. But I was no physicist. Not that you had to be to understand that the past is irrevocable. While he rambled on, I climbed reluctantly into the clothes he provided.

The twin lamps blinked furiously, slowed, changed to amber, and came gradually to a steady, bright green.

"The energy field will be established along the nexus," he said. "We should arrive about a mile and a half outside D.C., at nine in the morning, local time. That'll allow us to have dinner at the Congress Inn and travel to the theater at our leisure."

His fingers danced across the keyboard. Relays clicked, and somewhere in the walls power began to build. A splinter of white light appeared in the center of the torus. It brightened, lengthened, rotated. "Don't look at it," McHugh said. I turned away.

"You ready?" he asked.

I was pulling on a shoe. "I guess."

The floor trembled. Windows rattled, a few index cards fluttered off a shelf, a row of black binders fell one by one out of a bookcase. "Any second now, Gillie."

The general clatter intensified until I thought the building would come down on us. It ended in a loud electrical bang and a burst of sunlight. I could smell ozone. McHugh threw up an arm to shield his eyes. A final binder tottered and crashed. Then a blast of wind knocked me off my feet and across the mustard-colored divan. I went down in a hurricane of printouts, pencils, paper clips, and beer cans. Everything was being sucked into the torus. A chair fell over and began to slide across the floor. Windows exploded; the curtains flapped wildly. I grabbed hold of the divan.

A rectangular piece of clear sky appeared in the torus and began to expand. Everything not bolted down, books, index cards, monitors, you name it, was being blown through. "Got to find a better way to do this," McHugh shouted. He almost went too.

My senses rotated. I was looking straight down. Like out of a plane. I watched the stream of Mac's belongings drop toward a forest far below. A river ran through the forest. And in the distance, I could see green and gold squares of cultivated land. Something with feathers flapped in through a window, squawking, banged into a wall, and went out through the nexus.

The land was unbroken by highways or automobile traffic. But I saw a familiar white dome, gleaming in the sunlight.

"Gillie—!" He jabbed wildly in the direction of the dome. "Look. I told you—"

"Mac," I howled. "What the hell's going on?"

"We're *here*, goddamnit. Now what do you say?" He laughed and his eyes watered. He didn't seem to notice that the only thing between him and oblivion was the desk he was hanging onto.

"We must be at ten thousand feet, Mac. How do I close it?" He couldn't hear me. But I spotted what looked like the main power cord. I picked it up and yanked it out of the wall.

"You got one thing right," I told him as the windstorm subsided. "We were about a mile and a half from D.C. Straight up."

"Ready?" He stood beside the TDI. It was about two weeks after the first attempt.

"Should we wear seatbelts?"

He grinned. Very much the man in charge. "Have your little joke. But the adjustments will work. Don't worry. We'll be at ground level this time." The twin mode lamps on the TDI went to green.

"Same destination?"

"Of course." He hovered over the computer. "Ready?"

I nodded, positioning myself near the divan.

He touched the keyboard and this time a piece of darkness appeared in the torus. I tightened my grip. We got the electrical effects again and the ozone. And the sudden intoxicating bite of salt air. The strong winds were gone. "Caused by the difference in air pressure," he said. "All we had to do was get to ground level."

It was night on the other side of the torus. A lovely evening, broad dark sea, blazing constellations, and a lighthouse. A quarter moon floated just above the horizon. McHugh strolled over to the torus and stood gazing out across the scene. Surf boomed, and a line of white water appeared. "I guess we missed D.C.," he said.

I felt spray.

A large wave roared into the room. McHugh howled and ran for the computer. Water boiled around the walls, tossed the furniture about, smashed the windows. And shorted the power.

The hole collapsed.

※

"Here we go." Mac gave me a thumbs up. "This time we've got it right." There was no smile now, just jaws set and steely eyes straight ahead.

Everything was bolted down. The lab had been cleared of all furniture and nonessentials. I wondered whether we hadn't been lucky. What would have happened if the torus had opened in the depths of the ocean? Or under ten thousand feet of rock? "Mac," I said, "maybe we should forget it."

"Don't be ridiculous."

"I mean it. I get the feeling somebody's trying to tell us something."

McHugh pulled on his waistcoat and bent over a display. "Systems fully charged. We're all set, Gillie. You want to do the honors?"

Reluctantly, I walked over to the TDI, looked at him, looked at the torus. Looked at the keyboard. It was a new computer. He was trying to be casual, but it only made him look more rattled.

I pushed the button.

This time we got ground-level summer. Green meadows stretched toward a nearby line of wooded hills. Goldenrod, thistles, and black-eyed susans covered the fields. Afternoon heat invaded the lab. The air conditioner kicked in with a thump.

"At last." McHugh gazed through the hole. "Eighteen sixty-five." For a long time he didn't move. "Now, listen, Gillie: the nexus will close ten minutes after we go through. But it will open for ten minutes every twelve hours until someone shuts it down. Okay? Make sure you remember where we are. In case you have to find your own way back."

Without another word he stepped through. His image flickered, as if in a heat wave. On the other side, he raised a fist in triumph and gazed around. "Come on, Gillie." He produced a bottle and two glasses, filled them, and held one out for me.

I hesitated.

"It's okay," he said.

I stepped across. The air got warm. It was thick with the drowsy buzz of insects. I took the glass. "To you, Mac."

McHugh loosened his tie. "To the Creator, who has given us a universe with such marvellous possibilities."

The afternoon smelled vaguely of sulfur. I took my vest off. We stood in a valley on an open field enclosed by wooded ridges. The sky was hazy and dark. Nearby, a flag fluttered from a wooden gate. Occasional farm buildings were enclosed by fences and stone walls. I saw a wagon in one of the farmyards. A dirt road wandered through the center of the valley.

The buildings, the fields, the road, were all empty.

I fell in beside McHugh and we started to walk, in no particular direction. "Where is everybody?" I asked.

He ignored the question.

I mopped my brow. "It must be July or August. It's certainly not April."

He nodded, but he was satisfied to have arrived somewhere. *Anywhere*.

"It's quiet," he said.

The landscape was vaguely familiar. I had seen these ridges before.

Behind us, the torus hovered, McHugh's computer-laden lab vivid against the rolling hills. "Maybe," I said, "we should go back."

He removed his jacket. "You go back if you want to, Gillie." He fished his watch out of a pocket, looked at the sun, and shrugged. "Let's make it three o'clock." He set and wound the time piece.

I looked at the flag. It was the national colors, and I was trying to count stars when McHugh's breathing changed. He was staring over my shoulder, back toward the torus, toward the line of hills behind it.

"What's wrong, Mac?"

His lab still floated serenely in the afternoon.

"The woods," he said. "Behind the nexus."

Gray shadows moved among the trees. The sun struck metal.

My God. "What's going on?" asked McHugh. "Where are we?"

A bugle call split the afternoon.

A line of men came out in oiled precision. Bayonets gleaming. And a second line. And a third. They wore gray uniforms.

Drums rolled. The troops wheeled smartly into line and started quick-step toward us.

Behind them, on the hilltops, a gun roared. Something screamed overhead. I watched it tear across the sky and explode on the opposite ridge. And I got a good look at the standards. "Son of a bitch, Mac. It's the 24th Virginia."

I watched them coming up behind the torus. They maintained drill order, accompanied by officers with drawn swords on horseback. They seemed unaware of the device, which I suspected was invisible from the rear. There were thousands of troops.

I was getting a bad feeling. "Over there," I said. "The 7th Virginia. And up the line will be the 11th. My God." I was overwhelmed by the majesty of it. "You're right, Mac. We're *here*. Son of a bitch."

"Gillie, we're *where*?"

More missiles tore overhead. A long orchestrated crescendo shook the top of the ridge that had been hit a moment before. More projectiles raced in the opposite direction. "Down!" I screamed and threw myself on my belly and covered my head.

Moments later the ground erupted. Holes were blown in the ranks of the advancing men. Others hurried to fill the spaces. "This is *Kemper's* Brigade," I said. Mac was staring at me, not comprehending. "You've been dumped on again, Mac." I was getting to my feet. "We've got to get away from here."

The cannons were deafening. A gap was torn in the line of advancing troops, but they came on. Silent. Relentless. Into the jaws. Their generals didn't understand yet that war had changed. That you could no longer charge fixed positions.

"Stay down," screamed McHugh. "We'll wait it out."

"No. We can't wait *this* one out. We've got to get back before the hole closes."

"You're crazy. You'll get killed."

"Mac, we won't survive out here. You know what that is back there? It's Seminary Ridge."

McHugh was close to my ear but he had to shout anyway. "So what?"

"Pickett's Charge. We're in the middle of Pickett's Charge."

We got back moments before a cannonball roared into the lab, blew three walls apart, collapsed the front porch, and nailed Harvey Keating's Toyota, which was parked in his driveway.

The equipment was in ruins again.

Nevertheless, McHugh was exultant. "You see? It *does* work."

"Mac, you've made four attempts now. All four have been disasters."

"But we're *learning*. We're getting better. You have to expect a few problems." He looked at me for reassurance. "We know how to travel."

"That's what scares me." I pointed at the wreckage. "What are the odds against *accidentally* arriving at the exact time and place of a major event?"

He shrugged. "Slim, I would think."

"You've done it twice."

I knew he wouldn't quit, though. He bought more equipment and went back to work. "Making improvements," he told me. A few weeks later he was ready to try again, and he issued another invitation. "I want to say hello to Custer." I told him no thanks. He was disappointed in me.

But hell, I can take a hint.

So I wasn't too surprised when his newspapers started piling up. I waited a couple of days before breaking in.

The house was empty.

In the lab, his equipment was intact. Except for the TDI: A stone-tipped feathered arrow jutted from its polished black surface. It had lodged right between the mode lamps.

DEAD IN THE WATER

"Immortality?" I asked.

Armistead shook his head. "No. Not immortality. The child would not live forever. Nothing lives forever. He, or she, would be subject to accident, war, act of God, even a sufficiently unpredictable virus." He looked at me across the vast expanse of his desk and refilled his coffee cup. "Are you sure you won't have some, Catherine?"

"No. None, thank you. Please go on."

"All I can promise is that he would have a far stronger immune system than you or I, and that his cells will continue to divide indefinitely. Which is to say he will not age. His body will not betray him. At least at any time within the foreseeable future."

Under ordinary circumstances, Armistead would have been a man of amiable appearance. He reminded her of her father, white hair that refused to lie flat, warm brown eyes, genuine smile. His large ears and tendency to bob his head for emphasis suggested her Bassett hound, Toby. Yet the circumstances were most certainly not ordinary. Jeremy Armistead had it within his power to grant the most extraordinary boon.

"How much?" I asked.

He opened a folder but didn't look at it. "The program is partially underwritten by the Foundation or it would cost a great deal more than it does." He inhaled, glanced out through his French windows at the parking lot, where TV trucks recorded demonstrators carrying signs warning that Project Sunrise was an affront to Man and God. "One hundred thousand," he said. "I'm sure you'll agree it's a bargain."

It was a lot of money. But we could manage it. "Yes," I agreed. "It's not unreasonable. If it works. What sort of guarantee is there?"

"Unfortunately I can assure you only that we'll use appropriate methods. That there will be no negligence." He looked puzzled. "What sort of guarantee would you wish?"

"That at fifty he will still look twenty-five."

"Mrs. Cumberland, I'll be honest with you. We're just now beginning to use this method with humans. The technique has worked quite well with a number of mammals, and we can see no reason it will not work equally well with children. We could have waited and not made it available until we'd tried it out on some test subjects, but in that case you'd have to be patient for several decades. We have produced more than six hundred children so far, they have all tested as we expected, and none has shown any indication of defects or unexpected side effects. Of course, it is still very early in the process."

Outside, there was a burst of profanity.

He looked steadily at me. "We can't offer a formal guarantee of success. But it *will* work."

It was all very new to me, a concept I'd never thought much about until I'd watched a Biolab representative on the Morley Pinkston show earlier that month. Hal didn't like the idea much when I suggested we look into it. And I didn't know how *I* felt. But two of our neighbors buried a six-year-old recently, dead of an unpronounceable disease of the central nervous system.

"No. It wouldn't have happened to one of our children," Armistead said when I brought it up. "We don't know of any pathogens that would constitute a threat to *our* infants. Assuming of course that no one would deliberately introduce a hefty supply directly into the bloodstream. I wouldn't want to mislead you."

"No. Of course not."

"There *are* limits to what we can achieve."

"Yes. I understand." The light in the windows was becoming gray. It was going to rain. "But the child would be sterile." He nodded. "There's no choice in the matter. It's part of the licensing agreement we have with the authorities. Population being what it is, and so forth. If people are going to stop dying, we must think about birth rates."

I nodded.

"After all," he continued, "those who benefit by the procedure must be willing to act responsibly."

My child would never know what it meant to have a child of his own. How would he—she—react to *that*? What would he think of *me*?

"However, your offspring would have superior physical and mental capabilities. We would also, uh, tweak the happiness gene. Barring mistreatment in the natural environment, he would be far more stable emotionally than the average person, and consequently more able to deal with his, ah, differences." He looked down at the folder. "You have no children, is that correct?"

"No. None."

"Good."

I knew that only childless couples were eligible for the Sunrise Project. Once a woman had given birth, she was excluded from consideration.

"Mrs. Cumberland, are you aware that you will be required to agree to have no other children?"

After a long hesitation, I answered that I was. And that the project would supply me with one child only. The newslinks were speculating that the technique had been funded and developed because of population pressures, as a way to bribe people to discipline themselves.

"You understand also that the entire process will be handled in vitro. You will not carry the child."

"You don't make it easy, Doctor."

"Once again we have no choice." His glasses had begun to slide down his nose. "Nevertheless, it's something I wish my mother could have done for *me*." He laughed and adjusted them. "I wouldn't have to deal with *these* now."

"Can we choose the sex?"

"I'm afraid not," he said. "We will want to maintain a statistical balance, of course. And under the circumstances we think that would not happen if parents were allowed discretion."

"I see. You think they'd all choose boys."

"Most would. Many would think a life without children would be especially difficult for females."

"And wouldn't it?"

"We're creating superior humans, Mrs. Cumberland. I think they'll adjust quite nicely." Having disposed of that nettlesome topic, he settled back to await my decision.

"I need to think about it," I said.

"Of course. There's no hurry."

"Talk it over with my husband."

"Yes. I assumed you'd done that. We'll give you some material to take home. Information about the program, what you can expect, and so on. And some documents to sign, if you elect to come with us. Return them with a check in the full amount, fully refundable if you turn out to be pregnant, fifty percent if you change your mind. Once you've done that, we'll conduct an investigation to ensure your eligibility." He looked up. "You're *not* pregnant, are you?"

"No. Not that I know of."

"Good. Read through the brochures then, and perhaps we'll see you here again."

Outside, I received a security escort through the demonstrators. A TV reporter held up a microphone for me. Was I going to do it? Did I have any moral qualms? What did I think of the charge that this was just another way for the wealthy to suppress everyone else?

I mumbled some noncommittal answers, picked up an escort of security officers, and made for the street. On the way, pickets hurled insults and thrust pamphlets in my hands. Some predicted that the environment would be the first casualty of the program; others argued that Biolab was doing the work of the Devil. The Human Dignity League was out in force, maintaining that Project Sunrise would proliferate and that it was contrary to nature. Still others claimed that the cost of the service ensured elitism. I had to agree with that. Hal and I could consider it only because he'd come into a recent inheritance. (He didn't let me overlook the irony of that, by the way, when I proposed we use the legacy to pay for an enhanced child.)

One middle-aged man who looked as if he should have had more important things to do tried to conk me with a sign reading BIOLAB DESTROYS FAMILIES; a woman screamed that I was a killer. I didn't know what to make of that.

The security people turned me loose at the sidewalk, where a tall man with a thin blade of a nose and a long jaw fell in beside me. "Excuse me, ma'm," he said softly. "May I have a moment?"

He wore a dark business suit and a white carnation. I knew I should have kept going but something in his manner drew me back. "My name's Plainfield," he said. His eyes were dark and intense.

"I really don't want to talk politics," I said. "Or religion."

"Of course not." Despite the almost fearsome appearance, his voice was gentle.

"I apologize for the imposition, but I hoped I might persuade you not to cooperate with these people." He said it as if he were talking about a disease.

"I don't see," I said, "why it's your concern."

"It's everyone's concern." He glanced over my shoulder at the storm clouds that were rolling in from the west. Several people, acolytes, camp followers, whatever, were moving in and suddenly I was surrounded. "Imagine," he said, "imagine what will happen to all of us when this process becomes generally available. And there's only a trickle of babies coming into the world. When tired old men in ageless bodies have secured their positions. They will never step down. Not ever." His audience were nodding their approval. "What kind of world do you think *that* will be?"

"I didn't create the process," I said.

"No. But you, and people like you, will guarantee its success. Unless you're willing to sacrifice your personal ambitions for the common good, in which case you may help defeat it." He smiled at me as if he could look directly into my soul. "But it's probably already too late," he said. "Sunrise got this out of the bottle when nobody was looking, and now we have to find a way to put it back in. Unless you help, unless you join with us, we're not going to survive. *People* won't survive."

I tried to shake him off, to get away.

But he persisted. "They're going to replace all the generations of the future with a single wave of genetically-altered creatures. Who, by any reasonable standard, won't even be human. Is *that* what you support?"

"I don't agree that that's what's happening."

"Think about it. Sunrise, practiced on a wide scale, will guarantee that in a very short time, the human race will be dead in the water."

"That's absurd."

"Is it?" A mixture of sadness and anger burned in his eyes. "Put it on a personal level, Mrs.—?"

"—Marshall." I gave him my mother's maiden name.

"Mrs. Marshall, do you like your boss?"

"I have to go." I began pushing my way through. But the crowd moved with me.

"I hope so," he said. "Because in the world you're helping create, he'll never retire. Not *ever.*"

I broke away finally and hurried toward Ohrbach Avenue, where I'd parked my car so the crazies wouldn't trash it. I needed ten minutes to get there, and people followed me for a couple of blocks. But they'd disappeared by the time I got behind the wheel.

The talk shows seemed to have no other topic for the day. In fact, the Sunrise Project had been pretty much the sole subject of talk radio and

TV since the press conference. Callers seemed unanimously opposed to the process. Most wanted it outlawed, and others thought it sounded suspiciously like something Hitler would dream up. Many wanted to know who would decide what constituted 'enhancement.' One said that any woman allowing Biolab to take her child should be horsewhipped. The talk show host allowed that he thought horsewhipping might be a trifle extreme.

No one, not a single individual during the fifteen minutes or so that I listened, thought that gene manipulation should be used to lengthen the lifespan or to enhance physical, psychological, or mental capabilities.

My intention had been to return to work after the interview—I'm a clothing designer for Stratton & Mulberry Associates—but the experience had been more upsetting than I'd expected. So I drove around for most of the rest of the afternoon, and afterward I could not have told you where I'd been.

Hal had tried to discourage me from going. *It's not really something we want to do*, he'd said. *It'll be an emotional bath. Why put yourself through it?*

But he was unsure too. I knew that. It was in fact a terrible thing to confront the kind of possibility that had suddenly and without warning opened in front of us.

I was waiting in the living room when he got home. Hal was an architect, just beginning to move up in the firm. He was in his late twenties, a model husband in many ways, and he knew as soon as he walked in the door what had happened. "You went over to that genetic place," he said. It wasn't a question.

I passed him a cup of coffee. "Yes."

"How'd it go?"

I told him. I told him about a child who wouldn't know what it would be to see his, or her, body decline. Whose horizons would be literally unlimited. Who, even though death would eventually come, would never know debilitation.

Hal was just over six feet. He had blue eyes and a good smile and an inability to hide his emotions that, as much as anything, had been what I loved about him. It also made him a poor poker player. Now he looked worried. "It's hard to believe," he said. "Do you think they can really do what they say they can?"

"Well, that's one of the risks, isn't it?" I'd read everything on enhancement technology that I could find. It had worked fine on monkeys and rabbits and rats. And the test children were doing fine.

"But nobody really knows that these kids won't age, do they?"

"No. Not really, Hal. But if we wait until the evidence is in, we're going to be a little long in the tooth to start a family."

"I know." He eased down onto the sofa and I could see he was troubled. "I'm sorry any of this technology has been developed. I wish they'd just left things alone."

The government legislated against it for years, but interest groups had intervened, and I don't suppose there was any way to keep it from happening. Maybe you could move it back and forth on the calendar a little, but that was probably all.

"We get to pick the personality, right?" he asked.

"Within limits, yes."

"So we get a respectful happy kid who gives us no trouble?"

"Not *too* respectful. The booklets explain that they don't want to take a chance on producing a race of people who'll kowtow too much to authority. They feel a little rebellion's a good thing. Especially in the kind of world that might emerge."

"Great." Hal grinned. "So *that* at least won't change. And we can't have any other kids."

"Right."

"And the child can't have any at all. Ever."

"Right."

"I don't like that part of it either." Usually Hal was congenial, able to roll with whatever problems surfaced during the day without letting them work on him. But his face was drawn and pale, and muscles worked in the corners of his jaws. "We have to shelve all our plans. For somebody's else's pet ideas. How will we feel thirty years from now when we've had only the one kid and his hair starts receding? And he discovers he not only has developed allergies but he can't have a family because *that* part of the procedure worked? You really want them to experiment with *us*? With our future?"

No, I didn't. Of course I didn't. But we did not have the option of waiting several decades for the evidence.

"I think we ought to let it alone," he said. "Let somebody else put their kids at risk."

❋

The subject devoured the evening.

We wondered how lonely life would be for an enhanced child. How would he be treated by other kids? Or by other adults, for that matter? How many others like him, or her, would there be? At first, certainly, too few. The bulk of the human race would probably be off-limits. (Unless he pretended to be normal, hid who he really was.) It was hard to see how such a person could form anything like a permanent relationship. Who'd want to live with somebody who was going to watch you age?

Hal said he hated to agree with the Fundamentalists but he wasn't sure that indefinitely-extended life spans weren't somehow contrary to the divine plan anyhow. The remark surprised me. "I didn't think you believed in God," I said. "You never go to church."

"Neither do you, Catherine."

"But I'm not sitting here talking about divine plans."

"It just seems to me, the way we're designed, we're not supposed to go on indefinitely."

We switched sides and tried to look at all the implications. We kept coming back to what our child would think of us forty years down the road. *They took my family from me, and any chance of living a normal life.*

And if we declined, when he was suffering from heart disease, liver failure, or she had contracted breast cancer or meningitis, what then would be the verdict on our decision? *They played it safe.*

He would know. Everybody born from this day forward would know quite clearly that the opportunity had been there. Some parents, most, could say they did not have the money. We wouldn't have that explanation to offer.

I wondered how many other families were agonizing over the same issue that night.

We went to bed with nothing resembling a resolution, although we'd decided that, to discuss the thing rationally, we had to assume that Armistead and his colleagues could do what they said. That reduced the problem to more manageable, if still daunting, proportions. Would virtual immortality actually be a gift, purchased at the price of sterility? And perhaps of love?

Had Armistead suggested they'd make the child immune to such concerns?

Would I recognize such a child as my own?

I didn't sleep much.

✱

Next morning—It was a Friday—, I called in sick, wanting to take time to think about the issue that had taken over my life. I knew there'd be no peace until I'd sorted out how I felt. As he left the house, Hal said he was leaning toward forgetting the whole thing. People got along without the Sunrise Project until now, and they've done just fine. (That was completely off the point and he knew it. And anyway they hadn't done so well, had they? They kept dying.) He paused on his way out the door, and a look of frustrated anger came into his eyes. "If we go ahead with it," he said, "I don't think the child will thank us."

I didn't either. I didn't think we were likely to be thanked whichever way things went.

The TV reported that antiprotestors had arrived at Biolab and scuffles had broken out. It was going to get ugly, and I asked myself whether I wanted to run that gauntlet again. But that would be a cowardly way to arrive at a decision.

I decided that I needed to get away for a bit. Clear my mind. I got the Honda out and headed for the big cluster mall over on Alpine, passing an IHOP en route and wondering whether one of Armistead's subjects could pile on pancakes and bacon to his heart's content and never gain any weight. Not bother to exercise but still retain muscle tone?

The literature promised a marked increase in intelligence and creative capabilities. It was possible, within limits, to provide the child with predispositions in various areas: we could, for example, opt for ingrained musical talent. Whether the talent would develop, the booklets said, would depend on the environment and stimulation provided by the parents.

Talent to what degree? Nobody really knew yet. But genes contributing to a wide range of human abilities and tendencies had been identified. Biolab couldn't give you a world-class sculptor, but they could provide a running start.

Still, all that was irrelevant. The real issue was very clear: What would the child want? No: maybe what would be *best* for the child, a different question altogether.

And what did *I* want? Hal and I were being called on to sacrifice our own plans.

I got bored at the mall and drove through the morning. It was early September and the streets were thick with leaves. I passed an accident, a serious one off Cottonwood Avenue, one car crumpled and lying in a ditch, another on its side. An ambulance was there and a couple of police cars with blue and red lights blinking. Everybody was rubbernecking and traffic barely moved. The EMT's were trying to get someone out of the crumpled car. I remember thinking that Armistead's treatment wouldn't have helped any of the occupants. What would happen to an enhanced person severely injured in a collision? Might his body keep him alive and in pain when he might otherwise have died? It was another question to put to Armistead.

I drifted back to Biolab, parked in the street, and watched the commotion. The crowd was bigger and louder than it had been yesterday. And there were more police. Some people had been jailed. The radio reported a bomb threat.

I drove on, stopping finally at a playground where I watched mothers with their kids. A pair of twins, a boy and a girl about three, dominated the swings, giggling and laughing. Other children chased one another in endless circles.

An older woman, probably in her seventies, occupied a bench. I sat down beside her and we quickly found ourselves talking about families and child-rearing. She was interested that I had no children and assured me I had much to look forward to. She was frail with white hair and arms in which all the bones were visible. But her color was good, and her eyes were alert.

She'd had a good life, she said. Her husband was dead now, heart attack six years ago, her children of course grown and gone. A lot of grandchildren. Most lived out of town, but they came sometimes to visit.

"Would you do it again?" I asked casually. "If you had the opportunity, would you start over?"

She thought about it. "I wouldn't mind being twenty again," she said. I could sense the *but* lingering in there somewhere. "What an odd question it is." Her eyes stared past my shoulder. "No," she said, "I don't think so."

"Why not?" And, quickly, "I hope you don't think I'm prying or anything—."

"I just wouldn't want to go through it all again." She smiled. "It was a lot of work, you know."

I went into Westbrook Cemetery and watched a funeral. It's the only time in my life I've attended a burial service among complete strangers. One of the mourners was a young woman, pale and ghastly in black. She was swaying, virtually held erect by friends. And three kids wiped bloodshot eyes and held each other's hands. The cleric, who was a little man with red hair blown about by the wind, intoned the old phrases. "*In the sure and certain hope....*"

When hope is certain, doesn't it become something else?

A mourner told me the victim had died from a rare form of leukemia. One of the types they still couldn't do anything about. But the sort of thing, I assumed, Armistead would eliminate right at the gate.

After the service they drifted back to their cars. Some needed help; many were in tears. This, I thought, is part of what everyone calls our common heritage. It is what makes us human. It is how we achieve salvation, whatever that might be.

I stood watching the leaves swirl among the headstones. And a hand touched my arm. "Are you all right, Miss?"

It was the cleric. "Yes," I said. "I think so."

"Are you sure?" He was round-faced with deep-set gray eyes. Not much older than Hal. "I'm Father McMurtrie," he said. "From St. Agnes."

It had gotten cool. A gust of wind swirled around us. I told him my name and, when he offered his condolences, I explained I was a stranger. Had never met the deceased. Knew no one in the family.

"Really?" he said, and I saw that he'd concluded I was one of those deranged persons who get their entertainment from attending funerals.

So I explained why I was there, as best I could. As best I understood it myself. He listened and nodded and agreed that the decision was not an easy one. "I suspect," he said, "that some of the protestors might take a different view if *they* were being offered a prolonged youth, instead of the next generation." On the side away from the highway, the cemetery rose into low hills which in turn gave way to forest. He looked in that direction for a few moments. "Are you a Catholic?" he asked.

"I'm not even a believer, Father. Truth is, I don't think there *is* a God."

"I see."

"I mean, if there really *were* somebody looking out for us, all these terrible things wouldn't happen, would they?" I mentioned the accident I'd seen. And here was a young husband taken from his family. And every day the TV reported kids murdered by irritated boyfriends of the mother and sometimes by the mother herself. And all the tidal waves that were forever killing thousands in Bangladesh. And I threw in World War II and the Holocaust for good measure.

He turned his back to the wind. "So you've stumbled onto the great secret, have you?"

"I beg your pardon."

"Think you've got hold of something the rest of us have missed."

"I don't understand, Father."

He folded his arms and looked at the sky. It was slate. "You're probably right. There certainly doesn't seem to be anyone out there taking care of us. But that's really old news, isn't it?"

I was aghast. "Father, are you telling me you don't believe in God?"

He looked around to be sure we were alone. "I think His lack of engagement is self-evident, don't you?"

"I don't understand—."

"Of course, I wouldn't be saying this to you if you were a Catholic. As things are, though, I can't see that it does any harm. It's a relief, from time to time, to be able to tell someone what I really think."

"But you're a priest."

He nodded and his eyes were bright with an emotion I couldn't identify. "Whether He's there or not, Mrs. Cumberland, people need God. And if you're correct, I'm as close as many of them are ever going to come to finding Him."

"Oh."

We looked at one another for a long time, and he dropped his eyes like a kid caught stealing chocolate.

"So," I said, "where would the Church stand in all this? With regard to Project Sunrise, I mean."

"Oh, we'd be against it."

"I see."

"We're always more or less against things. Safety lies in maintaining the status quo, you know." His eyes sparkled and I realized he was enjoying himself.

"Seriously," I asked, "what would you do if it were your decision?"

"That's quite a different question."

"And your answer—?"

"You're talking about a body that stays young and healthy. What about the mind?"

"They tell me that the child would be quite stable."

"But will its mind continue to accept new ideas? Will it be flexible at eighty? Or at two hundred?"

"I didn't think to ask."

"*Ask.* It's very important. I'd say this: if they can assure me that the child's outlook would remain as young and energetic as its body, then I'd say *yes* without hesitation. Choose *life*."

"You're really certain, aren't you?"

A frown worked its way into his eyes and he looked out toward the canopy, which was struggling against the wind. Cemetery workers had arrived and were preparing to lower the casket. "Mrs. Cumberland," he said, "do you have any idea how many of these I've presided over? Or how many death beds I've visited? I'm tired of helping people leave this world. If there's a way to bar the door, even temporarily, I'm for it." And with that he touched his hat, told me he hoped he'd been of some help, wished me luck, and walked rapidly toward his car.

I was watching him drive away when I noticed a tall vaguely-familiar man in a dark suit studying a nearby tombstone. The method of the examination, the tilt of the body, the arms casually folded, the expression on the long face, told me his attention was really riveted elsewhere. When I started toward the Honda, his gaze followed me.

Plainfield.

He smiled, not unpleasantly. "Mrs. Marshall," he said. "What a surprise to see you here."

It was a bad moment. "I suspect the surprise is only on one side," I said. I looked around to make sure the cemetery workers were within range.

He nodded and smiled. "You have found me out. I saw you at Biolab earlier this morning."

And you followed me. My stomach began to churn.

"Please don't be frightened," he said. "I'm perfectly harmless. You can walk away any time you want, and you'll never see me again. But I *do* wish you'd give me a minute."

I started toward my car, which was parked about sixty yards away.

He made no move to follow.

So I stopped and turned back. "Mr. Plainfield," I said, "I'm only one woman. Why bother *me* about this?"

"*Dr.* Plainfield," he said.

"Pardon me?"

"*Dr.* Plainfield. My specialty is evolutionary biology."

I shrugged. "Why me?" I asked again.

"We have to start somewhere. Someone must make a stand. Why *not* you?"

"What can I do that you can't?"

"You'll have a forum," he said. "You can tell them what they need to hear." The good humor disappeared and I saw judgment in those eyes. "Have you any idea what would happen if everyone behaved as you're proposing to do?"

"I've no idea what you mean."

"Have you made your decision?"

"What makes you think I was ever in doubt?"

"I've watched you for the last couple of hours. You are very much in doubt. May I ask why?"

I scrambled for a response. "They want too much—." It was the wrong thing to say. It embarrassed me and I tried to call it back but once I'd started it was too late.

He appraised me and his eyes registered disapproval. "You've no philosophical position then, have you? Possibly a little later, when they run an end-of-year sale, you'll be able to manage a better deal."

"I think that's uncalled for."

"Yes," he said. "You're right."

"Anyway, why do you need me to speak? You're the expert. You tell them whatever the problem is."

"They won't listen to me. I'm just one more crank with a degree. But *you*. You're in the position of having looked at their offer. You have much to gain. Yet you can see the dangers along that road. So you've turned back.

"Of course it *does* require you to turn back. The issue we need to put before the public, Mrs. Marshall, is quite simple: *Sunrise* is the end of human development. The end of progress. We are going to turn our world over to a few power brokers, those who know how to maintain and extend their influence. The only protection we've had against these kinds of people is the course of nature. In time they *die*, Mrs. Marshall. But that is going to stop. Now they will go on and on, accumulating wealth, oppressing those who are less ruthless, and there will be no end to their reigns. The flow of new human beings, of new *ideas*, will cease. Even art will die.

"Death, whether we like to admit it or not, serves a real purpose: it helps erase old hatreds, heal old wounds. It clears the board for progress. It gets rid of the debris. Imagine a world in which almost no one had been born since, say, the sixteenth century. And those people, the popes, Henry VIII, Philip of Spain, imagine they were all here, and still running things. *That* is the world you propose to create." He pushed his hands into his pockets and glanced toward the cemetery workers. The coffin had now disappeared into the ground and they'd begun shovelling earth in on top of it.

"It doesn't have to be that way," I said.

"*Have to?* Perhaps not. But it *will* be. Human nature will take charge.

All the things that make life worth having will disintegrate. There'll be no families, because there'll be no children. Love as we understand it will become a poor thing; its most noble expression will be reduced to hollow acts of self-gratification."

"I really must be going," I said.

"What's your first name?" he asked. "*Mrs. Marshall* is so formal."

"Catherine."

"Catherine. A good Christian name. Are you a Christian?"

"Yes," I lied.

"I'm not. We live in a mechanical universe, Catherine. It doesn't care about us, one way or the other. So we need to be very careful. If we violate the rules, it will take its price. We do not occupy a special place; we have no protection."

It sounded like my conversation with Father McMurtrie. But I'd switched sides. "I know," I said, looking at my watch. "I'm late, Dr. Plainfield. I have to go."

"The problem is, nobody cares. Except a few crazies, right? It's all too far in the future." I was off and moving quickly across the curve of the lawn.

"We'll all be dead in the water," he said, his words blown about my ears by the wind. "Unless *you* do something."

He was still standing in the same place, framed against the tombstones, when I drove off.

I proceeded to get lost in the cemetery. I'd never been there before and there was a series of curving roads, all looking the same. I drove in circles for several minutes, and at one point passed the canopy again, which the two workers were taking down. The casket was gone. As was Plainfield.

I pulled out onto Wildberry Avenue, turned left, and started home.

I thought about heads rolling around the Tower of London and crusades setting out for the Middle East. I thought about how it had been to know that the next boy to come into my life might be *the* one. I thought of the innocence and the passion of being seventeen and in love for the very first time and wondered how such things would be possible in the Sunrise world.

The sudden blare of an airhorn caught my attention: I was halfway across Garden Avenue, sailing through a red light, and watching a tractor-trailer bear down from the left. The driver's face twisted with horror.

It was one of those moments that freezes, where the whole world squeezes down to a single piece of reality, to a little bulldog ornament atop the hood of that oncoming truck.

Then time resumed its flow, and I jammed down on the gas, stomped the pedal through the floor. Brakes screeched, and the street rolled overhead, the air bag exploded in my face, and my lights went out.

I woke up in a bed at Mercy Hospital with a broken arm, a lot of cuts and bruises, and several traffic citations. The truck driver, they told me, was okay. Not happy, but okay.

Hal shook his head and lectured me about being more careful. I described how the day had gone, and he said he'd assumed something like that had happened.

"Are you any closer to making up your mind how you feel?" he asked.

"Yes," I said. "Absolutely."

"You're ahead of me."

"I'd like to go for it, Hal. Give our kid a chance at the centuries."

"I thought you'd come down on that side," he said. "Was it the priest?"

"No. I don't think so."

"What then?"

I wanted to smile but I was swollen and the effort hurt. "I think I realized what I wanted when I looked up and saw the driver's face."

"His *face*?"

I replayed the moment. "It was contorted, like he knew he'd killed me. So I thought I was dead too." I looked at him and realized how much I loved him. "There's no advantage in being dead. Life is very sweet, and I can't see anything either inspiring or dignified about dying. If we can beat it, I say we go ahead. And do it any way we can."

Hal reached over and took my hand. "But the truth is," he said, "the looney, this guy Plainfield, has a point. Without new people getting born on a regular basis, we *will* become static. We *will* decay."

It was early evening. The sunlight was fading in the window. I looked at it for a moment. "Yeah, Hal. Maybe we will. But I think we've gotten so used to dying we think that's part of what it means to be human. I say we take over for the DNA and try it the other way for a change. See what happens.

HENRY JAMES,
THIS ONE'S FOR YOU

I t came in over the transom, like a couple hundred other manuscripts each week, memoirs of people nobody ever heard of, novels that start with weather reports and introduce thirty characters in the first two pages, massive collections of unreadable poetry from someone's grandmother.

They all go into a stack for the screeners, who look through them, attach our form rejection, and send them back.

Actually there's only one screener. Her name is Myra Crispee. She has one green eye and one blue eye, and a talent for going through the slush pile. She picks out the occasional possibility and gets rid of the rest. Every day. Love my job, she says. When I ask her why, she says it's because I pay her the big bucks.

Tempus Publishing isn't a major outfit, but we do okay. We don't specialize. Tempus will publish anything that looks as if it'll make money. But most of the manuscripts we see have already made the rounds at Random House, HarperCollins, and the other biggies. Some come in from an agent, but that has no effect on the way we treat them. Unless we know the author, they all go into the pile.

Sometimes we get lucky. We published a couple of self-help books last year that did extremely well, and a novel about Noah's ark that became a runaway bestseller.

Anyhow, the day it arrived was cold and wet. The heating system had gone down again so I was wrapped in a sweater. I'd just opened the office and had turned on the coffee when Myra came in, carrying an umbrella and a manuscript. That was unusual. She doesn't usually take these things home. "Hey, Jerry," she said, "I think we've got a winner."

"Really?"

She was beaming. "Yes. I was up half the night with it." She trooped over to her desk and sat down in front of what I thought was a second manuscript, but which turned out to be the rest of the submission.

"My God," I said, "that looks like a thousand pages."

She peeked at the end. "Twelve hundred and twelve. I've only read a few chapters, but if the rest of it is like what I've seen—."

"That good, huh?"

"I couldn't put it down." The magic words. We seldom saw anything that wasn't easy to walk away from. She leafed through the pages. "Incredible," she said. "Who *is* this guy?"

"What is it?" I asked.

"He calls it *The Long War*. It's about the war in the Middle East."

"Which one?"

"How many are we involved in? I didn't see the news this morning."

"It's been done," I said.

"Not like this, boss." She was still turning pages.

"Who's it by?"

"Guy named Patterson." She shook her head. "Edward Patterson. Ever hear of him?"

He was a stranger to me. "What's the cover letter say?"

She needed a minute to find it. "'Novel enclosed.'"

"That's all?"

"That's it."

We used to have a screener's box where she could deposit manuscripts that were potentially publishable. We dispensed with it because Myra rarely put anything in it. So she just brought the manuscript over and laid it on a side table. Then she walked back to her desk, pulled the next submission off the pile, and began turning pages. But I knew she was really waiting for me. Wanted me to pick up *The Long War*. "I'll look at it before I go home," I said.

She continued turning pages, sighed, and touched her keyboard. The printer kicked out a fresh rejection. "Okay," she said.

I was working on *Make Straight the Path*, an inspirational book by Adam Trent. It was pious and reassuring, loaded with anecdotes showing how the unbelievers get theirs. You wouldn't believe how his other books had sold. Penguin would have loved to have him.

I stayed with it, resisting the temptation to look at Patterson's epic. It *resembled* an epic. The manuscript obscured a coffee stain half a foot above the table. That made it official.

Now, lest you think I'm one of those editors who only cares how many copies can be moved, let me tell you that, while sales figures matter, it's always been my ambition to discover a new writer. Well, okay, all editors feel that way. But that's because we're generous and compassionate. So when Myra got up and headed for the washroom, I took a look.

Patterson lived in New Hampshire.

I lifted the cover page and glanced at the opening lines. That night I hauled it down in the elevator, the whole twelve hundred pages, and took it home.

I read it on the train. Read during dinner at Milo's. Read through the evening and took it to bed. In the summer of 2001, I went to the Army recruiting office with the young college student hero and cringed while he joined the Reserves. I rode with the UN inspectors while they played tag with Iraqi "escorts" and tried to surprise their hosts at suspect facilities. I sat in the councils of the president while his aides urged an attack on Saddam and constructed arguments they hoped the UN and the voters would buy.

The night got away from me, and I finally closed my eyes when the first light of dawn was hitting the curtains. I called Myra's voice mail a couple hours later, letting her know I'd be late. Called again around nine to tell her I wouldn't be in at all.

It wasn't simply one more war novel. This one had that cliffhanging quality, yes. But it was vastly more. It *owned* the war. Through the eyes of its characters the reader saw how it had happened, came to grasp the inevitability of the conflict. He understood what it had meant to ride shotgun on the convoys or to go house to house in Fallujah. He experienced what it was to fight an enemy who wasn't afraid to die. Who imagined killing to be a divine imperative.

I spent time with a group of insurgents, and came to understand what drove them. I carried stretchers through the burn wards of an Iraqi hospital when shattered bystanders were brought in. And finally I was with mothers in Ohio when the dread news came.

It had perspective, passion, fear, the determination of obviously flawed men and women in authority to get things right, the mounting frustration as those who had been liberated refused to throw roses.

I was holed up with it for six days. The outside world simply stopped until the last shots had been fired, and the fallout had begun to take its political toll.

It was a *War and Peace* for our time.

I had done better than find one more professional writer who could sell a few thousand copies of whatever. I had found a new Herman Wouk.

I finished late on a drizzly, cold evening, and sat staring out my apartment window at downtown Boston, thinking about Edward Patterson. On that night, only I, and Myra, knew who he was. Within a year, the whole world was going to know.

He lived in Laconia, at the foot of the White Mountains.

It was a quarter after ten. A bit late to be calling. On the other hand, this was a guy who, as far as I could determine, had never been published. I remembered my own reaction when the postcard had arrived from *Guns and Ammo* announcing my own first sale.

Myra, anticipating me, had gotten Patterson's number from information and printed it neatly above the title. I made myself a scotch and soda and reached for the phone.

"Wonderful," he said. *"Mr. Becker, that's great. You're actually going to publish it?"* He sounded younger than I'd expected.

"Yes, Mr. Patterson. Ed. Is it okay if I call you *Ed?*"

"Sure. Yes. Absolutely. Can you hold a second?"

"Okay."

He must have covered the phone. But I knew what was happening. He was passing the good news to his wife. Or girlfriend. Or whomever.

"I'm back," he said.

"Good."

"Mr. Becker, you have no idea what this means to me."

"I can guess," I said. "Ed, are you by any chance free to come into Boston tomorrow?"

He made a sound deep in his throat. *"I'm a teacher,"* he said. *"At the high school."*

"Okay. How about Saturday?" We don't usually open the office Saturday but in this case I was willing to make an exception.

"I can do that," he said.

"Fine. I'll have a contract ready, and we'll celebrate by going to lunch." The truth was that I wanted him signed and delivered before he found out how good *The Long War* was. If he realized what he had, I'd wind up having to deal with an agent. Or possibly even get caught in a bidding war with MacMillan.

❋

He was maybe twenty-five. Tall, with a nervous smile. Light brown hair already beginning to thin. Sallow cheeks, pale skin, watery gray eyes behind bifocals. He wore a fatigue jacket and hauled a laptop in a stitched bag over one shoulder. Didn't look much like Hemingway.

He turned the pages of the contract with long, thin fingers, not examining it, I thought, so much as admiring it. When he got to the advance, he stopped. "Twenty thousand dollars?" he asked.

I was about to say I'd be willing to go higher because I liked the book. I'd expected to go higher. But it was always best to start out with a conservative figure. You can always move up. "Seems like a lot," he added.

"Well," I said, trying to conceal my surprise, "Tempus believes in being generous." It didn't really matter. The book was going to make a ton, so there was no risk.

"It's certainly very kind of you." He smiled again. He looked like the kind of guy the other kids had picked on in the schoolyard. And I would never have believed him capable of the kind of rugged prose that informed *The Long War*.

I showed him where to sign, explained what we expected, that we'd want to be able to use his bio and likeness in promoting the book, that we might ask him to make a few guest appearances. I didn't mention that he was signing over all TV and movie rights, that he was giving Tempus a healthy share of any foreign sales, that we would also collect seventy-five percent of book club rights. And of course there was the option clause. "Normally, Ed," I told him, "we'd want to retain the right of first refusal on your next novel."

"But—?" he said, suddenly looking worried.

"I want to be up front with you, Ed. Is there going to be a sequel?"

"A sequel?" His eyes clouded. "There'll be another book."

"Okay. Good enough. Tempus is willing to forego the option. We'd like instead to sign you to a three-book deal. Beyond *The Long War*."

His eyes slid shut, and I was looking at the most beatific smile I'd ever seen. Paradise had arrived.

"We're offering a seventy-five thousand dollar advance for the three."

He put the glass down and stared at me. "I don't know what to say."

"Don't say anything," I said. "Just sign on the line." I showed him where.

I know what you're thinking. But we do not try to take advantage of our authors. We were providing a major service for Ed Patterson. We were giving him a chance to launch a new career, to break away from his teaching job, to fulfill a lifelong dream. When you've been in this business for a while, you discover that it takes a lifelong dream to drive someone to write a novel. Especially a big one.

He signed the contract. Four books in all. In triplicate. I put one copy in a manila envelope and handed it to him. "All yours," I said.

He was glowing.

"Now let's go celebrate."

We went across the street to Marco's. It's a quiet Italian restaurant just off the Common. It was still a little early for lunch, so hardly anyone was there. We ordered a decanter of red wine, and I filled both glasses. "To you, Ed," I said. "And to *The Long War*."

He wore a grin a mile wide. "Thanks, Jerry." He sipped the wine, made a face at it, put it down. "Strong stuff," he said.

I finished my own and refilled the glass. "I have to tell you, Ed, *The Long War* is pretty good. How long have you been working on it? Four years? Five?"

"I guess you could say ten or eleven. Somewhere in there."

"*Ten* years? You've been writing this since you were, what, fifteen? Do I have that right?"

"Oh, no, Jerry. I didn't *write* the novel. Max did."

"Max? Who's Max?"

"Ah," he said. "That's the *real* accomplishment. That's my surprise."

I finished the second glass in a swallow. "You didn't tell me there was going to be a surprise."

The waiter arrived. We ordered. When he was gone we picked up where we'd left off. "What surprise?" I demanded. "Who wrote the book? Are you his agent?"

"Hell, Jerry, anybody can sit down and write a novel. All you have to do is be willing to stay with it for, what, a year or so? Or five, I guess. Sit down and be willing to write every day. That's all it takes."

"What are you trying to tell me, Ed? Who's Max?"

He'd dropped the laptop onto the seat beside him. Now he set it on the table and opened it. Lights blinked on and the screen glowed cobalt blue. "This is Max," he said.

I stared at the computer, then at Ed. It was an ordinary HP model. Myra had one like it. Black case, the logo printed on the lid. "You said Max wrote the book."

"He did."

"Max is a computer."

"Actually, he's an artificial intelligence, Jerry." He leaned forward, breathless. "A *real* one."

"The computer wrote the book."

"He's an *AI*." He looked at me as if waiting for me to cheer. When I didn't a cloud crossed his face.

"I don't care what you call him," I said, "no machine could have written *The Long War*."

The big grin came back. "But he did."

"I don't believe it."

"A few years ago they were saying no computer would ever compete with a chess master. You look recently to see who's world champ?"

We sat staring at each other. The door opened and people came in. A family with a little boy. The boy had a pull toy.

"It took four days," he said.

"What took four days?"

"To write the novel."

A chill settled into my bones. I drank down more of the wine. Two plates showed up. Pizza for Patterson. Spaghetti and meatballs for me. But my appetite had gone south. "Four days," I said.

"Yes. Well, maybe a bit more. But not much." He took a deep breath and smiled modestly. "It took me almost as long to tell him what kind of book I wanted."

"It's just not possible."

"That doesn't include printing time, though."

"You're signed to do three more novels."

"Yes."

"I was expecting world-class stuff."

"They'll be good. Max was years in the making and has spent a long time analyzing the great books."

"How long?" I asked.

"How long what?" He was chewing on the pizza, obviously enjoying himself. But he looked as if he couldn't understand why I was unhappy.

"How long will it take to deliver the other novels?"

"Probably two weeks. It takes a while to run them off."

"Two weeks for another novel like *The Long War*?"

"Two weeks for all three. But they won't be like *The Long War*, although they'll be of comparable quality." He pushed his chair back and tried to look upbeat. "We've already decided on the next book. It'll be about the power and the downside of religious belief. Along the order of *The Brothers Karamazov*. But different, of course. Original."

I sat frozen. Yep, no problem for Max. You want something to make people forget *The Winds of War*? Have it for you Tuesday.

"You all right, Jerry?"

"I need some fresh air." Or maybe we'd get a new *Huck Finn*. This time around we'd take a hard look at anti-gay prejudice. I threw money on the table and headed for the door.

"Jerry, wait." He was right behind me.

Maybe a new Dreiser novel. By Max.

Or something in the mode of Scott Fitzgerald.

Traffic outside was heavy. Buses, delivery trucks, crowded sidewalks. "If Max wrote the book, why's your name on it?"

"Legal reasons. He's not a person. Can't sign checks. Can't really do anything."

"Except write great novels."

"You got it."

He stood in front of me and flashed an enormous grin. He had no idea what he'd done. This *child*, who was obviously very good with electronics, had canceled William Faulkner, Melville, Cather: What would their work be worth in the shadow of this *thing*? I assumed if he could do *Karamazov*, he could produce a new symbolic masterpiece in the spirit of James Joyce. Call this one *Achilles*, in which a man's life is driven by a search for control. Or maybe something to push *Remembrance of Things Past* off the charts. In eight volumes, delivered over the course of a month.

"I couldn't be sure it had worked," Patterson said. "I don't read that much. Not fiction. I didn't know whether it was any good or not. What Max wrote. You were the test. We'll put *his* name on the cover though, if that's okay."

"What's Max's last name?" I asked.

A bus was coming up behind him. It was a local, headed for Massachusetts Avenue. It had just picked up passengers at the corner, seen an opening, and was accelerating. It had broken loose from the traffic.

"Winterhaven. Max Winterhaven."

"Sounds pretentious."

"I thought it sounded literary."

Max Winterhaven was slung over his shoulder. I looked up at the bus driver, and I swear he knew what I was going to do before I did. I saw it in his face the instant before I gave Patterson his quick shove. His eyes went wide and he toppled backward. People screamed, the brakes screeched, and I either said, or thought, "This one's for Henry James."

I got clean away. The descriptions that showed up on CNN a few hours later sounded nothing like me. They also reported that the dead man had been carrying a laptop, but it had been smashed. Police were trying to reconstruct it, but I never heard anything more.

There was no widow, I'm pleased to say. I don't know who had been with him the night I called. *The Long War*, as we all know, has become an international best seller. We are sending the checks to the deceased's mother.

Literary authorities are on the tube almost weekly, decrying the loss of Edward Patterson, a man of incredible talent, who would have become a towering literary figure, had he only been given time.

TIME TRAVELLERS NEVER DIE

1.

Thursday, November 24. Shortly before noon.

We buried him on a cold, gray morning, threatening snow. The mourners were few, easily constraining their grief for a man who had traditionally kept his acquaintances at a distance. I watched the preacher, white-haired, feeble, himself near the end, and I wondered what he was thinking as the wind rattled the pages of his prayer book.

Ashes to ashes—

I stood with hands thrust into my coat pockets, near tears. Look: I'm not ashamed to admit it. Shel was odd, vindictive, unpredictable, selfish. He didn't have a lot of friends. Didn't deserve a lot of friends. But I *loved* him. I've never known anyone like him.

—In sure and certain hope—

I wasn't all that confident about the resurrection, but I knew that Adrian Shelborne would indeed walk the earth again. Even if only briefly. I knew, for example, that he and I would stand on an Arizona hilltop on a fresh spring morning late in the twenty-first century, and watch silver vehicles rise into the sky on the first leg of the voyage to Centaurus. And we would be present at the assassination of Elaine Culpepper, a name unknown now, but which would in time be inextricably linked with the collapse of the North American Republic. Time travellers never really die, he was fond of saying. We've been too far downstream. You and I will live for a very long time.

The preacher finished, closed his book, and raised his hand to bless the polished orchid-colored coffin. The wind blew, and the air was heavy with the approaching storm. The mourners, anxious to be away, bent their heads and walked past, laying lilies on the coffin. When it was done, they lingered briefly, murmuring to each other. Helen Suchenko stood off to one side, looking lost. Lover with no formal standing. Known to the family but not particularly liked, mostly because they disapproved of Shel himself. She dabbed jerkily at her eyes and kept her gaze riveted on the gray stone which carried his name and dates.

She was fair-haired, with eyes the color of sea water, and a quiet, introspective manner that might easily have misled those who did not know her well.

"I can't believe it," she said.

I had introduced him to Helen, fool that I am. She and I had been members of the Devil's Disciples, a group of George Bernard Shaw devotees. She was an MD, just out of medical school when she first showed up for a field trip to see *Arms and the Man*. It was love at first sight, but I was slow to show my feelings. And while I was debating how best to make my approach, Shel walked off with her. He even asked whether I was interested, and I, sensing I had already lost, salvaged my pride and told him of course not. After that it was over.

He never knew. He used to talk about her a lot when we were upstream. How he was going to share the great secret with her and take her to Victorian London. Or St. Petersburg before the first war. But it never happened. It was always something he was going to do later.

She was trembling. He really *was* gone. And I now had a clear field with her. That indecent thought kept surfacing. I was reasonably sure she had always been drawn to me, too, just as she was to Shel, and I suspected that I might have carried the day with her had I pressed my case. But honor was mixed up in it somewhere, and I'd kept my distance.

Her cheeks were wet.

"I'll miss him, too," I said.

"I loved him, Dave."

"I know."

He had died when his townhouse burned down almost two weeks before. He'd been asleep upstairs and had never got out of bed. The explanation seemed to be that the fire had sucked the oxygen out of the house and suffocated him before he ever realized what was happening. Okay, I didn't believe it either, but that was what we were hearing.

"It'll be all right," I said.

She tried to laugh, but the sound had an edge to it. "Our last conversation was so goofy. I wish I'd known——." Tears leaked out of her eyes. She stopped, tried to catch her breath. "I would have liked," she said, when she'd regained a degree of control, "to have been able to say goodbye."

"I know." I began to guide her toward my Porsche. "Why don't you let me take you home?"

"Thank you," she said, backing off. "I'll be okay." Her car was parked near a stone angel.

Edmond Halverson, head of the art department at the University, drew abreast of us, nodded to me, tipped his hat to her, and whispered his regrets. We mumbled something back and he walked on.

She swallowed, and smiled. "When you get a chance, Dave, give me a call."

I watched her get into her car and drive away. She had known so much about Adrian Shelborne. And so little.

He had traveled in time, and of all persons now alive, only I knew. He had brought me in, he'd said, because he needed my language skills. But I believe it was more than that. He wanted someone to share the victory with, someone to help him celebrate. Over the years, he'd mastered classical Greek, and Castilian, and Renaissance Italian. And he'd gone on, acquiring enough Latin, Russian, French, and German to get by on his own. But we continued to travel together. And it became the hardest thing in my life to refrain from telling people I had once talked aerodynamics with Leonardo.

I watched his brother Jerry duck his head to get into his limo. Interested only in sports and women, Shel had said of him. And making money. *If I'd told him about the Watch,* he'd said, *and offered to take him along, he'd have asked to see a Super Bowl.*

Shel had discovered the principles of time travel while looking into quantum gravity. He'd explained any number of times how the Watches worked, but I never understood any of it. Not then, and not now. "But why all the secrecy?" I'd asked him. "Why not take credit? It's the discovery of the ages." We'd laughed at the new shade of meaning to the old phrase.

"Because it's dangerous," he'd said, peering over the top of his glasses, not at me, but at something in the distance. "Time travel should not be possible in a rational universe." He'd shaken his head, and his unruly black hair had fallen into his eyes. He was only thirty-eight at the time of his death. "I saw from the first *why* it was theoretically possible," he'd said. "But I thought I was missing something, some detail that would intervene to prevent the actual construction of a device. And yet there it is." And he'd glanced down at the Watch strapped to his left wrist.

He worried about Causality, the simple flow of cause and effect. "A time machine breaks it all down," he said. "It makes me wonder what kind of universe we live in."

I thought we should forget the philosophy and tell the world. Let other people worry about the details. When I pressed him, he'd talked about teams from the Mossad going back to drag Hitler out of 1935, or Middle Eastern terrorists hunting down Thomas Jefferson. "It leads to utter chaos," he'd said. "Either time travel should be prohibited, like exceeding the speed of light. Or the intelligence to achieve it should be prohibited."

We used to retreat sometimes to a tower on a rocky reef somewhere downstream. No one lives there, and there is only ocean in all directions. I don't know how he found it, or who built it, or what that world is like. Nor do I believe *he* did. We enjoyed the mystery of the place. The moon is bigger, and the tides are loud. We'd hauled a generator out there, and a refrigerator, and a lot of furniture. We used to sit in front of a wall-length transparent panel, sipping beer, watching the ocean, and talking about God, history, and women.

They were good days.

Eventually, he had said, I will bring Helen here.

The wind blew, the mourners dwindled and were gone, and the coffin waited on broad straps for the workmen who would lower it into the ground.

Damn. I would miss him.

Gone now. He and his Watches. And temporal logic apparently none the worse.

Oh, I still had a working unit in my desk, but I knew I would not use it again. I did not have his passion for time travel. Leave well enough alone. That's always been my motto.

On the way home, I turned on the radio. It was an ordinary day. Peace talks were breaking down in Africa. Another congressman was accused of diverting campaign funds. Assaults against spouses were still rising. And in Los Angeles there was a curious conclusion to an expressway pileup: two people, a man and a woman, had broken into a wrecked vehicle and kidnapped the driver, who was believed to be either dead or seriously injured. They had apparently run off with him.

Only in California.

Shel had been compulsively secretive. Not only about time travel, but about everything. The mask was always up and you never really knew what he was feeling. He used to drive Helen crazy when we went out to dinner because she had to wait until the server arrived to find out what he was going to order. When he was at the University, his department could never get a detailed syllabus out of him. And I was present when his own accountant complained that he was holding back information.

He used to be fond of saying knowledge is power, and I think that was what made him feel successful, that he knew things other people didn't. Something must have happened to him when he was a kid to leave him so in need of artificial support. It was probably the same characteristic that had turned him into the all-time great camp follower. I don't know what the proper use for a time machine should be. We used it to make money. But mostly we used it to argue theology with Thomas Acquinas, to talk with Isaac Newton about gravity, to watch Thomas Huxley take on Bishop Wilberforce. For us, it had been almost an entertainment medium. It seemed to me that we should have done *more* with it.

Don't ask me what. Maybe track down Michelangelo's lost statue of *Hermes*. Shel had shown interest in the project, and we had even stopped by his workshop to admire the piece shortly before its completion. He was about twenty years old at the time. And the *Hermes* was magnificent. I would have killed to own that.

Actually, I had all kinds of souvenirs: coins that a young Julius Caesar had lost to Shel over draughts, a program from the opening night of *The Barber of Seville*, a quill once used by Benjamin Franklin. And photos. We had whole albums full of Alexander and Marcus Aurelius and the sails of the *Santa Maria* coming over the horizon. But they all looked like scenes from old movies. Except that the actors didn't look as good as you'd expect. When I pressed Shel for a point to all the activity, he said, what more could there be than an evening before the fire with Al Einstein? (We had got to a fairly intimate relationship with him, during the days when he was still working for the Swiss patent office.)

There were times when I knew he wanted to tell Helen what we were doing and bring her along. But some tripwire always brought him up short, and he'd turn to me with that maddeningly innocuous smile as if to say, you and I have a secret and we had best keep it that way for now. Helen caught it, knew there was something going on. But she was too smart to try to break it open.

We went out fairly regularly, the three of us, and my true love of the month, whoever that might be. My date was seldom the same twice because she always figured out that Helen had me locked up. Helen knew that too, of course. But Shel didn't. I don't think it ever occurred to him that his old friend would have considered for a moment moving in on the woman he professed (although not too loudly) to love. There were moments when we'd be left alone at the table, Helen and I, usually while Shel was dancing with my date. And the air would grow thick with tension. Neither of us ever said anything directly, but sometimes our gaze touched, and her eyes grew very big and she'd get a kind of forlorn look.

Helen was a frustrated actress who still enjoyed the theater. After about a year, she abandoned the Devil's Disciples, explaining that she simply did not have time for it anymore. But Shel understood her passion and indulged it where he could. Whenever there was a revival, we all went. Inevitably, while we watched Shaw's trapped characters career toward their destinies, Shel would find an opportunity to tell me he was going to take her back to meet the great playwright.

I used to promise myself to stop socializing with her, to find an excuse, because it hurt so much to sit in the awful glare of her passion for him. But if I had done that, I wouldn't have seen her at all. At night, when the evening was over and we were breaking up, she always kissed me, sometimes lightly on the cheek, sometimes a quick hit-and-run full on the lips. And once or twice, when she'd drunk a little too much and her control had slipped, she'd put some serious effort into it.

2.

Thursday, November 24. Noon.

The storm picked up while I drove home, reminiscing, feeling sorry for myself. I already missed his voice, his sardonic view of the world, his amused cynicism. Together, we had seen power misused and abused all through the centuries, up close, sometimes with calculation, more often out of ignorance. Our shared experiences, certainly unique in the history of the planet, had forged a bond between us. The dissolution of that bond, I knew, was going to be a long, painful process.

He'd done all the research in his basement laboratory, had built the first working model of his Temporal Occluding Transport System (which, in a flash back to his bureaucratic days with the National Science Foundation, he called TOTS) in a space between his furnace and a wall filled with filing cabinets. The prototype had been a big, near-room-sized chamber. But the bulk of the device had dwindled as its capabilities increased. Eventually, it had shrunk to the size of a watch. It was powered by a cell clipped to the belt or carried in a pocket. I still had one of the power packs at the house.

I would have to decide what to do with our wardrobe. It was located in a second floor bedroom which had served as an anteroom to the ages. A big walk-in closet overflowed with costumes, and shelves were jammed with books on culture and language for every period which we'd visited, or intended to visit.

But if my time-traveling days were over, I had made enough money from the enterprise that I would never have to work again, if I chose not to. The money had come from having access to next week's newspapers. We'd debated the morality of taking personal advantage of our capabilities, but I don't think the issue was ever in doubt. We won a small fortune at various race tracks, and continued to prosper until two gentlemen dropped by Shel's place one afternoon and told him that they were not sure what was behind his winning streak, but that if it continued, they would break his knees. They must have known enough about us to understand it wouldn't be necessary to repeat the message to me. We considered switching into commodities. But neither of us understood much about them, so we took our next plunge in the stock market. "It's got to be illegal," said Shel. And I'd laughed. "How could it be?" I asked him. "There are no laws against time travel." "Insider trading," he suggested.

Whatever. We justified our actions because gold was the commodity of choice upstream. It was research money, and we told each other it was for the good of mankind, although neither of us could quite explain how that was so. Gold was the one item that opened all doors, no matter what age you were in, no matter what road you traveled. If I learned anything during my years as Shel's interpreter and faithful Indian companion, it was that people will do anything for gold.

While I took a vaguely smug view of human greed, I put enough aside to buy a small estate in Exeter, and retired from the classroom to a life of books and contemplation. And travel through the dimensions.

Now that it was over, I expected to find it increasingly difficult to keep the secret. I had learned too much. I wanted to tell people what I'd done. Who I'd talked to. *So we were sitting over doughnuts and coffee on St. Helena, and I said to Napoleon—*

There was a thin layer of snow on the ground when I got home. Ray White, a retired tennis player who lives alone on the other side of Carmichael Drive, was out walking. He waved me down to tell me how sorry he was to hear about Shel's death. I thanked him and pulled into the driveway. A black car that I didn't recognize was parked in front of the house. Two people, a man and a woman, were sitting inside. They opened their doors and got out as I drifted to a stop. I turned off the engine without putting the car away.

The woman was taller, and more substantial, than the man. She held out a set of credentials. "Dr. Dryden?" she said. "I'm Sgt. Lake, Carroll County Police." She smiled, an expressionless mechanical gesture lacking any warmth. "This is Sgt. Howard. Could we have a few minutes of your time?"

Her voice was low key. She would have been attractive had she been a trifle less official. She was in her late thirties, with cold dark eyes and a cynical expression that looked considerably older than she was.

"Sure," I said, wondering what it was about.

Sgt. Howard made no secret of the fact that he was bored. His eyes glided over me, and he dismissed me as a lowlife whose only conceivable interest to him might lie in my criminal past. We stepped up onto the deck and went in through the sliding glass panels. Lake sat down on the sofa, while Howard undid a lumpy gray scarf, and took to wandering around the room, inspecting books, prints, stereo, whatever. I offered coffee.

"No, thanks," said Lake. Howard just looked as if I hadn't meant him. Lake crossed her legs. "I wanted first to offer my condolences on the death of Dr. Shelborne. I understand he was a close friend of yours?"

"That's correct," I said. "We've known each other for a long time."

She nodded, produced a leather-bound notebook, opened it, and wrote something down. "Did you have a professional relationship?" she asked.

"No," I said slowly. "We were just friends."

"I understand." She paused. "Dr. Dryden," she said, "I'm sorry to tell you this: Dr. Shelborne was murdered."

My first reaction was simply to disbelieve the statement. "You're not serious," I said.

"I never joke, Doctor. We believe someone attacked the victim in bed, struck him hard enough to fracture his skull, and set fire to the house."

Behind me, the floor creaked. Howard was moving around. "I don't believe it," I said.

Her eyes never left me. "The fire happened between 2:15 and 2:30 a.m., on the twelfth. Friday night, Saturday morning. I wonder if you'd mind telling me where you were at that time?"

"At home in bed," I said. There had been rumors that the fire was deliberately set, but I hadn't taken any of it seriously. "Asleep," I added unnecessarily. "I thought lightning hit the place?"

"No. There's really no question that it was arson."

"Hard to believe," I said.

"Why?"

"Nobody would want to kill Shel. He had no enemies. At least, none that I know of."

I was beginning to feel guilty. Authority figures always make me feel guilty. "You can't think of *anyone* who'd want him dead?"

"No," I said. But he had a lot of money. And there were relatives.

She looked down at her notebook. "Do you know if he kept any jewelry in the house?"

"No. He didn't wear jewelry. As far as I know, there was nothing like that around."

"How about cash?"

"I don't know." I started thinking about the gold coins that we always took with us when we went upstream. A stack of them had been locked in a desk drawer. (I had some of them upstairs in the wardrobe.) Could anyone have known about them? I considered mentioning them, but decided it would be prudent to keep quiet, since I couldn't explain how they were used. And it would make no sense that I knew about a lot of gold coins in his desk and had never asked about them. "Do you think it was burglars?" I said.

Her eyes wandered to one of the bookcases. It was filled with biographies and histories of the Renaissance. My favorite period. The eyes were black pools that seemed to be waiting for something to happen. "That's possible, I suppose." She canted her head to read a title. It was Ledesma's biography of Cervantes, in the original Spanish. "Although burglars don't usually burn the house down." Howard had got tired poking around, so he circled back and lowered himself into a chair. "Dr. Dryden," she continued, "is there anyone who can substantiate the fact that you were here asleep on the morning of the twelfth?"

"No," I said. "I was alone." The question surprised me. "You don't think *I* did it, do you?"

"We don't really think *anybody* did it, yet."

Howard caught her attention and directed it toward the wall. There was a photograph of the three of us, Shel and Helen and me, gathered around a table at the Beach Club. A mustard-colored umbrella shielded the table, and we were laughing and holding tall, cool drinks. She studied it, and turned back to me. "What exactly," she said, "is your relationship with Dr. Suchenko?"

I swallowed, and felt the color draining out of my face. *I love her. I've loved her from the moment I met her.* "We're friends," I said.

"Is that all?" I caught a hint of a smile. But nobody knew. I had kept my distance all this time. I'd told no one. Even Helen didn't know. Well, she knew, but neither of us had ever admitted to it.

"Yes," I said. "That's all."

She glanced around the room. "Nice house."

It was. I had treated myself pretty well, installing leather furniture and thick pile carpets and a stow-away bar and some original art. "Not bad for a teacher," she added.

"I don't teach anymore."

She closed her book. "So I understand."

I knew what was in her mind. "I did pretty well on the stock market," I said. I must have sounded defensive.

"As did Dr. Shelborne."

"Yes," I said. "That's so."

"Same investments?"

Yes, they were the same. With only slight variations, we'd parlayed the same companies into our respective fortunes. "By and large, yes," I said. "We did our research together. An investment club, you might say."

Her eyes lingered on me a moment too long. She began to button her jacket. "Well, I think that'll do it, Dr. Dryden," she said.

I was still numb with the idea that someone might have murdered Shelborne. He had never flaunted his money, had never even moved out of that jerkwater townhouse over in River Park. But someone had found out. And they'd robbed him. Possibly he'd come home and they were already in the house. He might even have been upstream. Damn, what a jolt that would have been: return from an evening in Babylon and get attacked by burglars. I opened the sliding door for them. "You will be in the area if we need you?" Lake asked. I assured her I would be, and that I would do whatever I could to help find Shel's killer. I watched them drive away and went back inside and locked the door. It had been painful enough believing that Shel had died through some arbitrary act of nature. But that a thug who had nothing whatever to contribute to the species would dare to take his life filled me with rage.

I poured a brandy and stared out the window. The snow was coming harder now. I couldn't believe anyone would think for a moment that *I* could be capable of such an act. It chilled me.

In back somewhere, something moved. It might have been a branch scraping against the side of the house, but it sounded *inside*.

Snow fell steadily against the windows.

It came again. A floor board, maybe. Not much more than a whisper.

I took down a golf club, went out into the hallway, looked up the staircase and along the upper level. Glanced toward the kitchen.

Wood creaked.

Upstairs.

I started up, ascending as quietly as I could, and got about halfway when a movement at the door to the middle bedroom caught my attention. The wardrobe.

One of the curious phenomena associated with sudden and unexpected death is our inability to accept it when it strikes those close to us. We always imagine that the person we've lost is in the kitchen, or in the next room, and that it requires only that we call his name in the customary way to have him reappear in the customary place. I felt that way about Shel. We had lunched with Cervantes and ridden with Washington and lived a thousand other miracles. And when it was over, we always came back through the wardrobe and out onto the landing.

He came out now.

Shel stood up there, watching me.

I froze.

"Hello, Dave," he said.

I hung on to the bannister, and the stairs felt slippery. "Shel," I said shakily, "is that *you*?"

He smiled. The old, crooked grin that I had thought not to see again. Some part of me that was too slow-witted to get flustered started flicking through explanations. Someone else had died in the fire. It was a dream. Shel had a twin.

"Yes," he said. "It's me. Are you okay?"

"Yeah."

"I'm sorry. I know this must be a shock." He moved toward me, along the top of the landing. I'm not sure what I was feeling. There was a rush of emotions, of joy, of anger, even of fear. He came down a few stairs, took my shoulders, and steadied me. His hands were solid, his smile very real, and my heart sank. Helen's image rose before me.

"I don't understand," I said.

Adrian Shelborne was tall and graceful, blessed with the clean-cut features of a romantic hero. His eyes were bright and sad. We slid down into sitting positions. "It's been a strange morning," he said.

"You're supposed to be dead."

He took a deep breath. "I know. I do believe I *am*, David."

Suddenly it was clear. "You're *downstream*."

"Yes," he said. "I'm downstream." He drew his legs up in a gesture that looked defensive. "You sure you're okay?"

"I've spent several days trying to get used to this. That you were gone—."

"It's true." He spaced the words, not able to accept it himself.

"When you go back—."

"—The house will burn, and I will be in it."

For a long time neither of us spoke. "Don't do it," I said at last. "Stay here."

"I can't *stay here*," he said. "What does that do to the time stream?"

Damn the time stream. I was thinking how candle-light filled Helen's eyes, how she and Shel had walked to the car together at the end of an evening. I was remembering the press of her lips against my cheek.

"Maybe you're right," I said.

"Of course I am. They just buried me, Dave. They found me in my bed. Did you know I didn't even get out of my bed?"

"Yes," I said. "I heard that."

"I don't believe it." He was pale, and I noticed his eyes were red.

My first ride with him had been to Gettysburg to listen to Lincoln. Afterward, when I was still trying to come to terms with the fact that I had really been there, he talked about having dinner with Caesar and drinking with Voltaire.

He must have felt my company to be of value, because he invited me to go a second time. I'd wondered where we were headed, expecting historic significance, but we went only to 1978 New Haven. We were riding a large misshapen brown chamber then, a thing that looked like a hot water tank. "I want you to meet someone," he said, as we emerged into streets filled with odd-looking cars. Her name was Martha, and she had been Shel's fiancée. Six hours after our arrival she would fall asleep at the wheel of her Ford. And Shel's life would change forever. "She and I had dinner last night at The Mug," he told me while we waited for her to come out of the telephone company building where she worked. "I never saw her again."

It was 5:00 p.m., and the first rush out the door was beginning.

"What are you going to do?" I'd asked.

He was in a state of extreme nervous agitation. "Talk to her."

I laughed. "Are you serious? What are you going to tell her?"

"I'll be careful," he said. Don't want to create a paradox. "I just want to see her again."

A light rain had begun. People started pouring out through the revolving doors. They looked up at the dark clouds, grimaced, and scattered to cars and buses, holding newspapers over their heads.

And then Martha came out.

I knew her immediately, because Shel stiffened and caught his breath. She paused to exchange a few words with another young woman. The rain intensified.

She was twenty years old and full of vitality and good humor. There was much of the tomboy about her, just giving way to a lush golden beauty. Her hair was shoulder-length and swung easily with every move. (I thought I saw much of Helen in her, in her eyes, in the set of her mouth, in her animation.) She was standing back under the building overhang, protected from the storm. She waved goodbye to the friend, and prepared to run for her car. But her gaze fell on us, on Shel. Her brow furrowed and she looked at us uncertainly.

Shel took a step forward.

I discovered I was holding his arm. Holding him back. A gust of wind blew loose dust and paper through the air. "Don't," I said.

"I know."

She shook her head as if she recognized a mistake and hurried away. We watched her disappear around the corner out onto the parking lot.

We had talked about that incident many times, what might have happened had he intervened. We used to sit in the tower at the end of time, and he'd talk about feeling guilty because he had not prevented her death. "Maybe we can't change anything. But I feel as if I should have tried."

Now, starting carefully downstairs, he seemed frail. Disoriented. "They think you were murdered," I said.

"I know. I heard the conversation." In the living room he fell into an armchair.

My stomach was churning and I knew I wasn't thinking clearly. "What happened? How did you find out about the funeral?"

He didn't answer right away. "I was doing some research downstream," he said finally, "in the Trenton Library. In the reference section. I was looking at biographies, so I could plan future flights. You know how I work."

"Yes," I said.

"And I did something I knew was a mistake. Knew it while I was doing it. But I went ahead anyhow."

"You looked up your own biography."

"I couldn't help it." He massaged his jaw. "It's a terrible thing," he said, "to have the story of your entire life lying at your elbow. Unopened. Dave, I walked away from it twice and came back both times." He smiled weakly. "I will be remembered for my work in quantum transversals."

"This is what comes of traveling alone." I was irritated. "I told you we should never do that."

"It's done," he said. "Listen, if I hadn't looked, I'd be dead now."

I broke out a bottle of burgundy, filled two glasses and we drank it off and I filled them again. "What are you going to do?"

He shook his head. "*It's waiting for me back there.* I don't know *what* to do." His breathing was loud. Snow was piling up on the windows.

"The papers are predicting four inches," I said.

He nodded, as if it mattered. "The biography also says I was murdered. It didn't say by whom."

"It must have been burglars."

"At least," he said, "I'm warned. Maybe I should take a gun back with me."

"Maybe."

"What happens if I change it?"

"I don't know," I said.

"Well." He took a deep breath and tried to smile. "Anyway, I thought you'd want to know I'm okay." He snickered at that. His own joke.

I kept thinking about Helen. "Don't go back at all," I said. "With or without a gun."

"I'm not sure that's an option."

"It sure as hell is."

"At some point," he said, "for one reason or another, I went home." He was staring at the burgundy. He hadn't touched the second glass. "My God, Dave, I'm scared. I've never thought of myself as a coward, but I'm afraid to face this."

I just sat.

"It's knowing the way of it," he said. "That's what tears my heart out."

I got up and looked at the storm.

"Stay here for now," I said. "There's no hurry."

He shook his head. "I just don't think the decision's in my hands." For a long time, neither of us spoke. Finally, he seemed to make up his mind. "I've got a few places to go. People to talk to. Then, when I've done what I need to do, I'll think about all this."

"Good."

He picked up the glass, drained it, wiped his lips, and drifted back against the sofa. "Let me ask you something: are they sure it's me?"

"I understand the body was burned beyond recognition," I said.

"There's something to think about. It could be anyone. And even if it *is* me, it might be a Schrödinger situation. As long as no one knows for certain, it might not matter."

"The police probably know. I assume they checked your dental records."

His brows drew together. "I suppose they do that sort of thing automatically. Do me a favor, though, and make sure they have a proper identification." He got up, wandered around the room, touching things, the books, the bust of Churchill, the P.C. He paused in front of the picture from the Beach Club. "I keep thinking how much it means to be alive. You know, Dave, I saw people out there today I haven't seen in years."

The room became very still.

He played with his glass. It was an expensive piece, chiseled, and he peered at its facets.

"I think you need to tell her," I said gently.

His expression clouded. "I know." He drew the words out. "I'll talk to her. When the time is right."

"Be careful," I said. "She isn't going to expect to see you."

3.

Friday, November 25. Mid-morning.

The critical question was whether we had in fact buried Adrian Shelborne, or whether there was a possibility of mistaken identity. We talked through the night. But neither of us knew anything about police procedure in such matters, so I said I would look into it.

I started with Jerry Shelborne, who could hardly have been less like his brother. There was a mild physical resemblance between the two, although Jerry had allowed the roast beef to pile up a little too much. He was a corporate lawyer in whose view Shel had shuffled aimlessly through life, puttering away with notions that had no reality in the everyday world in which real people live. Even his brother's sudden wealth had not changed his opinion.

"I shouldn't speak ill of the dead," he'd told me that morning. "He was a decent man, had a lot of talent, but he never really made his life count for anything." Jerry sat behind a polished teak desk, guarded by an India rubber plant leaning toward a sun-filled window. The furniture was dark-stained, leather-padded, highly polished. Plaques covered the walls, appreciations from civic groups, awards from major corporations, various licenses and testaments. Photos of his two children were prominently displayed on the desk, a boy in a Little League uniform, a girl nuzzling a horse. His wife, who had left him years earlier, was missing.

"Actually," I said, "I thought he did pretty well."

"I don't mean money," he said. (I hadn't been thinking of money.) "But it seems to me a man has an obligation to live in his community. To make a contribution to it." He leaned back expansively and thrust a satisfied finger into a vest pocket. "'To whom much is given'," he said, "'much shall be expected.'"

"I suppose," I said. "Anyway, I wanted to extend my sympathy."

"Thank you." Jerry rose, signaling that the interview was over.

We walked slowly toward the paneled door. "You know," I said, "this experience has a little bit of *deja vu* about it."

He squinted at me. He didn't like me, and wasn't going to be bothered concealing it. "How do you mean?" he asked.

"There was a language teacher at Princeton, where I got my doctorate. Same thing happened to him. He lived alone and one night a gas main let go and blew up the whole house. They buried him, and then found out it wasn't him at all. He'd gone on an unannounced holiday to Vermont, and turned his place over to a friend. They didn't realize until several days after the funeral when he came home. Unsettled everybody."

Jerry shook his head, amused at the colossal stupidity loose in the world. "Unfortunately," he said, "there's not much chance of that here. They tell me the dental records were dead on."

I probably shouldn't have tried to see how Helen was doing, because my own emotions were still churning. But I called her from a drug store and she said yes, how about lunch? We met at an Applebee's in the Garden Square Mall.

She looked worn out. Her eyes were bloodshot, and she showed a tendency to lose the thread of conversation. She and Shel had made no formal commitment, as far as I knew. But she had certainly believed they had a future together. Come what may. But Shel had been evasive. And there had been times when, discouraged that she got so little of his time, she'd opened up to me. I don't know if anything in my life had been quite as painful as sitting with her, listening to her describe her frustration, watching the occasional tear roll down her cheek. She trusted me, absolutely.

"Are you all right?" she asked me.

"Yes," I said. "How about you?"

The talk was full of regrets, things not said, acts undone. The subject of the police suspicions came up, and we found it hard to subscribe to the burglar theory. "What kind of intruder," I asked, "kills a sleeping man, and then sets his house on fire?"

She was as soft and vulnerable that day as I've ever seen her. Ironically, by all the laws of nature, Shel was dead. Was I still bound to keep my distance? And the truth was that Shel did not even care enough to ease her suffering. I wondered how she would react if she knew Shel was probably sitting in my kitchen at that moment, making a submarine sandwich.

I wanted to tell her. There was a possibility that, when she *did* find out, she would hold it against *me*. I also wanted to keep Shel dead. That was hard to admit to myself, but it was true. I wanted nothing more than a clear channel with Helen Suchenko. But when I watched her bite down the pain, when the sobs began, when she excused herself with a shaky voice and hurried back to the ladies' room, I could stand it no more. "Helen," I said, "are you free this afternoon?"

She sighed. "I wanted to go into the office today, but people get nervous around weepy physicians. Yes, I'm more or less free. But I'm not in the mood to go anywhere."

"Can I persuade you to come out to my place?"

She looked desperately fragile. "I don't think so, Dave," she said. "I need some time."

A long silence fell between us. "Please," I said. "It's important."

More snow was coming. I watched it through the windshield, thick gray clouds drifting toward us. Approaching cars had their headlights on.

Helen followed me in her small blue Ford. I watched her in the mirror while I considered all possible scenarios on how to handle this. Tell her first, I finally decided. Leave out the time travel stuff. Use the story I'd told Jerry as an example of how misunderstandings can occur. *He's not dead, Helen.* She won't believe it, of course. But that's when I get him and bring him into the room. Best not to warn *him*. God knows how he would react. But get them together, present Shel with a *fait accompli*, and you will have done your self-sacrificial duty, Dave. You dumb bastard.

I pulled through blowing snow into my driveway, opened the garage, and went in. Helen rolled in beside me, and the doors closed. "Glad to be out of that," she said, with a brave smile that implied she had decided we needed something new to talk about.

The garage opened directly into the kitchen. I stopped before going through the door and listened. There were no sounds on the other side. "Helen," I said, "I've got something to tell you."

She pulled her coat around her. Her breath formed a mist. "We aren't going to go into it out here, I hope, are we?"

"No," I said, as if the notion were absurd, and opened the door. The kitchen was empty. I heard no sounds anywhere in the house.

"It's about Shel," I said.

She stepped past me and switched on the kitchen lights. "I know," she said. "What else could it be?"

A white envelope lay on the table, with my name on it, printed in his precise hand. I snatched it up, and she looked at me curiously. "What is it?" she asked.

"Just a list of things to do." I pushed it into my pocket. "How about some coffee?"

"Sure. Sounds good."

"It'll have to be instant," I said, putting a pot of water on the stove.

"Do you always do that?" she asked.

"Do what?"

"Write yourself notes?"

"It's my to-do list. It's the first thing I do every morning."

She got two cups down and I excused myself, slipped out, and opened the envelope.

> *Dear Dave,*
>
> *I don't know how to write this. But I have to think about what's hap-pened, and figure out what I need to do. I don't want to jump the gun if it's not necessary. You understand.*
>
> *I know this hasn't been easy for you. But I'm glad you were there. Thanks.*
>
> *Shel*
>
> *P.S. I've left most of my estate to the Leukemia Foundation. That*

will generate a half-dozen lawsuits from my relatives. But if any of those vultures show signs of winning, I'll come back personally and deal with them.

I read it a half-dozen times. Then I crumpled it, tossed it, and went back to the kitchen.

She was looking out the window at the falling snow. Usually, my grounds were alive with bluejays and squirrels. But the critters were all tucked away now. "It's lovely," she said unexpectedly. And then: "So what's the surprise?"

Startled, I tried laughing to gain time. "Son of a gun," I said. "I went out to get it and came back without it." We strolled into the living room, where she sat down on the sofa. I hurried upstairs in search of an idea.

I've mentioned that the wardrobe was also a small museum. There were items of inestimable value, but only if you knew their origin. We had scrolls from the library at Alexandria, a sextant designed and built by Leonardo, a silver bracelet that had once belonged to Calpurnia, a signed folio of *Hamlet*, a pocket watch that Leo Tolstoy had carried while writing *War and Peace*. There were photos of Martin Luther and Albert Schweitzer and Attila the Hun and Charles XII of Sweden. All more or less worthless.

I couldn't bear to give away Calpurnia's bracelet to someone who would not understand its true value. I settled instead for a gold medallion I'd bought from a merchant in Thebes during the fifth century, B.C. It carried a handsomely-wrought likeness of a serpent. The Apollonian priest who joined me later insisted I had acquired a steal. At one time, he said, it had belonged to Aesculapius, the divine doctor, who had been so good he cured the dead. He backed up his view by trying to buy it from me, offering six times what I'd paid for it.

I carried it downstairs and gave it to Helen, telling her that Shel had wanted me to be sure she got it in the event anything happened to him. She glowed, and turned it over and over, unable to get enough of it. "It's exquisite," she said. And the tears came again.

If that thing had possessed any curative powers, I could have used them at that moment.

Snow filled the world. The stand of oaks bordering the approach to the house faded out. As did the stone wall along Carmichael Drive, and the hedges on the west side of the property. Gradually a heavy white curtain was drawn across the middle of the lawn. "I think we're going to get a foot before this is over," I told Helen.

She stood by the curtains, enjoying a glass of chablis. I'd started the fire, and it cracked and pocked comfortably. We added Mozart, and I hoped the storm would continue.

"I think so too," she said. A pair of headlights crept past, out beyond the stone wall. "I feel sorry for anybody out in this."

I stood beside her, and we talked inconsequentials. She had recovered herself, and I began to realize that it was her proximity to me, with all the baggage I brought to any meeting, that had triggered the emotional display earlier. I was not happy that Shel was still in the field. But during that afternoon, I came to understood that even if Shel were safely in his grave, I might still be the embodiment of too many memories. The decent thing to do would be to fade out of her life, just as Carmichael Drive and the outer grounds were fading now. But I knew I could not bring myself to do that.

She talked about looking for a break in the weather so she could go home. But luck held and the break did not come. The snow piled up, and we stayed near the fire. I was alone at last with Helen Suchenko, and it was perhaps the most painful few hours of my life. Yet I would not have missed them, and I have replayed them countless times since, savoring every movement. Every word. *I feel sorry for anybody out in this.* I was out in it, and I believed I would never find shelter.

We watched the reports on the Weather Channel. It was a heavy system, moving down from Canada, low pressure and high pressure fronts colliding, eight inches predicted, which, on top of yesterday's storm, was expected to shut down the entire east coast from Boston to Baltimore.

She talked a lot about Shel that day. Periodically, she'd shake her head as if she'd remembered something, and then dismiss it. And she'd veer off onto some other subject, a movie she'd seen, the latest political scandal, a medical advance that held hope for a breakthrough in this or that. There were a couple of patients she was worried about, and a few hypochondriacs whose lives were centered on their imagined illnesses. I told her how much I missed teaching, which wasn't entirely true, but it's the sort of thing people expect you to say. What I really missed was a sense of purpose, a reason to exist. I had that upstairs, in notes detailing conversations with Rachmaninoff and Robert E. Lee and Oliver Cromwell and Aristotle and H. G. Wells. Those conversations would make the damnedest book the world had ever seen, reports by the principal actors on their ingenuity, their dreams, their follies. But it would never get written.

We lost the cable at four o'clock, and with it the Weather Channel.

Gradually, the light faded out of the sky. I put on steaks and Helen made up a salad. Our timing was perfect because the power failed just as we put everything on the table. I lit a couple of candles, and she sat in the flickering light and looked happy. If the clouds had not dissipated, at least for these few hours they had receded.

Afterward, we retreated into the living room. The music had been silenced by the power outage, so we sat listening to the fire and the whisper of snow against the house. Occasionally, I glanced up at the door to the wardrobe, half-expecting it to open. I tried to plan what I would do if Shel suddenly appeared on the landing. I was caught in the ultimate eternal triangle.

It did not happen. We talked into the early hours, until finally she gave out and fell asleep. I moved her to the sofa and went upstairs for blankets. The heating system, of course, was not working, nor was anything else in the house. The second floor was already cooling off, but I had plenty of firewood.

I settled into a large armchair and drifted into sleep. Somewhere around two, I woke and lay for a time, listening to the silence. The fire was low. I poked at it, and tossed on another log. Helen stirred but did not waken.

The storm must have passed over. Usually, even during the early morning hours, there are sounds: a passing car, the wind in the trees, a dog barking somewhere. But the world was absolutely still.

It was also absolutely dark. No stars. No lights of any kind.

I pointed a flashlight out the window. The night had closed in, wrapped itself around the house so tightly that the beam seemed to plunge into a black wall. I felt internal switches go to alert. It looked like an effect out of a Dracula film.

I picked up the phone to call the 24-hour weather line. But it was dead.

"What is it, Dave?" Helen's voice was soft in the dark.

"You awake?" I asked.

"Sort of."

"Come take a look out the window."

She padded over. And caught her breath. "Where'd that come from?"

"I don't know."

We went outside. It was the thickest, darkest fog I'd ever seen. We didn't sleep well the rest of the night. At about six, Helen made toast over the fire, and I broke out some fruit juice. The lights were still off. More ominously, there was no sign of dawn.

I wondered about Ray White, my neighbor. Ray was a good guy, but he lived alone in a big house, and I thought of him over there wrapped in this goddamn black cloud with no power and maybe no food. He wasn't young, and I thought it would be a good idea to go check on him.

"I'll go with you," Helen said.

I got an extra flashlight, and we let ourselves out through the sliding door. I locked up, and we stumbled around until we found the pathway that leads down to the front gate. The flashlights didn't help much. The beams just got swallowed. There's a hundred-year-old oak midway between the house and the stone wall. It's only about ten feet off the walk, but we could not see it. In fact, I could barely see Helen.

We picked our way to the front gate. I opened it, and we eased out onto the sidewalk. "The entrance to Ray's house is across the street, about twenty yards down," I said. "Stay close."

We stepped off the curb. Her hand tightened in mine. "Be careful," she said. "Somebody might be trying to drive."

Carmichael is two lanes wide. It is blacktop, and bordered by a single line of bricks on either side, just below the curb. We intended to cross it in a straight line, and I warned Helen about the curb on the other side which, under these conditions, would be easy to trip over.

But we kept walking and never came to a curb. No curb and no sidewalk. After a while I was sticking out my foot, trying to determine what lay ahead. And then I knelt down and held the flashlight close to the road surface. "This is *rock*," I said, staring at the ground. Where the hell was there rock on the other side of Carmichael Drive? A patch of grass, yes, and some concrete. But not rock.

Something in my voice scared her. "You sure you know where we are?"

"Yes," I said. "Of course."

The rock was black. It almost looked like marble.

"Which way did we come?" she asked.

It was a bad moment. We stood in the street, on the sidewalk, wherever, and I had got turned around and had no idea.

"Stay," she said. I tried to keep her from walking off, but she just repeated the word.

After a minute I heard her voice. "Talk to me."

"I wish we weren't lost."

"That's good. Keep talking." Her voice came from my right, maybe ten yards away. I started chattering, and she said okay, don't stop. But don't move. She was circling me. Finally, in my rear, she said, "Okay, I've got it. Come this way."

As nearly as I could make out, the blacktop ended near White's side of Carmichael Drive. It just seemed to turn to rock. There was no distinct dividing line, but rather simply a gradual, uneven transformation from the one to the other.

I tried calling White's name. But no one answered.

"Are you sure we came out the right way?" Helen asked.

4.

Saturday, November 26. Late morning.

I woke up in a room lit only by a low fire. The powes was still off. "You okay?" Helen asked. Her voice was thin.

I looked at the clock on the mantel. It was almost noon.

She came over and sat down beside me. "I've never seen weather like this," she said.

I got up, collected snow, and melted it to make water. (It's amazing how much snow you have to melt to get a little water.) I went into the bathroom, and, with the help of a flashlight, brushed my teeth. I tried to draw the bathroom around me, as a kind of shield against what was happening outside the house. The shower. The medicine cabinet. A couple of bars of soap. It was familiar, my anchor to reality.

When I returned downstairs, Helen was putting the phone back in the cradle. She shook her head no. It was still out. We opened a can of meat, added some vegetables, and cooked them over the fire. No matter what happened, we were in no personal danger. That was good to know, but it did not ease my fears.

Helen said she wasn't hungry, but she ate well anyhow. So did I.

It had to do with Shel. I knew that beyond any doubt. We were in the presence of the irrational. I wondered whether we had already done irreparable damage, whether the old world had already receded beyond recall? I was terrified.

When we'd finished eating, I went upstairs to the wardrobe. Shel would be easy to find.

❋

He was standing where I knew he would be: on the slopes of Thermopolae watching the troops come in. He looked good. Tanned. Fit. Almost like a man on vacation. There were a few lines around the eyes, and I knew that, for him, several years had passed since the funeral.

"Shel," I said. "We need you."

"I know," he said gently. Below us, the Thespians were examining the ground on which they would fight. Out on the plain, north of the pass, we could see the Persian army. They stretched to the horizon. "I *will* go back."

"When?"

His eyes took on a hunted look. "When I'm ready. When I'm *able.* There's no hurry, Dave. We both know that."

"I'm not so sure," I said. "Something's wrong. We can't even *find* the rest of New Jersey."

"I'm trying to live my life," he said. "Be patient with me. I have a lot to do yet. But don't worry. You can count on me."

"When?"

"We have all the time in the world. Relax."

"Okay, Shel. Help me relax. If you're going to take care of everything, tell me what's causing the weather conditions back home? Why the power is out? Why I can't find my way across the street?"

"I know about all that," he said.

"And—?"

"Look. Maybe it has nothing to do with me."

The Hellenic squadrons were still filing in, their bright mail dusty from the journey north.

"I doubt it," I said.

He nodded. "As do I. But I've promised to go back. What more do you want?"

"Maybe you should do it now."

He glanced up at a promontory about a hundred feet over our heads. "What is *now* to you and me, Dave? What does the word mean?" When I did not respond, he knelt down and broke off a blade of grass. "Would you be willing to throw yourself from the top of that rock?"

"That has nothing to do with the business between us," I said.

"Not even if I pleaded with you to do so? If the world depended on it?"

I looked at him.

"What if it didn't matter whether you did it today or tomorrow? Or next month? Or forty years from now?"

"We don't *have* forty years."

"I'm not asking for forty of *your* years. I'm asking for forty of *mine*. I'll do it, Dave. God help me, I'll do it. But on my own schedule. Not yours."

I turned away from him, and he thought I was going to travel out. "Don't," he said. "Dave, try to understand. I'm scared of this."

"I know," I said.

"Good. I need you to know."

We passed ourselves off as traveling law-givers. We moved among the Hellenic troops, wishing them well, assuring them that Hellas would never forget them. We first glimpsed Leonidas sitting with his captains around a campfire.

People accustomed to modern security precautions would be amazed at how easy it was to approach him. He accepted our good wishes and observed that, considering our physical size, we would both have made excellent soldiers had we chosen that line of work. In fact, both Shel and I towered over him.

He had dark eyes and was only in his thirties. He brimmed with confidence, as did his men. There was no sense here of a doomed force.

He knew about the road that circled behind the pass, and he had already dispatched troops to cover it. The Phocians, as I recalled. Who would run at the first onset.

He invited us to share a meal. This was the third day of the standoff, before any blood had yet been spilt. We talked with him about Sparta's system of balancing the executive by crowning two kings. And whether democracy would really work in the long run. He thought not. "Athens cannot stay the course," he said. "They have no discipline, and their philosophers encourage them to put themselves before their country. God help us if the poison ever spreads to us." Later, over wine, he asked where we were from, explaining that he could not place the accent.

"America," I said.

He shook his head. "It must be far to the north. Or very small."

We each posed with Leonidas, and took pictures, explaining that it was a ritual that would allow us to share his courage. Sparks crackled up from the campfires, and the soldiers talked about home and the future.

Later, I traded a gold coin to one of the Thespian archers for an arrow. "I'm not sure that's a good idea," Shel said. "He may need the arrow before he's done."

I knew better. "One arrow more or less will make no difference. When the crunch comes, the Thespians will refuse to leave their Spartan allies. They'll die too. All fifteen hundred of them."

And history will remember only the Spartans.

We watched them, exercising and playing games in full view of their Persian enemies. Shel turned to me, and his face was cold and hard. "You know, David," he said, "you are a monster."

5.

Saturday, November 26. Mid-afternoon.

"This is not just heavy fog," she said. "It's *midnight* out there." Helen bit down on a grape.

I sat staring at the window, wondering what lay across Carmichael Drive.

She was lovely in the candlelight. "My guess is that a volcano erupted somewhere," she said. "I know that sounds crazy in South Jersey, but it's all I can think of." She was close to me. Warm and vulnerable and open. I reached out and touched her hair. Stroked it. She did not draw away. "I'm glad I was *here* when it happened, Dave. Whatever it is that's happened."

"So am I," I said.

She smiled appreciatively. And after a moment: "So what do *you* think?"

I took a deep breath. "I think I know what it is."

"I'm listening."

"Helen, there's a lot about Shel you don't know. To put it mildly." Her eyes widened. "Not other women," I added hurriedly. "Or anything like that."

That's not the kind of statement, I suppose, that gets any kind of reaction. Helen just froze in place. "I mean it," I said. "He has a working time machine." I was speaking of him in the present tense. With Shel it gets sort of confused.

"I could almost believe it," she said, after a moment.

I'd been debating whether to destroy my own unit. It would have been the rational thing to do, and the day after Shel's death I'd even gone down to the river with it. But I hadn't been able to bring myself to throw it into the water. Next week, I'd thought. There's plenty of time. "Here," I said. "I'll show you one." I took it out of the desk and handed it to her. It looks like an oversized watch. "You just strap it on, connect it to the power pack, here. Set the destination, and punch the stem."

She looked at it curiously. "What *is* it really, Dave? A notebook?"

"Hell with this," I said. I have to walk to keep my weight down. Three miles a day, every day. Other people walk around the block, or go down to a park. I like Ambrose, Ohio, near the beginning of the century. It's a pleasant little town with tree-lined streets and white picket fences, where straw hats are in vogue for the men, and bright ribbons for the ladies. Down at the barber shop, the talk is mostly about the canal they're going to build through Panama.

I pulled Helen close, brought up Ambrose's coordinates, and told her to brace herself. "The sensation's a little odd at first. But it only lasts a few seconds. And I'll be with you."

The living room froze. She stiffened.

The walls and furniture faded to a green landscape with broad lawns and shingled houses and gas street lamps.

When we came out of it, she backed into me. "What happened?" she asked, looking wildly around.

"We've just gone upstream. Into the past. It's 1905. Theodore Roosevelt is President."

She didn't say anything for a long time. Birds sang, and in the distance we could hear the clean bang of church bells. We were standing outside a general store. About a block away there was a railroad siding.

The wind blew against us.

Her breathing had gone somewhat irregular. "It's okay," I said. "It just takes a little getting used to."

It was late September. People were working in yards, talking over back fences. "We're really here, aren't we?"

"Yes," I said. "We are."

"My God." She took a long, deep breath. The air smelled of burning leaves. I saw hurt come into her eyes. "Why didn't he ever say anything?"

"He kept it a secret for twenty years, Helen. It was habitual with him. He wanted to tell you, and he would have got around to it in his own good time." I shrugged. "Anyway, no one else knows. And no one should. I'll deny this whole thing if anyone ever asks."

She nodded. "Is this," lifting a hand in the general direction of the town, "connected with the problem at home? Is that what you're trying to say?"

"I think so." Cabbage was cooking somewhere. I told her about Shel, how he had died but was still alive. Her colors changed and she moved closer to me. When I'd finished, she only stared straight ahead.

"He's still alive," she said at last.

In a way, he'll always be alive. "Yes," I said. "He's still out there." I explained about the funeral, and how he had reacted.

I could see her struggling to grasp the idea, and to control her anger. "Why didn't you tell me?"

"I didn't know how," I said numbly.

"You can take us back, right?"

"Home? Yes."

"And where else?"

"Anywhere. Well, there are range limits, but nothing you'd care about."

A couple of kids with baseball gloves hurried past. "What you're saying," she said, "is that Shel should go back and walk into that fire. And if he doesn't, the black fog will not go away. Right? Is that what you're saying?"

"It's what I *think*. Yes, Helen, that's what he should do." "But he's said he *would* do that? Right? And by the crazy logic of this business, it shouldn't matter when."

"But something's *wrong*. I think he never did go back. Never *will* go back. And I think that's the problem."

"I don't understand any of this," she said.

"I know." I watched a man with a handcart moving along the street, selling pickles and relishes. "I don't either. But there's a continuity. A track. Time flows along the track." I squeezed her hand. "We've torn out a piece of it."

"And—?"

"I think the locomotive went into the river."

She tried to digest that. "Okay," she said. "Grant the time machine. Dave, what you're asking him to do is unreasonable. I wouldn't go back either to get hit in the head and thrown into a fire. Would you?"

I got up. "Helen, what you or I would do doesn't much matter. I know this sounds cold, but I think we have to find a way to get Shel where he belongs."

She stood up, and looked west, out of town. The fields were brown, dried out from the summer heat. "You know where to find him?"

"Yes."

"Will you take me to him?"

"Yes." And, after a pause: "Will you help me?"

She stared at the quiet little buildings. White clapboard houses. A carriage pulled by two horses just coming around a corner. "Nineteen-five," she said. "Shaw's just getting started."

I didn't push. I probably didn't need her to plead with him. Maybe just seeing her would jar something loose. And I knew where I wanted to confront him. At the one event in all of human history which might flay his conscience.

"Let's go home," I said. "We need to do some sewing."

"Why?"

"You're going to need a costume."

She looked at me and her eyes were hooded. "Why don't we just shoot him?" she said. "And drag him back?"

"It seems that what you are really asking, Simmias, is whether death annihilates the soul?" Socrates looked from one to another of his friends.

The one who had put the question was, like most of the others, young and clear-eyed, but subdued in the shadow of the prison house. "It is an important matter," he said. "There is none of more importance. But we were reluctant—." He hesitated, his voice caught, and he could go no farther.

"I understand," said Socrates. "You fear this is an indelicate moment to raise such an issue. But if you would discuss it with me, we cannot very well postpone it, can we?"

"No, Socrates," said a thin young man with red hair. "Unfortunately, we cannot." This, I knew, was Crito.

Despite Plato's account, the final conversation between Socrates and his disciples did not take place in his cell. It might well have begun there, but they were in a wide, utilitarian meeting room when Helen and I arrived. Several women were present. Socrates, then seventy years old, sat at ease on a wooden chair, while the rest of us gathered around him in a half-circle. To my surprise and disappointment, I did not see Shel.

Socrates was, on first glance, a man of mundane appearance. He was of average height, for the time. He was clean-shaven, and he wore a dull red robe. Only his eyes were extraordinary, conveying the impression that they were lit from within. When they fell curiously on me, as they did from time to time, I imagined that he knew where I had come from, and why I was there.

Beside me, Helen writhed under the impact of conflicting emotions. She had been ecstatic at the chance to see Shel again, although I knew she had not yet accepted the idea that he was alive. When he did not arrive, she looked at me as if to say she had told me so, and settled back to watch history unfold. She was, I thought, initially disappointed, in that the event seemed to be nothing more than a few people sitting around talking in an uncomfortable room in a prison. As if the scene should somehow be scored and choreographed and played to muffled drums. Then she had grown interested while Socrates and his friends weighed the arguments for and against immortality.

"When?" she whispered, after we'd been there almost an hour. "When does it happen?"

"Sunset, I think," I said.

She made a noise deep in her throat.

"Why do men fear death?" Socrates asked.

"Because," said Crito, "they believe that it is the end of existence."

There were almost twenty people present. Most were young, but there was a sprinkling of middle-aged and elderly persons. The most venerable of these looked like Moses, a tall man with a white beard and expressive white eyebrows and a fierce countenance. He gazed intently at Socrates throughout, and periodically nodded when the philosopher hammered home a particularly salient point.

"And do all men fear death?" asked Socrates.

"Most assuredly, Socrates," said a boy, who could have been no more than eighteen.

Socrates addressed the boy. "Do even the brave fear death, Cebes?"

Cebes thought it over. "I have to think so, Socrates."

"Why then do the valiant dare death? Is it perhaps because they fear something else even more?"

"The loss of their honor," said Crito with conviction.

"Thus we are faced with the paradox that even the brave are driven by fear. Can we find no one who can face death with equanimity who is *not* driven by fear?"

Moses was staring at Helen. I moved protectively closer to her.

"Of all men," said Crito, "only you seem to show no concern at its approach."

Socrates smiled. "Of all men," he said, "only a philosopher can truly face down death. Because he knows quite certainly that the soul will proceed to a better existence. Provided he has maintained a lifelong pursuit of knowledge and virtue, and has not allowed his soul, which is his divine essence, to become entangled in concerns of the body. For when this happens, the soul takes on corporeal characteristics. And when death comes, it cannot escape. This is why cemeteries are restless at night."

"How can we be sure," asked a man with blond hair who had not previously spoken, "that the soul, even if it succeeds in surviving the trauma of death, is not scattered by the first strong wind?"

It was not intended as a serious question, but Socrates saw that it affected the others. So he answered lightly, observing that it would be prudent to die on a calm day, and then undertook a serious response. He asked questions which elicited admissions that the soul was not physical and therefore could not be a composite object. "I think we need not fear that it will come apart," he said, with a touch of amusement.

One of the jailers lingered in the doorway throughout the long discussion. He seemed worried, and at one point cautioned Socrates against speaking too much, or getting excited. "If you get the heat up," he said, "the poison will not work well."

"We would not wish that," Socrates replied. But he saw the pained expression on the jailer's face, and I thought he immediately regretted the remark.

Women arrived with lunch, and several stayed, so that the room became more and more crowded. In fact, no doors were locked, and no guards, other than the reluctant jailer, were in evidence. Phaedo, who is the narrator of Plato's account, was beside me. He told me that the authorities had hoped profoundly that Socrates would run off. "They did everything they could to avoid this," he said. "There is even a rumor that last night they offered him money and transportation if he would leave."

Socrates saw us conversing, and he said, "Is there something in my reasoning that disturbs you?"

I'd lost the train of the discussion, but Phaedo said, "Yes, Socrates. However, I hesitate to put my objection to you."

Socrates turned a skeptical gaze on him. "Truth is what it is. Tell me what disturbs you, Phaedo."

He swallowed to make sure of his voice. "Then let me ask," he said in a carefully neutral tone, "whether you are being truly objective on this matter? The sun is not far from the horizon and, although it grieves me to say it, were I in your position, I also would argue in favor of immortality."

"Were you in his position," said Crito, with a smile, "you would have taken the first ship to Syracuse." The company laughed, Socrates as heartily as any, and the strain seemed relieved for the moment.

"You are of course correct in asking, Phaedo. Am I seeking truth? Or trying to convince myself? I can only respond that, if my arguments are valid, then that is good. If they are false, and death does indeed mean annihilation, they nevertheless arm me to withstand its approach. And that too is good." He looked utterly composed. "If I'm wrong, it's an error that won't survive the sunset."

Simmias was seated immediately to the right of Moses. "I for one am convinced," he said. "Your arguments do not admit of refutation. And it is a comfort to me to believe that we have it in our power to draw this company together again in some place of God's choosing."

"Yes," said Crito. "I agree. And, Socrates, we are fortunate to have you here to explain it to us."

"Anyone who has thought about these issues," said Socrates, "should be able to reach, if not truth, at least a high degree of probability."

Moses seemed weighed down with the infirmities of age, and with the distress of the present calamity. Still, he continued to glance periodically at Helen. Now, for the first time, he spoke: "I very much fear, Socrates, that within a few hours there will be no one left anywhere in Hellas, or anywhere else for that matter, who will be able to make these matters plain."

"That's *Shel's* voice," Helen gasped, straining forward to see better. The light was not good, and he was turned away from us now, his face hidden in the folds of his hood.

Then he turned and looked openly at us. He smiled sadly at her. And his lips formed the English words *hello, Helen*.

She was getting to her feet.

At that moment, the jailer appeared with the poisoned cup, and the sight of him, and the silver vessel, froze everyone in the chamber. "I hope you understand, Socrates," he said, "this is not my doing."

"I know that, Thereus," said Socrates. "I am not angry with you."

"They always want to blame *me*," Thereus said.

Silence flowed through the chamber.

The jailer laid the cup on the table before him. "It is time," he said.

The rest of the company, following Helen's example, got one by one to their feet.

Socrates gave a coin to the jailer, squeezed his hand, thanked him, and turned to look at his friends one last time. "The world is very bright," he said. "But much of it is illusion. If we stare at it too long, in the way we look at the sun during an eclipse, it blinds us. Look at it only with the mind." He picked up the hemlock. Several in the assemblage started forward, but were restrained by their companions. Someone in back sobbed.

"Stay," a voice said sternly. "You have respected him all your life. Do so now."

He lifted the cup to his lips, and his hand trembled. It was the only time the mask slipped. Then he drank it down and laid the cup on the table. "I am sure Simmias is right," he said. "We shall gather again one day, as old friends should, in a far different chamber."

Shel clasped Helen a long time in his big arms. "It's good to see you again," he said. Tears ran down his cheeks.

She shivered. "What happened to you?"

A smile flickered across his lips. "I've been traveling a long time." He stood silhouetted against the moon and the harbor. Behind us, the waterfront buildings of the Piraeus were illuminated by occasional lamps. He turned toward me. "David, you seem to have become my dark angel."

I was emotionally drained. "I'm sorry you feel that way," I said.

A gull wheeled overhead. "Socrates dies for a philosophical nicety. And Shelborne continues to run when all the world is at stake. Right?"

"That's right," I said.

Helen was still trembling. "I don't understand," she whispered.

His lips twitched, and he ran his hand over the long white whiskers. He looked haunted. "I haven't seen you for forty years," he said. "You have no idea how many times I've gone to sleep dreaming of you. And you are even lovelier than I remember."

I put a hand on her shoulder. Steadied her. "He's been out here a long time."

Her eyes blazed. "What happened to *my* Shel? What did you do with him?"

"He's been living his allotted years," he said. "Making them count for as much as he can as long as he can. Before my conscience here—" lifting his eyes and targeting me, "before my conscience succeeds in driving me into my grave."

She couldn't hold back any longer. She burst into tears. And in that moment, I hated him.

"I've tried to go back," he said. "God help me, I've tried. But I could not bring myself to lie in that bed." Anger surfaced. I could not tell where it was directed. "Did you know that my skull was crushed?"

We knew.

He looked very old. And broken. He didn't seem to know what to do with his hands. The robes had no pockets. But he needed some kind of defensive gesture, so he folded his arms and turned to face the harbor. "I am not Socrates, Dave," he said. "I will not drink from his cup." His eyes locked on mine, and I could see him come to a decision. He drew us together, within the field of his Watch, and punched in a set of coordinates. "But I will settle the issue for you."

Helen shook her head no. No more surprises. And everything began to slow down. The harbor winked out, a ship's deck materialized underfoot, and the sky filled with fire.

We were on a Roman galley. The air was thick with powder and cinders, and the sails were down. We were pitching and rolling. The ocean broke across the deck, and men scrambled and swore at their stations. Below us, long oars dipped rhythmically into the waves. It was daylight, but we could not see more than twenty feet.

"How did you manage that?" I screamed at Shel over the hurricane of noise. The Watches had never possessed the precision to land people on a ship at sea.

"It's been a lot of years," he said. "Technology's better than it used to be."

"Where are we?" demanded Helen, barely able to make herself heard.

Shel was hanging onto a ladder. His clothes were drenched. "A. D. 79," he said. "Just west of Pompeii."

His eyes were afire. His silver hair was already streaked with black ash, and I began to suspect he had lost whatever anchor he might have had to reality. Time had become at last perhaps too slippery for him.

The ship rolled to starboard, and would have dumped Helen into the sea had the old man not grabbed her, and hung on, pushing me aside. "Isn't this glorious?" he asked.

"Why are we here?" Helen demanded, wiping her eyes.

The sea and the wind roared, and the dust was blinding.

"*I* will pick the time of my death," he cried. "And its manner."

I was having a hard time hanging on.

"I am uniquely qualified—."

We went down into a trough, and I thought the sea was going to bury us.

"—To make that choice," he continued, ignoring the ocean. "My death will be an appropriate finale to the symphony of my life."

A fireball roared overhead, and plowed into the water.

"Don't do it," I cried.

"Have no fear, David. I'm not ready yet. But when I am, this will be the way of it." He smiled at me and touched the Watch. "What better end for a time traveller than sailing with Pliny the Elder?" And he was gone.

"What was that all about?" called Helen. We dipped again and salt water poured across the deck. "Maybe we ought to get out of here too."

I agreed, and wrapped one arm around a stanchion, something to hold onto while I set the Watch.

"Wait," she said. "Do you know who Pliny the Elder is?"

"A Roman philosopher."

"I did a paper on him once. He was an essayist and moralist. Fought a lot for the old values."

"Helen, can we talk about it later?"

"He was also a naval officer. He's trying to rescue survivors. Dave, if Shel meant what he said, he'll be back."

"I understand that."

"He'll be older. But he'll be back."

"We can't do anything about that. I don't think we want to wait around here."

We were on the starboard side, near the beam. The sails were down, and a few shadowy figures were moving through the volcanic haze. (I would have expected to hear the roar of the volcano, of Vesuvius, but the only noise came from the sea and the warm dry wind that blew across the deck.) "Let's try the other side," I said.

He was there, on the port quarter, clinging to a line, while the wind howled. Even more ancient this time, frail, weary, frightened. Dressed differently than he had been, in slacks and a green pullover that might have come out of the 1930's.

Cinders stung my eyes.

He saw us and waved. "I've been looking for you." His gaze lingered on Helen, and then drifted toward the sea. His eyes seemed utterly devoid of reasoning. I wondered whether any part of the old Shelborne remained.

"Don't," I cried.

She let go her handhold and tried to scramble across the pitching deck.

He was hanging onto a hawser, balanced near the rail.

The ship pitched, went up the front of a wave and down the back. He raised his hand in a farewell gesture, and the sea broke across the deck. I was thrown hard against a gunwale. The night was filled with water.

When it blew off, Shel was gone. The rail was clear, and the line to which he'd clung whipped back and forth.

Helen shouted and pointed. I saw him briefly, rising over a swell, clutching a board and struggling to stay afloat, his white hair trailing in the water. But another wave broke over him and moments later the board popped to the surface, and drifted into the haze.

Something in the ship gave way with a loud crack, and the crewmen cried out. I pulled Helen close.

"Dead again," she said.

Maybe this time for good. I pressed the stem.

6.

Saturday, November 26. Mid-afternoon.

We returned to the wardrobe in separate, but equally desperate, moods.

Helen could not connect the wild man on the galley with Shel, or even the moody septuagenarian on the dock at the Piraeus. Furthermore, she had not yet accepted either the reality or the implications of time travel. Yet, on a primal level, she had seen him. And for the second time, she mourned him.

And I? I'd lost all feeling. How could I reconcile two graves? I collapsed into a chair and stared helplessly at the costumes, hanging neatly, marked off by period. Damn them. I remembered the planning and research that had gone into their creation. We had felt so well organized in those days. Prepared for anything.

I let it go.

And then I noticed that I was *seeing* the costumes. There was *light* in the room. It was gray, not bright, but it meant that the black mist was gone. I threw the curtains back, and looked out at a rain-swept landscape.

The trees, the grounds, the walkway, the garage, were visible, huddled together in the storm. The wall still circled the property. And beyond the wall, I could see most of Carmichael Drive. *Most of it.* But Ray White's house was missing. As was the world behind it. Carmichael Drive now skirted the edge of a precipice, its far side gone, broken off into a void. Beyond, I could see only gray sky.

Terrified, we went from room to room. Everywhere, in all directions, the picture was the same. On the east, where my property was most extensive, even the wall was gone. A seldom-used patio had been cut in half, and the stand of elms that used to provide shade for it now lined the limits of the world.

We opened a bottle of brandy and drew all the blinds in the house.

"Can't we replay that last scene?" she asked. "Go back and rescue him? I mean, that's the whole point of a time machine, isn't it? Nothing's ever irrevocable. You make a mistake, you go back and fix it."

I was tired and my head hurt and at that moment I hated Adrian Shelborne with every fiber of my being. "No," I said. "It would just make everything worse. We know what happened. We can't change *that*."

"Dave," she said, "how could we possibly make things *worse*?"

That was a pretty good question.

She eased onto a sofa and closed her eyes. "Time travel," she said, "isn't all it's cracked up to be, is it?"

Rain rattled against the windows. "We need to find a way to eliminate the paradox."

"Okay," she said. "What exactly is the paradox?"

I thought it over. "Adrian Shelborne has two graves. One out on Monument Hill. And the other in the Tyrrhenian Sea. We have to arrange things so that there is only one."

"Can we go back and stop the Friday night fire?"

"Same problem as trying a rescue on the galley. The Friday night fire has already happened, and if you prevent it, then what was the funeral all about?"

"It's like a big knot," she said. "No matter where you try to pull, everything just gets tighter."

We were still wearing our Hellenic robes, which were torn and soiled. And we both needed a shower, but there was no water. On the other hand, we *did* have rain. And as much privacy as we could ever want.

I got soap, towels, and wash cloths. She took the back yard, which was more sheltered (as if that mattered), and I stood out front. It was late November, but the weather had turned unseasonably warm nevertheless. Hot water would have been nice, but I felt pretty good anyway after I'd dried off and changed into clean clothes.

Then we sat, each in a kind of private cocoon, thinking about options. Or things lost. The rain continued through the afternoon. I watched rivulets form and wondered how much soil was being washed over the edge. Where? Where would it be going? When the weather cleared, I promised myself that I would walk out and look down.

"Who's buried in the grave on Monument Hill?" she asked.

"Shel."

"How do we know? The body was burned beyond recognition."

"They checked his dental records. We can't *change* that."

She was sitting on the sofa with her legs drawn up under her. "We also can't recover the body from the Tyrrhenian Sea. We have to work on Monument Hill. What can we do about the dental records?"

I looked at her. "I don't think I understand."

"We have a time machine. Use your imagination."

Chain-reaction collisions have become an increasingly dangerous occurrence on limited-access highways around the world. Hundreds die every year, several thousand are injured, and property damage usually runs well into the millions. On the day that we buried Shel, there had been a pileup in California. It had happened a little after eight o'clock in the morning under conditions of perfect visibility when a pickup rear-ended a station wagon full of kids headed for breakfast and Universal Studios.

We materialized by the side of the road moments after the chain reaction had ended. The highway and the shoulder were littered with wrecked vehicles. Some people were out of their cars trying to help; others were wandering dazed through the carnage. The morning air was filled with screams and the smell of burning oil.

"I'm not sure I can do this," Helen said, spotting a woman bleeding in an overturned Buick. She went over, got the door open, and motioned me to assist. The woman was unconscious, and her right arm was bent in an awkward manner.

"Helen," I said. "We have a bigger rescue to make."

She shook her head. No. This first.

She stopped the bleeding and I got someone to stay with the victim. We helped a few other people, pulled an elderly couple out of a burning van, got one man with two shattered legs off the road. (I was horrified. Shel and I had always maintained a strict hands-off policy.) "We don't have time for this," I pleaded.

"I don't have time for anything else," she said.

Sirens were approaching. I let her go, concentrating on finding what we'd come for.

He was alone in a blue Toyota that had rolled over onto its roof. The front of the car was crumpled, a door was off, and the driver showed no sign of life. He was bleeding heavily from a head wound. One tire was spinning slowly. I could find no pulse.

He was about the right size, tangled in a seat belt. When Helen got there, she confirmed that he was dead. I used a jack knife to cut him free. EMT's had arrived and were spreading out among the wrecked cars. Stretchers were appearing.

Helen could not keep her mind on what we were doing. "Your oath doesn't count," I said. "Not here. Let it go."

She looked at me out of empty eyes.

"Help me get him out," I said.

We wrapped him in plastic and laid him in the road.

"He does look a little like Shel," she said in a small voice.

"Enough to get by."

Footsteps were approaching. Someone demanded to know what we were doing.

"It's okay," I said, "we're doctors." I pushed the stem and we were out of there.

His name was Victor Randall. His wallet carried pictures of an attractive woman with cropped brown hair seated with him in a front porch swing. And two kids. The kids were smiling up at the camera, one boy, one girl, both around seven or eight. "Maybe," Helen said, "when this is over, we can send them a note to explain things."

"We can't do that," I said.

"They'll never know what happened to him."

"That's right. And there's no way around it."

There was also about two hundred cash. Later, I would mail that back to the family.

We carried him down to the garage and put him in the Porsche. I adjusted the temporal sweep to maximum, so that when we went the car would go with us.

7.

Thursday, November 10. Near midnight.

Mark S. Hightower had been Shel's dentist for seven years. He operated out of a medical building across the street from Friendship Hospital, where Helen had interned, and where she still served as a consultant.

I'd met Hightower once. He was short, barrel-chested, flat-skulled, a man who looked more like a professional wrestler than a dentist. But he was soft-spoken and, according to Shel, particularly good with kids.

We materialized on a lot down on Penrod Avenue, which was in the commercial district. The area was always deserted at night. Ten minutes later, we approached the hospital and pulled into the parking lot at the Forest Elm Medical Center. Hightower was located in back, well away from the street.

Victor was in the front seat, supported from behind by Helen. He was wrapped in plastic. He'd stopped bleeding, and we had cleaned him up as much as we could. "Are you sure you know how to do this?" I asked.

"Of course not, Dave," she said. "I'm not a dentist. But the equipment shouldn't be hard to figure out. How do we get inside?"

I showed her a tire iron. "We'll have to break in."

She looked dismayed. "I thought you could manage something a little more sophisticated than that. Why can't you just use that thing on your wrist and put us right inside the building?"

"Because it's not very precise. We could be here all night." I was thinking of Shel's trick in moving us from the Piraeus to the quarterdeck on Pliny's galley. If I'd tried that, we'd have gone into the ocean.

We put on gloves, and walked around the building, looking for an open window. There was none, but we found a rear exit that did not seem very sturdy. I wedged the tire iron between the door and the jamb, worked it back and forth, and felt the lock give. The door all but came off the hinges. I held my breath, waiting for the screech of a burglar alarm. It didn't come, and we were past the first hurdle.

We went back to the Porsche, got Victor out of the back seat and half-carried, half-dragged him around to the open door. Once inside, we set him in a chair. Then we turned on penlights and looked around. A half-dozen rooms were designated for patients, opening off a corridor that looped around to the reception area. I wandered from office to office, not really knowing what I was looking for. But Helen did one quick turn through the passageway and pointed at a machine tucked away in a corner. "This is it," she said.

The manufacturer's label said it was an orthopantomograph. "It does panoramic X-rays," Helen said.

"Panoramic? What's that?"

"Full mouth. It should be all we'll need."

The idea was that the person being X-rayed placed his forehead against a plastic rest, and his chin in a cup-shaped support. The camera was located inside a cone which was mounted on a rotating arm. The arm and cone would traverse the head, and produce a single panoramic image of the teeth. The only problem was that the patient normally stood during the procedure.

"It'll take six to eight minutes," said Helen. "During that time we have to keep him absolutely still. Think you can do it?"

"I can do it," I said.

"Okay." She checked to make sure there was a film cassette in the machine. "Let's get him."

We carried Victor to the orthopantomograph. At Helen's suggestion, we'd brought along some cloth strips which we now used to secure him to the device. It was an uncomfortable and clumsy business, and he kept sliding away from us. Working in the dark complicated the procedure, but after about twenty minutes we had him in place.

"Okay," she said. "He should be all right now. Don't touch him. Right?"

I backed away.

"Something just occurred to me," I said. "Victor Randall already has the head wound."

Her eyes closed momentarily. "You're suggesting the arsonist didn't hit Shel in the head after all?"

"That's what I think."

She considered that piece of data. "This keeps getting weirder," she said.

A mirror was mounted on the machine directly in front of the patient's face. Helen pressed a button and a light went on in the center of the mirror. "They would tell the patient to watch the light," she said. "That's how they're sure they've got it lined up."

"How are we sure?"

"What's the term? 'Dead reckoning'?" She punched another button. A motor started, and the cone began to move.

Ten minutes later we took the cassette in back, carefully leaving Victor in place until we were sure we had good pictures. The developer was located in a windowless storage room. Helen removed the film from the cassette and ran it through the machine. When the finished picture came out, she handed it to me without looking at it. "What do you think?"

The entire mouth, uppers and lowers, was clear. "Looks good," I said.

She held it against the light. "Plenty of fillings on both sides. Let's see how it compares."

The records were maintained in manila folders behind the reception desk. Helen found Shel's, and sat down with it at the desk, where the counter hid her from anyone passing outside.

The folder was filled with records of Shel's visits. "He goes every three months," she said. "That's not bad." (She also tended to talk about him in the present tense.) The results of his most recent checkup were clipped on the right side. In the middle of the sheet was a panoramic picture, like the one we had just taken, and several smaller photos of individual sections. "I think they call these 'wings'" she said. "But when they bring a dentist in to identify a body, they do it with *these*." She held up the panoramic and compared the two. "They don't look much alike in detail. And if they ever get around to comparing it with the wings, they'll notice something's wrong. But we should have enough to get by."

She removed Shel's panoramic, and substituted the one we had just taken. Then she replaced the folder. We wiped off the headrest and checked the floor to be sure we'd spilled no blood. "One more thing," said Helen. She inserted a fresh cassette into the orthopantomograph. "Okay. We've done what we came to do. Let's clear out."

"Wait a minute," I said. "They're going to know we broke in. We need to do something to make this look like a burglary." As far as I could see, there wasn't much worth stealing. Magazines. Cheap landscape prints on the walls. "How about a drill?" I said. "They look expensive."

She squeezed my arm. "What kind of burglar would steal a *drill?*" She went on another tour of the office. Moments later, I heard glass breaking, and she came back with a couple of plastic bottles filled with pills. "Valium," she said.

8.

Saturday, November 12. 1:15 a.m.

I had the coordinates for Shel's workshop, so we were able to go right in.

It was located in the basement of the townhouse, a small, cramped, cluttered place that had a Cray computer front and center, banks of displays, and an array of experimental equipment I had never begun to understand. Moments after we arrived, his oil heater came on with a thump.

Helen grumbled that we would have to carry the body up to the second floor. But I had done the best I could. The math had always been Shel's job, and the only place in the house I could get to was the workshop. So we dragged Victor up two flights of stairs to the master bedroom, dressed him in Shel's pajamas, turned back the sheets, and laid him in bed. We put his clothes into a plastic bag.

We also had a brick in the bag. Shel kept his car keys in the middle drawer of a desk on the first floor. We had debated just leaving the clothes to burn, but I wanted to leave nothing to chance. Despite what you might think about time travel, what we were doing was forever. We could not come back and undo it, because we were *here*, and we knew what the sequence of events was, and you couldn't change that without paying down the road. If we knew anything for sure now, we knew *that*.

I had left the Porsche at home this time. So we had to borrow Shel's green Pontiac. It had a vanity plate reading SHEL and a lot of mileage. But he took good care of it. We drove down to the river. At the two-lane bridge that crosses the Narrows, we pulled off and waited until there was no traffic. Then we pulled onto the bridge, went out to the middle, where we presumed the water was deepest, and dropped the bag over the side. We still had Victor's wallet and ID, which I intended to burn.

We returned Shel's car to the garage. By now it was about a quarter to two, thirty-eight minutes before a Mrs. Wilma Anderson would call to report a fire at the townhouse. I was a little concerned that we had cut things too close, and that the intruder might already be in the house. But the place was still quiet when I returned the car keys to the desk.

We locked the house, front and back, which was how we had found it, and retired across the street, behind a hedge. We were satisfied with our night's work, and curious only to see who the criminal was. The neighborhood was tree-lined, well-lighted, quiet. The houses were middle-class, fronted by small yards which were usually fenced. Cars were parked on either side of the street. There was no traffic, and somewhere in the next block we could hear a cat yowling.

Two o'clock arrived.

"Getting late," Helen said.

Nothing stirred. "He's going to have to hurry up," I said.

She looked at me uncomfortably. "What happens if he doesn't come?"

"He *has* to come."

"Why?"

"Because that's the way it happened. We know that for an absolute fact."

She looked at her watch. Two-oh-one.

"I just had a thought," I said.

"Let's hear it."

"Maybe you're right. Maybe there is no firebug. Maybe it happened a different way. After all, we already know where the fractured skull came from."

She nodded slowly. "Yeah," she said. "Maybe."

I left the shelter of the hedge and walked quickly across the street, entered Shel's driveway, and went back into the garage. There were several gas cans. They were all empty.

I needed the car keys. But I was locked out now. I used a rock to break a window, got in, and retrieved the keys. I threw the empty cans into the trunk of his Pontiac. "Wait here," I told Helen as I backed out onto the street. "Keep an eye open in case someone *does* show up."

"Where are you going?"

"To get some gas."

There was an all-night station down on River Road, only a few blocks away. It was one of those places where, after eleven o'clock, the cashier locks himself into a glass cage. He was a middle-aged, worn-out guy sitting in a cloud of cigarette smoke. A toothpick rolled relentlessly from one side of his mouth to the other. I filled three cans, paid, and drove back to the townhouse.

It was 2:17 when we began sloshing the gasoline around the basement. We emptied a can on the stairway and another upstairs, taking particular care to drench the master bedroom, where Victor Randall lay. We poured the rest of it on the first floor, and so thoroughly soaked the entry that I was afraid to go near it with a lighted match. But at 2:25 we touched it off.

Helen and I watched for a time from a block away. The flames cast a pale glare in the sky, and sparks floated overhead. We didn't know much about Victor Randall, but what we did know maybe was enough. He'd been a husband and father. In their photos, his wife and kids had looked happy. And he got a Viking's funeral.

"What do you think?" asked Helen. "Will it be all right now?"

"Yeah," I said. "I hope so."

9.

Sunday, November 27. Mid-morning.

In the end, the Great November Delusion was written off as precisely that, a kind of mass hysteria that settled across a substantial chunk of New Jersey, Pennsylvania, Maryland, and Delaware. Elsewhere, life had gone on as usual, except that the affected area seemed to have vanished behind a black shroud which turned back all attempts at entry and admitted no signals.

Fortunately, it had lasted only a few hours. When it ended, persons who had been inside emerged with a wide range of stories. They had been stranded on rocky shores or amid needle peaks or in gritty wastes where nothing grew. One family claimed to have been inside a house that had an infinite number of stairways and chambers, but no doors or windows. Psychologists pointed out that the one element that appeared in all accounts was isolation. Sometimes it had been whole communities that were isolated; sometimes families. Occasionally it had been individuals. The general consensus was that, whatever the cause, therapists would be assured of a handsome income for years to come.

My first act on returning home was to destroy Victor Randall's wallet and ID. The TV was back with full coverage of the phenomenon. The National Guard was out, and experts were already appearing on talk shows. I would have been ecstatic with the way things had turned out, except that Helen had sunk into a dark mood. She was thinking about Shel.

"We saved the world," I told her. I showered and changed and put on some bacon and eggs. By the time she came downstairs it was ready. She ate, and cried a little, and congratulated me. "We were brilliant," she said.

After breakfast she seemed reluctant to leave, as if something had been left undone. But she announced finally that she needed to get back to her apartment and see how things were.

She had just started for the door when we heard a car pull up. "It's a woman," she said, looking out the window. "Friend of yours?"

It was Sgt. Lake. She was alone this time.

We watched her climb the porch steps. A moment later the door bell rang.

"This won't look so good," Helen said.

"I know. You want to duck upstairs?"

She thought about it. "No. What are we hiding?"

The bell sounded again. I crossed the room and opened up.

"Good morning, Dr. Dryden," said the detective. "I'm glad to see you came through it all right. Everything is okay?"

"Yes," I said. "How about you?"

Her cheeks were pale. "Good," she said. "I hope it's over." She seemed far more human than during her earlier visit.

"Where's your partner?" I asked.

She smiled. "Everything's bedlam downtown. A lot of people went berserk during that *thing*, whatever it was. We're going to be busy for a while." She took a deep breath and, for the moment at least, some unconscious communication passed between us. "I wonder if I could talk with you?"

"Of course." I stepped back and she came in.

"It's chaos." She seemed not quite able to focus. "Fires, people in shock, heart attacks everywhere. It hasn't been good." She saw Helen and her eyes widened. "Hello, Doctor. I didn't expect to see you here. I expect you're in for a busy day too."

Helen nodded. "You okay?" she asked.

"Yeah. Thanks. I'm fine." She stared out over my shoulder. Then, with a start, she tried to wave it all away.

We sat down. "What was it like here?" she asked.

I described what I'd seen. While I was doing so, Helen poured her some coffee and she relaxed a little. She had been caught in her car during the event on a piece of rain-swept foggy highway that just went round and round, covering the same ground. "Damnedest thing," she said. "No matter what I did, I couldn't get off." She shook her head and drank the coffee.

"I could prescribe a sedative," said Helen.

"No, thank you," Lake said. She looked at me carefully. "I wonder if we might have a minute alone?"

"Sure," Helen said. "I should be on my way anyhow." She patted my shoulder in a comradely way and let herself out.

Lake turned her attention to me. "Doctor," she said, "you've informed us you were home in bed at the time of Dr. Shelborne's death. Do you stand by that statement?"

"Yes," I said, puzzled. "I do."

"Are you sure?"

The question hung in the sunlit air. "Of course I am. Why do you ask?"

I could read nothing in her expression. "Someone answering your description was seen in the neighborhood of the townhouse shortly before the fire."

"It wasn't *me*," I said, suddenly remembering the man at the gas station. And I'd been driving Shel's car. With his vanity plate on the front to underscore the point.

"Okay," she said. "I wonder if you'd mind coming down to the station with me, so we can clear the matter up. Get it settled."

"Sure. Be glad to."

We stood up. "Could I have a moment, please?"

"Certainly," she said, and went outside.

I called Helen on her cellular. "Don't panic," she said. "All you need is a good alibi."

"I don't *have* an alibi."

"For God's sake, Dave. You've got something better. You have a *time machine.*"

"Okay. Sure. But if I go back and set up an alibi, why didn't I tell them the truth in the beginning?"

"Because you were protecting a woman's reputation," she said. "What else would you be doing at two o'clock in the morning? Get out your little black book." It might have been my imagination, but I thought the reference to my little black book angered her slightly.

10.

Friday, November 11. Early evening.

The problem was that I didn't have a little black book. I've never been all that successful with women. Not to the extent, certainly, that I could call one up with a reasonable hope of finishing the night in her bed.

What other option did I have? I could try to find someone in a bar, but you didn't really lie to the police in a murder case to protect a casual pickup.

I pulled over to the curb beside an all-night restaurant, planning to go in and talk to the waitress a lot. Give her a huge tip so she couldn't possibly forget me. But then, how would I explain why I had lied?

The restaurant was close to the river, a rundown area lined with crumbling warehouses. A police cruiser slowed down and pulled in behind the Porsche. The cop got out and I lowered the window.

"Anything wrong, Officer?" I asked. He was small, black, well-pressed.

"I was going to ask you the same thing, sir. This is not a good neighborhood."

"I was just trying to decide whether I wanted a hamburger."

"Yes, sir," he said. I could hear the murmur of his radio. "Well, listen, I'd make up my mind, one way or the other. I wouldn't hang around out here if I were you."

I smiled, and gave him a thumbs-up. "Thanks," I said.

He got back in his cruiser and pulled out. I watched his lights turn left at the next intersection. And I knew what I was going to do.

I drove south on route 130 for about three quarters of an hour, and then turned east on a two-lane. Somewhere around eleven, I entered Clovis, New Jersey, and decided it was just what I was looking for.

Its police station occupied a small two-story building beside the post office. The Red Lantern Bar was located about two blocks away, on the other side of the street.

I parked in a lighted spot close to the police station, walked to the bar, and went inside. It was smoky, subdued, and reeking with the smell of dead cigarettes and stale beer. Most of the action was over around the dart board.

I settled in at the bar and commenced drinking Scotch. I stayed with it until the bartender suggested I'd had enough, which usually wouldn't have taken long because I don't have much capacity for alcohol. But that night my mind stayed clear. Not my motor coordination, though. I paid up, eased off the stool, and negotiated my way back onto the street.

I turned right and moved methodically toward the police station, putting one foot in front of the other. When I got close, I added a little panache to my stagger, tried a couple of practice giggles to warm up, and lurched in through the front door.

A man with two stripes came out of a back room.

"Good evening, Officer," I said, with exaggerated formality and the widest grin I could manage, which was then pretty wide. "Can you give me directions to Atlantic City?"

The corporal shook his head sadly. "Do you have some identification, sir?"

"Yes I do," I said. "But I don't see why my name is any business of yours. I'm in a hurry."

He sighed. "Where are you from?"

"Two weeks from Sunday," I said. "I'm a time traveller."

11.

Sunday, November 27. Late evening.

Sgt. Lake was surprised and, I thought, disappointed to learn that I had been in jail on the night of the fire. She said that she understood why I had been reluctant to say anything, but admonished me on the virtues of being honest with law enforcement authorities.

I called Helen, looking forward to an evening of celebration. But I only got her recording machine. "Call me when you get in," I told it.

The call never came. Just before midnight, when I'd given up and was getting ready to go to bed, I noticed a white envelope on the kitchen table.

My name was printed on it in neat, spare characters.

Dear Dave (it read),

Shel is back! My Shel. The real one. He wants to take me off somewhere, and I don't know where, but I can't resist. Maybe we will live near the Parthenon, or maybe Paris during the 1920's. I don't know. But I do know you will be happy for me.

I will never forget you, Dave.

Love,

Helen

P.S. We left something for you. In the wardrobe.

I read it several times, and finally crumpled it.

They'd left the *Hermes*. They had positioned it carefully under the light, to achieve maximum effect. Not that it needed it.

I stood a long time admiring the piece. It was Michelangelo at his most brilliant. But it wasn't Helen.

I went downstairs and wandered through the house. It was empty, full of echoes and the sound of the wind. More desolate now than it had been when it was the only thing in the universe.

I remembered how Helen had sounded when she thought she was sending me back to sleep with another woman. And I wondered why I was so ready to give up.

I did some quick research, went back to the wardrobe, scarcely noticing the statue, and put on turn-of-the-century evening clothes.

Next stop: the Court Theater in Sloane Square, London, to watch the opening performance of *Man and Superman*.

You're damned right, Shelborne.

Time travellers never die.